THEY STARTED IN NEW YORK...
AND DIDN'T STOP UNTIL HOLLYWOOD
HAD THEM IN ITS GRASP.

It was where Rebecca Parlato had fled to what she hoped would be a glorious future on Broadway.

...where the incredibly beautiful Shelby Cale wanted to win a beauty pageant and go on—quickly—to bigger and better things.

...where David Rau plotted his first entertainment triumph and the first step in the downfall of his wealthy film producer father.

...where Silver first discovered that under her outlandish clothes she had a voice that was pure gold.

...and where Erik Lungren saw and fell in love with the Southern born and bred Shelby Cale, whose perfect face and body would haunt him long after her love had faded.

Star Crossed

James Cass Rogers

WARNER BOOKS

A Warner Communications Company

WARNER BOOKS EDITION

The author acknowledges permission to reprint excerpts
from "As Time Goes By" by Herman Hupfeld, copyright ©
1931 (renewed) by Warner Bros., Inc., all rights reserved,
used by permission; and "You Can't Always Get What You
Want" by Mick Jagger and Keith Richard, copyright © 1969
by ABKCO Music, Inc., all rights reserved, reprinted by
permission.

Cover design by Gene Light
Cover art by Victor Gadino

Warner Books, Inc.
666 Fifth Avenue
New York, N.Y. 10103

 A Warner Communications Company

Printed in the United States of America

First Printing: March, 1985

10 9 8 7 6 5 4 3 2 1

With deep gratitude to all my family and friends who freely gave so much support during the slow evolution of this novel.

Bless the nurturers, especially four who rendered extraordinary assistance and spiritual sustenance: Phoebe Larmore, Elaine Markson, Tristine Rainer and Albert Zuckerman.

And with special thanks to Colin Higgins for sharing the story of the Raindance.

To mother and father,
whose love makes it all possible

It's still the same old story,
A fight for love and glory,
A case of do or die.
The world will always welcome lovers,
As time goes by.

Herman Hupfeld

You can't always get what you want,
But if you try sometimes,
You just might find,
You get what you need.

Jagger/Richard

Book One

1966–1967

REBECCA
July 1966
New York

She bent over the nude, masculine body and joked halfheartedly, "Hey, can I have your autograph?"

He did not stir.

On the mattress on the floor of her one-room apartment, his sandy-haired head buried into her only pillow, his ass barely covered by the sheet. "Hey, Erik Lungren," she said, overly bright. "I'm serious about that autograph. It's not every day I wake up with a famous writer in my bed."

A soft groan erupted from under the pillow.

She eyed the broad shoulders, noting for the first time a scar that puckered the skin under one blade. "Hey, come on, man. Rise and shine. Rise and shine."

Again he groaned, before flopping over on his back, one hand groping himself under the sheet, his eyes still welded shut. She cast an anxious glance at herself in the cracked mirror but it did nothing to offer assurance. Under her uneven, coal black bangs, her dark eyes were wide with concern. In her well-worn jeans and baggy T-shirt, she thought she looked as though she should be setting pins in a bowling alley.

She squared her small frame and sang out as carefree as she could, "Didn't you wanna get up at noon?"

His dusty gold eyelashes fluttered. "What the hell's the time?" His thick voice drove her backward into the middle of the high-ceilinged room.

"Noon—or maybe, five past if you want to be on the nose—of course, my damned old alarm clock could be off a bit, give or take say, five minutes, but it's got to be pretty close 'cause I just heard the noon siren on top of the firehouse—you know, the one over on Riverside? Near here, Ninety-sixth?" She took a deep breath to continue but his head rolled toward her.

"You always rattle on a mile a minute?" His hazel eyes squinted in the bright slash of sunlight, trying to locate her.

"Yeah, well, I do. Sort of. You know where I was raised—this was back in Lackawanna—you know Buffalo, don't you? Home of bad breath? Anyway, the kids on the block used to call me ol' motor mouth." She tried to chuckle but her throat was too dry.

"God almighty, it's hot," he grumbled and kicked off the sheet. "You got an air conditioner?"

"Yeah. The open window," she said, tearing her eyes away from his nakedness. "They say heat rises and, man, do I believe it. Already hot as Hades in here, ain't it?" Ducking her head, she blushed again. "Excuse me, 'isn't it,' I meant to—"

She fumbled for the coffee mug she had borrowed from her waitressing job. "You want some coffee? It'll have to be black though 'cause I've no sugar or cream. But you drank it black last night, right? At the diner?" She cast a furtive glance in his direction. "Remember? Mac's Diner where I was, you know, working behind the counter? You were pretty loaded when you—so do you remember anything about last night?"

"Not much. Got any juice?"

"I got an orange. You want an orange? It's cold. But I gotta warn you, it's been in the fridge a few days, maybe a week or two." She tore open the half-refrigerator and grabbed the orange, the only item on the top shelf. She spun to him. "Here. Catch." She tossed it overhand.

One of his big paws snatched it out of the air. "Nice throw," he said and tore into the skin. "Where'd you learn that?"

"Oh around," she said, suddenly pleased. She dumped the last of her instant coffee into the chipped cup. "A lot of hours at stickball."

"In the streets? Like the dead-end kids?"

"Yeah, but I got outta there, didn't I? Six months now. No more dead ends for me."

The thirsty sounds behind her gave her a momentary feeling of relief. At least with the orange, she had been able to satisfy *something* he'd wanted. Not like her humiliating debacle on the mattress the night before. The water in the aluminum pan boiled furiously. She turned off the jet of the hot plate on top of the small refrigerator.

"Where's your head?"

"My head?" she asked, then realized her stupid mistake. Busily, she filled the cup with hot water and waved one hand toward the toilet-closet. "In the corner. Not very fancy . . . in fact the whole place is kind of a sleaze-hole, huh? But cheap. Besides I plan to be out of here real soon."

Behind her, his bare feet slapped across the warped linoleum and into the tiny enclosure.

"The door doesn't close all the way," she said in a rush. "Probably one too many cockroaches squished in the hinges. But—"

A hard, steady stream of his water interrupted her. Amazed at the forceful sound and its duration, she felt a hot flash of embarrassment creep up her back under her T-shirt. Finally, she heard the sound of the chain being pulled, the toilet flushing.

Avoiding looking at him, she hurried to the bed, pulling up the sheet, fluffing the pillow.

"Hey."

The almost hard edge to his tone brought her to a standing position, clutching the pillow. "Yeah?"

"Turn around, will you?"

Her grip on the pillow tightened. Reluctantly she swiveled to partially face him. "Whatsamatter?"

Still nude, he was scratching one armpit, staring at her. "Haven't seen your face since I opened my eyes."

She dropped her head, cursing the color that flooded her cheeks. "Aw com'on, you don't wanna see my face."

"You said you're nineteen, right?"

"Oh sure, that I am," she lied and thought she had sounded fairly convincing. She sneaked a glance; his ruggedly handsome face was scrutinizing her with suspicion. She scrambled for her wallet under her clean T-shirts on the wall shelf. "I just look younger that's all."

She held out her birth certificate with the phony year. "See. Right there in black and white. Born March 14, nineteen forty-seven. That makes me nineteen. And a Pisces. What sign are you?"

"Gemini." He yawned.

"Isn't that a stupid question? Don't know why I asked it really. I'm sorry . . . it's just . . ." Flustered, she jammed her fake ID back into her wallet, feeling even more immature than her seventeen years.

"I still haven't seen your face," he said quietly.

She focused on her bare toes poking through her work sandals. "Just an ordinary, nonglamorous face, that's all. Nothing like those you date."

"How do you know who I date?"

She shrugged, hurrying to her pink waitressing uniform hanging on a nail by the tub. "Oh, you know . . . all those movie starlets I used to read about." She added lamely, "You know what I mean . . ."

"No, I don't," he said, a trace of annoyance in his voice. "Come here. Please."

She felt her body stiffen. Busily she turned to the sink with her uniform. "Got to wash the pits out of this. I sure as hell sweat a lot when I work at that diner. For a girl that is . . ."

"Hey, Rebecca . . ."

The sound of her name forced her to swing her eyes to him. The shaft of sunlight behind him silhouetted his over six-foot tall, well-formed body, the rays highlighting, like a golden aura, the hair on his arms and legs. She thought he looked like a Viking prince. An odd smile split the lower half of his unshaven face. "Put that damn dress down and come here."

She laid the uniform over the sink and moved slowly toward him, her head down. Painfully she came to a stop. He took her chin in one hand, slowly tipping it up. Desperately she tried to think of something to say. "Gorgeous, huh?"

Very gently, he brushed back her bangs. "Why do you hide behind these?"

"Hide? Who's hidin'? I'm standin' right here, aren't I?"

"Open your eyes," he said. "Look at me."

She looked into his eyes; they had greenish flecks in the soft brown. And they seemed to be twinkling. "You laughing at me?" she asked. Slowly he bent his head and kissed her on the lips. My god, she thought, he's really kissing me. And his eyes are closed! When he pulled back, she breathlessly said, "Thanks."

He laughed, a big, warm burst that engulfed her like a summer shower. "What are you thanking me for?"

She pulled away. "'Cause you didn't have to do that, that's why." She swung again to the sink and, turning on the water, began to scrub energetically the sleeves of the pink nylon uniform. "Hey, your novel *Bell of Donna* was the first hardcover book I ever bought in my life, no lie. My big brother, Tony, wrote me about it from Cornell. Said that all the kids were really into it. I had to save up for it, but geez, it was worth it. I laughed and I cried. Real sexy too. But when my ol' man read those parts, he threw your book out. Never forgave him for that."

She paused to gulp in air, rinsing the soapy water from the sleeves. "Do people still recognize you from that *Time* magazine cover? That's how I did, you know? Soon as you walked into the diner last night. That was a few years back, right? That *Time* cover?"

Wiping her hands on the back of her jeans, she dared a glance around. He lay on the mattress, smoking a cigarette, staring blankly at the sagging, pressed-tin ceiling.

"I'm talking too much again, aren't I?" she asked. "You must have a bitch of a hangover, huh?"

"Just trying to remember what the hell I did last night."

"Before or after you came into the diner?" she asked, hoping that he had forgotten *everything* about last night. Especially there on that mattress.

"Way before I met you," he said. "There was this Fourth of July party for Capote—"

"Truman Capote? Lordee, really? I just finished reading his new one, *In Cold Blood?* Wow, so you're rubbing elbows with the famous, huh? So tell me, who was there?"

He shrugged. "Who knows? I drank too much, too short of time. Got ripped to the tits. Made a complete ass out of myself."

"How?" she asked, daring to sink to her knees at the foot of the mattress, eager for inside news of that other world.

"Well, for one, I remember declaring loudly that all politicians were failed actors—and cited as example, old Senator Everett Dirksen on that Hollywood TV show, reciting that maudlin hit record and wouldn't you know it? There he was in the flesh, not more than five feet away."

"Oh, no," she groaned in sympathy. "Who else was there?"

He inhaled deeply and blew out three perfect smoke rings. Then he was looking directly at her. "Was I the first you tried making it with?"

"First? You?!" she exclaimed, suddenly flustered at the shift of focus to her. "Are you kidding? Oh no . . . really." It was all another major lie, but again she hoped her delivery had carried it off.

She started to bounce up from the mattress but one of his arms snaked out and he clamped onto her wrist. "Why're you always darting away?" He tugged her down flat beside him, bent his head and pressed his lips to hers. Through her nose, her breath escaped like from a punctured balloon. Her eyelids squeezed tightly shut, still he held the kiss, his tongue caressing her lips. His free hand roamed under her T-shirt toward her breasts. As his large, warm hand found its small, pointed goal, she shrank from his touch.

Oh my god, her mind shrieked, he's trying to do it again!

"Just relax," he breathed, the coarse stubble of his beard scraping her cheek.

Relax, her mind repeated numbly. Relax, dammit! Please! But it was impossible—the growing hardness protruding below his waist poked insistently into her side.

He pulled back slightly. "Hey . . ."

She couldn't open her eyes.

"You okay?" he asked.

She shook her head. "Sex in the morning makes me nauseous."

Laughing, he flopped on his back. She rolled to the far side and struggled to sit up. Her body felt weak, exhausted. "Your coffee's getting cold."

He glanced down at the dented alarm clock. "Hell, I've got to split. Meeting my editor after lunch." He bent to his jeans and pulled out a wooden kitchen match. "You didn't tell me you were an actress."

That brought her head up with a jerk.

He lit the match by striking it with a thumbnail. He smiled over the flame, lit a Camel from his nearly empty, crumpled pack and exhaled. "I found your photos and résumés on top of the tank in the bathroom."

"Oh no, not those ugly..." she said, wishing that she'd hidden them better.

He chuckled. "You forgot I'm taller than you. Saw 'em plain as day." He reached for his jeans. "You've had some good roles."

"Nothing in New York yet," she murmured, again aware of his nudity. "All were in summer stock. Haven't been cast in anything here yet."

"Is an actress who doesn't act still considered an actress?"

She stiffened. "Whadda'ya mean?"

He pulled up his jeans, stuffing himself into the fly. "Only that I feel when a writer isn't writing every day, he's not really a writer."

"Well, I don't know about your profession," she said, surprised at her own tone of defensiveness, "but being an actress is like an obsession. I'm taking as many lessons as I can afford and I'm thinking about my craft all the time. Like, I've got my first real Broadway audition tomorrow morning and I've been just crazed, hoping, praying practically every second I'm awake. Dreams can be an all-consuming thing, you know?"

A slow, easy smile formed on his square-jawed face. "'We are such stuff as dreams are made on,'" he quoted. "'And our little life is rounded with a sleep.'" His eyes held hers while he picked up his faded blue workshirt. "So what's your dream?"

She tugged at a hank of her hair. "Aw com'on," she said. "You know about dreams...they've got to be private. Like birthday-candle wishes."

Watching her carefully, he began tucking in his shirttail. "Anything to do with all these Broadway programs?" He nodded to the dozen *Playbill* covers dotting the buckling plaster walls—programs from *Mame* to *Royal Hunt of the Sun* which she'd picked up on the sidewalk after performances she couldn't afford to attend.

"I just want to be a working actress...that's all. And act 'til I'm seventy. Like Helen Hayes, or Ruth Gordon, or Lynn Fontanne. Then retire and write my memoirs."

"So you want to be a star?" He was sitting on the mattress, pulling on his boots.

For a moment, she stared at his Western boots, noticing how scuffed the toes were. "Doesn't everybody?"

"Damn right." He laughed, hard-edged and brief. "I think everybody in the whole goddamned world wants to be famous." He picked up his still burning cigarette from the improvised jar-lid ashtray, blew another ring and stared at her through the ash-colored smoke hanging in the bright shaft of sunlight. "Well, if you're serious about this success game, there're two big questions you'll eventually have to answer. The first is, how bad do you want it? And the second is, are you willing to pay the price to get it?" He paused to grind out the cigarette. "It's taken me a long time to come to some of those answers. Hell," he said. "I guess I'm still looking for them."

"You're so lucky," she sighed. "You've made it already."

The brightness in his eyes dimmed. "Babe, I haven't had a book published in six years."

She blinked back at him for a few beats. "You mean, after *Bell of Donna* there's been nothing? I thought I just didn't catch them. So how come?"

"Hell, I was twenty-three when that hit," he said, staring toward the window. "The youngest author ever to be a *Time* cover. Went right to my head and I craved every minute of it. I had more money and more loving and more fun. Shit, I didn't write a word for three years. Of course now, I realize I blew it all. Live and learn, right?" He rolled to his feet, chuckling dryly. "And here I am, a has-been at twenty-nine."

She was shaking her head vigorously. "No way. A has-been is someone who's given up. Have you? Aren't you still writing?"

He grinned. "Hell yes. I'm just polishing up my new novel now. It's over a thousand pages long."

"Really? Terrific—what's it called?"

"*Rogues and Scoundrels*," he said. "You like that?"

"Dynamite, really. What's it about?"

"Sort of a metaphysical action-adventure tale. Similar in genre to that Bogart movie, *Treasure of the Sierra Madre*. Well, mine's also an epic journey of three men in search of a dream," he explained intently. "A downed cargo plane in the upper Canadian Rockies, loaded with gold bullion. I'm hoping my editor will go with this last draft and bring it out next spring. Hey, I'll give you a signed copy."

"You will?" she asked, the hope in her voice nakedly revealing.

"Sure. Hot off the presses." He bent to retrieve his sand-colored corduroy sports jacket.

That action produced such a tug at her heart, she had to turn away. He was going to walk out and she'd never see him again. Oh, maybe on some TV talkshow, like Carson's or Mike Douglas's. But not in person. Not face to face. Not as close as they were on that lumpy old mattress. Lying next to his sleeping form after his brief but energetic efforts to induce her to make love, she'd watched his face all night in the soft glow from the street lights. She couldn't remember being so contented, so peaceful, so secure. As if she had been with him forever.

She bit her lip. She was nothing to him, just another warm body to take the chill off a lonely night. And she hadn't even been able to please him. Again, she damned her virginity. And her timidity.

His voice came again. "How the hell do you pronounce that last name of yours anyway?"

She turned, forcing a cheery smile. "Par-lot-o. It's Italian. Means to talk . . . a lot, right?"

"Never would have guessed," he teased.

"Oh, yeah sure," she bumbled on. "Actually I'm only half Italian. My old man's side. My mom's Jewish. That's where the Rebecca came from. So I'm half and half. Sort of a Jew-wop."

His grin widened. "Well little Miss Half 'n' Half, gotta go."

"Yeah, I figured as much. Hey, I'm real sorry I didn't have any food for breakfast."

"Will you stop apologizing?"

"Oh, yeah, really I know . . . it gets to be a real drag. I'm sorry." She caught herself with an exaggerated palm slapped to her mouth. "Whoops, there I go again. Awful, ain't it? *Isn't* it?"

"On you, I find it enormously appealing."

She shrugged, feeling her face turn a thousand shades of red. "Well . . . this is good-bye, huh?"

With two long strides, he was before her and his arms around her, pulling her to him in a big hug. It had happened so suddenly she did not have time to avert her face. Her nose crushed into a hard shirt button. Smothered against his burly, large frame, she felt like a tiny kid. He kissed the top of her head.

"Thanks, Rebecca," he said. "For taking pity on a stumbling drunk. And for not calling a cop when I insisted you take me home."

"Well, it wasn't like you were a stranger, you know? I mean I did know who you were, right?" she mumbled into his chest, liking his closeness too much to move. "And besides, it wasn't pity. You're a major talent, you know?"

He chuckled, squeezing her tightly. "You're a real sweet kid." He let her go and started for the door, then stopped abruptly. "Damn," he grumbled and yanked out his wallet. He checked the contents and turned with an apologetic, almost chagrined smile. "Hell, I hate to do this. Could I borrow a few bucks for a cab? I blew my last buck on coffee last night." His ruddy coloring deepened.

"That happens to everyone, huh?" she said, hurrying to her own wallet on the shelf. "Will five be enough? I've got a little more." She held out the bill.

"This isn't going to strap you?" he asked, taking it.

"Oh no, I'm on night shift again. I'll get some tips, you know?"

Carefully he folded the bill and slipped it into his shirt pocket. "Think you can call in sick tonight?"

"Me? Sick? I haven't been sick in ages."

"Thought you might want to come down to my place this evening."

She blinked once and suddenly sagged against the counter with exaggerated "malaise," one hand flopping weakly to her chest. "A devastating case of flu just struck."

He laughed and patted his coat pocket. "Got a pen?"

Her feet did not seem to touch the floor as she flew to the box on the shelf. "Have I got a pen, he asks? You're the only one who writes? What color would you like? Blue, red, black, green . . . one for every mood." She offered them with a grand, theatrical swoop of a bow.

Chuckling, he grabbed one and scribbled on a piece of paper torn from the deli sack. "I'm in the Village. Right off Waverly Place."

"What time?"

"That's the problem. I could be holed up with Max, my editor, until late. Hammering out this last section. Wait a sec." He pulled a ring of keys from his tight jeans and began removing one. "This opens both doors. Just let yourself in anytime. I'll be back whenever, okay?"

She took the offered key as if it were the one promising total happiness. "You can trust me, Erik. I won't rip you off."

He chuckled, shaking his head. "You're something else, Rebecca." He opened the door. "And don't mind my housekeeping—it looks like it's been hit by one of those H-bombs missing off Spain."

"Won't bother me. Who are the tidy people of the world anyway?"

"About six-thirty? I'll phone you there if I'll be later." He threw her a wink and headed into the hall, started down the stairs. "Bye, Rebecca. Catch you tonight."

"Bye, Erik," she called out. She stood there, listening to his bootsteps descending until she heard, very faintly, far below, the vestibule door closing. From some apartment a radio played, Sinatra was singing a very appropriate song, she thought, "Strangers in the Night." And her heart would not stop pounding. She spun into the middle of her room and began twirling around and around and around, her arms outspread, faster and faster, singing along loudly, "Do-bee dobee do . . ."

Abruptly she stopped, her eyes popping open. Damned if she hadn't forgotten all about her audition the next morning. Her debut—her very first Broadway audition. For the first time since arriving in New York, she was surprised to find herself actually looking forward to a talent tryout. Lordee, lordee, lordee, was she going to knock them on their asses!

ERIK
July 1966
New York

Traffic was so congested, Rebecca's five bucks got him only as far as the Plaza Hotel. He climbed out of the taxi and began walking jauntily toward Lexington Avenue with thirty-seven cents in his jeans.

In spite of the muggy, relentless heat, his spirits soared. He was remembering Rebecca, vividly. How vulnerable she was, yet exhibiting the bravado of a street-wise survivor. He fell to thinking how he might describe her physically in writing. Maybe something like, "Raven-haired, with an ivory, cameo face, she did not trust her own beauty, but her luminous black eyes were fired with magic." He started mulling over where he'd take her for dinner that night. O'Casey's maybe—if Max sprang for another advance.

On the busy, lunch-hour sidewalk, Erik paused in front of Doubleday's, frowning at the displays for the Number one and two *New York Times* Bestsellers, Susann's *Valley of the Dolls* and Robbins's *The Adventurers*. His mind's eye brushed aside the annoying displays, replacing them with stacks of his own *Rogues and Scoundrels*. He was so close to finishing it that he allowed himself the luxury of projecting that far ahead. His novel had been such long, painful struggle. Months and months and months, over three years of discipline and self-denial.

In addition to his own critical voice pounding away at the pages, his long-time editor had been tough, demanding, meticulous, brilliant. But that was why Max Lerner was considered the best. Certainly top man at Schuman & Croft. And it had been Max, seven years previously, who had bought, edited and served the same midwife role on the first book.

Bell of Donna, Erik's only published novel, had been a fictionalized comedy drama, based on his first major love affair; he'd been nineteen, she thirty three; he'd been a bouncer in a Cheyenne, Wyoming, poker parlor and she'd run the illegal game. He had written and rewritten the tale over a period of four years while on the road, bumming and odd-jobbing around the states. Within weeks of publication of *Bell of Donna,* Erik had reached what had been his most fanciful dream ever since winning a local, junior-high, short-story contest in Coos Bay, Oregon. *Bell of Donna* had been a huge bestseller, garnering an enviable collection of reviews and being nominated for several major prizes, including the National Book Award. And he had been only twenty-three years old.

Suddenly he had been swept into a totally foreign world. For the first time in his life he had been able to afford all those luxuries which always had meant "success" to him and he had spent money as if he would continually have an endless supply. A handcrafted Ferrari in L.A., which he had totaled two nights later on the Pacific Coast Highway racing Sinatra's Masaratti. Erik's next toy had been a sixty-foot yawl docked in the Mediterranean, but not long after, he had gambled it away in Monte Carlo.

Erik had lived hard, spent foolishly and had loved being a celebrity—the best tables in the best restaurants, his name in gossip columns linked with beautiful women, the flattery of university professors whose books had been part of his own self-education. Despite Max's warnings to ignore the hoopla and get back to work, Erik had not written. He had been having too grand a time. Besides there had always been tomorrow.

Within a very short three years, tomorrow had come. His bank account had dwindled to nothing. But worse, he had been no longer "hot." High-society folks, college students, people on the streets had found newer heroes. The "literary lumberjack," as Erik had been tagged, was old hat. Invitations had dried up. People whom he once considered close friends had begun avoiding him. His phone had stopped ringing.

He had fled to the shores of Maine and had holed up in a fishing shack. Only then had he begun back to work. Fighting the castrating fears of whether he would be able to find his talent once more. Struggling with the necessity of having to produce—not only to regain his reputation, but to pay the bills to survive. But he had done it. And none too soon. Seven years was a hell of a long time between books.

The twenties-styled building on Lexington which housed Schuman & Croft was like the publishing company itself—old, venerated, elegant. In the elevator on the way up, Erik slipped on his corduroy sports jacket and ran his fingers through his unruly mane of hair. It was not until he stood before Max's door that he realized that he was on the wrong floor. Max had been recently promoted to editor in chief. Quickly Erik hit the fire stairs and ran up two flights. The receptionist motioned him cheerfully down the hall. As he approached, Max's matronly secretary looked up from her typewriter with a wry smile. "Well, don't you look like you've swallowed the canary."

"What's to complain about today? Unless it's this damn movie actor running for governor of California." He tapped the *New York Times*'s front-page article on Ronald Reagan's political campaign. She laughed politely and buzzed the intercom.

As soon as Erik stepped into the large, masculinely appointed office, the graying, bespectacled figure bounded up from behind his desk, asking, "Did you have a good Fourth, my boy?"

"'But what creates the most surprise. His soul looks out through renovated eyes.'" He reached for Max's outstretched hand.

Max pumped his vigorously. "You and your damn Keats. What brings on these newly renovated eyes?"

"This girl I just left."

"Ah, should have known."

"Max, this one's really special."

"Weren't they all?" Max chuckled. "Sit down, sit down. Sorry I had to cancel lunch on you. Would you believe, I haven't had lunch at the Algonquin since that last time with you."

Erik sank into one of the leather wing-back chairs before the cluttered desk. "You not eating at the Algonquin is like trying to imagine LBJ not having grits for breakfast."

"I'm having food sent in lately." The intercom interrupted him. Answering it, he waved a hand toward the bookcase bar and was immediately engaged in a serious dicussion, some problem in the distribution department.

Erik poured a Scotch on the rocks, watching Max's spirited responses. As usual, Max was wearing one of the three suits he owned, a summer-weight poplin. Erik recalled when both of them had endorsed heartily Thoreau's warning to be wary of any undertaking which required new clothes. Obviously Max still held by that belief.

Taking his drink back to the chair, Erik's thoughts returned to Rebecca. What was it that so attracted him to her? He could not remember being so affected, so viscerally touched by a girl after just one night—especially one he hadn't made it with.

Max had hung up and was smiling benignly. "Daydreaming again?"

"It's this girl, Max. Honestly, I feel so energized by her. Like—" He felt a pang of distress. Max had glanced at his watch. He couldn't remember Max ever doing that before in his presence. "Am I keeping you from something?"

Somewhat guiltily, Max looked up. "Oh, I am so sorry, my boy. Just doesn't seem to be enough time in the day anymore."

"Comes from being such a damned good editor." Erik eyed the narrow, bookish face behind the black, horn-rimmed spectacles. He raised his glass. "Congratulations, Max, on your new position. Couldn't go to a more deserving guy."

"Thank you, my boy."

He said it with such sincerity, Erik felt a tightening in his throat. He sensed there was something going on behind Max's friendly gray eyes. Something beyond the opening banter.

Max, in his cordovan leather desk chair, folded his arms across his striped rep tie. "What do you want out of life, Erik?"

The question took him by surprise. He hesitated briefly before answering. "To be the best damned writer in America, of course."

Cautiously, Max proceeded, "If you could choose another writer's career, alive or dead, whose would you select?"

"No question there: Jack London."

Max nodded thoughtfully. "Interesting you would choose a writer who was enormously popular and critically accepted."

Erik grinned, shifted his weight. "Yeah, well, you know me. Always want the whole cake."

"If you could have only one . . . popular or critical success. Which would it be?"

"Hell, critical acceptance, of course."

"Are you sure you could do without all that mass adulation?" Max leaned his elbows on the desk. "Isn't that what you got off on the most after *Bell of Donna*? All those people idolizing you. Calling you the new Kerouac? That avocation of being a celebrity?"

Erik felt uncomfortable with the direction of the questioning. "Sure, I got off on that. But I'd rather have a rave review from Christopher Lehmann-Haupt in the *Times*." He swallowed half his drink. "Why'd you ask?"

"Because, after rereading your last draft this weekend—twice in fact—I've reached the unfortunate conclusion that your novel does not work, mainly for the reason you're trying to ride both those horses at once: wanting a big popular success and a critical one at the same time."

"Which sections don't work?"

Max held his gaze, before answering quietly, "All of it."

"All of it? What the hell's that mean?" Erik swallowed with difficulty. "Haven't I done everything we talked about?"

His editor was silent for a few moments. "Erik, I know it's a shock. Hell, I'd give anything not to have reached this decision. But the damn thing just doesn't work. I honestly feel the novel's murkier now than it was before." He sighed and gestured with the palms of his hands. "The spontaneity is lost. What was instinctive and joyous has become mannered and tedious. I take my share of the blame, I should've seen it earlier."

Erik took a moment to study his boot toes, then looked up with a self-conscious shrug. "So we'll rewrite it."

"I'm afraid that's impossible, my boy."

He felt his face redden. "What do you mean? Of course we will, I mean, hell, I'll go back to step one again. I'll take the germ of the idea and start over."

"If you want to, that's up to you, my boy. I'm sorry, but I feel I just can't do anything more for it. Already I've spent too much time."

There was a tinge of gruffness in his voice that Erik had never heard before. As though Max were angry at him for something. "Max, you assigning me another editor? Is that it? Well, hell, I understand. A lot of new responsibilities and——"

"It's true," Max interrupted quietly. "I don't have time to ride herd over this anymore."

Erik reached for his glass and downed its contents in a gulp. "So who'll it be? Steiner? Burden? Hell, not Valency, okay?"

"I'm sorry if you misunderstood." Max hesitated, paling. "I'm dropping the book, Erik. Schuman & Croft will not publish *Rogues and Scoundrels*."

A ball of fire exploded in Erik's gut, cutting off his air.

Max rose and came around to the front of the desk. He sat on the edge. "Hell, you have your whole life ahead of you. Remember, in writing, as in life, it's not the destination, it's the journey that brings the true joy. The doing. You've a lot of fine books in you. I don't doubt your talent, Erik. You've a great gift. A born storyteller, an ear for the natural. But on this one, you're thinking too much. Not feeling enough."

Max tugged off his glasses and rubbed the bridge of his nose. "I suggest you take time off from this one. You've been on the road, drifting, a loner too long. Maybe take one of those academic jobs you were offered. Get married, have a family. At least develop a long-term relationship with one of those innumerable ladies. You could use those experiences. It would help your writing."

Erik tried to focus his eyes on something other than the pained expression on Max's graying face.

"I know this is a stunner, Erik. I wish there were an easier way. Honest to God, I do. But there isn't. I can't accept the novel. I honestly don't feel, in my professional judgment, *Rogues and Scoundrels* is worth continued rewriting."

Erik took a deep, painful breath. "I'm not a quitter, Max."

"My friend . . . being mature is also knowing when to call it quits. When to walk away and know you've given your best shot for now."

Erik shook his head, trying to clear it. "Max . . . Max, I need this one. I've got to get this one out."

Wearily, Max rose from the desk's edge. "Of course, you're free to take it elsewhere. Hell, Erik I'm not infallible. I could be totally wrong on this. We both have been so close to it. I urge you to get other opinions, by all means. But it's not for Schuman & Croft. I'm sorry . . . really I am, my boy."

The intercom buzzed. Openly relieved, Max reached behind him for the phone. "Yes," he said into the receiver. "No. I'll take it." He raised his eyes. "I'm sorry, Erik. My call to London."

Erik nodded vaguely and pushed himself out of the clubchair. "I guess that's it then."

"Afraid so." Max's face was a pallid mask of a very tired, drained, old man. "I'll be in touch later."

He searched Max's eyes, trying to find something to latch onto. Some hope. Some future. There was only resignation. Erik could not find any words. He reached out and squeezed Max's shoulder, then dropped his hand. Leadenly he forced his boots across the carpet and out of the office.

SHELBY
July 1966
New York

"Crossed off the list?" Shelby tossed her waist-length, straight blond hair, an impatient dismissal. "There's been a mistake."

"No mistake," said the beefy guard barring her entrance. Emphatically he jabbed a stubby finger at the typed page on his clipboard. "This here is the revised list. Just got it this morning. Your name ain't on it. So I can't let you in." He flipped over a page. "It was on yesterday's. But today it's crossed off. See?"

There on the paper, plain as his badge, was SHELBY CALE with a line through it. Next to hers, another name had been inked in.

She crossed her bare arms over her white cotton sundress and locked eyes with the squat ugly man. She was standing in the gilded lobby of the Odeon Theater. A large, ornate display stood nearby, announcing in an elegant, silver script—*The American Beauty Pageant*—Presented by *Villa Caesari Cosmetics*. Behind her, outside, the incessant traffic noise of Broadway, mid-Manhattan. In front of her, the padded-leather, double doors muffled sounds of hammering within the auditorium.

But she was aware only of the fat red face of the guard.

Her spine lengthened and she drew herself up to her full five-feet ten-inch height, knowing she presented a commanding presence in spite of her youth. "I'm not leaving until I speak with someone in charge." She recognized the tone of her voice and felt heartened. It was one of imperious command and she used it when angry with a servant back at Oak Hills.

He scowled back. She did not budge. Finally, he turned to stomp away, muttering scornfully for her to hear. "Spoiled Southern bitch."

Without moving, she watched his portly frame descend the carpeted stairs leading to the lounges. When he disappeared, her eyes swung back to the elegant lobby display. Just under the world famous logo for Villa Caesari Cosmetics, a gray velvet drape dropped to the floor. Unable to control her curiosity, she glided to the velvet curtain and lifted the corner high.

Beneath a bold, silver sign asking, "Who will be *Sunny*?" there was a full-color photo of the pageant's television hostess, Cara Noor. Critically, Shelby judged the image of the renowned movie star. Despite the gauzy effect and the airbrushing to remove the wrinkles, Shelby thought Cara Noor was definitely showing her age. Ancient, way over forty. And some movie star! Hasn't made a film in at least five years. Still, Cara Noor was attractive—in a cheap, Hollywood sort of way.

Shelby glanced beneath the photo to the twenty-five empty picture frames, each bearing the name of a contestant. Quickly she scanned the rows of names, looking for hers. It wasn't there! She *had* been crossed off the list.

She tossed her head defiantly and let the drape fall back in place. So she was a day late for the sign-in. What's one little day, after the months and months of planning and dreaming? If they only knew what she'd had to go through just to get this far. The schemes she had devised. The lies she'd had to improvise.

But now, as she paced the black and white marble squares of the lobby for the dozenth time, Shelby felt frustrated, angry and impatient and something she had rarely experienced in her eighteen years. She felt a strange balloon of uncertainty expanding in her chest, a growing fear. All her plans and boldness would be dashed to pieces if she were not admitted to the pageant.

That's all she wanted, not to win, only to be admitted. She did not need the guaranteed hundred-thousand-dollar modeling contract going to the winner. Shelby was born into money and had private income of her own. Her deceased grandfather, on her mother's side, Colonel Edwin Arlington Porter, had willed Shelby one third of his revered horse-breeding farm, Oak Hills, outside of Middleburg, Virginia.

Nor did she seek the fame which would be heaped on the winner selected to represent Villa Caesari's new line of *Sunny* cosmetics. The only reason Shelby wanted to be admitted was that the pageant offered her the most direct escape from a predestined life. Her maternal grandmother, Evangeline Boullifant Porter, ruled over Oak Hills with such total dominance that in Shelby's life every decision, from choice of clothes to boyfriends, always had been Evangeline's. Shelby wanted only to be free, to live her life, *her* way. She knew from years of devouring New York and world fashion magazines exactly where she stood on the beauty scale. This pageant could land her an independent modeling contract. Of that she had no doubts.

Hearing a street door open behind her, Shelby turned and blanched.

Giorgio Caesari, Villa Caesari cosmetics *himself,* was walking directly toward her, eyeing her intently.

She tried to smile, to be nonchalant, but the closer he came, the more dizzy she felt. His eyes were boring into and through her.

Much handsomer than the pictures she had seen, his patrician face, heavily tanned with a rich bronze luster, was frozen, ageless, unreadable. He was dressed all in soft gray, the suit darker than his dove gray silk tie, his shirt an even softer shade, almost a pearl gray. Not a jet black hair on his aristocratic head was out of place. And still he came toward her without a smile or flicker of warmth.

Two feet away, he ceased moving and stared hard at her face, studying it pore by pore, as if under a microscope. Suddenly he reached out with a hand, grabbed her chin and tilted her head toward the overhead light. Holding firmly onto her jaw, he maneuvered her face in the harsh light.

"H-hello, Mister Caesari," she stammered into his palm. "I'm Shelby Cale."

Without acknowledging that she had spoken, he dropped her chin and stepped back. Finally, he said, "Yes."

Yes, what? she wondered. Hadn't she read that he personally had selected the top twenty-five contestants? Her hopes soared. Fumbling for something to say, she automatically turned on her most radiant smile, a million-dollar asset that always achieved results. "I'm a little late, aren't I?"

"Turn around," he said. It was a blunt command.

Hesitatingly, she did so, feeling a flush creep up her neck. She turned to meet his hard stare and tried to guess his age. Maybe fifty, she thought.

"Put your purse down." There was the merest trace of an Italian accent.

Immediately, she laid her white straw bag on top of a radiator.

"Walk to the far end and back."

Disconcerted, she slid past him, the skirt of her white sundress brushing against his knees. She started down the lobby, remembering to place one foot in front of the other as she had learned at Miss Wright's Finishing School for Young Women—shoulders back, head high as if an invisible wire were gently pulling her up from the crown of her head.

"Slower," the voice behind her ordered.

She eased her pace. Conscious then of her height, she felt awkward, her knees rubbery. The lobby's end was an interminable distance, but she finally reached it. Then, with a well-practiced maneuver, she rose slightly onto the balls of her feet, one arm brought waist high and bent gracefully at the elbow, her wrist tracing the turn in the air as she swiveled back to face him.

The return walk was excruciating. But she kept smiling and smiling, her eyes riveted onto his. But he was not watching her face. He was concentrating on her body now, the way it moved under the thin cotton of her sundress. She felt that he had undressed her completely, as if she were parading nude before him. It gave her a strange sensation, a tingling warmth between her legs that crept upward until her cheeks felt hot. She stopped before him.

His manner cold, impersonal, he asked, "Why are you late?"

She hesitated. "Family problems."

"No phones on the farm?"

She glanced away, her mind flicking off reasonable excuses. "I . . . I couldn't get away."

"Punctuality is an absolute prerequisite for my *Sunny* girl. You have failed your first and consequently your only test."

Flustered, she felt her head rising stiffly, anger bubbling within.

But he continued coldly, "Your shade of lipstick is atrocious. Too orange. Try my 'Desert Nectar.' And you have tons too much hair."

"I've never had it cut. Not once," she said with heated pride.

"Obviously." He strode to the double doors, then paused. "And get rid of that hideous dress and those ridiculous gloves. You look like a silly sixth-grader going to tea at grannie's." He pushed open the swinging doors and vanished inside.

For a moment, she could only stare at the doors, then began trembling uncontrollably. She wanted to run far away, to flee the hideous embarrassment of ever having to see that dreadful man again. Blinded by hot tears, she spun around and ran down the stairs to the ladies' room.

The acrid smell of disinfectant greeted her. She tore at her gloves, ripping them from her hands, and threw them violently into the trash receptacle. She leaned both hands on the nearest sink, dropped her head and wept, her heart broken. Her sobs echoed off the tiled walls, hollow and empty as the life ahead of her. She was doomed.

"Why don't you just scream?"

Her head snapped up, one hand clawing to part the hair before her eyes. Reflected in the mirror was a short, heavyset woman with shaggy auburn hair and a round, open face. "Go on. Does me a lot of good."

"Will y'all go away," Shelby cried. "Leave me alone."

"I would, but as my kids say, I have to make a wee-wee." She marched into the nearest stall. "Don't mind me." She shut the door with a snap.

Shelby straightened her back and howled.

"Atta girl," came the voice.

Noting the tinge of sarcasm, Shelby yelled into the mirror, "Will y'all shut up!"

"Well, excuse me, your highness."

Shelby was livid. How dare that woman take that tone. As if I don't have enough to deal with. She turned on the faucet and cupping the water in both hands, bent to rinse her face. The liquid cooled her hot cheeks and stinging eyelids. She checked her eyes, the light sea green of her pupils was surrounded by new threads of red.

Above the running water, she heard the toilet flush behind her, and then the lock being opened. She would ignore that nasty woman. She turned off the water and with face dripping, moved to the paper towel dispenser, jutting her head forward so not to drip on her dress. The dispenser was empty. The next one was also without towels.

"Not too well organized, are they?" the woman said. "No towels out here, no toilet paper in the booths."

Shelby reached into her purse and found a Kleenex. The roundish woman was lighting a cigarette. Shelby sighed, her patience overtaxed. "Do y'all mind smoking that outside? Cigarette smoke makes me deathly ill."

"Gee, that's tough," the woman said and inhaled deeply.

Shelby turned to stare coldly. She figured the bitch to be about forty. Large mouth, prominent upper teeth, shaggy auburn hair that looked self cut. Dressed in a plain brown, box-jacket suit, the skirt too tight over her full hips, the woman wore no jewelry, and as far as Shelby could tell, no makeup. No hint of style or glamor. Obviously didn't work for Caesari.

"So what happened yesterday?"

"What?"

"You didn't show."

"Y'all with the pageant?" Shelby asked, disbelieving.

"Well, I'm not here to check the johns." The woman chuckled huskily. "We contacted every Cale within fifty miles of Middleburg."

"I live with my grandmother," Shelby said quickly.

She had too much to hide and this woman was striking dangerously close to the elaborate network which Shelby had devised to cover her entry into the pageant. For her home address, she had put the address of a girl friend's aunt who was abroad. But there was something else Shelby had to conceal. Only seventeen when she had mailed in the form, she was supposed to have obtained her parents' signature of approval. Shelby had forged her mother's.

Nervously, she dug out her brush and began attacking her long, straight hair.

"Caesari thinks you've got too much hair."

"Well, I think he's got too much rudeness. So there." She was counting strokes to herself. Eighteen, nineteen, twenty . . .

The woman guffawed in a short burst of air through her nostrils. "That's damned accurate for sure." She paused, then added, "You're one helluva lucky girl."

The brush suspended in midstroke. "Y'all're kidding?"

"Would I kid someone who takes this all so seriously?" The woman doused her cigarette under a running faucet.

"What'd he say?"

"If you're done, we should be going." The short legs started for the door. "You were being replaced by an alternate from Des Moines but Caesari likes your look." She opened the door.

"*He does!*" Jubilation raced through her like a brushfire.

"By the way, I'm Mo Engle. The TV producer. So don't be late again, or I'll can you myself. Understand?"

Shelby nodded, not really listening. I'm in, I'm in! She was singing to herself. She was free!

When she stepped into the large rehearsal hall, her joy deflated in another flash of uncertainty. Never in all her born days had she seen so many radiantly beautiful girls. And it seemed everyone had stopped talking at once. Shelby paused in the doorway, surveying the competition. As the other twenty-four contestants sized her up, Shelby began to smile, turning on the dazzle, feeling no animosity, only certainty. She always knew where she stood in any room with women. She walked toward the nearest contestant and stretched out a friendly hand. "Hi, y'all, I'm Shelby Cale from Oak Hills, Virginia."

DAVID
July 1966
New York

Through the smoky haze, he again checked his gold Cartier watch, frowned and surveyed the small nightclub's sparse audience. Someone wasn't doing their job, David thought. Even with this unknown performer, there should have been some publicity, handouts, posters. The only reason he'd heard of her was because the bartender at the Village Gate down the street had raved that she was such a comer. So where the hell was she? The midnight show was already twenty-eight minutes late. Amateurs. All of them.

Finally the lights on the small platform up front blinked and went off. A rustle of movement, footsteps on the wooden platform, a stumbled *thud* and a girl's voice saying, "Shit," followed by a guttural laugh, anxious yet cocky.

The spotlight snapped on revealing an odd-looking girl sitting precariously on a high wooden stool, her boots searching for the top rung, a large, black Gibson guitar across her lap. "Hi, folks. Sorry to keep you waitin'." She chortled again, a dry rasping sound. "Had some heavy matters to attend to."

God, she was weird. And seemed loaded. David quickly crossed her off his list. He turned to find the waiter for his check.

"My name's Silver an' you came to listen an' I came—period."

She tilted back her head and roared with laughter, this time deep-throated and dirty. There were a few embarrassed chuckles from the audience.

"Yup," the performer was saying, her large mouth cracked wide. "Silver's my name, singin's my game." She struck a solid chord on her guitar and immediately launched into an old Bessie Smith song, "Wasted Life Blues."

Poor choice for an opening number, David assessed. Should've been something more upbeat, have to wake these people up after their long wait. He checked again and couldn't find the waiter. His gaze came back to the singer.

In a strapless, forties, full-length, black velvet formal, Silver had a leanness that made her bare arms look like pieces of tight sinew. Her skin was the palest of whites, set off all the more by the black dress. Her hair was a mass of frizzy tight curls which formed a bushy pale halo, its whiteness a shade short of being albino. Hell, maybe she was. He couldn't tell by her eyes. They were hidden behind darkly tinted, wire-framed sunglasses.

But it was her voice that he'd come to hear. And he'd already given up on her. It was tinny, unsure, no breath support. He was half standing to leave, pulling from his velvet blazer a five-dollar bill to toss on the table, when her singing shifted swiftly into a higher gear. Her body coiled like a tight spring and she threw herself into a driving, upbeat, gospel-influenced rendition. He sat back down and hunched his small, intense frame over the table, unconsciously running a hand through his short-cropped, dark hair. He listened with every fiber of his being.

Her voice now was deep, throaty, rich, full-bodied. The more she increased the beat, the more power she seemed to be able to draw from some inner source of raw, gutsy strength. She was belting it out, building and building the wrenching sound until it became the howl of an enraged beast. She reached the final sustained note, nearly shrieking. Her face contorted, her head thrown back on the frenzied bellow. She held it and held it and held it. When there was no breath left, she cut it off with a final slap on her guitar.

There was an infinitesimal stirring in his coccyx, a tingling rare and therefore respected. David turned and signaled the waiter for another beer. He'd stay one more song.

An hour later, he was waiting impatiently for her again, this time on the dark, deserted side street outside the club. After what seemed like ages, he heard the service door open. She stepped out into the muggy air. She'd thrown over her shoulders an ornate fringed shawl which looked like the one that used to be on his mother's grand piano in the upstairs music room. In one hand, Silver lugged her guitar in a cheap, imitation-leather case.

Trying to control his eagerness, he stepped forward. "Silver?"

"Yeah?"

"I'd like to talk with you."

She peered over the top of her glasses. "Wha' about?"

"I'm going to make you famous."

She grinned expansively. "Shit, man, you done said the magic words. Who you with?"

"Only me."

"No label?"

"No label." He noted with some irritation that although his assessment of her on stage was that she was short—beside him, she was about his own five-foot seven-inch height.

She started up the street to the bright lights of Sixth Avenue. "You be an agent?"

"No," he said, joining her. "My name's David Rau."

"Never heard of you."

"Never heard of you either."

"You *will*, baby, you will."

"Not if you keep audiences waiting like tonight."

She stopped to squint at him. Before she could speak, he jumped in. "You take drugs?"

"Hey, man, you be a narc?" Her face pinched into a scowl.

In spite of himself, he laughed. "No, I'm not a narcotics officer. I'm a producer-manager."

"So what's a front man got to do with me?"

"I'm putting together a band."

"Just what the Big Apple needs. Another fuckin' band." Again she started walking. Her high-heeled boots clicked determinedly.

"Not here," he said, catching up with her, "Out in Frisco."

"You're lookin' for a chick singer and you want me, huh?"

"Right on."

"Tough shit." They had reached the corner. Opposite them the Waverly Theater's marquee announced, SHOP ON MAIN STREET. She turned north toward the Women's House of Detention.

David matched her measured stride. "Let's talk about it first, okay? Before you make up your mind?"

"Talk all you want, man, but I be a solo act. Don't wanna sing with no band."

"Not even with the best?"

"The Beatles lookin' for a chick?" She cackled at her own humor.

Irritated, he walked in silence beside her for a moment. Damn, one tough little bitch. But it had taken him three months of a coast-to-coast, sixty-five-clubs-and-twice-as-many-chicks search to find the right voice. He sure as hell wasn't going to pull out now. He changed tactics.

He started telling her about the four experienced musicians he had already lined up out on the West Coast—a keyboard man, two electric guitarists (one lead, the other bass), and a drummer that could play circles around Ringo. He paused dramatically after each name to see if she recognized any of them. The space cadet hadn't. Some musician. Judging from the songs she'd sung, she mainly knew folkies like Odetta and Baez.

But by the time they reached Eighth Street, she was listening openly as he described the kind of music he was after—a unique sound that was different from any being produced, a hard-driving blues rock that would combine the wail and soul of the old masters like T-Bone Walker and Ivory Joe Hunter with the stomping, electric back beat of Chuck Berry's rock 'n' roll. All wrapped up with some new electronic gear and the emerging West Coast harmonies. Feverishly he launched into why he felt such a group was a potential goldmine.

David had become so wrapped up in selling her that he had not noticed that they'd stopped walking. They stood before a mod-shoe store on Eighth. The windows displayed an incredible array of the latest, gaudy styles for men—clunky, high-heeled, square-toed shoes in garish colors.

Silver stood, gazing raptly at his face. "Man, you got spit on your chin."

Self-consciously, he ran a hand over his face. When he got excited, drops of spittle did spray from his mouth.

She was chuckling. "Wanna come up?"

He glanced at his watch. It was after three. "Sure."

She led him up two flights of dark stairs which smelled of boiled cabbage and urine. Unlocking a door in the rear of the building, she opened it, bent, brought out a candle and lit it, striking a match on the door frame. "Better than electricity," she explained. "More romantic, dig? Cheaper too."

She shut the door behind him.

He stared in amazement. The two-alcove apartment was swathed everywhere with old fabric—lace tablecloths draped the doors, chenille bedspreads swooped overhead, the walls were covered in antique velvet draperies which were flounced and swagged. It was like being inside a child's makeshift tent. The heat was oppressive, the smell musty, as if an old trunk just had been opened up. He felt trapped.

Silver was lighting more candles. "Clear a spot over there and park your butt."

He moved to the sagging couch-bed and started making room for himself. "You're into old movie magazines I see." He placed a pile on the floor next to still another towering stack and lowered himself to sit.

"I was raised on them," she said, putting her guitar case on the mantel of the false fireplace. "My mom worked in a beauty shop. Brought home all the ol' ones. Back in Bountiful. Ever hear of it? Bountiful, Utah?"

He shook his head with a minimum of movement.

She laughed huskily, plopping herself on the floor to pull off a scruffy boot. "Only thin' bountiful in my life was the fan mags. I dreamed on 'em. Wanted to grow up just like Doris Day. Or maybe Cara Noor."

He shifted uncomfortably.

"'Cept Noor was always too sexy. I wanted to be clean-cut, wholesome, just like Doris Day. Can you dig that?'' She giggled and yanked off the other zippered boot. "Shit, wish I had me a number to smoke. I'm so flat-assed broke, can't even afford that.''

"I don't like getting stoned.''

"Well, hell, man, no wonder you're so uptight. Just look at you. Sittin' there like a bomb's tickin' under your ass.''

It was true. He was feeling unbelievably tense. He wanted to get on with persuading her, but he was trying to cool it for a while. He knew at times he had a tendency to push too hard. But dammit, he always knew what he wanted and until it was his, nothing else mattered.

She scooted on her buttocks across the faded carpet toward him. "You got the prettiest brown eyes. And the nicest olive skin. Natural California tan, huh? Hey, how old are you?''

"Twenty-three.''

"You raised in California?''

"L.A.''

"L.A.'s a big town. Where 'bouts in L.A.?'' She took off her glasses and leaned forward. The bodice of her black gown fell open, fully exposing her small white breasts. They were pointed like funnels.

He pulled his focus from them, answering reluctantly, "Beverly Hills.''

"Honest to gawd, really? Oh wow! Know any movie stars?''

He squirmed, looking toward the door. "A few. Assholes all.''

"Like who, huh?''

"I don't want to talk about that crap.''

"Aw, com'on. Give a girl a thrill, will ya?'' She squeezed his knee, causing him to look at her face.

Her eyes were the palest blue he had ever seen: striking, unique, arresting; set in a pale, angular face that was not unattractive, just different. "Hey, Davey, how come you don' wanna talk about them movie stars?''

"I hate the place, that's all.''

"What was your last name again?''

"Rau," he said.

"Like in 'wow?' "

"Yeah. Look—"

"The Wow Girl! You any relation to her? She was big in the forties. Pretty lady, dark, exotic-looking, like you. She was 'Rau' too... Hey, Davey, don't pull away. I won't bite." She placed both arms on his knees and leaned her chin on them, peering up, pinning him down. "Oh, yeah, I remember now. Nedra... Nedra Rau. She was one of my mom's all-time favorites. You any relation to her? That Nedra Rau?"

He did not want to answer. Why should he? Why tell this spacey chick things he'd never dared tell anyone? And yet, she did seem to get off on all that Hollywood bullshit. He cleared his throat and said, "Nedra Rau was my mother."

"Gawdamn," she roared. "Imagine that! Nedra Rau's son. Right here in my very own livin' room. My mom would bust a gut. Hey, wasn't Nedra Rau married to some big hot-shot producer? Wha'ever happened to her anyway?"

"She died." He pushed her arms off his knees and stood. "Look, I want you to sing with my band. There's a music explosion going on out on the Coast. Record companies are snapping up groups right and left."

"I'm a single. Just gettin' started here," she said and stood, gathering the folds of her long black skirt in one pale hand. "Want some vino? Think I got me some left."

He nodded absently. "Nothing will happen here for you."

"Says who?" She was in the front alcove, bending into the refrigerator, grabbing a half full bottle of red wine.

"I know the music scene backward and forward. I grew up in sound studios. I've been reading the charts since I was nine. I know what sells and what's going to sell. Solo folk acts are dead."

"Tell that to Dylan." She grabbed a couple of small jam jars.

"He's yet to sell a million units, did you know that? That whole genre has been played out. People want a change, something gutsy, less esoteric, something immediate, that hits them in the groin, not the head."

"Sounds like you're pushin' roller derby." She began pouring.

"*Goddammit, I know what I'm talking about!*" He grabbed the offered jar of wine. "You think I'd risk my whole future by making wrong choices? Believe me, I've done my homework."

She shrugged, sipping from her glass and sinking cross-legged onto the rug. He paced the far end of the room. "You want to play in asshole joints the rest of your life? How many people did you reach in your two shows tonight? Give me a rough estimate." He halted to take a swallow. The wine was sour, flat.

"Who cares how many?" she asked. "I get off on it anyway. Don't make no diff how many people hear me. *I* hear me."

"Don't give me that shit. You want to be a star. You know damned well you do. You want to play to packed auditoriums. Five, ten, fifteen thousand screaming fans hanging onto your every note, your every move. Record albums with your name splashed all over them. Stacked by the hundreds in stores across the country. Limousines at your beck and call. The best hotel suites. Champagne, instead of this cheap rotgut." He flipped his jam jar and the remaining wine shot out, splashing into the false fireplace.

Her eyes flicked back from the red droplets. "You always so fuckin' dramatic?"

"Damn right I am," he said, his voice rising in pitch. "It galls the hell out of me to see a great talent like you wasting away, playing shitty guitar, singing shitty songs in a shitty hole. You have the best damn rock voice of any chick I've heard. And believe me, for weeks now, I've been schlepping around to every cheap club on both coasts trying to find it. Silver, you've got what I want. And when I want something, I get it, come hell or high water."

She did not move, merely stared back as if watching a show.

In a burst of anger, he gripped her bare arms and yanked her to her feet, spilling her wine. "Dammit, listen to me. How much are you making? Answer me. How much did you make tonight?"

"Eleven bucks."

"Eleven bucks! I can't believe it. You want to go on playing to a handful of people for a lousy eleven bucks a night?"

She looked down passively at his hands which still clamped her upper arms. "That hurts, man."

He let go and began pacing again. "I just don't understand people like you. It's like you're *afraid* of making it. You feel more comfortable sitting on your ass dreaming about it. Hoping. Like a bolt of lightning. Zap! You're a success." He whirled to face her, his complexion darkening even more, his eyes shooting sparks. "Well bullshit, baby, bullshit! Nobody gets there without working and sweating and crying and making it happen. You get there by fighting, clawing, stomping your way up. You get there by taking chances, putting yourself out on a fucking limb, knowing when to play by the rules and when to break them. But you get there. Whatever and however you do it, you get there, because, baby, there isn't anything else."

She rubbed her pale arms, hugging them close to her lean, stringy body. He could tell she was close to tears. When he spoke again, his voice was purposely calm, almost gentle.

"You need me, Silver. I can do all the fighting and squawking, the pushing and shoving, the planning, the choices, the deals. It takes all that to build a career. To make it happen and make it last. There isn't anything I don't know about the business of making it. And I'm going to make it. I'm going to be the biggest motherfucker in the whole goddamned music world. I've always known it, believed it, trusted it. I want you to trust it too."

He reached out and touched her shoulder. She shuddered slightly. He forced a smile, again softening his voice. "I can make you a star, Silver. Bigger, brighter, more famous than anything you ever dreamed of in Bountiful-pissing-Utah." He ran his hand gently down her arm. "Want to be a star?"

She gazed at him without blinking. "I want you to fuck me." Her hands crossed to her opposite shoulders. With one push on the bodice straps, the gown fell to the floor with a soft hiss. She was totally nude.

His eyes moved down the pallor of her thin body. From the circle of black velvet at her feet, her frame rose like a white stamen out of the petals of a dark flower. Other than the large contrasting circles of dusky pink around each nipple, there was no other color on her entire body. Not even between her legs. The protruding fullness there was pale, hairless, shaven clean.

He hesitated. "Silver, I . . . this sure as hell isn't any way to start a business relationship."

She lay down on the black circle, reaching up for him. "I don't do business with no strangers."

He appraised her, coldly, objectively. "And I never fuck the help."

Laughing throatily, she dropped her arms. "Hell, man, I ain't workin' for you yet."

"You *will* be."

"Depends on how good you is." Her bony fingers kneaded her already erect nipples.

Jesus, what he had to go through to get what he wanted.

He unbuckled his Gucci belt.

REBECCA
July 1966
New York

"Next!"

Each time she heard it, she wanted to turn and flee, but forced herself to move forward. One more pace, one step closer to the stage—and the agony.

She tossed a quick glance over her shoulder. The line of girls stretched behind her, zigzagging out to the alley, around huge pieces of scenery parked until the next performance. *What suckers we are. Some producer dangles a role and look what happens. Hundreds of us, all hoping, praying—as if we'd die if we don't get it. The pits.*

"Next!"

She inched around the corner of the giant red-carpeted staircase aware that on it, Carol Channing had become a legend as Dolly. Now Ginger Rogers was getting the standing ovations. And Rebecca was reminded that she'd never become a successful, working actress unless she could make it through an audition. And as tough as it was, auditions were becoming a hell of a lot easier than facing her life as a seventeen-year-old nobody.

"Next!"

That jarred her so, without thinking, she took a step ahead with the others. Concentrating on those girls she could see, she tried reading their faces. Did they have it more together than she did? Dammit, most of them looked like finalists for Miss America. How could she possibly compete with them? Like the redhead in front of her. Stacked, huh? I could play her kid brother.

Rebecca tapped the redhead on the shoulder and whispered, "Do you think he's out there?"

The lovely redhead turned and stared down. "Who?"

"Mister Broadway . . . David Merrick?"

"That's what I hear," the redhead said, her voice a melody.

"Never thought I'd make it this far. Kind'a scary, huh?"

The beauty smiled calmly. "Nothing to it. They just want to take a look at us. See how we move and talk, that's all."

"You've been through this a lot?"

"Not in New York. I just got in from Cleveland yesterday."

Rebecca blinked back in amazement. "You did? I mean, wow, you seem so cool, you know?"

The redhead with the creamy complexion smiled confidently. "What's to be nervous about? It's not an audition. It's an interview. They don't want to see talent now. Just if you look the part."

Rebecca smiled gamely. "Well, if they want gorgeous, you've got it for sure. If I weren't so talented, I'd be jealous."

Behind her, an alto voice piped up. "It's already cast by now anyway."

Rebecca whirled in disbelief. "No way!"

Coldly the blonde's pencil-thin eyebrows arched upward. "This is just sop they throw Equity to meet their union contracts. They already know who they want."

"Next!"

Rebecca moved up to Number-two spot. An icy hand was squeezing her intestines. Quickly she closed her eyes and said a prayer. Please, please, please, let me do my best, huh? Let me knock

Merrick's heart in his mouth. Let him see that I'm perfect for the part . . . nobody but me. Let me be so good, so special he'll say— "That's the one. *That's* the one I want."

A flash interrupted her prayer—a sudden image of Erik Lungren picking up the *New York Times* and reading Walter Kerr's review: "A blazing new star was born last night on Broadway. Rebecca Parlato totally eclipsed the rest of the superb cast." *That* would show Erik wouldn't it? Then he wouldn't dare treat her like last night.

"Next!"

With eyes tightly closed, she stepped forward to become Number one.

"You okay?"

"Wha'?" Her eyes popped open.

A boyish-looking man stood before her. "You feeling all right?"

"Yeah, sure," she mumbled.

"Just walk out to the mark by the light and speak up." He smiled encouragingly at her.

She nodded and tried to return it, but he disappeared again. She felt like a silly child caught playing an adult game. Like last night at Erik's. Furious at herself for thinking of it, she took a small step forward, forcing herself to peer out onto part of the darkened stage. She could only see a half moon of yellow light falling on the floor, in its center the elongated shadow of the redheaded girl. She heard a rumble of a voice ask a question, then a low, melodic response.

A spasm wrenched her insides. It was one thing to go out there and act, but totally different to stand out there and be herself. What the hell would they ask? What'd they be looking for? Dammit, how could she possibly convince them she was talented . . . just by talking?

Holding her green-cloth book bag straight out, she squatted and did a couple of deep knee bends. Despite the cold hand clutching her stomach, she felt calmer. Despite her pounding heart and the dryness in her throat, she was ready as she would ever be.

"Next!"

She took a deep breath and stepped out into the darkness. The pool of light flickered briefly as the previous girl walked out of it and vanished. Like a moth to a flame, Rebecca moved toward the brightness. It came from a single yellow worklight in a wire-mesh basket on a metal stand.

Silence all around her. She entered the warm circle of light, found the mark in masking tape on the floor and put both feet firmly on it. She raised her head, one hand brushing back the bangs from her eyes.

Blackness. Silence. Except her pounding heartbeat.

"Rebecca Parlato? Am I pronouncing that correctly?"

The deep, rumbling voice from the darkness startled her. Was that Merrick? It'd sounded exactly like Erik. Oh, God, no! It couldn't be Erik. Not after last night. She couldn't face him after last night. Not after he stood her up! She opened her mouth to answer, but she was so frightened, so confused, an iron door slammed on her consciousness. Her mind went blank. Totally blank.

"Well? Am I saying your name right?"

The light next to her was blinding. She blinked rapidly, struggling to latch onto something, anything inside her head. Desperately she sensed this was wrong, terribly wrong. But her head was a vacuum. There wasn't a word, a thought, a memory.

"Rebecca? Answer me, please."

Her legs were like soft rubber. She felt she was going to pitch forward onto her face.

"Please. Just tell us your name."

Tears started flowing down her cheeks. She could feel them but not name them. She opened her mouth. As if from a distance, she heard a pitiful, moaning sound.

"Jerry, help her off, okay?"

Someone was at her elbow, pulling her. She took a step backward, out of the light, stumbled, almost falling onto the arm that tugged her.

"*Next!*"

Like a switch suddenly turned "on," her mind snapped back, flooding her with the vivid, terrifying reality of the moment. Oh my god, oh my god, what've I done? Wrenching free, she started to run. A red exit light was before her. A door beneath it. She slammed against it. From somewhere came a burst of laughter. The door would not open. The wave of nausea began to rise from the pit of her stomach until it was choking the back of her throat. Again and again she slammed her shoulder against the metal.

Suddenly the door flew open and she spilled out into the alley.

For hours, she wandered the sweltering, muggy, dense streets of midtown Manhattan, trying to wipe out the horror of her double-dose of humiliation, first at Erik's, then at the Saint James Theater. But tears streamed on until she could not cry anymore. When the ache in her throat became unbearable and her heart about to collapse from pressure weighing on it, she worked up enough nerve to seek out a kindred soul.

In a small patch of welcome shade, she stood across from NBC's Studio Forty-seven, scrutinizing every exiting person, hoping that she had not missed him after his daily taping. When finally he appeared, "Hey, Robby!" she shouted at the top of her lungs. Darting into the street, she dodged the front of a honking taxi and ran toward him. He had stopped in front of the glass doors, squinting at her, a puzzled expression on his elfish face. "Robby," she called out again, slowing to a walk. "It's me, you little pisher."

"Becks?!" he hooted and she felt a flood of warmth at his old nickname for her. Rushing to her with outstretched arms, he caught her in a full embrace and they whirled around in circles in the middle of the sidewalk until she was dizzy.

Releasing her, he stepped back grinning openly. "I thought for sure you were some rabid soap opera fan. Yelling like that."

"Oh, you and your fans, Mister Big-time," she bubbled. "Aren't they all little old ladies with blue hair?"

"You'd be surprised. Some are very young indeed."

"Indeed, is it?" She grinned affectionately. "Same old Robby."

And it was true. Incredibly, Robby looked much the same as when, several years earlier, he'd left Buffalo for Broadway. Even smaller than she, he was blessed with a gorgeous head of light blond hair which hugged his head in a mass of tight ringlets. And eyes as blue as robins' eggs. Though he was only nineteen, his face was an odd mixture of youth and age—like an ageless elf of the Black Forest, she thought.

"So Becks, what're you up to? It's been months and months. Why didn't you call again like you promised? I thought for sure you'd died, or worse, gone back to Lackawanna. You Equity yet?''

She ducked her head, glancing down at his glossy brown loafers with the bright, shiny pennies, remembering that his mother always polished his shoes every night after he went to bed. ''I've been trying, really, you know? It's just...oh hell, Robby, I don't know...''

He took her arm, steering her toward the intersection. ''Becks, you're too talented not to be working. Remember that kids' play we did in that Buffalo park? Even then, you had that special something.'' He laughed. ''I always did have an eye for talent.''

''Especially your own,'' she teased.

''Well, as they say, if you don't toot your own horn, no one else will.'' He stepped smartly to the curb, raised an arm and signaled an approaching cab. He tilted his blond head to her. ''Come on, I'll give you a lift, Where you going?''

''My digs. Near Broadway and Ninety-eighth.''

''About as close to Buffalo as you could get, huh?'' He threw open the passenger door of the taxi and motioned her forward. ''I'll drop you off at Columbus Circle.''

Gratefully she slipped into the cab. As it pulled out into traffic, she realized how much she had missed his energy. It seemed to radiate out of his pores like a powerful scent. Even as a kid, he'd had that effect on her, and now, once again, that energy was filling her own very drained cup.

His eyes sparkled with a mischievous twinkle, like any second he would do something really outlandish, maybe even devilish, yet thoroughly enjoying himself the whole while. ''When was your last audition?''

The rawness around her heart began anew. ''This...this morning.''

''Oh yes, the new Burrows comedy at the Saint James. How'd you do?''

''Zilch.''

''Why?''

''Who knows?''

''If *you* don't, no one does,'' he snapped. ''Spill it.''

She hemmed for a moment, scooting down into the seat on her tailbone, not wanting to relive that horrible experience. ''I froze.''

"Why?"

Again she shrugged, pretending to be absorbed in the cab's route.

"Rebecca," he began, all business. "You've got to learn to be objective about these things. How are you going to grow if you don't examine and study what you're doing and how you're doing it and why you're doing it? That's part of our craft too."

He sounded as if he were angry with her and she remembered how mad he used to get at her for being unprofessional even when they'd been kids. Then he had left for New York to become a working actor, and had been at it since the age of eight. Now he was pinning her down with demanding eyes. "So what happened, Becks?"

"Well to tell the truth," she started, searching for words. "It...see, I met this guy."

He groaned, flopping back into the seat.

"Robby, please, don't hate me for this...it...well, it was something really special, you know? I'd never felt that way before ...ever. Like I'd known him before. And the guy's really famous and—"

He sat up, suddenly all ears. "Who?"

She shook her head. "I can't. Not fair to him, you know?"

"Come on, Becks. No secrets, remember?"

She hugged her book bag for protection. "I can't. Really, who the guy *is* doesn't make any difference. It was just...well, last night, we had a date...and he didn't show up. I waited six hours for him at his place, practically going crazy, and—"

"What's he famous for?"

"He writes," she hedged.

"Norman Mailer," Robby said, as if he knew.

"No way. Look it was just a one night thing, you know? But I got kind of silly about him. And—"

"Tom Wolfe?" he cut in eagerly. "Salinger? Not Philip Roth?"

"Dammit, Robby, will you listen to me? I'm trying to tell you what happened."

"It's fairly obvious what happened," he said with a large degree of sarcasm. "You let your personal life interfere with your career."

Silently she twisted the strap of her book bag, her defensiveness melting. "I suppose you're right," she finally said. "You know, I should've realized I was wasting my time by the third phone call."

"From the mysterious writer?"

"No. From those women who kept calling his place." She paused, before adding dryly, " 'Chippies' my mom would call them."

His laugh was infectious. She basked in it, turning her face toward the warmth as if it were the sun. It made Erik and the Saint James seem far, far away. She moaned broadly. "Guess I'll never learn. Anyhow, I was so bummed out, I just couldn't keep my head straight."

Robby leaned forward to adjust his suit jacket. "Everyone's scared at auditions, Becks. Some just hide it better. Each one you go through will get easier. Hey, I'm up for a really big part in a legit Broadway musical."

"Really? That's super. You must have a terrific agent."

"A real schmuck. I'm the one who does the hustling. And Mother, she's a real whiz at sniffing out the scene. I don't suppose you have an agent yet, do you?"

"Are you kidding? You can't get an agent without having a part locked up and you can't even get *into* most of the auditions without an agent. Vicious circle, huh?"

"I'll see if I can help you out on that."

"You will? Robby, that'd be sensational, really."

He beamed at her. "Didn't I promise you—someday, we'd be stars? Well, it'll happen, Becks. You've got to start believing that again. I swear it'll happen. For both of us." He squeezed her hand reassuringly and leaned toward the driver. "You can let me out on the next corner and take her on up Broadway."

"Oh, Robby, no . . . I can catch the subway really. It's faster. Cheaper, too."

He jerked to her. "You're going to do as I say from now on. Now listen, Zack, my acting teacher, is tops. And he's starting a new term next month. I think you better be in it."

"Geez, Robby, if I have to audition, I'll probably blow it."

"*See*, that's the attitude that defeats you. You have to want something so bad, you persevere until you overcome all your insecurities. Now, do you want it?''

"Yes, yes! I want it. Boy, and how do I want it. I want it so bad I can taste it. Phew! It tastes like dead flies, but I want it."

He laughed outright. "Okay, I'll put in a good word for you with Zack. He adores me."

"Who doesn't? You're so damned cute it makes me wanna puke."

His pixie face beamed. "Ain't it the truth. Here..." He reached into his coat pocket and drew out some bills. "For the cab." He leaned over, kissing her cheek loudly. "*Now* you going to tell me who's the writer?"

She made a frightened face, recoiling like a heroine from the villain in a silent movie. "My lips are sealed, sir."

"All right for you, Becks. I won't forget this," he growled with mock menace, then threw her a gleaming smile and bounced out of the taxi.

"Bye, Robby," she called out, slamming the door. She rolled down the window. "Thanks. I love you, you little pisher you."

He waddled away like Chaplin. The cab moved into the mainstream of vehicles. She waved until he was out of sight, then swiveled forward, still holding the bills. With each block that zipped past her window, his encouragement echoed in her ears. Her body began tingling with excitement, new hopes generating deep within by his enthusiastic support.

She glanced down at the fist of money. Quickly she counted the bills. Fifty dollars! He'd laid all that on her for a five-buck cab ride. Her excited whoop startled the driver. She waved the money at him until he was laughing too.

ERIK
July 1966
New York

He was swaying. He could tell because the view of his boots kept shifting back and forth. The toes hung out over the edge of the curb. From the dimmest regions of his mind, consciousness flickered. It wanted to know where he was. The rest of his mind was too numbed to answer. He raised his eyes and blinked in the harsh sunlight.

He found himself standing on the east edge of Washington Square. Across the street was a graystone building of New York University. Students streamed up and down the front steps. How appropriate to end up here, Erik thought. How bloody appropriate. Watching that same doorway was an end of a circle that had begun years before. Ironic.

Shifting his gaze upward, he located the sun. It was far behind him in the west. Late afternoon. He had lost a whole day. The movement of his head abruptly exploded fireworks of color before his eyes. He winced. Yet before that pain had subsided, another took its place. Only this one was not in his head. It felt like icy needles were stabbing his heart. He had remembered what he had been trying to forget. Max Lerner had dropped him. His longtime editor and friend had told him that *Rogues and Scoundrels* was not worth piss, let alone publishing.

He leaned back against a tree trunk and lowered his large frame to sit on the dirt. To keep his mind off the consuming pain, he studied the students. He envied them at that moment. He had not been able to stay through high school—after the death of his father, he had had to quit in order to pay off debts as the sole surviving Lungren. His education had been entirely from the thousands of books he had read—and five years of bumming and working around the states at jobs ranging from logging in Alaska to coal-mining in West Virginia, from being a shrimp tender

45

in the Gulf of Mexico to a barker in a strip joint in Chicago.

And dammit, he thought suddenly, his *was* the superior education. He wouldn't trade places with these kids for anything. He hated his bouts of self-pity and the booze that always brought it on. He stood up and found a drinking fountain, momentarily quenching his thirst. The sun beat down. He tore off his sweaty corduroy coat. Try as he might, he could not remember much after leaving Max's office the previous afternoon. He did recall a bar somewhere. A Village bar. He must have taken a subway downtown—yes, now he could place it, the White Horse. Dylan Thomas's old haunt. How apropos. Getting blind drunk in a bar made famous by a blind drunk.

He closed his eyes, remembering himself under that very tree seven years earlier. Only twenty-two then, his hair sun-bleached by a harvest sun, his skin deeply tanned. He had just hitchhiked straight from the Kansas wheatfields. At his feet then was his knapsack with everything he owned, but most importantly his polished manuscript of *Bell of Donna*. That time so long ago, Erik had also been waiting, watching, for the same man. A man he had hoped would help him.

Erik had first heard about Michael McKitrick in Ann Arbor at a poetry reading by Allen Ginsberg. The beat poet had called him a nurturing writer and teacher, better than any agent. When Erik had arrived in New York, determined to be published, determined to make a name for himself in the literary world, he had come straight to NYU to find McKitrick.

Each day Erik had encamped on this very spot, waiting until McKitrick's English classes were finished. Each day, Erik had pestered the man to read his novel. Eventually McKitrick had promised to read it just to get rid of him. Less than a week later, McKitrick himself had taken Erik to meet Max Lerner. Michael McKitrick had been indispensable as a critic on the first novel and had stayed on to become his best friend.

Now, that afternoon, Erik felt cold sober by the time he spotted Michael, walking down the steps with the bent-shouldered stoop of a man too long over a desk. Michael was almost frail-looking, with straight, longish brown hair receding sharply at the temples. He dressed as casually as the students and his boyish face was creased with a perpetual frown as if he had forgotten something important.

Erik stood with an effort and stepped forward. Michael, cutting across the street, saw him and hurried up. "Holy Mother of God, you look like warmed-over death." He shifted his books to the other hand and offered the free one.

Erik slapped it halfheartedly and they headed into the park. An odd pair, he thought, the younger one, big and broad; the older, small and frail—the younger defeated; the older still fighting.

"Max called me yesterday morning," Michael began, trying to keep up with Erik's long strides. "Said it was the toughest decision he's ever made."

"Wish you had forewarned me."

"He asked me not to. Wanted to tell you personally. He sounded pretty upset."

"That makes two of us."

"No, three, Erik."

Erik looked away quickly. The rush of warmth for his friend at that moment engulfed him. They were rounding the circular fountain; the splash of its water was drowned out by street musicians improvising a bongo-based riff. Erik waited until the sound of the percussive jazz began to fade. "Seven times I was in his office . . . nothing but encouragement—how great it was going, how pleased he was with the progress. Then suddenly he throws it in the trashcan."

They reached the other end of the park. Michael glanced both ways and steered him across the street. "Look, everything boils down to economics. Publishing is just another business. His decision probably has nothing to do with your book. Set it aside, get some distance. Come at it fresh."

Stepping up on the sidewalk, Erik stopped. "Michael, I don't know if I can."

"Listen, my friend. Talent doesn't just dry up and blow away. It's there—all the time. It merely gets buried. And you know what by? Fear. Plain, simple fear."

"Yeah, I'll admit it. I'm terrified. Do I have it in me?"

"You're pushing too hard. You can't lay all those expectations and needs on the end of a creative piece of work. It's hard enough without all that."

Erik noted Michael's concern and, wanting to lighten the mood, feigned a right hook to his friend's chin. Suddenly he felt exhausted. It swept over him like a north wind and numbed him to the bone. His arms dropped. "Michael, would you read it for me? Let me know what *you* think? If you think it's worthless, I'll dump it."

"Been waiting for you to ask me."

Some of the tension eased out of his chest and hope flickered alive. Michael shifted his books again. "Did you read what that retard Nixon said yesterday?" Erik shook his head and Michael continued wryly, "The *Times* quoted our illustrious ex-vice president as urging LBJ to increase the number of GIs in Vietnam to five hundred thousand. God spare us from such leaders."

Erik grunted, lost in his own thoughts, staring across the square at the shadowed marble arch. Michael said quickly at his elbow, "Listen, I don't have to read your novel to know one thing. You're a terrific writer. So don't fight it. If this book needs work. Stop stewing. It'll come. They're all born in their own timing." Michael waved up at the large brownstone apartment building before them. "Come up for some coffee. Maureen will be home from rehearsal soon."

"Naw . . . I don't feel like dumping in your living room."

Michael chuckled. "Lately, it's been Maureen dumping the loads. Her TV job is driving her around the bend. Come on up. The twins would love to see you."

He arched his back. Tenseness knotted his shoulderblades. "Thanks, anyway, Michael." He started to move away, then paused to cuff Michael lightly on the shoulder. "Thanks, buddy. I'll get you a copy of my last draft." He turned to go.

Michael called after him. "There's a peace rally in Bryant Park on Saturday. Want to join me?"

Wearily Erik waved an arm, but did not turn back.

In the vestibule, he unlocked the mail box and dug out his mail—mostly bills. At the bottom, he saw a key. Perplexed, he picked it up. It looked like his own. Checking his keyring, he remembered. That girl—he'd given his key to that black-eyed actress, Rebecca. Hell, he had forgotten all about her. And he had told her to wait for him.

The phone was ringing when he let himself into his apartment. He hurried to the bedroom to answer it and stopped short. The room was spotless—bed made, clothes picked up, books stacked neatly. A note was on his pillow. The handwriting small, controlled.

Dear Mr. Lungren,
While you were out, the following called:

1) Ginny at 6:42 PM
2) Carole at 7:19
3) Carole again at 10:35

I told them I was your housekeeper.

Yours truly, A Fan

P.S. You're out of sink cleanser.

Erik sank back on the bed. Damn, damn, damn, he hadn't once remembered her. So wrapped up in himself. He struggled to recall her last name. His phone was irritatingly insistent with its rings. Hoping it might be Rebecca, he picked up the receiver. "Hello?"

"Erik?" The woman's voice was plainly exasperated.

"Oh hi, Mo. Just left your husband."

"Erik, you sonofabitch, where're the rewrites?"

He rubbed his face, thinking, then remembered his former promise, given in a burst of drunken goodwill. "Damn, Mo. I just haven't gotten around to it."

"Look, Erik," she said, making no effort to cover her irritation. "If you remember correctly, it was *you* who asked me if I had something you might do to pick up a few extra bucks. Well, I came through on my end. Last week, if you remember, I gave you a check for two hundred and fifty dollars. Just for a simple polishing job. The other half was guaranteed when you delivered. Am I right so far, Erik?"

"Yeah, Maureen, I know. I promised. But something heavy's been going down and I . . . I'll get it to you."

"When?" It was a crisp demand. "This ex-movie queen, Cara Noor, is driving me bananas bitching about her lines. Not to mention her husband, Irving R. Dyer—who happens to be one of the heaviest turkeys I've ever dealt with. He made us paint her dressing room twice before allowing her to come to rehearsal. He threatened to fly Gore Vidal in from Rome but I told them we already had a damn fine writer polishing them.''

"You didn't mention my name?"

"Don't worry, Erik," she said with more than a tinge of sarcasm. "Your precious reputation is inviolate. However, Dyer's about ready to yank Noor as hostess from this damned meat parade unless I come up with some witty, bright remarks for her."

Using his feet, he slipped off a boot. "Okay, okay, got the picture. I'll get them to you as soon as I can. I promise."

"Baby, you come through and I'll personally get one of these bimbo beauties to give you the best head you've ever had."

"Bread's harder to get."

She laughed. It was full, husky, warm. "Someday, if you ever want to write a book about a beauty pageant, believe me, I've got stories that'd turn your curly hair straight. See you tomorrow morning, okay?"

"I'll try . . . "

"Do more than that, huh? Do it for Michael, and the twins, and for God and for country and for Villa Caesari. But most of all, for me, okay? Eleven years I've bugged Caesari—let me produce something big. So this is it, my big break. I can't afford to blow it."

"Maybe I *will* ask for my pick of the beauties."

"Settle for the bread. It'll last longer." She clicked off.

He replaced the receiver and fell backward on the bed, staring blankly at the print on the wall of *Venus Rising from the Sea*. What had he done with Mo's silly script?

The final chapter. Maybe that's what had thrown Max. The climax too obscure. Not concrete enough. Perhaps a fresh approach. He pushed himself up and walked into the front room to his desk. His body felt like he had just rowed to Maine and back, but he sat down before his typewriter. He rolled in a clean piece of paper. The last chapter . . . where to begin?

He silently repeated his favorite Hemingway writing maxim, the one that had seen him through many a bleak, barren spell of creativity: "You have always written before and you will write now. All you have to do is write one true sentence. Write the truest sentence you know."

He thought carefully. The truest sentence he knew. Then his
fingers curved over the keys and he typed:
    I want to be a winner again.

DAVID
July 1966
New York

With a hand on the small of her back, he pushed Silver ahead,
allowing her to go first into the dimly lit, enormous, green and gold
restaurant in the sky. Tables covered in white, glowing softly under
individual green-shaded lamps, terraced a parquet dance floor. On two
sides, the glass walls, draped by heavy green velvet, offered a stunning
panoramic view of Manhattan by night, but David was not only
unimpressed, he was pissed. In spite of his fifty-dollar tip to the maître
d', they were being led to a table all the way in the rear, right next to
the kitchen's swinging doors. Tensely, he kept his eyes on the waiter's
back, extremely aware of the titters their entrance was causing.

And why not? Silver wore a full-length, thirties evening gown,
once silver lamé, now tarnished and tacky looking. On her pale arms,
long black opera gloves, but with several buttons missing; on her halo
of white hair, a cheap rhinestone tiara. But nobody could have
mistaken her for the duchess of Windsor.

They arrived at their designated table. The big doors nearby
swung with a steady *thunk-thunk* as waiters constantly arrived,
disappeared and reappeared with full trays. "Enjoy yourselves," the
waiter said coolly and vanished.

"Ain't you glad we came?"

"No."

"Well, thanks a heap, man." She bent forward to read the menu
over the top of her dark glasses. "Wow! Top-dog prices, huh, man?"
Thunk-thunk. Thunk-thunk, went the door behind him.

"Order anything you like," he said, attempting to be pleasant. Carefully placing the menu aside, he glanced around as casually as he could. People were still staring.

Well, why not. She's a freak. A goddamn, genuine, one hundred percent, twenty-four-carat freak. But hell, if she causes this much attention just walking into a joint, imagine what the kids will do when she sings. They'll tear the fucking walls down.

"You mad at me?" She was pulling off her gloves.

Thunk-thunk. Thunk-thunk.

Her plaintive tone irritated him. "Look, Silver, you wanted the Rainbow Grill. Here it is. I hate the goddamn place. I hated seeing the musical *Man of La Mancha* but you dig that stupid song, "The Impossible Dream" so I took you. I hated the Circle Line Tour of Manhattan. But you wanted to go on a boat ride. I told you, anything you wanted, this is your day, Silver. But I'm warning you. I leave for San Francisco on the red-eye."

Their waiter was approaching so David changed the subject. "Have you decided what you want?"

"What're you havin'?" She sounded like a child.

"Steak sandwich and a Coke."

"I'll have a cheeseburger an' a Bloody Mary."

David gave the order curtly to the waiter who departed into the kitchen. *Thunk-thunk.* He tried a smile, his features set into a quasi-agreeable mode. "Why'd you pick this place anyway?"

"Since I was a lil' knob of a girl back even before Bountiful, in Arkansas, my granddad tol' me 'bout it a lot, he was here durin' the war, always called it the top of the line." She glanced up quickly over her glasses to see his reaction.

He felt like laughing, but kept his face straight. "So, you wanted to be a singer here?"

"Yeah . . . that's why I done come to New York in the first place. To sing at the top o' the line. First thin' I done when I got off the bus was to come up here. But they wouldn't even let me in to look 'round."

"Why not?"

"No bread, I guess. Or maybe, I was too young. I forget."

"How old were you then?"

"Eighteen."

So that made five years, he thought. Five shitty years she's been kicking around this town trying to make it as a singer. His anger was subsiding. She was kind of pitiful, not knowing in which direction her true talents lay. With her "belt 'em out voice," she wanted to chirp like Doris Day.

One of the *thunks* from the swinging doors produced their order. The plates and drinks were set before them. Silver immediately poured steak sauce all over her sandwich, then attacked it with a ravenous gusto.

He cut a small piece of steak and chewing it thoughtfully, looked away, out through the far window at the twinkling lights of the George Washington Bridge. "I guarantee within six months," he said, "we'll be making money. With no sweat. That is, if everyone listens to me and does what I tell them." He forced himself to look at her. "That's in the contract too, remember."

She nodded without looking up from her plate. With those damn glasses he found it impossible to read her eyes anyway. He leaned back in his chair, holding his drink. "Silver, you're going to have to make up your mind. My flight leaves in less than four hours."

"You spring for my plane ticket out?" She gulped some of her drink, washing it around in her mouth before swallowing.

"And back. If you don't work out."

Her fork froze halfway to her mouth. "Wha' the fuck's that mean?"

"If, by chance, the vocal balance with the rest of the group isn't right. I don't want any standouts or stars, just a solid—"

"You mean, I could drop everythin' here—my career, my pad, my friends, everythin', an' go all the way the fuck out there, an' you could dump me. Jus' like that?" She snapped her fingers loudly. Heads turned.

"My professional hunch is you'll work out just fine." He tried to smile reassuringly.

She frowned, turning toward the bandstand. A man was turning on the lamps of the brass musicstands. "They're gettin' ready." She held out a hand. "Look, I'm so excited my old bod's shakin' like a dog shittin' prune pits."

"What do you say, Silver? Sing top of the line joints with us?"

"I gotta take a pee." She was up and out of her chair.

Dammit, she's playing games. The bitch. Gimme, gimme, gimme. A full day's entertainment, a free meal, and then so long, sucker. He watched her weave through the tables causing people to stare after her. He saw their smirks as they joked about her. Phonies. As weird as she was, Silver was genuine. He longed to get out of there, out of New York, back to the one place he felt at ease, where he could pursue his far-ranging plans.

Shortly, he glanced up. Silver was hurrying back to the table, her pale face flushed and excited-looking. "My gawd," she moaned, plopping breathlessly into her chair. "Guess who's in the ladies' john?"

"Lawrence Welk."

"Naw, Cara Noor! No lie. She was at the mirror talkin' to some lady 'bout some beauty pageant. I was so goosed I 'bout peed on the floor."

She prattled on, unaware of the sudden change in his attitude. At the mention of the star's name, David involuntarily had sat bolt upright, straining to see the entrance to the room. Silver went on and on about Cara Noor, but he was not listening.

Jesus, he thought, if she's here, then *he's* got to be here too. Of all the places in the whole goddamn country, on the same goddamned night!

Silver had paused. "What'sa matter, David? You look like a rat croaked in your shorts."

The lights began to dim. The band struck up a loud fanfare as the master of ceremonies moved to the microphone. David was oblivious. If he were going to make a move, it had better be now. He leaped to his feet and grabbed her wrist forcefully. "We're leaving."

"Wha'?"

He gave her arm a hard tug, nearly dragging her up. "I said we're leaving. *Now!*" He pulled the startled girl to her feet and began yanking her down the aisle.

"But Da-a-a-vid!" she protested above the blare of music. Someone hushed her as they passed a table.

He didn't care if he were making a scene, all he wanted was to get out of there, as fast as possible. With each step, a fierce headache rocketed up the ladder of his spine. He kept his eyes locked on the entrance, determined to get there before he caught sight of the familiar figure.

The band finished an exultant fanfare and the MC oozed into the PA system, "Ladies and Gentlemen, before we begin our final show, it is a great privilege and honor to welcome back to the Rainbow Grill one of our all-time favorites—in town to be the TV hostess for the American Beauty Pageant this Sunday night...Ladies and Gentlemen, *Miss Cara Noor!*"

David's grip on Silver tightened and he quickened his pace. The crowd had burst into a surprised "Oohh!" and were now applauding loudly. All were looking toward the entrance. A spotlight swung to the doorway. The aging but still glamorous, blond star appeared, in form-fitting beige chiffon gown encrusted with sparkling beads, a white fox fur thrown casually over one shoulder. The applause became deafening. She laughed and waved graciously. The MC yelled into the microphone above the applause, "And with her, her husband, famed movie producer, *Irving R. Dyer!*"

David's timing was piss-poor. He realized he should have stayed at the table. The one person he never wanted to see again—the one person who had brought so much pain and anger into his life—the one man who had created a living hell for him—stood directly ahead. But it was too late to turn back. David lowered his head and kept plowing forward, hoping against hope that he would not be seen.

Irving R. Dyer, short, balding, with his trademark long, thick cigar stuck in his mouth at a jaunty angle, strode into the spotlight like he had just won big at the track. His wife, Cara Noor, paused dramatically on the landing leading to the lower floor, milking the applause. Dyer swiveled his head appreciatively to survey the crowd's reaction. His gaze came to rest on the tiara in the bushy white hair of the lady being pulled through the crowd beside him.

David, out of the corner of his eye, could see Dyer's head turned in his direction. His temples flamed with an intense pain, near blinding in intensity. He stumbled into the throng at the main entrance, shoving through into the outer foyer. Behind him, an all-too-familiar voice rasped loudly, "Davey?"

David raced into the foyer toward the down elevator, Silver clutched his hand and streamed along behind, a blur of white and tarnished lamé. The doors on the elevator were closing. His arm shot out, slamming into the narrow space between the doors, forcing them open. He squeezed through the opening and with a strong jerk, yanked her into the crowded elevator, jamming people roughly toward the back.

Across the foyer, through the startled observers, Dyer, his cigar waving in the air, hurried toward the closing doors, crying out, "Davey, dammit!"

Slowly the doors came together, cutting off Dyer's astonished expression. A clammy shudder swept through David.

"That was most uncalled for, young man."

"Fuck off, lady," he shot over his shoulder.

"Well, I *never* . . ." said the shocked matron.

"Well, you should," Silver retorted. "It's a heap o' kicks."

The remainder of the short descent passed in strained silence. His head pounded, sending shockwaves that left him weak. He was aware vaguely that Silver was looking at him out of the corner of her glasses, an expression of shock arching her faint brows.

At the bottom, as soon as the doors opened, he dropped her wrist and careened out into the lobby. She followed close behind, her high heels clicking in staccato bursts on the marble floor.

Outside, the stagnant night air hit him, and he gulped it through his mouth in gasps. His head reeled. Behind him, Silver cried, "Wait! Wait for me, David!"

He did not look back. He was walking swiftly, heading toward Fifth Avenue, shoulders hunched, hands in his slacks' pockets. Now in stocking feet, Silver rustled to his side, carrying the hem of her long skirt and her silver sling-back high heels. "That li'l man with the fat cigar," she began, out of breath. "We runnin' from him?"

He didn't answer. His steps firmed.

She scurried alongside excitedly. "He's that big hot-shot producer, ain't he? I seen him on the Oscars, ain't I? He knows you too, don' he? He called you, Davey! Wow!" She danced ahead, bouncing backward before him. "That's real excitin'. Big Hollywood hoedad like him. Somethin', somethin' Dyer, right? Irving! That's it. Irving R. Dyer! Wait'll Mom hears. She'll mess in her drawers she'll be—"

Silver fell silent and he passed her. A few paces more and she still had not reappeared beside him. Not losing his forward momentum, or moving his head any more than necessary, he swiveled his shoulders to seek her.

She stood in the middle of the sidewalk some distance back, her mouth open, her dark glasses pushed high on her forehead, her eyes large with discovery.

"Come on," he ordered. She did not move. He slowed. "Silver," he warned. Still she did not respond, merely stared at him openmouthed. He stopped and slowly turned. "Goddammit, *come on!*"

She lumbered forward. "I 'member now . . ." Her tone was that of a surprised little girl. "That Dyer guy. He was married to that Nedra Rau, wasn't he, Davey? He's your pa, ain't he?"

He could not control himself. His hand shot out, catching her full across the cheek. Her glasses were knocked askew. She whimpered, falling back. He raised his hand again, checking it at the last instant. "If you ever repeat that to anyone," he said, straining for control. "*Anyone*, you hear me? So help me God, I'll kill you."

Her fingers rubbed the red blotch appearing on her cheek, her light eyes fogged, but her mouth had snapped shut.

After a few stony beats, the rigidity with which he had been holding his slight frame eased and a smile brightened the dark cloud of his face, making him look boyish and charming. "Hey, did I tell you how pretty you look tonight?"

ERIK
July 1966
New York

Backstage of the Odeon Theater, in a small, cluttered office, Erik glanced again at the full-page ad taped to the wall above the TV set.

Someone had torn it from that morning's *New York Times* and it read: *Who will be Sunny? Tonight the world will find out. Nine P.M. Channel 8. Brought to you by Villa Caesari Cosmetics.*

The secretary's voice shrilled outside, "Mo, thank God you're back!" Expectantly, he stood, listening to the hurried exchange in the hall. Soon the office door opened and Mo strode in like a field general. Seeing him, her plain, round face wreathed in surprise.

"How's it going, Mo?"

"Six hours to live on-air and *Herr* Caesari decides the opening segment lacks pizzazz. He wants it revamped completely." She tossed a full clipboard onto her overflowing desk. "*That's* how I'm doing." She yanked off the box jacket of her rust-colored suit and flung it carelessly over the back of the chair. "Switch on the set. No sound."

He reached out and pulled the ON button for the portable TV monitor which sat on a cardboard packing box. The bright, color picture began to fade in. He looked again at Mo—her small eyes were dulled with anxiety, yet her manner was as breezy and as cocksure as always—he was genuinely fond of her; she was a good match for Michael's quiet intellectualism. Erik grinned. "Thought being a big-time producer for Caesari would rate you an office more befitting your position."

She dropped into the chair behind the desk and snorted a burst of ironic air through her nostrils. The phone next to her began ringing. She ignored it, staring at the rehearsal on the monitor with a professional detachment. The TV showed a long shot of the entire stage. Erik thought the metallic silver set with its swooping, graceful ramps looked like a mockup for a futuristic airport terminal.

"Mo," her secretary called in. "Irving R. Dyer again on line two."

"Oh lord, not that son of a bitch again. Tell him I'm following his advice and getting fucked." She lit a cigarette and picked up Erik's rewritten script. "Bless you my son bringing these."

"Sorry they're so late," he began but she was already reading his revisions. He returned his gaze to the monitor. The contestants were being led on stage by a slight, fey-looking man in tennis sneakers. The girls were wearing rehearsal clothes, many had their hair in curlers. The shot was from too far back for Erik to see any of their faces clearly. However, their ripe, young bodies held his interest.

The camera shots became tighter on the girls now. Even without makeup or fully coiffed, it was clearly evident that Caesari had hand-picked each of the contestants. Each seemed lovelier than the last.

Suddenly, Erik was leaning forward. The young woman on the small screen was so spectacularly beautiful he was unaware that he was holding his breath. With light blond hair swept back tightly off her face, high, sculptured cheekbones and almond-shaped, startling green eyes, she reminded him of the print of Botticelli's Venus hanging in his bedroom—classical yet vibrantly alive. As she stared boldly into the camera, she was at once the embodiment of total innocence and seductive sensuality.

His breath expelled in a rush. "Damn, who is *she*?" he asked, not taking his eyes from the screen. The beauty was prancing down the ramp in a bright yellow, stretch jumpsuit like a frisky thoroughbred colt. Her thick braid of blond hair—the color of golden ripe wheat under a harvest sun—bounced against the delicious curve of her buttocks. Her legs were long, her frame willowy, more on the athletic side than the gaunt, *Vogue* image, her breasts were high and surprisingly large for a model. They bounced provocatively under the stretch material.

"What's her name anyway?" he asked, turning to Mo.

"Who?" Mo was bracketing with a black felt pen the new speeches.

"That incredible blonde."

"We have fourteen blondes," she said dryly, not looking up.

"That one with the long braid."

"Shelby," she snorted, as if disapproving. "Shelby Cale. Our wardrobe mistress calls her 'the rich bitch from Virginia.' "

"Damn is she something else to look at."

"Just a piece of eye candy. She's only eighteen, too young for you." Mo stood, dismissing the topic. "Do me a favor and I'll approve your second payment in a flash."

Reluctantly, he brought his attention back to the script. "The rewrites are okay?"

"You may have just saved my ass from the permanent shit list of Irving R. Dyer." She grinned toothily. "You do have an easy, natural way with words. Cara's going to love them. Will you take them to her?"

He shook his head. "I get uptight around stars."

"Even fading ones?"

"Cara Noor was a heavy sexual fantasy of mine—long before I even knew what sex was."

"Tell her that. She needs a boost."

"Why would she need anything I tell her?"

"Because she's married to a turkey who gives her only grief, because she's forty-nine, going on fifty and absolutely terrified of falling on her face in front of forty million viewers in exactly five hours and thirty-eight minutes. And you're a good-looking, if somewhat sloppily dressed, under-thirty stud, that's why. Besides, she's going to love your writing."

He eyed her warily. "You palming her off on me?"

She snatched up her clipboard, voicing huskily, "Erik, baby, would I lie to you—my husband's best buddy, the hero of my twins?"

"If need be."

She burst out with a short, hard laugh. "Just do it, huh? I've a zillion and one things before air." She tore open the door and paused, holding out the script to him.

He raised a flat palm. "One condition. I soothe Cara, I get an introduction to Shelby."

"Stick with Cara, baby. *She* know's what she wants."

Reluctantly Erik knocked on the theater's "Star" dressing room door. An elderly black maid answered and asked his name. "Erik . . . Watson," he quickly improvised and explained the purpose of his visit. In too short of a time, he and Cara Noor were left alone together in her luxurious dressing room. Awkwardly, he stood across the bright yellow and white room. The smell of fresh paint hung in the heavily perfumed air.

Cara had barely greeted him before sinking to a white wicker chaise longue full of plump yellow pillows and diving into his rewrites as if he had just offered water to a parched survivor of Death Valley.

While she read, he surreptitiously scrutinized her, trying to find something about the woman which would evoke the feelings he'd had for her when he was a daydreaming adolescent. Yes, she was still enormously attractive reclining there in her pink satin dressing gown with matching pompom slippers. Even with the heavily sprayed hair and the small pair of reading glasses, which she had put on almost shyly, the fabulous face which had graced a dozen or more of her husband's movies looked like an expertly touched-up photo of her former self. The full-breasted body which had fed his pubescent fantasies was even more endowed now, giving her a squatter, less well-proportioned silhouette. Her whole manner, in fact, seemed forced, rehearsed, as if she were doing a whiskey-parody of herself.

He glanced away to cover his disappointment. Somehow fantasies were not supposed to age, he thought—by their definition, a fantasy should remain unaltered by time, unaffected by the humdrum, petty pains of life.

Cara placed the script aside and slipped off her glasses. She leaned seductively on the side cushion, crossing her legs so that the satin robe fell open, discreetly revealing a tanned calf muscle. Unabashedly her eyes traveled up his long frame, pausing ever so slightly on his crotch before moving up to meet his gaze. "My, my, my," she murmured. "You're better looking than some of my leading men."

For a moment, he wondered if she really expected him to believe that. To cover his discomfort, he scratched his neck under the collar of his blue workshirt. "What'd you think of the rewrites?"

"Oh, those," she said, then flashed a tantalizing smile. "Positively charming, darling. Witty, warm. You may have just rescued me from the greatest humiliation of my life."

"My pleasure, ma'am," he mumbled, unsure of what was in the air.

"Darling, I've been waiting for over two months for something as good as this. Really, you have a lovely talent," she said hurriedly and rose. "I haven't really thanked you properly yet for coming up with such amusing things for me to say."

She moved slowly past him—so close he could smell the spray which lacquered her champagne blond hair into an unmovable mass, also the unmistakable odor of gin. Only when he heard her click the lock on the door behind him did he understand the purpose of her staging.

He watched Cara glance into the three-sided vanity mirror on her return to the longue, as if checking out her own desirability at that moment. She sank languidly onto the cushions and looked up through her thick, false eyelashes. "Come here, Erik," she whispered. He hesitated. "Well, come on," she urged softly. "Don't be shy." He advanced a couple of steps, trying to think of a quick way out. "Closer," she whispered.

One more step brought the toes of his boots under the chaise. He realized he was grinning foolishly. A small hand reached out and touched the heavy, silver buckle of his belt. "That's pretty. Navajo, isn't it?"

"Yes. Won it in a poker game in Taos when I was eighteen."

One red-lacquered fingernail traced the primitive design and paused as she tilted her head upward. "How does it open?"

The question was so innocently asked, so demure in tone that he found himself reaching to show her the hidden catch. A non-innocent stirring erupted to life in his groin.

"How clever, those Indians," she said softly, the open buckle in her small hands. "Here . . . let me try it." She slipped the worn leather belt back inside the buckle and closed it again. "Like this?"

Feeling his mounting tumescence, he watched the red-nailed hands undo the buckle. "Yeah . . . like that."

"Well, now," she said, taking a deep breath, expanding her breasts suggestively. "Let's see how big a fan you really are." With a deft twist, she unbuckled it again and flipped open the top button of his jeans.

She was just getting down to business when, behind him, the door knob rattled loudly. "Cara," a male voice growled. "Open up dammit."

She jumped to her feet, her face paling under the layers of makeup. "Coming, darling," she called out. Throwing a more-than-guilty glance at Erik's hurried buttoning up, she stalled by fumbling loudly with the lock and then threw open the hall door.

Irving R. Dyer breezed past her, a small whirlwind of crusty energy and instant suspicion. Reeking of expensive cigar smoke, he fixed a hard glare on Erik. "Who the hell are you?"

"This is the new writer, darling. Erik . . . Erik, what'd you say?"

"Who gives a shit what the hack's name is," Irving snapped. "Why the hell was the door locked?"

"Vera must have," Cara responded innocently.

"She's out in the hall. It was locked from inside, dummy."

"I locked it," Erik offered. "Didn't want to be disturbed on the rewrites." He smiled politely, observing the hyper-energized little man. Decked out in Savile Row finery, a dark blue suit cut expertly to camouflage the middle-aged paunch, Dyer looked like a lower East Side deli owner who had suddenly come into a lot of money. His features were coarse, gray eyebrow hair protruded like tufts of unmown lawn. A large diamond twinkled on a pinky finger.

Dyer snapped his fingers toward Erik. "So where's the goods?"

Over an hour later, Erik finally managed to satisfy the petty demands of Dyer, who had insisted on innumerable "fine tunings" in Cara's speeches. Exhausted by the unexpected encounter and burning inwardly with a pentup anger, Erik knocked on Mo's downstairs office door. He strode in, throwing her a "you-owe-me" look.

Mo was on the phone and frazzled. "So forget the cops in back. Tell 'em we need 'em out front. And *pronto*!" She slipped the receiver back into the cradle and raised her head to Erik. "Have you seen what's happening out front? Madness! Must be at least two thousand people already. Eager to stand *four* hours just to catch a fleeting glimpse of someone famous." Clucking to herself, she stood. "So? How's by you and Cara?"

Angrily, he lit a cigarette. "Irving R. Dyer, the big asshole himself, made me rewrite some a half dozen times. But, he's finally approved them all."

"There is a God. Bless you son." She stepped smartly to the open door, yelling out, "Get the new monologues from Cara and have them made up for the teleprompter. Pronto."

Just as she was closing the door, an urgent shout echoed down the hall. "Mo! Get Mo! On stage!"

Mo plunged through her doorway and took off at a trot. Erik followed. His long strides brought him to the stage door first and he yanked it open, stepping aside for her to barrel on through.

Mo hit the stage almost at a dead run, her short legs pumping beneath her stocky trunk. Erik was right behind. They slowed to a ragged stop.

In the bright TV lights, two, well-dressed matrons were trying to pull an enraged Shelby Cale into the wings. Digging the heels of her tennis shoes into the polished stage floor, she was crying out, "Y'all can't make me! I won't go!"

"What the hell's going on?" Mo demanded as Shelby disappeared.

The stage manager huffed, "Those two women just barged in and started hassling her."

Mo started moving into the darkened area off stage, both the stage manager and Erik alongside. "How'd they get past the guard?" she asked.

"I don't know," the stage manager said.

"Want me to stop them?" Erik offered.

"Yes! At least find out what's going on!" she yelled after him.

Erik loped around the stage wing just in time to see Shelby being pushed through the stage door leading to the back street. He hit the closing door at a dead run and blasted out onto the sidewalk. The glare of the late afternoon sun momentarily blinded him. By the time he could focus properly, Shelby had been hustled into the backseat of a waiting cab. One look at her stricken face propelled him forward. "Hey! Hold on there!"

The older of the two women, an erect, gray-haired aristocrat, spun to face him. "This is none of your concern, young man," she said, the tone haughty, condescending.

He tore the cab door from her grasp and reached in to grab Shelby's wrist. The touch of her soft skin was like a jolt of high voltage. It prickled the hairs on his arms. She raised her astonishing eyes which flooded both with renewed tears and instant gratitude.

"Unhand her," the older woman ordered behind him. But he was frozen with delight, lost in the sea green mysteries of Shelby's eyes.

The other woman, much younger than the first, already seated on the far side of Shelby, had a firm grasp on Shelby's other wrist. "Let me go," Shelby cried to her, trying to scramble out on his side. She threw him a helpless, pleading look—it wrenched something deep within him. At that moment, he would have lain down in front of a freight train if it would have assisted her.

From the sidewalk, Mo's voice barked, "What's going on?"

With one forceful tug, Erik hauled the girl out of the cab. Shelby righted herself and he drank in her golden beauty firsthand, barely listening to the argument between Mo and the older woman.

"What do you mean, it's none of my concern?" Mo shouted. "You come barging in, disrupting my show, kidnapping one of my girls! She's *my* responsibility. I'm the producer!"

The aristocratic older woman stiffened her back visibly. "If y'all would be so understanding, please," she uttered with a noticeable drawl. "Shelby Ann is *our* responsibility. I am her grandmother, Evangeline Boullifant Porter and my daughter, Elizabeth, there in the taxi, is Shelby Ann's mother. So if *you* all excuse us, this is a family matter."

He could not tear his gaze from Shelby's eyes. Through a veil of tears, their almost translucent green stared back at him openly. He felt tangibly that somewhere, someplace, some time before, they had stood side by side like this, lost in each other's gaze. It was more than *déjà vu* for him—it had a reality, concrete and vivid.

Mo changed her tone. "Look, Shelby and the rest of us go on the air at nine P.M. sharp. Can't you—"

"Not Shelby Ann," the grandmother cut in coldly. "We would never permit her to participate in such a degrading display."

"Well, somebody had to have given their permission," Mo challenged. "Who signed the parental release forms?"

Shelby ducked her head, giving herself away only to Erik.

"Release forms?" the grandmother repeated disdainfully. "I'm sure I don't have an inkling as to what y'all're referring. Shelby Ann, perhaps you would care to explain?"

Shelby's head drooped even further. He wanted to reach out, hold her, comfort her, protect her, take her far away with him.

"Young man, out of my way," the grandmother ordered brusquely.

He looked at Mo, who shrugged her confusion. Not wanting to, yet not having any choice, he slowly stepped aside, freeing the cab door.

"Get in, Shelby Ann," Evangeline Boullifant Porter ordered with a crisp authority.

Helplessly, Shelby began to cry again. With a defeated sag to her shoulders, she moved to slide into the rear seat. As she ducked inside, she murmured for his ears alone, "Thank y'all . . ."

His heart belly-flopped off a high dive.

"Can't we discuss this?" Mo asked, placating. "Our entire blocking, all our timings, the whole show depends on having twenty-five contestants."

The sharp profile of the older woman did not turn as she bent stiffly into the cab's rear seat next to Shelby and slammed the door. A curt order was issued and the taxi pulled away from the curb.

Mo's hands flew to her hips. "Well, I'll be . . ."

Erik stood staring at the end of the block where the cab was last seen. "You just lost the real winner. Damn . . ."

SHELBY
July 1966
New York

For every block the cab drove her further away from her dreams, her sobs increased. She wished she could will herself to die—right there in the back seat.

"Shelby Ann," her grandmother warned, "if you do not cease this infernal racket, we will leave for Oak Hills this very night."

"But why can't I be in the pageant?" she wailed.

"No Boullifant woman has ever paraded in such a vulgar display."

"But y'all just don't understand. Y'all *never* do. This pageant isn't like Miss America. We're not judged in bathing suits. Only expensive *haute couture* clothes by Yves Saint Laurent and just . . . everybody. Why Giorgio Caesari himself selected the gowns."

Shelby's mother turned in surprise. "I had no idea Giorgio Caesari had anything to do with this."

Sensing an opening, Shelby jumped in, momentarily forgetting her tears. "Why, mother, it's all *his* pageant. He's sponsoring and producing the whole thing. Why, Mister Caesari's spent millions to find a girl to represent his new cosmetics. *Sunny,* he calls them. Haven't y'all seen those ads in *Vogue, Harper's Bazaar, Seventeen?* —'Who will be *Sunny?*' They're calling it the biggest search since for Scarlet O'Hara."

Beth Ann, as Shelby's faded rose of a mother was known, glanced across to Evangeline. "Why, yes, I do recall reading about that, I think. Mother, did y'all realize—"

"I will not permit her participation," Evangeline said. "And *that* is *that.*"

Shelby recognized the tone. It was an abrupt dismissal of the topic. Anything further that might be said was futile. She began to weep silently into her hands.

The tears did not diminish until she was alone in the bathroom of her grandmother's suite at the Waldorf-Astoria. Slipping off the white jersey robe, stepping into the tubful of pink bubbles, she noticed again how long and fit her legs looked, fit without being muscular. "Runner's legs" was how one beau had put it. Not one of the girls in the pageant had legs like hers. That remembrance brought on a new wave of anguish and she sank tearfully into the frothy pink bubbles, scented with rose petals.

What was she going to do?

Oak Hills—those monotonous, rolling green fields dotted with twisted, grotesque old trees—the endless cycle of thoroughbred colts being bred, born, trained into winners, groomed to perform, kept to breed, penned in by endless, white fences . . . just like herself.

She longed for the freedom to live her own life, far away from the dull, stupid, boring people of Middleburg, Virginia, and surrounding environs. She longed to meet and know exciting people whom she'd discovered in the pages of *Harper's Bazaar* and *Vogue* and *Life* magazines. The fabulously successful few who had broken through, who had triumphed—extraordinary people who came and went as they pleased and with whom they so desired—people who were *somebody*. Sophisticated models, glamorous movie stars, famous politicians, leading sports figures—anyone and everyone at the top of their profession and on top of the world.

And the places she dreamed about...cliff-perched villas overlooking azure waters; gleaming white yachts bobbing in secluded coves; exotic, mysterious bazaars teeming with strange people and rich delights; new adventures in foreign capitals—London, Paris, Berlin, Tokyo, Rio—the ultrasophisticated hangouts of international jetsetters, the well known and the very wealthy; places where the unexpected happened, where unforeseen pleasures abounded—places as different from her own confining world as she could possibly dream. But now, she could foresee nothing in her future but Oak Hills....

A soft tap at the door opened her tearful eyes. Her mother entered, drawn and wan-looking, still wearing the severely tailored beige suit. Beth Ann closed the door quietly behind her. "I think it's time we two had a little chat."

With a groan, Shelby rolled her head to the wall.

"Shelby...why? Why did y'all run off like that? How could y'all do that to us? To the family who loves you? I was terrified; your poor grandmother was so upset, I thought she'd have a stroke."

Shelby had to bite the inside of her cheek to keep from screaming, "I wish she had!" She detested it when Beth Ann was motherly like this.

A cigarette lighter clicked and Shelby glanced over her shoulder. Beth Ann must be upset for she rarely dared to smoke in so close proximity to her forbidding mother. She exhaled bitterly. "Why, Shelby, just tell me, why."

"Oh, mother, please," she moaned, turning her whole body away to the wall and drawing up her knees. "Y'all just don't understand."

"I'm trying, Shelby, really I am."

"No, you're not," she retorted over her shoulder. The tears had ried up. In their place, a deep anger kindled within. "Y'all're just rying to make yourself look good . . . so y'all can tell Evangeline, well, I tried, mother, I honestly tried.' "

When her mother finally spoke, the tone was again its more usual distant and brittle. "Y'all've never forgiven me for what happened with your father."

"Daddy has nothing to do with this."

"Oh, yes, he does," Beth Ann replied. "Y'all think y'all can just run off like he did, and to hell with everyone else."

Shelby rolled over to a sitting position and reached for a washcloth. 'Daddy didn't run away," she said with barely controlled venom. 'You and Evangeline *drove* him off."

Beth Ann's cigarette halted in midair. "Billy Jay was an alcoholic and he ran off with his secretary after having an affair with her for *two and a half years*. Need I remind you?"

"Who made him an alcoholic?" Shelby challenged. "If I had to listen to Evangeline putting down my bloodlines every ten seconds and working for her like a darkey, I'd turn to drink too!"

Coldly, they measured each other, until Beth Ann rose to her feet. "I won't have y'all blaming mother or me like this." She threw the half-finished cigarette into the open commode. "Y'all were too young then to know the true Billy Jay."

"I was nine and I knew him better than any of you."

"Hush up," Beth Ann hissed. "Y'all will wake your grandmother from her lie-down."

"Who cares?"

Beth Ann swung around, her cheeks flushed. "Y'all're just like him. Vain, stubborn, willful, selfish—"

"I'm glad! I'm glad I'm just like him," Shelby cried.

A muffled sound silenced her. For a second both of them stared at the closed door. Someone was knocking on the outer hall door. Evangeline could be heard calling out, "Who's there?" A male voice answered, indistinct, but subservient.

Quickly Beth Ann flushed away the incriminating cigarette, grabbed an atomizer of gardenia scent and sprayed the air, before opening the bath door and ordering Shelby, "Y'all get out of that tub right now.

We're leaving in jig-time." She shut the door behind her. Shelby was once more alone.

And the tears began streaming down her cheeks again. "Oh daddy, daddy . . ."

Almost at once, the door flew open, startling her. Beth Ann flurried in, carrying a long-stemmed yellow rose. "Get up! Get up out of there this very second," she said, flying to the mirror.

Shelby stared at her mother's reflection. Something had happened. Beth Ann was positively glowing.

"Did y'all hear me?" Beth asked into the mirror. With her cuticle scissors she snipped the yellow bud from its stem. "Get up and get dressed. Right now, honey." Her voice had lost its hard edge. Now it was breathless, almost girlish.

"What's the matter?" Shelby asked in a monotone, slowly rising from the tub and reaching for a towel.

"Honey, y'all won't believe who's downstairs. Waiting for *us*!"

"Who?"

Her mother slipped a bobby pin into the bun to hold the yellow rose tight to her head. She stepped back to survey the results before turning and announcing triumphantly, "Giorgio Caesari himself."

A shower of sparks flew outward to every pore of Shelby's skin. "Mister Caesari?"

"He had the bellboy deliver this lovely rose on a silver tray," Beth Ann rhapsodized. "And on the back of his calling card, he wrote: 'I'm waiting in the lounge to make your acquaintance.'"

Evangeline appeared dourly in the doorway, tying the belt of her emerald green bathrobe. "This is pure folly, Beth Ann."

"Oh, mother, come now," Beth Ann said, deftly applying a pale pink lipstick. "How often do we get a chance like this? To meet someone as well known, as world famous as Giorgio Caesari?" His name rolled off her lips as though she were tasting rare wine.

Feverishly Shelby began drying herself.

Evangeline arched her long neck. "Y'all know perfectly well what he's after."

Beth Ann smiled enigmatically. It was her own special smile, reserved for the rare occasions she went against Evangeline's wishes. "Oh, mother, what harm would it do to meet him? He's not going to change our minds," she said, smoothing her eyebrows. "It'd be sort of fun, won't it? Like meeting a movie star or something. I mean, my goodness, the girls at the club will be positively green with envy. I can't wait to tell them. It will make this whole dreadful trip worthwhile."

"Elizabeth Ann," Evangeline said sternly. "Y'all're mooning on like a silly schoolgirl."

Shelby was amazed to hear her mother actually giggle. She couldn't remember ever hearing that before. It sounded so foreign to her, so fresh and disarming, for a brief moment, she thought she could see what her father must have seen twenty years earlier.

Beth Ann fluttered to the door. "Oh come-come, mother. Let's show him what southern graciousness is all about. After all, he's made this special trip to find us. My goodness, the least we could do is be hospitable enough to hear him out."

Clutching her robe, Shelby's eyes flicked back and forth between them. For once in her life, she was rooting for her mother. Evangeline drew herself up stiffly, turned and marched into her adjoining bedroom.

"If y'all won't come with me," Beth Ann sang out after her, "I guess I'll just have to go down by my lonesome. I am not going to miss this opportunity. It's a highlight, a positive highlight."

Shelby kept her face emotionless, but she was holding her breath, waiting for Evangeline's response. "Oh, for heaven's sake, Elizabeth Ann," came the testy reply.

And Shelby knew that her mother finally had won a round.

Noiselessly the elevator doors slid open on the lobby floor revealing the trio from Oak Hills. The first out was Evangeline Boullifant Porter, her bony shoulders thrown back under a short mink cape, her chiseled head held high on a long neck which looked surprisingly young for the over seventy-year-old woman. While Evangeline looked like she were striding into the national horseshow finals with tickets for the best box seat, Beth Ann, behind her, gave the impression she was late for a vital appointment. She appeared flushed, with bright spots of deep rose accenting the high bones of her cheeks. In her white straw hat and gloves, Shelby's mother was still attractive, though there was a tired tension in the lines filigree-ing the corners of her eyes. She tossed a look over her shoulder at her daughter.

Dressed in a pale blue cotton-silk shirtdress, Shelby hesitated in the open elevator doors. A fear so strong swept over her that she felt faint. She couldn't face him. He would know in a glance that she was not worth the effort, nothing more than a stupid, silly teenager from a hick southern farm.

One of Beth Ann's gloved hands shot out, grabbing hold of her arm. "Now stop this, y'all hear? Y'all got yourself into this mess, young lady. Now y'all get yourself out. Y'all owe Mister Caesari a sincere apology." And Shelby was tugged unceremoniously into the lobby.

As soon as they entered the darkened interior of the cocktail lounge, Shelby spotted him, sitting alone in the half-circle booth. Her shoulders drooped and her cheeks flamed.

With a slight bow, he rose, expensively tailored, darkly attractive, smiling graciously. "Obviously Shelby's beauty is inherited from her mother's side of the family."

"I can't tell you what a sincere pleasure this is," Beth Ann said, just short of gushing. "Positively. We've used all of your lovely products for years and years."

Shelby glanced up from the floor, amazed both at the outright lie and the silly tone to her mother's voice. Beth Ann sounded like the girls at Mrs. Wright's school when they'd panted about Paul McCartney—and her mother's southern accent was now thicker than magnolia leaves.

Caesari waved a hand to the cushioned booth seats. "Won't you please join me for a moment?"

Evangeline ignored the invitation. "Shelby Ann, isn't there some-thing y'all wanted to say to Mister Caesari?"

Shelby felt her cheeks blanch. "Mist—Mister Caesari," she stammered, not daring to look at him. "I'm afraid . . . I . . . I can't be in your—"

"Please," he interrupted, stepping back to make room for them. "Just a few moments of your time." He stared directly at Beth Ann with a heavy-lidded gaze. "It would be an honor and a pleasure to be surrounded by such exquisite samples of southern pulchritude."

Evangeline's hand briefly fingered her timepiece broach beneath her fur cape, then a thin sigh escaped her lips. "Very well . . . but only for a moment."

"Excellent," Caesari said, beaming, and turned to Shelby. "Please, excuse us. Would you mind waiting in the lobby?"

As soon as Shelby walked stiffly into the lobby, the willpower which had been holding her upright vanished with a *whoosh*. She sank into a high-backed, carved wooden chair and tried to imagine what was being said around that booth table. Five minutes passed, then ten. She was so absorbed in her own dilemma, she did not see him approach.

"Come," Caesari ordered.

Unsteadily she followed him back into the lounge. If anything, Beth Ann looked more flushed and Evangeline even more stoic. Unnerved, Shelby slid in next to her mother, folding her gloved hands in her lap, her head bent.

"Sit up," Evangeline said sharply.

Shelby pushed her spine up against the cushion. She searched their faces for some clue while Caesari sat elegantly opposite her. "I must say," he began, all charm and half-lidded eyes, "you are fortunate to have two such concerned relatives looking out for your welfare. I have promised them that *if* they allow you to participate this evening, and *if* the judges should choose you, every aspect of your career will be handled by your family's lawyers. Furthermore, I personally have given my word that everything you or your likeness will appear in will embody all of the high principles by which you were so obviously raised."

Her pulse seemed suspended in midbeat. His black eyes seemed to have wedded to hers.

"However," he continued, his tone cooler. "*If* you do not win, you *must* promise to return home tomorrow and pursue your own life. As I explained, I have no say in the final selection. It's up to the panel of celebrity judges. You must take your chances with the other girls."

There was such joyous singing in her head she momentarily lost track of his words.

"Shelby," her mother was speaking. "Don't you have something to say to your grandmother?"

"Thank you, grandma . . . thank you."

Evangeline tugged on a white glove. "Far be it from me to stand in your way, Shelby Ann. I want you to remember that when we all return to Oak Hills tomorrow."

"I will, grandma, I promise I will . . ." But her fingers were crossed under the table.

Barely four minutes to airtime, a newly shorn Shelby was rushed to her off-stage position by one of Caesari's assistants. Her last hour and a half had been filled with such frantic activity she barely had time to breathe, let alone think. On the exciting limousine ride back to the theater, Caesari had insisted that she *must* cut her hair if she wanted to be one of the top four finalists.

Too scattered to protest, she had been whisked to a private room backstage, away from the other contestants. There he had personally overseen the shearing by his top hairstylist, a slight, young man named Carlos. Nearly twenty-four inches had been whacked off until her hair just grazed the top of her shoulders. Next, while her hair had been given a quick body wave, another young man, whose name she had never caught, applied a delicate blending of makeup, concentrating especially on the areas around the eyes. Again and again, Caesari had corrected any tiny detail which did not meet his standards. He'd been so exacting, Shelby had been ready to scream with anxiety. With less than fifteen minutes left before airtime, Caesari had finally given his approval and had slipped out of the room for her to dress. He hadn't even wished her good luck.

Now, standing on the steep ramp in line with half of the contestants, Shelby was so unsure about her appearance her knees were trembling uncontrollably.

For years and years, she had prided herself on her own personal trademark—her waist-length, perfectly straight hair. Now it flipped off her shoulders and bounced around her face. It looked too saucy and perky under the wide-brimmed straw hat with the long yellow ribbons. Dressed in her first outfit, a soft yellow organdy afternoon dress by Givenchy, she felt, for the first time in her life, insecure about her looks. She wished that her father would whisk her away to safety. She squeezed her eyes shut and prayed.

"Shelby, you look sensational!" The deep voice startled her. Her eyes popped open, and focused down on him.

It was the big, sandy-haired guy who had tried to pull her from the cab and the clutches of Evangeline. In a rough, outdoorsy sort of way, he was good-looking, very rugged. And he'd appeared so suddenly, as if her prayers had been answered.

With one easy movement, he grabbed the railing and hoisted himself up before her. "I was just in the control booth and noticed something I think's important." He leaned forward, lowering his voice, smelling of Dentine, cigarettes and alcohol. "The panel of judges—from where they're sitting on the main floor—they can't see the first entrance of any of the contestants on this side. *But* they've each got a small TV monitor in front of them. So . . . when you walk down the ramp, don't play to the audience, play directly to the camera at the bottom. You know . . . make believe it's your best fellow, make love to it with your eyes. That way, the judges will immediately see you at your best."

"Aren't y'all going to tell the others?" Her voice was annoyingly thin with tension.

He winked, as if sharing a secret and whispered, "Nope."

"Why?"

" 'Cause you're definitely the most beautiful girl here."

She felt a spark ignite in her breast. "Really?"

He smiled—it was a wonderful smile, open, friendly, warm. It made the corners of his eyes crinkle up in the cutest way. "Shelby, with that new hairdo, you're the most beautiful damned creature I've ever laid eyes on. Like a painting by Gainsborough. You're—"

"Hey!" came the angry man's voice below. "Who the hell're you?"

Her stranger frowned down at the beefy security guard. "Friend of the producer."

"I don't give a damn if you're Mayor Lindsay, get out of here."

"Right," the stranger said, hopping down beside him. He called up. "Trust yourself, Shelby."

Before she could respond, he was hustled out of sight. Damn, she hadn't even thanked him.

"Thirty seconds to air, everyone," the loudspeaker blared. It was the producer's voice, brisk but motherly. "Good show, everyone. It's going to be just dandy, I know."

An expectant, tense hush fell. Suddenly there was a dramatic, almost ominous roll on the timpani drums and an announcer's full-bodied voice boomed out over the speakers, "Live from New York City and the famed Odeon Theater—Villa Caesari Cosmetics proudly presents . . . The New American Beauty Pageant!"

It seemed to Shelby that it took no time before, above the orchestral accompaniment, Cara Noor's breathy voice sang out her first introduction, "Now here's a southern belle who will ring your chimes—from Virginia, Miss Shelby Cale!"

Releasing a deep breath, Shelby took the long step that brought her out into the white, hot lights and into view of the audience. She navigated the turn at the top of the swooping silver ramp and headed down. The glare of the lights was blinding. For a second, she could not locate the camera with the glowing red light. Finding it, she concentrated on it for all she was worth, zeroing in on it with a generous smile, aiming to be as natural yet as seductive as she could. At the bottom of the ramp, on a whim, she reached up and whipped off the wide-brimmed straw hat, gracefully turning in a complete circle, holding the hat out so that the long, satin ribbons floated in a shimmering yellow arc around her. She might have been imagining it, but she thought she heard an audible gasp of pleasure coming from the audience. That perked up her spirits considerably. With one last, lingering look—an over-the-shoulder, through-the-lashes, smoldering look directly into the "on" camera, she glided effortlessly to her assigned position on the wide stairs next to the girl from Florida.

For the first time, she had a chance to see out into the darkened auditorium. Only the first few rows were visible in the light spilled from the stage, but it was enough to confirm her glowing expectations.

She had never seen such an assemblage of elegant people in her life. The gentlemen, all in tuxedos, the women, in stunning evening dresses, obviously only the elite of New York and international society had been invited. Shelby could pick out several well-known faces—Angela Lansbury, who was currently starring in the musical *Mame*, sat in the second row and just behind her, Wilhelmina, the well-known model and over there, Richard Avedon, the famous photographer who'd just been featured in *Life*.

A warm glow of pleasure began to fill Shelby. With a rush of recognition, she felt, at last, she had come home.

The next seventy-two minutes was a breathless whirl of barely controlled chaos. During the commercial breaks, the contestants broke ranks and rushed to the large, curtained-off stage area to change into their next outfits. There was much scrambling, screaming, tears and curses as each tried desperately to be back in place in time for the next entrance. Zippers broke, accessories were lost or "borrowed," shoes mismatched, hairstyles drooped, mascara ran with nervous perspiration. And yet, somehow, miraculously the nationwide TV show proceeded without a hitch and without even the live audience out front knowing of the backstage traumas.

With each of her entrances, Shelby's confidence grew and she playfully presented a different image with every introduction. For her Courreges sports outfit—a creamy white golfing ensemble with box-pleated culottes—she chose a jaunty athletic walk with the golf putter flung rakishly over her shoulder. For the working-girl section, her outfit was a demure, forest green suit by Chanel and she adopted a studious expression, broken at the end by a smile of delighted surprise. For her last ensemble, the evening-wear segment, she projected a dreamy, romantic image in her Yves Saint Laurent gown—a backless, shoulderless, empire-waist dress of soft rose silk. She floated behind her the hand-painted floral panels like a train of colorful butterflies.

Only when the time came for the top four contestants to be announced did Shelby become fully conscious again of the serious-ness of the proceedings. Her heart began to pound so loudly, she was positive the front of her gown was revealing its rhythm to the audience. Through the calling of three other names, she smiled and smiled, suspended in anticipation.

"... and our last finalist," Cara Noor announced, "... Shelby Cale."

Instantly, Shelby's smile broadened and she stepped down the tiered levels, moving through the twenty-one less fortunate contestants who were applauding graciously, until she stood on the designated spot. A camera moved in to pan the four lucky girls. When it came to her, she suddenly remembered her father—he might be watching out there in Wisconsin. She wished she had thought earlier of wiring him or something. Her attitude changed visibly and she felt it was the most genuine smile she'd mustered all night.

During a commercial break, all but the final four left the stage and the lighting changed dramatically. Bright pin spots picked up the finalists, showing the rush of the makeup assistants who'd appeared to dab at the faces of each. Nervously the four girls stood before the live, buzzing audience and waited for the show to resume.

During that awkward and tension-filled moment, her mind flew to her grandmother and mother. She wondered where exactly in the audience they were sitting; Mister Caesari had told her he'd given them a pair of special seats. She gazed out at the indistinguishable rear of the house, hoping with all her might that they, especially Evangeline, would see by her presentation that she was a natural model, different from the world they came from, born to higher aspirations and gifted with special talents they never dreamed of. Even if she didn't win, they just *had* to allow her to stay in New York to pursue a modeling career.

Again the pageant was on the air; the climax approaching swiftly. One by one the names of the bottom two girls were called out and Shelby's name was not among them. Now, there were just the two left, she and the lovely girl from Florida. They stood side by side, Shelby the taller. She closed her eyes and waited. . . .

When her name was called out as the winner, her long lashes fluttered briefly, then parted revealing wide, astonished eyes. Pandemonium broke out among the large corps of press and photographers being held off stage. Waves of applause washed over her and still she stood, frozen with the absolute bliss of the moment. It overwhelmed her with its intensity, as if she'd just been charged with thousands of watts of electrical energy.

Tears filled her eyes as she accepted from Cara Noor the single yellow rose, symbol of the new *Sunny* logo. Behind her, twinkling lights in large script letters the entire height of the stage spelled out S-U-N-N-Y. Holding the rose like a scepter, her high cheekbones glistening, Shelby listened to the appreciative roars of approval and to the closing theme music, "The Most Beautiful Girl in the World," lushly played off stage by a fifty-piece symphony orchestra.

She'd won! She'd made her escape. She was *free*. And in her mind, she shouted to her grandmother, somewhere out there in the cheering audience, "I'll never, ever have to go back to your damned Oak Hills again, you stuffy old bitch! *Never—ever—again!*"

REBECCA
August 1966
New York

Zachery Butterick stood before his new term students, his eyes raking over their expectant faces, his voice richly theatrical, "As actors you are *all* going to fail. And you deserve to." He paused, his eyes coming to rest on Rebecca sitting in the last row.

She concentrated on his open-to-the-waist, black buccaneer's shirt.

"Those of you new to my class," Butterick continued, "may find my words disturbing. Good. After today, you may not want to return. That's also good. There is a glut of actors on the market as it is. And *all* of you will fail because you're second-rate."

Her insides were fast becoming a block of ice.

Butterick stroked the narrow, black band of his beard, a half smile aimed at Robby. "My only hope is that *one* of you—just one—will be so incensed by what I've just said, that you will prove me wrong."

Zachery Butterick was the best in the city Robby had insisted, because the man *made* one grow as an actor. Five minutes into the first session, Rebecca felt—if intimidation were Butterick's secret, he'd already succeeded with her. But she'd show him, she'd show them all. Maybe not today, she agonized, but one day.

"As we have two new apprentices this term," Butterick said, "I think we should get to know them by asking them to do a little something."

Her grip tightened on the seat of the chair.

"Let's do something really easy," Butterick went on. "A private moment. Something of your inner self so that we may better understand you as an actor."

Frantically she searched her mind for a glimmer of hope, an idea, *anything* that she might be able to present in front of all these strangers . . . and him, up there, already judging.

"This is the only exercise all term that will go uncriticized by all of us," he continued. "It's an intimate, revealing moment between strangers whom you'll never meet again." Grandly, he lowered himself into his school-desk chair. "Let's begin with Rebecca Parlato. Show us what you've got."

"Not much," she said under her breath and made her way forward. She crossed the hardwood floor and faced the brick wall, squeezing her eyes shut. Concentrating her energies, she focused on the incident she'd chosen at the very last moment. Gradually, through massive effort on her part, all sounds in the room receded for her and her breathing steadied.

Her posture collapsed, becoming that of a very young girl, and she turned, eyes wide with mischief and adventure.

She was alone in her parents' crackerbox house, in their bedroom, outside the window the noises of the busy Buffalo cross-street were muffled by tall banks of sooty snow. She scurried to her mother's closet, stood on tiptoes, reaching for her mother's only party dress—it was blue velvet, soft to the touch as she pulled it over her head, fastening the belt tightly around her waist and bunching up the skirt so it just skimmed the floor. Teetering in her mother's high-heeled, gold sandals, she artfully applied lipstick and rouge, watching herself with delight in the full-length mirror. Stepping back, she held out the edges of the skirt and bobbed a low curtsy.

Suddenly another figure appeared in her mirror. Whirling, she moaned, "No, daddy..." and backed away. He lunged, grabbing her in both arms, sinking to his knees, his beery lips crushing against hers. She squirmed free and fled, wiping her mouth.

Far away, she heard someone giggle.

With a jolt, the class came back into her vision. Startled, totally losing her concentration, she ducked her head and hurried back to her chair, the silent reaction of the class confusing, unbearable. Finally she brought herself to look over at Robby. He was grinning at her, giving her the "A-okay" sign.

Vastly relieved, she sank back and took her first, long look around. The other new student was being called up. His name was Scooter Warren. He swung to face the class and she shrank down, out of his line of vision. The guy was just too damned gorgeous—real star quality—tall, dark, brooding, like a young Montgomery Clift, she thought.

He was slicking back his long hair, crouching as if in front of a mirror and there was apprehension, nervousness. Evidently not pleased with his reflection, he shrugged in resignation and reached for an imaginary door, passing through it. The way he walked clearly indicated that he was going somewhere he had two minds about—part of him wanted to, the other kept holding back.

She was fascinated by him. His choices were so clean, so precise; the way he used his body so fluid, so controlled. There was no doubt in her mind—this actor was truly extraordinary. Contrary to his youthful features, he was displaying a talent well matured and starkly vivid.

He paced, tortured, working up enough nerve to enter somewhere. Then, abruptly giving up, he whirled, running back to his starting place. He slammed the door, trembling with rage and a deep, obvious pain. He stripped off his T-shirt and looked at himself in the mirror again like a rejected little boy. He appeared so thin, vulnerable, she felt total empathy. That feeling, however, was short-lived, for the actor peeled off his jeans and stood, facing them, totally nude, examining his body as if in front of a full-length mirror.

Embarrassed, she lowered her head and when she dared raise her eyes again, a hot flash of mortification singed her face. The naked young man, his hands roaming his body, was staring directly at her.

Four hours into her nightshift, Rebecca was still upset. She ran back and forth behind the long counter of Mac's Diner, balancing greasy plates, collecting dirty dishes, working the cash register, giving change, putting away tips in a big, empty mayonnaise jar on the shelf to be divided up later, not that many customers left tips and not that Mac was so honest in his division.

On top of stewing about that flakey actor, she worried about her finances. Ever since the previous Monday she had owed seventy-five bucks on her sleaze hole of an apartment and she wouldn't be paid until the following night. And Butterick's class, which she was determined to stick with regardless of what happened that morning, cost fifteen bucks more a month than her previous teacher, not to mention the added subway fare to and from the Village. Then there were the planned new photos and creatively expanded résumés both of which Robby had insisted upon as absolutely necessary. And to make matters worse, the jukebox kept playing Sinatra's "Strangers in the Night," the same song that had been on when Erik Lungren had walked in that night. To escape the memories, she ducked into the kitchen, only to hear the radio blasting a news bulletin about some sniper killing a dozen people from a University of Texas tower. In horror, she ran back behind the counter and quickly said a prayer.

Shortly after two A.M., Rebecca finished her chores, changed into her jeans and a T-shirt in the ladies' room, stuffed the ugly pink nylon uniform into a paper sack to take home to rinse out, and slipped wearily out the side door into the dimly lit side street. Just under a block away, the lights of Seventy-second Street blinked and she started for them, her legs aching from being on them close to seven hours straight.

Muffled noises up ahead brought her to an abrupt halt: from the alley, scuffling sounds and solid thuds. More thudding again, then a distinct groan. Her heart launched into her throat. Somebody was being mugged! Not wanting to run past the alley opening or out into the exposure of the empty, open street, she crouched, peering forward, one hand groping around for a weapon. Remembering all too well the radio's report of the random, senseless violence from that tower in Texas, she shrank against the wall, unable to find her breath.

"Aggah!" the victim's cry came to her, pitifully weak.

Something moved into the half light—a man silhouetted. Then another man. Still another was beating on someone behind a large garbage container. Three against one! Her sense of justice boiled over.

Her hand landed on something hard—a glass beer bottle. Clutching it, she searched the same area, finding a whole six-pack of empty bottles. Grabbing the container, she mustered all her courage, said a quick prayer and filled her lungs. Cocking her arm, she aimed and threw a bottle with all her might, directly at the shadowy figures. As soon as it left her hand, she started screaming at the top of her lungs. The bottle crashed against a far wall, shattering loudly. Still yelling, she threw another, then the third and fourth. They exploded like gunfire.

Shouted voices—deep, startled—then footsteps running. She could make out three forms hightailing toward Seventy-second. Encouraged, she started after them, hurling the last two bottles in quick succession, screaming like a banshee, "Run, you chickenshits, run!"

Seeing them zip around the far corner and out of sight, she slowed, at once very frightened. Shakily she turned to locate the victim. His weak groan led her to the side of the trash container. She knelt, reaching out in the dark for the crumpled body. "Hey, man, you okay?"

Another groan erupted and he pushed up into a sitting position. "Think Butterick would've liked my entrance?"

"Scooter!!"

His beautiful face smeared with blood, he grimaced bitterly in the dim light. "For my next number, I'd like to do the assassination scene from *Julius Caesar*."

"Any blade cuts? Wanna doctor? The police?"

He shook his head. "Naw, just want to get home. Will you help me?" He raised a hand.

She eyed him for a moment. "Where do you live anyway?"

He wiped his cut lip on the sleeve of his baggy sports coat and smiled ruefully. "Hell's Kitchen area. See me home?" Again he offered his hand.

Not making eye contact, she clasped it and leaning back on her heels, she tugged him upright. Wavering, he sagged on her and patted her shoulder. "Hell, for a little tyke, you sure are one tough woman."

She staggered under his weight, not knowing what to say. She'd never been called a woman before, and for some reason, it touched her really deep inside.

By the time they struggled off the IND downtown and to his dingy apartment house on West Forty-sixth near Tenth Avenue, Scooter was managing fairly well, at least he'd stopped groaning with every step. Following him carefully up the grimey interior stairs to the second floor, she remembered. "Oh Hell's bells," she muttered. "I left my uniform sack in the alley. Mac'll can me for sure."

"Tell him you were mugged by a transvestite."

"What'd those guys get off you anyway?" she asked.

"Nothing to get. Guess that's why they were so pissed." He unlocked and opened a door with a Number Five.

She followed him into the narrow hall, hesitating just inside the entrance, watching him hobble into the bathroom at the far end. "What were you doing in the alley anyway?"

Studying his face in the mirror, he said, "Hell, there go auditions for a month." Grimacing, he struggled out of his sports jacket, letting it slip to the cracked tile floor. Leaning against the sink, he turned on the tap and looked back at her. "I was waiting for you."

She glanced into the room off the hall. "You a Dylan fan, huh?" The walls of the starkly bare room contained only one large, full-color poster of Bob Dylan, smiling, tipping his hat.

"Master poet, master teacher," he said. "Sure hope he recovers from that motorcycle accident. I've been bummed out for weeks on account of it." He was trying to get his T-shirt over his head, but couldn't raise his arms high enough. Giving up, he grabbed the front and yanked, tearing the flimsy material away.

The sight of his thin torso brought back vivid memories of his "private moment" that morning. She blushed and turned away.

"Close the front door," he said and bent over the sink.

Heart hammering, she hesitated, then shut the door. "Those punks," she muttered. "Wish I was the size of my big brother— I'd've beat the shit out of 'em."

He started to laugh, but gasped, grabbing his side. "Oh god, no comedy, huh?" Switching out the light, he shuffled toward her, bent over like an old man. "Think I could get some character roles out of this?"

With the blood washed from his face, he did not look so gruesome. She inched backward toward the door. "Guess I'll be going."

"Come on in till I mellow out. I'm all jacked up."

She brushed the bangs out of her eyes, and felt some dried blood on her forehead. "Let me wash up first, huh?"

"Don't hide in there all night."

She scurried into the bathroom and closed the door. Not really understanding why she was trembling so, she used the tail end of his T-shirt to scrub the blood off her face and arms. Hating the dark circles under her eyes, she fluffed up the sides of her hair and stood uncertainly for a long time, not knowing what she was feeling. Finally she opened the door, and ventured out.

Dylan's "Man of Constant Sorrow" was playing in the other room. She paused in the doorway, not seeing Scooter in the subdued light from the street windows. A small, portable stereo sat on an old steamer trunk, the record revolving slowly, a whole stack of albums on the spindle. "Scooter?"

"Up here."

A large loft bed reached by a wooden ladder stretched across the end of the small room, a tiny kitchenette tucked under it. Scooter sat on top, leaning against the wall, his long legs out in front so that his bare feet hung over the edge. "Come on up."

"Better be going," she said. "I'm bushed."

He waved a small tube. "Could you put this on my cuts?"

She shrugged, debating with herself. Finally she figured he was too pooped for any funny business and awkwardly climbed up the homemade ladder. "Wow, this is neat. Ever fall out?"

"Nope. Been pushed out though," he said with a lopsided grin.

Thinking the smile made him look more like James Dean than Montgomery Clift, she took the tube of ointment, noting the cardboard box-top in his lap. He was rolling a cigarette. At first, she assumed it was tobacco, but then, with a start, thought she recognized it. "Maryjane?"

"Perfect end for a not so perfect day," he said, lighting it.

Sitting on her knees, the ceiling a scant one foot from her head, she carefully observed him take a long drag. His straight, mink brown hair hung limply past his ears. The eyebrows were thick, the nose aesthetic looking, his eyes, deepset and the color of dark sable. She couldn't remember seeing a face so handsome—just short of being down-right beautiful. It made her extremely self-conscious of her own looks.

Pulling the joint from his lips, he held it out, offering it.

"Don't need it, you know?" she murmured, and put a little of the greasy ointment on her fingertips. "Close your eyes," she suggested and leaned forward to apply gingerly the medicine to the cut over one eyebrow. Her hand shook and his skin felt hot, almost feverish.

He flinched and pulled back. "You ever try reefer?"

"Oh, yeah, sure," she mumbled, vividly conscious of his bare torso. A small patch of brown hair nestled between his two tiny nipples like a baby tarantula. She edged toward the ladder.

"Jesus," he muttered. "You're one uptight chick."

"Oh, yeah?"

"Yeah. I could tell by just looking at you this morning during your scene. Uptight was written all over you—especially the way you used your body."

"I was nervous, you know? Some of us more sensitive performers get that way before doing a scene."

"Not talking about nerves." His gaze hardened. "Why the hell do you think I stripped this morning? To turn on Butterick? Because I get off on shocking people?"

Feeling cornered, she focused on the fat candle burning on the shelf over his head.

"See how uptight you are," he said. "You can't even bring yourself to talk about it."

"It disgusted me, that's why."

"So why?"

"Geez," she sighed, irritated both at him and with her confusion.

"This morning, I did that for *you*. To show you what's *wrong* with your acting."

"Wha'? *Now* I've heard everythin'."

"You know what I noticed about your memory bit? You didn't touch yourself once. Not one goddamned time. Not even accidentally."

She jerked her head up. "What's that got to do with anything?"

"Everything." He leaned back against the wall and took a long, hard look at her. "You still have your cherry, don't you?"

Without responding, she reached for the ladder, but his foot shot out, kicking it away from the edge. It landed on the wood floor with a crash, bouncing the record needle, causing Dylan's voice to skip.

"Go ahead. Jump," he taunted. "Run away. But the more you run from it, the more it pursues you."

"What the hell's 'it?' " she snapped.

"Sex."

"Geez, have *you* a one track mind."

"Just trying to help you as an actress."

"I don't intend to star in skin flicks, you know? What's sex got to do with acting?"

"Everything. Unless you're sexually free—in tune with your body, all its responses, your acting is going to suffer. You'll keep on acting with only a tiny part of yourself. Like you did this morning."

"I think you're full of asphalt."

He reached for the box-lid again. "You've got a real great face for being an actress, Rebecca. It constantly changes. Just like the ocean. One second it's gray, then the sun comes out and bingo!—it's totally different. Yeah, supersensitive face, all right. Too bad you don't support it."

"What do you mean, support?"

"Your body doesn't support your face. It works against it." He paused to lick the rolling papers. "You ever been nude with a guy?"

"Geez, there you go again. Back on the same track."

"Huh-uh," he muttered, frowning. "Not talking about sex. Talking about nudity. Big difference." He lit the new joint, savoring a lungful. "So I take it you've never been nude with anyone before."

"Sure, my mom," she said, as caustic as she could.

A small smile twisted his swollen lip. "Touch your tits."

She recoiled. "Man, you're too weird. I'm splittin'."

"See how uptight you are?" he threw at her. "You don't think that shows in your acting? You can't even touch yourself in front of someone else."

Her hands flew to her breasts, grabbing them hard. "See?! Big fuckin' deal, huh?"

"Didn't ask you to maul 'em to death," he said easily. "I asked you to touch them ... intimately."

Her hands dropped. "More jollies for you, huh?"

"Don't flatter yourself, kiddo. I couldn't care less."

"So *you* say." Her arms crossed over her chest and for what seemed like ages, they did not speak. Dylan launched into "Desolation Row."

"Give me some of that stuff," she finally said.

"Knock yourself out." He passed the joint.

She held it like a pencil, smelling the rich, sweet, pungent aroma. Slowly she raised it to her lips, shutting her eyes tightly as she sucked the smoke in. Instantly she was coughing. "Strong, huh?"

He shoved her hand away. "Try another." She waited until her chest had cleared, then took a small drag.

Ready to burst, she exhaled. "Where you from anyway?"

"The Bronx. Nowheresville."

"Geez, I'd have never known. Where's da Bronx accent, huh?"

He smiled. "Worked my ass off to get rid of it."

"Scooter your real name?"

He nodded. "Don't ask why, because I don't know. My old man liked it, that's all."

She giggled. "Scooter sounds kinda silly ... you know, for a stage name." The joint was in her hand again and she took another puff.

"Christopher's my middle name. I use that."

"Christopher Warren," she murmured. "Nice. Could do Shakespeare with a name like that."

"Shakespeare's okay, but I like contemporary stuff better. Williams, Genêt, Brecht. I'm waiting to get into the Actors' Studio. Study with Strasberg, Gadge Kazan. The best actors come from there."

"What do you think of Rebecca Lawrence as a name?"

He shrugged, handed her the joint.

"How 'bout Rebecca Addler?"

"Why don't you stick with your own name, Parlato. It's real."

"Well, even Dylan changed his name, right? From Robert Zimmerman? And he's real, right? Besides I don't want anything connected with my old man."

"Why not?"

She took another puff, deliberately ignoring his question. The stereo was playing "Don't Think Twice, It's All Right." She wondered if Scooter were orchestrating something. Though she had heard the song frequently, she felt now she was hearing it for the first time—every word, each verse was fresh, powerful, full of meaning and longing.

She closed her eyes, leaning her head back against the wall, listening with her whole body, becoming a part of Dylan's voice, the guitar on which he played, the girl to whom he was singing. . . .

Lazily she opened her eyes. Scooter was observing her, but this time she did not feel like looking away. Relaxed, she watched the shadows flickering over his face. He smiled off-kilter.

Abruptly she sat up and with one, clean motion, pulled her T-shirt over her head. Feeling bold, adventuresome, she locked eyes with him, throwing back her shoulders. "This was not meant as a sexual act, you know? This is merely to prove that I'm not as uptight as you think I am."

"Or as *you* think you are," he corrected, his eyes holding hers.

She could not believe how exhilarated she felt, as if it were not the shirt she had peeled off, but a layer of some unexplainable burden. Slowly she raised her hands and still watching his reaction, she gently touched her breasts, caressing them timidly, then with more freedom.

Surprised by her own actions, she glanced down at her fingers moving tentatively over her dark nipples. "Not much to look at, is there?"

"Anything over a mouthful is a waste."

She giggled. "I'll have to remember—" Suddenly a ball of self-consciousness slammed into her stomach. She fumbled for her T-shirt, trying to recover her breath, her shoulders dropping forward.

"Don't," he said quietly.

She couldn't raise her head. "I feel terribly . . . you know, brazen."

"So now you know how 'brazen' feels. Use it sometime acting."

"Maybe," she mumbled, fumbling for the front of her shirt.

"So you're bare-chested and so am I. As you said, big fuckin' deal."

Again she giggled, feeling foolish, immature. "Me and my garbage mouth. Mom used to wash my mouth out with soap if she—"

"Take off your jeans."

Tensing, she lowered her head, shaking it from side to side.

"Why not?"

"My panties have holes in 'em," she said, barely audible.

"So take them off too. I won't look at them."

"But you'll look at me."

"So? Isn't that what this exercise is all about?"

She hesitated. "Promise you won't try anything?"

"Hey," he said softly. "I'm an invalid."

Her hands began to tremble. Welding her eyelids together, she undid the fly button of her jeans and with a huge gulp of air for support, leaned backward and stripped everything off at once, kicking both panties and jeans free from her feet. Rapidly she sat up, knees together, hugging them, covering as much of herself as she could. Painfully, she listened to her own heartbeat, feeling the swift pulsations sending reverberations through her whole body.

"Open your eyes."

She shook her head tightly.

"Why?"

"'Cause I'll see you and get so-o-o embarrassed, you know?"

"Nothing to be ashamed of," he said casually. "Tens of thousands live year around like this."

"Not in Buffalo," she said. "In the winter, they'd freeze their tushies off." She blinked open her eyes to see his response and plotzed.

Scooter was nude too, his long, thin frame like an exclamation point not three feet from her. He grinned amiably. "Know what I like most about my skinny body?" he asked, touching his ribcage.

"No," she breathed.

His hand moved lower. "I've a big cock." He flipped it over on his leg, appraising it as if it were a recently purchased salami. He turned his eyes on her. "There you go again, getting uptight. I'm just talking about it, not demonstrating it."

She did not raise her head, her face felt on fire. "I think I could use some more of that stuff."

He handed her a new joint, his fingers grazing hers softly.

They shared the complete jay, passing it back and forth from opposite ends of the loft, silently listening to Dylan. Gradually she felt more and more relaxed, forgetting for long stretches of time about their nudity and coming to the sweet awareness of how much they had in common, their goals, their dreams.

But she was dying to know more about him. Dozens of questions bubbled into her mind but she could not find her tongue to express them. She lay on her side, knees up, her breasts covered by an arm. The low, nasal singing on the stereo fanned her like a gentle, tropical breeze.

She felt a movement beside her. Scooter lay stretched out, his gorgeous face close. "How are you feeling?" he asked gently.

"How'd you know where I worked?"

"Called Robby."

"I should've known."

"Tell me about your old man?"

"Wha'? Why?"

"You seem to have hangups there, that's all."

"*He's* the one with problems, not me."

"What kind?"

"Naw . . ."

"Come on, I want to know you better. Understand you. I can't if you hold back. Resistance creates barriers. Barriers inhibit actors."

After several long, agonizing moments, she began shakily, "Angelo's a crude slob, really. Usually drunk. Works night shift at Bethlehem Steel. Worships my brother, Tony. Ignored me. Until Tony went away to Cornell on a football scholarship. I love Tony . . . wasn't his fault."

"What wasn't?"

"Please . . . I'd rather not."

"What happened after Tony went away?"

She squeezed her eyes shut, trying to block out the memories. "He . . . my ol' man . . . started, you know . . . coming on to me."

"Sexually?"

She nodded grimly.

"Did your mother know?"

She rolled her head away, feeling her eyes liquefy. "Mom's kinda high-strung. Has a hard time coping with things. Takes gobs of Valium . . . puts plastic covers on everything in the house. You know the kind—a pink flamingo statue out in front? Kinda space city, you know . . . wasn't ever aware of much at all. Angelo threatened to beat me up if I told her."

"So what happened?"

A tear wet her cheek. "Got pretty heavy . . ."

". . . and?"

She gulped some air. "One night . . . Mom was zoned out . . . Angelo drunker than usual . . . cornered me in my room . . ." She broke down, crying softly. "It was horrible . . . tried to . . . I tried to fight him off . . ." She sobbed, unable to continue.

"Did he do it?"

Defiantly she shook her head. "No, 'cause I began screaming . . . he hit me hard. I kneed him in the gonads. Got away. Out of the house." She wiped her face, sniffling. "Waited until . . . you know, he'd passed out. I snuck back in for some things. Took enough bread from his wallet for busfare. Split. Came here. Haven't been back since. Won't ever . . ." She tried to smile. "Just your average daily soap opera, huh?"

He was silent for a long while, staring at her, his eyes limpid pools of compassion and understanding.

She rolled her head away. "I . . . I never told that . . . to anyone before. Don't know why I did. Always felt, you know . . . it was my fault, somehow.''

"You're lucky, Rebecca."

"Me? Why?"

"You're young enough to work it all out. Through your acting. It's a huge reservoir of untapped resources waiting for you to draw on.''

"You gotta suffer to be artistic, huh?"

"That's why we're different, us actors. Special folk. So much to give.'' He laid a hand on her bare stomach. "I want to give to you, Rebecca. To help you over this hurdle . . . please. Close your eyes.''

Warily she did, but she was too conscious of his touch. His hand felt so big on her. It moved slowly upward, brushing softly against her breasts. She heard her breath quicken—and cursed the part of her that wanted to flee, yet trembling at the thought of what might happen. Suddenly embarrassed by the size of the breast which he massaged, and by the hardening nipple, she attempted to push away, but he pressed her flat, throwing a leg over her.

"Hey," she said. "Thought you were an invalid?"

"I'm in bed, aren't I?"

One of his fingernails flicked the tips of her breasts. She could feel his hot breath blowing on her neck, like a dry wind. It smelled fruity, tart like an apple. Slowly his hand moved down her trunk, rubbing her hip bones, then her thigh. She tried closing her legs, but he forced his hand between them, touching her there, pressing hard, then soft. He pushed her legs apart, stroking the insides of her thighs.

She felt dizzy, as if the bed were spinning so fast she'd be hurled from it at any moment. All consciousness of time slipped from her and she floated in a state of suspended weightlessness—as if on a white, puffy cloud separated from both earth and sky.

His warm fingers were probing her deeper until she gasped, recoiling from his touch, then pushing herself back into his hand to find that same sensation. Her body felt on fire, her skin tingled everywhere, the delightful excitement in her groin growing, enlarging, engulfing her, sweeping her up into a fevered pitch.

Again and again he caressed her there expertly, raising her higher until her thighs were moist. He was between her legs now, pushing at her with his hardness. She tried to wiggle out from under him but his weight held her down.

The pain was unbearable. Rolling her head from side to side, she moaned, "No, no," in rhythm with his movements, faster and faster, waves of pain and pleasure washing over her, inundating her, taking her higher and higher until she felt she'd explode into a million pieces, never to be put back together again.

"Oh god," she cried out, rising and then falling back on the sheet drenched with sweat, weeping uncontrollably, until he stopped moving completely. Only then did his lips seek hers, sealing their act with a long, tender kiss.

And on the record player, Dylan had fallen silent.

DAVID
October 1966
San Francisco

In the dull gray light, David whirled from the window of his Mission District warehouse loft and flung aside the purple madras spread dividing the living area from the rehearsal space. He frowned at the still sleeping form and jostled the side of the cast-iron bed. "Hey, get up."

The slight form did not stir. "Silver," he said louder and jiggled the bare shoulder which poked over the old quilt like a vanilla Sno-cone. "Move it, Silver," he said. "The guys'll be here soon."

"For Chrissakes," she grumbled into the covers. "Give a girl a break, willya?"

"Get up and maybe I will."

She rolled over flat on her back. "I'd settle for a fast fuck."

"Jesus," he moaned, sniffed again and headed for the small kitchen area near the rear emergency exit. He slammed the teakettle under the sink's faucet and began filling it with water.

"David," she called out sleepily. "Did you give some thought to lettin' some o' the street kids crash here at night. We got all this here space, dig? An' there's so many out there on the streets. It'd—"

He cut in, "Going to make some pretty heavy changes today."

"We was that lousy last night?"

"Judging from the audience, I'd say you guys sucked." He slammed the refrigerator door.

Shortly she appeared beside him, her sinewy body shivering noticeably under a ratty pink kimono. "You won' come down too hard on the guys, will you?" she asked throatily. "Man, they've been bustin' their asses to please you."

"Not hard enough."

David did not greet the rest of the band members as they stepped off the open freight elevator which serviced the warehouse's upper floors. Stonefaced he waved them to chairs he had formed in a half circle in the center of the long brickwalled loft and made them listen to the reel-to-reel tape he'd made of their performance. The raucous, driving music poured from the large, hanging KLH speakers, his top-rated Fisher amplifier putting out forty watts of power.

His back to them, David balanced his checkbook at his desk near the shelves filled with his extensive record collection—over twenty-five hundred albums chronicling the history of rock music from its roots. He'd always spent a lot of bread keeping abreast of what was being put on the market. But what was eating up his bank account most was subsidizing the members of the band. He frowned and pocketed the checkbook. Three months, maybe four, then his mother's trust fund would be completely wiped out. It was time to launch an all-out attack on the music world.

Without turning, he waited until the final note of the last song had faded away and the audience—what little had stayed on until the finish—had offered their spiritless acknowledgment. Switching off the tape deck, he swiveled his chair to stare at them. Only Hawk met his gaze, the others looked away, uncomfortable, perhaps even apprehensive.

Finally Hawk pulled his lanky body upright. "Okay, man, just spill it, why don'cha? We know what it's goin'a be, dude."

"Do you?" David asked.

"Damn right," Hawk snarled. "I think we wailed last night. Best ever. But you don't, now, do you?"

"Not the best, but not the worst either." He paused, watching Hawk, the lead songwriter and guitarist. "Why do you think you bombed?"

Hawk's lips formed a tight line under his beaklike nose. "You're pushin' us in the wrong direction, man. Twistin' me and Larry's songs. Foulin' up their purity, makin' 'em too slick, too commercial, too A.M."

Larry stopped picking a pimple to add sullenly, "And you've rehearsed the spirit out of us, man. Day 'n' night. For months now. It ain't no fun playin' for a dude that's never pleased."

David let the remark slide, eyeing the other members. Zisk, the keyboard player with the teen-throb face which David had so carefully selected, studied a paint stain on the wood floor and Peter, the young drummer, who had some of the goofy charm of a Tommy Smothers, nervously chewed on a wad of gum. Silver was listening from the kitchen area where the smells of her baking handiwork were the most intense.

David popped to his feet, pacing in front of them. "Okay, hear me out. On tape you guys sound fine. The songs are catchy, tuneful, the arrangements solid, lyrics inane enough to be considered meaningful. The backup vocals are more than adequate, your instrumental work proficient, if Pete could beat off on time." As no one laughed, David continued, "But something's lacking. White Meat, as good as it is on tape, is just too bland in person to excite anybody. We've no flash, no style, not different enough visually."

"Speak for yourself, man," Silver joked, bringing in a plate of warm oatmeal-and-molasses cookies.

"You're damned right," David said with enthusiasm. "You *are* the only ingredient that makes us special."

"Yeah, bleached white flour." She cackled briefly at her own humor and held out the plate.

He waved it away. "What I'm driving at is simply this . . . from this moment on, I'm shifting emphasis. The songs, arrangements, backups, everything remains the same. But Silver will carry the majority of the solo spots."

Like a delayed chain reaction, the announcement hit each before him. Silver's mouth widened in disbelief, Peter's gum came to rest on the tip of his tongue, while Larry's probing fingers froze on his cheek. Zisk raised his head in shock.

Hawk did not move a muscle. "What the fuck?"

"Just what I said," David replied evenly. "Sound wise we're right up there with the best. Visually we're as exciting as watching two solo sets of Buffy Sainte Marie. With Silver doing the leads, the group will receive more attention. She's the hook we need. Let's face it, who can resist looking at her? I should've never kept her in the background. Now, as far as lyric changes, I want—"

"Just one fuckin' minute," Hawk bellowed, his forehead flushing crimson under his headband. "They're my songs—mine and Larry's. *We'll* do the singin'."

"White Meat will feature Silver," David said tightly. "Like the Airplane features Slick. Like Big Brother features—"

Zisk broke in, "I thought it was a 'no-stars' band. Just five musicians balancing each other. That's how you sold us."

David tried to keep it light. "Where would Jagger be without the Stones behind him? Just another pretty face."

"So what'll we be called?" Larry asked snidely. "Silver *and* White Meat? Silver *with* White Meat? Or just plain fucking *Silver*!"

Hawk jumped to his feet. "I ain't playin' no backup for nobody," he voiced sharply and glanced down at her. "Nuthin' 'gainst you, Silver, but I ain't cut out to be no backup man. Had my fill of that."

"That goes for me too," Larry said, also rising.

"Look," David hurried to say. "The group is still White Meat. You'll each get time at the solo mike. But I'm telling you, it's a goldmine. It'll get us some notice."

Hawk stormed to his guitar case and snatched it up. Larry quickly followed suit. David lowered the level of his voice. "She'll make us unique, that's all. She's our ace in the hole. Listen, Colton, the club's manager, right? He said last night that—"

Hawk jerked around, his prominent nose jutting into the air derisively. "Don't give a rat's fuck what Colton said. No chick's doing *my* songs."

"You're under contract," David countered.

"You done just ripped it up."

"Hey, mellow out," David said. "Let's discuss this rationally."

The bell, tinny and distant, pinged as the warehouse service elevator rose up the iron-grated shaft. Hawk glared with Larry by his side. David said, "Those guitars you're carrying belong to me."

Silver leaped up. "You're all actin' like a bunch of babies. Nobody's asked me wha' I think."

David ignored her, concentrating acidly on Hawk. "I also own every song of yours. You signed them all over to me for five grand."

Silver flew between them like a white butterfly, her wool-blanket skirt rustling like the beating of wings. "Aw, I don' wanna be no soloist, David. I wanna keep it like it is."

He held his ground. "I repeat, Hawk. If you walk out, your instruments and your songs remain with me. They're my property."

Hawk hurled his case to the floor. "Take the fucker, man. And keep the goddamned songs. Me and Larry can turn out two a day easy, right Larry?" Nodding glumly, his partner set his guitar case down. Behind the metal grating the top of the elevator came into view, its pings louder. Close to tears, Silver wailed, "Hey, not after all the hours we put in. We can't bust up . . . we just can't."

The complete elevator slid into view and the pings stopped. Hawk tore open the metal fence and stepped inside, looking back at the silent two by their chairs. "Zisk? You an' Pete comin' with us?"

Zisk hesitated, then strode to the elevator, leaving the youngest member standing forlornly, chomping on his gum. Abruptly Peter dashed to join the trio in the elevator. Hawk, a satisfied leer on his face, slammed closed the metal grate and hit the button. "See, man," he taunted as the elevator began to descend. "You've got wha'chew wanted now: one lead singer . . ."

The top of the elevator sank toward the loft's floor. David leaned down, shouting, "You don't think you mothers can be replaced? Bullshit for brains, bullshit!"

The heads of the quartet disappeared. He grabbed hold of the grate with both hands, screaming, "You schmucks are a fuckin' dime a dozen, you hear? Not one of you has the talent or guts to make it!" He shook the metal bars, rattling them loudly. "You couldn't land a gig playing for free in a fuckin' whorehouse!"

Silver rushed forward, grabbing his arm, trying to pull him away from the wobbly grating and the open shaft just beyond. He shook her off and stalked to the narrow front windows. Their cold, gray light caught the fear on her face. Warily she followed, but she bellowed ferociously, "You dumb fuck! You jus' blew the whole trip. Down the tubes, man, down the tubes."

He struggled to raise one of the windows, his whole body shaking. The sash was stuck. He grabbed a wooden crate, dumped the albums onto the floor and, using the box as a battering ram, smashed it into the window. The glass shattered, sending splinters flying. He stuck his head out into the cool, damp air and spotted the quartet, six stories below, exiting the warehouse onto the long-idle loading dock.

"You flamin' assholes!" he shrieked down. "You're nothing without me! Nothing but amateur bullshit!"

Vehemently, Hawk flipped him the finger.

A siren exploded in David's head, piercing like sharp needles into his skull. He snatched up the heavy crate and hurled it out the window. It spun through the air, end over end, and crashed harmlessly onto the street, splintering into kindling.

He snapped his head back inside, the siren still screaming. He blinked in the direction of Silver—but the image that came back was blurred, fuzzy. His eyes were not focusing. He could only make out that her mouth was agape, and that she looked flushed.

They stared at one another, silently, as if two species of cats had run accidentally into each other on the same jungle path. Wavering, he took a conciliatory step in her direction. She recoiled, peddling backward. "Silver," he attempted to say, but it came out strangulated, unintelligible.

She flinched at the sound, then, spinning on her heel, fled toward the rear, her long skirt billowing out behind like a small dark parachute.

"Wait a sec," he groaned, trying to reach her. "My head . . ."

"You're fuckin' crazy," she tossed over her shoulder and hit the iron bar across the fire stairs' door. She pushed through it and, like a frightened rabbit, slipped away.

Stumbling to the bed, he crumpled onto it, curling into a tight ball. He waited for the inevitable, knowing from past experiences what was coming. At the peak of the pain, just at its most unbearable, the siren shut down and total blackness descended.

The dull, steady throb in his temples—like a continuous backbeat to an unheard song—pounded him slowly awake. His eyelids shifted upward. Near darkness greeted him.

And silence.

Only in his father's Beverly Hills house had David known such silence . . . the plushly carpeted halls and stairs, the thick walls, the thirty-odd rooms which easily absorbed the handful of servants. And outside, the dense vegetation secluding the ten-acre estate and splashing fountains, all swallowed up sounds, ridding the air of anything human, reducing it to an unearthly silence, a tomblike eeriness.

And then he remembered what had triggered the rare migraine attack: White Meat was no more. Time was running out, along with his money. He hated to admit it, but a pet phrase of his father's seemed applicable—the time had come to shit or get off the pot. With a sharp groan, he rolled to the edge of the bed and swung his feet to the floor. Even before the first wave of dizziness had crested, he was making plans.

The first part of his three-pronged attack took effort—a hard-driven business arrangement with Colton, the night club's manager, that would cost David some big bucks. Pleased with his powers of persuasion but concerned about betting so much on one throw of the dice, David hurried out of the Matrix and hesitated on the sidewalk in front of the popular nightclub. Part two of his plan required finding Silver. Knowing her penchant for the bizarre, the obvious place to begin looking was the Haight-Ashbury District, an area he usually avoided.

Mechanically, David buried his hands deep inside the pockets of his Roos-Atkins car coat and began walking. His energy level was disastrously low, but he was determined. Reaching the outer edges of the Panhandle, a narrow strip of green that ran into Golden Gate Park, he tensed—the freaks were out in full force. Hordes of them, milling about in the gaudy array, looking like refugees from some Fellini flick, he assessed. "Hippies" the mass media had begun to call them, but to him the street people were just stoned freaks— couching their nonproductive lifestyles in catchall phrases of pure bullshit. Flower children, the peace and love generation, psychedelic dropouts—all of it reeked to David of hype and hypocrisy. They were all just trying to get laid or stoned.

He hurried on, pushing through the throng on the corner, trying to reach the other side. "Acid, acid!" some chick yelled. "Get your free Owsley White Lightnin'! Guaranteed Enlightenment in Six Hours!" Wrapped in an American flag, the spaced-looking young woman thrust a grubby hand to him. Unable to avoid her, he shook his head. She persisted, grabbing his hand to drop something into it. He jerked away, scattering the tiny pills onto the sidewalk. Instantly, a short-haired kid wearing a plaid sports jacket dove for them. David stumbled over him, pushing on, feeling a rising anger.

He broke through and darting across the far street, moved steadily into the crowded sidewalks of Ashbury Street. Keeping an eye out for Silver's bushy head, he shoved past the brightly lit, psychedelically painted storefronts, garish in their Dayglo colors. To him, the store owners were nothing but a new breed of hucksters, selling "hip" merchandise geared for the new scene: intricate "trip" posters, love beads, leather belts and stash purses, glass and plastic bongs and other dope paraphernalia. Purveyors to the whole sick scene. Out for a fast buck. Just like everyone else.

Amplified rock music came to him, The Byrds singing "Turn, Turn, Turn." David slowed, changed his direction, making a quick detour to the large discount record store in the next block. It was one of a nine-store chain in the Bay Area and therefore a major source of information. This was part of his off-hours routine. When he was not totally absorbed in making music to sell, he was out researching what kind of music actually sold. Keeping his fingers on the pulse of the entire music industry was his homework and he took it damned seriously.

Ducking inside the store, he quickly surveyed the merchandising layouts, making note of which label was getting the most space and which artist the most push. Columbia was the big winner that week with Simon and Garfunkel's new album, "Bookends." The big, elaborate, moving display was eyecatching in its graphics and damned expensive, he valued.

Listening to the Lovin' Spoonful launch into "Rain on the Roof," David browsed through the new-release bins until the manager behind the counter got off the phone. "Hi, Zeke," David greeted.

"Oh wow, it's the big-time producer," the fringed-vested manager said caustically. "My lucky night. I was hoping I'd missed you this week. So don't tell me, okay? You're still negotiating, right? Big label, right? You're holding out for more bread, right? Months now and I don't see nothing, Rau. You talk a good game, but you ain't produced squat."

David concentrated on the new Top 40 list on the countertop. He tapped the list. "How's my pick of the week doing?"

"Okay, wise guy, so you guessed lucky. Seventy-nine units I sold of the Association's "Cherish" just yesterday. Now here's my pick, The Trog's new one."

For another twenty minutes, David milked for information. Zeke knew the rack and jobber end of the game better than anyone in the city. Then, after receiving a fairly solid breakdown of the records sold that week in the Bay Area, David slipped out into the streets. "Spare some change, man?" asked a teeny-bopper with a painted butterfly on her cheek. "Get a job," David growled, once again eager to locate Silver. Four hours later, close to one in the morning, he finally found her.

Numb from the cold, sick of the whole dirty, ugly, tawdry scene, David slipped into a storefront offering herbal teas and health food munchies. Silver's raspy, unmistakable voice came to him from the back of the narrow, crowded room. Singing "Empty Bed Blues," she sounded hoarse, exhausted, as though she'd been at it for a long, long time. Under the harsh fluorescent lighting, she looked like a faded white lily draped over a black guitar.

David elbowed his way through the crowd. He had only to glance at their faces to know she held her audience completely. Their rapt attention bordered on the worshipful as she wrung out every ounce of pathos from the lyric. The rough graininess of her voice added to the open wound of pain being expressed. Again the future flashed before his mind like a blazing comet.

Her last note faded away and he put down his cup to applaud loudly. He was the only one to do so. The others merely nodded, a few clicked their fingers to demonstrate approval. Heads turned, faces frowned at the intruder who did not know the ground rules. "Say, peaceful, bro," an Afroed black guy sighed. "Keep it cool, man, can you dig it?" an obese girl in a gingham grannie dress offered with a buttery grin. David clapped even louder and said to the fat girl next to him, "Hey, I'm doing *my* thing. You do yours."

Over the top of her dark glasses, Silver zeroed in on him. Avoiding his gaze, she slid off the stool and handed the guitar to an aging beatnik with a graying Maynard G. Krebs goatee. Groans of displeasure burst out but Silver muttered something about the "vibes being too heavy" and scooted out the backdoor.

David caught up to her in the alley, matching her long, booted stride. "Hey, let's talk it out."

"Nothin' to say to you, man," she said, not looking at him.

"You sounded terrific back there. The best I've heard you."

"Ol' Bessie's my style, dig?" She threw him a meaningful glance over her shades and rounded the corner into the street.

"Blues are definitely your forte. We *should* do more pure blues."

She pulled up short. "What's this *we* shit, Tonto?" she shot at him like a whip. "From now on, I'm goin' to sing what *I* wanna sing . . . dig?" Snatching off her dark glasses, she shoved them into a pocket of her baggy, handmade skirt. "An another thin', I done got me a new pad already. I'll pick up my stuff tomorrow, okay? Late. Real late."

He shrugged his only response. As if surprised by his silence, she jerked away again, heading up Masonic Avenue. For a few steps, he followed a pace behind, watching her struggle to pull her arms out of the sweater's sleeves. Under the shapeless gray wool, she wrapped her arms around her middle, hugging her thin waist.

He yanked off his carcoat and draped it around her shoulders. She halted, her head lowered. A shudder trembled her back. She muttered with clenched teeth, "You damned, sonofabitchin' cocksucker. Wha'chew do tha' for?"

"You looked cold."

"I *am* cold, dammit," she growled. "An' I've been cold for two months now an' you ain't never done nothin' 'bout it before. You jus' want somethin' from me? Huh? That it? You only bein' nice 'cause you want somethin'?"

"Yeah, I want something from you. I want you to come back with me." Seeing her head rise warily, he added in his softest voice, "I missed you, Silver."

She did not believe him—it was etched all over her pale face like black brushmarks. He steered a new course. "I admit, Silver . . . I'm a raving Viet Cong at times. Like this morning. I couldn't have killed everything better if I'd blown it up with Napalm, right?"

She nodded, scowling, distrustful.

"I need you," he continued with soft urgency, "to keep me on the right track."

"You never listened before. Why should you start?"

"Because I see what happens now . . . I lose everything I want . . . especially you."

Silver did not move. "I don' know, David. You scare me sometimes awful. I never know when you're gonna explode."

"I can't promise I won't blow up now and then. It's my nature."

"Ain't askin' for no promises, man . . . all I want's a little honesty."

"I'm being as honest as I can, Silver."

"Yeah, but how honest is that? You want *me* back or my voice?"

He did not hesitate. "Both."

"Meanin' you want me to sing for you?"

"Right."

"An' if I won't?"

He locked eyes with her. "I'm going to tell you something I've never told anyone before. The last time I saw my mother alive . . . I'd just turned eight, she was moving out of the house after the divorce and I begged her to take me with her. But she said, she couldn't. That her life was not her own. 'Not until I reach my goals, Davey,' she said." He paused, then continued slowly, "I understood then. And I'm still just like her. My life is not my own until I reach my goals. Regardless how much I may personally feel, I can't take you back, unless you're part of the plan."

She sniffed, eyeing him with renewed curiosity. "Well, if that don't pucker my butt, nothin' will."

He laughed with a boyish urgency. Shaking her head sagely at him, she took his coat from her shoulders and held it up. "You better wear this then, man. I got me a heavy sweater on."

He took her back to the loft, removed her several layers of clothing and, on the quilt, tried to make love to her. But love was damned difficult for him to express and he knew it. So he ended up just screwing her, paying as much attention to her pleasure as he could. Afterward, he realized he need not have worried. Of all the chicks he'd been with, Silver was the easiest to make come.

While her breathing normalized, he kept his eyes on the old Irish lace tablecloth she'd rigged overhead as a canopy. The wavering light of the fat candle on the floor revealed the many rips and tears in the lace.

"Colton wants us back," he said quietly.

"He does!" she squealed, jumping to her knees, the patchwork quilt falling from her bare shoulders. "Hot shit, why didn'cha say somethin'?"

"Because you won't dig the conditions. He wants you to sing lead." He looked up at her. "Said it was the only way he'd let us have another crack at it."

The statement was far from the truth. Colton only agreed to the group's return if David fronted all the publicity money, paid for the other band and kicked in something under the table. David now studied her stoic reaction.

It was many moments before she spoke. "What 'bout the other dudes?"

"Who needs them? We got the songs, have the equipment. Best of all, we've got you."

She frowned, nestling into her side of the bed. "You know what your problem is, man? You don't think o' others, dig? You jus' sort o' barrel on through an' then you act surprised when some cat jumps up an' yells, 'Hey, man, I don't dig that.'"

He wiggled his jawbone a few times. "Posters for the new gig are already at the printers. If Hawk and the others are here before I hire replacements, I might consider taking them back. Otherwise . . ."

She wrapped a lanky leg over his middle. "But is it fair to them, man? Seems kind of cold an' hard-nosed. Gotta consider the karmic repercussions, dig?"

"You're the important factor, Silver." He yawned. "Don't forget that. You're going to hit bigger than the opening of the new Metropolitan Opera House. Now let me crash while I can . . ." He turned into her, wrapping her in his arms, tightly hanging on. Phase two, accomplished.

SHELBY
November 1966
New York

"Tilt your chin a hair to the left—too much. Back. Up a bit. Hold it. Think sexy, Sunny, keep it coming, keep it coming."

The camera clicked and whirled. In three seconds, the top-rated photographer shot seven exposures. "Okay, okay, relax," Teddy said, making a lens adjustment.

With a *whoosh*, Shelby expelled the air she had been holding.

"Dammit, Sunny," the hairdresser moaned in exasperation. "Now you've messed the wave."

"Oh, I'm so sorry," Shelby murmured. A stocking-footed hair assistant darted into the light, her smoke blue smock bearing the silver logo of Villa Caesari. The errant lock of hair was carefully prodded back into place with the tail of a sharp-ended comb.

Moving only her eye muscles, Shelby tried to locate her boss beyond the bright lights. "How much longer?" she asked plaintively.

"Until I know Teddy has it," came his voice.

God only knows when that will be, she thought. Caesari's suite of offices lay just down the hall. An endless relay of secretaries and assistants streamed in and out of the studio in order that he could run his mammoth cosmetic empire while overseeing every detail of each Sunny ad. He was so demanding, a scheduled hour would stretch interminably into three—often four and more. And Caesari expected that she appear as fresh in the last minutes as she had in the first. That was not so difficult for some print ads or commercials for which she could move about while being shot. For this photo session, however, she had to remain totally immobile. Her lower back, her arms, everything ached from being held stiffly for so long.

She caught a glimpse of Caesari leaning forward into the white light, his darkly tanned face frowning noticeably.

"How long's this smudge been here?" He jabbed a well-manicured finger at the product bottle suspended on an invisible fishline. "Replace this."

"May I take a break then?" she asked.

"But of course," Caesari said, his annoyance evident.

She broke the pose, dropping her arms and standing straight. At once she felt relief in her strained muscles. Gratefully, she slipped out of the gold heels and leaving them, lifted the heavy gold lamé skirt of the Grecian-styled gown and stepped off the white roll of paper, out of the hot, glaring lights.

Caesari, totally occupied with the phallic-shaped bottle, did not acknowledge her. In her stocking feet, she walked quickly to the phone on the side counter and dialed her service number. "Hi, it's Shelby," she said when the lady had answered. "Any word from my father?"

"No," the friendly voice responded. "But an Erik Lungren has called three times today."

The name sounded vaguely familiar but Shelby couldn't place it with a face. "What'd he want?"

"No message, but he left his number. Want it?"

"Y'all're positively, absolutely sure my father hasn't called?" Again the answer was negative. Fighting her disappointment, Shelby collected her other messages—one from her lawyer, two from the accounting firm, something about a lost W-2 form, and a call from *Women's Wear Daily* requesting a follow-up interview. "Hold all those and if my father phones, be sure to connect him here, immediately."

She hung up and stood tiredly for a long moment before heading for her dressing room at the far end of the two-storied space.

"You're not planning on sitting in that?" Caesari's voice asked.

She turned. "Honestly, Giorgio, how else is a girl to go?"

"You'll have to have wardrobe remove the gown first." He stepped forward, looking like a fashion page from *Gentlemen's Quarterly*.

She let her posture droop. "Forget it. I'll wait 'til we're through." She paused, adding grimly, "If my bladder bursts, just bury me in ol' Virginny."

"I'm certain your grandmother would be quite pleased at your return. Dead or alive." From an inner pocket, he removed and checked a thin datebook. "We've dinner at seven-thirty. *Le Pavilion*."

"Giorgio, my father is coming in tonight. Remember, I told you."

One of his black eyebrows rose. "When?"

"He said he'd be here by dinnertime."

The eyebrow arched higher. "No. *When* did you inform me of this?"

"Just after I heard from him. Monday . . . Tuesday, maybe."

He closed his calendar. "My car will call for you at seven."

"Giorgio," she cried. "I can't. I haven't seen my father in over three years. It would be—"

He cut her off by an almost imperceptible narrowing of his eyelids—a warning to which she'd become all too accustomed. "Very well," he sighed, "if you insist. Bring him along." He dismissed the subject by spinning toward the shoeless crew replacing the besmirched bottle.

"Teddy," Caesari said, "can't you get more highlights on that side? Like the sun itself."

Shelby felt like screaming, he made her so mad.

So what if the Sunny line, within three months of hitting the market, was the most successful and profitable introduction in the history of the cosmetic industry? So what that he had made her, almost overnight, into the most recognizable face in all America? So he was a genius . . . she wouldn't deny him that. But none of these factors mattered when it came down to his callous treatment of her.

Snuggling deeper into the lynx fur coat, an exhausted Shelby stepped out of the Villa Caesari building into the bitter cold of Fifth Avenue. Christmas lights and decorations were already in place over the street and in the store windows; the cathedral bells of nearby Saint Patrick's chimed carols. She hurried to the silver limousine at the curb.

When she was let off in front of the Sutton Place Towers, she eagerly stepped to the uniformed doorman. "Did my father arrive?"

" 'Fraid not, Miss Cale."

Her spirits sagged. "Damn," she murmured, walking through into the marble-floored lobby of the luxury high-rise. "Oh, Miss Cale," the doorman said behind her. "This came for you a short time ago."

"How nice," she said, absently accepting the long white box which bore a florist shop's name. In the elevator, to the accompaniment of piped-in Muzak playing a schmaltzy rendition of "Moon River," she opened the box of long-stemmed yellow rosebuds. The enclosed card read simply: "Looking forward to your return call." A phone number was included just under the signature, *Erik Lungren*.

Briefly she stared at the bold, masculine handwriting, trying to remember where she'd met the man. There had been so many in the last few months—dozens and dozens—all giving her the rush. There was no way she could keep track of them. Besides, she had no desire to. She'd know when the right one came along, purely on instinct.

Entering her apartment on the eighteenth floor, she dropped the box on the foyer table and hurried into the white carpeted, sparsely furnished living room. There was no message from her father with the answering service.

Stewing, she pinned up her hair and bathed. She wished she could stay longer in the hot tub but she knew Caesari's driver would arrive promptly at seven. Reluctantly she climbed out, toweled herself, donned her full-length cashmere robe and sat at her vanity table.

Her image shocked her. The creamy smooth complexion on which she prided herself had vanished. The hot lights of the all-afternoon session, in combination with the heavy makeup, had blotched her face horribly. And to top it off, an angry, red pimple had begun to form on her brow.

Snatching up the receiver, she rang Caesari's office. His private secretary answered. "Sugar, this is Shelby. Contact Giorgio and tell him I can't make it tonight. My face is hideously broken out," she moaned. "I wouldn't go to a darkey's funeral looking like this."

Within minutes the phone rang. Caesari demanded to know what was going on. "Giorgio, I promise not to breathe a word to Leonard Lyons," she said. "But I'm afraid I'm allergic to your products."

"Nonsense," he replied. "You've been wearing my makeup for months. It must be something you've eaten."

"I've been starving to death," she said, her tone rising.

"I'm coming over to see for myself."

"I'm appalled that y'all think I'm lying." But he'd hung up. Sputtering with anger, she slammed down the receiver.

Slowly time ticked by and her apprehension grew. Long before, she found it not only totally impossible to read Giorgio's thoughts or feelings, but even more disconcerting—he seemed impervious to her charms. His lack of sexual interest frustrated and even confused her. His coldness made her feel weak and his disapproval reduced her to a state of fear.

The intercom buzzer beeped. She flew to the entrance foyer and instantly told the doorman to let him come up. She dashed to the bathroom to scrutinize her face one last time—the marks were there all right, but certainly not any disaster. She slapped her face a couple of times, urging the splotches to look more alive.

Shortly her doorbell chimed. She mentally crossed her fingers and opened the door.

A big, sandy-haired stranger grinned down at her.

In utter confusion, she stared back, then glanced down the carpeted hallway. Caesari was nowhere in sight. She partially closed the door. "Yes?" she asked, pulling her white robe tighter.

His smile faded some. "You don't remember me?"

"Should I?" Before the stranger could reply, she added, "Did y'all just ring downstairs?"

"Yeah." His ruggedly good-looking face clouded. "You're expecting someone else?"

She frowned. "Yes . . . if y'all don't mind . . ." Her voice trailed off as she took a closer look at him. "Say, I *do* know you, don't I?"

He smiled again. "I'm Erik Lungren. We met at the pageant. I gave you sort of a—"

"—a *pep* talk," she finished for him. "Of course, *now* I place y'all. I'm so sorry. Erik, is it? Please, forgive me. It's just . . . well, I was expecting Mister Caesari any moment." She watched his soft hazel eyes register disappointment.

He glanced down at his thumbs hooked into his belt, then back at her. "I realize it's sort of presumptuous to arrive without an invitation. Just thought I'd chance you being in."

"I am, but barely," she said, feeling some of his awkwardness. Opening the door further, she checked out the far elevators. "Would y'all like to come in for a spell?"

"I'd like that."

She stepped back to let him through, then closed the door softly. "I must look a fright," she said, leading him into the living room.

"On the contrary," he replied, eyeing her. " 'To one who has been long in city pent, 'Tis very sweet to look into the fair, And open face of heaven.' "

The way he said it made her feel he was quoting someone, but she did not want to ask who. Regardless, the words pleased her and she tilted her head. "My face? See? Horribly blotched."

He leaned down to examine closely. "Hardly noticeable. You look flushed, that's all." Before she was aware of any movement, a broad hand lay on her forehead—gentle, cool, steady. Instinctively, her eyes closed. "Doesn't seem you have fever," he said, his voice low, quiet.

For a moment, she relished his touch, but more his concern. Her eyes opened and she looked deep into his. They exuded a warmth and attentiveness she had not experienced for some time.

"Oh, I'm not running a fever," she said with a light laugh. "It's just that makeup and hot lights wreck havoc on a girl's skin."

Slowly, he took his hand away and it dropped loosely to his side.

"Obviously yours is extrasensitive. In fact, it's so creamy you don't look like you've ever been out in the sun."

She laughed again and moved to the table lamp at the end of the off-white, deeply cushioned couch. "My grandmother always forbade going out uncovered—insisted that snow white skin is a sure sign of pure bloodlines." Switching on the lamp, she turned to him, aware that her hair was now backlit effectively. "She's very big on that—bloodlines."

"Yes, a strong aristocratic type. I could tell that afternoon they came to the pageant to fetch you."

"*Fetch* me?" She trilled another laugh, tossing her hair. "That's putting it mildly."

He laughed with her and it made her feel warm and comfortable. And then there was that softness in his eyes. They were observing her every move like a farm animal—one of Evangeline's horses, or perhaps a field dog, friendly, expectant, yet somewhat cautious.

He pulled a hardbound book out of his baggy sports coat pocket. "I brought you a copy of my first novel."

"A writer?" she asked, very surprised, and accepted the book. "*Bell of Donna*," she murmured, reading the title. "A novel by Erik Lungren." She raised her eyes. "How impressive . . . really, truly."

"I wrote an inscription for you."

"You did?" She thumbed to the inside cover, reading aloud, "To Shelby, with grateful thanks for her inspiration." He had signed it, *With Love, Erik.* She lowered the book. "Inspiration? What inspiration?"

"I've your picture over my desk. Since I put it up, I've gotten a new publisher for my present novel. Your smile makes bearable the whole tedious process of writing."

The way he said it produced a short flurry of gooseflesh all over her—he sounded sort of shy, hesitant, but *very* respectful. "How thoughtful, really. Thank y'all, muchly," she said. "I'll try to read it this weekend. I promise. If my time's not all booked up." She laid the novel on the endtable, laughing gaily. "And I thought y'all were one of the stagehands or something . . . but a writer, I had no idea. Looks can be deceiving, can't they?"

He jerked his wavey head toward the entrance foyer. "See you got the flowers."

"Oh, my goodness, I forgot all about them." She hurried to retrieve them. "I only just got back myself," she sang out and picked up the long box. "Why don't y'all come into the kitchen while I put them in water." Throwing a quick glance into the foyer mirror, she moved to the kitchen. "How did y'all know where I lived? Thought Villa Caesari guarded that information like a military secret."

He ambled in and leaned against the counter, crossing his thick arms across the pearl buttons of his cowboy shirt. "My friend, Mo, got it for me. Remember her... Maureen Engle? The pageant producer?"

Her hands hesitated over the open box of yellow buds. "Y'all a friend of hers?"

"Yeah ... super lady."

"I ... I guess I really didn't get a chance to know her too well," she said, hedging her true feelings. "These are so lovely. Yellow roses are my very all-time favorite." She opened a cabinet, searching. "Now, what to put them in? I don't think I've got a single vase yet."

"Doesn't look like you have much of anything."

Moving on to another cabinet, she laughed. "Honestly, it's worse than living at a hotel. At least *there* I had room service."

"How long have you been here?"

Discouraged at not finding a suitable container, she shut the last cabinet door. "Couple of months. Caesari's office found it for me, but—"

The buzzer sounded in the entrance foyer. Instantly she shivered. "Oh, my god, that must be him." She dashed to the intercom. "Hello?" she called into it, then hearing Caesari's name, added, "Yes, please, send him up." She let go of the button and thought frantically. Giorgio had made it clear that *all* personal dates would have to be cleared with him first—just as a precaution against any freeloaders or gigolos.

Hearing water running, she returned to the kitchen. Erik had filled her stainless steel coffee pot, minus all its internals, and was putting in the roses. He glanced up. "Want me to go?"

"No," she said quickly. "Not especially, but..."

"But...I probably should?"

"Why don't y'all just wait in the bedroom," she suggested. "He shouldn't be long, I'm sure. He just wants to see my blotches."

"Well, if that's what he came for, he'll be disappointed."

"Well, I'm *not* going out tonight and that's final." She turned. Erik, with an amused smile, was watching her from the kitchen. "Well, I'm not," she repeated. "He can't make me."

His broad shoulders shrugged. "I always say—what's fair's fair."

"Y'all are so right." A soft bell from the hall elevator whirled her toward the front door. "That's him. Hurry." Erik swiftly moved into the living room, cutting across to the bedroom. "Don't close the door," she whispered. "I'll get rid of him as fast as I can."

"Sounds good to me," he said quietly from the other room.

Her doorbell chimed. In front of the hall mirror, she pinched at her face until she winced, then hesitating a few seconds, opened the door. Immediately, Caesari, dressed in formal dinner attire, appraised her face. He frowned and strode past her. "Come here."

She closed the door and moved to him. He snapped on the bright, overhead hall light. "Raise your face," he ordered. Doing so, she crossed her fingers tightly behind her back and closed her eyes. Unexpectedly he touched her cheek, causing her to flinch. Unlike Erik's cool hand, Giorgio's was moist and warm.

Pulling away, she looked at him icily. "*See*, I wasn't lying."

"Hardly the catastrophe you implied."

"Y'all should have seen them right after my bath—big ugly red marks all over my face."

Without commenting, he walked into the kitchen, noticing at once the yellow roses on the counter. "Who are those from?" he asked, rinsing his hands in the sink.

"A friend," she said.

"Who?"

"Oh, for heaven's sake, Giorgio, aren't I allowed to have my own friends? Or is that also covered in the small print of your contract?"

He took his time drying his hands on a paper towel—like a surgeon, she thought, overly cautious of germs. "Get dressed," he said.

"I'm not going anywhere tonight. Not with my face like this. Besides, I still haven't heard from my father."

"Tomorrow morning, nine sharp, you have an appointment with my dermatologist." From his black satin vest, he pulled out a white business card. "He's the very best."

"I'm sure he is," she murmured coolly.

"He assured me that light layer of foundation would not harm."

"Good," she responded. "Let *him* wear it then. Tonight my face is taking a vacation." She snatched up the coffeepot of roses and strode into the living room, setting them on the endtable next to Erik's book.

Erik's book! Quickly she stuffed the novel under the end cushions of the couch.

"Who's Erik Lungren?" Caesari's voice asked behind her.

She spun, her eyes flicking past the open bedroom door. "Who?"

"Erik Lungren," he repeated, brandishing the florist card.

Flustered, angry at him for having fished the card out of the box, she said, "Just a writer friend."

"A writer? Of what?" he asked incredulously.

"Novels," she said, trying to remember the title. "He's a friend of Maureen Engle's."

One of his eyebrows arched toward the ceiling. "Where did you meet him?"

"At the pageant," she offered and plopped herself onto the couch, hugging the end cushion. "Anything else y'all'd like to know?" she asked, overly sweet.

Giorgio studied her for a long moment, his chiseled features set. She forced herself to hold his gaze and not glance toward the darkened bedroom doorway just beyond him. He slipped the florist card into the watchpocket of his evening vest. "What happened to the furniture I ordered?"

"Sent it back."

"Why?"

"Didn't like it," she said boldly. "Just this couch."

"When did you do this?"

"The same day it arrived."

He started walking toward the floor-to-ceiling drapes at the far end. She tensed as he passed the bedroom door. "You plan to live like this for long?" he asked, and yanked on the cord, opening the heavy damask drapes. Gradually, through the sliding glass doors leading out onto the balcony terrace, the garland of lights on the Fifty-ninth Street Bridge came into view. Across the street, a gaily lit Christmas tree on a terrace twinkled in the night breeze.

"Until I get bored with it," she responded. "I sort of like all this emptiness . . . matches my life."

He stood with his back to her, apparently looking out at the view, but she had the oddest feeling he was observing her reflection on the glass. "Are you not happy being Sunny?" he asked.

Nonchalantly, she reached out and touched the nearest rosebud, trying to control the sudden quavering she felt at the back of her throat. "I have so little time to myself, y'all've got me booked so much. Your whole staff orders and pushes me around like I'm a servant or something. And you . . . y'all treat me like I'm a product that can be replaced if I don't measure up. And I don't have any real friends of my own." She had the feeling Giorgio was not listening.

He did not turn but ordered softly, "Come here."

Briefly she debated whether to defy him more openly. Gathering the soft folds of her robe's skirt, she rose from the couch and walked to him. He turned to her, his metal-colored eyes moving minutely over every centimeter of her facial skin. "These are the only blemishes?"

"Yes."

"You're positive?"

"Of course."

"Let me be the judge of that."

She hesitated, a question forming.

"Open your robe."

She felt a bubble of rebellion lodge in her throat. "Why?"

"Because I told you to."

Her head rose. "Am I to do everything y'all tell me?"

"Yes."

"Well, I won't."

His eyes narrowed almost imperceptibly and he did not speak for several moments. "Either you open your robe and let me see for

myself, or get dressed immediately. I will not keep the head of my
Paris office waiting.''

Her back stiffened. ''I am not lying, Giorgio. These blotches are
only on my face.''

''Prove it.''

A groan of anger burst from her throat and her hands tore open the
sash belt. She yanked apart the front of her robe, her eyes closing.
The silence in the room was unbearable. A warm finger touched
lightly at her lower abdomen, causing her to recoil. ''What's this?''
he asked.

''Birthmark,'' she said, clenching her jaw.

Then the oddest thing happened—she heard a sharp intake of
breath. When he spoke again, his voice was thick, soft. ''Drop the
robe.''

Curious to see a chink in his armor, she opened her eyes. His face
appeared drained of blood, making his tan look as if it came from
out of a bottle. But it was his eyes that gave him away. Focused
below her stomach, they no longer reminded her of metal—in fact,
they looked soft, almost vulnerable. As they traveled up her body,
however, the hardness returned. By the time they reached hers she
could detect nothing out of the ordinary.

''Do we have to do this in front of the whole world?'' she asked,
terribly aware of the opposite apartment tower. In response, he
grabbed her robe and yanked it from her shoulders. It fell to the
carpet. Wrapping her arms around herself, she shuddered and her
head drooped forward, her eyes stinging with unshed tears. It
seemed an eternity before she heard him complete his circle of her.
''Satisfied?'' she managed to ask.

''It is very apparent you've gained weight through the hips,'' he
said crisply. ''You're getting a fat ass.''

She reacted as if he had burned her with a lit cigarette. Bending
quickly, she grabbed her robe, holding it to her front, her lower lip
trembling. ''You . . . you bastard!''

Through her tears, his face blurred, but his voice came with a
clipped precision. ''I'm canceling next week's shootings and making
an appointment for you with a weight specialist. I will not have my
Sunny as broad through the hips as a Long Island matron.''

Stunned, she struggled to find words to express her rage. The phone rang next to the couch. Before she barely registered it, Caesari had answered and said, "One moment, I'll see if she's in." She pulled on her robe as he covered the mouthpiece. "Are you in for your father?"

"Daddy?!" She rushed forward, grabbing the receiver. "Daddy, where are you?"

"In Chicago," came the familiar voice, sounding very far away. "You can't believe the damned mess here. It's taken forever standing in line to get to a phone."

"Oh, daddy, daddy," she repeated, unable to stop the tears.

"Baby, you weren't worried about me, were you?"

"I waited all day," she sobbed, sinking to the couch.

"Oh, poor baby," he drawled in his soft Southern accent. "I'm really sorry but it's been a damned crazy day."

"When y'all coming?"

"Baby, that's why I called. This damned blizzard has fouled up my whole schedule and—"

"Y'all're not coming?"

"Sugar, I'd love to if I could. But the airport's closed indefinitely so I guess I'll just postpone this trip for a while and return home as soon as I can."

"Oh, daddy . . ."

"I know, I know, baby . . . I'm disappointed, too. Believe me. But we'll make it another time. Soon, I promise."

"Can't y'all give me a little hint? To have something to look forward to?"

"Wish I could, baby. Really. But we'll have to see how things develop with my boss on this merger thing. You'd . . ." His voice faded out, a crackling sound interfering.

"Daddy? I can't hear you," she shouted. The static increased, sharp, staccato, then diminished, his voice emerging like a figure in a snowstorm. ". . . we're all so proud of you, sugar. Little Curtis has a wall full of your ads and Laura's just dying to meet you. Had her hair cut just like yours. They all send their love, sugar."

She wiped her eyes with the back of her free hand. "Oh, daddy, I miss y'all so much. I just—"

"Baby, this connection is terrible. What'd y'all say?"

"I miss y'all," she cried out.

"I love y'all too, sugar. I'll be in touch. Y'all be a good girl and we'll talk real soon. Bye now, baby."

The line went dead, buzzing rudely in her ear. She stared at the receiver in her hand as if it were an unrecognizable object. Feeling a horrible cloud of loneliness blanketing her, she tried to find the phone cradle through the haze of tears. A large masculine hand gently took the receiver from her and replaced it.

Erik stood before her, jacket off, looking down from what seemed an incredible height. She had forgotten he was there. She jumped up, looking about, whispering, "Where's Caesari?"

"Gone. Right after you got on the phone. I heard him go."

Relieved beyond words, she dropped to the couch, suddenly unable to stop the tears. She felt the cushion sag next to her and a warm, protective arm around her shoulders, pulling her close. His action came as such a welcome surprise, she could only sob more. "Y'all must think I'm a complete idiot," she cried into his chest.

"Not at all," he said softly. "But you're right about one thing." She looked up tearfully, searching his face. "Caesari *is* an A-Number-One bastard," Erik said. "It took every ounce of willpower to keep me from stomping in here and decking him."

The very thought pleased her. "Oh, my god," she breathed. "I'm so glad y'all didn't. He'd probably have fired me on the spot."

"He treated you like a slab of meat in a butcher shop. Why do you put up with that?"

"What choice do I have?"

"Hell, Shelby," he groaned, then pulled away, holding her shoulders. "You could walk out of that contract any time you choose. And right into any top modeling agency in the world. Or be your own agency, go independent."

Her eyes widened in alarm. "Oh, I wouldn't want to give up being Sunny. It's the very best thing that's ever happened to me in my *whole* life. I adore it, really, truly . . . I can't walk anywhere without someone recognizing me. And I'm meeting the most fabulous people. At the premiere party for *Who's Afraid of Virginia Woolf?* Giorgio and I sat at the very same table as Elizabeth Taylor and Richard Burton. Had such a good time, we laughed all night. Things like that make it all worthwhile. Y'all know what I mean?"

A pained expression filtered his slow nod. "Yeah, I know what you mean. I've been there."

His understanding and sympathy was so unexpected, his concern so evident, she felt like crying again. She pulled away slightly to collect her emotions, not wanting to appear as young and foolish as she felt.

For a moment, both were silent. He reached into his shirt pocket, withdrawing a pack of Camels. He hesitated, asking, "Mind if I smoke?" She shook her head. He lit a wooden kitchen match by scratching a thumbnail over its end. Her eyes flared in wonderment. "You know," he began again. "You are blessed . . ."

For want of a quicker response, she lowered her long eyelashes and looked up through them. "Why do y'all say that?"

"To be so close to your dad. Like I was."

"Oh, yes," she agreed, vigorously. "I *am* blessed that way. Blessed to have the most wonderful daddy in the whole world. And the finest horseman in Virginia . . . well, once upon a time anyway. He doesn't ride much anymore. Not year 'round, anyway."

He was smiling, tilting his head.

"What do y'all find so amusing?" she asked, tossing her hair provocatively.

"You," he answered, his tone playful. "I find you endearing."

She was touched by the mere sound of it but, because he was staring so raptly at her face, she longed to slip away for needed repairs. "Would y'all like some champagne? I'm just dying of thirst." Before he could reply, she swiveled her knees off to one side and rose in one graceful motion. "It's in the fridge. I was depending upon my daddy to be here to open it, but . . ." Her voice trailed off and she moved into the hall. "There're glasses on the top shelf next to the sink. I'll rejoin y'all shortly," she said enticingly and closed the bathroom door.

Her eyes swept over the incredible array of bottles, jars, tubes, and brushes jamming the shelves and layering the top of the vanity table. Swiftly she chose what she would need. It would be only the bare necessities for she did not want to suddenly reappear with full makeup. Expertly she set to work, her fingers moving deftly over the routines learned so well, a blush here, a highlight there. The last thing before washing her hands and turning off the vanity lights, she slipped her diaphragm into place.

Erik stood by the windows overlooking the bridge, sipping from one of the elegant Baccarat glasses she'd purchased at Tiffany's especially for her daddy's arrival. On the table next to the yellow roses, he had set the open bottle of champagne on a paper towel next to her glass. She paused in the doorway, holding the pose until he turned. She could tell by his eyes that her preparations met his approval.

He strode to the table and poured the other glass. She glided nearer to the window wall and waited for him to come to her. Slowly, he did, not taking his eyes off hers. He handed her the glass and raised his. " 'Truth is beauty, beauty is truth,' " he said softly and touched the rim of his glass to hers.

The soft clink of their glasses meeting, the lovely words he had uttered, the way his eyes stared longingly over the rim of his glass as he sipped—all these sent a shiver of delight down her back. She wrinkled her nose at the bubbles and laughing, as if to herself, she abruptly turned from him, moving to the small portable radio on the endtable. She switched it on, and turning it low, searched leisurely for an appropriate station. She settled on one of her favorite songs, "Born Free." Taking another sip from her crystal goblet, she eyed him openly. "Are y'all close to your father?"

"Dad died when I was sixteen—just a year after mom passed away."

She did not know what to say so asked, "How'd they die?"

"Dad, at sea. A few miles out of Coos Bay, that's in Oregon. A fisherman. Just disappeared overboard one night." He hesitated. "About a year earlier, my mother went fast too. One minute she was playing the piano in the parlor, the next, she was gone. Cerebral hemorrhage."

"I'm so sorry." She moved closer to him. "How'd y'all become a writer?"

"Started as an avid reader. Mom got me a library card when I was six. Made certain I used it every week. Each night, she read to me before I went to sleep—Twain, Kipling, London, Dickens. She had a beautiful voice, soft, melodious. Much like yours.''

A lump welled in her throat and she felt the tears forming in her eyes. She did not know why she was crying again; she thought maybe it was because she felt somehow that they were both orphans in a way, alone in the world. The only thing she knew for certain was that she wanted him to come and put his arms around her, to hold her tightly.

He frowned at the portable radio, it was playing "Winchester Cathedral." He switched it off and without a word, crossed to her, enveloping her in a tender embrace. He kissed her cheeks and she felt his warm, rough tongue licking the tears that slipped from her eyes. Gently he rocked her back and forth, murmuring in her ear, "It's all right, Shelby, it's okay." Again and again he kissed her face, then her neck and hair, retracing his steps over and over until her breath quickened.

She raised her arms, locked them around his neck. Tears forgotten, she searched for his lips and pressed hers on them. She held there, her mouth partly open, breathing in his warmth, feeling a growing excitement. Slowly his tongue explored, pushing softly into her mouth, running the tip over hers, snaking deeper, raising her pulse sharply. One of his hands fumbled for the opening of her robe and she arched back slightly to free it. His fingers traced her shoulder to the neck, then down, cupping over a breast, covering it completely, sending a shower of shivers shooting down her legs.

A small sigh escaped from her throat and she rubbed the tight shirt material over his chest. Locating a pearl snap, she pulled on it and the shirt popped open to the waist. She ran her fingers over his mat of sandy chest hair, loving the kinky softness, feeling his heart hammering deep inside and the hardness growing in his groin, pushing at her stomach.

Abruptly he bent and with one arm under her, one around her back, lifted her off the floor as if she were a mere child. Holding her tightly, he carried her into the bedroom. She was overwhelmed with the ease by which he transported her—she could not remember being carried by anyone before, except by her daddy. . . .

Laying her on the green satin comforter, he kissed her eyes

closed, moved to her nipples, flicking them with his tongue until she felt like they would burst with pleasure. Gradually he moved down her stomach, pushing open her robe as he descended, until he reached her thighs.

His touch was so tender, yet so strong, so sure, she felt like he were lighting small, intense fires on each spot he landed. The heat rose within her as he licked the insides of her thighs, nuzzling his nose against her, until he finally probed her with his tongue. Instantly he locked onto the most sensitive spot, causing her to gasp. She clutched at his head, pushing it down harder, grinding her hips, small moans escaping from deep within her. He matched them with his own rumbling growls. The flames erupted, lashing at her skin until she was writhing with an exquisite agony. He pulled back and rolled off the bed, tearing at his clothes.

Quickly she pulled the robe from under her, yanking it off, not taking her eyes from him as he dropped his jeans and bounced stiffly before her. He was big and burly, his legs and forearms covered with sandy hair to match that on his broad chest. Sitting on the edge of the bed, he began struggling to slip off his boots. As he grunted with the effort, she reached up, tugging at his shoulders until he fell back flat. She scooted over closer and lowered her head, putting her mouth over the head of his erection.

She took in as much of him as she could, moving up and down, feeling his pulsations, tonguing the hard ridges. She raised her eyes to his. He seemed astonished at her skill. She winked and pulled back to look closer at him as he struggled to free his feet from boots and jeans.

His skin was the color of pale tropical sand. Several scars stood out prominently, of various sizes and colors. She traced one on his ribcage, wondering how he got it. She could hear his breath erupting irregularly. Lying flat, she held out her arms. He lowered his weight onto her. She pushed her breasts into his hairy chest, rubbing them back and forth, titillated by the roughness. She opened her thighs and waited expectantly. He gazed raptly into her eyes and whispered, "Soft voice, sweet lips, soft hand and softer breast..." His eyes closed, his lips met hers passionately and with one sure thrust, he was inside. She wrapped her long legs around his waist, locking her ankles over his broad back, matching every move he made with one of her own.

Bucking and twisting, their tempo increased, the mattress bouncing beneath her, the soft clang of metal, the brass headboard hitting the wall with each stroke. His face buried into the crook of her neck, the coarse texture of his shaven whiskers exciting her even more. His groans grew with zest, his breath rasping hoarsely, mixing with hers. . . .

Before all thought ceased and pure exhilarating sensation took over, she had one last realization—this guy was good . . . goddamn was he good.

REBECCA
March 1967
New York

The banging of metal on metal awoke her. Instantly remembering what day it was, she rolled to the edge of the loft bed and peered over.

The steam radiator was reluctantly gurgling to life, sounding like someone was hitting it with a ball-peen hammer. The apartment was freezing, frost silvered the panes of the windows. In the dirty, cold daylight, Scooter was nowhere to be seen. For the second night he hadn't come home. Not even to wish her Happy Birthday.

It took her over an hour of crying before she could move out of his bed. She scrambled down the ladder and ran through the still crisp air into the bathroom. A steamy hot shower warmed her body but did not thaw the ice that coated her heart.

Later that morning, she sat layered and numbed in the beanbag chair, holding that week's *Time* magazine with the Redgrave sisters on the cover. She had been trying to read about the stars of *Georgy*

Girl and *Blow Up* but had been too upset by Scooter's absence to concentrate.

The phone rang and she leaped for it. A woman's voice asked, "Rebecca McKenna?"

For a fleeting moment, she was about to say, "No," before she remembered her new stage name, "Yes, this is her . . . she."

"Ralph Shawzin's office calling. He'd like you to come back and audition again. For the part of Susie? Tomorrow morning at ten?"

"Really? Oh wow! That's terrific, really . . . whew!" She jotted down the necessary information, hung up and stood in a state of suspended animation. A callback! Her first, legitimate callback. A momentous step forward. She couldn't wait to tell Scooter. And Robby. With a start, she glanced at her dented alarm clock. Almost noon. Lordee, she was going to be late.

Battling the March winds, Rebecca fairly flew down Forty-fifth, making swift progress despite the awkwardness of her new high heels. Robby had bought her the pair for auditions, to give her added stature on stage; plus he'd sprung for the burgundy, paisley, long-sleeved dress she was wearing, to make her look more mature, he'd said. She clutched the bulky white letterman's sweater to her and darted beneath the sedate but welcoming canopy of Sardi's.

"Good afternoon, miss," the stout, maroon-coated doorman greeted, opening the glass doors for her. "Thank you . . . sir," she said, stepping through. "Bye." Inside the enclosed alcove, she hesitated, uncertain whether she should have tipped the man or not. She yanked off her brother's high-school sweater and folded it over one arm so the big, blue-felt "L" was concealed. She raked her fingers through her hair, then throwing back her shoulders, opened the inside door and made her tentative entrance.

The interior was warm, wood-paneled and with an air of subdued energy. And the wonderful smells, mouth-watering. She stood just inside the door, barely breathing, absorbing like a sponge, trying not to gawk. The small line of beautifully dressed people diminished rapidly and soon she was facing a goateed gentleman behind a podium.

"I'm here to meet Robby . . . Robin Rhomann for lunch," she said, unable to search the islands of faces beyond him. "This way, please," the man responded and turned. She followed close on his heel, watching the carpet.

"Well, it's Rebecca McKenna," Robby greeted embarrassingly loud, as if they hadn't seen each other in ages. In smart blue blazer and tie, he stood up beaming, the picture of exuberance. His tiny, bespectacled mother sat beside him, bobbing her head with a blue straw hat.

Rebecca slipped gratefully into the chair being held by the maître'd. He said politely, "Enjoy your lunch."

"Thanks, Jimmy," Robby bubbled.

"Hello, Rebecca," Mrs. Rhomann said, blinking rapidly behind her thick glasses. "Happy Birthday."

Quickly Robby echoed his mother, adding, "May your eighteenth year be your best so far."

"Thanks," she said, her eyes on the water goblet in front of her.

"Becks, you look sensational," he whispered.

"Yes, very nice, dear," Mrs. Rhomann concurred.

"I feel a little underdressed."

"Nonsense," Robby said. "Becks . . . raise your head. This isn't a solemn high mass."

She straightened up and froze in wonderment. "Oh, my God, that's Lee Remick." The lovely actress sat at an opposite small table for two.

"Stop staring," he hissed. "You want everyone to think you're a tourist or something? The secret is to pretend you belong . . . old hat, and all that. Hey, guess whose table we're sitting at? Anytime he comes in, this is his very own special table." Robby winked mischievously. "Orson Welles."

"Gee, is it big enough for him?"

Both Robby and his sparrowlike mother laughed. Rebecca blushed with pleasure, unfolded the large, pink cloth napkin and sat up straighter.

Mrs. Rhomann did not stay long, wanting to take advantage of a sale at Bullocks. But before leaving, she made certain Robby had enough money, then cautioned, "Robin—your rehearsal's at three." She tilted her head and smiled brightly. "Remember, always be punctual. And cheerful as the spring robin. I'll be waiting for your dinner break.''

"Gotcha, Mom," he said and pecked her on the cheek.

After Mrs. Rhomann had bobbed away and Robby had expertly ordered for both of them, Rebecca sprang the good news. "That's fantastic, Becks!" he exclaimed. "Your *first* callback. I knew you'd do it soon, didn't I?"

Basking under his praise, she wiggled in her chair. "I never could've done it without you, Robby. Really, I owe it all to you."

"That's poppycock. Of *course* you could've done it on your own. You have the talent, that's why." He paused, adding with a puckish grin. "All I did, was help with the packaging.''

Lunch was glorious, her Nicoise salad scrumptious, the ambiance stimulating, and Robby's company, as always, entertaining. He rambled on with witty stories of the rehearsals for his Broadway musical, the temper tantrums of the aging star, the plans for their New Haven tryout and the likelihood of a new solo number being written for his own expanding role.

Soon he asked, "Have you told Scooter yet? About the callback?"

"I just got the call before I came here. Scooter had left already." Conscious that Robby was studying her, she smiled quickly. "But I know he'll think it's a gas."

Robby toyed with his spoon. "Becks . . . mind if I ask something that's been bugging me? What *do* you see in him? I mean, granted he has a pretty face—that is, *if* he got his hair cut. But beyond that?"

Taking her time, she rubbed her palms over her knees, feeling the thin material of her skirt. "Well, geez, Robby . . . I mean, I think he's sensational on all counts. He's such a gifted actor, really dedicated to his craft. He's studied just about as long as you have. And . . . he's a scream sometimes. That night we went up to the Lincoln Center rep? Scooter had me in stitches the whole night tearing apart Jason Robards's performance. And last week, we saw *Macbird*. Talked all night about it. He knows a lot about politics, much more than I do. So he caught more of the real satire of the piece—stuff like, which character was Bobby Kennedy and who was

Robert McNamara. And Scooter is . . ." Her voice petered out, her posture sagged.

Robby smiled hesitantly. "When you first moved in with him, I thought . . . give it a week, maybe two. *Then* you'd see him through some reality glasses. But, ye gawds, Becks, you've been there over two months. And you keep telling me you love him, but I *still* don't know why."

"Why does anybody love anyone?"

He threw his small hands up into the air. "I don't know. I'm asking you. Other than you and mother, I've never loved anyone before."

"Well hell's bells, Robby, this is all new to me too."

"So what's it like?"

She jiggled one foot. "What?"

"Being in love."

She searched her mind, trying to find something that would capture the essence of what she felt. In frustration, she gave up. "I don't know. I just think about him all the time."

Robby slumped in his chair. "That's what I was afraid of."

"Whaddaya mean?" she challenged.

He measured her deliberately. "Only that if you're thinking about Scooter, you're bound to blow your callback tomorrow."

"I knew it! I just knew you were going to say something stupid like that. Geez, Robby, give me a little credit, huh? I mean after all, I'm eighteen. I know what I'm doing."

Defiantly they eyed each other and for a second she had the image of them as kids, sparring just like this.

"Look, Becks, if you're happy, *I'm* happy. But somehow every time I'm with you lately, I get this real strong feeling, you know, that you're not really happy."

"But I *am* happy," she protested meekly. She wished she could really level with him. But she had always felt that he was prejudiced against Scooter for some reason . . . maybe jealousy.

He reached over and patted her hand. "That's good enough for me. I just don't want anything to get in the way of your career, Becks. You're too talented to end up some damned housewife out in Hackensack. See those caricatures?" he asked, indicating the hanging rows of framed cartoons of famous theater people. She nodded, sweeping her eyes over them for probably the thousandth time. "Someday, Becks, ours will be up there. Right where everyone coming in will see them. That's *our* dream, Becks. Your audition tomorrow could be the beginning of a very long and successful career."

"From your mouth to God's ear," she quipped.

Robby grinned slyly and signaled for the check. "Well, like this Adam Clayton Powell keeps saying, 'Just keep the faith, baby . . . keep the faith.' "

But by eight o'clock that night, Rebecca was finding it difficult to have much faith in anything, especially herself. She had not seen Scooter for over forty-four hours. That alone was a rising tide of anguish. And her meat sauce would be a disgrace to the Parlato side of the family. Dumping more garlic salt into the long simmering pot, she heard the front door opening. Scooter was back! Whisking the script out of sight under the sink, she checked her impulses to run and greet him with a hug, instead called out, "Hello, hello."

He sauntered into the room, sniffing the air. "Damned, if you don't look like Beaver Cleaver's mother," he said, removing his heavy parka.

Still wearing her burgundy dress and heels, Rebecca beamed and smoothed the front of her white apron. "Oh, yeah, that's me all right, slaving all afternoon over a hot stove." She tried to read his mood.

He selected an album and plopped it on the turntable, switching it on. Dylan's voice started singing nasally "Subterranean Homesick Blues" and Scooter climbed up to the loft. "What're you making besides spaghetti?"

Pleased he was interested enough to ask, she opened the refrigerator. "Salad, french bread with garlic butter—got a bottle of wine, that rosé you like—and some dessert."

"What kind?"

She hesitated. "Oh, just some cake, that's all."

"Cake? With noodles *and* bread? You trying to get me fat?"

"You? Fat?" She laughed tensely. "Man, you'll get fat when Mama Cass gets skinny."

That made him chuckle. She grinned to herself, peeling the oily, thick skin from a cucumber. So far, so good, she assessed.

Dinner surpassed her wildest expectations. Paying his highest compliment, Scooter stored away plates of spaghetti, finished off all the bread and salad, downed nearly all the wine himself. She wondered if he'd eaten for days.

She grew uncomfortable under his silent steady gaze, which reminded her of those cheap paintings of Jesus for sale in Times Square—the ones where the eyes followed her regardless of where she moved.

"Ready for some cake?" she asked, heading backward down the ladder while balancing the dirty plates. "I made it myself."

"What kind?"

"Double-fudge devil's food," she said, lifting it from the hiding place on the bottom shelf. Critically she surveyed her first attempt at baking and found it woefully lacking. Even the wording on top, over which she'd sweated, looked like it'd been lettered by a three-year-old.

Noiselessly he appeared behind her, leaning over her shoulder to read aloud the words on her cake, " 'Break a leg.' Hey, what's up?"

"Oh, nothing much," she said. "It's just, well . . . you know last week when I went down to that audition at the Cherry Lane?"

He shrugged, taking a piece of cake before she could supply a plate. She inhaled deeply and dove in, "Well, guess what, Scooter? They called me back—no lie! They want me to come back tomorrow at ten to try out again."

"Mazeltov. You got any milk?"

"Oh, shoot, I'm sorry. Yeah." She threw open the refrigerator, grabbing the gallon container. "So I went down this afternoon and picked up a copy of the script." She poured a large glass, continuing, "The part's perfect for me. No lie—not very big, but it's juicy. As they say, no small parts, just small actors, right?" She handed him the glass and bent to retrieve the script from behind the garbage sack. "This is it . . . a comedy, sort of . . . real black humor though. Called *The Conquest of Mars and Other Trivial Matters*."

"Not crazy about the title," he said, climbing back up with his cake and milk.

"Yeah, but it's not a bad script, really. And the role is something I know I could do." Her voice faded. "Wanna cue me, Scooter? I'm only in three scenes..."

"You're talking like you've got it already."

"Just thinking positive, that's all." She took a bite of cake, but it tasted like sawdust. "Robby says one's attitude is everything in auditions. Like he says—"

Scooter cut her off sharply. "What's he know about acting—*real* acting, not that musical-comedy crap."

"So Robby's in a Broadway musical," she flared. "You gonna hold that against him?" The smell of marijuana wafted down to her and she relaxed some—at least he was going to stick around for a little while.

She hesitated, then said, "I'm going to kill the light, okay?"

"What for?"

"Too glaring, man. Light a candle."

She doused the bright overhead light and waited expectantly for the flare of his match on the candlewick. Seeing it, she hesitantly undid her belt and pulled the dress over her head. Wearing only her green tights, she shivered in anticipation.

For over three weeks, Scooter had not shown any interest in her physically. She thought it was because he was bored with her sexually. So now, yearning for that intimacy herself, she quietly climbed the ladder in the warm glow of the single candle on the wall shelf above his head. She was ready, even eager to prove her love—willing to do things he long had tried to instruct and interest her in, things that because of her own timidity she had never been able to bring herself to even attempt. Tonight, however, would be different. It would be her birthday present to him. And a "welcome-to-womanhood" present to herself.

Wearing only a faded pair of bellbottom jeans, he lay on his back, staring at the movie ad he'd tacked to the wall of Jane Fonda in her *Barbarella* costume. Rebecca crawled self-consciously next to him and stretched out, sharing the same pillow, her heart pounding so loudly she was afraid he'd hear. He gave no indication she was there. Timorously, she reached out and laid a trembling hand on his bare, flat, lean stomach. Carefully watching his face, she began to move her fingers in tight little circles, gradually widening their circumferences until they included the very top of his jeans. Her breath quickening, she grew bolder and moved her fingertips lower until they passed gently over the soft, full mound at his crotch. Continuing the circular motion, she moved her hand back up his stomach and around, down again, this time pausing to press more firmly, flattening her palm, cupping him.

With a jerk, he grabbed her exploring hand. "What the hell're you doing?" He scrambled over her and pushed himself off the edge of the loft. His feet hit the floor with a heavy crash, rattling the dishes in the sink. "I'm sorry, Scooter . . . really, I just . . ." she moaned into the pillow, curling tightly into a ball.

He stomped across the wood floor. The sound of the zipping up of his parka brought her head up swiftly. "Don't go . . . not tonight. Please . . ." she begged. "We don't have to—"

"All this crap about Robby. And break-a-leg cakes and scripts and callbacks and turning out the lights. I can't think straight here." He started for the hallway.

She heaved herself to the ladder, barely finding breath to speak. "So I'll cool it. I'll shut up, okay? Me and my big mouth will just cool it for the night. All right? I won't say zip. I won't *do* zip. You won't even know I'm here."

By the hall doorway, he turned back. "You're so jacked up about this callback of yours, you can't even think what *I* might be going through." His voice dropped to a harsh whisper. "I got my *own* head to deal with. It just so happens that at eleven in the morning, I've a damned important audition of my own. My *last* chance to get into the Actors' Studio." He stalked into the hall. She struggled to find words, feeling defenseless, guilty as accused. She flew down after him.

He was fumbling with the deadbolt lock on the front door. Throwing it open, he whirled. "Lady, I've got *one* objective in life. Just one. To get into the Studio. That's what acting is all about. *True* acting. And it's *all* I want." He tore open the door.

"Scooter, please . . . I didn't know . . . let's—"

He slammed the door behind him.

Her legs would not support her anymore. Pressing her bare back to the wall for support, she sank to the linoleum. Her sobs broke the stillness of the long hallway.

At six A.M. the following morning, Rebecca stumbled down the loft ladder, numb and exhausted from the endless cycle of self-accusations which had kept her tossing in pain all night. Stiffly she fixed a pot of coffee and stared at the pages of the script. The lines of dialogue which she had memorized the previous afternoon now seemed completely foreign to her. Where was he? Why hadn't he come home? Why does he do this to me?

Close to eight, still not dressed, she felt even more jangled, hyped-up on all the coffee. When the phone rang, she dove for it, answering hopefully. Robby's cheery voice greeted her. She attempted to follow his words, but they jumbled together in her head.

"Becks? You all right?"

"Sure, sure," she mumbled. "Big day today, huh?"

"You're going to knock 'em all dead, Becks."

"If they're *all* dead, who'll cast me?"

He laughed. "My rehearsal's not until four. Promise to call me as soon as you're out?"

"Yeah, sure, Robby . . . gotta go now."

"Hey, buck up, kid, you sound drugged or something. Positive everything's fine and dandy?"

"Super, really, catch ya later."

The receiver seemed heavy in her hand. She let it slip back into the cradle and stared at Dylan on the wall, trying to think where Scooter might have gone. With a new burst of grief she realized she had scant idea of what his life was like outside of his apartment.

She showered and dressed mechanically, pulling on the paisley dress. Absently brushing her hair, she decided to forgo wearing makeup like she had the last time. Robby had sent her to a makeup expert to learn some tricks, but now she saw no reason for the extra effort.

The air outside was crisp and cutting, despite the bright sunshine. She shriveled into the heavy sweater and caught the downtown IND on Eighth, standing the whole way to the Village, holding the script loosely in one hand. Surfacing on Sixth Avenue, she trudged west, dreading each step that took her closer. How could she go through with it? She felt so energyless, so scattered—the whole thing would be one big waste of time. Maybe she could get a postponement, arrange to come back later . . . another time, another day.

She spotted a phone booth up ahead. Hurrying to it, she was about to slip in to dial the theater, when she stopped short. She had not realized where she was.

Three doors down the side street, in front of the entrance to his apartment house, Erik Lungren was helping a gorgeous girl into a cab. The blonde, bundled up in a hooded fur coat, looked very familiar, but all Rebecca took in was Erik—barefoot, rugged, touseled as though he had just gotten out of bed—bending to plant a lingering kiss on the girl's lips. At that instant, a terrifying thought raced through Rebecca's mind—he would see her! Think she was following him, spying on him, wanting to make contact again.

Rebecca began to run, sprinting toward Sheridan Square, not looking back, trying to put as much distance as quickly as possible between them. Two blocks away, she slowed her pace, attempting to still the nerves which crackled like overloaded electrical circuits just under her skin.

The Cherry Lane Theater, tucked into the crook of the street, appeared deserted—not like the first day she'd shown up when dozens of actresses milled about, waiting for their chance to audition. The street's emptiness underscored how exclusive her callback was. There would be only a handful returning. She was one of the lucky ones.

In front of the box office, she stopped, remembering she hadn't brought her hairbrush. Spiritlessly she ran her fingers through her hair.

"Rebecca . . ."

The sound of his voice spun her around so quickly she could not locate where it had come from.

"Over here," he said and stepped out of a doorway.

"Scooter!" she cried, dashing to him with such a rush of blood to her head she felt stoned. He caught her in his arms and lifted her completely off the sidewalk. Half laughing, half crying, she hugged his neck, burying her face into the fur trim on the hood of his parka.

"You turkey, what're you doing here anyway? Where've you been, huh? No, you don't have to answer that. Oh, God, how I've missed you."

She did not want to let go, but his grip loosened on her back and she slid down his thin body until she stood, peering up at him. "Scooter, I'm so sorry about my behavior last night, really I am. I should've known something important was going on. I just didn't..."

His unshaven face looked haggard in the harsh sunlight and his eyes were bloodshot, anxious. "Just wanted to wish you, break a leg."

Her breath caught in her throat. "Oh, thanks Scooter... I can't tell you what that means."

He was digging in his parka's pocket and pulled something out. "Wanted you to have this—combination break-a-leg and belated-birthday gift. Sorry, I forgot. Guess, I've been a little zoned out, huh?"

She looked down at the furry object in her hand. The beady, glass eyes of a tiny toy monkey gleamed back at her. The dark fur had been rubbed off in places and one leg bent askew but to her it was the most beautiful gift she'd ever received. "Oh, Scooter, thanks, it's terrific."

"Suppose I could tell you I've had it for a long time, but I found it over on the docks around sun-up. Sort of reminded me of you."

She wiped her eyes, grinning foolishly. "Hey, thanks, it's a great boost, you know? To be compared to a monkey... a stuffed one at that."

He smiled lopsidedly and her heart soared like a helium-filled balloon, high over their heads. "Hey," she said, squeezing his narrow waist. "Big day, huh? For both of us."

"Yeah," he said, looking over the top of her head. "It's almost ten. Don't want to be late, do you?"

"No, I sure don't... not now, huh?" She studied his exquisite face for a moment, trying to memorize it, wanting to take it inside with her. *This* was the Scooter she loved. And had, from that first night together. "Hey, you're gonna do it, Scooter. You're gonna make 'em wish they'd taken you the first time. I just know it." She gave him another quick hug. "Thanks, Scooter... for coming, really." She backed away slowly into the street. "Man, oh man, do I love you."

"Hey, hang onto that monkey . . . it's full of magic."

She planted a kiss on the monkey's nose and bounced up onto the sidewalk. With one last grateful wave, she turned for the theater entrance, and purposely walked headlong into the door, kicking it with her foot to make a loud crash, but reeling back, holding her head. Staggering, she looked at the toy monkey in her hand, shrugged and reached for the doorknob. Scooter's laughter buffeted her joyfully inside.

Four hours and thirty-three minutes later, she burst through the same door, tears streaming from her eyes so thickly she could hardly see. She tumbled to the phone booth on the corner and shakily dialed Robby's number. He answered. "Becks?"

"*I got it!*" she shrieked. "Robby, Robby, *I got it!*"

He screamed a hoot of approval. "Becks, that's sensational!"

"I must've read six, seven times. And each time, I thought, that's it—thank you very much, but no thanks," she rattled on breathlessly. "Until I was so crazed I thought I'd crawl up the proscenium, but then the next thing I know, the director is sitting right next to me, telling me the rehearsal schedule. No lie, I thought I'd died and gone to heaven."

"So when do you start?"

"Tomorrow afternoon—there's a read-through with the cast," she said. "Oh, Robby, it was just like we dreamed . . ."

"You got it because you were the best, Rebecca, think of it."

"I can't, I can't, I'm flying out of here this instant," she said in a scramble. "Broadway, next stop!" She plopped down the receiver and jiggling from one foot to the other, tried her home phone. The line was busy. Not wanting to wait any longer, she tore out of the booth, heading for the subway.

Two at a time, she raced up the stairs. Inserting her key, she realized that too much elation on her part might be contrary to Scooter's mood. Deliberately, she tempered the incredible high to a more controllable state and opened the door.

The first thing she noticed was that Dylan's grinning face no longer greeted her from the wall; the second was that the phone receiver lay nakedly on the floor, off the hook. "Scooter, you home, man?" she called up to the loft and darted halfway up the ladder. The mattress was empty. And his hand-carved stash box was missing from the shelf.

Mystified, she climbed down and turned to survey the room. Everything else seemed to be in place. The closet door stood wide open—only her few articles of clothing hung there, pushed off to one side. On his side, empty metal hangers. . . .

For an agonizing moment, she could only stare at them, her first thought that they had been ripped off. Finally her feet began to move, taking her to the bathroom. All of Scooter's toilet articles had been removed, even his shaving kit.

She took down every item on the bookshelf, looking for a note where he sometimes left one, unaware that the small frightened animal noises came from her own throat. Only when she had finished did the full force of the reality strike her.

Scooter had split without so much as a note good-bye.

A sickening, nauseous feeling welled within her until she was propelled into the bathroom. Again and again she retched into the toilet until there was nothing left in her stomach—but still the dry heaves erupted, leaving her spent and sweaty.

She collapsed into the beanbag chair, crying until there were no tears left, her heart booming inside, an empty drum covered by skin.

At dusk, Rebecca found herself wobbling along upper Times Square near Forty-eighth, not far from the second-floor studio where Robby was rehearsing. Too early for the dinner-and-theater crowd, the sidewalks still bustled with hookers and pimps, johns and tourists. In front of the Mark Hellinger Theater, where Melina Mercouri was starring in a musical version of *Never on Sunday,* called *Illya Darling,* Rebecca stalled, blindly studying the production stills before she worked up enough nerve to go bother Robby at work. But Rebecca knew if she did not talk to someone soon, she would be a basketcase before morning. Just off Seventh, she trudged up the long flight of narrow stairs and knocked timidly on the landing's first door.

A balding man, built like a dockworker, opened the door part way. "Closed rehearsals."

"I've *got* to see Robby Rhomann," she implored. "It's an emergency, honest."

The man gave her a hard look. "What's your name?"

"Rebecca Parlato," she answered automatically. The door closed and it seemed ages before Robby opened it again and stepped out, looking not very pleased. The tears started again, but she bit her lips to hold them back. When she began to explain what had happened, Robby nodded.

"I know," he said grimly.

"You knew?"

"Scooter called my place during lunch, asked to come over."

"Where *is* he?"

Robby glanced at his wristwatch. "Right now, I'd say he's deep into Pennsylvania."

She tried to blink back the tears. "Why? Why's he there? What happened? What'd he say?"

"You know him, doesn't mumble much. Only that he was giving up acting and—"

"Giving up—?"

"And that he wanted to borrow some money. I loaned him—"

"—borrow? What for? What'd he want it for? Tell me, please."

He motioned for her to keep it down, throwing a concerned look at the closed studio door. Muffled sounds of a piano and singing voices held his attention for a moment. "Look, Becks, I tried to tell you about him. I told you he was no good for you . . . that he was too selfish to think of you and your—"

"Where's he going, huh?" Her voice sounded shrill in the high-ceilinged hallway, but she could not help it.

"You've got to forget him, Becks."

She grabbed the sleeve of his sweater. "Where's he going, Robby?"

"San Francisco," he said quietly. "By bus."

"Scooter's going to California? And you didn't try to stop him?"

"What could I do, Becks? He was all wound up. Besides—"

"Wha'd he say? 'Bout me? Did he give you a message for me?"

He shook his blond head, hammering another nail into her coffin. "He did say something about the Actors' Studio . . . pretty negative. Called it an elitist clique." His eyes locked on hers. "Scooter's not worth all this, Becks. Look, you're so upset you've even forgotten about your triumph this afternoon. Your first New York production. It's a time for celebration, not—"

"How could you've given him the money to split?" she whispered but with the force of a shout in its concentrated fury. "You . . . of all people! I thought you were my buddy. I thought you were on my side."

"I am," he snapped. "That's why I did it."

She stared in disbelief. "You wanted him to go?"

For the first time since she'd known him, Robby's countenance threatened her, his face becoming hard, jaded as he said, "He was nothing but a big drag on you—taking your attention off your acting."

"Robin," she warned, "my career has nothing to do with this. I'm talking about my *life*. Scooter's my life, dammit!"

Robby sighed wearily. "Things will all look differently once you get into rehearsals."

"You're crazy if you think I can take that part now."

"You're not serious?"

"I've never been more serious," she said with conviction. "Scooter's more important to me than any role ever written."

"I didn't hear that. You didn't say that."

"You think I could go on rehearsing as if nothing has happened? The show must go on and all that crap? I couldn't, Robby . . . I just couldn't."

"That is the most unprofessional defeatism I've *ever* heard."

"Man, you just don't get the picture, do you? I mean, if Scooter did fail his audition, it certainly wasn't because he's *not* talented enough. He failed because *I* got in the way. I blew his concentration, interrupted his flow. It's *me* . . . I'm the one to blame."

"Poppycock," he snipped. "If you blame yourself for his incompetence, you don't *deserve* to be an actress. Let alone a star."

Her jaw opened and closed as she vainly searched for a comeback.

He lowered his voice, but the brittleness remained. "If you continue to think like this you'll stay Rebecca Parlato from Seventh Street in Lackawanna. A *nobody* who threw her whole life away for a big, no-talent schmuck!"

"You can go get screwed, Robby," she said and started down the steep stairs. "I love him. And Scooter is too talented to give up his acting. *I* believe in him. I'm going to find him and bring him back."

At eleven-forty that night—after writing a resignation letter to her producer, packing up everything in the apartment, carting the boxes to the basement where the manager said they could be stored, and after pawning the new birthday wristwatch her brother had sent—Rebecca caught the Greyhound bus heading west for San Francisco. Clutched grimly in her hand as the bus pulled out of the Port Authority building, she held the tiny, worn toy monkey. Scooter's last words kept coming back to her, over and over, "Hang onto that monkey, it's full of magic . . ."

Book Two

1967–1968

ERIK
April 1967
New York

Up at Columbia University, he climbed behind the wheel of Michael's old Chevy coupe, hollered, "Thanks" to Michael, waved a listless good-bye to the twins and steered out into traffic heading back downtown. On the car's scratchy radio, Country Joe MacDonald sang out, "One, two, three, four, what are we fighting for?" Erik couldn't answer that one. In fact, he had damned few answers about anything anymore.

Back at his apartment, Erik found a telegram from Paris. It was from Shelby. "Arriving home at noon after glorious adventure. Have ordered car for us. Pick you up around six P.M. Can't wait. Love you."

He stared at the message. After the initial burst of enthusiasm, several questions stubbornly arose. If she were returning so early, why the long delay until six? Surely Caesari hadn't planned an extensive debriefing period. And how could she have forgotten? He'd told her numerous times that he would borrow Michael's car for the weekend. What the hell was he to do with it now? Michael would be tied up all morning, perhaps all day as one of the organizers of the Spring Mobilization, that weekend's planned anti-war demonstrations.

Erik poured a half glass of Scotch and dialed Mo's office. He was surprised to learn that she had gone home already. Receiving a busy signal on their home line, he downed the glass and grabbed the car keys, heading for Mo and Michael's Washington Square apartment.

Mo answered his knock still wearing her brown cloth streetcoat. Before he could say hello, she marched back into the living room.

He swore it looked like she was crying. "I brought the keys," he explained, following her. "Won't be needing the old bomb after all." He heard what sounded like a sob. "Mo, you all right?"

Her back to him, she lit a Gauloise and tossed her head back to inhale. Whirling, she let the smoke out in a rush, a single tear rolling down a plump cheek. He was stunned. "What the hell's happened?"

"Goddamn Caesari," she rasped. "Close to twelve years I've slaved in his TV department. Getting half the pay, working twice as hard as the goddamn men. And what thanks do I get? I make a pitch to him for this new V.P. of Development and the sonofabitch has the gall to tell me—'Women are not cut out to be executives.'"

She stubbed out her cigarette in the coffee-table ashtray. It was an angry, violent gesture.

"I threatened to quit unless he promoted me and that—that douche-bag says, 'You're expendable.'" She fumbled in her coat pocket, brought out a used hankie and blew her nose. "So here I am—over forty, overqualified, and out of work."

"You quit?"

"Damn right I did. I wouldn't work another minute for that—that Dago pimp." She sniffed again and turned to the windows.

"You'll find a new job," he offered lamely. "Or maybe you'll want to stay home with the kids, play housewife for a while."

"Are you bonkers?" she snapped. "Lord, Erik, you can be so damned dense sometimes. I've already started looking for a new job." Not knowing how to respond, he laid the car keys on the coffee table. She blew smoke through her nose in a soft snort. "Hell, I'm sorry. You caught me at my worst. I haven't cried since the twins were born." She moved to the front door to let him out, putting on a false cheerfulness. "So look, you have a hot weekend with America's favorite blond. But may I suggest? Get over this silly infatuation. What you need is a *real* woman."

He let the remark slide, as he often had to do with Mo and started to give her a sympathetic hug but she pulled away with typical reserve. In spite of it, he felt enormous warmth and concern for her.

Back at his place, the afternoon dragged on and still no word from Shelby. He tried reaching her several times at her private New York

number but her answering service insisted she had not arrived back
from Europe.

Growing more despondent, he sat looking around his cramped,
book-cluttered living room. Other than the used office desk in the
corner, there was not a piece of furniture that was his—most were
cast-offs from Michael and Mo. Each time he induced Shelby to
spend time there, he felt embarrassed by its meagerness. He was
more than ready to move on, but where? And with what? He
replenished his drink and fell to worrying about the chances for
Rogues being a success, hoping for an economic security that, this
time, he was positive he would not blow away.

By six-thirty-eight, the gloom hung over him like a low pressure
weather front. He forced himself to concentrate on the *New York
Times* interview with the surgeon Dr. Christiaan Barnard, who was
astonishing the world with his heart transplants. Erik reached for the
bottle again, thinking ruefully that he certainly could use a whole
new heart. He seemed to have worn his out along the way, too much
pain felt, too much booze drunk, cigarettes smoked, and passions
spent.

He barely heard the car horn blaring outside his street-level
apartment. He dove for the window. A gleaming, white '67
Thunderbird—its black convertible top up, concealing the driver—
was double-parked in front. He grabbed his canvas flight bag and
hurried out.

Shelby, in huge sunglasses, waved from behind the wheel. He tore
open the door on her side and hungrily pulled her up into his arms.
Kissing her, warmth flooded his body like a high tide. She broke
loose with a delicious pout. "Shame on you, y'all've been drinking.
So early in the day? And y'all're not wearing those ol' jeans? Y'all
look like a truck driver."

He grinned, tossing his bag into the back seat, feeling suddenly
lighter. "Once I was. An honorable profession." He pulled her to
him again and smothered her mouth with his, the warmth in his
groin bursting into a full blown hard-on.

She untangled herself with a knowing, teasing smile. "Well, hop
in, sugar. *I'm* driving." Before he could protest, she slipped behind
the wheel. She glanced at the straining front of his faded jeans.

"And for heaven's sake, do something about that nasty ol' thing before someone sees."

"I don't care who sees it," he joshed and slammed her door. "I want the world to know I love you." He leaned in through the open window to kiss her again.

"That's not love, that's lust."

"My heart loves you, my peter lusts you." With a wink, he withdrew to walk around to the passenger side.

Once he was inside, she put the rumbling engine in gear and gunned the car recklessly out into the street. "Miss me, sugar?"

"You know I did."

"I know nothing of the sort," she said flippantly. "For all I know, y'all could've been shacked up the whole time, or maybe with a different girl each night."

"I only finished the galley proofs this last Monday. Fourteen, sixteen-hour days. I've been totally celibate."

"Celebratin'. Y'all've been celebratin'?"

"Celibate," he corrected. "Means complete sexual abstinence."

"Really? What a lovely word."

Barrelling the powerful auto toward the Lincoln Tunnel, she talked animatedly, relating her exciting experiences abroad. In spite of her erratic driving, he could hardly keep his eyes off of her. In a tan twill, tailored pants-suit and leaf green silk blouse, she looked like a debutante going to the club for lunch. But she was so damned beautiful, his throat ached.

Stepping on the accelerator, she glanced over. "Why so sour, sugar? Having second thoughts about spending an entire weekend alone with little ol' me?"

"Hell, babe," he began dryly, "when're you going to drop all those trite, Southern girl phrases?"

She tossed her head and shot the car in front of a cab. "Well, little ol' me, happens to adore little ol' phrases like little ol' me. I'm proud to be from the South, sir. And Dixie's still my national anthem."

"No wonder they loved you in France."

"A one-girl happening, Giorgio called it. I was mobbed everywhere.

'Sun-nee! Sun-nee!' they shouted. And the press..." Entering the tunnel heading for New Jersey, she became very busy steering.

He reached over and laid his hand across the back of her neck. Her skin felt soft and cool to his touch. "I do love you, babe."

"My, my, my," she purred, arching her head back into his hand. "So damned attentive now that your ol' book is done. But you seem sort of, I don't know... like quiet."

He squeezed her neck. "It's just this post-partum blues, hon. Handing in the novel and all. I feel kind of deflated... empty."

"But what on earth for?" she asked, knitting together her delicate brows. "Seems to me you should be absolutely joyous. Y'all're *free,* sugar. Certainly for the first time since I've known y'all. Fussing and stewing about it all the time. I declare, sugar, it got to be a bit much at times."

"Writing's the very core of my life."

Her mouth turned downward. "That surely doesn't leave much room for me, does it?"

"Hell, you're my muse of fire. And right now, all I want is to get my sweet muse into bed."

"Sugar, that's going to make me drive all the faster. Hang on!" Laughing wickedly, she stepped on the gas.

When the threatening sky began to pour, somewhere deep in southern New Jersey, Erik took over the wheel and Shelby started to unwind, coiling languidly in the passenger seat. He asked, "Did you keep your promise?"

"Which one, sugar?"

"Telling Caesari about us?"

"I didn't promise I would," she said. "I said I'd *try.* But the opportunity never came up. We were on the go like crazy over there. Must have done over a hundred photo sessions and—"

"—thought we agreed," he interrupted, trying to control his irritation, "it would be better all way around if you were out in the open about us. I'm damned tired of sneaking around like we're doing something immoral or illicit."

"Actually isn't it kind of fun? Putting one over on that ol' prig?"

The windshield wipers slopping back and forth filled the strained silence. Finally she scooted over as close as she could in the bucket seats and entwined an arm around his shoulders. "Please, sugar, don't be angry with me . . . I just couldn't bear that. I'll tell him when the time's right. I promise I will." She leaned into him and kissed his neck. Then she was sitting bolt upright, staring straight ahead.

He had seen it the instant she had. Out of the rain, an ominous red glow seemingly in the middle of the highway. He pumped the brakes. Her arms flew out, hands clutching the padded dash, her eyes locked on the blurred outline of a large vehicle on its side across the highway. They were heading for it on a collision course. She began to scream.

Beyond a row of flares, two stationary police cars materialized, red lights flashing. He jerked the wheel to avoid them, throwing out his right arm, slamming her back into the seat, holding her there. Again he pumped the brakes. The T-bird began to skid sideways. He tried to aim for the far side, away from the police cars.

The car careened into a complete spin. He let go of the wheel and threw himself across her, a split second before their car slammed broadside into a telephone pole. The entire driver's side exploded inward, showering glass and bits of chrome, the cloth top ripping open, the sound a deafening cacophony in his ears.

His next awareness was the cold rain pelting his back, the intense pain in his right thigh. She was whimpering under him. He cried hoarsely, "Babe?! Babe?!" And fought to free himself from the tangled metal weighing on his hip.

The next few minutes were an anxious blur—helping hands reaching through her broken window, her door being forced open, Shelby pulled out from underneath him. Then he was extracted and standing, swaying unsteadily in the pouring rain, a blanket thrown over his shoulders. Shelby, weeping hysterically, was unhurt but shaken to the marrow of her bones.

Ambulance sirens, flashbulbs going off, white, stricken faces, staring at them, the rain pelting mercilessly, more police, more questions, mumbled responses. He and Shelby ended up in the back of a squad car, soggy, cold. She shivered in his arms, her blond hair matted against her cheeks. More flashbulbs outside the open rear door; someone calling her name. He buried her face deep into his chest, waving away questions, uttering denials.

On the side of the overturned bus banners hung limply, forlornly in the driving rain. The smeared letters were still legible as the squad car pulled past: WAR IS GOOD BUSINESS! INVEST YOUR SON!

In the antique four-poster, deep in the goose-down bedding, he gradually awoke, drifting in and out of sleep. Next to the head of the bed, a dormer window with lead-framed panes offered a sunlit view of thin pine trees on a rocky steep bank across the river gorge. Shelby slept on beside him, a small crease worrying her brow, her hair dry but matted from the rain.

For a long time, he lay on his side, watching her, listening to her quiet breathing, feeling warm, contented, grateful that the doctors at the small local hospital—after quite thorough examinations—had found nothing wrong with her. Even the deep muscle bruise on his own thigh, he'd been told, would disappear in a few weeks. He gently kissed the frown on her brow, not really wanting to wake her, but sort of hoping he would. And at that moment, desire flared so intensely, he had to force himself out of bed. It had been over three weeks since they'd been together.

Five minutes later, in damp jeans but a fresh flannel shirt, he hobbled downstairs, across the lobby's plank floor of the restored eighteenth-century coach house, looking for a cigarette machine. His eyes fell on the counter. Immediately his desire to smoke vanished.

The headlines announced boldly: RAIN WRECKS SUNNY. Underneath was a large news-wire photo of them in the back of the patrol car. Clinging to him, Shelby looked wet and miserable. He appeared angry, glaring at the camera for its intrusion.

Swearing to himself, Erik went back up the stairs, reading about the series of multiple accidents, starting with a busload of anti-war demonstrators heading into New York for the Moratorium Rally. The lead article was short on facts and long on innuendo—playing up the involvement of the T-bird, rented by Villa Caesari for Shelby Cale, age eighteen, but driven by Erik Lungren, age thirty.

The four-poster was empty. He could hear the shower running behind the closed bathroom door. He placed the newspaper on the top shelf of the closet and sat in the hoop-back Windsor chair, staring into the cold ashes of the fireplace. When Shelby emerged, fresh, glowing, wrapped in a China blue silk robe, he was smoking his third cigarette.

"Mornin', sugar," she said cheerfully and rummaged in her Vuitton suitcase. She brought something out and hid it behind her back, coming to him. She handed him a small gift-wrapped package. "I brought y'all this from Paris."

"How're you feeling?" he asked, smelling her clean-scented hair.

"Sensational . . . really. Open it."

He tore off the wrapping. "You're sure? No pains anywhere, no stiffness? Headaches, blurring of vision?" She shook her head, eyeing the blue velvet box in his hands. He opened it begrudgingly. Inside a pair of gold cufflinks—made from authentic Napoleonic coins. "Thank you, love. They're terrific," he said, already too aware that she had insisted on paying for the whole weekend. And now these expensive cufflinks. "Too bad I don't have a shirt with French cuffs."

She threw back her head and laughed—sultry, breezy, with a hint of lasciviousness bubbling underneath. The kind of laugh he'd expect to hear coming from a barn's hayloft on a hot summer day. "Well, it just so happens," she began, "back at my place, a dozen silk shirts await thee. Made especially in ol' Pa-ree. *All* with French cuffs, *trés bien, oui*?"

She reached for her riding clothes laid out on the bed's quilt. "I've got the whole day planned, sugar. We're going to have ourselves a grand ol' time." Brooding, he watched her lithe, firm, tantalizingly ripe body disappear under a layer of clothing.

All through breakfast in the antique-filled dining room, he wanted to tell her about the news article. But she was in such effervescent spirits, he hated to destroy the mood. She ate ravenously and afterward, they walked hand in hand along the winding riverbank, following the wellworn path through the scrubby pines to the riding stables.

She made a great show of selecting just the right two horses and soon was cinching up the saddle on a frisky roan. He followed suit with the large bay she'd chosen for him. Shortly they were riding along the narrow trail which forded the river and led up into the nearby hills.

Shelby proved to be an expert rider and he let her lead up the steep incline between the thin pines. She sat well in the saddle, her back straight, the reins held loosely but firmly in one hand. She brooked no nonsense or shirking on her mount's part and dug the heels of her boots firmly into his flanks to urge him on faster.

Erik tried to get the feel of being on horseback again. It brought back memories of one five-month stint on a Montana cattle ranch—long before his first novel had been published. The sun felt warm and strong on his shoulders. The heavily scented air smelled of pine, damp earth and drying rocks. He began to feel extraordinarily free, burdenless, bursting with energy. He felt damned lucky—not only to be alive, but to be there, at that moment, watching her pert ass bouncing in the saddle in front of him.

At the top of the crest, she dismounted, waiting for him to reach her. Together, they led their horses off the trail, along the bluff overlooking the meandering river. Far below, the small, white clapboard inn sat in a grove of pines like a small dollhouse. Tying off the horses, he grabbed the wool stable blanket and took her hand.

"Where we going?" she asked, untying her scarf and shaking loose her hair—it surrounded her face with a soft, golden glow.

He grinned but did not answer. He led her further into the deeply wooded hillside until he came to a likely spot—a small clearing of sun-drenched grass nestled at the base of giant boulders. The ground was drier here, protected by the large outcropping of rock. Spreading out the red plaid blanket, he grinned mischievously. "Ever make it outdoors?"

"Like the animals?"

"Ain't we all?" he teased.

"Sugar, some may be, but not all of us."

He pulled her to him and kissed her eagerly, pressing his hips into her. His erection was immediate and full. He felt her breath quicken and he lowered his hands, slipping them down inside the waistband of her slacks under her panties. As soon as he touched the soft curve of her buttocks, she pulled away. "Now don't y'all go getting any funny ideas, Mister Outdoorsman," she voiced. "I, for one, prefer beds."

"Then it's high time you were initiated into the unexpected joys of outdoor screwing." He tugged her back close and sank to the blanket, pulling her down with him. "Sunlight and mountain air on your skin, the smell of crushed pine needles beneath you, the pure sensation of being part of the earth."

"Erik," she cautioned, but he cut off her protests, smothering her mouth with an eager kiss. Arms around her, he snaked his tongue between her teeth, pushing it deeper. He brought up a knee between her legs, pressing his thigh against her. Pulling free her blouse, he opened it fully. Running his tongue down her neck, he began concentrating on her perfect, full breasts, flicking at the flat-topped, cylindrical nipples, sucking them, standing them upright like hard, pink erasers. Hurriedly he rolled over her and tugged at his belt, shucking down his jeans.

Warily she eyed him, then with a quick glance around, she raked her long fingernails, tracing his length. Her expertise had surprised him the first time they'd gone to bed; somehow he had not expected such an angelic-looking girl to be so knowledgeable about carnal subjects. Later, she'd admitted screwing since age fourteen—having been initiated by one of her grandmother's young stable hands. Her sexuality was one of the major reasons Erik found her so damned alluring—she was a mesmerizing combination of child and woman. At once both innocent and erotic.

Now, there on the wooden hillside, deep in the shadows obliquely cut by sharp angles of sunlight, he unzipped her slacks, pushing them down carefully to leave on her pale pink panties. He ran his hand over the silky texture, loving the softness encasing her softness. Her panties were always old-fashioned, high-waisted, sensible. He loved them, their feel, their look, their chastity.

He did not want to hurry. He desired to linger over her body, become reacquainted with all the wonderfully familiar but still arousing nuances, to feel the incredible smoothness of her unblemished skin, to taste her ripe sweetness. Slowly he rolled down her panties, gradually unveiling her.

He kissed the tiny, dusky brown birthmark set low on her abdomen like a faint thumbprint; a beauty mark just above the soft, thin growth of golden brown hair. He breathed in her musky sweet odor, tonguing her. Her cries of pleasure frightened out of concealment a mother quail and her several chicks. The alarmed chirps, as the birds scampered away into the rocks, startled Shelby. She opened her eyes, rolling her head toward the sounds. Her face blanched. "Someone's up there," she hissed.

He spun his head, following her horrified stare to the giant gray boulders above them. "Where?"

"He's got a camera!" She clutched the blanket to her.

Still searching, he rolled to his feet, tugging up his jeans, stomping his feet deeper into his boots. "Where?!"

"Below that dead tree," she whimpered, frantically pulling at her blouse, her face now flushed a deep magenta.

He spotted him—or rather the telephoto lens. It must have been a foot long. "Hey, you!" Erik roared and began to run, trying to fasten his pants at the same time.

Like a mountain goat, the man scrambled up the rocks and disappeared. Erik hit full-stride on the slope at the base of the boulders. He burst through the underbrush and vaulted onto the first outcropping of rock, then pulled himself up onto a ledge of the largest rock. He could hear loose stones clattering up ahead, then he could see him again.

The man, a camera bouncing from a strap around his neck, ran toward a Ford sedan parked on a fire trail. Erik lowered his head, poured it on, gaining on the guy, reaching him just as the car door was opened. "You dirty sonuvabitch," Erik panted and lunged for the camera.

The solidly built man swung out with a fist. Erik blocked it, slamming a return punch into the guy's gut and catching the drooping chin with a sharp uppercut. The man reeled backward, falling against the car. Erik snatched at the camera, tearing it from the strap. He hurled it with all his strength toward the rocks below. Far away, it crashed with a satisfying completeness.

Erik cocked his fist again. "You bastard—you want more?"

The swarthy-skinned man shook his head; his lower lip was split and blood dropped onto his white shirt.

"Then get your fuckin' ass out of here."

As soon as Erik entered the clearing by the horses, Shelby—dressed and obviously shaken—ran forward, throwing her arms around him, burying her head into his shoulders. "Why?" she sobbed. "Why would anyone do such a thing?"

Reluctantly, he told her about the morning headlines and photo. She recoiled, ashen. "Oh my god, Caesari will skin me alive." He started untying the horses, muttering, "We better split. No telling how many damned reporters are nosing about."

They rode back to the stables in silence. Wasting no time, they walked along the river trail. Beyond the back entrance of the inn, Erik spotted a knot of men, smoking and talking. Erik hustled her forward and slipped her up the backstairs unseen. At the landing to the second floor, they both halted in one movement.

Giorgio Caesari sat in a straight-back chair facing them. Impeccably dressed in a three-piece dark gray suit, he stood very slowly. "We'll go to your room." His tone was flat and as unreadable as his face.

"That's up to her," Erik replied evenly. Her eyes were dulled but she nodded, then darted ahead, scurrying to their door. "I've got the key . . ." Erik began, but the door was unlocked. She ducked inside.

When he and Caesari followed, she had already shut herself in the bathroom. Erik glanced around—all their personal items had been removed. Erik rubbed his raw knuckles where he'd hit the cameraman and asked, "What's on your mind?"

"You disgusting degenerate," Caesari spat out.

"Because I'm getting what you want?" For a second, Erik glimpsed under Caesari's mask—a flash of fury. Erik grinned, pleased that he'd touched a raw nerve. "Look, we're all adults here. I—"

"Shelby's *not* an adult," Caesari broke in.

"Couldn't prove it by me."

"I know all about you, Mister Lungren. Ever since you first sent Shelby a bouquet of yellow roses, I've collected a rather extensive file on your previous escapades: a certain matter of a hashish arrest in June of sixty-three; a paternity suit in the fall of sixty-four, settled out of court for thirty-five thousand dollars; a personal check signed by you in June of sixty-five to a documented abortionist." He paused, his voice firming. "You are a degenerate and belong behind bars."

Erik laughed. The idea that someone, anyone, would go to all the trouble of collecting a file on him struck him as patently absurd. Shelby chose that moment to reenter the room. She'd brushed her hair, applied a light layer of fresh lipstick. However, she appeared so terrified, Erik moved to her. She looked to Caesari through lowered lashes. "I'm so sorry . . . really, truly."

"You have lied to me. Deceived me at every turn," Caesari said. "You swore to me you weren't seeing anyone. Imagine my shock to have to read about my suspicions in the morning paper. Your escapade made the front page of every newspaper in the country. The implications of you being with this . . . this man are scandalous and—"

"Aw, cut the shit," Erik exploded. "Your moral outrage smacks highly of materialistic considerations. All you're concerned about is your goddamn investment."

Caesari whirled. "Leave us alone! There's a car waiting downstairs with your bag. The driver will return you to the city."

"I'm not going anywhere unless it's with her."

"Please, Erik," she said softly. "Just let me speak to him alone."

"He doesn't *own* you," Erik muttered, but she wasn't listening. He eyed both for a moment then strode to the door. "I'll be just outside in the hall." But neither looked at him.

Erik stepped into the hall and shut the door, stalking to the end of the hallway. He was so worked up it took him a while to register what was going on beneath the window. The inn's parking lot was jammed to overflowing. He could pick out three station wagons with network TV insignias. A knot of newsmen, complete with movie and still cameras, milled impatiently near two large panel trucks stationed at the far end. On the sides of each was a familiar logo reading MOVIEMOBILE. Damned media, he railed silently, leaping on an insignificant crumb of news like this. Damned scavengers!

He rolled away from the window and returned to the room's door. He could hear a muffled voice beyond the door—Caesari's, then Shelby's wail, "But I said I'm sorry, what more can I say?"

Erik threw open the door, surprising them both. "What the hell do you want from her?" he shouted to Caesari and, stepping into the room, slammed the door. "You goddamned sadist—can't you see she's upset? Leave her alone for Chrissakes!"

"Get out," Caesari ordered.

"You're goddamned right I'm getting out. With Shelby." He reached to take her hand but Caesari stepped between them. The action exploded the powderkeg inside Erik. Reason fled and pure, animalistic aggression shot to the surface. He grabbed the startled man's shoulders, spun him around and slammed him, face forward, up against the wall next to the fireplace. A blue-and-white Wedgwood plate jarred off the mantel, crashing to the floor. Twisting Caesari's arm, Erik leaned his weight on the frightened man's back.

"No, Erik, don't," she pleaded. "Please..."

Taking his time, Erik released his hold and Caesari slipped away, straightening his tie, as if he had been jostled in an elevator. *"Cara mia,"* he said thinly. "I suggest you redo your face. Less eyeshade, more lip gloss." He preened, the epitome of elegance and élan. "The two of us are going down to greet the gentlemen of the press."

"Oh, I couldn't," she breathed, one hand swooping to her face. "Giorgio, really, what would I say to them?"

"That you are here in these lovely hills to shoot a sixty-second commercial for our new Blush Divine. Mister Lungren was kind enough to volunteer to drive you out last night as we were to have begun this morning at seven. Unfortunately... the accident... you are thankful that no one was seriously injured. Credit the state pol—"

"That's why those Moviemobile trucks are out there," Erik broke in. "For this damned phony commercial?"

Ceasari stared stonily. "It goes before the cameras in an hour."

"Pretty expensive coverup."

"I suggest you take me up on my offer for the driver and the car. Your services are no longer needed."

"Services?"

Caesari smiled, a tight, victorious gloat. "You are officially listed as the writer of this commercial."

It took a beat for Erik to recover. "I don't belong to that union."

"Oh yes. As of this morning. My chauffeur is holding your card for you. Would you care to see your script?"

"What the hell's with all this? You think this is going to smokescreen the whole thing, fool anybody?"

"No one outside of this room will know the truth," Caesari said.

"How about the night clerk? I checked in as Mister and Missus."

"Miss Cale's booked in room six downstairs," Caesari explained, overly patient. "Every other empty room in the inn has been booked by Villa Caesari. Four in all."

Caesari smoothed his black hair on one side. "*Caramissa,* please. I promised them we'd be down shortly. I want to hit the evening news."

Her eyes wavered to Erik and back, helpless confusion registering. "Couldn't I speak with Erik alone? Please . . ."

Caesari glanced at his diamond encrusted Piaget watch. "Very well. Five minutes. No more."

"What if I take six?" Erik threw at him. "You have us shot?"

Imperially, Caesari walked into the hall. Erik bolted forward and slammed the door, spinning to her, trying to get a grip on himself.

She stood, weeping silently into her hands as if too ashamed to look at him. Her image struck him as so forlorn, so goddamned helpless, so needing of protection, he moved swiftly to her, enveloping her in an embrace, kissing her wet cheeks again and again.

"I'm so sorry," she sobbed into his shirt.

"Nothing's your fault, babe," he murmured, lifting her face. "Just an unfortunate series of circumstances." He hesitated, then spoke what had been on his mind from the moment he'd first seen the morning's headlines. He wanted something from her so much, he was afraid he would blow it. He began slowly, "There is another way out. You could quit. Come away with me. Out of the city.

Somewhere where we can breathe. Where it's just us. Maybe we could even think about getting married."

She scanned his face. "Oh sugar, some day, yes . . . I'd love to marry y'all . . . But not now. Not while I've got everything going for me . . . and you're . . . you still—"

He tried to recover from the blow to his solar plexus. "Not successful enough? Is that it? *If* I were rolling in bread, on top of *my* world, would you say, yes?"

"That's not fair," she cried and pulled away. "I didn't say . . . I just . . . I can't toss this all away. Sunny's all I've got . . . that's me—"

He stared at her tearstained face, the hollowness returning to his gut. He forced himself to nod. "Well, then, we better get on with this charade." He started for the door. Her voice stopped him. "I do love you, Erik." He tried to smile and said, "That's something then, isn't it?" He opened the door, stepping through and closing it quietly behind him.

In the hallway, Caesari stood by the window overlooking the parking lot. He did not bother to turn around as he spoke. "The car is in back. For Shelby's sake, please refrain from any comment whatsoever, now or in the future, about this." His voice was thicker than usual, and when Caesari turned, his face sagged like a sail without wind. "Never in the twenty-eight-year history of my company has anything come so close to tarnishing my reputation. I will not tolerate any further incidents, Mister Lungren." He drew himself up. "To leave her alone . . . how much? Name a price to never see her again. Ten thousand? Twenty?"

Not believing the pathetic, tawdry scene playing before him, Erik shook his head. "I'll see Shelby as long as she wants me. And something else. You treat her well, or you'll have to answer to me, personally." Erik made certain the message was received and understood, before he turned to stomp down the stairs. Yet even before he reached the rear of the inn, the heavy weight of failure rounded his shoulders.

DAVID
May 1967
Beverly Hills

Driving too fast to make the turn, he hit the brakes and squealed the tires to an abrupt stop before the ornate cast-iron gates. Instantly the gates, his rented Chrysler and both occupants were bombarded with crossbeams of high-intensity floods, and the imposing driveway curving out of sight up the hill was simultaneously lighted by low, stone footlights which bathed the Italian streetstones in a warm, welcoming glow. Like a yellow brick road to Oz, he thought, and this Oz also has no wizard, only another fraud behind a curtain.

"This is it, huh?" Silver piped, the excitement evident in her voice. "Kinda spooky, ain't it? Like they sure as hell don' want no strangers pokin' about."

He stared up at the familiar lion motif interwoven at the very top of the gate's intricate ironwork. He could not bring himself to reach out through his open window and push the button on the intercom box.

"David? You shakin'? Or are we in one of them L.A. earthquakes?" She laughed quietly, then fell silent for a moment, watching his profile.

"What'samatter, David? Don'cha think you can handle it?"

He closed his eyes. No one in the group knew how desperate he was. His bank account was down to nothing, he'd been forced to sell his own personal stereo system, plus his entire record collection. He had borrowed heavily, at exorbitant interest rates, with IOUs signed practically in blood, with promises to pay back within forty-eight hours, and the IOUs held by some heavies who would love to see him eat shit. So, not only everything he'd been working for in the last three years, meaning White Meat and Silver, but also his own future and present ass, was on the line.

"Goddammit to hell," he exploded, startling Silver severely. He reached out, finger punching the box's button just as she hit his arm with a solid thwack. "Damn you boy, don't scare me like that." The intercom voice squawked, "Yes?"

He couldn't place the voice. "David Rau for Cara Noor," he said into the box. He worried whether he was risking too much, counting on something, which at best was based on a slim memory from his tumultuous boyhood.

The gates clicked loudly and began to swing open. "Oh, wow," Silver sighed and continued to coo softly, all the way up the drive as she took in the lighted Greek and Roman marble statues and baroque fountains dotting the grounds. Without the headlights, making the turns by rote, David sped the car under the tall spires of towering palms lining the drive, palms which had been tall when he was a boy and which had grown up with him, for again he had that sense of being small, and that only augmented the unease he had been feeling ever since landing in Los Angeles.

Rapidly the large three-storied Mediterranean-styled house came into view—its red-tiled roofs dark against the night sky, the pink stucco walls awash in a soft glow from the directional floods hidden behind lush ferns. Silver's mouth dangled open. "Talk about bein' born with a silver spoon up your ass."

"Just shut the fuck up for a while, will you?"

Her mouth snapped closed but her eyes grew larger. He swept the car into the interior courtyard before the main entrance, swung around the large circular fountain, past the tiled steps to the towering double doors and stopped in the shadow of the east wing. Switching off the motor, he looked over at her.

On the way from the airport, she had changed clothes in the back seat, into her "fancy duds"—a used navy blue sailor's suit, a scarf of old lace around her neck and on her head a sequined sailor's hat. He thought she looked like a Tenderloin transvestite ready to party.

"I'm going in alone," he said and opened his door. "You wait out here."

She grabbed his arm. "Now hold on, boy. I didn't come all the way down here to fuckin' Beverly Hills to wait outside in the goddamned car. When you asked me to come along, the first thin' you said was, 'Wanna meet Cara Noor.' Don' you go denyin' it.''

"I've changed my mind."

Her grip tightened. "You sack o' shit, you couldn't make this trip alone. You promised. An' here I am, lookin' slicker than spit on a slate rock.''

He wrenched himself free and stood outside. "I also promised you guys I'd get you a record contract by the end of this month. Well that's this weekend. So that's what I'm busting my balls to do. Besides I just have to pick up something in the library.'' Ignoring her outburst of sour curses, he slammed the car door and strode toward the main entrance under the tiled portico. He could smell the night-blooming jasmine—jasmine his mother had planted over twenty years earlier. He hurried up the stairs, already beginning to feel smothered by the unearthly silence.

Before he could ring the bell, the door flew open revealing Cara in a low-cut, pink chiffon evening gown, diamonds flashing at her throat and earlobes. A bejeweled finger was frozen to her painted lips, indicating broadly for him to be silent. Quickly she glanced behind her, then motioned him forward. David squeezed through the narrow opening.

"He's on the phone, upstairs,'' she whispered. David pushed past her and across the marble squares, hurrying into the book-lined library. His eyes swept over the room—nothing had changed except the large painting over the fireplace. It was now a still life by Renoir. He figured it cost upward of half a million dollars. Irving was doing all right for himself.

Forgetting Cara, David moved swiftly to the books behind the leather chesterfield. He began scanning the rare-book titles, anxious but methodical.

"What on earth are you doing?'' Cara asked huskily and closed the library doors. "Darling, you promised you'd be here for dinner. We're ready to leave for the premiere now.''

He was immersed in the classical literature section—Moroccan leather, the titles in gold printing. He was positive this was where his mother had placed it. But where the hell was that Melville collection?

Rustling her skirt, Cara strode toward him. "Davey! What the hell are you looking for? Is this why you called me? You wanted a goddamned book?" She spun to the liquor cabinet. "I should've known. You were always the strangest, most obsessed child. . . . I thought it was bizarre of you to phone. You haven't communicated with us for years."

Methodically, he moved to another shelf, his fingers racing over the bindings of the books. "Thought you said this was some sort of anniversary party?"

"Our sixteenth," she said warily over the rim of her glass. "After the premiere of *Revenge* tonight. It's our seventh film together. And Irving thinks it's our best. He's throwing me a tent party at Chasen's. That's really where I wanted you to come." She let out an exasperated sigh, "Davey, what in God's name are you looking for? You're driving me bananas."

Bending low to read the bottom shelf of leather-bound books, he glanced over at her. He decided that all the peroxide and face lifts and emerald-cut diamonds could not conceal the fact—she was a lousy actress. Always had been. His mother could have acted this tramp off the screen by just standing still. "What a shame I won't be able to see your latest failure," he said flatly. "I'll be on a return flight." He started on the top row, wanting only to escape. "If you're up in San Francisco tomorrow night, call the Winterland box office. I'll leave you a couple of comps. I'm having a small party of my own. Probably only five thousand or so. My new group will entertain. You free?"

Cara began to play the "misunderstood innocent" to the hilt, sagging against an upholstered chair. "You promised on the phone you'd stay for the party. I should've known. Even as a child, you were like this, so vindictive, vicious. You made my life hell."

"I'm pleased to hear there was *something* successful about my childhood." The title of the first book on the third shelf leaped out to him. With a barely suppressed cry, he yanked out *Moby Dick*. Immediately he fanned open the gilt-edged pages, holding the oversized book upside down, shaking it. Cara edged closer to him, watching with a fanatical fascination.

The flat manilla envelope slid out and fluttered to the Persian carpet. He swooped down and picked it up, the book forgotten on the floor.

"What is that?" Cara demanded harshly. "This is Irving's house, Davey. These are his books and things. You can't come barging in here. What is that? Answer me, you putz," she shrilled.

He could feel the cardboard thickness of the eight-by-ten package and fought to control the emotions which were erupting by the memory of his mother placing it there. On the very day she had been forced to move out, Nedra had taken him into the library and secretively, theatrically, whispered to him that the envelope was only for dire emergencies for either of them, then she had kissed him and walked out of the house for the last time. Three months later, she was dead. David spun for the door.

In his path, Cara eyed him with hostile suspicion. "I'm calling Irving down. He should—"

"—just a letter I remember my mother putting there," David interrupted, reaching deep for a boyish smile. He held out the envelope. "Just sentimental value. I only remembered it this last week." He thrust it at her, knowing she was blind as a bat and too vain to reach for her glasses.

"Cara!"

The gruff voice in the hall stunned them both. David felt the skin tightening over his skull. The door shot open and David had to step to the wall to avoid being hit. From behind the door, he watched Cara's last face lift being tested by a patently artificial smile.

"Come on," Irving ordered, beyond David's view. "The car's here."

"Darling, just a moment," she began dramatically. "I've arranged a little surprise for your anniversary present."

"Later," Irving said, his tone sharp, irritated. "The car's waiting."

Behind the door, she reached for David and latched onto his arm. Before he could jerk away, she had pulled him into view with startling strength. Irving, in evening clothes, was striding away, toward the front doors, his bald pate thrust forward, his shoulders hunched for battle. David yanked free of Cara just as she called out.

"Happy Anniversary, darling!"

Irving whirled, his eyes landing on David. His bushy brows slammed together. David fought to hold the gaze.

Cara rushed on, "Isn't this wonderful, darling? Davey's here to wish us 'happy anniversary.' Don't you just love my surprise?"

"How come?" Irving asked harshly.

She shot a glance at David and lied badly, "Because I called and invited him."

"I asked him." Irving locked his deep-set eyes on David. "Well?"

The curt inflection, the implacable stare, the demanding manner were so repellent David could not find his voice. He had been hoping that he could slip in and slip out before this encounter could take place. Now Irving blocked the front way out. David turned on his heel and headed for the library's French doors leading to the terrace.

"So why're you here?" Irving demanded behind him. "You need money? Got law troubles? Need a smart mouthpiece?"

"No." David tried the handle to the first terrace door. Then the next. Both were locked. He started across the rug, heading for the front hallway again.

Irving, squat and solid as a bowling pin, stepped in his way. "So you went and legally changed your last name to Nedra's? That supposed to make me feel bad? Me? I couldn't be happier."

David tried moving around him but Irving sidestepped in front again. "My sources also tell me you're managing one of those screeching shithole rock-and-roll bands. That's music?"

"It's going to make me more money than you ever dreamed."

"By the time you get it—*if* you get it—you'll be stone deaf and crazed on drugs."

Trying a diversionary tactic, David walked to the fireplace and nodded to the Renoir. "What happened to that big oil of Nedra? In her riding clothes? It disappeared the moment Cara walked through the door."

Irving chuckled, a rattling chest noise. "Had it burned. Well, you know how funny girls can be about such things. I didn't want to hurt Cara's feelings. Not on my goddamned wedding night.''

"But you didn't give a damn about mine, did you?'' The accusation hurled rawly from the back of his throat.

Irving studied him as if he were numbers in a debit column. "I figured you'd be man enough to take it. But you sure as hell proved me wrong. You were kicked out of every fakachtah school I put you in. From that military prep school all the way up to Stanford. Hell, you couldn't wait to do something rotten to get expelled. Especially if it could drag my name into the papers.''

"Maybe that should have told you something,'' David retorted.

"Yeah. That you were an ungrateful sonofabitch.'' Irving's temper surfaced. "You were a mama's-boy from day one. Nedra spoiled you rotten. Turned you into fucking crybaby. I never forgave her for that.''

"You asshole,'' David railed. "You fucked her over from the moment you met her to when you killed her.''

Irving shook his head. "Nedra was a weak-livered sobsister and she turned you into one. Biggest mistake of my life marrying that fag hag. You're going to end up just like her. And she died of an overdose!''

David twitched, dangerously close to losing all control. He turned blindly for the hall door.

It opened before he reached it. Cara, swathed in a full-length ermine cape, stammered uncertainly, "There's a young . . . person—''

"Hi, David,'' Silver squawked, anxiously stepping into view. "Jus' wanted to see what was takin' you so long.''

He groaned audibly, ready to lash out. However, he caught sight of Irving. The stunned, disbelieving look on Irving's puss was well worth the price of admission. David began to feel almost exhilarated. "Silver, you're too much. You meet Cara?''

"Sure did. Boy, ain't I the lucky one,'' she said, awestruck. "Wait 'til my mom hears 'bout this. She'll scream her tits off. Oh, 'scuse me, ma'am.''

David moved forward to take Silver's arm. "Good night, Cara. Thanks for letting me in.'' He pulled out the flat manila package and waved it triumphantly. "This is part of Nedra's legacy to me. And I claim it now in front of all you witnesses."

David couldn't help but laugh at the confusion on all their faces. He flourished the envelope and swept a gawking Silver out of the house.

In the car, once outside the iron gates of the estate, David pulled over and gently opened the envelope. He slipped out the small cardboard-backed, tissue-wrapped, piece of stiff paper. He folded back the tissue, exposing the simple line-drawn figure of a clown on a unicycle. Silver leaned over it and cried in disappointment, "That's what you came back for? A kid's drawing? Hell, I can do you up one better than that."

He laughed, repacking carefully. "It's a genuine, authenticated Picasso. Irving gave it to Nedra on their fifth anniversary." Resealing the envelope, he tossed it nonchalantly into her lap and gunned the engine. "Looks like we'll have our bash after all."

San Francisco

The Picasso sketch, sold to the prearranged art dealer, brought in a quick ten grand. By the following evening, all but some loose change had been spent. Survival Saturday, as David privately had labeled the concert, was do or die. If White Meat didn't get signed that night, he had made it clear to all concerned: He would disband them.

With the concert in full swing, the band rocking, the crowd bopping, David hustled up the vertical ladder to the follow-spot platform high above the crowded dance floor. He poked the kid hard on the shoulder. "You asleep or stoned?" he shouted above the din of White Meat playing full out on two giant banks of amplifiers on either side of the stage.

The acne-scarred kid shrank sheepishly. "I'm straight, man."

"Barely," David hollered. "I want Silver covered at *all* times. If she moves, you move. You're two goddamned beats behind. Shape up!"

Scrambling down the ladder, David surveyed the orgiastic sea writhing below on the dance floor. It was a wall-to-wall, undulating

carpet of dirty, freaked-out hippies. On the sides, the raked auditorium seats were crammed with the zoned-out; in the aisles, some were
humping, some passed out. The strobe lights continually froze the
action into stop-frames; the brilliant white bursts flashed on the
rococo gilt of the former ballroom, adding more pizzazz to the
festivities. But for him it was no party. It was the biggest, most
important production of his life.

On the way back to the stage, one of his assistants collared him.
"Fire chief's looking for you," the guy screamed. "Madder than
hell."

"What was our last head count?"

"Over forty-four hundred."

David leaned into the kid's stringy hair to be heard. "Tell the
chief we're closing the doors. No more admitted." He paused, a
tight, pleased smile appearing briefly. Over forty-four hundred.
More than enough. After all, the freaks were only background extras
for his broader scheme. "What about the guest list?" The kid
shrugged in response to the question. David grabbed him. "You
think this is for the brotherhood of man? Give the freaks a free
show? I want to know who's checked in on the VIP list, asshole.
That's what we're here for."

A chick in a medieval gown waved him over to the food stands.
Wearing a pin-on button that read MCNAMARA IS A WAR TOY, she
lamented, "They were just pigs. Clawed at the cake with their
hands. I thought this was the sharing generation—we're all pigs! I'm
splitting."

He caught her arm, shouting. "Not until all that rental stuff is
cleaned and reboxed. That's your gig too." He shoved her back to
the free refreshment stand which still offered punch and ice-cream
bars.

Listening hard to the balance of sound, David made a beeline for
the mixing-board operator hunched over the slide buttons and dials.
"Bring up the bass, man," David urged. "I want the floor to shake.
That's it, that's it. The San Francisco earthquake of sixty-seven!"

Backstage, he grabbed a bottle of beer from the crew's ice chest
and stood in the wings, assessing the band's performance. They had
started shaky, tentative, they knew what was at stake all too well.

But now they were really beginning to cook. Hawk, on lead guitar, slid effortlessly into a blistering riff, while Larry dug in with a driving line that was straight out of Charlie Christian. Zisk filled it out with solid, two-handed chords on the keyboard and Peter provided a funky and a very dirty backbeat.

Silver, on the other side of the stage, was taking a breather, banging a tambourine hard on one thin thigh. Just before the concert, she had whacked off the long skirt of her old silver lamé formal so it now was the briefest of miniskirts. She caught him staring at her and winked at him over her dark shades.

Behind the band the movie screen was a constant flow of psychedelic patterns and colors, blobs and patterns melting and oozing into each other, the best and most expensive light show in town. David's long-haired assistant appeared with the VIP list. The raucous, near-deafening noise did not interfere with David's concentration on the clipboard of names. His all-out, month-long assault on the record labels had produced results. Reps had signed in from RCA, Capitol, RPM, Elektra and MGM. Still missing were Decca, Columbia, Bell and a few smaller, chickenshit labels.

Someone grabbed his arm and he looked up angrily. The beefy biker glared down at him. "My bread now, sonny."

David shook the meaty paw off and glanced around apprehensively. "Told you not to come near me."

"I don't give a dirty fuck," the guy shouted, the purple tatoo of a skull and crossbones bulging on his heavily muscled bicep. "I want my bread. Or I'll bust your head open and use the goo to grease my boots."

David hustled the big-bellied guy to an isolated corner behind the projection table. "Did you do it?" he asked.

"Hell, yes," came the hairy growl. "Enough Mellow Yellow to guarantee good times by all. Now pay up, you little puke."

"Let go of me," David yelled. "And I'll pay you."

The biker withdrew his hand and hitched up his greasy jeans. David set his beer bottle between them on the railing and from his wallet, carefully counted out one hundred bucks. "Remember, you don't know who I am."

The biker grinned widely, displaying a gap of missing front teeth.

"Ain't never seen you before in my sweet life." He lumbered away, counting his bucks.

David grabbed his beer bottle, took a healthy swallow. The LSD in the free fruit punch had been a last-minute inspiration. He knew it was risky, but he wanted to insure that the crowd's reaction was so far out that the label reps would sit up and bark on cue. From the looks of the frenzied mob out front, the acid was doing its number.

Finishing his beer, he walked to the side curtains for a better view of the stage. The quartet was ramming home the last verse of "Pacific Coast Highway," one of their best all-out rock numbers. The close three-part harmony sounded the tightest he had ever heard. Peter's backbeat was solid on the drums as they reached the bridge segueing into Silver's solo on the last verse.

She strode into the white light and grabbed the mike from the stand as if she were going to strangle it. Her pale hair was flattened with perspiration and her lean arms glistened with moisture. She kicked off her high heels straight into the crowd, then hunched over the mike, bringing forth such a howl from her bowels that all eyes were drawn to her.

As the shriek increased in intensity, she straightened with it, until she stood, legs splayed, pelvis thrust forward, head reared back, screaming her guts out. Just when the audience began to scream with her, she jerked forward, launching into the last verse, machine-gunning the lyrics: "Travelin' down Pacific Coast Highway/ You an' me and a cat called Free/ Thumb truckin' down Pacific Coast Highway/ Highway One to the sun." As she sang, she charged the lip of the stage, clawing the air for the hands outstretched to touch her electrical magic.

Her frenzy mushroomed, her jerky awkward dance becoming more frantic as she pushed for the climax. Hitting the last line, spasms wracked her body, her neck tendons bulged. Abruptly, on the last beat of the song, she jammed the mike head into the V of her crotch and collapsed into a heap onto the stage floor. As startled as anyone, David hurriedly signaled the head light man to kill all the lights.

Instantly the stage and ballroom plunged into total darkness. The response from the audience was overwhelming. He had never heard anything like it. The bellow rose as one voice, the roar of a single, giant beast that wanted more. It was the most satisfying sound he had ever experienced.

Thousands of feet began stamping until the entire building shook with a steady, demanding beat. The on-stage lights dimmed up and Silver was nowhere to be seen. A cry of disappointment broke out. Hawk and the rest of the band stood awkwardly grinning at the mob. David felt a tug on his sleeve. Silver, wet with sweat, her body bent and throbbing, struggled for breath, her face aglow with excitement. She grinned up at him hugely. "Pretty hot, huh, man?"

Hawk was looking over with a questioning shrug. David thought quickly. The prearranged order of songs would have to be changed to bring the crowd down again. He made an appropriate selection and signaled for the guys to launch into one of the few slower numbers, one that did not feature Silver. Over the still clamorous crowd, the song started.

Next to him, Silver wiped her face on a towel, still heaving for breath. He frowned. "You're peaking too soon." He was already noting that the crowd had begun to lose interest in the band without her out there.

"Ain't that jus' like you, man," she said. "I'm raisin' a fuckin' riot an' you're tellin' me I'm peakin' too early."

He bent to her angrily. "I've carefully structured the set to build. Stick to the game plan. How can you keep topping yourself?"

"Jus' watch, man," she said, the energy sparking from her like lightning. "You ain't seen nothin' yet." She tossed him the towel and bounced out onto the stage. The crowd roared its approval, drowning out Hawk's vocal solo. David started to yell to her to get off, when he noticed the top rep for MGM showing his backstage pass to the roadie on guard at the stairs. David knew the real action was finally ready to start.

"Okay, Rau, you win," the rep said, approaching. "You've been honking this group for months. Tonight, I finally see why. That Silver is outta sight."

"Took you long enough," David replied, feeling a warm glow of well-being.

"Okay, don't rub it in. I'm prepared to make an offer. Ten

upfront, five percent royalty. Two for you as producer. Standard five-year contract. Renewable each year. Ten albums a must.''

David waited. "That's it? What about *my* contract?"

"I can't give you what you're asking. Our label doesn't have in-house producers.''

"That's bullshit," David spat out. "You want my act, I get a separate contract to produce other groups. No discussion on that point.''

"Be reasonable, Rau," the rep said with a placating smile. "You're just starting out. Frankly, I'm impressed. You seem to have what it takes. But one step at a time. Take my offer. If this group hits, then you can make your demands.''

David shrugged, an odd sensation forming behind his eyeballs—it felt like they were slowly elongating in their sockets. "No deal, Wilson. I want twenty-five upfront for signing the group and seven percent royalty. Plus three for me. I know your label—you give away to the wholesalers—two free albums for every ten they order. You don't give royalties on those freebies. And you know it.'' He could tell he had the guy stymied.

"Well, think it over," the rep offered lamely.

"Don't have to," he snapped. "Now, excuse me. I see Elektra's knocking at my door." He strode away toward the other rep, the strange feeling growing behind his eyes. Everything was beginning to look like it was through the wrong end of a telescope. He joined the Elektra man.

"Solid gig, David. Real solid." This rep was a younger, more hip and more likely to spot incredible potential. They chatted together for a few minutes, listening to the band. Soon, however, David felt a compelling gritty urgency to get on with the business at hand. "You want to make an offer or shoot the shit?''

"Yes and no," the rep said. "Dig your group. Think we could do big things for them. However, my boss won't go for a separate contract for you. No one fresh in the business has a *carte blanche* deal like that. They won't take the risk.''

David had to look away—the disappointment combined with the strange, wavering sensation, as if the floor were rocking gently—made him unsure of his response. He struggled to remain on top.

"MGM just offered me an A-and-R position. Plus twenty-five for the group and seven royalty. Can you top that?"

The young rep frowned thoughtfully, as if considering whether it were a bluff or not. "I'm authorized to go fifteen and six. No more."

"Let me think about it," David mumbled. "But I'm not signing unless I have a contract too. Put that in your fucking hopper and see what comes out." Abruptly he walked away, rubbing his eyes. Things were not in focus. What a fucking time to get sick, he thought and sank to an upturned drum case.

While he remained there, unable to find the strength to get up, two more label reps approached him. The staid, middle-aged head of a small label called RPM came up to David and droned on and on about wanting to expand his middle-of-the-road stable but he did not come forth with a substantial offer. Wearily David waved him away, the numbness in his shoulders making any movement a difficult chore. The number two West Coast rep for Decca came up and said he was considering David's demand for a separate contract, he liked the group that much. David started to laugh. "You look like a fuckin' billy goat." He giggled and shot to his feet, feeling a blazing burst of restless energy. "No fuckin' goat's goin' to chew my ass." He left the startled man.

At the bottom of the rear stage stairs, he stumbled, pitching forward, falling hard into giant, hairy arms. It took him a while to recognize the biker. The beefy face was laughing, pressing close, and small pink snakes were crawling out of the gaps between his teeth. "Dig your acid, man. I put a couple hits in your beer. You sure as hell paid for it. So now enjoy it, man." He shoved and David flew away for what seemed like miles, mumbling, "Acid, acid, who's got the acid?"

The colored moving lights, rays of rainbow gelled beams danced into his awareness—the intricate patterns of light and color, the flashing bursts of white swept him up into a state of near ecstasy. He had never seen anything so beautiful—the thousands of shades, the particles of dust and smoke that hung in each beam, how the colors transformed faces into a kaleidoscope of ever-changing emotions.

Somewhere over him, around him, in him Silver was crooning,

the lyrics etching deeply into his stoned brain: "Baby/ when you're feelin' low/ an' the floor's comin up to greet you/ when there ain't no softness/ no pillow for your head/ I'm always there to meet you/ Baby, I'm your mama/ I'm your papa/ An' I'm your sister too/ So come an' get it/ just' grab hold of/ Your sweet mama's love."

Enchanted out of his mind, he wandered the dance floor among the gyrating bodies, turning in all directions, his mouth slightly open, his entire being listening to the song with an intense absorption. He was jostled, bumped and crashed into, even thrown to the floor at one point, but still he moved on, undaunted, lost in the music, the lyrics, and the ever-changing phantasmagorical fantasy enmeshing him.

And then he saw her—standing in a golden haze, gazing at him with so much tenderness and love, he began to weep. Through his tears, he moved to her, overwhelmed that she was before him once more. All else faded. Even the music. It was just he and his mother, meeting on a gauzy plane of shimmering golden light. Her eyes, dark and magnetic, exuded such sensitivity, such delicacy of spirit, such compassion, he was once again a mere boy.

He held out his hands to her and the cry that burst from his lips came from the deep well of loneliness within. "Moma," he sobbed and reached out, wrapping his arms about her, drawing her close, burying his face into her. For that one instant, an instant that stretched into a blissful eternity, he felt peace, he experienced the forgotten pillow of security, the longed for expression of need and love.

Suddenly it all shattered. With a cry of scorn, she wrenched free and melted into the wall of colors. At once, the golden haze dissolved into a confused palette of cold, depressing hues. Terror engulfed him. He had lost her again. He sank to the floor and cried like a baby.

REBECCA
May 1967
San Francisco

It was a nightmare. She tore herself out of his tenacious grasp and fled. Hurtling blindly through the maze of strobe-lit, writhing bodies, Rebecca ran from the stoned-out freak who had called her Moma.''

The rock music blared out over the dance floor so loud, so overwhelming, she could not separate her own heartbeat from the pounding rhythm of the song. The air was foul with the smell of sweat and unwashed bodies, mixed with the sickening sweet aroma of incense and marijuana.

Out of the garishly colored haze, a policeman materialized, solidly real in his blue uniform. She darted toward him and spotted the exit door. With a rush of relief, she pushed through the crowd and escaped.

The cool, damp night air was a blessed tonic. But she forced herself to keep moving, away from the mob still trying to get into the free concert bash for a new band called White Meat. Once off the teeming sidewalk and into the street, she slowed, looking back, checking carefully if she were being followed by that "Moma" freak. Not seeing him, she edged to the far side and gratefully sank against the hard metal of a psychedelic, gaudily painted VW van. She would watch for Scooter there. On the street corner a radio was playing Jimi Hendrix full blast, the angry defiant music served as a background score for the amazing, ongoing scene.

Her eyes swept over the young people in their outlandish costumes parading the sidewalks. Despite the chill in the air, many were barefoot. Guys sported beards and beads, ponchos and feathered hats, tie-dyed T-shirts, military coats, sashes and tasseled scarves tying off brightly patched jeans below the knee. Girls, some in mini-skirts, others in full-length dresses, wore fringed shawls and witches' capes, jangling beads and tinkling bells, many had wreaths of flowers woven into their hair, or carried bunches of daisies, handing out single flowers to all they met. Others daintily accompanied their meanderings with Tibetan finger cymbals, some had ornate cheek designs in day-glo colors.

Wherever Rebecca looked people had that blissful, beatific look on their faces—a look which she had begun to accept in the many weeks of coming to the Haight-Ashbury. It was just part of the scene. They smiled benignly to themselves and to each other. Stoned, she figured, watching the clusters around the street dealers—joints for a buck, an ounce of Acapulco Gold for fifteen, a hit of acid for a buck fifty: Purple Haze, Sunshine, Windowpane, Chocolate Mescaline, whatever.

It seemed that each time she came to the area there were more kids, but the one face she longed for was not among the colorful stream. For a long while, she had believed in her heart of hearts that Scooter was there, that this would be his scene. But now, after weeks of searching, she was not certain of anything anymore. *Scooter, where are you, huh? Are you here at all?*

Disheartened, she pushed herself off the car and trudged ahead, searching on, attempting to dispel the cloud of gloom that had hung over her since leaving New York. She was afraid she might walk right past him and not even know him. Looking so openly at people created its own problems. A lot of the guys and some of the chicks read it as an invitation for contact. More than once, she had to dart around some space-eyed freak who asked if she wanted to "get it on" or "did she have a pad to crash in," or did "she want to get high," or "higher?"

"Spare some change?" a barefoot kid of no more than fifteen asked cheerfully in front of her. He was wrapped in a scrungy-looking blanket and his face was ravaged by pimples. He looked so pitiful, she went against her usual principle and dug into her jeans pocket for a hard-earned quarter. He took it from her with a soft, "Groovy." She started on, but the youth fell in beside her. "I've been here three days already," he said proudly. "Think I can last the month?" Not wanting to encourage him, she shrugged, avoiding his eyes by watching the flow on the sidewalk.

"Man, people are so beautiful here," he continued dreamily. "Wish the whole world could be like this, don't you?"

She walked on silently, stealing looks at the guys on the corner from underneath her long bangs. "My ol' man has a warrant out for me," the kid boasted. "But he won't find me. Hell, I can live on nothing here and no one will turn me in. Turn me *on*, yeah." He giggled. "I'm crashing at the Diggers Free Store and eating their stew handout in the park. Where're you crashing?"

"I'm sharing a place with a great old lady near North Beach. Kinda deaf but sweet," she replied, having decided the kid was perfectly harmless. "Hey, aren't your feet cold?"

Still shuffling, he looked down at his bare, dirty feet as if to find out. "Kind of, yeah. I traded my shoes for this blanket. That's the way the whole world should be run, right? No money. Just barter for what you need."

She dug her hands deeper into the pockets of her letterman sweater, feeling like a lost outsider, like the book she was reading, *Stranger in a Strange Land.*

"Isn't that the pits about Ali?"

Confused, she glanced over at the kid. "Cassius Clay?"

"Yeah, the bastards took away his title today. For not going into the army. Damned if I'm going either."

She let his statement ride in silence, too confused about the Vietnam war to have any opinion one way or the other, except that it was creating divisions among more and more people. And it saddened her to think that young people, like these around her, were over there, fighting a raging war, while in the Haight, kids were tripping along in fantasyland. She and the tagalong kid passed a pine coffin on the sidewalk. Inside were a boy and girl, sitting upright, arms wrapped around each other. As she passed by, Rebecca heard the girl say softly, "No, I like Baez better than Collins, but Judy has prettier eyes."

"Sure hope I get laid soon," the kid beside Rebecca said, casting a hopeful eye in her direction. "Sixteen years is a long time." He laughed boisterously at his own joke.

"Maybe you should go back home."

"Never," he said, then asked plaintively, "You don't want to love me a little? Pass it around?" She shook her head.

Shrugging with disappointment, he flashed the peace sign and ambled away, his blanket trailing behind like a tattered shadow. She forged ahead, seriously considering for the millionth time whether she should follow her own advice. Maybe she should give up and return to New York.

A few weeks earlier, she had splurged for a copy of the *Village Voice* to read the review of the opening of *The Conquest of Mars*. The effusive praise for the actress who had replaced her had set Rebecca off on a crying jag; she had wept off and on for several days.

Now Rebecca took one last, long look around the infamous corner of Haight and Ashbury streets, shivered and headed for the bus stop. She did not belong in this city—she couldn't understand what the hippy movement was all about. They all seemed so aimless, with no goals except immediate satisfaction. The news media was calling it "Fort Lauderdale for Hippies." The sheer number of kids made it all the more impossible to find Scooter; each day, her hopes sank further. If she did not find him soon, it would be too late. He would be lost from her forever.

Three nights later, Rebecca was on the Number Five bus leaving the Haight district after another fruitless night of searching. Halfway up the steep street, the electric bus lurched around a parked Greyline tour bus. She peered in curiosity at the conservatively dressed tourists clustered at the corner of a small park and wondered what could be holding their interest. As her bus pulled ahead, she saw in the center of the tour group a band of raggedy-dressed hippies performing some sort of street theater.

Her heart leaped into her throat. The tallest performer—she was positive! She shot out of her seat, pulling on the cord, shouting to the driver, "Stop! Stop! I've got to get off!" The bus continued up the hill. "Please," she cried. "Please, stop. It's an emergency." Twisting around, she bent to watch the performers in the park grow smaller and smaller. "Stop, dammit!"

At last, the bus pulled over at a designated stop and ever so slowly the rear door opened. She jumped to the sidewalk and began running downhill. "Scooter!" she screamed, drawing close to the group of startled tourists. They parted to let her through and she slowed to a stop, her eyes locked on the bearded and even gaunter-looking Scooter.

He turned to her. For a fleeting instant, she wondered if he'd be glad to see her. But in the next, her doubts vanished. A wide grin broke across his gorgeous face and he held out his arms to her. She rushed into them, her heart exploding with so much love she felt it would burst. He wrapped his long arms around her, drawing her closer. She buried her face into his thin chest and cried joyfully.

The next few hours blurred in a haze of delicious emotions. She couldn't stop herself from touching him, from watching him, from wanting him. But even from the beginning of their reunion, there on the crowded sidewalk, she had to pull back from him, give him his space to do his own thing. Scooter had insisted that the performing group finish their "entertainment" for the tourists. She stepped aside to watch, joining the tour bus group on the fringe. The "troop," as he had called them, consisted of one other male and two very attractive females, one tall with bug eyes, the other short with large breasts. The troop's performance was primarily pantomime, a series of satirical set pieces designed to evoke laughter but each sketch had a strong point of view. The most successful was a depiction of a robotlike family, where simple daily life was turned into mechanical and emotionless gestures.

With a mixture of pride and envy, Rebecca watched the ease and fluidity with which Scooter, as the husband and daddy of the family, executed the precise movements. By far he was the most accomplished of the group and invariably his routines were applauded the most. He closed the performance with a solo encore, a bit that tickled her the most, where he pretended to be in an ever diminishing glass box—he ended up confined in a tiny space, sucking his thumb in terror.

After the troop's bows and the passing of a squashed felt hat, Scooter was in an expansive mood—they had netted close to thirty-three dollars. He herded them into a taxi and with their newly acquired funds, treated them all to a many-course dinner in a tiny restaurant down in Chinatown. It took her most of the night to become accustomed to his new appearance—his dark, full beard added a certain strength to his face and enhanced his velvety brown eyes, the intensity of which had not diminished since their separation. Though he appeared even thinner than she'd remembered, when he undressed to take her to bed in the troop's two-room pad just outside of the Haight, she could tell his body was tighter, harder than before—a fact he attributed to his "survival" lifestyle.

Apprehensively, she peeled off her own clothing, desperately wanting to please him, but embarrassed by the lack of privacy in spite of the relative darkness. Scooter's mattress was a scant six feet from the bed shared by the three other members. She tried to forget about them, to respond openly and freely to his hurried actions, but every time a noise of pleasure escaped from him, she felt frozen with embarrassment.

Fortunately, the deed was over with rapidly and he fell asleep without comment almost at once. Only then did she relax, listening to his deep breathing, holding him tightly, overjoyed at her fortune but plagued by questions she longed to ask, like, which one of the girls had he been sleeping with? Eventually she drifted off to sleep, entwined in the long leanness of her love.

In the morning, Rebecca awoke before any of the others and was stunned by the filth and clutter in the two rooms. She slipped into her jeans and T-shirt and suddenly remembered. She was to have been at work at nine and it must have been way past that. Hurriedly she made her way downstairs and out of the large, dilapidated, wooden house. Relishing the sensationally sunny morning, she found a phone booth down the block and rang the coffee shop, apologizing profusely for having to quit at once. Hanging up, she thanked her lucky stars that she had been paid in cash the night before. At least she had enough to get her by for a week or so.

She ran to a small grocery store nearby and bought some oranges, coffee, a dozen eggs and a can of Comet cleanser. She scampered back to the apartment. No one had stirred since her exit. Quietly she set to work cleaning the kitchen. She wondered what the troop ate, for all she found was a sack of long-grain brown rice, a few onions and a container of some black paste labeled Miso.

She was down on her hands and knees in the bathroom scrubbing around the toilet, when the smaller girl, whose name was Bambi, walked in totally nude. Obviously a natural redhead with the largest, most perfectly formed breasts Rebecca had ever seen, Bambi made no attempt to cover herself, smiling warmly. "Mornin', I gotta piss."

"Oh, sure . . . excuse me," Rebecca replied and withdrew in spite of Bambi's protests that it was "cool." Walking into the front room, Rebecca stopped dead. Scooter was still crashed out, but the remaining couple on the other mattress was heatedly making love without even a blanket over them. Before Rebecca could avert her eyes, the girl, who called herself Space, waved cheerfully over her partner's shoulder. Blushing, Rebecca darted back into the kitchen, avoiding looking at Bambi, who sat on the john, before the open bathroom door, brushing her teeth. Rebecca moved to the far wall and busied herself at the sink. The impassioned noises coming from the front room increased and she began humming to herself, "Hang on Sloopy, Hang On," louder and louder to block them out.

Shortly, the noises ceased and with great relief, Rebecca turned just as the couple strode nude into the kitchen, the chubby, homely-looking guy still in a semi-erect state. She whirled back to the sink, washing her hands for the tenth time that morning.

"What was your name again?" the guy asked behind her.

"Me? Rebecca," she supplied without turning. "And yours was . . . ?"

"Stash," he responded and stepped into the open bathroom.

"That's 'cause he's always got some goody tucked away somewhere," the girl called Space explained. "Just when we think we're out of stuff, ol' Stash here whips some little number out. What's this icky stuff?"

"Supposed to be coffee," Rebecca said. "Couldn't find anything else to make it in."

"That's 'cause we don't drink coffee," Stash said from the bathroom, urinating loudly, his hands on his hips. Bambi was brushing her hair right next to him, her big boobs jutting out over the sink.

"How come?" Rebecca said, not knowing where to look.

"It's an artificial stimulant," Space said, her slightly bugged eyes landing on the bowl of oranges. "Ah, Space sees fresh fruit."

Anxiously, Rebecca handed her one. "Guess you guys aren't into any other artificial stimulants then—you know, like drugs?"

Stash hooted from the bathroom joined by the two girls. "There are artificial stimulants," Space explained. "And then there are *natural* stimulants."

"Yeah . . . but," Rebecca began, handing an orange slice to Bambi, "isn't coffee natural—comes from a bean, right?"

Scooter's voice growled from the front room. "What's all this gawdamned jawing about? I'm trying to sleep."

"Tough titty, man," Bambi replied, grinning at Rebecca. "We're just getting acquainted with your chick, that's all," Space added.

"Hey, Rebecca," Scooter growled from the front room. "Come here. My dick's hard and I'm horny as hell."

She felt her face flame under the amused gaze of the nude trio before her. Scooter called her name again, this time more forcefully. Agonizing, she ducked her head and with eyes on the floor, walked past them into the front room. Slowly she raised her head, fearing the worst. Scooter sat cross-legged on the mattress, fully clothed, smiling broadly as he rolled a jay. "Don't you look like the terrified mouse," he teased. "Did I say horny? Meant, hungry."

"Me too," she sighed in relief. "I've got some—"

"Who wants to eat out?" He stood and lit the joint.

It had been clear to her from the beginning that Scooter was the boss of the impoverished troop—what he said, went; what he wanted to do, all wanted to do. As much as she wanted to spend some time with him alone, she realized she would have to wait for that luxury. She stood by the bay window while the others grabbed clothes from a large steamer trunk; whatever their hands landed on, they dressed in hurriedly. In their haphazard array, the trio known as Space, Stash and Bambi looked to her like a band of ragamuffin chimneysweeps. Scooter, at least, had on an old sports coat which added a certain dignity to his long frame.

In short time, he led them to a small café on the edge of the Panhandle for a breakfast of omelettes, French toast and hashbrowns. She noted they all ate like there was no tomorrow. She, herself, was too happy to be hungry and picked at her Danish, watching Scooter's every move and nuance. He was in a cheery, up mood, talking continually of the troop, how they had banded together and what mime was all about. "It's the purest form of acting in the world," he said at one point to her. "Has been since man first got up in front of the campfire to tell his tribe of his hunt that day. Using only your body to relate the experience, you become the very essence of that experience. Your communication with the audience is immediate, direct, unfiltered by words or symbols which mean different things to different people. You saw how those Greyline tourists ate it up."

"Thirty-three bucks worth," Stash said. "The square suckers."

Smiling lazily, Scooter reached for the bill. "We'll have to get your things. Where've you been staying?"

The troop swept her up and piled onto a crosstown bus heading for her digs in North Beach. Walking to the rear of the crowded bus, Scooter suddenly transformed into a blindman with a severe case of hiccups. Every time he hiccupped, he stumbled into someone "accidentally." Giggling with embarrassment, Rebecca led him to a seat and sank next to him. She wished he would stop clowning so they could grab this moment away from the others to talk seriously, but he continued his routine for several blocks. Eventually his attack was "cured" and he calmed down. She leaned into him, speaking softly, "So you want me to move in with you guys?"

"Don't you?"

"Well, yeah, I guess so, sure," she said, not too enthusiastic about living with a bunch of skin-freaks. But still, if that were the only way she could be with Scooter until they left for the east, she'd have to get used to it somehow. "How long do you plan to stay out here?"

His brow furrowed. "You got any place better in mind?"

"Well, yeah . . . sure," she said, not feeling too secure. "How 'bout New York?"

"New York?" he repeated disdainfully, loud enough for a few heads to turn. People were beginning to catch on that he really wasn't blind. She wished he would talk quieter. "*This* is where it's at," he continued. "The whole world will change because of what's happening here . . . right now in the Haight. And this is only the beginning. The whole revolution starts here."

She tilted her head up at him, whispering, "You mean everyone's gonna stop bathing?" She regretted it as soon as it left her mouth.

"I'm talking about people's values," he said sharply. "Their priorities. Whether having two cars in the garage and a split-level home is really what's it all about. That whole success syndrome. Like having to make it to the top. That there're only winners and losers—winning is the only thing that counts. That kind of jock, rah-rah, football mentality that runs this country. But here, in the Haight, it doesn't make any difference what you are—or how successful you are in monetary or career terms. People don't give a damn about your past. Or your future. It's who you are at that moment. How you relate to others and to yourself. And to the whole earth and the protoplasmic consciousness. *That's* what's important."

She scanned his intensely beautiful face, trying to absorb what he'd said. "But what about your acting career?" she asked, her voice giving away her uncertainty. "Don't you want to be an actor on the legitimate stage anymore?"

With a sigh of extreme frustration, he sank back, as though she'd failed to grasp the easiest essentials. It made her feel very dumb and she couldn't think of anything to say to offset it. He crossed his arms and began to speak without looking at her. "I *am* an actor on the legitimate stage," he muttered as if his jaw were frozen. "The *streets* are the only valid stage left to us. The streets belong to the people. Not some asinine bureaucracy of capitalistic money-mongers. Like Broadway. That's nothing but establishment money producing establishment-supported theater. It's bourgeois capitalistic propaganda. The only good thing, it doesn't reach anybody except the monied upper class of a very small area. And what does it reach them with? Hackneyed old formula musicals like your sweet friend Robby's in right now. Or drippy meaningless bedroom comedies, like *Cactus Flower*. Pap and pablum for an overfed minority."

The strength of his conviction pinned her against the window. Yet, it stirred something deeply within her. She had never thought of Broadway in those terms—to her, it had always been the end of the rainbow, the pot of gold waiting for the industrious few and the

tenaciously talented. Yet there was something quite satisfying about
his idea that the streets were for the people—like theater should be.
As little as she knew about theatrical history, one thing had always
struck her—no matter what period of classical theater, the plays that
endured down through time, Aristophanes, Molière, Shakespeare,
all had been supported in their time by all the classes, from the
highest lords to the lowest serfs.

After collecting her one suitcase of belongings and after her
hurried but heartfelt good-byes to her landlady they headed back to
the pad. On the way, the others chatted and laughed with Rebecca,
making the whole excursion like a holiday outing. After virtually
being alone for so long, she began to enjoy the company of her
ready-made 'tribe' as Scooter called them.

Once back, he ceremoniously dumped the contents of her suitcase
into the large trunk, announcing solemnly for her benefit, "What's
yours is ours, what's ours, is yours." She felt a twinge of protest
deep inside as a red wool sock disappeared into the pile. Inside that
sock was stuffed the toy monkey Scooter had given her. She made a
mental note to retrieve the talisman before anyone found it.

They all plopped down on the mattresses and smoked a few joints
which Stash whisked out, much to the delight of the others. While
they talked of where they would perform that afternoon, to pick up
dinner money, Rebecca took a small puff on a passing jay, now and
then. She hadn't been stoned since Scooter had split New York and
had wanted to keep that special feeling for the two of them alone.
But everyone was in such good spirits and she so wanted to fit in, to
belong, to please Scooter.

Soon he was on his feet, developing a new routine with Bambi. It
was based on his "blindman with hiccups" bit on the bus, and
Rebecca watched, both fascinated at seeing his talent develop and
enrich the episode and jealous that he had not chosen her.

Again they hit the streets, this time heading for Golden Gate Park
and the Botanical Gardens. There, on the wide sidewalk leading to
the interior displays of exotic plants, the group formed a half-circle
and began to perform. Gamely she watched from the sidelines.
Before long she was amazed at the number of people drawn from all
over that area, an odd mixture of hippies, old people, young

executive-types with their "office" girl friends, mothers with their children and a group of Japanese tourists with their snapping cameras. She was fascinated by how easily everyone got into the spirit of the event and how the troop's routines transcended all the barriers, creating laughter for everyone—especially the children. She ached to be a part of it all and realized that the creative side of her nature, a side that she had nurtured privately for years, was yearning for a release, an outlet.

Longingly, she observed Scooter work with Bambi on the new "blindman" piece and felt, deep inside, if given a chance, she could do it better than the little, stacked redhead. Bambi was cute as a button and sweet as hell—even if she did have gaga-eyes for Scooter—but she lacked the ability to become the character, always stood outside of it, commenting in some manner upon the role. This distracted from what Scooter was creating.

When the applause and laughter reached a peak, Scooter approached Rebecca and handed her the old, green felt hat to pass around. Pleased to be included, she danced before the crowd, clowning it up but making certain she approached as many as possible, holding out the hat for donations, grandly thanking anyone who made a contribution by bowing with a flourish. With the Japanese giving the most, the "take" of the less than half-hour performance was just under twenty dollars. Scooter pocketed it with a flourish and took off running, actually skipping over the green grass. His troop, along with Rebecca, followed, laughing at their mutual success. He reached a knoll and flopped on his back, arms spread out like a kid ready to find animals in the clouds overhead. The others followed suit. She lay as close to him as she could without touching him.

The sky was a bright brilliant blue, plump white clouds rolled in quickly from the sea, the air smelled of spring, freshly mown grass and budding leaves. The sun warmed, filling her with a golden glow. The sounds of the city were muffled. She could hear children at play, laughing, and someone was playing a flute, its soaring, improvised melody winged over them like a bird, drifting higher and higher, then swooping low, making lazy circles.

She closed her eyes, listening, smelling, feeling—she was part of that hill, that sprawling childlike troop, a part of Scooter. The agony and loneliness, the guilt and fear seemed far away. Like from a bad dream, she had awakened and found herself surrounded by love and companionship. She felt at peace with herself, with Scooter, the others, even the very earth upon which she lay. And God, was she stoned.

Something brushed her lips and fuzzy hair tickled her chin. She opened her eyes. His gorgeous bearded face hovered over her, his eyes melting her with an exquisite tenderness. His lips touched hers again and his warm breath mingled with hers. "So you want to join us?"

She wrapped her arms around him and pressed him to her, resting his head upon her breasts. She couldn't remember being happier, ever.

SHELBY
September 1967
New York

Settling gracefully into the luxurious gray leather cusions, she turned away from her father bending into the limousine beside her. Unexpectedly the bald spot in his graying, short-cropped hair had winked into view. It produced a sad tightness in her throat.

Her father waited until the chauffeur had closed the rear door before stating forcefully, "Brainwashed! That's what he said. That he'd been brainwashed by our military in Vietnam. Now what kind of talk is that? And from a man who used to head one of America's largest corporations."

"Who?"

He glanced at her and she knew she hadn't been listening attentively enough. "Senator Romney," her father replied, none too patiently. "Mighty disappointed in that man. Here I was hoping he'd run for president. But he's blown that for good with that kind of pacifistic garbage.''

She leaned into him. ''I just can't believe y'all're here.''

''Honey, I can't either,'' Billy Jay Cale drawled and patted her hand all too briefly. ''The last time I saw you, in that blue-and-white school uniform? Like a little golden angel. And now . . . well, now y'all're such a grown-up, successful young lady, I feel kind of like a bumblin' ol' fart.''

''Daddy,'' she admonished lightly, smiling despite her discomfort. She didn't want to hear that he felt awkward with her, because that was exactly how she'd been feeling all day.

''Where to now?'' he asked, watching the chauffeur maneuver the sleek long auto expertly into the midtown traffic.

She hesitated, eyeing her father's profile—that thankfully had not changed. In spite of a slight puffiness under his eyes, the sharp angles of his brow and nose were perfect, she thought, like a college athlete's.

Billy Jay smiled at her. ''What's my beautiful little girl got next on the agenda?''

She slipped her arm through his. ''Well, daddy, we've got a choice. There's a . . .''

He was frowning. ''Sugar, don't y'all think nineteen's a little old to be calling me 'daddy'?'' He must have seen her disappointment for he added quickly, ''Why don't y'all call me, Billy Jay? Like everyone else. I'd surely love that.''

''But, y'all are my daddy,'' she said, conscious of the pout in her tone. ''And I just never had the opportunity to say it much before . . .'' She had to glance away for fear he would see the welling tears.

The intercom phone buzzed at her elbow, startling her. Grateful for the diversion, she picked up the receiver. ''Yes, Alfred?''

Beyond the glass window partition, in his livery suit and cap of Villa Caesari gray, the young chauffeur eyed her boldly in the rearview mirror. ''Miss Cale, do you wish to follow your itinerary?''

She considered the alternative. The late summer air was far too muggy for the hansom cab ride in Central Park. That would have to wait until after dinner. That left only the shopping. But she really didn't feel like fighting gaping crowds ogling her—not when she wanted to be alone with him. He already had seen her effect on strangers. At lunch, the Russian Tea Room had come practically to a stop the moment she had walked in with him. Heads turned, voices hushed, everyone gawked. Over an order of exquisite Bellini, Billy Jay had told her that he was so proud to be seen with her he could "bust." His praise had left her strangely disquieted. Somehow she felt it was not Shelby that was making him proud, but Sunny—and Sunny was nothing more than a smiling face in a commercial, an image in a print ad.

"Proceed as planned, Alfred," she said into the receiver and hung up, longing for a tall cold drink.

"Baby," her father murmured, "did I hurt your feelings?"

"Of course not," she said brightly.

"Baby, if y'all want to call me 'daddy,' y'all just go right ahead. After all, y'all're still my little girl, now aren't you?" He threw an arm around her shoulders, squeezing her warmly. "Remember that time you squashed Evangeline's prize roses?"

Brightening at the memory, she laid her head on his shoulder. "I didn't squash those damned ol' things . . . Charger did. He's the one that fell."

"Why, you little vixen," Billy Jay joshed. "Y'all did it on purpose and y'all know it. Looking like a champ. Hurtling over the hedge. Straight onto Evangeline's fifty-year-old bushes."

"I meant him to jump those ol' things too."

"Like hell you did," he teased solemnly. "I saw y'all jerk the reins. Y'all'd been clearing that high a jump for months."

At that moment, she felt closer to him than she had all day. "I'm so glad y'all didn't punish me that time. It proved above everything else that you loved me more than them."

He pulled away slightly. "Of course I punished you. I always seemed to end up doing what your gawdamned grandmother wanted."

"But you didn't. Don't y'all remember?"

"I recall it all quite clearly, Shelby Ann. I marched you up to your room. Whipped off my belt and beat the daylights out of—"

—"*the bed*," she finished for him. "Remember? You whipped the bed and I screamed after each stroke."

"Oh, no," he said firmly.

"Oh, yes," she insisted. "We were laughing so hard, trying to cover it up, afraid that the others would hear."

He eyed her strangely. "Shelby, I never did any such thing."

"Daddy, I recall it like it just was yesterday. Y'all whipped the bed, not me—then went downstairs and told them I'd begged for forgiveness."

His head drooped and for a brief moment, his eyes clouded. "I must have been in my usual state at Oak Hills—inebriated beyond all pain, all consciousness."

She adjusted the skirt pleats of her mauve silk dress—a Dior original she'd puchased specifically for these precious daylight hours with her father. "I never could tell when y'all'd been drinking."

Billy Jay returned his gaze to her. His eyes gave him away. As much as he wanted, he did not believe her. And that disturbed her even more.

Shopping for gifts filled the better part of their afternoon and took away some of her ache. Shelby insisted, over his strongly voiced objections, that she purchase presents for his new family out in Madison, a ready-made family that Billy Jay had married into several years earlier—people she'd only seen in his annual Christmas card photo. They always looked like such a happy, all-American family, Shelby envied the two young children.

At Tiffany's, Henri Bendel's, and F.A.O. Schwarz, she carefully selected outlandishly expensive gifts for each, ignoring her father's pleas for fiscal conservatism and graciously signing a few autographs for flabbergasted fans. Later while he was explaining a new tax shelter that he felt appropriate for her, Shelby lured him into the men's department of Saks Fifth Avenue. She persuaded him to try on a deep maroon velvet smoking jacket with black satin lining and trim. She thought it made him extremely distinguished-looking. "I'll feel damned silly lounging in front of the TV with this on," he grumbled good-naturedly. She bought it for him anyway, saying she wanted to picture him in it whenever she thought of him.

Dutifully, Alfred followed behind them out of the store, carrying the packages. She dismissed him with a curt, "Front of Scribner's in a half hour."

"A bookstore?" Billy Jay queried as they walked up to the antique facade on Fifth.

"I want y'all to meet...an author acquantance of mine," she replied and noted that the front display window had only a small pyramid of copies of *Rogues and Scoundrels*. Instinctively she knew, Erik would find the display far too insignificant. Especially next to the mountains of a book she'd never heard of, nor would she ever read because of its title, *Lord of the Flies*.

Inside the elegant paneled store, the smell of freshly bound books rushed to greet them in a cool blast from the air conditioner. While she surveyed the hushed sales area, her father took her elbow, whispering, "Is this acquaintance someone special?"

"Oh heavens no," she replied, her eyes landing on Erik, a good head taller than the others in a rear alcove. "Just a passing acquaintance, that's all. His new book is officially published today, but actually it's been out for a couple of weeks."

Erik had not seen her yet. Dressed in the new dark blue corduroy suit, white shirt and wide tie, all of which she'd bought as presents, he looked damned uncomfortable and somewhat surly. Nearby, a small easel with a placard announced his presence from one to four P.M. to sign copies. He was autographing one at the moment for a short roundish woman.

"Hi, y'all," Shelby greeted him with just enough casualness. He swung to her, then immediately sized up her father. She made the introductions hurriedly. Her father politely offered his hand but Erik shook it in what she thought was a rather cursory manner. She rushed to cover the slight. "We were wandering by and I thought I'd drop in to get an autographed—"

"Hello, Shelby," the plump woman at Erik's elbow said.

"Why, Miss Engle, what a surprise. I didn't recognize you."

"Couldn't miss you," Mo said. "You look like a million bucks."

"Why, thank you. This is my da- my father, Billy Jay Cale. Miss Engle was the producer of the Sunny pageant."

Erik had been drinking! Shelby could smell it on him. And after she had specifically warned him that very morning that her father was an active member in the Madison chapter of Alcoholics

Anonymous. She could tell by the way her father was appraising Erik that he had also smelled the alcohol. She searched her mind for a quick remark but Erik beat her to the punch. "Smashing debut, eh what? Score another victory for the vociferous critics."

Mo snorted—a sound Shelby considered vulgar and unladylike— and said, "Who cares what those jerks say? I've bought copies in every store within walking distance. If enough are sold, the publisher'll start pushing it anyway."

Angrily, Erik stared over the tops of their heads at the main entrance. "Not exactly a rush. Including yours Mo, I've signed seven in two hours."

Mo struggled to lift her plastic shopping bag with three of his books. "Lord, I'd have bought more but who can carry the mothers?"

"I'd like to get a copy for my father and his wife," Shelby said sweetly. "Would y'all autograph one for them?"

"Give the buyer what they want. Hell, you should know that by now, Shelby," he said. "God knows how many units you've sold."

She continued to smile brightly but was fuming internally—it doesn't take anything to be civil. She leaned into her father, saying proudly, "It's for Billy Jay and Linda . . . and say something especially nice."

Mo asked, "Tell me, Shelby, how's Herr Caesari treating you?"

"Why just fine, thank you. Giorgio's awfully considerate really. And a real gentleman in all matters." She directed that last little barb in Erik's direction. He was pretending he didn't hear, busily writing his inscription.

Mo's shaggy head lowered and she began fumbling in a bulging purse. "If you ever get tired of modeling and want to give acting a try, give me a jingle." Mo brought out a bent business card and handed it over. "I'm with the Hendricks Talent Agency now. You never know with Caesari when you'll be out of a job."

Shelby stared at the card to cover her growing distaste. "I have a whole long year left on my Sunny contract, thank you," she responded, proud of the mature coolness in her voice. "But I'm sure I wish y'all the best in your new line of employment."

Again Mo made that coarse sound through her nose and gathered the heavy bag to her broad bosom. "Gotta run, Erik. My new line of employment calls," she said pointedly. "Come for dinner this week, okay? The twins keep bugging me to ask. And buck up, maybe I can land you a part in a beer commercial."

Shelby was astounded that Erik actually laughed. And as Mo trudged away, she noted that Mo's slip hung down in back a good two inches. Pity the poor talent agency she represents, Shelby judged silently.

"I dig that woman," Erik muttered, "even if you don't."

"Daddy, we have to run," she said, deliberately giving Erik a cold shoulder. "I'll have to change before dinner. We're going to Lutece," she announced. "Won't daddy love that?"

"If he likes prissy French waiters fussing over him all night."

"Why, I declare," she flared, "Lutece is the most famous French restaurant in the country. Giorgio's very favorite."

"It's overpriced, overstaffed and overstuffed," Erik rumbled and suddenly lurched backward, his arm knocking a tall stack of his books. The noise of all those heavy, thick volumes hitting the floor broke into the subdued atmosphere. He bent to retrieve them and his suit jacket ripped loudly. "Goddammit to hell," he growled, righting himself to glare at her. "I told you my old jacket was good enough."

She slipped on her dark glasses and grabbed her father's arm. "Come on, daddy. We'll be late." Quickly she began steering him away, but he said to Erik, "Thanks for the inscription. And good luck." They hadn't walked halfway to the cash register when Erik's voice boomed out behind them, "The book's on me, babe."

She marched directly to the street doors, her father keeping step beside her. "Kind of an artistic temperament, isn't he?" Billy Jay said, once they were on the sidewalk. "Is his book any good?"

"How do I know? I couldn't get through the first chapter."

It was not until they were once again in the limousine, heading up Sixth Avenue toward the Hilton Hotel that her father read the inscription. Billy Jay stared at her with a puzzled expression. "What's with you two anyway?"

"What do y'all mean?"

In response, he handed her the book open to the inside front cover. There, in the recognizable bold script, the letters large, hurried, almost childlike, Erik had written: *To Billy Jay Cale, with humble thanks for your beautiful creation. Gratefully, Erik Lungren.*

All through dinner at Lutece, Shelby was miserable. Not even the new gown from Yves St. Laurent's fall collection—a shimmer sea of sand-colored satin with large puff sleeves and plunging neckline, a design she knew positively to be one of the most flattering gowns she'd ever worn—did not make her feel any better. Billy Jay rambled on and on, all through dinner and back to his hotel—every detail about some boring business merger he was negotiating. Her good nights were hurried, strained, her kiss on his cheek, dry and dutiful.

She had a splitting headache by the time she stepped off the elevator opposite her Park Avenue apartment. She felt more confused than ever about her daddy—and couldn't shake the odd, empty feeling that somehow he had abandoned her again, left her on her own, just like before.

Unlocking the door, all she desired was a long soak in a hot fragrant bath. She hadn't counted on Erik being there. In the bedroom, shirtless, in faded, torn jeans, he was propped up against the brass headboard of her bed, a beer can in one hand, in the other, a cigarette with ash ready to drop on her antique Chinese comforter. "Erik!" she cried, her voice thin with outrage. She hurried to slip a crystal ashtray under the dangling burning ember. "What're y'all doing?"

Her eyes swept over the large, nearly all-white room. It was a shambles—newspapers and magazines littered the white plush-pile rug, beer cans crushed and flattened formed a minefield around the wastebasket. His new blue suit and shirt were twisted and strewn about. The TV was tuned soundlessly to the "The Beverly Hillbillies" and the room was sticky hot, thick with blue smoke and smelling of beer, cigarettes and sweat.

He blinked blearily. "Jeez, am I glad you're home early."

"Look what you've done to my room!"

He surveyed the room slowly, as if focusing for the first time. "Oh shit, I'm sorry . . ." he mumbled and threw his legs over the side to get up. In doing so, he knocked a full ashtray off the bed onto the spotless white plush carpet.

"God, Erik," she cried. "Y'all're such a pig!" She stormed across the room and into the bathroom, her heavy skirts cracking like a sudden wind in the desert. She kicked shut the door behind her, slipped out of her heels and tried in vain to get the zipper down the back of her gown. Frustrated and too angry to ask for help, she grabbed the bodice of the thirty-two-hundred-dollar original and yanked hard, ripping it from her with repeated jerks. She stepped out of it and flung it from her, striding to the tub in her pantyhose.

The floor was sloppy wet. And even more disgusting, dark brown pubic hairs littered the tub bottom. He *was* a pig. She turned on the faucet and with his hairbrush, swirled the offending matter down the drain.

She had just stretched out into a fresh tub of hot, fragrantly oiled water when his knock came at the door. "Made some java," he said quietly on the other side. "Want some?"

"No," she said, closing her eyes. She just wanted to be left alone. It couldn't have been two mintues later when he knocked again. This time, not waiting for a response, he walked in.

Without opening her eyes, she said, "Get out."

"I wanna read this to you," he said thickly from somewhere near the end of the tub. "It hit the newsstands just in time for the commuters."

"I don't want to hear a word," she said, her jaw tightening.

"A review of *Rogues*. From the *Post*. Under the headline SECOND NOVEL JINX."

She wanted to drop below the surface of the water, submerging her ears with an impenetrable barrier. If she hadn't remembered the eight o'clock booking the next morning, she would have willingly gotten her hair wet with bath oils. "Erik," she said, "I'm not in the mood to hear a thing."

"Jus' listen to this. Only take a sec." He began to read. "Erik Lungren's second novel, *Rogues and Scoundrels*, is another prime example of the jinx that has plagued many a promising writer in America's literary history. This new, thousand-page monstrosity is a hybrid of—"

"—Erik," she warned, her eyes still tightly closed.

"—every literary device since the birth of the modern novel . . ."

She sat bolt upright, her eyes popping open, the water slapping the sides of the tub. He stood near the sink, scratching the hairs on his stomach, holding the paper out from him as if it were a dirty diaper. And he continued reading, ". . . confuses deliberate obscurity and leaden prose with intellectual depth and literary merit."

She clenched her fists into two tight balls on either side of her thighs, pressed down against the bottom of the tub with all her might and began to scream, "Get out! Out! I want you out. *Out* of my bathroom. *Out* of my apartment. Now! Get! *Out!*" Trembling with bottled up fury, she bent her head, a hank of thick hair falling over her brow. She waited for either his explosion or sounds of his exit.

His impassioned, hoarse voice jarred her to look at him again. "We've heard what you want," he said. "Now hear what I want. I want a little understanding from you. Just a little. As to what I might be going through at this particular point of my life. I have worked for four years, spent four, bloody hard years to give birth to this book. And it is a bomb. Stinko . . . El Puke-o. And I'm in pain, dammit. Can't you see? Not once have I heard a word of concern for my state of mind. Not an offer of moral support. Or encouragement. Nor a caress that I haven't initiated. You run around in your own goddamned, screwed-up, little world and you don't realize that there are whole other beings out here—dying of pain. And where *are* you, Shelby?" His voice broke and he hardened it into a cutting edge. "Out flitting around as a ludicrously overpaid shill for Caesari."

"I was out with my daddy and y'all know it!"

"Ah yes, the aging boyscout," he said snidely. "With his jock crewcut and green polyester suit with the metal American flag on the lapel."

"That does it!" Like a whip, she snapped to her feet and stood, water streaming off as she pointed regally to the door. "I want you out. Now! And don't bother calling until you hear from me 'cause I just might not let you come back. I'll have to seriously give some thought to your boorish behavior." Not looking at him, she stepped out of the tub and stretched for a fresh, terry-cloth bathsheet on the shelf above the commode. Her footing slipped on the wet tiles and she pitched forward helplessly.

His strong, bare arms caught her before she crashed headlong into the sink cabinet. "Whoa down," he gulped. She wrenched way from his grasp and righted herself, the shock of coming that close to a facial disaster nearly crumbling her resolve.

"I'm not going to say thank you," she said, her lower lip beginning to quiver. "If y'all hadn't come in here bothering me with your self-centered ravings and drunken ramblings, I wouldn't have slipped." She snatched the towel out of his hands. "Now I mean it, get out."

Briskly she began drying her legs. When she turned and found he wasn't present in the bathroom, she felt triumphant. Gathering herself in the floor-length, wool-jersey robe, she carefully tiptoed across the slippery tiles and peered into the bedroom, expecting him to be sprawled on her bed sulking.

The bedroom appeared empty—the beer cans had been picked up and general order restored. Only a gray, smudged area in front of the bed remained from the spilled ashtray. Not hearing anything except the hum of the air conditioner—now turned on and clearing the air—she stepped into the room. He was reflected in the mirror of the ceiling-high, eighteenth-century mahogany armoire. He had pulled on his shirt and was bent over, tugging on a boot. He glanced up and caught her watching him in the mirror. His normal ruddy coloring had paled and his eyes were dulled with a sullen pain.

She broke his gaze and marched directly to her side of the bed, yanking back the gold-embroidered comforter. She snapped on the chrome, Art Deco bed lamp and said in a monotone, "Turn out the hall light on your way out, please." Dropping her robe, she stretched her long, supple body, thrusting out her breasts, undulating her spine, rolling her hips to work out the lower back tension. Aware that he was watching her gave her a tremendous surge of elation, a sense of power, knowing that he was hungering for her. That he was always hungering for her. That he couldn't get enough of her. Now that he wasn't writing. Well, it was about time he paid for his former negligence.

Finally, the hall light snapped off and she glanced toward the unlighted hallway. She could not tell if he were standing there in the darkness, still watching her under the soft glow of the pink glass-shaded lamp. Deliberately unconcerned, she climbed into the bed, pulling only the black silk sheet over her body, arranging it casually to better outline her form under the clinging softness.

The distant front door clicked shut. He was gone. He hadn't been watching her after all. She turned out the bed lamp. Damn, she'd left the bathroom light on. She closed her eyes. He'd gone. Walked out on her. Didn't love her enough to stay and fight. Talk about concern for others—did he have an inkling what she had been through that day?

She fell to wondering if she should let him come back, even if he crawled over broken glass. She concluded that maybe, if no one else better showed up in the meantime, she might consider taking him back, if properly wooed, but certainly not until he'd learned a lesson or two.

In the near darkness, she heard herself sob, "Daddy . . ." and it so startled her, she rose quickly to turn out the bathroom light, not knowing why shc was crying.

REBECCA
November 1967
San Francisco

She threw herself into the solo mime with a determined attack, focusing all her energy. Dressed in black tights and T-shirt with red suspenders holding up baggy shorts, her long hair tucked up under a knit watch cap, Rebecca concluded the bit of hijinx, the last explosion of hiccups knocking her flat on her fanny. She hopped up, oblivious to the cold and her hunger, wanting only to please the handful waiting in a knot on the corner.

The bus pulled up. She rushed to the chilled, boarding passengers and thrust out her knit cap. In less than thirty seconds, she slunk back to the barren tree where she had stashed the now grungy gray letterman's sweater. Wracked with discouragement, she yanked it on. She had to face it. Her solo act wasn't working. Sixty-eight cents! She'd be insulted if it weren't so damned humiliating.

She trudged up the Panhandle section of the park and ducked into the nearest coffeeshop to warm up. Sitting at the counter, half-listening to the "Ode to Billy Jo" playing on the jukebox, she disconsolately nursed her coffee loaded with sugar and milk. She was failing Scooter, she just knew it. But what was worse, she had no idea how to help him out of his severe tailspin.

The jukebox changed hits. Slowly she tuned into the blues-like song, recognizing it. She'd heard it first that night at the Winter Garden. Sung by that strange-looking girl with the whitish hair and the powerful voice. Rebecca moved closer to the sources of sound, the lyrics deeply sinking into her: "Baby/when you're feeling low/ An' the floor's comin' up to greet you/ When there ain't no softness/ no pillow for your head/ I'm always there to greet you." Rebecca began to sing along softly, thinking of Scooter, aching for him.

Later, outside on the corner, she did not know which way to turn. The bleak, gray overcast skies seemed appropriate for the changes that had come to the Haight. Gone was that naive glow of enthusiasm, the hints of new beginnings. Gone was the teenage invasion for the "summer of love." What remained was a frightening, hard-core element.

Like that knot of dudes on the corner, she thought, who were eyeing her boldly, daring her to walk past. Heavy dopers, she thought and moved quickly across the street.

A kid sauntered up wearing a stovepipe hat, tilted at a rakish angle. He held out a huge white chrysanthemum. She could tell he was a newcomer—still believed in the peace-and-love message. For a second, she was about to tell him to buzz off, but something checked her. It was his infectious grin. It reminded her of Robby's. And she felt a twist of longing for a kindred soul.

Slowly she accepted his huge flower and put it up to her face, dipping into a deep curtsy. He laughed and clapped his hands like a child. Promptly he plopped his tall black hat on her head. "Bravo," he shouted, and scampered away, hatless, flowerless.

Curious to see how she looked with the musky scented mum to her face, she found a window of a wildly painted headshop. After a few petals were plucked, what greeted her was a walking white flower, crowned with a whimsically tilted stovepipe hat. She stared at this strange but beguiling creature. And loved it. A lot.

In a corner of Golden Gate Park, Rebecca selected an open area where several paths converged. There she launched into all of her routines, the large white flower firmly tied to her head, covering all but her eyes. Within minutes, she had attracted a sizable crowd. Her creativity flourished and she concentrated so fully on her performance, all sense of time and place vanished. She luxuriated in the joy of making people laugh.

The "crying child" routine evoked such response, she expanded it on the spot, improvising new schtick. She scurried to a bench and plopped down next to a matron in a fur stole, a pet poodle on a leash in her lap. The little, black dog started yipping in a frenzy. Rebecca rolled her head back, sending her mute howls heavenward, kicking her legs fiercely back and forth under the bench. Solid laughter reached her ears and she jumped up, swept off her tall hat and bowed, soliciting.

The first guy dropped in a buck, the second gave her fifty cents. From behind a sailor in uniform, a small white hand came forth with a folded bill. Rebecca caught a glimpse of an unknown president before the bill disappeared into the hat. Thinking it was play money, she pulled it out and stared at the green engraved face. It wasn't a president. It was Benjamin Franklin. Holy smokes, a hundred-dollar bill!

She raised her head and looked directly into a pair of striking pale-blue eyes that exuded warmth and an open curiosity. Instantly, Rebecca recognized her. With that mass of white, frizzy hair, she could only be Silver—the lead singer of that rock group, the one she had just heard on the jukebox. Suddenly shy, Rebecca held out the bill. "I think you must have made a mistake, ma'am."

The rock singer chortled. "Ma'am? Shit, honey, no one's done called me ma'am in my whole born days." Silver's hand clasped hold of hers, squeezing it closed over the bill. "It's yours, if you take off that big ol' flower an' let me take a squint at your face."

Rapidly, Rebecca untied the ribbon and pulled the flower away. Silver began to smile again, her thin face wreathed in good humor. "If you ain't the prettiest lil' thin'... what's your name?"

"Rebecca."

"Howdy, Rebecca. Mine's Silver."

"I know. I saw you at the Winter Garden."

"No crappin'?" the singer asked, unabashedly pleased.

Rebecca nodded, suddenly liking this person a whole lot. "I thought you were just terrific. And I hear that song all the time now. You know, 'Mama's Love'? You are so talented, no lie."

Silver patted her arm. "Honey, I been watchin' you for a good half hour. Talk 'bout talent. You got it up the ol' yin-yang."

Rebecca laughed. Silver put on her dark shades. "I mean it, honey, you're a gawdamned chunk of genuine, forty-carat talent and I think you deserve the rest of the day off. Wanna come with me?"

Rebecca nodded enthusiastically and Silver said, "Rebecca, you an' me is gonn'a be real tight friends. I jus' feel it in these ol' bones. An' they ain't been wrong yet."

In the taxi Silver hailed, Rebecca began shivering. She was damp with perspiration from the physically demanding mimes. Silver peeled off her mangy white fur coat and draped it over their fronts, scooting down close. Gratefully, Rebecca pulled the scraggly fur to her chin feeling a rush of warmth just from the thoughtfulness. "What's this kind of fur anyway?" she asked.

"Ain't it a beaut? Rabbit I think, but I ain't sure. Could be bleached skunk for all I know. But shit I don' care. I done seen it hangin' in this second-hand store an' I just had to have it."

"Must be wonderful to buy what you want."

"Honey, money don' buy happiness. But it'll buy a Cadillac to drive around in until you find it."

"And making it so big like you have, you know?"

"Ho," Silver chortled. "Ain't made it so big yet. The album's only seventeen in *Billboard*. But it's got one of them there bullets."

"Bullets?"

"Yeah, ya know, honey . . . they put one o' them lil' bullets besides them albums movin' up real fast. We entered the charts at sixty-three an' have been climbin' purty steady. David . . . he's our producer an' manager, he thinks we should hit gold by the end o' the week. An' he should know. He's one helluva smart cracker. He's the one raking in all the bread."

"How about that single?"

" 'Mama's Love'? Shit, honey, that there's number nine. When it goes number one, then we done made it to the top."

Rebecca felt awed to be in her presence. "You guys just exploded haven't you? I mean, it was only a few months back that I saw that concert. Never heard of you before that."

Silver rasped a good natured laugh. "Right after that gig, we done signed with RPM that very next week. An' David's been pushin' the deejays like crazy ever since. He sure makes thin's snap, crackle and pop."

"RPM?"

"Revolutions-Per-Minute label. Sounds hip, don' it? It ain't though. Been 'round for years. White Meat's their first rock group. 'Course David wanted Columbia or Epic, one o' them biggies. An' he won' cop to it, but I think he done blew the negotiations with them others. He got blasted on acid—you know, that night o' the concert? Blew his fuckin' mind. Hell, he gets uptight now if we smoke a doobie in front o' him."

The cab dropped them off in front of a towering white clapboard Victorian house perched precariously on a steep lot and reached by sharply inclined, narrow cement stairs. Trudging upward behind Silver, Rebecca glanced up at the tall, round tower rising at the corner of the gingerbread-style house. "I done named this here place, 'The White Castle,' " Silver was saying proudly. "Ain't it jus' like a fairy tale? David rented it for all o' us. He's got a room here too. Keep us more like a family, he said. But sure as hell, he jus' wants to keep us in line. That dude don' trust no one, no how."

Inside off the main entrance hall, Rebecca could see into several partially furnished rooms. All were empty of people. Following Silver up the sweeping wood staircase to the second floor, she asked why there was no one about. "Down at the warehouse," Silver replied, heading for the tower wing. "David's done booked us a cross-country tour. Thirty-eight cities in forty-five days. Won't that be a gasser though? We done got us a rehearsal at four. Hey, you wanna come down an' see us sweat?"

"Sure, why not?"

On the third floor, Silver opened a door, stepped into a room and waited for her to enter. The room was totally round, except for the one flat wall which held the door. Old fashioned windows with thick, curved glass swept around the room, offering a stunning view of the Bay Bridge far below leading to Oakland. "Wow," Rebecca breathed, entranced.

"This here is mine," Silver said, as though it were her prized possession. "Ain't it out o' a movie?" A white, filigree-iron, four-poster bed stood in the center of the room, covered on all sides by long swags of white lace tablecloths. "I got me a room next door jus' for my clothes." Though it was blatant bragging, Rebecca did not begrudge her new friend. There was an air of childlike delight about the singer which was open and engaging. Silver threw the fur coat on a curved-wood clothes tree. "Wanna bath an' a change o' clothes?"

"Oh, man, yes, 'deed I do."

"Follow me, honey." Off her bedroom, they entered the largest bathroom, Rebecca had ever seen. White tiles with a white marble sink and an enormous, white cast-iron tub standing upright on giant bear claws. "Oh, man, it's beautiful," she sighed, moving to the tub.

Silver indicated the bottles of shampoo and conditioners. "Help yourself, honey. I'll go find you some fancy threads."

Rebecca unsnapped her suspenders, a question forming. She asked it hesitantly, "How come you're being so nice to me?"

Silver smiled, her form like a pale shadow in the doorway. "Them big, dark eyes of yours. They got so much pain in 'em. I get me my heartbreaks out through my singin'. I wanna help you get rid of yours. Ain't that what friends is for? No you enjoy tha' bath."

The hot bubble bath was a genuine luxury. Though Rebecca could have spent all afternoon in the comfortable, big old tub, she didn't want to keep Silver waiting. She wrapped herself in a large bath towel and scurried back to the tower room. Silver handed her a black jumpsuit with a large exposed brass zipper. "This here is too small for me, but it'll look swell on you, I bet."

Rebecca shyly turned her back to drop the towel. "Aren't you going to be late?"

"Nope . . . besides, can the muthers start without me?" She chuckled again, watching Rebecca zip up the jumpsuit. "Say, that fits jus' dandy, don' it? Looks real sharp too. You sure got the cutest lil' figure. Hey, I got me a scarf that'd do that up real purty." She popped off the bed and began pawing through a rainbow array of scarves hanging on hooks between the windows. "Say, you with that bunch of performers I used to see down in the park all the time? With that tall, dark, good looking dude?"

"Yeah," Rebecca answered softly. "That's Scooter."

"Gawdamned, ain't he purtier than Tyrone Power?" Silver brought a gold silk scarf and began tying it around Rebecca's neck. "So how come you're doin' a solo act?"

Rebecca glanced down at the white-as-dough hands. "The troop's sort of . . . taking a vacation right now."

"Stoned on what?"

Rebecca felt a flicker of relief at the singer's perception. "This time it's reds. Last week, Purple Haze . . . then there was chocolate mescaline and crystal meth and nothing real hard, understand . . . just . . ."

"Even if he's stoned, tha' pretty boy treat you good?"

Rebecca fingered the scarf at her throat. ". . . sometimes . . ."

Silver nodded gravely. "Now we're gettin' to some of that pain. Honey, promise me tha' we'll always be this honest, okay? Sisters?" She held out her hand.

Rebecca clasped it and shook it firmly, sealing something she felt instinctively. And like Silver's grip, it was strong and true.

They were in the back seat of a cab heading down to the waterfront when Silver suddenly sat up. "Hot shit! I jus' had me a helluva' idea. White Meat needs somethin' special to open our first concert over there in Oakland. That's the big kickoff for the tour. Could you dig playin' for ten thousand freaks at once?"

"You mean the whole mime troop?"

Silver considered briefly, then said with enthusiasm, "Hell, if David sees some of your stuff he might spring for signin' you guys up for the whole shebang tour."

"All of us? The whole tour?"

"Hell, don' see why not. He's always sayin' you gotta be different if you wanna make it big. An' I sure as shit don' see no rock 'n' rollers travelin' with no mime troop as an openin' act."

A block from the piers, in front of a row of deeply shadowed abandoned warehouses, the taxi pulled over. Rebecca was so keyed up she had difficulty getting out. She followed Silver through a side door neatly labeled *Rau Enterprises* and into a giant, whitewashed space, brightly lit and buzzing with noisy, bustling activity.

At the far end of the open, block-square, two-storied building, a crew of longhairs struggled to assemble a portable stage. Several feet high, steel tubing bolted together like giant tinkertoys, covered by white plastic sheets. In another area portable lighting grids stretched across the cement floor, several guys attaching Fresnels and Kleig lights. Two motorized forklift trucks hoisted banks of amplifiers onto either end of the partially sheathed stage.

At the closest end of the noisy cold warehouse, in an area defined by an large old Mexican rug and some Salvation Army living room furniture, Rebecca recognized the other members of White Meat, lounging with their instruments, drinking beer, a couple playing cards. Two frazzled young women, looking overworked and underpaid, covered their ears to talk into phones in a desk area behind a bulletin board. On that corkboard was a large map of the United States, with colorful little flags pinned on the thirty-eight cities of the tour. In the whole building, there must have been thirty people, each busily involved in some specific task. Very organized, she thought—an urgent efficiency everywhere. Like a touring theatrical show. What an adventure. And what an audience for Scooter's talents.

She swiveled to find Silver. Her heart skipped a beat, then sank to the pit of her stomach. Silver was talking with none other than the "Moma" freak from the Winterland concert.

There was no mistaking him. Wearing the same leather sports

coat. Slight, dark, a compressed energy. It poured out of him unchecked. As though he were overamped. He was everywhere at once, his hands jabbing the air as he barked commands. Silver danced sideways to keep up with him. He looked more like an uptight college kid, Rebecca thought. And he gave her the willies. She turned for the door, her fantasies of helping the troop plummeting in flames.

"Rebecca!" Silver's gravely, hearty voice broke above the din. "Come here an' meet David."

Head lowered, Rebecca forced herself to turn and walk back.

"Don' be shy, chil'," Silver said. "He ain't goin'a bite'cha. This here's David Rau. The head honcho behin' the group. We owe it all to this cat, ain't that right, David?"

From under her bangs, Rebecca tried to meet his stare. Black and hard, his eyes appraised her with a gritty coldness and then flicked away. "Watch it, Dingo!" he shouted to one of the forklift operators. "That's forty-grand worth of amps in your lap."

Silver took her arm, whispering, "Loosen the fuck up, silly. His bark's a helluva lot worse than his bite."

Rebecca forced a smile, but her face felt encased in plaster. He eyed her again, briefly. "Silver claims your act's a gas. Let's see what you can do."

Only because Silver was right there, offering encouragement with a friendly arm around her waist, was Rebecca able to find her voice and then hated the tentative timbre, "Oh, I couldn't . . . not without the others."

"Thought this was a solo act," he shot at Silver.

"Go on, honey. Put on your posy an' do somethin'."

Again, Rebecca hesitated, not wanting to blow the opportunity but hating the unexpected pop quiz, the unprepared-for audition, the classic actress's nightmare.

One secretary ran up to him, thrusting out a full clipboard—something about a late cancellation of the Philly accommodations. He grabbed the board and shook his head at Silver. "I don't have time for this shit." He threw a withering glance at Rebecca. "You blew it, baby." He spun away.

"Now wait a damned minute," Rebecca heard herself shout.

Though it surprised the hell out of her, she felt compelled and too worked up to stop. He swung back and she plunged on determindedly, "I didn't blow anything. *You* did. You're passing up a real unique opportunity. The troop I'm with is extraspecially talented. We even got a rave in Herb Caen's column. We'd be thrilled to audition for you. But not here. Not with all this noise. And not with you thinking of a hundred different things." David looked startled, as though he were not used to people yelling at him, especially chicks. She cooled her outburst and smiled her friendliest. "Just say where and when and we'll be there. I know for sure you won't regret the time spent."

He tossed an impatient look at Silver, who seemed to be enjoying the whole scene. "Don't bitch that I never listen to you," he groused to her. "Set something up." He stalked away, yelling at someone else.

Silver roared with laughter, slapping her on the back. "Honey, I sure don' know where the hell it came from, but the ou'burst sure done caught the man's ear. Ain't you the hellcat pushin' that troop o' yours. How come you ain't got tha' fire pushin' yourself?"

"I just didn't like his damned arrogant attitude."

"Honey, no one does," Silver said. "That's jus' his 'Linus blanket.' But you sure as hell can't argue with success, can you?"

"I don't know," Rebecca murmured. "Never tried before."

Balancing three overloaded sacks of groceries, Rebecca burst into the communal pad, barely able to contain the excitement exploding in her chest. On the stereo, the played-to-death, beat-to-shit, new album of the Beatles, "Sgt. Pepper's Lonely Hearts Club Band." In the smoky, stale dimness, she surveyed the sprawling, zoned-out assemblage—most she recognized, it looked like one baby-faced dude hadn't moved from the armchair all day. There were a handful of strangers, that was the norm, no one offered to help her with her sacks, that too was normal. Rebecca navigated the bodies and made the kitchen, cleared the table of litter with a swoop of her arm. From the corner, Stash looked up from his "Fabulous Furry Freak Brothers" comic book. "Humungus munchies. Got anything sweet in there."

"Help yourself but the steak's for Scooter," she said, unpacking and looking around. "Where is he?" Then she spotted him, watching her from the loft bed over the tub. She pretended she hadn't seen him and announced loudly, "Hear ye, hear ye! Good news for the acting troop, if you are within the sound of my voice. And in *this* hemisphere. We have a legitimate audition tomorrow afternoon. To insure our being there, I was given a hundred bucks." She paused dramatically and dug out the wad of bills, casting a glance under her long bangs up at Scooter. He was listening with more attention now. She unscrewed the Mason jar piggy bank and stuffed in the money. "After the grocery bill, sixty-four dollars!"

"Someone laid a hundred bucks on you? For what?" Bambi of the big boobs, as Rebecca now referred silently to the little redhead, appeared out of the bathroom. "Our Rebecca of Sunnybrook Farm, doing pornos? Who'd have thought?"

Rebecca grimaced sweetly in her direction and continued, "It so happens that the audition is for the position of opening act to White Meat in concert. Maybe even for their whole tour. If we're good enough." She looked up fully at Scooter. He was leaning on one elbow, settled into his hand, but he seemed focused on her.

"White Meat with Silver?" Space asked, her fish eyes blinking with discovery. "She is so-o dyn-no-mite!"

Even Stash rolled up from the corner with new respect in his voice, "For money? They'd pay us and everythin'?"

Scooter remained silent and Rebecca wondered why. Had he tuned into what she'd laid at his feet? Some of her anger vented as she said to the others, "But I don't think you guys are ready for a shot at something big. You've tuned in and dropped out, all right. Some revolutionaries you turned out to be. Hell, you assholes aren't any different than what you're supposed to be against. My ol' man, Angelo, zonks out with beer, my mom with downers and television. How're you guys different? As far as I'm concerned, you're all a bunch of chickenshits. Just ask yourself, what are you doing for the cause? You're not reaching anybody with your all-important message.

Hell, you're not even reaching each other." She locked eyes with Scooter and decided to shut up before she pushed him too far.

Moving deliberately, he took his time to reach the center of the room, taking centerstage, Rebecca assessed. He picked up the Mason jar and shook the bills and change cynically. "Well, it looks like we've got some rehearsing to do, don't it?"

The others hooted their approval but Rebecca wanted only some acknowledgment from Scooter. But he was hugging Bambi.

Around noon of the following day, in their favorite hollow just inside Golden Gate Park, all of the troop, dressed in their black turtlenecks and dark jeans, limbered up with some Hatha-Yoga stretching exercises led by Space. Not one of the troop seemed any worse for wear after their all-nighter of rehearsing—except for Rebecca. She was dead-tired and overly anxious. And to make it even worse, Scooter had not talked to her in private all night.

Now in the park, she watched him select as an opener one of their favorite routines, the Mechanical Society. All of them launched into it with verve, going through the robotlike motions, faces frozen into inhuman masks. Soon they attracted a healthy-sized crowd of onlookers.

The appreciative applause of the crowd keyed up the troop all the more, but as the scheduled time for the audition approached, then passed, Rebecca nervously began paying more attention to the flow of pedestrians in and out of the area. After nearly an hour, the troop exhausted their repertory and Scooter called a break. Not bothering to pass the hat, they regrouped under a eucalyptus tree.

"Maybe they were just fuckin' with your head," Scooter remarked. "Having a few kicks." "No way," she said, her posture tensing. "Silver wouldn't do that to me." Scooter asked, "How come you're so damned sure? Hell, you only met the chick yesterday."

Rebecca drew herself up. "Some people you know right away. And I know Silver will show."

All at once, the others started offering their opinions, arguing among themselves. Rebecca's insides were churning. She offered a silent plea to the trees towering overhead and turned to the deflated, suspicious troop. "Well, com'on you guys," she offered with a display of gung-ho enthusiasm. "Let's start from the top. If they haven't shown up when we finish, let's call it a day."

One by one the others joined her—all but Scooter. Standing by the trunk of the tree, as rigid as one of its branches, he eyed her with a hostility that bordered on contempt. Her heart ached for a sign of reconciliation. He had been so damned short with her, downright mean sometimes, ever since the drugs had started to be the troop's only activity. Twisting away now from his line of vision, she again asked herself why she was staying on with him. The same answer came back to her. He needed her, even if he wasn't aware of that. And she needed him. And that she couldn't forget, even under the nerve wracking circumstances of a seemingly doomed audition. But her spirits perked up some when Scooter hunched his shoulders and transformed into the lead robot character. Knees stiff, feet shuffling along, with jerky movements of arms and head, he moved expertly into the routine. She made herself focus on her performance and kept her distance from him.

Halfway through their second set piece, she spotted the snowy Afro bobbing down the sidewalk. Without dropping a beat, Rebecca moved into the center of the troop and whispered, "Here they come." She could almost feel a charge of excitement sweep through them. Even Scooter seemed to redouble his efforts.

The piece they were performing was one of their most politically oriented, their only routine requiring props. All but Scooter wore a small, paper coolie hat. They were a band of Vietnam guerrillas, brandishing imaginary rifles as they stalked through the jungles. Suddenly Scooter jumped out from behind a tree, wrapped in a large American flag. Waving it over them like Dracula's cape, he mowed them down. Rebecca dropped to the ground, "dead" and caught a glimpse of Silver in her ratty fur standing next to David. He was frowning sourly.

Crowing jubilantly but silently, Scooter stood, legs spread over the massacred Cong unit and whipped the star-and-stripes like wings. Behind his back, Bambi crawled to him with her last gasp, stuck a rubber dagger into his shoulder blades. He collapsed on top of Stash and died. After a few beats, he popped to his feet and bowed to the startled onlookers and the troop rose with a flourish, also bowing. Rebecca was watching Silver. The rock singer appeared to be arguing with her producer, holding onto one of his arms. David jerked away and started to move off. Rebecca stopped and her inaction soon brought the rest of the troop to a standstill. All of them stared at Silver trotting after the producer. "What's with them?" Space asked. Rebecca shrugged, her skin turning clammy and cold. "Let's keep going . . . or we'll lose the crowd."

"We were only doing it for those two," Scooter said sharply. The troop's inactivity had begun to dissipate the onlookers.

Unexpectedly Silver reappeared at the crest of the sidewalk, David in tow. Rebecca hurried to meet them. Silver grinned under her dark glasses. "Honey, hell I'm sorry. I overslept." David looked like he'd eaten nails for lunch, Rebecca thought. She nodded to him. "Want see some more of our stuff? We have a whole bunch of routines. If you'd like, we could—"

"What the hell's going on?" Scooter's voice broke in.

"Where's your posy?" Silver asked her.

Scooter appeared by her side and glared at David. "Thanks for showing up on time."

Rebecca leaped in quickly. "Scooter, this is Silver and—"

"Come on," the producer snapped at Silver. "We don't need them." He turned to move away. Instantly Scooter had a hold of David's arm, swinging him around. "Who the hell do you think you are? Ed Sullivan? Give us a fair chance for Chrissakes."

"Scooter . . ." Rebecca pleaded.

"Shit, man," Silver said, startled. "Let's jus' cool it, okay? Groove with it all."

"Get your fucking hands off me!" David wrenched free.

Scooter towered over him like an enraged scarecrow. "Mister Big-Time Hot-Shot Rock Producer. Going around ripping everyone off. Exploiting musicians—the whole movement. Charging inflated prices for the very people who're making rock 'n' roll a hit."

Rebecca turned helplessly. Silver slipped off her dark glasses, staring in amazement. David arched his neck up at Scooter. "You

Commie bastard,'' he spat out. "I saw that American flag bit." He grabbed Silver's arm. "This group sucks. Bunch of pinko faggots."

Scooter lashed out, a fist catching the producer with a solid punch to the chest. Rebecca yelled in shock. David reeled backward. He regained his balance. "I'll have you arrested, you asswipe!"

Scooter lowered his head as if to charge, but Rebecca threw herself on him. "No, Scooter, please," she pleaded, holding onto him in spite of his efforts to throw her off. "Let me at him," he choked out. "I'll kill the mutherfucker." He threw her to the ground, but David had already retreated. She looked up just in time to see the producer disappearing over the top of the rise.

"Are you satisfied now?" Scooter screamed down at her. "Trying to commercialize us? Hook us up with a ripoff punk like that? You don't know shit what we're about."

For a second, she thought he was going to kick a foot out at her. She threw her arms up to protect her head. "Lay off, you big ape," Silver bellowed, the raw power of her voice startling him. "She was only tryin' ta help."

"I don't need her fucking help," he muttered, his fists clenching. "None of us do. We were doing just fine until she showed the fuck up." He strode away to the gawking troop.

Rebecca managed to push herself up to her feet and began to run. Sobs broke from her chest. Racing blindly, she burst through the underbrush on the far side of the clearing and kept going. Branches slapped at her and she tripped, fell flat out, her head burrowing into a musty, dank pile of leaves. She lay there, her fingers clawing at the earth as if she were trying to bury herself.

A hand touched her shoulder and she flinched, pulling away. "Don'cha cry, honey." It was Silver's voice gentle as rainwater.

"Please, please, leave me alone," Rebecca sobbed.

"Honey, I ain't leavin' you," Silver replied and sat down in the dry leaves beside her. "If you feel like bawlin' go right ahead."

So Rebecca did and then raised her head to wail, "And the absolute worst part of all this? I still love the bastard. I do."

Silver reached down and pulled her to a sitting position, offering a tissue to wipe her nose. "Honey, an' I love that asshole, David. Oh, he pretends he don' know it. An' I have to put up with more crap from him than a mangy dog with a family o' fleas."

"Why?" Rebecca sniffed. "Why do we put up with it?"

Silver shrugged, pulling her close. "Well, honey, the way I see it, it's my shit-bag theory o' life. See, I figure nothin' is perfect. No relationship. No gig. All of them dish out some shit now an' then. But if you're still diggin' most of the relationship, then you have to store that shit away someplace. I sorta see mine as a big plastic garbage bag, dig? You stuff the bad away an' get on with whatever it is that's gettin' you off. But one day—that shit bag's gonn'a be full. Then you gotta figure it out. Do you wanna get a bigger bag an' keep on goin'? Or is it time to say—hey, the shit bag's full. No more shit. I've had enough. So if your shit bag's full, honey, walk away—real fast like. An' don' look back. See? We always got us that choice. Life ain't worth livin' unless we got choices. And we do, honey. We do."

Rebecca felt a small glow of warmth bursting to life within her cold shell. Tearfully she hugged Silver back. The two of them rocked softly in the shelter of the bushes and Silver began to croon softly: "Baby, I'm your momma/ An' I'm your papa/ an' I'm your sister too/ So come an' get it/ Jus' grab hold of/ Your sweet mama's love..."

DAVID
January 1968
San Francisco

"Take seven," the engineer said into his mike, laying it on the reel for editing reference. The boisterous, boogie-beat music blasted again from the large speakers suspended on either side of the control panel. David leaned back in his swivel chair listening intently. He was satisfied—for eight bars. Frowning, he flipped forward to his mike, hitting the talk-back switch. "Cut, dammit," he said, his voice transmitted to the band members over both the studio speakers and their individual "cues," headphone sets. "Peter," he directed to the drummer, "you lost it going into the bridge."

"Sounded solid out here," Peter's voice whined into the booth.

"I don't give a damn what it sounds like out there. The beat wavered in here and in here is where it counts." David and his sound engineers were enclosed in a soundproofed booth that housed all the recording equipment. Through the front window, he could see clearly all the musicians except Silver. Only the crown of her scarf-covered head was visible above the temporary wall baffleboards which isolated her vocals.

After conferring hurriedly with his main sound specialist, David switched on his mike. "Take it from the pick upon the two fives," he ordered, referring to specific chords. "And Peter, I want the backbeat dirtier. No frills, understand? All right, let's finish this turkey."

The tape rolled again. "'Stompin' the Grapes'—take eight, third verse," the engineer laid on the reel. Hawk counted out the beat in a surly monotone and broke into an angry, heated solo that segued into the bridge. David leaned into the man at the soundboard. "Too hi-fi. Make it funkier." The top-flight engineer twisted a few dials until David nodded.

At any given moment, David was listening for problems in tempo, attacks and releases, the arrangements and executions of solos, the harmony of the backup voices and the quality of the sound itself. When he sensed something wrong, he considered various psychological or technical methods of rectifying it. It was exhausting work and he strove to remain on top of it all, not allowing himself even a moment's lapse in concentration.

Sipping bitter black coffee from a styrofoam cup, he kept an eye on the control panel's needles indicating volume and balance of each instrument. Simultaneously, he was aware of what the delays were costing him. By the sixteenth take, he knew they were not even close to finishing the cut. Already, that one song was a good five grand overbudget.

He groaned, slapping his forehead. Silver's voice had cracked horribly halfway through the last verse. "Cut," he said into his mike and waited for the musicians to wind down. "Goddammit, we don't have time to piss this session away," he began heatedly. "When I order 'cut,' you stop. Otherwise we'll be here forever."

"Shit if it don' feel like it already," Silver's voice joked.

"We're takin' a break," Hawk announced, his guitar already unstrapped. David glanced at the the wall clock—it was just after ten P.M. The session had started at five and already the band had been given over an hour in break time. David sighed, under protest, and said, "Be back in fifteen."

"Thirty," Hawk announced and strode out of view.

David crushed the styrofoam cup and chucked it, missing the trashbasket by a yard. Silver tapped on the glass, a glare of white against the pane. Firing off a list to the two engineers on what section to pull from the last master reel, David slipped out into the overly air-conditioned studio.

Silver waited in the corner, her acoustical Gibson around her neck. She smiled wearily. "You been promisin' all week to hear this. Worked it up with Hawk."

"We got two full sides," he explained again.

"I think this one's real importan'. We can drop tha' seaside ditty. Never liked it anyway. Too Beach Boys." She lifted her guitar.

"Hawk put you up to this?"

"Jus' lissen, man, will you? We all think it should be cut."

"Jesus, Silver," he sighed, but she began to strum a simple folk-chord vamp. She broke into a Dylanlike twang: "It ain't right/ it ain't fair/ big ol' us/ bein' over there./ With all our power/ with all our might/ still don' make/ the damn thing right./ No more war/ no more killin'/ helpless people/ like women an' chil'ren."

David attempted to hold it in but by the second verse he couldn't control it. He burst out in the first real laugh of the day. Her face dropped into a scowl and she stopped altogether. "It's relevant, ain't it? Me an' the dudes think—"

"—Relevant, schmellevant. It's totally out of sync with the rest of the cuts."

"Sez you." It was Hawk's voice.

David turned. Hawk and the others were clustered just inside the doorway. "Yeah, says me," David began. "The tune's insipid and the lyrics inane. Told you before, White Meat's not going to join any movements. We're a rock group. Period."

"We want it on the album," Hawk said and ripped off his beaded headband. His black hair dropped limply past his shoulders. David swung his gaze to Zisk, the moderate of the group. "You in on this too?"

"I like it, David," Zisk said, his teen heartthrob features serious. "It'd be one out of twelve cuts. Give us a certain credibility."

"A credibility we're lackin'," Larry added snidely. "Right now, I'd say we rank just a cut above The Monkees."

"Listen," David said, his ire rising, "the only credibility worth having is airplay. You think that piece of shit will make A.M.?"

Hawk folded his arms across his chest, his beaklike nose jutting into the air. "Fuckin' A.M.—me an' Larry turned out four jingle-ditties for your gawdamned A.M. Ain't that enough?"

"Barely," he said. "You guys should realize by now—for every A.M. hit, we see another hundred thousand units. If not more."

"I'm for selling less," Hawk snarled. "And sayin' more."

"Something that *needs* to be said," Peter joined in.

David scanned the semicircle before him. They had planned it down to the timing, knowing full well he'd have to compromise to get on with the night's schedule. "The cuts on the album remain the same," he said icily. "Now let's finish this." No one moved—not even Silver. She eyed him boldly over the rim of her dark glasses. "I won't take this for long," he continued. "I've two other groups that can wipe your asses off the charts faster than you can spit. Now, either do things my way or you don't do it at all." He surveyed them individually, meeting only resistance. He spun to the nearest overhead mike. "Can you hear me in there?"

"A-okay," the engineer signaled inside, waving behind the glass.

"That's a wrap." Without looking back, David walked out of the studio.

Instead of returning that night to the large Victorian house he shared with the group, he followed his usual routine of late. He went straight by cab to his office in the RPM headquarters, three floors of a fifties hi-rise building on Van Ness. The clerical side of his job as Artist-and-Repertory representative of the small label was always the most tedious and time-consuming.

Unlocking his door, he noticed a light on in the president's office. That was odd—usually the old man was the first to leave for the day. Curiosity aroused, David tapped lightly on the glass door. Hearing no response, he tried the knob.

The large corner office was empty but in a terrible state of disarray—legal papers were strewn across the usually neat desk and file folders were scattered on the floor chairs. He noticed a fifth of Johnny Walker Red on the desk, the bottle less than a third full. He walked behind the desk to examine the contents on top. "Won't do any good," a voice slurred behind him.

David whirled. The graying president of the label leaned against the lavatory door and smiled bleary-eyed. "It's no use trying. The ship is sinking. In fact, it's sunk. Abandon ship." He laughed sardonically and rolled heavily into his office in shirtsleeves, the vest of his suit unbuttoned, tie askew.

"Kind of late for you, isn't it, W.H.?"

"Later than I thought." The president's pasty face was puffed with drink, his gray hair mussed. He fumbled through some papers, extracting one. "Might as well be fully informed. This'll be on all desks first thing in the morning anyway."

David read it quickly. It was short and to the point. RPM had been purchased outright by Allied Industries Incorporated and W. H. Neihardt, president, was resigning effective immediately. David felt a flush of anger and shock.

"Yes, sudden, isn't it?" W.H. slid into the leather chair behind the desk. "Nineteen years I've been with RPM. Seventeen of them solidly in the black. Then comes rock..." He sighed and rubbed his eyes.

"What the hell happened? You were solvent when I signed on."

"I just told you: today's music."

"My White Meat album was a smash. The two albums by my other groups made a substantial profit. I could have produced more."

"Hindsight, David. Perhaps I should have listened. You were insistent enough..."

"Who'll replace you?" David asked. The president raised his palms vaguely. David felt incensed by the gesture. He struggled to recall what he knew about Allied Industries. The only item that came to mind was the giant international conglomerate was consistently in *Fortune* magazine's top twenty U.S. corporations. "What the hell does AII know about the music business?" he demanded. "And where does this leave me?"

W.H. shrugged disinterestedly. "Where does it leave any of us?"

"Goddamm it, W.H., you promised my contract would be valid for—"

"No guarantees in business, David."

"You were a blind fool not to take advantage of my abilities. If you'd given me a chance, I would have turned RPM around."

"Perhaps . . . well, good luck, David," W.H. mumbled. "I never cared for you personally, but I admire your business instincts."

David headed for the hall. "You were born a loser, W.H."

Far into the early hours of morning, David paced his office, trying to assess the damage to his future. On the wall behind his desk was the framed gold record for "Meet White Meat"—the one possession he was most proud of—a testimony to his own tastes and drive. Next to it was a framed blowup of the *Cashbox* article for December 1967, headlined SMASH WHITE MEAT TOUR. Two other framed articles hung below—one from the new music rag started over in Oakland, Rolling Stone, which touted the debut of another of his groups, Tunnel and the other a *Billboard* Top 40 list showing Cobalt Blue's single as being Number four for two weeks.

Personally, he had made a healthy bundle from his percentages of both record sales and box office receipts. What concerned him was where he was going. If he left RPM, he would have to go without any of his groups. He would have to start over again at another label and that prospect appalled him.

By noon, the floors occupied by RPM were in chaos. Half the staff had been pinkslipped, the warehouse containing all product had been padlocked, along with all financial records and legal documents. Even the president's office bore a large seal on the door and Neihardt was reported on his way to Honolulu. Contracts with all groups and artists were up for review and one memo ordered that all albums in production were now on hold. Immediately David called the head of the sound studios to insure the master reels of White Meat's album were safe. He was informed that lawyers for AII had issued a writ of injunction, only qualified personnel would have access to an RPM product. David's name was not on the approved list. No amount of screaming on his part would release the tapes.

At two-thirty, he received a call. The male voice was polite but restrained. "This is Dixon Shaw's office calling. The chairman would like to meet with you at three today. In the presidential suite at the Mark Hopkins Hotel.''

David could not control the sarcasm in his voice, ''Am I assuming correctly that Shaw in the chairman of Allied Industries?'' Hearing a polite confirmation, David said he'd work the meeting into his afternoon.

Shortly before three, he presented himself at the doors of the hotel suite and was ushered into the elegantly furnished living room by a buttoned-up young male assistant who informed him, ''Mister Shaw will be with you presently.'' Alone, David waited impatiently, mentally reviewing the information about the chairman he'd been able to dig up.

Dixon Shaw was only forty-four years old, *summa cum laude* graduate of both Yale Law school and Harvard Business School. He'd been vice president of AII's Penrand Chemicals, one of the major suppliers to the U.S. Army for napalm. At thirty-six Shaw had been elevated to president and at thirty-nine brought up the board of directors of AII. He'd been named chairman of the entire Corporation at forty-one, and since then, net profits had soared a staggering thirty-two percent.

Shaw's credentials were damned impressive, but no more so than Shaw in person. When the chairman strode into the room, he exuded the strength and confidence of a man in charge of twenty-two unrelated companies whose total assets were well over the nine billion mark. Round face, with thinning red hair and a thickening body deftly camouflaged by a hand-tailored, pin-striped suit of a conservative cut and a wide silk tie, Shaw looked to David like a successful divorce lawyer for some Boston suburb.

After a firm but brief handshake, the chairman sat in an easy chair and launched the topic with the zest of a coach, ''I'm most impressed by your achievement at RPM during your short tenure there, David. It is my opinion that you have the makings of an extremely capable executive. One who will help turn a profit for the company. I'd like to have you as vice president of all Talent and Product. Does that appeal to you?''

''Only if I have complete autonomy. Run my own shop.''

''Then the position is yours. On two conditions only. I do not want to lose your obvious gifts in the studio. We'd like you to continue in your producing capacities, personally supervising as many albums as you possibly can. Of course, you can expect fair compensation in royalties."

"I'm expensive," David offered with a knowing smile.

"You'll be amply rewarded, rest assured. Which brings us to the main condition. When RPM was presented as a possible acquisition, to a man the entire board was extremely concerned about one factor of the record business today. I'm speaking of the subvervise nature in a great deal of the music aimed at the younger buyer. The 'rock-and-roll' market."

David nodded, suppressing a smile. "I understand."

"Our researchers presented a comprehensive study of the lyrics of many hit records. I can make a copy of it available if you'd like. The bottom line was that a great many songs contain a distinct flavor of anti-US, antigovernment, antibusiness, anti-involvement in the war in Southeast Asia. I will be blunt," Shaw said, running a palm over this thinning hair. "Allied Industries is a thoroughly red blooded American corporation. We want no songs or groups advocating the use of any drugs or the overthrow of any of our traditional American and Christian values. And no lyrics or group comment that is in opposition to the united war effort of our government. Do I make myself clear?"

"Perfectly," David said. "I'm a firm believer in the old Goldwynism, 'You wanna send a message, call Western Union.'"

The chairman laughed politely and stood. "Welcome aboard, David. Have your lawyer contact my office in New York."

"It's my pleasure, sir," he replied, shaking Shaw's hand.

Walking him to the hall door, Shaw asked, "You follow pro football?" David shook his head "No" and the chairman continued, "That Broadway Joe Namath of the Jets—my kind of quarterback. Unpredictable, a real scrambler. Never gives up. We could all learn from that."

It wasn't until David was in the elevator on the way to the lobby that he realized he'd called Dixon Shaw, "Sir." He couldn't remember being that deferential to anyone before. But then he couldn't remember being as impressed either.

Halfway down the block from the Mark Hopkins, on impulse, David stepped into a real-estate office. While the theme for "Mission-

Impossible'' played on the office radio, David rented the first furnished penthouse apartment the agent described. Within fifteen minutes, he had signed the contract and written a check for four grand—first and last month's rent plus two thousand security. Keys in his pocket, he took a cab to a Jaguar dealership near the RPM headquarters and bought off the display floor a new 1968, gunmetal gray XKE convertible. While the nonplussed dealer verified the personal check written for the full amount, David walked back along Van Nuys Boulevard. His step was light, a general sense of well-being pervaded his system. He was back on the track again.

At his office, his secretary informed him that Silver had called three times. But there were more pressing matters and David concentrated on his new responsibilities. He memoed instructions to Business Affairs to prepare cost figures for buying out the contracts and dumping a third of the RPM talent roster. He also restructured the A-and-R department with the remaining reps Shaw had not had fired. As second-in-command, David selected a bright, but not too bright, young man who'd been there less than a month. He liked the guy's South Bostonian street toughness and figured it would help in holding the hyenas at bay. Silver kept calling. David kept busy with his new duties, knowing he'd see her at the scheduled studio session that night.

An hour before leaving for the recording studio, he was hitting full stride in the energy department. He'd juggled the factory's pressing of three new albums he wanted out right away and was listening on his office speakers to a demo tape for a girl with a voice sounding like Melanie.

"Shaw on line two,'' his secretary said in the doorway. He punched the button. "Rau, here.''

It was the young male assistant's voice and there was a quiet urgency to it. "The chairman wants you to tune to 99.8 F.M. Immediately.'' Before David could ask why, the secretary clicked off.

David dialed his set behind the desk. The voice coming out of the speakers was unmistakable. It was Silver, backed up by the whole damned combo and she was singing plaintively, "It ain't right/ it ain't fair/ big ol' us/ bein' over there . . .''

Instantly the phone receiver was to his ear, his finger tracking down the list of the control-booth phone numbers for every disk jockey in the city. He found the call numbers and dialed. The line was busy. He bolted from his chair, running toward the door, hurling at his assistant, "Keep trying that station. And get that damned tape off the air!"

David sprinted the two blocks to the car dealership. He demanded and received the keys to his new Jag and hopped inside, revving the engine and roaring into the street with tires squealing. Hunched over the wheel, he tried to hit the green lights on the boulevard. He missed one and slammed on his brakes, taking the moment to switch on the radio. He dialed the station. The deejay—a sloppy fat slob David loathed—was rapping hoarsely away, ". . . so far you guys' response has been terrific. But keep those calls coming. Like I said, White Meat wants to know what you think. And remember, it's an exclusive on KQAC F.M.—your feelin' groovy station . . ."

Arriving in front of the two-storied brick building, David double parked, ran inside the lobby and past the startled receptionist. "Wait!" she yelled after him. "You can't—" But he barged through the swinging doors, down the hall to the glass-paneled control booth. A cut from the Stones' new release, "Their Satanic Majesty's Request" was playing in the hall and over the airwaves.

At the end of the hallway, behind the glass walk, the bearded paunchy deejay rose with a cheery wave. David froze him with a withering look. The deejay lumbered to open the door. "Hey man, hear there's big changes at your label—"

"Give it here," David fired at him, snapping his fingers.

"Hey, Rau, I assumed you'd cleared it."

"Give it to me. *Now*!"

The saggy, hairy jowls jiggled and the deejay slid his paunch to the tapedeck, removing a reel. "What can I say, man? Except I had to take the phone off the hook. They're digging it out there. The most."

David snatched the tape from him and recognized the childish scrawl marking the label in black-felt pen. "Silver give this to you?"

"I thought it was cool, man. What can I say?"

"How many times did you air it?"

"Just twice, man. Honest Injun."

"You make a copy?"

"No . . . I wouldn't do a—"

David pushed past him to the tapedecks. A second reel was racked up. He hit the rewind button. Behind him, the deejay sat again, over his microphone. "I'm on now," he rasped and turned on his mike as the Stones faded.

David slipped the second reel off and with both tapes firmly under his arm, left the booth. Returning down the hallway, he could hear the deejay broadcasting, "For those of you who missed a sneak preview of White Meat's new anti-war song . . . well, I'm sorry. What can I say? You missed it, that's all. A real heavy song, by a very heavy group, produced by a heavy . . . *heavy* cat . . ."

He waited for Silver in his new digs on top of Russian Hill. He knew she'd show up eventually. He'd left word at the recording studio canceling the White Meat session and that he was available only to Silver at his new address.

The first call he made after leaving the F.M. station was from a phone booth on the corner. After a considerable wait, the chairman had come on the line, his voice cool with disappointment. David hurriedly explained the situation and promised such reprehensible actions would never occur again under his jurisdiction. "I sincerely hope not," Shaw had replied formally. "For your sake."

Those last three words now kept ringing in his ear as David unpacked his large leather suitcase he'd brought over from the White Castle. Into the oak chest of drawers and the deep walk-in closet of the master bedroom suite, he methodically arranged his few clothes.

From the bottom of the suitcase, he brought out the last and most important item and carried it into the living room, looking around for an appropiate spot. He tried several locations, under different lighting, before being satisfied.

He turned out all the lights but the crystal table lamp and sat down staring into the magnetic, sympathetic eyes of his mother. In a simple, flat-gold frame the eight-by-ten, black-and-white, studio portrait was the very last taken of Nedra. He had been only seven at the time and had carried the photo with him ever since. Her delicate oval face had always given him strength and rededication to his life's goals. Tonight was no different.

He turned off the lamp and sat in the dark, barely aware of the panoramic view through the walls of glass, from the Golden Gate Bridge outlined in bright orange lights to the dramatic skyline of the city by the bay.

A buzzer sounded harshly, shattering his sanctuary. It took him a few moments before he located the intercom box in the hall. The doorman in a perturbed tone announced Silver's arrival and David told him to send her up. He unlocked the door, the only one on the top floor, opened it and returned to the living room, found an overstuffed chair and sank into it, lost in the shadows. Shortly, he heard her voice in the entry way. "David? You in here, man?"

"Yeah."

She inched around the corner, feeling the wall, her dark glasses in one hand. She was wearing that ratty, white fur coat that had become her trademark in the media. "Where are you, man? Damn, its darker in here than a nun's hole. Why don'cha have the lights on? Holy shit, look at the view!" She bumped into an armchair and whined, "Oh hell, man. Turn on a damn light for Chrissakes. You tryin' to scare me or—"

He snapped on a table lamp next to him. Blinking and squinting, she fumbled to put on her dark glasses. "Wow, man . . . what a score. Who's this pad belong to?" When he didn't respond, she turned from the terrace's glass wall. "Gawdamned, if it don' look like Joan Crawford should be livin' here. Does it belong to that rich dude who snatched the label? He lettin' you use it? Wait'll the boys see this. They'll cream in their jeans."

"They'll never see it."

"But why, man?"

"I don't want them here. Ever."

"'Fraid they'll trash it an' the owner'll get pissed?"

"It's mine. Take a look around if you'd like. It's the last time you'll see it." If he had kicked her, she probably wouldn't have looked any different than she did right then. He moved to the coffee table, picked up the reel of audio tape and lobbed it at her feet. Startled, she bounced backward. He could tell she recognized it and his anger flared again. "You think you're pretty fucking smart, huh?"

"We jus'...jus' wanted to see—"

"I know what you wanted," he cut in acidly.

"Oh, David," she moaned, taking a conciliatory step forward. "I'm sorry, man. I tried an' tried gettin' you by phone. But you never called back. Then we heard wha' happened with the label, it bein' sold an' all. I figured we'd all been dropped or somethin'. Tha' it wouldn't make no difference if we tried sellin' tha' song. I swear on my grannie's grave..." She was close to tears, her cheeks blotched with red.

He glared. "Sorry isn't good enough, Silver. I've had it with you. You, Hawk, the whole fucking circus. After all I've done for you. Put you where you are. To have you turn around and stab me in the back. That's it. No more."

Tears slipped from under her sunglasses but he had just gotten started. "You guys think with one hit you've got it made? That you can do it again without me? Do you? Answer me, goddammit!" She shook her head, her mouth trying to form words. "Fuckin' Hawk," he growled. "Let's see how he does on his own. He and Larry. As of now, they're out of the group. I'm not taking their shit one minute more."

"You can't do tha', man," she cried. "Where'll we get the songs?"

"I've a dozen songwriters under contract. Any six would be better than Hawk and Larry. Let's see how those two motherfuckers like being back on the street."

"Don', please don'," she sobbed, coming toward him. "Please don' do this. It was all o' us, man, all o' us. Not jus' Hawk an' Larry." Still crying, she reached out, started to put her arms around him. He yanked them away. His head was splitting from all the yelling.

"Man...I love you," she cried. "Please don' do—" Seeing his eyes, she shrank back. "I ain't tha' ugly, am I?"

"You want the truth?"

Her head swiveled back and forth on her thin neck. She didn't want the truth. No one ever wanted the truth. She turned to flee, stumbled and caught hold of the endtable to maintain balance. The table tipped, sending its contents tumbling. The glass-fronted photo crashed, shattering on the parquet floor. "Goddamn you," he yelled.

The gold frame had popped apart. Carefully with his fingertips, he lifted the black-and-white glossy photo and blew off the glass shards. With his free hand, he picked up the pieces of the frame. He had forgotten Silver. "It's your mother, ain't it? How come I never seen this—"

"Get out, Silver. Just get the hell out."

She backed away, nodding, then turned, running into the entrance foyer. He called after her. "We've still lots of hits to record, you and I." She slammed the door and he was alone. He propped the photo against the lamp. His mother smiled at him wistfully.

SHELBY
March 1968
New York

"What do you want?" Mo asked, the foul-smelling cigarette clenched in her teeth. Erik, tipsy, withdrawn, studied his cards.

Shelby's fingers drummed her own cards, sending signals to him that she was bored, bored, bored. She had been for weeks, hating the drudgery of being Sunny and the dreary sameness of her regimented life. That evening, she had wanted to see the film *Elvira Madigan* and later go dancing at Arthur—instead Erik had dragged her here to Mo and Michael's drab apartment to play poker, a game she detested. What he liked about this mismatched couple was beyond her. Political discussions *ad nauseam*, especially about the North Korean detention of the U.S.S. *Pueblo*. It was times like this when Shelby wondered why she had ever taken up with Erik again. But she knew there was something special about him worth hanging on to, an honesty, a loyalty, a sweetness, even when he'd been drinking heavily. Like that very evening.

"You should see this talented kid I yanked away from William

Morris today," Mo continued, raking in the pile of change. "An actor named Robby Rhomann. Going to be a star—blond curly hair, cute little pixie face and talent up the ol' whazzoo."

"Sounds like a fairy to me," Michael said.

Mo threw him a sour look. "Very funny, Michael. You should try writing for *Screw*."

"Only if you'd represent me," came his testy reply. He turned to Erik. "Forty-two percent of the New Hampshire vote. Eugene could wrestle the nomination away from that fat Texan."

Mo lit another cigarette. "Michael," she began, as if talking to one of the twins, "LBJ got forty-eight percent. All write-in votes."

"But no one predicted McCarthy'd do that well," he insisted. "And it's just the first primary. By August, he could have it all sewn up."

Shelby scooted back her chair. "Erik, sugar . . . do you mind if we go? I've a splitting headache."

"Why didn't you speak up sooner, babe?" He lumbered to his feet.

"Well, I was having such a good time."

While Michael dragged Erik into the hall for her mink coat, Shelby dutifully thanked Mo for the evening and complimented her on her "adorable" twin sons, who had been such disruptive terrors before going to bed.

"Just like their father," Mo joked. "Crazy 'Laugh-In' nuts." She hesitated. "Erik's taking it pretty hard, isn't he?"

"Y'all mean this book? Honestly, sometimes I wish he'd become a teacher or something. Write for television. Anything. He just mopes around all the time with nothing to do. It's driving me crazy."

"He'll snap out of it. But he needs a lot of support right now."

Shelby turned to the hallway. "Y'all coming, sugar?"

Though Erik lived only a few blocks away, Shelby preferred waking up in her own bed. In the cab on the way to her place, the cabbie's radio was playing the Fifth Dimension's "Up, up and Away" and Erik was mute, sullen. She snuggled closer, resting a hand gently on his thigh. "Sugar, want to know what I'm thinking?"

"Uh-huh . . ."

She whispered into his ear the most raunchy expression she could think of—a preview of coming attractions. He mumbled, "That's nice . . ."

Damn, he hadn't even heard her. She let her hand slip inside his thigh, caressing upward. He opened his legs, granting her more freedom, but the reaction was so automatic, she wondered if he were really aware of her rare boldness. "Erik," she began again, remembering something he had mentioned casually over dinner. "Y'all really considering leaving New York and taking off for a spell?"

"Maybe," he replied, finally looking at her.

She rested her head on his shoulder. "I'd just die without y'all. Really. I don't know what I'd do without having y'all around."

"Oh, I'm sure you'll find some little ol' thing to play with."

She couldn't tell if he were making fun of her or not, so she removed her hand and joined his silence for the remainder of the taxi ride. In front of her Park Avenue apartment tower, she was shocked to hear him tell the driver to wait. "Y'all not spending the night?" she asked when he had joined her under the glass canopy.

The sharp wind from the river ruffled the sandy waves of his hair. In the sheepskin car coat she'd bought him for Christmas, he looked so ruggedly sexy she ached for him to hustle her upstairs.

He threw an arm around her and started walking her toward the glass doors. "Can't tonight, babe. Michael wants to meet for a drink."

She halted, pulling away. "Y'all mean to tell me that after drinking and talking to him all evening, y'all're planning to do more of the very same thing? Right now?"

"He asked and I agreed. Something's on his mind, babe."

"Well, I'll be damned," she breathed and tossed her head.

He shrugged. "He's pulled me out of many a tailspin. If I can reciprocate, then—"

"Well, y'all just go right ahead. Don't pay any attention to me." She flounced for the door. Rather than stopping her, as she'd hoped, he called out, "Hey, I thought you'd understand."

"Oh, I understand. Y'all just don't love me."

"You know that isn't so," he answered, taking a step forward. "I'll see you tomorrow night . . . and all this weekend."

"Maybe. Maybe not." She swept through the doorway.

In her big brass bed, she tossed. She was seething. Damn Erik's book. If it had succeeded like he'd wanted, everything between them would be different. She was positive of that. It just wasn't fair—here she was really falling in love with the big ox and it was like he was a million miles away. Unreachable, unapproachable.

Before drifting off to sleep, she resolved it was time for some new tactics to charge up his interest in her. But damn, she couldn't think of any that she hadn't already used.

In the morning, a miraculous phone call awakened her early. "*Cara mia*, I've canceled our bookings for the whole of next week," Giorgio announced breezily. "Come fly with me to the Caribbean. We'll take a much deserved vacation on my yacht."

Shelby was ecstatic. This was a card she had yet to use on Erik. "Giorgio," she trilled, "when do we leave?"

His chauffeur picked her up within the hour and drove her to LaGuardia where Caesari was waiting inside his private Lear jet. The flight south was uneventful. She was too exhausted from her fitful night's sleep to pay much attention to her employer. She did note, however, that Giorgio was in exceptionally high spirits, a rarity that made him most attractive in his white turtleneck and dark blue blazer. He spoke amiably about his plans for expanding the Sunny line to include suntan oils and lotions. She barely listened. She kept wondering what Erik's reaction would be when he recieved her message on her service.

Upon landing in St. Thomas, balmy breezes greeted them, further lightening her heart. "Oh, I love it already," she exclaimed as Caesari ushered her to another limo for the short jaunt to the harbor.

The moment the craft was pointed out to her, she stopped in amazement. It wasn't like any boat she had ever seen—more like a small cruise liner. Over one hundred and fifty feet long with a raked smoke funnel, it rose majestically white and glistening from the clear azure water. She read aloud the name printed in gold on its bow, "*Circe*."

"No, *bellissima*," he corrected. "It's *Sir-see*. After the enchantress in Greek mythology who turned every man who approached her into a beast. All except Odysseus. He'd drunk a special potion making him immune to her spells. She so marveled at this unique man, she fell madly in love with him.''

"How romantic," she said, dreamily.

Aboard was a surfeit of splendors—six double staterooms, a huge salon aft complete with a movie screen concealed behind a large, gold-framed Matisse painting, a dining room big enough for a sitdown dinner for twenty, a freshwater swimming pool that could be covered in inclement weather and what seemed to her like acres of teak decking. In her bathroom, the sink and tub fixtures were gold and her huge, plush-carpeted stateroom, delicately hued in soft mauve and pink, came complete with its own sauna and private sundeck. "Oh, Giorgio," she enthused. "It's spectacular. I may never want to leave."

He actually laughed. "Why don't you take a small nap, *cara mia*. I'll have one of the stewards knock on your door an hour before dinner. By the way, it will be formal."

"But Giorgio," she cried. "Y'all told me not to pack anything but my toothbrush and swimsuit."

As if he had been waiting for the cue, he swept to the triple, full length, mirrored doors and opened them. A row of stunning haute couture gowns shimmered before her. She gasped with delight. He moved to the open hall door. "I'm certain you will find something you like. Pleasant dreams, *cara mia*." Softly he closed the door. Not bothering to undress, she collapsed on the bed and soon was deliciously asleep.

She awoke to a soft tapping at her door. "Dinner in an hour, Miss Cale," came the pleasant male voice. The faint throb of powerful engines indicated that the *Circe* had left port and was underway. "Thank y'all so much," she called out and bounced off the bed. Running to the full-length windows of her sundeck, she pulled back the heavy brocade drapes. A breathtaking sunset filled the sky, a riot of pinks and golds over the expansive blue green sea. Delighted by the prospect of an entire week of freedom in such beauty, she luxuriated in a hot tub, redid her nails, applied a minimum amount of makeup and swept up her hair into a modified French roll, leaving long curls, Grecian style, on either side of her face.

Selecting a gown was extremely difficult; each one she tried on was more beautiful than the last and every one of them fitted her as if it had been handmade for her. Obviously Giorgio had been preparing for her arrival aboard for some time—even the matching row of shoes were in her size. She finally decided on a pure silk, sari-type dress that fell from one shoulder in soft folds of iridescent greens. Low-heeled, matching gold sandals completed the exotic outfit.

Eager to meet the other guests, knowing they had to be fascinating or Caesari would not have invited them, she took one last look in the triple, full-length mirrors and left to find the action. Wrapping the silk shawl loosely around her shoulders, she entered the main salon.

She looked around in surprise. The large, elegant room was empty, except for the luxurious furnishings all in a monochrome of soft gray—the large, deep-cushioned pillow couches and chairs were upholstered in suede like the walls. Recessed, indirect lighting in the ceiling spotlighted the several Impressionistic oil paintings in ornate silver frames. On a parson's table, a silver bucket of chipped ice held a bottle of Crystil champagne.

"May I pour you a glass?" A strange, hoarse voice brought her around. A powerfully built bull-of-a-man stepped into the subdued light. Dressed in a white, double-breasted nautical suit with gold braid on the shoulders, the man was totally bald and heavily tanned. A deep scar puckered one cheek, drawing up the side of his mouth into what looked like a perpetual sneer. There was no mistaking the glint in his eyes. Checking her out from stem to stern, he was letting her know he heartily approved of his survey.

She felt disconcerted. "Yes, please," she said without warmth, drifting to the far side of the salon.

"Allow me to introduce myself," he began and strode to the champagne. "I am Captain Burge. Captain of the *Circe*."

"*Enchanté*," she replied and pretended to study the still life of wildflowers above one couch—the signature was either Monet or Manet. The loud pop of the champagne's cork caused her to jump. Angry with herself, she turned. "Where are the others?"

"Others? There are no others," the captain said. "Only you and

Signore Caesari." He approached with a full glass extended. "Were you under the impression there would be others, Miss Cale?"

She did not care for the tone of his voice—it was at once both gruff and far too personal. She took a sip of the cold, gold champagne, trying to still the confusion he was generating. "I don't believe it's any of your business."

There it was again, the mocking half-smile below the jagged scar. "As you wish, Miss Cale," he replied with a slight bow of his smooth head.

"Ahh, I see you two have met. Bravo," Giorgio said, entering in black tie and tuxedo. Enormously relieved, Shelby glided to him trailing the shawl out from her. "Oh, Giorgio, this gown is divine."

"*Bella donna*," he praised. "Are you hungry?"

"*J'ai trés faim.*"

"The sea air," the captain said, but she pretended not to hear.

Despite the forbidding presence of the captain at the far end of the glass-topped table, dinner was surprisingly congenial. Giorgio was more relaxed than she had ever seen him. Gone was the stiff formality which pervaded his business dealing with her and in its place, a chatty buoyancy kept her amused. The multicoursed dinner, quietly served by three young men in white jackets, was delicious, especially the *veau de cordon bleu*.

By the time dessert arrived, a delicate lemon souffle, all the fine champagne and rare wines, a different one with each course, had begun affecting her. Even the captains's brutal facade seemed less threatening and he fascinated her with several sea stories of his adventures aboard some of the world's most famous private yachts. One in particular, about Onassis and Maria Callas making it atop a grand piano, she found titillating, in a gossip-column kind of way. But she also could not help feeling the gossip was telling it just to see her reaction.

After dinner, the captain bowed formally and bid her good night, leaving Giorgio to take her for a stroll around the gently throbbing decks. The glistening stars were out in force and the sea was flat and still, the air intoxicatingly gentle and warm, smelling faintly of tropical flowers. Caesari was quiet as they stood by the rail, staring out over the glistening water.

"Giorgio," she began softly, "what would happen if I got married?"

The question was so unexpected it caught him completely off-guard. She studied his patrician face in the light of the half-moon as he tried to recover. "To this Erik Lungren?" he finally questioned.

"Nobody's asked me, if that's what's worrying you." She laughed. "I'm just curious what would happen to my Sunny contract with that silly clause and all."

"Sunny is America's ideal of new feminine independence," he said with his business tone. "As much as I would hate personally to lose you, I'd have no choice. Why this topic all of a sudden? We just renewed your contract for another three years."

"Yes, I'm very aware of that," she teased and took his arm. "I was just feeling so romantic here in the moonlight, I got to thinking about honeymoons and such." She leaned her head on his shoulder, closing her eyes, waiting for him to kiss her, wondering why he never had.

"Tomorrow early we dock at St. Croix," he said deliberately. "You had better retire now."

She stood upright, stung but smiling languidly. "Good night, Giorgio. It's really been divine . . ."

She slept soundly that night, lulled by the steady throb of the engines and the gentle roll of the *Circe*. Her dreams were all of Erik—but in one, he had an ugly jagged scar on his cheek.

In the morning, they anchored just outside the harbor of Christiansted and took the small, motor launch in to dock. She and Giorgio toured the colorful town by foot, shopping in the quaint little stores. He bought her a wide-brimmed straw hat to keep the sun off her face. They lunched in a charming little five-star restaurant high up overlooking the yacht-dotted bay. Giorgio talked extensively of his boyhood in Parma and his meteoric rise in the cosmetic world based on his grandmother's peasant cold-cream, made from goat's milk. Shelby had heard it all before.

That afternoon, back again on the sea dotted by green-fringed islands, Caesari refused to allow her to be out in the sun. He did agree to her swimming in the pool, but only after the captain had steered a new course so that the shadows of the upper deck covered the pool area. Dinner that evening was again just the three of them, another lovely gown to wear, another fabulously delicious meal and too much wine to drink. Again, the captain annoyed her by staring—this time continually at her breasts.

After four days of this never varying routine, Shelby was bored out of her mind. The *Circe* stopped at every island—Anguilla, St Maarten, St. Barthélemy, St. Kitts, Barbuda. The disembarkings with Giorgio in the motor launch, often accompanied by the increasingly boorish Captain Burge, became monotonous. The glaring sun, the similarities of the isolated coves and harbors, the sameness of the tourist-filled towns, the same cheap "native-made" junk for sale in the shops—it all seemed so damned repetitious.

Even though Giorgio remained cordial and pleasant, he was constantly laying down rules—watching not only what she ate but how she put the food in her mouth, limiting the amount of alcohol, insisting she be covered from head to toe when out in the sun.

She felt a prisoner in a water palace. And guilt for leaving Erik so suddenly began to fester. Though she knew the *Circe* had a ship-to-shore telephone on which Giorgio kept hourly track of his cosmetics empire, she was also aware it too was off-limits. The one time she tried phoning Erik from a hotel lobby in Barbados, Caesari had unexpectedly appeared and she had to disconnect before it rang.

On the morning of the fifth day, she had no desire to get out of bed. Appearing topside only to complain of "women's problems," she sneaked a bottle of vodka from the bar back to her stateroom. She began to drink—at first mixing it with fruit juices from her own refrigerator but soon by taking slugs straight form the bottle, hissing with open mouth until the burning stopped. She'd only been really bombed a couple of times in her life—and now she went at it with a vigor. The more she drank, the more she missed Erik. In the previous weeks, they had been together almost constantly. She missed waking up and going to sleep beside his huge frame.

She thought it was terribly unfair that she could not make love to him right that moment. She began rubbing her hands down her nude body, flattening her breasts, then pushing them up, pinching the

nipples until they hurt. She smoothed her belly and caressed her
hips, bringing her palms around up inside her thighs, lightly touching herself, pressing, releasing. She scooted up to see the reverse of
herself in the mirrors.

She moaned and took her hand away. It just wasn't any good.
Finding the half-full bottle, she raised it and gulped the fiery liquid
greedily. She gasped, choked, coughed, cleared her throat and
suddenly felt wonderful. Bold and adventuresome. She located a
secret purchase made while Giorgio's back was turned in a little
shop off a crowded town square. A black topless Rudi Gernreich
bathing suit. She struggled into the tiny pieces, stumbled into the
bathroom, grabbed the brush and attacked her hair. She concocted a
wild mane, like Baby-Jane Holzer's and smeared a bright gloss over
her lips. And rouged her nipples lightly.

Unsteadily she weaved toward the aftdeck. Cutting through the main
salon, giggling to herself at the thrill of adventure, she was drawn up
shortly by the sight beyond the partially draped windows. Caesari,
bronzed and slenderly built in a brief black bikini, frolicked poolside
with some of the crew. He looked so boyish and having such a good
time, she paused, leaning against a chair for support, fascinated by the
odd sight of her employer in such an unguarded moment. Slowly she
focused on the young men. Each seemed strikingly handsome, all had sun-
bleached hair and their hard, brown bodies glistened with oil and water.

She gathered her composure and slid open the glass door, stepping
out of the air-conditioned dimness into the blazing sun. The blinding
light made her dizzy. She squinted, trying to regain her equilibrium.

One by one the crew noticed her and became like statues.
Climbing out of the pool, Giorgio spotted her. "Shelby! Where's
your hat?" He came at her with a large, white towel. "Your skin.
Think of your skin. And where did you get that tacky suit?"

"I bought it," she said airily and danced out from under the towel.
Keenly aware that she was the focus of his crew, she teetered to the
edge of the pool, pointed high her bare breasts and poised to dive.

Suddenly her head erupted, her vision blurred and she felt herself
keeling to one side. Strong, brown arms caught her—the skin
slippery, the sweet smell of sweat and sunning oil filled her nostrils.
She inhaled deeply, trying to clear her head but only felt dizzier. She

tried to resist the massive pair of arms which pinned her but in the next moment she was being carried out of the harsh sun, into the cool, dim passageway. Floating effortlessly through the air, cradled in iron hard arms, her head resting on the bare skin of a granite hard chest, she craned her neck to see who was carrying her. She chilled with a sudden fear.

Bald head glistening with sweat, the jagged cheek scar a bruised purple color, his mouth cruel with an amused sneer, Captain Burge ignored her brief, helpless flurry to extricate herself and kicked open her cabin door. He dumped her, sprawling and squealing, onto her bed.

Outraged, she glared up at him. He was wearing only black lederhosen and his body was that of a serious weight lifter, his muscles sculptured and bulging.

She was aware also that his eyes were raking over her own naked limbs and a surprisingly lustful thought flashed through her groggy mind. With a teasing, sensuous move, she rolled to one hip, one hand raising to cup an exposed breast. Sultry-eyed, she reached out to touch his leather pouch.

With a grunt, he slapped her hand away. "You're trash," he rasped, then strode out the doorway, his leather-covered buttocks tight and full. Before she could think of a cutting retort, he slammed the door on her.

Some hours later, after the ship had settled down for the night, Shelby was brimming over with curiosity and determination—she had to find out, one way or the other. Wearing only a gossamer, chiffon peignoir, she crept out of her cabin and ran lightly down the carpeted hallway to the aft passage leading to Caesari's master suite. Reaching his door, she quietly tried the brass doorknob. It was unlocked. Glancing over her shoulder, she gathered the skirt of her peignoir and slipped inside.

In the center of the master cabin, under a dim pool of light and on a raised-platform bed, Caesari lay, covered by a gray chinchilla spread, a black velvet sleeping mask over his eyes, his thin bare arms outside the covers, palms up. She thought he looked like he were sacrificing himself on an altar of fur.

Noiselessly, she slipped out of her nightgown and crawled under the double-sided fur throw. He did not stir. Lying on her side, she reached for his groin. As if he had been waiting for her, he was already hard and his length strained against her hand. She ducked under the fur and put her mouth on him. His hands touched her head.

He gasped and his body jackknifed into a sitting position. The next thing she knew, Caesari had thrown off the fur and she was rudely shoved aside by his feet. Dumbfounded she struggled to sit, watching him tearing off his mask, his face a deep magenta of shock and embarrassment. "Shelby!" he croaked and covered his wilting crotch with a pillow.

She fought for an air of decorum. "Well for heaven's sake, who'd y'all think it was? Captain Burge?"

"Go back to your cabin at once."

"Well, I've never..." Her arms flew over her breasts, she rose stiffly from the bed. "I should've guessed long ago when y'all didn't make a pass at me. I'll get out, all right. Just see how far." In all her glorious nudity and righteous anger, she marched for the door, pausing to sweep down and snatch her fallen nightgown from the carpet.

His voice, once again cold and authoritarian, stopped her at the door. "Reread your contract. You're mine, but I'm not yours. *Capiche*?"

"Don't count on it, you...you greasy ol' queen." Head held high, she strode out, her bare breasts swaying with indignation.

ERIK
March 1968
New York

"Doc Spock is right you know," Michael declared, rummy-eyed but still loquacious on the stool next to him. "The enemy is not the

Vietcong—the enemy is Lyndon Baines Johnson. Business as usual for the military-industrial complex. More war. More deaths. More destruction. Unless we get us a president who'll stop it."

With a few exceptions, it had been nearly a nonstop talk-a-thon and drinking match since after their poker game with Mo and Shelby. Michael had done the most talking, topics had varied little, either politics and the war, or Mo's inability to become involved in his concerns. Erik knew his buddy was leading up to something. Until it came, all Erik could do was hang on to whatever bar and wait. Listen and nod, drink and wait.

Outside, dawn was opening, revealing more distinctly the tawdry interior of the present bar and its clientele: winos, street hustlers, junkies, East Village flower children, some reminding Erik of Dickenslike street orphans.

The jukebox switched from The Archies' "Sugar, Sugar" to the Mamas and Papa singing "Monday, Monday." "What the hell day is this anyway?" Erik mumbled, his tongue thick and coated.

"How the fuck should I know? Thought you were keeping track."

"I gotta call Shelby." He slid off the stool. "I think I promised we'd get together this weekend." He started for the back hall. "Too late, sucker," Michael hooted. "The weekend's gone bye-bye."

"Shelby Cale's residence," answered her phone service. When Erik explained who was calling, there was a message for him: "Cruising with Caesari, ciao," he repeated dully. "Ahh, shit. Hey what day is this?"

"For those of us who have to work, it's Monday." She cut him off by hanging up. He stood cursing. He'd blown it. Shelby had split on him. And with that arrogant sonofabitch. Cruising. Where for Chrissakes? Long Island Sound? The Mediterranean? With Caesari's bucks, it could be anywhere. Leadenly, Erik made his way back to Michael and sunk to the stool.

"Television has changed it all," Michael said at once. "Bringing it right into our living room. Every night Cronkite, Huntley, Brinkley—bodycounts, jungle footage. That's why there's so much dissension. Too many people are seeing the real truth for once. Hell, if they'd make it a TV-series for ABC, the war'd be cancelled in thirteen weeks, right?

"She left town on me."

"Ohhh, she'll be back you lovesick pukeface." Michael put his feet on the floor and stood. "Let's blow this joint. Get some breakfast."

Sullenly, Erik followed Michael to a coffee shop near Thompkins Square. Run by an elderly Polish couple, it was full, despite the early hour, with old-timers soaking up the steamy warmth. Hunger, though, was the last thing on Erik's mind. Time, he figured, to sober up. Face the realities in the harsh, winter light of day. Everything he touched lately seemed to fail—his book and now his relationship with Shelby. Only that had been keeping him going lately—his love for her, his need, his desire. But now . . . "Cruising with Caesari, *ciao*."

"Small gunfire, Erik," Michael said over his eggs.

"Now what the hell're you talking about?"

"The reviews on your book. Just small gunfire."

"Easy for you to say, you mick prick."

Michael grinned like a kid and sopped up some egg yolk with his toast. "Critics," he sneered. "Hemingway called them 'lice that crawl on literature.' They don't mean shit. Small gunfire."

Erik stared into his muddy coffee. "If that barrage leveled at me was small, I'd hate to see the big stuff."

"Enlist. Go to Nam, buddy. *That's* the big stuff. That stuff can kill you."

"I don't know if I could write again even if I could try."

"You'll write again," Michael answered firmly. "Because nothing else is important except your writing."

Erik disagreed quietly, "There is something else . . ."

"So goddammit, quit farting around," Michael said and slapped the table. "Get a hold of her, plant her by your side and get on with it."

It wasn't until, for old times' sake, they'd walked over to the West Village to have a morning eye-opener at the White Horse Tavern on Hudson that Michael finally dropped his bombshell. "I'm leaving Mo," he said, as though his mind were made up.

Erik sputtered into his Scotch, "Wha' the hell?"

"Now buddy, don't get all worked up about this. I've thought about it a great deal and have decided it's the best for all concerned. She's so wrapped up in this talent agency crap and I'm light-years away. It's slowly killing us."

A new pain began coagulating inside Erik. "What about the boys?"

"That's the damned hard part," Michael said, looking away. "It's going to be rough on them, but they're established in school now. And I figure—with me gone, Mo'll have no choice. She'll have to pay more attention to their needs, give more of herself." He paused, then added caustically, "She's so damned career-driven. I rue the day her ol' man taught her poker. No shit, I do. He raised her to think like a man and look what's happened."

Erik tried to smile. "Gloria Steinem and friends would raise a few arguments here."

"Fuck 'em. And fuck Mo too. She's a good egg, but hell, I've been both father and mother to the twins. It's her goddamned turn."

He waited until Michael had cooled down, before asking, "What're you going to do? Get a place of your own?"

"Hell, no. I'm splitting the whole routine. Already handed in my resignation at the university. I'm heading out to California. Help RFK win that primary. It's the last one before the convention and I've a hunch Bobby will come out there fighting like the champ he is."

"Does Mo know any of this?"

"No," Michael answered and rose. "Guess now's as good as time as any. Come with me, buddy? She doesn't leave for the agency until ten."

The walk over to the apartment was painfully quiet. Erik felt awash with conflicting emotions. Without Michael, life in New York would be very flat—like stale beer: no kick, no bite, no high.

Mo met them at the front door, dressed for the office and only tolerantly amused. "Ah, the literary warriors home at last from the battles. Or is it, vanquished vagabonds home from the bottles?"

Michael took her arm gently. "Let's talk, Maureen." He propelled her toward the rear hallway. She cast a confused, questioning glance at Erik. He had to look away.

He roamed the living room. Wishing he were elsewhere, he avoided looking at the photos of the twins, tow-headed and freckled, grinning mischievously from the sofa wall like Norman Rockwell covers. The full-time housekeeper, arriving back after dropping off the boys at school, asked him, in her lilting Jamaican accent, if he wanted breakfast or anything. He declined and she waddled into the kitchen.

Soon Mo appeared in the hall doorway. Shock was carved on her round face like knife cuts on a pumpkin. Angrily she lit a cigarette and moved to the windows. "He wants you to drive him to the airport."

"Now? He's leaving now?"

She nodded, not meeting his eyes. The silence became oppressive. The ash on her forgotten cigarette grew long, dangling at the end like a tired finger. Suddenly she looked up, her eyes accusing. "You sonofabitch, why didn't you tell me he was miserable?"

"I didn't know . . . honestly, I didn't."

"Isn't that something?" she snapped. "His wife of nine years and his best friend didn't even know. The damned, melancholy black Irishman . . ." She choked back a sob, turned and lit a new cigarette with the butt of the old. "How could we've been so goddamned blind?"

Erik shrugged helplessly. She snubbed out both cigarettes in a full ashtray, muttering, "I'm going to be late for work. And I'll be damned if I'm giving that up—Michael or no Michael." She grabbed her brown wool coat and marched to the front door. Opening it, she hesitated. "Tell him . . . tell him for me . . . oh hell, I'm no good at exit lines. You think of something appropriate." Forcefully she closed the door behind her and was gone.

With Erik driving the old family Chevy, Michael stopped at the nearby grade school and disappeared inside to say good-bye to his sons. Double parked on the narrow Village street, Erik sat at the wheel, staring ahead, seeing nothing, thinking too much. He could hear the shrill, excited screams of the school kids playing behind the brick wall in an open courtyard. They sounded so carefree.

Soon a sober-faced Michael hurried down the steps and climbed into the passenger seat. "Holy Mother of God, what am I doing? What am I doing?" His head sank against the door's window and his eyes closed.

Erik started the car and pulled forward toward Seventh. "I don't know, Michael—what are you doing?"

"I'm dying inside."

"Welcome to the club. The only one I know open to everyone."

The drive to JFK Airport passed too quickly for him. Thoughts tumbled around in his brain like sodden laundry in a clothes dryer. Erik could not find words to express any of them. Michael tuned into the radio and watched the building pass while Judy Collins sang Joni Mitchell's "Circles." By the time they reached the front of United's terminal, Michael was trying damned hard to lighten the mood. "It's the start of a great adventure," he said unconvincingly. "Christ, how many times do we get a chance to start over?"

Erik pulled into a three-minute parking zone and switched off the engine. "I've half a mind to come with you."

"Hey, do it then, man. What a gas that'd be. The two of us? In sunny California. Lounging around the pool. Batching it. Wild times, Erik. It could be wild times." His voice petered out, as if he realized the futility of pressing that daydream. "No . . . you've got to get back to work. Start something. Anything. Just get back to your writing."

"There's Shelby too . . ."

"Ah yes. The golden goddess. The mythical American beauty."

"I love her, Michael . . . more than I've loved anyone."

"Yeah . . . I know you do." He reached behind the seat and pulled up his battered, imitation leather suitcase. "Look at this piece of crap. I came to New York in 1947 carrying this mother. Took it on my honeymoon to Atlantic City in fifty-eight. And here I am in sixty-eight, leaving with the same goddamned bag. Life's little circles, eh?" He slipped out of the car.

Erik joined him on the busy sidewalk before the glass fronted terminal. "Damn, this all happened so fast, it still hasn't sunk in."

"Our paths will cross again soon, buddy. And I want some nice fat letters, you hear? Something to collect over the years: *The Correspondence of Erik Lungren and Michael McKitrick*—two misfits on the highway of life." Tears welled up in his eyes, bringing them quickly to Erik's. They stood, grinning foolishly, awkwardly at each other. "A couple of old softies, aren't we?" Michael groused and grabbed him in a warm hug.

"I'm going to miss you, buddy," Erik said thickly.

Michael pulled away, reaching for his bag. "Well . . . so long."

"Thanks, Michael . . . for everything."

Soberly, Michael walked away a few paces, then turned. "I love you, buddy." He dove through the crowd and disappeared.

On the way home, Erik bought a quart of Tequila Gold and made arrangements for a new bottle to be delivered every noon until otherwise notified. He locked himself in his apartment, turning up the steam heat and began methodically to polish off the bottle. Toasting again and again, his multiple losses. Good-bye book, good-bye Shelby, good-bye Michael . . . .

On the afternoon of his fourth straight day of self-torment, his phone rang. Even in his stupor, hope flared that it would be Shelby, blithely announcing her return. A stranger asked, "Is this Erik Lungren?"

"Yes," he groaned, hopes dashed.

"Western Union here. We have a telegram for you. It reads, 'Darling. Stop. Help me. Stop. Desperate. Stop. Have fled. Stop. Am hiding. Stop. Need you at once. Stop. Room 302 Bluebeard Hotel, Falmouth Antigua.' The telegram is unsigned. Would you like a copy?"

Immediately upon hanging up, Erik attempted to reach her by phone. It took precious time to contact the hotel in Antigua. There was no Shelby Cale registered and no one answered in Room 302. He demanded someone go check the room and waited impatiently. The clerk eventually returned to annouce that there was no response to his knock and he refused to open the door until the manager arrived that night. With growing panic, Erik fired off a return telegram to the occupant of Room 302: "Am on my way. Hang on. I love you."

It was after ten P.M. when his plane landed in balmy Antigua. In front of the low-keyed terminal, Erik hailed the first cab in line and slipped the black driver a twenty, promising another just like it if they made it to the Bluebeard Hotel in under ten minutes. The frantic, but speedy ride took closer to fifteen. Erik slapped another twenty into the upturned, pink palm and scrambled out, almost forgetting his flight bag.

The spotlighted hotel, a rambling, whitewashed stone affair, sat among towering palms on a secluded sandy beach. In the courtyard lobby, he hurried to the front desk. After rapid inquires, the answers of which only increased his anxiety, Erik demanded and received direction to Room 302. He ran from the startled desk clerk, through the outside colonnade, around the pool and up two flights of exterior stairs.

Room 302 was at the end of the corridor. He pounded on the door. "It's Erik," he shouted. "Open up!"

There was no response. His fist hammered again. "Shelby!" he called out. Pressing his ear to the door, he could hear nothing. He took three steps backward and ran at the door, hitting it with his shoulder full force. The door groaned on its hinges but held firm. Again he backed off and charged, grunting at the force of the blow. The door splintered and burst open, hurling him to the carpet.

The curtains waved lightly in the breeze from the open window, only a filtered greenish light from the pool area below illuminated the room. But it was enough to see by.

On the large bed, Shelby lay under a sheet, pale and still, her hair covering the pillow like a silken scarf. Rushing to her, he grabbed her naked shoulders. They were cold, lifeless. He yanked her upright—her head, like a heavy stone, dropped back on her neck and his heart leaped from his chest, lodging in his throat. He lowered her to the pillow and snapped on the lamp on the night table. His eyes landed on a brown plastic, pharmaceutical bottle. Instantly he recognized it—her Valium prescription. The one she kept filled to help her fall asleep after a nerve-jangling day. The bottle was empty.

He fell to his knees, tearing the sheet from her. She was wearing a white, gossamer nightgown. He pressed an ear against her left breast, straining to hear, listening through the soft mound for a sign, an indication of life. At first there was nothing, then faintly, dully, he heard a distinct thump. Then, after what seemed an eternity, another beat.

He snatched up the phone receiver, clicking frantically for the hotel operator. A woman's voice answered. "Emergency," he rasped. "Get a doctor to Room 302. Now!" He slammed the receiver down and tore off his jacket. He had to get her under a cold shower. He bent to lift her.

She stirred in his arms, her eyes partially opened and a faint smile tugged her lips. "Y'all have come. How sweet," she murmured and stretched arms above her head as if waking from a deep restful sleep.

A cautious relief flood him. "How many pills did you take?"

"Three, maybe four. I just couldn't sleep. Oh, Erik—"

"The bottle's empty—you're positive how many you took?"

"Of course I am," she insisted drowsily. "I had only a few left."

He looked closely at her pupils—set like bits of gold in a sea of light green. Tears were beginning to flood over the color. "I'm all right," she whispered. "I swear, sugar. I'm fine. Now that y'all're here."

He took a deep, unburdened breath and sank, sitting on the edge of the bed, wrapping his arms around her, pulling her close. "I thought . . . I thought . . ." He couldn't finish.

"Oh, sugar," she cried, her tears wetting his neck with warmth. "I'd never kill myself. Not while y'all still love me." She broke down into a series of soft sobs, burying her face into his shoulder.

"It's okay now, babe," he murmured into her sweet-smelling hair. "I won't let you go. Not now. Not ever."

"Please excuse. You called for a doctor?" a refined voice inquired. In the broken doorway stood an impeccably dressed, elderly, tiny Oriental man carrying a black case. Behind him in the hallway, a handful of guests in their bedclothes clustered in curiosity. "Yes," Erik responded, not releasing her. "Come in, please. I'll fix that door."

Despite her protests, Erik had the doctor thoroughly check her over—taking her pulse, listening to her heart with a stethoscope, testing her reflexes. "I told y'all, I was okay," she yawned when the doctor was finished. Erik thanked the kindly gentleman and gave him the last twenty from his wallet. The doctor bowed formally and withdrew. Erik slipped the chain into the lock to hold closed the splintered door.

"Honestly, sugar. I was just asleep."

"Pretty heavy sleep, babe," he said, toeing off his boots. He suddenly felt exhausted himself. "Your telegram had me expecting the worst."

She tugged him down beside her. "I'm so relieved y'all're with me." She kissed his lips.

His body surged with new energy. "What is it, babe? What happened?"

As if too ashamed to look at him, her eyelashes fluttered, then dropped. They lay on her cheeks like strangely beautiful exotic insects. "It was horrible," she said and at once tears flooded her lashes.

"Don't, babe . . . don't even think about it then."

"I can't help it," she cried. "I felt . . . so humiliated."

"What? Tell me please."

"Shhhh, not another word until you make love to me."

He felt like insisting she tell, but he also ached with desire for her. Slowly he stood, watching her as he removed his clothes. She appeared eager, revived, strangely energized as she pulled off her sheer nightgown. He laid beside her and she was all over him, taking the lead, going down on him, thrusting herself at his tongue urgently until he rolled her over and entered her. He fought to control himself, to prolong the incredibly sweet sensation of being inside her once more.

But she wanted it hard and fast, urging him on with her hips. Lying face to face, one of her legs thrown over him, they rode quickly excited toward their ultimate destination. He waited until she began climaxing then stopped moving altogether, letting her violent internal contractions squeeze and milk him to completion. He came with a deep, contented, fulfilled sigh. "Delicious," she breathed and kissed him passionately.

He returned the kiss, feeling wiped out, heavy with the lack of sleep and the residue of so much booze still in his system. However, he was resolved not to slip off until she had explained her mystery.

As if reading his mind, she said softly, "Y'all will hate me if I tell you."

"How could I, when I love you so much?"

She clung to him for a long time before speaking. "Do y'all really want to know?"

"For God's sake yes, but if you don't want to tell me..."

"I do...and I don't. I'm afraid what your reaction will be."

"If it's painful to say, it'll be painful to hear..." He waited impatiently, determined not to press, fearing the unknown.

"Promise me something."

"Anything."

"Y'all won't blame me for what happened."

"I won't."

"Promise?"

"I promise." He wished the light were on so he could see her face.

A sob broke across the pillow. "Giorgio raped me. It was horrible, I felt so ...so degraded."

It was like she had plunged a hot poker into his chest. He was off the bed, stumbling across the room in the dark before he was aware of his movement. He fumbled for the light and switched it on. She lay curled on her side, tears gushed form her eyes like blood from open wounds.

Rage raked his spine. He exploded with a fist slamming into the wall, crashing his knuckles through the plaster. A brief howl broke from his chest and trying to shake the pain from his hand, he knelt before her and swept her into his arms.

"I'm all right, really, truly," she insisted. "I wasn't hurt physically. It didn't last long. I had too much to drink, had been bored for days. Y'all know I can't drink. I'd laid down to take a nap. I awoke with him...him..."

"Don't...don't say anymore," he said. "You're safe now."

She wept against his chest. "I hate him. Loath him. I never want to see him again in my whole life."

"You won't have to. Never again. If you want, we'll press charges. Have the bastard locked up for good."

"Oh no . . . I couldn't do that. But I'll have to see him," she sobbed. "We just renewed my contract."

Hurling himself away from her again, he stormed to the other side of the room, holding his throbbing right arm at the wrist. "Your Sunny contract's torn up. And if he threatens litigation, I'll kill the sonuvabitch."

"Oh, no . . . no. Then I'd lose you."

"You're not losing me, babe . . . I'm right here. I won't leave. Ever."

"Y'all promise?"

He threw a steel net over his anger and pulled it deep inside. He held her again, forcing himself to speak softly, "Babe, I promise on my mother's soul, I won't leave you. I won't let you be hurt again."

Her lower lip trembled. "But what'll I do if I'm not Sunny?"

"Well . . . for one, you could be my wife."

Her sobs stilled and she raised her head, her eyes growing wide. "Are y'all asking me to marry you?"

"You're damn right I am," he said, surprised at the suddenness of it all. "Marry me, Shelby. I'll do my damnedest to make you happy."

She brightened and wiped her cheeks with her fingertips. "Y'all mean, I won't have to get up at six in the morning and go off for some stupid session while y'all're lolling around in bed?"

"We'll loll together," he said, liking the idea very much.

Laughing lightly, she propped herself up on one elbow. "When do you want to get married?"

"When?"

"How about tomorrow?"

"As soon as we wake up."

She threw her arms around his neck. "Oh yes, yes. That'd be divine." She hugged him close, whispering wetly into his ear, "Mrs. Erik Lungren. Hmmmm, I just love the sound of that."

She laughed easily again and he kissed her hard, marveling at her recuperative powers—how much like a child she was in so many ways. Bouncing back after such a traumatic and degrading experience. God, how he loved her for that.

REBECCA
July 1968
San Francisco

Cross-legged on the buckled linoleum, Rebecca unpacked the box, peeling the newspaper from the mismatched utensils and chipped cups. Her eyes landed on a news photo and her fingers stiffened.

The burly, handsome face of Erik Lungren grinned at her. In a white, double-breasted suit, he looked very tanned and excessively happy. Clinging to his arm was that gorgeous Sunny girl, blessing him with a dazzling smile. She, too, was all in white with little white flowers in her hair. And disgustingly beautiful.

The bottom of the news photo was missing—torn jaggedly just above Erik's right hand which, for some reason, was in a cast. Rebecca began pawing through the crumpled papers, looking for the lost piece. Not finding it, she turned over the ripped page and tried to locate the missing section by matching the movie advertisement for *Bonnie and Clyde* on the back. Near the bottom of the stack, she located it. With a sinking, queasy sensation in her stomach, she read:

SUNNY MARRIES, LOSES TITLE

Shelby Cale, twenty, better known as the Sunny girl, was wed yesterday on the island of Antigua to author Erik Lungren, thirty-one. Today, Villa Caesari announced Mrs. Lungren's contract as *Sunny* had been terminated. It is the first marriage for both.

Rebecca had difficulty reading the date at the top of the photo, her eyes were swimming so with tears. March 21—just seven days after her own nineteenth birthday. Erik had been married for four months and she hadn't even known.

She found herself on her feet, moving toward the room which Scooter had claimed as theirs. In her hand was clutched the news photo. She walked through the living room where Bambi and the new girl were hanging the Che Guevara poster, passed the front bedroom in which Stash, Floyd, and Scooter were weighing out on a small scale a new pound of weed, breaking it into ounces to be sold for twenty bucks a lid. She entered the back bedroom and softly closed the door which was her favorite feature of the new apartment. It offered her much valued privacy in an all too communal lifestyle.

She fell facedown on the bedspread, her head seeking the hollow of her arms. Immediately she began to cry. She did not know why she felt so empty, so alone, but the tears seemed to have found their own reason and kept flowing, dampening the sleeve of her sweatshirt.

The last two months had been such a bummer—not only her relationship with Scooter but the general state of life in the United States seemed to be fast deteriorating: the ongoing war in Vietnam dominated more and more the conversations of the troop and the young people for whom they performed; then there had been the two senseless assassinations in less than two months. Martin Luther King's in April which had triggered those horrendous riots in the black ghettos, then Robert Kennedy's—just hours after he had swept to victory in the California state primary. The photo of his sprawled body in that hotel kitchen had horrified Rebecca. She couldn't understand what was happening in her country or why. It all seemed so hopeless now—idealism, standing up for what one believed, to oppose the mainstream of political thought . . .

She heard the hall door open and quickly tried to swallow her sobs. "What're you bawlin' for now?" Scooter asked behind her. She shook her head, wishing he would just leave her alone for a while.

"What's that?" His hand snatched the news clipping from her.

"Give it here," she demanded, scrambling for it.

"Who's this lovely couple? Lord and Lady Shit-eating Grins?"

"Scooter . . . I'm warning you. Give that back." She rose from the bed, reaching for the piece of newsprint. He dangled it in front of her, taunting, "You know those two? Is that it, huh?" He paused to take a closer look at the photo. "Damned if they don't look like they should be selling sangria in a fuckin' TV commercial."

She ceased her efforts and sat on the edge of the bed. "Scooter, you can be such a royal pain in the ass."

His dark hair in a ponytail, a bushy, full beard obscuring his features, he casually lit a match and intoned, "Thou shalt not have graven images before thee." He set the piece of paper aflame.

He was watching her expression, so she made it as blank as possible, but inside, she hated him at that moment—destroying the one picture she'd ever had of Erik. She rose and headed for the hall. He stepped in front of her and closed the door. "I want to talk to you," he said, his expression solemn.

"I don't feel like talking now."

"Well, I do. You don't feel like doin' anything lately. Moping around here like a spoiled little brat."

"I'm surprised you even noticed."

"Don't get wise ass."

As he was blocking the exit, she returned to the bed and sat cross-legged on it, folding her arms across her middle. She wasn't going to say anything—not as long as he was using that tone. She looked on the bare floor for the ashes of the newsprint.

"Don't ignore me, Rebecca. I'm talking to you."

"You're talking at me. I can't remember the last time we had a real conversation. You always end up yelling, dig?"

"You ever think you might be giving me good reason?"

She glared at him defiant and angry. Just once, she wished she could shout back at him without fearing reprisals.

"There you go again," he sneered. "Withdrawing on me."

"I'm waiting for you to say what's on your mind so I can go take a shower."

He nailed her with a harsh gaze. "I want to start ballin' the others."

"You gotta be kiddin'," she struggled to get out. "But somehow I know you're not."

"Damn right I'm not," he said. "You realize the whole time you've been with us, you haven't once gotten it on with any of 'em?"

"Just you, Scooter. That's enough for me. That's all I want."

He stopped before her and for a second she thought he might slap her again like that horrible night. His eyes narrowed. "Everyone's going down in the whole world with everyone else. And you are still hung up. Like you got some precious jewel jammed up there that no one else can touch."

"Only you Scooter," she said quietly, holding his gaze.

For a while he did not speak and she could tell he was making a real effort to calm down. That raised her hopes. She tried thinking of the good times they'd had together—the evening he'd taken the troop to see *The Graduate*, where the two of them had laughed and necked in the darkness like high-school kids; or that one glorious afternoon which they'd spent all by themselves—window browsing the exclusive shops of Maiden Lane, listening to the Black Panthers harangue the whites in Union Square, having gooey, scrumptious ice cream Sundaes at Blums, talking theater—the roles they'd like to do, the plays they'd like to see performed and by whom.

Now, Scooter sat on the edge of the bed and when he spoke his voice was the gentlest she'd heard since that day. "Look, Rebecca, you're just not getting into the swing of all this. Love is where it's at. You gotta loosen up. Show people you love 'em. Prove to the others you're part of the whole trip. That you're one with the universe. The cosmic consciousness of it all. Otherwise, it's just not going to work out. Life's too short to be hung up on all those hypocritical, bourgeois standards of what's right or wrong. If it feels good, it's right. You just haven't given it a chance."

He looked so forlorn, his narrow shoulders hunched forward, the need oozing out of him like sweet syrup from a bottle, she wanted to reach out and hold him. But she couldn't bring herself to do it. She was afraid he would take it as a sign of her acquiescence. "I do love the others," she said. "Bambi and Sylvia ... even the new guy, Floyd ..."

"And Stash?"

"Yeah," she said begrudgingly, not meaning it—the sight of Stash's porky body with his foul odor turned her stomach. "But not like you, Scooter. None of them like you. My love for you is different. Gimme a break, will you?" She touched his shoulder, yearning for him to turn and hold her.

He did not move. "I want you to come in the front room with me," he began, deadly quiet. "And strip down and join us. Initiate the new members and christen this new pad."

"It's the middle of the afternoon, for cripessake."

"You're undermining the whole spirit of the tribe." Abruptly he stood and she flinched, drawing back. "I'll give you five minutes," he said. "If you're not out then, I'm comin' to get you. We'll show you how much fun your missing." He tossed a meaningless smile and opened the door. "Gotta get rid of these damned doors," he mumbled and walked away.

She sat immobilized, hearing the others laughing in the front room. Stash's ever-present radio turned up high to Steve Miller's "Children of the Future." And the tears started again. Scooter should not ask this of her—not if he really cared for her. Maybe she'd been fooling herself—like she had with Erik.

She pushed herself off the bed. Grabbing her letterman sweater off the nail on the wall, she opened the window to the fire escape and slipped out, closing it behind her. Quietly she climbed down the rusty iron steps and dropped noiselessly the last eight feet to the alley below.

Winded from the steep climb, she pushed the doorbell. From inside, the Byrds were blasting "Eight Miles High." Shortly, the door popped open and Hawk peered down his beak at her, a sly grin forming. "Well, chickee, hello," he crooned. "Whadda ya want? Autograph or ball?"

"Is Silver here?" she asked, uncertain.

"Yup," he replied, his grin fading rapidly. "Well, ya comin' in or goin' stand out there like a refugee from Biafra?" He turned and walked away. She followed him inside, shutting the door behind her. She hesitated in the entryway, the music pounding her eardrums.

Hawk threw a vague finger in the direction of the back of the house. "She's doin' her Earth Mother routine in the kitchen," he shouted, then squinted at her. "Hey, didn't I see you at that Family Dog bash last weekend? You performed, right?"

"Yeah," she yelled, pleased. "I'm with the No-Name Troop."

"Oh yeah, righteous. You get bored back there with mama you come join us." He winked suggestively and sauntered into the big room.

She could see several spaced-out kids lounging about on big, Afghanistan mirrored pillows and recognized some of the members of the band. A few chicks with Cleopatra eye makeup stared back at her competitively. She ducked her head, walking on, led by the smell of cooking food.

Silver, barefoot, in a floor-length grannie dress, was stirring something in a big aluminum pot on the stove. Rebecca warmed at the mere sight of her. "Hi," she greeted from the doorway.

"Hot shit," Silver exclaimed and waved the wooden spoon like a wand. "Jus' in time for breakfast."

"Breakfast? It's almost time for supper."

Silver laughed and dumped some spices into the pot. "Only for straights. Us rockers are jus' gettin' up."

Soon, Rebecca was absorbed in the food's preparations and the constant stream of chatter from her friend. Silver was in an ebullient mood. Early that morning White Meat had wrapped up the last cut on their third album. The record was going to be pressed the following week and released just in time to coincide with their upcoming cross-country tour.

"Gotta hand it to him," Silver chortled. "David sure as hell knows what he's doin'. This time, he's lined up only the big joints. We're even doin' Madison Square Garden. Can you dig it? Me singing' for twenty thousand freaks in the big Apple? Top o' the line, huh?" She hauled the big pot of her "Utah stew" to the long pine table and placed it on a metal trivet. "Hey, you wanna come 'long? Wouldn't that be a gas? I'd love havin' someone to talk to. Half the time I can't relate to the cats in the band. 'Specially on the road. They get so weirded out. It's all that free nookie bein' thrown at 'em. Them groupies make 'em think they're King-Kong or

something. Me? All I get is cats wantin' me to record their song.''
She paused, eyeing her over heart-shaped shades. ''I'm serious,
chil'. Wanna come with me?''

Rebecca shook her head slowly. ''Thanks, but I couldn't let down
the troop. We're picking up paying gigs all the time now.''

''You okay? Seem kinda down. How thing's with that Scooter of
yours?''

''Not so hot . . . I guess . . .''

Silver grabbed a couple of red tin plates and started filling them
from the big pot. ''You an' me is going' for a lil' soul to soul.''

Upstairs, in the bright afternoon sunlight, the two sat on the
curved windowseat of Silver's bedroom and polished off their plates.
Rebecca was surprised at how much she ate and was grateful not to
have to hide her feelings. She spoke openly about what had happened
back at the new apartment and how much it had upset her.

Silver patted her hand. ''Sometimes I think the only thin' that
governs men is their cocks. David is the only dude I know who
ain't.'' She laughed slyly. ''Course, his *other* head keeps him
screwed up.'' She reached into a small, ivory-inlaid box, pulling out
a fat joint. ''Wanna cool out?''

''Oh, I don't think so. Thanks.''

Silver lit a kitchen match by striking her thumb over the end.
Rebecca grew suddenly very focused on the flame. ''I used to know
a writer that could do that,'' she said softly. Thinking of Erik and his
new bride made her insides feel queasy, so when Silver passed the
jay she took a drag and screwed up her nose. ''Whew! This tastes
funny.''

''Hash oil,'' Silver explained. ''The very essence of the very
essence that get's you high. I got me a lil' bottle of it. Cost a fuckin'
fortune but gives good jollies. Anyone can coat the outside of
anythin' an' smoke it an' be sillier than Spiro Agnew on acid.''

They howled for an explosive moment, then fell to serious
smoking in silence, passing the joint back and forth, each curled up
on the tapestry-remnant pillows. The thick glass of the old windows
behind them distorted the picture-postcard view of the city below
and the bay beyond. The sun was low in the sky and peeked in over

Silver's shoulder, backlighting her and bouncing over to brush Rebecca's eyelids.

She leaned her head back against the sill, a drowsy heaviness overtaking her. The Turtles singing "Happy Together" filtered up from somewhere in the house, seemingly from a very far distance. Silver's nearly round room was a perfect retreat, high up in the sky, as if on the side of a mountain—like lying in the hot sun in a meadow of tall grass. Something sweet and aromatic, like spring flowers, hung in the air.

Silver was shaking her shoulder gently. "Com'on, chil', I gotta treat for you."

With difficulty, Rebecca pushed her heavy limbs into a standing position. Her feet felt like weighted lead as she followed her friend out and into the hot steamy bathroom. It smelled like she had walked into a tropical greenhouse—honeysuckle was rampantly in bloom. The huge cast-iron bathtub was full, hills of white froth bubbles oozing over the sides and onto the white tiles like slow-motion lava. In the window, a large piece of antique stained and beveled glass refracted the sunlight, scattering tiny bright rainbows over the tiled walls and floors.

Silver handed her a tall bottle of imported bath oils. "You soak a spell while I check on the boys." And then she disappeared, floating away amidst the rainbows of glowing colors and white tiles.

Moving with great deliberation, fighting to maintain her balance, Rebecca kicked off her jeans and stepped into the hot water, sinking into the frothy whiteness until only her head poked out. The intense heat took her breath away. Slowly growing acclimated, she opened her eyes.

Silver grinned at her from above. "Keep one paw dry," she said, handing over a small blue towel. She lit another joint and sank to sit on the edge of the tub. Rebecca giggled and leaned back, feeling more relaxed than she could remember. It seemed that the heat of the water seeped into her very bones, easing out all the tenseness and drawing away anxieties.

Silver's hand softly passed the joint. Rebecca took another deep puff and forgot the jay was in her fingers. It slipped into the bubbles and sank like a stone. Rebecca frowned with disappointment. "You got a face mask?"

That broke them both up and they laughed hysterically, then fell quiet. Silver was staring down at her with great affection, yet with obvious concern. "Chil', you are so beautiful. You have no idea at'll. I jus' hope the fuckin' you're gettin' is worth the fuckin' you're gettin', if you catch my drift, can you dig it?"

"Rebecca," she heard Silver say from far, far away but could not open her eyes to reply. She was back in the meadow of tall grass again, smelling growing things all around, the sun's heat enveloping her nude body. All was peaceful. From far away, as if at the end of a tunnel, she heard a guy shouting, then harsh, ugly, angry words being yelled back and forth, then pounding footsteps coming upstairs.

"Wha' the fuck's goin' on?" Rebecca heard Silver yell.

Rebecca tried to open her eyes but could only manage a small slit. Dazzling flashes of color momentarily sidetracked her concentration. With a bone-chilling suddenness, a shriek shattered the meadow's silence. It sounded like a wounded animal screaming in pain. Concerned, wanting to help, she raised her head, trying to seek the source of the sound. Dimly she could make out a familiar shape at the far end of the white foothills of bubbles. His beard-fringed mouth was open wide. Again the awful sound shattered the air, assaulting her eardrums. It raised the hackles on her arms.

"Goddamn you, Rebecca," he screamed. "Goddamn you to hell!"

She sat up, terrified. It had been Scooter's voice. She was positive. But here was no one there anymore. The rainbows bounced around the room. Her panic mushroomed. She had to get out of the heat. She tried standing but slipped on the wet porcelain.

"Honey, it's all right. It's cool," Silver reassured from nearby. "Jus' your crazy ol' man. Don' know how'n hell he got up here without one of the dudes stoppin' him. You okay, hon?"

Rebecca whimpered in her frustration to find the way out of the white, frothy water. She threw a wobbly leg over the edge. "I gotta find him," she said. "Something's hurt him bad."

By the time she made it back to the new pad, her anxieties had crystalized into sharp slivers of fear. Still stoned but fighting to maintain control she flung open the door. The first thing she saw was Bambi crying, curled up in a fetal position in front of the cold fireplace. The new black chick, Sylvia, sat lotus-style in the corner looking very blissed out. Stash and Floyd knelt at the coffee table counting out small stacks of paper money.

Scooter did not look up. He sat stiffly on the couch, his head bent toward a stranger—a hard-faced dude with short blond hair cut military fashion. The stranger was speaking earnestly in a low voice, pointing a finger at a piece of paper. Rebecca's first impression was that Scooter was making a dope sale. She stepped forward, closing the door behind her. Scooter glanced in her direction and his expression flickered, then darkened, turning over her stomach with its grim blackness. The stranger had to be a narc—a narcotics officer was busting Scooter!

"What's happening?" she heard herself ask in a small voice. Everyone ignored her and terror kept her from repeating the question. She inched forward.

". . . once there," the hard-faced guy was saying in a dry monotone "contact the last name on the list. Memorize the whole thing and then destroy it. We can't take any chances of it falling into the wrong hands."

Scooter nodded and reached for the larger stack of bills Stash had counted out. He handed it to the stranger and both stood. They shook hands solemnly and the short-haired guy said, "Power to the people." He turned and walked past her without so much as a look. The door opened and shut behind her. Scooter scorched her with another glance and walked out of the room.

"Stash," she whimpered. "What's going on?"

Bambi raised her head to cry mournfully, "He's been drafted."

"Scooter drafted?" Rebecca echoed blankly.

Stash nodded and pocketed the remaining cash. Floyd announced simply, "He's going underground. Tonight."

"Underground?"

Sylvia lurched out of the corner, a vapid gaze in her eyes. "Buddha said, 'Never in this world can hatred be stilled by hatred. Only by non-hatred, this is the law, eternal.' "

Rebecca looked from one to another. This had to be a nightmare—
it wasn't real. It wasn't happening. She was just too stoned to realize
she was still dreaming. She stumbled into the hall. The door at the
far end was closed. She pushed it open.

Scooter's head jerked up from the canvas knapsack on the bed.
"Get out," he ordered. "I don't ever want to see you again."

"Wha'? Scooter, what's wrong, man?"

Turning his back, he grabbed a pair of wool socks and stuffed
them into the knapsack. He started rolling up a pair of patched jeans.

"Scooter? Talk to me, dammit. What's going on?"

Angrily he forced the jeans into the mouth of the knapsack. She
ran forward, grabbing his arm, trying to get him to look at her. He
jerked free, whirling with such ferocity, she fell back.

"You goddamned starfucker," he snarled. "Wouldn't get it on
with your own people. Oh no. But you'll go and fuck someone with
a big name."

The pain was so intense she could barely breathe. "What're you
talkin' about?"

"How long've you been going over there, huh? Behind our
backs? Ballin' all the rock stars." He grabbed the straps of the
knapsack and threw it over his shoulder. "Shit, if Stash hadn't
followed you and seen you going into their big fuckin' mansion, I
wouldn't've known where the hell to track you down." He swung
back to her, accusing. "Just to tell you what's been dumped on me.
A goddamn draft notice! And what do I find when I get there? A
goddamned stoned starfucker flashing her stuff in the tub. Were you
waitin' for the band to join you? Goddamned fuckin' hypocrite!" He
plowed out of the room.

She ran after him. "It wasn't like that. Scooter . . . you gotta
believe me."

In the living room, he threw open his arms, drawing the others to
him. Even Stash had tears in his eyes. Scooter hugged them and
broke away.

"Peace, brother," Stash mumbled, flashing two grubby fingers.
Bambi sobbed, "We'll follow you." Scooter shook his head violently.
"Too risky. We'll all get busted. This is my trip. Stay here.

Continue with the troop." Sylvia pressed something into his hand. "My Tibetan amulet," she murmured. "It will ward off evil spirits."

"Scooter," Rebecca moaned, moving to him. He avoided her, heading for the door. He was through it before she could reach him.

She darted into the outside hall, her head swimming, her chest constricted. "Wait! Scooter, wait!" He did not look back as he loped down the stairs. They reeled before her, swaying like a rope bridge over a deep chasm. She forced herself down them, hanging onto the wooden banister for support. "Scooter!" she screamed.

Far below, she heard the street door slam. Struggling for balance, the walls pressing in on her, she scrambled awkwardly down the last flight and rushed for the main entrance.

Outside, the sidewalk was crowded, the lights of the storefronts blinding. For a horrifying moment, she thought she had lost him. Then she spotted his ponytail swinging in the distance, disappearing rapidly toward the corner. She tried to run, but she kept stumbling into people. Her eyes were clouded with tears, blurring everything into a grotesque mirrored funhouse, confusing her, terrifying her all the more. She had to get to him. To explain. To attempt to rid herself of the overwhelming sense of guilt and shame that weighed down her shoulders, impeding her progress.

She reached the corner and rounded it. A half block away, he was about to board a city bus. "Scooter," she shouted, racing for him. Her fingers skimmed his jacket as he stepped up through the opening. "Please no . . . no," she pleaded. "Oh God, don't do this to me. Please, don't . . ."

He shifted forward without looking back and the door closed in her face. "Scooter," she screamed. It tore from the depth of her bowels wrenching her insides, doubling her up.

The bus pulled away, leaving her on the curb. Her last glimpse of him was the back of his head, his ponytail swinging as he sat down. Her breath abandoned her. She sank to the pavement, a gaping emptiness where her heart had been.

DAVID
August 1968
San Francisco

In his corner office, he eyed his chunky assistant in the tight Nehru jacket. "You get the release dates for Cobalt Blue worked out with distribution?"

Artie nodded his double-chins. "And with the art department."

"I don't want it coming out on top of White Meat's live one." Without removing his hands from his pockets, David sank into his desk chair. "How about the gross for last night's gigs?"

Artie handed him neatly typed column of figures. David leaned over them, calculating, judging the total box-office receipts for three of his groups' concerts the evening before: Cobalt Blue raked in $93,000 in Detroit; Home Free tallied $67,000 in Philly, while the Tunnel/White Meat joint concert in Phoenix came in with a satisfying $112,000. He looked up, a frown creasing his brow. "What the hell happened to Home Free? They should've been closer to eighty." His intercom buzzed and he snatched up the receiver. "Yeah?" His secretary informed him that Dixon Shaw was on line two. He hit the button. "Good morning, Dixon. Where are you?"

"London," came the reply.

"Then I should've said, good evening," David said smoothly, putting his feet up on his desk. "What can I do for you?" He and Dixon had become quite intimate in their dealings lately. The headman for AII had been more than pleased by RPM's remarkable financial turnabout.

"I have a report in my hand that I find most disturbing," Shaw said, his voice as clear as if he were in the next room. "I consider it a serious breach of our working relationship."

David lowered his feet to the carpet. "What is it?" With growing anxiety, he listened to his mentor, then said in his most deferential manner, "Dixon, I swear I knew nothing of this. I'll handle it at once and get back to you."

"File a report with my assistant," Shaw said coldly and rang off.

David shot out of his chair, barking, "Goddamned Silver. I want to talk to her. Artie where're they?"

"Dallas. The Sheraton."

David relayed the information to his secretary and waited for her to buzz him back. He walked to the window and snapped the venetian blinds closed, plunging the room into semidarkness. "That bitch," he muttered. "Know what she did last night? From the stage in Phoenix? Urged the kids to burn their draft cards and actively demonstrate against the war. Instead of an encore, she got them chanting, 'Hell no, we won't go.'" He thought for a moment, then exploded anew, "What kind of screwed-up organization is this? How does Shaw all the way fuck over in London hear about this before I do? Somebody's ass is going to burn for this, Artie. Believe me."

His secretary buzzed. "I have Silver's room in Dallas. There's a Rebecca on the line."

He grabbed the receiver. "Where the hell's Silver?"

"She's resting right now," a quiet voice answered. "She's wiped. I don't think she can make it tonight, David."

"Who the hell are you? Do I know you?"

"Yeah . . . we've met a couple of times," Rebecca responded. "I'm a friend of Silver's."

"Well, look, Rebecca . . ." He tried to place a face to the name. "I want to speak to Silver. Like now. Put her on."

"She just got to sleep," the chick answered, her voice like a child's. "I'm not kiddin', she's in rough shape. I think she's burned herself out. Twenty-eight concerts in less than three weeks is just too much. If she could just get a full night's sleep—"

"She's booked for tonight," he cut in. "And this afternoon. We're recording both concerts today. A live, double-album. Besides, she's not even half through the tour. When it's over—then she can sleep. I don't want to ask you again. Put her on."

"I can't. I just can't wake her. She hasn't slept more than six hours in the last four days. If I—"

"Goddammit! I want to talk to her."

There was a long silence on the other end and he thought he'd won. However, the chick came back with a thin, determined tone, "I'll have her call you as soon as she wakes up. I'm sorry."

"Not half as sorry as when I'm done with you," he shouted and hung up loudly. "Goddamn chicks!" He threw open the door, startling his secretary in her alcove. "Book me the next flight to Dallas."

It was during the afternoon flight that David read of his father's promotion. On the front page of the *L.A. Times* provided in first-class section, under the lead stories of the Soviet invasion of Czechoslovakia and the Democratic convention in Chicago, there was a touched-up photo of Irving with the headline: DYER TO HELM PACIFIC.

David quickly read the article. Irving had been upped by Pacific Pictures' board of directors, from senior executive world operations officer to president of the board and the studio. Irving was quoted as predicting a rosy future for the smallest of Hollywood's major studios.

David carefully refolded the newspaper and stuck it out of sight in the cloth pocket before him. It galled the hell out of him to think of Irving's achievement while he, himself, was still having to kiss ass with Shaw. He was all too aware that Silver's latest rebellion had dangerously jeopardized his own career. Allied Industries—after the recent Republican party's convention in Miami—was listed as a major contributor to Nixon and Agnew's record-breaking, campaign war chest.

Upon landing at the Dallas' Love Field, David took a cab the seventeen-miles to Fort Worth's Tarrant County Convention Center. On the way, he mulled over various strategies he might have to use with Silver. Although he knew the afternoon concert had already started, he was unprepared for what greeted him backstage.

His live album was going down the toilet. White Meat's sound was sluggish, spiritless and what was worse, Silver's singing was abysmal—it lacked vitality and punch, as if she were singing under the influence of downers. David pushed closer to the drape wings of the stage.

Centerstage, the mike cord wound around her like a snake, Silver hung on to the mike stand, her body lifeless under the black lamé pants-suit. Sweat poured off her and her dark sunglasses kept slipping down her nose. She repeatedly shoved them up with a nervous gesture. And her voice appalled him. Gone totally was that magical power and strength which had captured legions of admirers, young and old.

She was trying to belt out above the band, a bluesy talk/ jazz song; "Which of us ain't thrown the first stone?/ Which of us ain't stoned the first throw/ And which of us ain't had the guts/ the courage to stand up an' shout/ I love you, man/ That's/ What it's all about."

David was vividly conscious that above her the suspended microphones were capturing her every breath on eight-track audiotape in the 18-wheel soundtruck outside. Seventy-five grand it had cost him to insure that only the very latest and best equipment with the industry's top sound engineers would record these two concerts. And what were they getting? Worthless, amateurish crap.

The band, led by a sour-faced Hawk, struggled valiantly to punch home the final chorus, but the result was pathetic—as if they had been infected with the same lethargic virus Silver had caught. The song ground to a ragged halt and was over. He checked out the audience visible inside the light bouncing from the stage.

Instead of the usual crowd pressing, flesh on flesh, against the raised stage, only a handful were present and they looked so wasted, he figured they didn't care if Silver sang the Supremes' hits in Swahili. Beyond them, the first rows were visible. Those faces reflected keen disappointment and their applause was as perfunctory and dulled as the performance. A few loud boos erupted above the clapping and some bold hecklers were loudly jeering. One redneck-looking teenager jumped on the arms of his seat, yelling, "Rip off!" Others echoed it.

With a defiant pout, Silver leaned against the wall of amplifiers near David and eyed the crowd over the rims of her dark glasses.

Her chest heaved with deep arrhythmical breaths. She raised the hand mike, rasping into it, "And the same to you motherfuckers." That only increased the amount of booing. Irate whistles, shrill and discordant, swept the huge, circular hall, topped by the stamping of thousands of feet. The audience's anger, hostility and frustration began to peak.

David called to the stage manager, "Get her off. This concert's over."

The jeers, boos and stomping feet increased as the band hustled off stage. Silver dragged herself into the shelter of the curtain wings, caught sight of David, and immediately crumpled to the floor like a broken sack of flour.

A melodramatic cop-out, he thought at once. She's too ashamed to defend herself. Out of the circle of curious on-lookers, a face, vaguely familiar to David appeared. The chick, with straight, long, raven black hair and beaded headband, looked as though she wanted to be an American Indian. Kneeling she threw a supporting arm around Silver and locked eyes with him in open animosity.

The audience coutinued roaring. David jerked his head to the stage manager. "Get Silver back to the hotel. And I want the band out of here in two flat."

"Shouldn't we cancel tonight's concert?"

"Like hell we will."

David had to knock loudly four times before anyone answered Silver's hotel room door. The small-boned, hippie-Indian chick opened it, her cheeks darkening with blood at the sight of him. He brushed past her into the foyer and swung back. "You're Rebecca, right?"

She nodded, eyeing him apprehensively through the fringes of her bangs. He got the distinct feeling she did not trust him. From the bedroom, behind him, he could hear a television set playing quietly. He jerked his head to the closed door of the two-room suite. "How's she doing?"

Rebecca shrugged. "You saw for yourself. She's wiped out." Her voice, though small, was filled with challenge.

He met her steady gaze, trying to determine how he could use her to get what he wanted. If she were Silver's close friend, she might come in handy. He tore his eyes from her and entered the dimly lit bedroom.

Her head raised by a pillow, Silver lay flat on her back on one of the two large beds. Her still-damp hair was slicked back against her head. She wore only a puce-colored chenille robe, her feet pointing upward like two pale signposts. She kept her eyes on the color TV set opposite her. At the Democratic convention, Eric Severeid was interviewing a delegate with an Ohio button.

"I want to talk with you," David said to Silver. "Alone."

"Have no energy to listen," she droned.

Like a dark shadow, Rebecca slipped between them and sat on the side of the bed. "She can't go on tonight. She needs rest."

"Let me be the judge of that," he said and pulled a slip of paper out of his white-linen sports coat. He held it out to Rebecca. "Do me a favor, kid. Run down to the lobby and call this doctor. Mention my name and tell him to come check Silver out. Right away."

Rebecca hesitated, not taking the phone number. Silver waved it away with a limp hand. "I ain't havin' no strange sawbones checkin' me out. I jus' wanna sleep. But I can't."

"Maybe you should see him," Rebecca said quietly. "He might prescribe something to make it easier."

"She's right," David added. "Won't hurt to find out what's wrong."

"I know wha's wrong," Silver muttered. "It's ain't no fun singin' for a bunch of freaks who don' appreciate wha' you're doin'. You starve for years. Everybody loves ya. You start makin' it an' they scream you sold out. Well, fuck tha' shit."

"What the hell are you talking about? Who says that?"

"Didn'cha read *Rollin' Stone*," Silver said, her eyes rolling to look at him for the first time. "Their review of our L.A. gig?"

"Who the hell cares what they say? Critics always dump on success. Makes them feel pure and powerful."

"I care," Silver wailed, her feet locking together at the toes.

Rebecca stood, her hand out. "I'll make that call."

He gave her the slip of paper and waited until she had gone.

Without her in the room, for some reason, he felt more sure of himself. He went to the TV and switched it off.

"I was watchin' that," Silver said tightly.

"And I want to talk," he countered.

"So talk. But I warn you . . . my ears're kinda stuffed up."

He chose his words and tone carefully. "You've let me down again."

"I'm sick, man. Can'cha see?"

"The doctor will determine that. What I'm talking about is potentially more destructive." He moved on to complete the circle of the room. "Remember how you begged me not to fire Hawk and Larry? How you pleaded with me for days to keep them on? How you promised you would follow everything I said, to the letter, from then on if I reconsidered?"

"I ain't done nuthin' wrong," she said with a noticeable quiver.

"You've deliberately defied me."

"For Chrissakes, stop pacin' aroun'. You're makin' me seasick."

He halted at the foot of the bed, letting her have it with both barrels. "*The Phoenix concert*," he thundered. "You led them chanting, 'One, two, three, four' we don't want your goddamned war' for fifteen minutes!"

She flopped over on her side, her knees drawing up to her chest. She hugged them, her back a thin rack of bones under the old bathrobe.

He leaned over her. "How can I trust you anymore?"

She began to weep, heavy, deep, convulsive sobs wrenched her. He let her continue for a moment then walked around to the other side of the bed, squatting down so his face was level with hers. "*I want an answer, dammit!*"

She pulled back, her eyes popping open, wide with fright. "Awlright," she sobbed. "I did it. I did it. An' I'm sorry, David. I won' do it no more. I promise."

He stood wearily, lowering his voice but not its intensity. "What can I do except disband the group?"

A bright vivid red began raising up her neck, like a thermometer. "Please, please don' break us up. I'll go on tonight. I promise man . . ."

"Actions, Silver . . . actions weigh more than words."

"Oh gawd, David, I feel . . ." She fell back flat on the bed, clutching the robe closed. "So empty . . . empty inside. The well is dry. I can't go to the well no more . . . nuthin' to draw from . . ."

"That's bullshit and you know it."

"It ain't, it' ain't. I jus' don' have it no more." She stared bleakly overhead. "An' if I have to look at one more spangled cottage-cheese ceiling like this—I'll jus' curl up an' die."

He signed in exasperation and settled himself into the armchair beside the bed. The room was dreary—like all other hotel and motel rooms across the country. He knew from accompanying them on their first tour, how monotonous and draining life on the road could be; airpot terminals, limo rides, interchangeable streets, hotel lobbies, motel rooms and junk-food diets. But it was all a means to an end. A necessity. To him, anything was bearable as long as it got him closer to what he wanted. Just a point of view.

He began talking softly, as if to himself. "The only thing I admire in this whole damned business is a professional—a pro. Someone who does the job the best to their ability time after time after time. Never sluffing off. Giving their all. Demanding as much from themselves as they do from others. Even more from themselves. Someone who delivers the goods regardless of their personal or emotional state. That's a pro. And they're damned few of them in the business. Look at all the groups—the singers who've come and gone in a flash. One hit and that's it. Because they didn't have the discipline, the taskmaster inside, the hunger. Amateurs. Gutless amateurs who deserve to fail." He hesitated, shifting modes.

"You can call me hard-nosed, testy slave driver," he continued, learning forward on his knees. "But I deliver, I'm a pro, Silver. I take pride in that fact. I drive myself harder than I push others. And if you can't take it—if you don't want to be a pro—if you want to slip on down the backside of the ladder we've climbed together—go back to being a crybaby amateur—then you better tell me, right not. Because I am not going to coddle you anymore, or nurse you along every step of the way. From now on, you have to pull your own weight. You're either a pro or not. Which is it?"

She was staring at him with eyes so full of tears their blueness was all but washed away. "I wanna be a pro," she cried. "I do. I really do." She gulped in air to wail, "But I ain't got no more energy."

"Energy comes from the mind, Silver." He tapped his skull slowly. "The mind. Now you either get your head screwed on straight or we'll call it quits right now. I don't have time to play these games."

The sobs began again in earnest and he cursed silently her weakness. He was ready to wash his hands of her, to cancel the rest of the tour, to disband the group and concentrate on the other performers in his stable of talent—the pros. She must have realized his seriousness for she sat up, rubbing her eyes with two fists. "Help me, David," she said between sobs. "Jus' this once. An' I'll never let you down again, I swear."

He waited in the foyer while the hip, young doctor in the mod-golfing attire examined Silver. Afterward in the hall outside, the long-haired Texan gave his report for David's ears along—Silver was suffering from acute physical and mental exhaustion. David made a discreet inquiry, received the answer he was looking for, handed over some money and made arrangements to meet the doctor backstage just before White Meat's concert.

A half hour before their scheduled appearance, David, who had been keeping track via telephone of the progress of the warm up band, Tunnel, hustled a still listless Silver out of the hotel lobby and through the mob of fans who had been unable to obtain concert tickets. At the sight of the rock queen, they pressed forward, calling her name, flashbulbs exploding, autograph books stuck out aggressively. He waved them away and shoved ahead, one arm gripped tightly around her reed-thin waist. He deposited her inside the rear of the first limousine and checked to see if the rest of the group were piling into the second. Satisfied, he ducked inside next to her. She came alive for a brief flurry. "Where's Rebecca?"

"Here I am," the black-eyed girl said, scrambling in to pull down one of the jumper seats facing them. "Sit next to me," Silver insisted and slid over against him. "Move it," he growled to the driver. The fans were pressing up against the windows, calling,

waving, jostling the heavy vehicle. The car inched forward following the police motorcycle escort. With sirens screaming mournfully
in front of them, the limo began picking up speed. He looked
behind. The second limo was on their tail. So far so good.

Throughout the whole twenty-minute trip to Fort Worth, Silver
leaned on Rebecca's shoulder, eyes closed, like she were a survivor
of Auschwitz, he thought. Via the limousine radio phone, David was
able to time their own arrival just as Tunnel started their first
encore.

At the convention center's rear stage entrance, inside the police
barricades and the eight-foot-high wire mesh storm fence, David
handed over Silver to the stage manager to take to the subterranean
dressing room while he checked the set up in the mobile recording
studio. Those details absorbed him totally until the last possible
minute.

Then, as scheduled, David met the young doctor in the corridor
outside the dressing rooms. A local deejay had referred the doc to
David and had indicated that the recent returnee from Nam and the
Army Medical Corps was understanding, with-it and would keep his
mouth shut. David greeted the medic warmly, noting that in his
fringed-buckskin outfit the Doc looked like a hip Wyatt Earp.
Together, they walked down the long corridor under the stage. The
muffled roar of the enthusiastic audience above echoed down the
cement block walls. The pungent smell of marijuana smoke lingered
everywhere. He rapped once on Silver's door and entered.

She and her friend sat hunched before a portable black-and-white
TV set. Silver looked up with a shocked, bewildered expression.
"David, come here an' check this out," she said in a rush. "There's
a fuckin' police riot goin' on in Chicago."

"I can't believe it, I can't believe it," Rebecca kept repeating,
transfixed by the tube's action. Her face was drained of color.

"We've got five minutes," David reported, glancing at the set.
Helmeted police were charging into a taunting herd of chanting,
young demonstrators, many of whom were wearing football and
motorcycle helmets. He nodded to the doctor. "Get it ready."

The bare, antiseptic dressing room suddenly reverberated with an
explosion of grief from Rebecca. "Oh, my God," she groaned,

doubling over, hugging herself. "Did you see that? That cop? He billyclubed that kid from the back. Knocked him right down. Did you see it? Look . . . look! That kid with the ponytail on the ground. That cop's still hitting him! I can't believe this is happening . . ."

"Reminds me of the Selma days," the young medic drawled and stuck the hypodermic needle into a small, glass vial.

Silver patted Rebecca gently. "Honey, don' fret. He's not there. Jus' keep tellin' yourself that. Scooter ain't there."

"But he could be," Rebecca moaned into her hands. "He could be. My God, aren't they going to stop this?"

"Silver," David called. "Come here."

"What's that?" she asked. "I don' like no needles."

Rebecca swiveled in her chair, her mouth popping open with disbelief. "You're not going to shoot her up?"

"Roll up your sleeve," David ordered.

Silver approached, eyeing the needle apprehensively but baring one thin, pale arm.

Rebecca piped up, "Silver, you're not going to let them do this?"

"Shut up," he snapped.

"It's just a Vitamin B-twelve combo shot," the doctor assured, dabbing moist cotton on Silver's forearm. "Nature's pick-me-up."

"Silver," Rebecca pleaded. "You don't know what's in that. Are you going to take their word for it?"

"I told you to shut up," David said. "If not, get out."

Silver smiled uneasily. "Honey, it's cool. Jus' a few vitamins to git my energy up. Ain't that so, doc?"

Rebecca suddenly darted forward, grabbing the doctor's arm. "No. You can't do this!"

"Hey, easy, sister," the young medic said.

David clamped a hand firmly on Rebecca's wrist, yanking her away. "I told you to shut the fuck up." He held her until the needle had entered the vein and the plunger had been pressed all the way down. Silver's eyes closed and an odd smile parted her lips. Rebecca jerked free, darting forward again. She swiped at the needle, clasping it, then licking her fingers.

"That's speed," she hissed at David. "You asshole! You going to shoot her up in New Orleans too? And Miami? You going to have a

Doctor Feelgood waiting in the wings every time she steps off stage? Is that your way of helping her?''

"You don't listen very well. I told you twice to shut your trap. This is none of your goddamned business.''

Silver laughed, a low smoky, dirty cackle. Carefully she rolled down the white sleeve of her minidress, chuckling to herself. "Man, oh, man, is that some stuff. Mother Nature helpin' ol' mother earth herself.''

The doctor smiled, packing away his equipment into the small leather case. "How do you feel, Miss Silver?''

She grinned lewdly. "Slicker than hammered pig shit. Hey buck-skin Doc, you're as cute as a baby's butt. Wha'cha doin' after the show?''

Rebecca was watching her with an expression of great sorrow, then turned slowly away and moved to sit in front of the TV set, riveting her eyes on the screen, her posture wooden. David shook hands with the doctor and slipped him a couple of tickets to prime box seats. "Thanks, doc.''

"Anytime, my friend," he replied and winked at Silver. "Give 'em hell, baby. That's what they came for." He started for the door.

She winked suggestively. "You stick aroun' afterward an' I'll give you some hell too.''

"I brought my wife." He waved and ducked out.

"Hell, bring her too, if you ain't chickenshit," she called after him, then leaped to the mirror, grabbing a hairbrush. "Look at this ol' puss. She looks a fright." She began attacking the mop of frizzy hair with enormous gusto, singing softly to herself.

David smiled at her reflection and, with one last sour glance at Rebecca, ducked out to check if everything was ready.

Pleased with the crowd's reception of his opening band, David decided backstage to give Tunnel one more encore, they deserved it, they were pros. Next he accompanied them to the sound truck to hear a test recording of their last numbers. He jawed with them for a moment, riding on their energy for a while, then when all was ready and the crowd ripe with anticipation, David returned down the underground passageway to the dressing rooms. Opening her door, he heard Silver screaming hoarsely, "Them mutherfuckers! Them gawdamned, shit-eatin', mutherfuckin' pigs!"

She crouched over the TV set, wildly gesturing her arms. The night scene on the tube looked to him like an eerie battlefield on a Hollywood movie set—bright lights flooded a city street bordering a park. Rows of shield-bearing, gas-masked police marched down the center of the street, advancing on a group of rock-throwing demonstrators. Clouds of tear gas wafted over them. "Get them dirty pigs!" Silver shouted, waving a fist at the screen.

"Silver, you're on!"

She sputtered at him, a steely, unnatural glint in her eye, "It ain't right, David. Our people are gettin' hurt out there. They're jus' kids, man. An' it's a fuckin' war. The revolution has done arrived!"

He snapped off the set and took her arm. "I want no bullshit up there," he warned. "Not one word about this, you understand?" He squeezed her arm sharply to drive home his point.

Rebecca jumped up. "Silver, you've got to stand up against this. Send your support to those kids in Chicago. Let the kids here know what's going on."

He tightened his grip on his star, shoving her toward the door. "Get out," he yelled at Rebecca. With difficulty, he managed to steer a bewildered but feisty Silver into the corridor, moving her down it quickly.

"Silver," Rebecca cried behind them. He could hear her running footsteps catching up to them. He pushed through the double-doors and roughly pulled Silver up the stairs to the backstage area. Milling people held back their progress, gawking at them—sound men, roadies in charge of the equipment, lighting men, press, local deejays, chicks already stashed away for fun-and-games after the concert. Out front the keyed-up audience clapped in unison, chanting, "We want Silver! We want Silver!"

The closer they walked to the source of the sound, he could feel in her arm an electric energy beginning to pulse. Hawk appeared beside them, matching their steps. "How ya doin', mama?"

"Hot, man," she rasped. "Hot as a pistol an' ready to fire."

Hawk grinned, "Jus' lead the way, mama. Jus' lead the way."

The pitch and intensity of the audience's shouting sent palpable waves of energy backstage. David shoved the dark glasses into Silver's hands. She was slipping them on, jiggling on one foot, when Rebecca showed up. "Silver," she begged. "You can't ignore what's goin' down in Chicago. This is a turning point . . . they need our—"

He lashed out, pushing Rebecca away and shoving Silver to the wings, facing the stage. He stood behind her, hands on her hips, speaking into her ear. "They're waiting for you, Silver. Listen to them. Your fans, Silver. They love you. They're with you. You're a pro. You won't disappoint them."

Her body coiled under this touch, her head bobbed. "I hear 'em, man. Jus' listen to 'em. I'm ready. Let me at 'em."

He signaled and the stage plunged into darkness. Quickly the other members of the band rushed on, plugging in their instruments. The audience roared in anticipation. He held onto Silver who strained to be released. "Ladies and Gentlemen," the stage manager shouted into the backstage mike, "WHITE MEAT!" The lights shot up, the band hit their first powerful chords, the audience screamed as one.

Only then did David let her go. She rushed out, a deafening roar shook the stage. She grabbed the mike from its stand, tossed the cord over one shoulder and bounced forward grinning. She pranced in rhythm to the driving beat of the band behind her and danced to the stage lip. Right on the nose, she threw back her head and let forth a piercing shriek. It soared over the band and the clamorous crowd, then dipped magnificently into the first verse: "Hey, all you chil'ren/ hey, all you fiends/ We're here to rock/ an' to feed your dreams!"

A glow of satisfaction began to effuse him. This was the old Silver—packing an incredible wallop with each gut-wrenching note. She was bouncing around the stage like a live wire, her hips wiggling shamelessly under the tiny mini-skirt. She was electrifying. And the sound of the band was gutsy, raw, dirty, powerful.

He turned to handle one last bit of annoying business. He found her huddled on the steps leading to the basement passage. He tapped her on the shoulder. She looked up with huge, questioning and hostile eyes. "You're off the tour, as of now," he shouted over the din.

"But Silver—" Rebecca began in protest. He cut her off. "This is my show," he yelled. "And I don't want to see your face ever again. You're a drag on my star. I want you out. Now!" He pulled her roughly to her feet and shoved fifty dollars into her hand. He manhandled her toward the backdoor. Offering only token resistance, she tried to catch a glimpse of Silver through the curtains.

The haunted look in her eyes as Rebecca disappeared left him with a strange, disquieting feeling. It took several minutes in the box office counting out the hefty gate receipts before he could shake it.

Book Three

1971–1973

SHELBY
February 1971
New York

Breezing through the lobby of the Plaza Hotel, she yanked off the beige mink hat and tossed her head impatiently, freeing her hair to tumble to the shoulders of her matching fur coat. She paused at the entrance to the Palm Court, surveying the assembled diners until she spotted her. Sitting alone at a far table under a drooping palm frond, her mother tensely held a cigarette in one hand, a highball in the other. Shelby hurried to her, ignoring, but aware of, the stir her entrance was creating.

Beth Ann smiled wanly. "Hello, dear. You're late."

She sank into the opposite chair. "Today is absolutely impossible. I wish y'all'd give me more notice next time. I have to be back by two." She shucked off her mink and picked up the menu. She was famished.

"You've gained weight, haven't you dear?"

Shelby made a point of smiling disinterestedly and studied her mother. Beth Ann looked marvelous—for her age. The little tucks to get rid of the bags under the eyes and chin had worked wonders. The severe French roll had been replaced by a softer, shorter wave, the gray disappearing with a lighter, overall tone. But Beth Ann's eyes were anxious, reproachful.

She was explaining to Shelby, "There was a cancellation at the Columbia Clinic. Evangeline insisted we fly up to take advantage of it."

Dutifully, Shelby asked, "How is she?"

"If she were one of her horses, she'd have herself shot." Her mother broke into a self-conscious laugh and ordered another bourbon and branchwater.

Shelby made no further inquires about Evangeline. Her grandmother had not seen, spoken to or communicated in any manner with Shelby since the marriage. At least Beth Ann made an effort once a year, but only out of a sense of maternal obligation, Shelby felt.

Throughout lunch, Shelby kept up her side of the boring, meaningless conversation, the recent earthquake in L.A. which had claimed so many lives—Beth Ann insisted it was six hundred or more, Shelby recalled it was closer to sixty—to how much Alan Shepard's wife, on TV after his moonwalk, looked like Cousin Naomi.

Shelby refused to volunteer any information about her life, although she did speak at length about the extensive remodeling of the house she had purchased in Connecticut after landing the highly lucrative Lincoln/Mercury TV commercials.

While Beth Ann picked at her food, Shelby polished off her Oysters Rockefeller, then glanced at her Rolex diamond wristwatch. "I've got to dash. It's been so sweet seeing y'all again."

"Shelby," Beth Ann said hurriedly. "I had breakfast this morning with Giorgio. He's in an absolute snit."

"Isn't he always?" She pulled on her fur.

"Y'all know how terribly fond he is of you. How he always looked after your interests." Beth Ann took another nervous sip of her drink.

"His interests, mother." She prepared to stand. "I've really got to run. We have to finish this shoot today."

Beth Ann bent and brought up a folded newspaper. "He showed me this," she said gravely and handed it over.

Shelby glanced at the indicated column. "I never read Suzy Knickerbocker. Silly gossip."

"I suggest y'all read it now. Before it's too late."

Shelby sighed and quickly read the lead paragraph. She glanced up with a look of hurt and disappointment. "Surely, mother y'all can't believe this refers to me? I'm happily married, thank you, very much."

"Are you?"

"But of course," she replied, a little too forcefully. "And I resent

Giorgio's implying this...this trash is about me." She stood. "Mother, I'm twenty-three years old. I'm perfectly capable of taking care of my own life. Without interference from anyone, especially Giorgio Caesari."

"We're only concerned for your welfare, Shelby Ann."

"Yes, I'm sure y'all are." Shelby bent to peck her mother's newly tucked cheek. "Now, don't worry, I'm doing fabulously, y'hear? Bye-bye." She tossed a small wave with an accompanying smile and strode away. At the lobby's newsstand, she bought a copy of the same newspaper and reread the item several times in the cab. By the time she reached the commercial film studio on Ninth Avenue, she was seething.

She marched directly into the large studio abuzz with activity and sped up the backstairs. She found him bent over a moviola machine with the film editor. She switched on the overhead light.

Jacques swiveled in annoyance, his mature, handsome visage softening. "Our princess has arrived," he began, oozing his more than ample charm. "Come, look. See how beautifully I have captured you."

"I want to speak with you," she said and waited for the editor to slip out of the room. She closed the door behind him and slammed the folded newspaper on top of the moviola. "You bastard, you promised."

Jacques perused the lead paragraph and swung back, all innocence. "*Ma chérie*, I have no idea."

She snatched up the paper, reading aloud, "According to her famous director, a super model is rehearsing in the wee hours while hubbie slaves away in hibernation." Again she slapped down the paper. "You swore you wouldn't breathe a word."

"*Chérie*, I haven't. Believe me. That item could be referring to a half-dozen models, no?"

"How many super models do you know with a husband who slaves away in hibernation?"

His face was a putty of confusion.

"It's finished with us," she said, biting off her words. "We're going downstairs now—wrapping up today's shoot as if nothing has happened. But I'm warning you, Jacques, I won't work with you again."

"But, *chérie*, we're both contracted for three more."

"I'm contracted for three," she said. "Need I remind you, I have approval of all my above-the-line personnel." She pranced out.

True to her word, Shelby sailed, seemingly carefree, through the rest of the day's filming. She joked with the crew, teased the hairdresser, flirted with the account exec, handled her professional duties with her usual style and aplomb, being appropriately seductive before the carmeras in her bugle-beaded Ungaro designer gown. Jacques remained deferential throughout and shortly after six, he called a wrap of her second commercial for Chanel perfume. She returned to her dressing room with Larry, the dapper account exec from the advertising agency.

While she changed into her street clothes, behind a folding screen, Larry waxed on and on how wonderfully everything was going and how much he was looking forward to next week's shooting. She let him continue until she was ready to leave then bussed him lightly on the cheek. "I'm afraid we'll need a new director for the remaining three," she said sadly. "I find Jacques terribly difficult to work with. I'm sure we can find someone more sensitive. Have a fab weekend." She left Larry dumbfounded.

The 6:48 train from Penn Station to Darien was bitterly cold, dirty and crowded with commuters. In a rancid smoking car, she sat bundled in her fur coat and cap, hair tucked up out of sight, dark glasses further helping her from being recognized. In agitated discomfort, she smoked—a habit she'd picked up since living with Erik—watching the snow-covered scenery pass, listening to Wall Street executives discussing with surprising heat Nixon's announced trip to China.

She cursed herself for not hiring a limousine to drive her home and then blamed it all on Erik. He was such a stickler when it came to money, insisting they live on the meager advance for his new novel, allowing her only to carry the house payments and maintain her apartment in the city for the nights she could not make it home. But deep down, she stewed about Suzy's column, hoping against hope that he had not seen it. But he was such an avid newspaper reader.

The taxi from the Darien train depot entered the rows of barren maple trees lining the long drive. Soon the headlights picked up her blue gray clapboard house. Built in 1814, remodeled many times, it sat back in the surrounding wooded five acres like a sturdy farmhouse. But it didn't look welcoming. Erik hadn't bothered even to turn on the porch light and the only lighted window was his upstairs study. She paid off the driver and let herself in the front door. "I'm home, sugar," she called up the massive oak staircase. She dropped her overnight bag. "Sugar?" she tried again.

The house was freezing. She turned on the furnace and walked into the living room she had carefully furnished—with the aid of a top New York decorator—in nineteenth-century antiques indigenous to the region. Bitterly, she switched on every light and lamp in the room. She had not been home in four days. Was he even aware that she'd been gone?

Upstairs, she opened his study door. He had not heard her. In dirty T-shirt and jeans, he sat, his shoulders bent over a yellow legal pad on his desk—an antique English law conference table that was her housewarming gift to him. The book-lined room was thick with cigarette smoke and smelled disturbingly of sweat.

Wrinkling her nose, she hesitated—the week's newspapers were strewn around the upholstered easy chair. "How're y'all doin', sugar?" she asked softly. As his head rose with a start, she slipped her arms around him from behind, kissing the back of his neck, breathing into him, "I've missed you."

He leaned back into her. "Babe, is it that late?"

"Y'all forgot your promise," she pouted and withdrew his arms.

"Nope. See. I wrote a reminder." He pointed to a slip of paper taped to the wall above his desk. It read simply, *Make Dinner*. "I'm real sorry, just lost track. You hungry?"

"Famished." She searched his eyes for a telltale sign.

"Let's go to that fish joint," he said, turning back to the legal pad. "But a bit later, okay? Just want to noodle this section a bit."

"Fine with me," she said briskly, moving toward the door. "I want to noodle a bit in a hot tub. You could use one too. *And* a

shave. The kitchen's a shambles. Didn't Juanita come in today?''
But he was already back into his work. Hurriedly she picked up all
the newspapers and took them with her. Locked in the bathroom, she
tore out Suzy's column and flushed it away. Then took all the papers
down to the backporch for the incinerator.

It was close to nine that night before Shelby could drag him away
from his desk. During the drive to the local restaurant, Erik asked
only perfunctory questions about her week. His mind seemed on
other matters. When he was withdrawn like that, it unnerved her.

"Do you think I've gained weight?'' she asked over her crab
salad, which had too much lettuce and not enough meat.

"Well . . . not really. What do the scales say?''

"I never get on them anymore,'' she replied, watching enviously
as he dipped another piece of juicy white lobster into the cup of
melted butter. ''Besides I really don't care. Giorgio starved me for
so long.''

He sipped his bottle of beer, looking over her shoulder at the
boisterous bar section. Every place they went, he always chose a
table in a corner where he could sit with his back to the wall. He
insisted that he like to observe people, but she couldn't help but feel
that her company was not enough to stimulate him through an entire
meal. She swung her head to follow his gaze, wondering what could
be holding his attention. All she saw were working class types, out
for a night on the town.

Fish joint was right. The small cafe was crowded, nosiy, too
brightly lit for her tastes and the jukebox played too loudly, at that
moment it was Gordon Lightfoot singing, ''If You Could Read My
Mind.''

She returned to her salad, longing for the hot garlic bread. ''Beth
Ann mentioned my weight over lunch.''

"Your mother was in town?''

"Didn't I tell you?'' she responded, perhaps too quickly. ''Well,
she was. We lunched today. She's drinking too much. Three in an
hour. Wouldn't that be something if she became an alcoholic? And
after Evangeline drove daddy out for that?''

He signaled the waitress with the bouffant hairdo for another beer and then asked Shelby, "Do you think they'll ever be reconciled to us?"

"Who cares?" she replied and lit her own cigarette. She squinted in the smoke. "Do y'all realize it'll be three years next month?" The beehived waitress replaced his bottle with a full one. Shelby noted aloud, "For what you're spending on beer, we could've had a lovely meal elsewhere."

He grinned. "For our anniversary. I'll take you anywhere you want for dinner."

"Tahiti."

His grin faded and for a moment he looked very tired. "Within reason, I meant."

"Well, Tahiti's within reason," she replied stiffly. "My reason anyway. Honestly, Erik, we never go anywhere or do anything that's really fun."

"We went sailing off Maine last fall, didn't we?"

"Fun for you, maybe," she said, blowing smoke over his head. "I was wet, cold and miserably seasick on that leaky ol' tub. The whole week." When he laughed at the memory, she couldn't resist glaring. "Well, I was."

"Sorry 'bout that," he responded, still smiling. "I though we had a grand time."

She dunked out her cigarette in his melted butter and dropped it into the ashtry. "I'm longing for a little sun and sand."

"When the novel's done. Anywhere you want."

"I want to go now. I'm tired of waiting around for you to finish. You said it'd be done last summer. Then it was Christmas. In another month it'll be Easter. I could die of old age before you're done." He laughed again and she suddenly became quite angry. "Well, *it's true*. Honestly, you have no idea how *itchy* I am."

"Yes, I do," he said. "I read that column piece."

Beyond her control, she felt her face flush. Her eyelashes batted a defense. "Y'all don't believe that . . . that trash, do you?"

"Should I?"

Before she could respond, someone was leaning drunkenly on their table, breathing beer fumes down on her like hot blasts from an open furnace. "Say, you're Sunny, ain'cha?" Flustered, she looked up into a broad, coarse face with bulbous crooked nose. Thick stubby fingers grabbed her arm. "Com'on over an' meet my buddies."

Erik reached across the table and jerked away the stranger's hand. "Excuse us. This is a private conversation."

"I ain't askin' you, buddy," the big-bellied man said. "I'm askin' Sunny here. Com'on, sweetheart. Have a few laughs." Again he clamped a paw on her arm.

"No thank you," she said, extracting herself and smiling as sweetly as she could. "I'll stop by on our way out though."

"Naw, com'on now," the man persisted. "We're fans of yours. Me an' my buddies." Wavering unsteadily, he swung a hand toward the bar. She ducked to avoid being hit.

Erik threw down his napkin. "I asked you politely, now I'm telling you. *Leave us alone.*"

The drunk hitched up his workpants. "Why don'chew get lost yourself. Let a real man care for this sweetie."

Heads turned in the small restaurant and a hush had descended. "Erik . . ." she tried to warn, but he was on his feet. "Erik, please," she pleaded. "Let's just leave."

"I haven't finished my beer," he said heatedly. "Now, as for—"

The drunk punched him hard in the stomach. She moaned, finding herself on her feet. Erik straightened up, his eyes on fire. He lashed out with a fist, catching the man under the chin, lifting him momentarily off the floor and driving him backward into another table. Dishes crashed, and the startled patrons scrambled out of the way.

She tugged at his sleeve. "Please!" He shrugged her off just as the drunk lowered his head and charged, bellowing like a bull. He hit Erik full force in the chest, knocking him down. She shrieked, "Stop it! Stop it!"

It was too late. Erik rolled to his feet, his clenched fists raised into a quasi-boxer's stance. He threw one, then two quick jabs into the man's face. Blood began spurting from the pulpy nose, but the man retaliated with an uppercut which cracked Erik's jaw. With a flurry of fists, they began in earnest.

Helplessly, she looked for someone to break it up. Everyone just stood and watched, like they were all enjoying the evening's diversion.

Sickened, she grabbed her fur and purse, running for the rear door. The crack and crunch of bones on flesh followed her into the parking lot. Fumbling in her purse, she located her set of car keys and trembling, climbed in behind the wheel of her white Continental.

Back at home, she switched on the kitchen light. Look at this mess! Imagine his giving Juanita the day off just because she said her child was sick. He didn't even bother checking. Hasn't an inkling how to deal with hired help.

She marched upstairs and slipped into a sheer nightgown. Lying in the darkness on the king-sized bed, she smoked one cigarette after another, thinking back over her marriage.

It had begun divinely. Being fired from her Sunny contract had granted her immediate freedom to do as she wished. She'd been signed at once by the Ford Modeling Agency. Three times in her first year freelancing, she had been on the cover of *Vogue*, twice on *Harper's Bazaar*. Offers for television commercials had continually poured in and she'd had her pick of the best.

For that first year, Erik had been by her side, willingly jaunting first class to many of her around-the-world location sites, Morocco, Bali, Peru. He had delighted in being with her under any circumstances and had been devoted, caring, loving, worshipful—only complaining about the money she spent from her accounts. She had learned a vast amount from him—in St. Moritz how to ski, in the Mediterranean how to sail, in the South Pacific how to skin dive, in the Rockies how to camp out and "rough it." He had taken her to museums, plays, rock concerts and smoky clubs for jazz. She could not have wished for a more satisfying or complete life.

Then, Erik had begun his third novel. Suddenly he had been no longer available to her. For the entire last two years, he had been holed up in this house. She could not remember the last time he'd been into the city with her. He had become moody, withdrawn, often testy and curt. She had had her first extramarital affair one week the year before—in Berlin with a German film director of some note. After that, there had been an Argentine banker, a Canadian Air Force captain, a brief fling with a halfback for the New York Jets, and a Southern senator had captured her fancy for about two weekends. The list was not that extensive; she had always discreetly terminated each relationship before it had become sticky or no longer just fun. Erik never knew—or let on he did. But now she was not so sure.

It was after two A.M. when the sound of an arriving car drew her to the bedroom window overlooking the front drive. Erik was clambering out of an unfamiliar, battered pickup. He loudly thanked the driver for a "helluva" time and waved as the vehicle roared off down to the road. He stumbled on the porch step.

She slipped back between the sheets, hearing him bumping up the main steps. She feigned sleep. "Shelby?" he asked in a slur and switched on the table lamp. She felt the bed give as he sat on the edge, then a cold hand on her shoulder. He shook her gently. "Babe? You awake?"

"I am now," she muttered without turning.

"Can we talk?"

"You're drunk."

"Yup. That I am. S-s-sorry."

She rolled over to show him the extreme displeasure she felt.

His right eye was nearly swollen shut and his upper lip was cut, a bloody scab already formed. The knuckles of one hand were bruised and split. The collar of his shirt was half torn off and he was grinning like an ape.

"You look a mess," she said.

"Should see the other guy," he boasted. "I was going to invite him in but figured it was kind of past bedtime. Man, we—"

"He drove you home? That . . . that pig?"

"Helluva guy. Had a solid right too," he said, rubbing his chin.

"I don't believe it! Y'all were fighting each other like dogs—then he turns around and drives you home?"

"Well . . . we had a few beers first," he said sheepishly. "We pooped out pretty fast fighting. Fairly evenly matched. Had plenty of time to cool off. He apologized. I said I was sorry. We fell to talking. He trucks fresh farm produce to the cannery. A background of all gristle and sweat." Erik stood unsteadily and struggled out of his shirt. "Why'd you run out like that?"

She shook her head. "I don't understand you, Erik. I really don't.

One minute you're ready to kill the slob and the next—you're drinking buddies. What is it with you?"

He shrugged, smiling broadly and slapped his hairy belly. "Just a low-class clod at heart, huh?"

"Well, y'all certainly act like it at times. I was never so humiliated in my whole life. You were grinning, Erik. When I ran out, you were actually grinning—enjoying beating on that fat pig."

"Ah, now . . . that's a bit of exaggeration, isn't it? A bit of artistic license?" He smiled crookedly and shucked off his jeans. Nude and wavering, he headed for his side of the bed.

"Not without a shower," she said firmly. "You smell like a brewery locker room."

"Ah, come on, babe. I'm beat as hell." He threw back the quilt.

"Erik," she warned. "I'll sleep in the guest room."

"Ah, shit," he grumbled and scratched his groin. "Can't a man come home drunk once in a while? Hell, I haven't blown off steam like—"

"For *three* hours, I sat here worrying what happened to you. Did you once consider me? You could have called at least."

"And *you* could have stayed," he countered sharply. "Not taken the car. Run off in the night like some prissy missy afraid of getting her hair mussed."

"I am not accustomed to public brawls," she retorted.

"You like 'em private, eh?"

The way he was looking at her made her uncomfortable—as though he were referring to that gossip item. "And another thing," she said quickly. "I will never, ever go back to that fish joint again. If you can't take me someplace decent, you can go by yourself."

He began to laugh, a deep, rumbling growl which bounced his testicles and made her even all the more angry. "I mean it," she said.

He quieted down, nodding with a silly smirk. "I'm sure you do, babe." He started for the adjoining bathroom. "As of tonight. The fish joint is off-limits to married folk." He paused in the doorway like a granite mountain of winter-pale flesh. "See how you always get what you want?" He winked and withdrew.

Tense with indecision, she lay, not knowing what she wanted. She closed her eyes, wishing things were different—that his novel were finished, that they were free to escape somewhere as before, to have him totally focused on her again. She heard the shower cease and shortly his bare feet padding across the carpet. He switched off the lamp and crawled heavily into bed. She could smell the soap he used, the shampoo, even the toothpaste. For what seemed like ages, he did not move toward her and she had the awful feeling he was slipping off to sleep.

When his hand began caressing her back, she turned into him. He wrapped her in his arms, whispering, "Lord, I hate it when we fight."

"Me too."

He kissed her lips and she began to relax even more. "Sugar," she began softly, loving the touch of his fingers on her breasts.

"Hmmmm?"

"Y'all really didn't believe that ol' thing in the column?"

"Not for a minute," he murmured.

She could feel him hardening. "I would just die if you did," she said and raised her hips so he could free her nightgown.

"Just one of the prices of public life," he mumbled into her neck, doing wonderful things with his fingers between her thighs.

"Oh, sugar," she breathed, the heat intensifying within. "I do love you so . . ."

"Shelby, my beautiful Shelby . . . my love . . ." He eased into her.

DAVID
April 1971
Los Angeles

"No, No," the matronly wife of AII's senior vice president insisted over dessert. "The sixties ended brutally in sixty-nine with the Charles Manson murders. For me, anyway, that was the ultimate end of the decade.'' She smiled at their host. ''Even if, as you insist, Dixon, that technically the decade didn't end until this past New Year's.''

The chairman, at the head of the crystal and silver table, leaned forward. ''Indeed sixty-nine was a tumultuous year. Everything from Chappaquiddick to Neil Armstrong on the moon; from Woodstock to the death of Judy Garland; 'Sesame Street' to the first X-rated film winning a Best Picture Oscar.''

David cleared his throat to speak one of the few times all evening. ''*Midnight Cowboy* won in 1970. But it was released in sixty-nine.'' He shifted in his chair, feeling trapped inside his tuxedo.

Shaw nodded, stiffly polite, as if he did not like being corrected at his own dinner party. He lifted his champagne glass, smiling graciously at his other guests. ''As I was not out here for New Year's, may I propose a belated toast? To the New Decade, the Seventies. May it bring prosperity for all.''

''And peace,'' a French actress added forcefully.

Ignoring that small breach of etiquette, everyone drank. David took a small sip, squirming. He detested social functions like this. Boring chitchat, knee-jerk opinions, faked conviviality. Everyone kissing the chairman's ass, deferring to his concepts, his politics. The only reason David had accepted the invitation was the simple fact that he, like all the others present, wanted something from Shaw. He wanted to be named the new president of the record label. For that, he would have sat through almost anything. But enough was enough.

Thankfully, Dixon had to be in Hong Kong the following day, which curtailed the evening's forced festivities. David was among the first to make his way toward the front door. Shaw leaned into him confidentially. ''Stick around. We'll have a nightcap.''

David paced the spacious living room, aware of, but uninterested in Shaw's impressive collection of nineteenth-century American Western art, including four large Remington paintings, and a half-dozen Russell bronzes. In his mind, David ticked off the points he intended to make and the strategy of his presentation.

''Brandy?'' Shaw asked, appearing in the doorway.

''Whatever you're having.''

Shaw returned holding two large crystal snifters with a judicious amount of amber-colored liquid in each. "Let's get comfortable," he said and loosened his dress shirt's collar.

David did likewise, sizing up Shaw. In the few short years since being named head of AII, the chairman looked aged by a decade, his reddish hair thinner, his paunch more pronounced. Wearily, Shaw lowered himself to the couch in front of the blazing hearth. "Sit, David. We haven't touched base in a long while."

"If you don't mind," David began with clubroom grace, "I prefer standing. Tonight was the longest I've sat still for ages."

"As you wish," Shaw responded, then continued in a reflective tone, "Was it a mistake? AII taking over Pacific Studios? You were raised in the heart of this industry. You have demonstrated an uncanny sense of having your finger on the pulse of American youth. With the majority of filmgoers being under the age of twenty-five, I'm most interested in your views of our newest acquisition."

David hesitated, wanting to ask, if his opinion were so greatly considered, why hadn't he been asked before the purchase. Now he chose words carefully, "In today's market, any movie-making is a risky venture. The cost of the product rises as the buying public decreases. However, as in any business, find the right product, the profits are there. Look at Fox and *Easy Rider*—minimum investment, gargantuan returns."

"Another more delicate question," Shaw began. "Would you consider your father, as head of Pacific, capable of turning out such product?"

David stalled, taking a sip of the Courvoisier. "Irving's from the old school of studio filmmaking. Spend a fortune to buy a well-known property, cast the biggest stars you can get and pray for a hit."

"Irving has done fairly well with Pacific."

"But times are changing faster than he is. Take a hard look at his development list. Not one viable project for the youth market." David took a moment to sip his brandy and then slid smoothly into his opening gambit. "I'm considering an expansion into films. For that very market my records reach."

"I think that unwise," Shaw said with a slight frown. "You'd be overextended. Besides, RPM needs your creative drive and business acumen. You've turned it around in three short years." He paused, chuckling. "For which we've made you rich as Croesus, correct?"

By the blazing hearth, David stood silently studying the flames, then looked over. "I'll level with you, Dixon. I've been unsatisfied lately. Turning out pop hits has become a game too easily won. I'd like to take on some additional responsibilities—try my wings in new areas. I need the stimulation. Now, of course, if you made me president of the label, I wouldn't need to look further."

With a vexed wave of his glass, Shaw said, "I haven't made up my mind who I want. Perhaps next week. But rest assured I'm giving you every consideration."

"Just wanted you to know where I stood. As you remember, my contract is up at the end of this month."

"I'm fully cognizant of that fact," Shaw said, his tone now businesslike. "To be frank, I am not certain whether the board is ready for a 'rock 'n' roll' president of the label. The corporate image and all that. They still like Jerry Vale."

David dug up a boyish smile. "Not pressuring—just aware of my own worth."

"As we all are," the chairman said and tossed the remains of his brandy into the fireplace. The resulting flame burst high and died just as quickly. "Now, if you'll excuse me, Helen and I have an early flight." He headed for the front entry. David followed. At the door, Shaw paused, as if to make a conciliatory gesture. "How're the new headquarters working out? Pleased with the move down here from San Francisco?"

"Fine, just fine," David lied badly. "Very convenient to the new sound studios."

"Congratulations. You've given us a very impressive plant. Good night."

The door closed and David found himself outside in a light spring rain. Turning up his collar, he sprinted to his convertible Excaliber. The red leather seats were wet—he'd left the top down. Not bothering to put it up now, he hopped in and gunned the car toward the street.

Reaching the west gate of Bel Air, he idled the engine, briefly debating whether to head out to his new Malibu Colony beach house or back up Sunset to the new RPM tower. His office won again.

As he sped east, David was again aware of the hatred he had for L.A., and how it was getting in the way of his work. Everything was drudgery now. Everything tedious. Just the day before he had blown a contract with a promising new group with a Crosby, Stills and Nash kind of sound because he had forgotten to follow through on a previous promise so small it had slipped his mind altogether. It irked him that he was no longer on top of his professional duties. If he weren't a pro, he didn't know what the hell he was.

Cursing again the corporate decision to consolidate all RPM divisions in Los Angeles, near a brand new complex of "state of the art" sound stages, David parked in the underground garage of RPM's Sunset Strip tower, took the elevator to the tenth floor and entered his expansive corner office, not bothering to turn on the lights. The rain pelted against the glass walls as he hurriedly disrobed, throwing his damp tuxedo into the closet. His desk was piled high with matters to be attended to, but he had no enthusiasm for burning the midnight oil for yet another night. Pulling the blanket from the top shelf of his closet, he lay down on the couch, wrapping it around him. He lay in the darkness, waiting for sleep.

The loud *click* woke him with a jolt. In shock, he stared into the gleaming point of a six-inch switchblade. It aimed directly, not an inch from his nose.

"Wake up, ya mutherfucker," the all-too-familiar voice croaked. "Get your ass up! We got us some business to attend to."

"What the hell?!"

"Get up! But don' go tryin' no funny business or I'll slice your beak quicker than a grasshopper spits."

"Silver . . . what the fuck?!" He struggled to a sitting position. She crouched low, the pearl-handled knife wavering an inch from

his face. "Son of a bitch! I ought'a slice you up jus' for the hell of
it. Like you done me."

"What the hell're you doing? You're supposed to be in Saint
Paul."

"Well, I ain't, am I? I jus' had me a hunch you'd be here an' I
was right, my ol' ESP in tune, dig?" She straightened up but the
blade held its target.

Behind her, through the glass walls, a dull pinkish light was
breaking over Griffith Observatory. The pink tinged Silver's matted
hair. She looked like a bag lady, her unpressed, black slacks stained
with what looked like dried pizza sauce. Her gaunt frame shook with
minute vibrations. Her pupils were dilated to their fullest and they
had a steely, inhuman glint, unnatural and unnerving.

"What're you on?" he demanded.

"None of your fuckin' beeswax. Stand up!"

Slowly he rose to his feet, the blanket dropping to the carpet. She
took a step backward and began to cackle, a hollow, brittle sound
that sent chills racing up his ribs. "Well, ain't you a cute piece o'
tail. Shit, if you ain't the only dude I know still wearin' jockey
shorts. Hell, man, don'cha know? You supposed to let it all hang
out." She cackled again, her breathing belabored. Suddenly she
rasped, "Take 'em off."

"Silver . . ."

"You heard me. Take 'em off before I cut 'em off. Let's see wha'
you been hidin' for so long. Come on!" The blade jabbed at his gut.

He jumped back, sucking in his stomach. Quickly he slid his
shorts off, watching uneasily.

"I have me half a mind to rape you," she said, her mouth twisted
into a half-smile. "'Cause that's wha' you done to me, man. You
raped me. Used me to git wha' you wanted. Tossed me out like a
sack o' trash. Fucked with my head so much I don' know if'n I'm
comin' or goin'."

"How'd you get up here?"

"Shit, man, haven'cha heard? I'm a star, man. I'm famous. My
ol' puss is so recognizable I jus' have to flash it an' doors open. I'm
a genuine rock-'n'-roll queen." She frowned darkly. "I should cut
off your pecker for doin' that. Man, I should've never listened to

you. Back there in New York? I should've stayed on. Done my own thing ..." Tears began gushing from her eyes. "Why'd'cha dump me, man? Why? Didn't I do my tricks like you wanted?" She sobbed brokenly and her arm dropped.

He lunged for her knife hand, his fingers grabbing her wrist, twisting. She bellowed in pain, but would not drop the blade. They struggled fiercely—her strength amazed him. Her arm was like steel. she kicked his bare shins with the toes of her boots, clawing at his face with the fingers of her free hand, low, animal noises erupted from her chest as though she were possessed.

Unexpectedly, her arm went limp, her fighting ceased, the knife, slipping from her grasp, dropping silently to the rug. He snatched it up and backed away, holding it protectively in front. She moaned in defeat and collapsed into a messy heap near the couch, her head buried in her arms on its seat cushions. Her thin back heaving under the baggy ski sweater.

Warily, he eyed her and tried to quiet his own breathing. He palmed the blade closed and, not turning his back on her, went to his closet, pulling off the rack a silk Hawaiian sports shirt and a pair of slacks. He dressed hurriedly behind the desk and unlocked the bottom drawer, put in the knife and relocked the drawer, pocketing the key. Only then did he begin to relax. He sank into his leather chair behind the desk and leaned back, his focus not straying from Silver crying hoarsely across the room. What a waste, he thought. One of the truly great rock voices—hailed from London to Tokyo—reduced to this . . . this freaked-out sack of bones. What a goddamn waste.

He spotted her large tapestry purse on the chair by the door along with a bright orange oil-cloth rain slicker. Hustling to it, he brought the purse back to the desk, dumping out the contents: a horrendous amount of junk fell out, tampons, candy, a wooden toothbrush, three pairs of dark glasses, loose paper money—tens, twenties, fifties, a couple of hundreds, gobs of change—wadded used Kleenex, slips of papers with names, a mismatched pair of knee socks, a dog-eared paperback, *Naked Came the Stranger*, a silver art nouveau container with five neatly rolled joints, a small glass vial of white powder—probably cocaine—and enough pills to stock a small pharmacy—red, yellow, white, uppers, downers, Quaaludes, acid. He looked up in disgust. Angrily he swept it all back into the purse and tossed it on the floor.

The sound startled her. She raised her face, dark circles under her eyes stood out like dirty thumbprints. "I weren't goin'a hurt you, man," she sobbed. "Really, I weren't . . ."

He sat again in his chair. "How come you're not with the band? In Saint Paul? You've got a gig there tonight."

"I quit, man," she cried. "No more White Meat for me. I've done had it. Those muthers can go fuck themselves. You know what they done? They got me stoned an' then stripped me. Locked me out of my own room. My own fuckin' room! An' all them straights laughin' at me. In the hall. I was jus' tryin' to get back into my own room. An' I'm the one gets thrown out of the hotel."

"So you quit? Just like that."

"Yeah, jus' like that," she sobbed defiantly. "I won' sing no more with 'em. No how." She pushed up and wobblingly started for her purse.

"Stay away."

"I jus' need a lil' somethin', man. Quiet me down, like . . ."

"You've had enough. More than enough. You disgust me."

She threw back her head and glared. "I do, huh? Well, kiss my sweet ass, boy. You disgust me. Dumpin' us in second-rate joints. No promotion. No crowds. Makin' us travel by bus. *By bus*, man!"

"Give me a monster and you can have your limos back."

"An' why haven't we had no hit, huh? 'Cause you're too damned busy makin' hits for some other group. Look at all these damned Grammys," she growled, waving an arm at the collection on the bookshelves. "Not one for us, man. Why? 'Cause you haven't produced our last two albums, man."

He touched his fingertips together. "I can't produce for every group on the label. You guys have to pull your own weight." His mind raced ahead. There was no way he could pull her back together enough to have her make the concert in Minnesota that evening. He'd have to think of a replacement.

"David," she said, whining irritably. "Can I do a solo, huh? Jus' me? Give me my own band, David. Please. Not askin' for much.

Jus' some dudes who'd be proud to back me up. Not hasslin' me all the time.''

"What makes you think you could make it alone?"

"'Cause I'm good, man." She edged closer to the desk, scratching one arm like crazy. He wondered if she were shooting dope on top of everything else. "Jus' give me my own lil' band. Let me start small, dig? I know I can make it on my own. I jus' know it."

The sun had risen over the San Gabriel Mountains—it was so clear he could see all the way to the horizon of the china blue ocean.

"Look at me, David. Fer gawdsakes, please, huh? I know I'm kinda fucked up now, but I'm a pro, David. A real pro. I can pull it together if you jus' give me a lil' hand. 'I can get by with a lil' help from my friends,' " she singsonged and dropped heavily into the chair at the corner of the desk. "I don' wanna end up like Janis. An' Hendrix. Wiped out. Weren't the dope. Fuckin' fame killed 'em, man. It's a life-sucker. I don' wanna end up like them. Please, help me, man."

He studied her for a long moment, searching his mind for a way out of this mess. "Okay," he said slowly. "Where're you staying?"

"Tropicana," she answered brightly, then sank sourly. "Ain't that where they found Janis? Bummer karma. I better boogie out of there. Can I stay at your pad, huh, please?"

Behind his desk, he unlocked the bottom drawer, removed the switchblade, slipping it into her purse. "You go back there and wait for my call." Handing her the bag, he put his arm around her waist and began walking her to the elevator. She sagged against him like a windless banner.

"I knew you wouldn't let this good ol' girl down. You an' me go back a long ways, huh? Thicker than blood in December, right?"

"I'll call the guard to get you a cab."

"I really weren't gonna slice you, man. Jus' goofin', dig?"

"Yeah, sure." He pressed the button and the doors opened immediately. "Get some rest. I'll give you a jingle later today."

She leaned forward unsteadily and pecked his cheek—she smelled of cheap wine. "In spite of all your shit, I love you, man, really, I do . . ." The doors began to close. She held them open, sniffled and wiped her nose on a sleeve. "We're gonna hit it big man, jus' like ol' times. I feel it in my ol' bones." He pried her fingers loose and the doors closed on her.

In his office telephone directory, he looked up a number and dialed, waiting impatiently for an answer. "Hello?" he began, consciously disguising his voice. "I want to report a drug violation. Never mind my name. And a concealed weapon. Yeah. It's all in her purse . . ."

Around seven that evening, David emerged from RPM's sound studio number three and immediately was accosted by several newsmen waiting in the parking lot. One shouted, "Give us a comment on Silver's drug bust?"

David feigned surprise. "Her what?!" A porta-pack TV camera was thrust toward him, the local ABC newswoman speaking into a microphone. "She was busted for possession at the Tropicana around noon. Surely you knew that? Wasn't she your protégé?"

David frowned seriously. "I've been holed up all day mixing Cobalt Blues' new single. Left strict instructions not to be interrupted. What's happened?"

The woman reporter relayed the story which had broken nationwide that afternoon—the narcotics division of the LAPD, acting on an anonymous tip and armed with a search warrant, broke into Silver's motel room and found among her personal possessions a large quantity of illegal substances. As well as a concealed weapon. Reported to have been under the influence of drugs at the time, Silver had been subsequently arrested, booked and was now being held in Sybil Brand, the local women's jail.

David pushed through the reporters, heading for his Excaliber, making it plain that he was clearly astonished and upset. Another reporter asked loudly, "According to an RPM press release this morning, you fired Silver *yesterday* and yanked her from White Meat. Why?"

David climbed into his convertible. "Because she was not fulfilling the terms of her contract." He started the engine, warming it up. "I will add, I'm extremely sorry for her. But we had warned her. It is RPM's expressed policy that none of our performers abuse our national and local drug laws."

A young male voice shouted, "What about White Meat?"

David smiled. "White Meat will continue its tour with our new singing sensation, Kay Lee Reed. Dynamite voice. But nobody will replace Silver. Ever. Good night.'' He drove off, pleased with his performance.

Over the next few days, David made no effort to contact Silver or arrange for a lawyer to handle her case; he ignored her phone messages and offered no help in placing her in an appropriate drug rehabilitation program. As far as he was concerned, she no longer existed. She had failed the test of remaining a pro.

On the following Monday, long after the sensationalistic news about Silver had faded away, replaced by the fast-breaking story of the largest anti-war demonstration on record gathering in the nation's capital, David was in a regular weekly A-and-R conference meeting, listening to that month's releases when his secretary brought in a memo. With a falling sensation, he read the short communication. The chairman had just named Alan Leonard, former head of RPM's law department, as president of the label.

David shot to his feet and left the conference room. He slammed his office door and snatched up his phone, dialing his lawyer's private line. ''Ian? I want you to break off all existing negotiations.''

''I just heard about Alan Leonard. Listen, we've got AII over a barrel now. They'll have to sweeten the pot to keep us happy.''

''Are you listening? I told you I want all *existing* negotiations suspended as of now. And I want you here in my office—now.''

Within the hour, David had laid out in detail his new strategy for his conservatively dressed lawyer. Ian frowned across the desk. ''But there's no precedent. RPM and Pacific are completely autonomous. AII may be the parent, but they are separate children from entirely separate marriages.''

''If Dixon wants me to stick to RPM, he'd better come through.'' David stood, giving notice the meeting was over. ''One other thing—let this out on the streets. I want to see how dreamland reacts.''

The next morning's trades—both the *Hollywood Reporter* and the *Daily Variety*—carried reports of his new contractual demands. Pissed that both articles stressed his relationship to Irving, David sat back, waiting for the phone to bring him a response from the outside world. He didn't have long to wait. Irving's office at Pacific was the first. The ice-toned secretary informed him that Irving wanted a meeting "at once." David chose a non-industry bar in Santa Monica and said he would be there at three P.M.—for one half-hour only.

At five after three, David showed up, walking into the dimly lit cocktail lounge off Ocean Avenue. Irving was already seated in a back booth, like a fat cat ready to pounce.

As David approached, Irving began heatedly, "What are you? *Meshuggeneh*?"

David smiled, seating himself across the red-checked tablecloth. "Yeah . . . like a fox."

"Lions eat foxes for hor d'oeuvres."

"Have to catch them first."

"Hell of a lot of traps to catch foxes."

"Only the old ones, Irving . . . only the old ones."

Irving glowered and jammed a long, thick Havana cigar into his mouth. David leaned back to avoid the ensuing smoke. "Still sucking on those phallic things?"

"Listen, don't tell *me* about Freud. I know all about Freud. A cocaine addict. Living and working out of the same house his whole life? That's healthy? Fuck Freud. We're talking about *you*. What the hell do you think you're up to? That rock music softened your brain? My eyes, I couldn't believe this morning. Had to call Hank Grant. See if he were blowing it out his ass. And he tells me it's the gospel. Straight from your own mouthpiece. So I ask again. And answer me this time." Irving bent forward, cocking his nearly bald head to one side. "What are you? Crazy? You'll never get it. Why even try?"

"I'll get it."

"Over my dead body."

With a faint smile, David folded his arms across his chest. "Well, whatever . . . I'm going to get it."

"What makes you so damned sure?"

"RPM folds if I split."

"You think you run that show?"

"I know so."

"*Tsuris* of the colon, believe you me."

David couldn't keep the grin off his face. Irving's reply was his favorite rejoinder when cornered. "If I'm so crazy, Irving, how come you're here? Admit it. I've got you by the balls."

His father faked a derisive choke on his cigar and shook his head sadly. "Boy, are you one green sonofabitch."

David looked up at the waitress in the miniskirted tunic. "Tonic. On the rocks. Twist of lime."

Irving threw him a scornful glance as if that were a pansy drink and ordered a straight whiskey, then settled back into the green leather cushions. "What makes you think you know anything about making movies?"

"You serious?"

"So you hung around a few sets as a snot-nosed kid. Making them is a whole different league."

"We'll see, won't we?"

"If you happen to get this—and note I said if—'cause if you ask me, you've got a fag's chance of screwing Raquel Welch—but let's just say, for sake of argument, you do happen to con Shaw into this . . . you're going to fall on your goddamned ass."

"You said the same about my chances in the music business."

"Making rock and roll and making movies is hardly comparable." Irving stubbed out the end of his cigar into the ashtray, snapping the remaining length in two, as though hating the idea of someone finding half of a five-dollar Havana.

David once again leaned onto the table. "Want to compare bank accounts? How about stock portfolios? Or tax shelters? Real estate? Do you have any idea how much *I'm* worth?"

"A spoonful of spit," Irving growled. "Who gives a shit how much dough you've got? You think money's a judge of talent? Helluva lot of asshole millionaires around. How many are geniuses?"

"Don't have to be a genius to make movies, Irving. Take a look at yourself."

His father jerked forward at the waist, his bushy gray eyebrows colliding. "Always a wiseass. A babe in arms, and you were a wiseass. Now get one thing straight, Mister Wiseass. I'm running that studio. Me. Not Dixon Shaw. I make the rules. I decide who's making pictures at my studio. Not Dixon Shaw. And if you think you can waltz into a corner office on my lot—for a hands-off, *carte blanche*, three-picture deal—you're not only a wiseass, you are one helluva *crazy, sonofabitch wiseass!*"

David sipped the tonic water, deliberately taking his time. "I'm not asking for an upfront three-picture deal. Just *one* guaranteed upfront. If that brings in a healthy profit for Pacific, I get another one, double the first budget. If that clicks, another double the previous budget. You can't lose, Irving. I promise you, my first one will be your biggest hit of the year. It'll only make *you* look good."

"Listen, not even Mike Nichols has a deal like that. Or Kubrick."

"Producers at every studio in town have a multipact deal."

"One or two. But they have *proven* track records. What've you proved? Only that kids today will buy any crap you put on wax."

"Those same kids are the majority of the box-office bucks. Even Dixon knows that. That's why I'm going to win. He's a *very* smart man."

"He don't run *my* studio."

"It's not *your* studio. You're just a hired hand."

"We'll see who's hired and who isn't."

"Yes, we will." David stood, throwing down a ten. "Drinks on me. See you at Pacific." He walked out. In his mouth, the taste of victory was sweet. Oh, so goddamned sweet.

REBECCA
December 1971
New York

Deep in New Jersey, the Greyhound bus let her off in front of the intimidating gates of the state institution—solid brick columns supporting iron bars. Rebecca shivered in the freezing air, her breath crystalizing, and yanked the stocking cap over her ears. She trudged up the cement path in the shoveled snow, eyeing the huge brick building. With its barred upper windows, it seemed ominous and imposing, like a medieval fortress. It gave her the willies just looking at it.

Inside the main reception area, the smells almost gagged her—a pervasive scent of ammonia mixed with steamed institutional cooking as well as urine, vomit and sweat from the overheated building. At the information desk, a starched nurse told her to wait in the solarium.

In the long, narrow, glass-enclosed porch, the windows steamy, the air muggy from the radiators, Rebecca peeled off layers of thrift-shop sweaters and sank into a sagging rattan chair beside a tired Boston fern. She waited, filled with apprehension.

At least fifteen minutes passed before an aged-looking woman entered. With a start, Rebecca recognized her. Like a ghost, Silver shuffle-walked forward in pink felt slippers, her white hair shorn, the angles of her face like slabs of pale rock.

"Hi, Silver," Rebecca greeted and stood. She held out the small gift-wrapped package. "Merry Christmas."

Absently Silver took the gift and collapsed into an opposite chair, pulling tight the long green cotton bathrobe. "Ain't this the fuckin' merriest?"

Rebecca indicated the forgotten gift. "There's a real pretty card inside. A dove of peace. By this artist I'm folding for. You know, cutting and folding his silk-screened cards? In this giant, drafty loft down by the Hudson. It's colder than—"

"Why'd you come? I was hopin' you'd give up tryin'."

"I . . . I've wanted to see you for ages."

"How'd you know I was here?"

"I tried all over the place when I heard what went down," Rebecca began softly. "I wrote the RPM offices in L.A. several times. Then directly to David Rau. But no reply. So finally I took a longshot and wrote to Bountiful, Utah. I . . . I didn't know your real name so I just addressed it to 'Silver's Mother.' And you know? I got a real sweet note back from your mom about a month later. I felt terrible not knowing your real name."

"Sara Jane Schermerhorn," Silver said in a monotone. "Can you see that in lights?" A rasp in her throat rattled briefly, then died.

"Sara Jane's a nice . . ."

"Stinks like a crapper in August an' you know it, girl." For a second, the pale blue eyes twinkled to life, before dulling rapidly.

"You should see some o' the freaks they got in this joint. Space city, believe you me. Makes you sleep with the lights on."

"Pretty bad, huh?"

Silver raised her frail shoulders and let them fall. "My shrink tells me to think positive. But it sure as hell ain't easy. Some turkey keeps stealin' the bottoms of my p.j.s. Snitched four of 'em. These is the only ones I got left."

"I'll send you a couple or three pairs."

Silver's eyes watered and she glanced down. "You was always the best, Rebecca." In her lap, her hands twisted together like writhing snakes. "I heard James Morrison bit the big one too. In Paris. Cried all night when I heard that. Guess I was the lucky one, huh?" She looked up with a sly smirk. "Did I tell you I balled him once? God, was he beautiful. Like a dark angel or somethin'."

Swiftly Rebecca moved to her, kneeling, wrapping her arms around her. "Oh, Silver, I missed you so much. I just couldn't believe you wouldn't okay my visit. I thought maybe they had you in a padded cell or something. I'm so glad you let me come." A hand stroked her hair absently. "Can I do anything for you, Silver? Other than the p.j.s?"

"Sweet lil' Rebecca. Them eyes are still filled with such pain. I almost forgive you."

"For what? What'd I do? Tell me ... please ..."

"For leavin' me that way. When I needed you so bad. Dallas? The night o' them riots in Chicago?"

"But ... I didn't want to."

"That's awlright, honey. I got over the hurt. You splittin' with tha' roadie. I un'erstand. You was hurtin' too."

"Roadie? What roadie? I didn't split. I was *thrown* off the tour. David chucked me out on my ass."

"Run tha' by me one more time. You say, David kicked you out?"

"Said I was a bad influence on you."

"Why tha' two-bit mutherfucker. He fed me all this crap. Hell, I should've known you wouldn've left me. Tha' David ... he's one cold snake-sucker. He's the one who got me busted."

"*He what?*"

"Sicced the pigs on me. He was the only one knew I was back in L.A. Took me a long time to figure tha' one out. An' I haven't heard hide-nor-tail of him since. After all them millions I made for him."

"I don't think there's anyone I know more hateful."

"Don' waste the energy. He'll get what's comin' to him. Karma, dig? What goes 'round, comes down. 'Sides, if it wasn't for him, who the hell knows where'd I'd be by now? My shrink says I should thank ol' David."

"When . . . when will they let you out?"

"When I'm rehabilitated."

"What's that mean?"

"No longer self-destructive, I guess . . ." Silver scratched her burr-cut head. "Ain't it purty? Sorry I chopped it off now. Wish I had me hair like yours. So long an' straight an' shiny. Wha'cha been doin'?"

"Surviving," Rebecca said.

"You ever hear from tha' gorgeous man?"

"Scooter? No . . . not a word."

"You're still carryin' a hot torch for him, ain'cha?"

Rebecca nodded, then brightened. "But I'm a working actress. With this theater group called Real Amerika—spelled with a 'k,' you know? And we have our own theater. Do shows four nights a week. The *Village Voice* calls us the best political theater in the city." She fell silent for a moment, then took the pale hands again in her own.

Silver squeezed back. "You're the only one I ever heard from. You won't forget ol' me?"

Rebecca bit her lower lip. "Never. All the help . . . the support you gave me out west. I'm so grateful, Silver . . . I only wish I could repay you somehow . . ."

Silver looked at her gently for a long moment. "Honey, you already have . . . jus' by bein' you."

A male nurse with long sideburns to his chin arrived to take Silver back to her ward. When Rebecca hugged her close, Silver whispered in her ear, "You jus' hang on out there. It'll get better. I jus' know it. You got the purest karma I know."

Emotions overflowing, Rebecca watched her friend being led away, then turned to hurry toward the front exit.

The return trip to Manhattan seemed endless. In the back of the bus, she tried finishing the paperback edition of *The Pentagon Papers* but a black kid with a cassette tapedeck played "Bye, Bye Miss American Pie" over and over until she knew the whole song by heart.

On Christmas Eve a driving snowstorm hit the city. Snowflakes lashed her unprotected cheeks and stung like bits of driven glass. The wind fairly blew her into the vestibule of the East Village apartment building. Shaking all over to rid herself of the thin layer of snow, she climbed up four flights and unlocked the door.

"That you, Rebecileh?" came the cheerful call. "I'll be out in a sec. I made some cinnamon rolls."

Led by her nose, Rebecca had already found them. Gratefully chewing one, she plopped on the daybed and pulled off her cheap plastic boots. She rubbed her frozen toes, trying to keep her eyes off Ada's open suitcase on the bed in the alcove. It was already packed, ready to go.

The bathroom door opened, letting out both steam and her plump roomie, dressed only in panties and bra. "Better hurry, kid."

"These rolls are terrific, Ada. Do I have time for a bath?"

"Are you kidding? We should've left fifteen minutes ago." Ada began tugging on a pair of tartan-plaid wool slacks. Rebecca watched her enviously—Ada Grotosky, forty-two years old, a working actress for twenty of them, always seemed to know where she was going and attacked everything with the same zestful enthusiasm— be it her acting or her Marxist ideology. Rebecca adored her and was challenged by Ada into defining her own political views, somewhere to the immediate right of George McGovern.

Ada's dyed orange-red hair emerged from her sweater like a tossed carrot salad. "Well, com'on, kiddo. Josh won't hold the final curtain."

Rebecca pushed herself off the daybed. "Have you and Josh decided where you're spending the holidays?"

"Yeah." Ada grinned, grabbing a hairbrush. "You ready? Bermuda! Talk about bourgeois fantasies. We're flying out right after the show."

Rebecca darted to the bathroom. "Why Bermuda?"

"Josh knows the head of a workers' commune down there," Ada sang out. "They want to organize a strike against the exploitative corporation that owns the majority of farms. Josh and I are going to lend a hand."

"Mixing a bit of business with pleasure, huh?"

"Can I help it if the commune happens to be on a gorgeous sunny tropical isle? It was either that or going up to Newfoundland to picket the fisheries. And who the hell wants to freeze their asses off when we can be burning them off for the same common good?"

Rebecca laughed. "I love your practical politics. When'll you be back?"

"Sometime after the twentieth," Ada responded and snapped closed her suitcase. Her aging, kewpie-doll face grew pensive. "Gee, kid, I wish you could come along. Hate to think of you up here, all by yourself."

Struggling into a fresh cotton turtleneck, Rebecca said, "My brother invited me out to Trenton for both tomorrow and New Year's. Anyway I've got to find a new job. That'll take time." She didn't want to admit she'd decided already not to take Tony up on his holiday invitations. She didn't enjoy being around Tony's defensive and standoffish wife.

Ada came forward holding out a gift-wrapped small package. "Here's a little something for my dear comrade," she said warmly. "I'm usually not one for observing decadent religious days but let's just say this is a token of my love and admiration."

Rebecca was touched, and more than embarrassed. "Oh, Ada . . . I didn't get you anything. You insisted that—"

"Good," Ada said firmly. "That way I don't have to cop to Josh I accepted one." Ada gave her a warm hug. "Open it whenever you like, but don't you dare tell Josh. He'd think I'm backsliding."

Rebecca squeezed the generous bulk in the fake fur. "Ada, for a commie, you sure are a sentimental ol' thing."

Ada pulled back in mock anger. "Old? Why you little—I'll show you who's old. Come on. I'll race you to the theater!"

They tore down the stairs like a couple of kids, pushing and shoving each other out into the piercing wind. Squealing like kids,

they ran all the way to the small storefront theater on Second Avenue
which served as their alternate home. Rebecca let Ada win.

For close to two years, Real Amerika had been Rebecca's personal salvation. She had stumbled across it almost the first week she'd
arrived by bus from Dallas. Starting as an assistant propperson,
working up to apprentice performer, then understudy and finally a
full-fledged acting member of the small ensemble, Rebecca firmly
believed that the group and the work had given her life new meaning
and purpose. And had helped to fill the terrible void.

Backstage now, in costume for the opening number, listening to
the six-man pit band warm up out front, Rebecca looked around at
the faces of the group. Each was an old and trusted friend. She felt
her heart tug, she would not be with them for six long weeks.

The show's overture began with a brass fanfare and once again
Rebecca got that excited stir in the pit of her stomach. Around her,
the acting members were going through individual techniques and
rituals to loosen up. She stretched nervously. Raphael, the nineteen-
year-old acting apprentice, sought her out, his puppy-dog eyes
worshiping her. "Have you seen *The Godfather* yet? Want to go
tomorrow?"

"Give me a ring tomorrow at Ada's, okay?"

"We've sold out again," he sang, jive-dancing to the overture.

She joined him in the impromptu dance. "Seems kind of silly to
close when we're doing such good business."

"Well, you know Josh. We're not in this to make money, but—"

"—to enlighten the masses," she finished with him, laughing.
She adjusted the wire hoop that stuck out from her body like an open
umbrella and winked at Raphael. "Good show."

Josh turned to whisper loudly, "Places, please."

She took a deep breath, listening to the whizz-bang conclusion to
the upbeat overture. The stagelights blacked out. The final performance of *We're Not in Kansas, Toto* began.

The first number performed by the cast of ten was called the "Attica Gavotte" and it was danced and sung before a backdrop painted to resemble a garden terrace of the New York governor, Nelson Rockefeller. The cast, dressed in burlesqued finery, represented the moneyed upper class at a garden party the afternoon of the Attica prison massacre. The song was a direct parody of the famous "Ascot Gavotte" from *My Fair Lady*, but the message was in keeping with the whole tone of Real Amerika, a biting satire on the political and social mores of the United States.

"Oh Rocky, dear Rocky/ you've done it again/ you've shown us how to make/ mice into men/ Send in the choppers, the tear gas and cops/ kill all those Jews, niggers and wops." With precision, the performers executed the formal dance steps, their noses haughtily in the air.

"Everyone who should be there is here," they sang. "Everyone who doesn't care is here/ Why should we worry and give a fig/ if those rats are killed/ by our own dear pigs?" Repeating the chorus, they brought the number to a stately close. The audience response was immediate and strong, applause sounding ten times the mere ninety-nine paying customers.

Again the lights blacked out and swiftly the backdrop was rolled up to set the scene for the first comedy sketch—a scathingly funny condemnation of the "house arrest" justice handed down by the military courts to Lieutenant William Calley for his part in the murder of twenty-two civilians in My Lai, Vietnam.

Rebecca's only solo number came close to the end of the ninety-minute, fast-paced musical-comedy revue. Much to her surprise, her first attempt at singing publicly had turned out to be one of the true highlights of the whole show—garnering her special notice. Several reviews had praised her comedic singing, one calling her a truly special mixture of Judy Holliday and Gwen Verdon.

In darkness, she now scurried on stage with a wooden stool, placed it on the glowing *X* and sat with her back to the audience. A single white spot picked her up and the piano vamped the introduction. Looking over her shoulder, she began to sing lugubriously: "Here I sit/ All broken-hearted/ Paid my dues/ but can't get started./ My wages have been frozen/ by my overeager boss/ But what about the cost/ of everything I eat?/ And my rent keeps raising/ with the price of heat./ Who's to blame/ for my dire predicament?/ Can I point an accusing finger/ Without fear of imprisonment?''

Slowly she swiveled and stood, revealing a huge, padded belly under her bathrobe, making her look nine months' pregnant. The audience howled with laughter. With her hands on the small of her back for support, she launched into the chorus in her low, Gravel Gertie voice, "Nixon's the one/ There ain't no other/ He got me this way/ Him and Big Brother/ I've got the awful feeling/ There's nothing I can do/ So you better watch out/ Or he'll screw you too!''

After two quick verses and another chorus, her comedy lament concluded. The audience ate it up. Every night it had been like this—stomping, cheering, whistling and such applause the show had to be stopped until the demand was met—one more chorus of "Nixon's the One." Knowing that this would be the very last time she would sing the number, she could hardly find breath to get through that night's obligatory encore.

All too soon, she was back onstage with the entire cast performing the closing number—a protest against the 7,000 arrested "illegally" in the nation's capital in the previous May's anti-war rally.

Again and again they sang the last chorus, building it to a rousing, old-fashioned musical-comedy finale, complete with cut-time, chorus-line unison kick step. Red, white, and blue bunting dropped in from above and a giant American flag unfurled from the floor, completely covering the rear of the stage. Blinking, moving lights outlined the proscenium as the men fell to one knee and the women stood behind, arms raised high on the last note. Black out. The audience was on its feet, cheering and clapping at the same time.

The lights came up. Rebecca joined hands with the others and stepped forward. Together they all bowed, then stood applauding the audience who returned in kind. Everyone seemed to realize that something extra special had come to a close. The audience would not let them go. Waves of applause swept over the performers.

Josh stepped forward, chubby, magnetic. The audience quieted to hear his words. "This show may be closing, but Real Amerika will be back in the spring with a whole new format. Until then, thank you and remember—we're all in this mess together. Keep the faith. We *shall* overcome.''

Rebecca looked out over the faces of the audience which cheered and clapped again. True to form, the audience was an odd mixture of the hip young and the conservatively dressed, upper- and middle-class types. Something drew her eye to a lanky, short-haired figure standing in the rear of the house. Her heart sank to her stomach and then skyrocketed.

It was *Scooter*! Smiling lopsidedly at her in the same, shy, boyish way, his handsome face tanned and lean. He was pointing to the side exit of the theater. She nodded repeatedly. Barely able to contain her excitement, she edged to the wings and slipped off stage, running to the stage door, the applause still flowing. She burst through into the darkened, snowy alley and slowed, her chest near suffocating.

He appeared at the far end, silhouetted against the bright street light, wearing a long overcoat, surrounded by softly falling snowflakes. He moved to her, limping slightly. Immediately concerned, she darted forward. He stopped and waited for her. She drew up. ''Well, as I was saying, before we were interrupted, I just . . .'' Her attempt at a joke ran out of steam and stopped.

''Hi, Rebecca,'' he replied, solemn and shy. Awkwardly they stood, three feet from each other, as though each were afraid to move first.

''Where've you been?'' she asked, then added quickly, ''No, you don't have to answer that.'' She shivered, wrapping her arms around her damp costume.

He came to her, opening his long, wool overcoat. She moved into him and he enveloped her with the coat, pulling her into his trunk. She felt stiff, wooden. She wanted to lean into him, to feel his warmth, but something held her back.

''You were very good in there,'' he said quietly over her head. ''You've really grown as an actress.''

''Thanks,'' she said, pulling back to look up at his face. The eyes seemed sadder, the pretty boy coarsened. He even smelled different. Perhaps it was the baggy old coat, but there was a distinct odor of a stranger about him. ''I gotta get back in,'' she said.

''I'll wait here for you, okay?''

"Sure. Why not?" She pulled away, hurrying to the stage door, feeling chilled both from the cold night air and this stranger whom she thought she still loved.

Rattled, Rebecca changed out of her costume, hugged everyone, wishing Josh and Ada "*bon voyage*" and said her good-byes to all. With one last cheery wave, she grabbed her car coat and slipped out into the silent alley. He stood where she had left him. She could not see his eyes and moved to him, wanting to ask too many questions.

Silently they walked through the new snow. A bright pool of light at the intersection drew her on. "You hungry?" she asked at the corner. "There's a cheap spaghetti place we could . . ." Her voice faltered. He kept staring at her. "I'm starving," she continued and looked down at his thick work shoes. "Always too nervous to eat before the show, but man, stand back when the curtain rings down. It's real pork-out time."

He shrugged noncommittally. Confused by his reticence, she stepped off the curb. Traffic was light on the avenue, very few people on the sidewalks. The snow had stopped and everything looked coated with powdered sugar. "How come you showed up tonight?" she asked. "Did you know I was in the show?"

"I read the *Voice* review," he said, his breath a chilled fog.

Hopeful but overwhelmed, she murmured, "Man, am I hungry."

Inside the tiny Italian cafe, she ate hungrily, grateful that it gave her something to do. Scooter picked at his salad, sitting stiff and tall. "Where's your appetite?" she asked. He shrugged. "My sister cooked a big dinner before I left."

"You've got a sister? Where?"

"Staten Island. I've been staying with her."

"For how long?"

"Couple of months."

She stared at him, wondering if he'd made any effort to find her. And then remembered that the *Voice* review had been out for weeks and weeks. He'd waited until the last performance. She felt her stomach cramping up and pushed away the half-eaten plate of lasagne.

He smiled oddly. "Your eyes were always bigger than your stomach."

"Yeah? I always figured it was my mouth." She tried to laugh but couldn't find the right button to turn it on. "Mind if I ask you one question? Just one, I promise." His short-cropped head tilted expectantly, so she barged ahead, "What happened to your leg?"

"I broke it trying to hop a freight," he began matter-of-factly. "Compound multiple fracture—the fibula. Had to set it myself. Didn't do such a hot job."

"Couldn't afford a doctor for something important like that?"

"There weren't any around."

"Where was that?"

"The Yucatan."

"Mexico? No wonder you're so tan. I thought most guys in the underground hit Canada. I figured you were up there."

He shook his dark head and she waited for him to expand his story. He didn't. She grabbed the bill and stood. "Well, you're just a bunch of information." She moved to pay the check.

He left the cafe and waited outside. Once she'd joined him again in the cold, he said, "Thanks for the salad. Couldn't chip in. I'm broke."

She shrugged it off, feeling her anger ebb, wondering what was next. Part of her wanted to take him back to the empty apartment, another part wanted to say good-bye, let bygones be bygones, let the dream lie shattered. He took her arm gently. "Going to ask me home?"

She looked into his eyes, liking what she saw. "It's Christmas Eve, right? Gotta be room in the inn."

Rebecca unlocked the door and switched on the ceiling light and stood back, watching him silently survey the meager living space. He paused before the large subway poster for *Hair*. She wondered if he'd seen yet the first 'nudie' rock musical. She started talking to cover her nervousness. "Ada . . . she was the funny, orange-haired lady? This is all her place. But she stays over a lot at Josh's, the chunky guy who made the speech at the end of the show? So it's worked out real well. You'll like her a lot. I do . . ."

He threw his overcoat on the daybed and eased down, sitting beside it, stretching out his leg stiffly.

"I'm sorry about your accident," she said. "Real sorry."

He cracked a halfhearted smile. "One good thing—it's made me 4-F. Don't have to worry about running and hiding anymore."

"That's great. It's all official? The feds not hassling?"

"Nope."

"So now you can get back to your acting. Bet you're burning to hit the old boards. There's a lot of exciting theater going on. Schechner's group down at the Performance Garage and—"

He was shaking his head, side to side. "No acting. No more."

Stunned, she could only stare at him.

"Not with this." He slapped his leg. It was an angry, defeated gesture.

She moved to him. "Scooter, you're too talented to let a little thing like that get—"

"Little thing?" he interrupted, his voice harsh, bitter, like the old days. "How many actors do you know with a gimp leg? You want me to try out for Chester on *Gunsmoke*?"

She sank to her knees next to him. Staring up at him, her eyes watered. She struggled to find words that would console or inspire. But she was too confused about the tangled web of emotions tugging her every which way. Unexpectedly, he reached out and touched her head.

"I like your hair that long," he said. "Looks real good on you."

She couldn't remember him ever complimenting her appearance before and it completely threw her. "Scooter, I . . ."

"No. Wait a sec. I have something I want to get off my chest." He twisted a hank of her hair around his long, thin fingers. "Been trying to say it since the alley, but it's not easy. Since I split on you I've had lots of time to think. Too much time. Too much thinking. There were weeks at a stretch—months—holed up in the mountains, fighting major bouts of malaria and dysentery, never getting enough to eat. Always suspicious of anyone I met—Was this the guy who'd rat on me? The old paranoia blues." He stopped fiddling with her hair and his hands dropped to his lap. She folded her hands over his, moved beyond words.

"Rebecca, you kept me going off the deep end. I thought about you all the time. How you came out from New York to find

me . . . what that meant. How I was scared of that. Down in Halachó,
I ended up living with a bunch of gringos, political refugees, some
SDS underground, including several women—very strong, independent women. They turned my head around. Wouldn't take any of my
male-type games. Shot me down in flames time after time. And each
time, I came back to thinking about you. I treated you badly. And I just
want to say . . . I'm sorry. And especially sorry for leaving you that
way. I was jealous. Hurt. Couldn't get it out any other way. Words
get in my way . . . like now, huh? But what I'm trying to say is . . . I
still love you, Rebecca. I wanted you to know that. Regardless of
what happens.''

She bent and kissed his hands, forgiving him, feeling at peace,
and very womanly. She pulled him to his feet and wordlessly led him
to the rear alcove. In the dim recess of the room, she undressed
him and laid him on the bed. She removed her clothes and lay beside him, conscious of his thin, twisted leg. When he tried to turn
into her, she pushed him back, murmuring, ''No . . . this is my gift
to you.''

She covered his mouth with a kiss, feeling his heart beat beneath
her. She ran a hand down the hard ridges of his body, tracing him.
Raising her head, she looked down at his beautiful, sensitive,
broken-spirited face. ''Merry Christmas, my love . . . merry, merry
Christmas.''

ERIK
March 1972
New York

Straining with effort, Erik finished the last set of ten situps and
panting, fell back flat on the white pile rug which stretched wall to
wall throughout Shelby's Fifth Avenue duplex.

He checked the gold Baroque clock. She had promised to phone if the ad-shoot would run past three. It was now after four and still no word.

At five, he called Shelby's modeling agency; they put him in touch with Avedon's studio. The session had been over since three. Erik returned to his editor's notes, forcing himself to block out everything else.

At ten after six, he was worried. In the spacious living room, on the white cushioned couch, he sat staring at the smeared red lips of Andy Warhol's Marilyn Monroe over the baby grand, trying to recall if Shelby had mentioned other plans.

He found the Four Seasons' number, dialed and cancelled his reservations for dinner. He loped up the carpeted stairs to the master bedroom suite, and took a quick shower. After shaving, he dressed in a new dark blue pinstriped suit by Bill Blass. In the triple floor-length mirrors in her huge walk-in closet with its row upon row of gowns, dresses, furs and racks of shoes, he tightened the knot of the dark maroon silk tie. He couldn't remember the last time he'd worn a tie, let alone a suit. With its nipped-in waist, big lapels and flared trousers, he thought he looked like a longshoreman putting on the ritz. He walked into the bedroom.

She stood in the doorway in astonishment. "Mister Lungren? My, my, my, is that really you?"

She looked like she had just stepped off a *Vogue* cover, all gold silk and green tweed. He gave a welcoming hug. "Babe, you said you'd call by three. We've missed our dinner reservations but if you hurry we can catch—" The phone rang on the nightstand. She started for it. He waved her away. "Let it ring, babe. Take your bath."

"Aren't you raring to go," she teased and turned for the bathroom, the phone still ringing. "Damn that service. Answer it, will you, sugar? Pretty please." She blew him a kiss and disappeared.

He heaved a sigh and picked up the receiver. "Yes?"

"Miss Cale, please."

"You again?"

"I understand Miss Cale's home now," came the brusque voice. "May I speak with her?"

"What are you—following her?" Erik jerked loose his tie and unbuttoned the collar button. "I'll give her your message. Now—"

She appeared in the bath doorway, mouthing, "Who is that?"

He covered the mouthpiece. "Some ass who's been calling all afternoon. I've got his name downstairs."

"Well, for heaven's sake, don't use that tone," she said, moving to him. "You sounded just horribly rude."

"Hell, he's a pushy sonofabitch." He reluctantly handed her the receiver and slouched into the brocade armchair, listening.

"Why, I'd love to read it," she was saying as she pulled off a gold clip earring. "Just send it over in the morning and I'll read it at once and call you. Thank y'all so much for thinking of me. Bye, now."

He waited until she'd hung up. "Well?"

"Just some ol' movie producer," she replied and yawned, speaking through it, "He's sending over a script."

"To be thrown on the pile in your closet?"

"Who knows?" She slipped off her shoes and eased back onto the pillows of the bed, her arms over her head.

He eyed her languid pose. "I've tickets for Lily Tomlin tonight at the Palace. Fifth row center. Can we make it?"

"Oh, sugar," she sighed.

He hesitated, trying to curb his disappointment. "Thought you were dying to see her?"

"I am . . . but not tonight. Horrible day. Richard shot me until I thought I'd drop." She propped up on one elbow, a cascade of blond hair falling over her shoulder. "How sweet of you to make all these plans."

"I wanted the whole evening to be a surprise."

"I'm just bowled over—you look so debonair and all. We'll have to put that suit to good use soon, won't we?"

"Does your husband have to book you too?"

Her fuller lower lip projected into a sultry pout. "All of sudden, y'all're as skittish as one of Evangeline's colts."

"Let's just go out for a drink. Anything, okay?"

Her torso lengthened. "I recall waiting months and months for you to poke your ol' head out of your study," she said and rose, striding to the bathroom with an enticing rustle of nylon-encased thighs. "I'm dying for a long soak and that's all."

He watched her teardrop ass sashay out of sight. She was right, he knew he had neglected her. But dammit, now he felt like making up for that and celebrating a little. And she hadn't even asked why.

He yanked off his clothes and wrapped himself in the dark blue velour robe. It had been one of three gifts she had presented him on his thirty-fourth birthday the year before. The other two were a new Jeep, "just for the country," and a rare first edition of poetry by Keats. All he had been able to afford for her birthday was a sexy negligee ordered from a national catalogue. She had never worn it.

He tuned in the color TV in the corner, selecting a local news program and sat on the bed, smoking one of the jays he'd rolled for the evening's festivities, half-listening to a report on the indictment of Clifford Irving on charges stemming from the fraudulent biography of Howard Hughes. Erik was more pissed by the half-million-dollar advance from the publisher than he was by the fraud. He had only gotten fifty thousand for his new novel.

Forty-five minutes passed and Shelby did not emerge. He tapped lightly. "*Entré, monsieur,*" she called out. He walked into the steamy, black-and-white tiled room, holding up the chilled bottle of Dom Perignon and two champagne glasses.

Up to her neck in bubbles, her hair piled loosely on top of her head, she was carefully studying her reflection in the magnifying side of a hand mirror. "Sugar, do you think I should get a nose job?"

He had to laugh. "Course not."

"You just don't take me seriously, Erik. That's the problem."

"Problem? We have a problem here?" He sat on his haunches and popped the cork, quickly pouring a glass. "Not me. I had a very successful meeting with my editor this morning. He said the book was an extraordinary achievement. That the prose 'glimmers.'" Erik held out the glass.

She shook her head. "When'll it be out?"

He took a sip, wishing she'd join him. "Some time this fall."

"Goodness, that's a long time to wait," she replied and lifted one leg to examine it.

The sight of her sleek, glistening wet limb tightened his throat. He ran a finger down the calf. She shivered in annoyance, lowering it back into the suds. He winked. "When was the last time we made it in a tub?"

"I told you sugar, I'm pooped. Besides we messed around this morning, didn't we?"

He stood slowly. "Are we on a quota system now?"

"Oh, sugar, don't take it so personally."

"How the hell am I supposed to take it? I've been waiting all day to celebrate."

"Celebrate what?" Her eyes opened wide with genuine surprise.

"I just told you. My editor loves the novel. Predicts big things for it. And I'm virtually finished with it."

"How divine."

"Let's take a couple of months off," he suggested, pouring another glass full. "Go out west. To Oregon. Let me show you where I was raised. Where my novel is set. Then go sailing up on Puget Sound. You'll love it out there. Clean and green. Good people. Honest folk."

"Oh, sugar," she moaned. "I'd surely love to, but the timing is just all wrong. Remember that contract with Kodak? In a week, we start shooting a series of four commercials."

He stood. "Well, hell, Shelby, when are we going to get together again?" He left the bathroom and stomped down to the library to have a drink to calm down.

Later when he returned upstairs to apologize, she was already asleep on her side of the king-sized bed. Doffing his robe, he slipped in beside her and lay watching her delicate profile, wanting to hold her, but afraid of waking her.

The next morning, he was jarred to consciousness by the intercom buzzer. The doorman informed him of a messenger-delivered, registered package. Erik groggily told him to send it up. On the living room mirror, he found a note reminding him of her appearance on the *Today* show at nine. Swearing to himself for missing it, he answered the doorbell and signed for the package. Idly he opened it while listening for the coffee to perk. It was the Hollywood hoedad's film script. The producer had enclosed a note urging Shelby to get right back with her response. The title printed on the bright yellow cover read *Fool's Gold*. The screenwriter's name was unfamiliar.

Over morning coffee, toast and four scrambled eggs, Erik began to read a few pages out of curiosity. By page seven, he was completely engrossed. It was a simple story of a group of teenagers in a mountain town who attempt to resurrect an abandoned mine for their own profit. The kids run into local opposition from the town's fat cats, resulting in violence but eventual victory for the underdogs. Finishing the screenplay, Erik went upstairs to shower and dressed to attack his rewrites.

Shelby showed up around one P.M., looking dewy-eyed, radiant and in an expansive mood. "Did you see me?" she asked. He explained his late arising. She pouted playfully. "Well, I really had fun with it. Hugh Downs was so nice. I felt I'd known him for ages. Is that the script?" She picked it up.

"It's surprisingly good," he said and pulled her onto his lap for a little squeeze. "Sorry I missed you, babe. Any chance of reruns?"

"Why do you say 'surprisingly?'" she inquired, opening the script randomly. "Do you think all film scripts are lacking in literary merit?"

He chuckled, nuzzling his nose against her hair it smelled of the outdoors, fresh wind and sun. "The ones you've been offered, yes."

She frowned. "What's my part like?"

"Read it."

Sighing, she stood and tossed the script onto the side table. "Not now. I had to be up at six." She started to move off. He grabbed her arm gently. "You promised the producer you'd get back to him."

"That was just to get rid of him."

"I don't want him calling here again. Either notify him now you're not interested. Or follow through on your promise."

She puffed out her cheeks, blowing out an exasperated burst of air. "Honestly, Erik . . . sometimes you're so . . . such a boy scout!"

He waggled his eyebrows. "And I'm after your cookies, girlie."

She smirked and exited, the script tucked under her arm.

Back at his desk, he soon forgot that she was even in the apartment until some time later that afternoon he heard her in the doorway. Looking vaguely troubled, she sank to the loveseat. "Well, sort of effective story, isn't it?" He nodded, not wanting to offer any further opinions until he'd heard hers. She curled her stocking feet under her. "I couldn't do it though. Those two nude scenes..."

He shrugged. "Depends on the director. Could be minimal flesh and maximum eroticism."

"I'd have to know before I got involved."

"Did you like the girl's character?"

"Sort of... yes. Kind of a sweet bitch actually."

"Well, then, why don't you meet with this producer and see what his ideas are?"

"Certainly the best role I've been offered, isn't it?"

"By far..." He did not speak for several moments. "Well...?"

"I don't know if I want to be an actress."

"You've complained about being nothing more than a high-priced product-pusher since I've known you. Acting is one option you've talked of exploring. Nothing to lose by meeting the guy."

She shrank against the wall, suddenly an insecure child. "Will you come with me?"

The following afternoon with Shelby on his arm, Erik knocked on the producer's suite door of the Sherry-Netherland Hotel. She let go of his arm to straighten her picture-brim straw hat. Wearing a spring suit of white silk, she looked so serene that he felt only he could tell how nervous she really was.

Almost at once, the door swung open revealing a short, dark-haired, intense-faced young man. His black eyes darted over Erik and brightened when landing on Shelby. "Come in," he said and stood back. "In case you're wondering, I'm the producer." He closed the door behind them.

Taking off her hat, Shelby flashed her trademark smile. "So pleased to meet you, Mister Rau."

"Call me David," he offered with a satisfied smile and ushered them to a floral-print couch. "Sit. Sit." He waved them down vigorously.

"I hope y'all don't mind my bringing my husband."

"Not at all," Rau replied but Erik had the distinct feeling the producer was annoyed by his presence. "So what'd you think of my script? You were pretty vague on the phone."

Erik said, "We wouldn't be here unless we felt it had merit."

"It's the best damned script to come out of Hollywood in years," Rau said as though offering an undebatable fact.

Pacing around the room, his silk shirt open several buttons, a good chain flashing on his tanned skin, Rau began a very hyper but well-presented sales pitch. Why the script was so good and how he knew Shelby was perfect for the role of Gretchen. "I turned on the tube one night last week—out in Malibu—and there you were. In a perfume ad. The way you moved, your voice, your look—the whole package was Gretchen. Yes, more sophisticated, yes, more glamorous. But the essence was there—the innocence, the intelligence, the independence, and of course, the right look, the beauty. I haven't shown the script to any other girl. I won't. I want you."

"I'm very flattered, David," she replied, her voice soft, womanly, evocative. "But we have serious reservations." She leaned into Erik as if showing solidarity of opinion from the couch.

"Such as?"

She glanced at Erik and he believed she wanted him to voice her objections so he said, "We're concerned about the nudity."

"Is that all? Well, don't be. If I land the director I want, the least you'll get is an Oscar nomination."

"Who?" Erik inquired.

"I'm not at liberty," Rau said with a darting glance at him, "to discuss that at this time. But he's internationally renowned. Won several major festival awards. Nominated three times for an Oscar."

"What about you, then?" Erik countered amiably. "What have you produced, that sort of thing."

"I have a *firm* three-picture commitment from Pacific Studios. That alone is a major achievement."

"So this is your maiden voyage?"

For the first time, Rau sat down. He placed his elbows on the arms of the wing-back chair and started speaking in a low, confidential tone. "If you would like I can give you a printed résumé of my experience in the entertainment industry. It is *quite* extensive."

Shelby crossed her legs and smiled brightly. "I remember Pacific

Studios. My daddy took me to Hollywood when I was a child—seven or eight—and somehow, I forget why, he arranged a tour of Pacific. I was thrilled. Honestly, I was. We got to see them filming some Bible movie, lots of camels and costumed crowds. Even an elephant. I remember that the best.''

Erik looked at her in amazement. He'd never heard that story before and wondered if it were one of her gracious fabrications to smooth over any tensions. Rau, however, appeared to be quite taken by her remarks. He bent to her eagerly. *"The Sins of Bathsheba.* That would have been the summer of fifty-five. I was on the lot then too.''

''Y'all were?'' she exclaimed. ''Why, y'all must've been a kid too.''

Inwardly Erik smiled. He had seen Shelby don this fantastic Southern girl act so many times he knew it by heart. Sitting beside her through too many dull dinner parties, cocktail shindigs, theater openings, interviews—he had filled his time most satisfactorily by just watching her do her thing. She was marvelous at it. She could turn on the glamor, the Southern graciousness, the irresistible charm like a magical tap.

Like the way she now sat, leaning forward, ankles locked together off to one side, her whole body language saying, ''I'm utterly captivated.'' She was sensational with her eyes—they did most of the talking for her, they hung on every word of the other party, everything was found to be delightfully original, intimate, perceptive. She had the extraordinary ability to make men around her sparkle. It was a quality he dearly loved and he sat there now, observing that unique brand of bewitchery, aware of its power and at the same time, captivated by it. As was Rau.

The producer was transfixed by Shelby's allure. Gone was the serious frown which had been so locked into place. Rau now looked like an enthusiastic kid. But he was too perfectly coiffed for Erik's tastes and too casually elegant in his faded designer jeans and velvet blazer. And by far, too damned cocky.

Trilling one of her special laughs, Shelby tossed her hair. ''Well, David, it's been a real pleasure meeting y'all. But I am really not all that convinced. I—''

Rau butted in, "But you're not saying, 'no.'"

"No . . . I'm not." She unwound her legs and stood, holding out her hand. "I will promise to think about it."

Popping to his feet, Rau hurried to take her hand, holding it loosely like a foreign object. "That's good enough for now. But I warn you . . . I'm very persistent until I get what I want."

She laughed again. "A fair warning."

By her side, Erik shook hands firmly with the producer, trying to lock eyes with him. But Rau avoided anything more than a cursory acknowledgment. In the elevator on the way down, Erik kissed the top of her head. "Are you interested?"

Shelby leaned tiredly against his shoulder. "I loathed him."

During the following week, while Erik wrapped up his rewrites and edits, David Rau—true to his "fair warning"—persisted in badgering Shelby to accept the role. He left dozens of messages, every morning sent a bouquet of red roses; he mailed long typewritten letters—*Memos from Rau*, Erik began calling them as some ran over ten pages—explaining every aspect of the upcoming production from the sound track album to how he wanted her photographed like Julie Christie in *Darling*. He telegrammed short messages of encouragement and pleas to trust him, that he only had her best interests at heart.

Though by midweek, Erik was completely fed up, he was surprised to note that Shelby seemed to find the heated pursuit flattering and even amusing. She appeared to blossom under the barrage, becoming playful and coquettish and bubbling with a newfound energy. Erik chalked it up to just one more mysterious aspect of this tantalizing creature. But something about it all made him uneasy, and disturbed his sense of balance.

On Friday morning, over a leisurely breakfast in the windowed alcove facing the bright morning sun, Shelby suddenly shot to her feet, thumping down a section of newspaper. "Check out Earl Wilson," she said and flew out of the kitchen. Erik picked up the page. Under a photo of her, Wilson had written, "Rumor has it that famed glamor queen, Shelby Cale, is seriously considering a *nudie* movie offer by one of Hollywood's hottest young producers. Now there's a flick I wouldn't take my wife to.''

Erik located her upstairs, dumping the last vase of Rau's roses down the incinerator chute in the bathroom. She whirled to him. "If that doesn't read like a plant straight from the horse's ass.''

"Why don't you call him and tell him to kiss off.''

Her eyes lit up with agreement. She strode purposefully across the room, reaching the white phone by the bed just as it rang. She snatched it to her ear. "Hello?''

He watched her face drain of color, then flush rapidly. She fumed into the receiver, "Gi-Giorgio, this is none of your damned business.'' She sat down on the bed, her back rigid as though in the center ring of a horseshow. "Even if it were true, which it isn't—not by a long shot—you're overstepping yourself.'' She paused, her spine lengthening further. "Kiss off, Giorgio,'' she said bitingly and slapped the receiver down. "That bastard! Imagine him ordering me not to accept the role. That it would be irrevocably damaging to his Sunny image.'' She poked a cigarette into her mouth and lit it as though it were an effigy of Caesari.

She looked up and blew smoke past him in irritation. "What're you doing?''

"I'm calling Rau and telling him we want a retraction or he faces a goddamned lawsuit.'' He found the number of Rau's hotel.

Her hand flew to his. "Don't,'' she said in an odd tone of voice and then forced one of her smiles. "Let's just keep calm about this for a while. Maybe he had nothing to do with it.''

Erik did not understand her hesitancy. She offered a fresher smile, a finger raised to trace his jaw line. "It's rather amusing, don't you think? Here we are, all worked up over . . . over what? Just a couple of childish men. And a tacky bit of gossip. Haven't we been through all this before?''

He filled his chest with air to stall for time and finally nodded his agreement. She pecked him on the cheek.

That evening, while in the study, he answered the phone, a call for Shelby from Oak Hills. He yelled up the stairs for her and promptly hung up his extension, trying to concentrate on his work.

Some minutes later, she came into the room, white-faced, shaking with barely controlled fury. "That sonofabitch called Beth Ann."

"Which one?"

"Caesari, who else? She ranted at me like I was in grade school. She's sounding more like Evangeline all the time. Must have said 'I forbid' a dozen times. That Evangeline would have a stroke. I should be so damned lucky."

He tugged her close. "I think this whole thing's gone far enough. Let's call this hot-shot, Hollywood-yo-yo and tell him to get off the track. Right now."

She tilted her head, searching his face with clouded eyes. "But I haven't decided yet . . . I've half a mind to do it—just to spite ol' Caesari and mother. Serve them right."

"That hardly seems a reason to commit to anything."

She wiggled free of his grasp. "Well, there may be other reasons."

"Like what?"

"Well, for heavens' sake, how long do you think I can go on modeling? Each day there's a new face on the rack—fresher, younger. I'm sick of dieting and being treated like a dumb blonde. And look what this city's air has done to my skin . . ." She shoved her face close to his, closing her eyes as if he would see the damage more clearly.

He kissed the tip of her nose, trying to pull her closer. She squirmed away. "Your friend, Mo? She handles these kind of negotiations, doesn't she? My agency doesn't."

"Thought you didn't like Mo that much?"

"She's smart though. So's David Rau. Just keeping my options open—as you always say." She gently pulled his head down and thrust her tongue into his mouth. He inhaled her. But he had a sodden lump in his gut that told him she'd already made up her mind.

That next afternoon, Erik climbed the front stairs of the brownstone townhouse on East Fifty-fourth. The brass plaque on the door read *The Hendricks Talent Agency*. He was ushered by a chic-looking secretary into Mo's cluttered, dusty office and at once felt saner. Mo always had that effect on him—she was solid and unassuming. He regretted not seeing her more often since Michael had split. Hugging her, he noted a large tear under one arm of her smocklike dress.

She settled behind her paper-stacked desk and lit a Gauloise. "This David Rau means business. I checked with my L.A. contacts. Evidently Rau's three-picture deal is firm. But Pacific didn't give it to him. Rather the head of AII which owns Pacific."

"Why?"

She snorted and flicked her cigarette on the carpet. "Because Rau made a fortune for AII's record label. And you want to hear the real capper? Irving R. Dyer, president of Pacific, is Rau's father."

"No kidding?"

She smiled toothily. "But evidently Dyer fought this deal all the way to the top. So much for blood being thicker than water."

"So Rau's legit?"

"For now. The grapevine out there is laying four-to-one odds he'll fall flat. He's stepped on more toes than the National Organization of Women."

"What do you think?"

She puffed heavily for a moment. "Hollywood's a whole different ballpark from New York. But the game's the same. You play to win. Rau's been a winner before. He could do it again. He sure as hell won't be playing to lose." She paused to inhale deeply. "Still . . . I don't know if I'd put any money on him. I understand he and Irving hate each other's guts. And you remember what an asshole that Dyer can be. On the Sunny pageant? Making us do all those rewrites for Cara Noor? Lord, I thought I'd kill the bastard."

"I don't know if I want Shelby getting caught in a crossfire between those two. When it comes to those games, she's defenseless."

"Hell, Erik, don't be love blind. Shelby has the greatest defense system in the world—she's goddamned beautiful."

"That *can* be a liability."

Mo studied him openly. "Want your wife in the movies?"

"I don't really know if I can answer that," he said and meant it. "She's been so damned bored with modeling. I know she's restless as hell. Acting could broaden her horizons, give her new challenges, help her whole outlook on life." He paused, thinking deeply. "To be truthful, Mo, there are times I'm afraid I'll lose her—she'll up and run off, just to change the scenery."

He picked a brown leaf off the azalea. "Think she can act?"

"With a face like hers, who needs to act? Much."

A commotion erupted in the reception room. She sighed broadly, "School's out."

The door burst open and in scrambled her eleven-year-old twins, identical twisters of energy, one in a Yankees' baseball cap, the other in a Dodgers', hollering first at Mo, then seeing Erik, veering paths, changing targets. "Where've you been? Been locked up?" one jeered. The other punched his chest. "You mad at us or something?"

Erik groaned, "Man, oh man, have you two squirts grown. You're Tommy, right?"

"Wrong, you jerk. I'm Timmy. He's—"

"I'm Tommy," the other chimed in and made a glum face. Erik stood back to look. Their hair had gotten darker; their faces had lost some of the cherubic innocence. More and more they looked like Michael and it pained him that his friend was not seeing them grow up.

They fired questions like a double-barreled shotgun, switching topics, wanting to know if he'd heard from their "old man" and which team he was betting on to take the World Series, even though spring training had only begun, and what he thought Bobby Fischer's chances were for winning the World Chess matches against "that Russian."

"Enough, enough," Mo soon ordered. "You've tons of schoolwork. I'm not paying for that fancy prep school for nothing."

"Ah, mom," they groaned in unison.

"Get to it," she said. "I mean it. Now git."

As she pushed them out of the room, they sang together, "Jeremiah was a bull frog!" and danced ahead of her into the hall.

She slammed the door, shaking her head. "If I ever lay eyes on Michael again, I'll kill the little mick runt."

"I haven't heard a damned thing from him. How about you?"

"A postcard last month to the boys," she snorted. "He's still up in Montreal. Helping the draft dodgers." She plopped heavily into her chair. "How in all consciousness he can help other people's kids and neglect his own ... the boys need a dad, badly. I was only kidding about killing him. I still miss him. Mainly when I crawl into bed."

Erik walked the entire twenty-some blocks back to Shelby's apartment tower, pondering each step of the way. Unlocking the front door to her duplex, he heard someone playing the piano. He paused in the doorway of the living room, watching her. In the gathering darkness, Shelby sat at the white piano, intent over the sheet music, wearing only a sleek, moss green jersey robe. She looked like she had just emerged from the bath, free from makeup. Her playing was tentative but earnest. With a start, she saw him and her hands rose off the keys.

"Go on," he said. "My mom used to play that."

"'Humouresque,'" she said and stood, moving to the couch. "Seven years of mandatory lessons and I can't play worth a damn." She collapsed onto the cushions with a dejected slump. "What'd Mo say?"

"Only that Rau seems legit and she'd be happy to handle the negotiations if you'd like." He put his arm around her, pulling her close. She rested her head on his shoulders. For a long while, neither spoke. He was filled with uncertainty, knowing what was coming.

"Sugar," she began seriously. "Do you want me to do it?"

"I've told you, babe ... that's entirely up to you."

"But what if I can't act? I could make a fool of myself."

"Won't know unless you try. Can't be afraid of trying things."

"But I'd be away for three whole months," she wailed, suddenly emotional.

"Only a plane ride away."

She jerked back from him. "You *do* want me to do it, don't you?"

"Shelby, I ..."

She pushed off the couch. "You don't really care if I'm gone that long. You want to get rid of me so you can mess around."

"Stop it! You don't mean that and you know it." He couldn't help the anger in his voice—she always seemed capable of pushing the right button to get a rise out of him.

"You don't love me anymore. You want me out of your life for good. You're just sitting there dying for me to take this part so . . . so you can be free again. You've got a new book coming out. You want to be able to cat around like you used to. You don't fool me. I can read it in your face." She began to weep, her shoulders shaking under the thin material, her breasts heaving, straining against the front of her robe.

He crossed swiftly to her, held her tightly. He groped for words. "I love you, babe . . . I'm behind any decision you make. But I can't make it for you. I'm sorry, I can't . . . I won't. It's up to you."

SHELBY
July 1972
Montana

Under the broiling sun, the clapper boards slapped together in front of her nose. "Scene Twenty-two; take eighteen," the young man said and moved, clearing the camera's range of vision.

Shelby, trying not to squint in the sun's glare, began again as directed. She stared sorrowfully after the lone figure on the dirt road that wound among the thinning pine trees. And tried to think of the saddest of all possible thoughts.

"Anytime you're ready," came the slightly accented voice of the director. Though soft-spoken, there was an unmistakable edge of irritation.

She attempted to conjure up the morning she had learned her father was never going to come home again. No tears came.

"Cut," the director ordered. Immediately the camera stopped

rolling and there was a buzz of voices as the crew broke and began milling about, talking; someone laughed softly.

Out of the corner of her eye, she was vividly conscious that Werner Sturhm, the director, was once again being lectured by the producer. Their heads were bent together but David Rau stared hard directly at her as he spoke. She felt like sticking out her tongue at him.

The sun beat on her relentlessly. She detested the perspiration soaking through the back of the cotton sundress. David Rau was angrily gesturing to the surrounding mountains. She pretended not to look in that direction but she did note quickly that rainclouds were building in the west. The elderly director hurried to her.

"What seems to be the problem, Miss Cale?" he asked in his slight Austrian accent.

Deliberately she turned away, seeking the shade from a nearby, low-hanging pine bough. She caught a glimpse of David eyeing her as though she were a piece of malfunctioning equipment.

"Miss Cale, I must know if we can get this shot soon," the director was saying, overly patient. "It is such a simple, little moment. I *am* not asking for buckets. A mere moistening of the eyes."

"I *am* trying," she sighed, both weary and angry.

In the background, David Rau turned away, muttering just loud enough for her to hear, "Get an onion to shove under her nose."

She bristled, staring at his back in disbelief.

Werner quickly interceded. "We're losing the sun. See? Rain on the horizon."

"Then film that and get your damned tears," she said and marched away. She went straight to her trailer, kicked her wardrobe girl out of the air-conditioned coolness, slammed the door, locked it and fell full out onto the couch-bed. She fought the desire to scream.

God, she hated that bastard, Rau. From the first day of rehearsal he had been pushing her, needling her, forcing his decisions upon her, making her repeat each shot endlessly until he was satisfied. Werner Sturhm wasn't directing, David Rau was and she loathed his dictatorship.

There was a brisk knock at her door. "Go away," she shouted, rolling into the rear cushions. A muffled voice pleaded with her to come out. She recognized the drawl—the assistant director, a trim, roving-eyed Texan whom she liked better than anyone on the whole crew. "I'm not coming out," she yelled. The silence outside offered some satisfaction, at least someone was taking her seriously.

Shelby flopped onto her back, unconcerned that her costume was being wrinkled. She raised a bare arm, checking out the skin—bright pink and beginning to tingle. That alone made her furious.

She rose and quickly slathered a thick layer of protective cream over both arms and her bare shoulders. Noticing the cream was getting on the straps of the sundress, she yanked the pale, yellow garment over her head and tossed it over a chair. Wearing only a silk Teddy, she sat staring at her reflection in the mirror lined with bulbs. She looked horrendous—the curly poodle-cut was so cutesy-pie it revolted her. Bitterly, she began brushing out the curls which had taken the hairdresser over an hour to arrange.

Her eyes landed on a newly delivered envelope propped up against the mirror. It was from Erik. Hurriedly she tore into it, and began to read. Halfway through the first page, she lost interest and let it slip from her fingers. Just the same old business about the novel's publication and why hadn't she written or called? She had tried writing. But what was there to say? If he only knew what she were going through just because of him.

The door handle rattled behind her. "I'm not coming out," she yelled. Unexpectedly the door flew open. The producer stood there, pulling an extra key out of the lock, nailing her to the chair with an accusing glare.

His voice was ice. "These tedious little tantrums of yours are damned expensive."

"If things don't change around here, you *will* see a tantrum."

Abruptly he stepped up into the stairwell and slammed the door shut. His hand jerked the sundress off the back of the chair. "Look what you've done to your costume. What the hell's with you anyway?"

She crossed her arms over her lacy bodice. "If you'd let Werner direct this film, you might have something to be proud of."

"He's not getting a damned thing out of you."

"And you are? You don't want an actress, you want a machine. I tried all day to please you and what do I get in return? Threats, ridicule, aspersions cast on my talent. Well, I've just had enough of you for one day."

His eyes flicked on her and away. "If you were a true pro, you wouldn't give a damn whether you liked me or not. But obviously you have a helluva lot to learn about being a professional."

Her neck elongated. "I have been a professional since I was eighteen. Which, if I remember correctly from your overblown, self-serving résumé, is at least three years before y'all started. It is *because* of my professionalism that I know what I'm talking about." She paused and then said bitingly, "You don't know what the hell you're doing."

The skin tightened over his cheekbones. "And you do?"

"Enough to protect my own interests. It's clear no one else will."

He shot her a triumphant glance. "What do you think I'm trying to do? Make a fool out of you? I'm looking at the whole picture and you're stuck so on yourself, you can't see beyond the mirror." He leaned in and venomously said, "If you don't shape up, I may recast and start again. I'd rather be two weeks behind schedule with a cooperative actress, than to put up with your spoiled shit for another day." He tore open the door, preparing to leave.

"Then *do* it!" she shouted. "I don't have to put up with this . . . this injustice any longer."

"You selfish cunt," he hurled at her and stalked down the steps, slamming the door behind him.

She erupted to her feet, the jar of cold cream in her hand. She threw it with all her might at the door. It struck with a resounding crash in the small aluminum trailer, showering bits of glass and globs of white cream, creating a sticky, gooey, sliding mess all over the door. But it did not satisfy any sense of release from her shock and revulsion. Never, ever had she been called that before in her whole, entire life.

She crumpled into the vanity chair and collapsed over her bare, greasy arms. Her eyes overflowed and in surprise, she raised her head, looking at her tearful image. "Dammit to hell," she cursed and grabbed her brush.

Moments later, once more in costume, she emerged into the glaring sunlight, the tears still streaming. She strode purposefully to her position, tossing to the director, "Let's get this fiasco over with."

The director and the stunned crew leaped to action. She successfully completed the required sequence on the first take. But the producer was nowhere to be seen.

It was later that evening, in her room under the eaves of the old brick hotel back in the village, when she learned where David had gone. She had just finished the dinner she'd had sent up from the small cafe and was chatting on the phone with the friendly Texan who bunked in a motel out of town. He mentioned that the producer had left to fly to New York and wouldn't be back for a couple of days. "Why'd he do that?" she asked.

The A.D. said, "Something to do with his record business. You know he's riding two horses at once. And he's also trying to find an actor for the psychotic kid. That's the only part not cast yet—plenty of time. Won't get to that sequence for several weeks."

She took a small bite of the sourdough roll. "You'd think he'd have cast that by now. And it also appears to me he's involved in one too many projects at once. No wonder he's such a hyper little megalomaniac."

The Texan laughed. "Hey, did you hear the latest about Fonda? Left for Hanoi today to talk to the Cong."

"Henry or Peter?"

"Jane," he said with another laugh. "They're already calling her Hanoi Jane."

"Honestly, y'all'd think she'd have learned by now to keep her mouth shut. She just doesn't have a head on her shoulders, does she?" Shelby yawned. "What time are y'all making me get up in the morning?"

"Five. Sorry about that."

She groaned, said a quick good night and hung up. She lay for a long time wondering why she felt so upset. For some reason, the news of Rau's sudden departure disturbed her more than she wanted to admit.

Over the next few days, Shelby's workload was minimal and she

had a great deal of time on her hands. Bored with the small
mountain town and the location film crew, she kept to her room,
trying to write another letter to Erik but giving up in frustration. She
fell to worrying about the producer's choices. Especially the director,
Werner Sturhm, old world charm, always kissing her hand and treating
her like a Viennese bon-bon to be packed away in a box when not
needed. How Rau had ever imagined this director was capable of
handling a subject so innately American as the film's story continually
perplexed her. In fact, every choice Rau had made on this project,
she did not understand—including her own casting. Her character of
Gretchen was supposed to be a small-town, all-American tease—no
sophistication, no glamor, no understanding of herself or her boyfriend.
She began to wonder whether the whole project was doomed from
the start because of Rau's blindness to the ingredients he'd assembled.

She placed a call to Erik in Darien, waiting interminably for the
hotel's antique switchboard to make the connection. Finally his
voice boomed in her ear—it sounded so close, so much like him, she
began to unwind.

"I was hoping you'd call," he said. "Purposely stayed in tonight."

"If you hadn't, where would you've gone?" she asked, giving
him a bit of the kittenish quality she knew he loved.

"Don't know . . . out," he replied vaguely. "Hate hanging around
this big old place without you. How's it going?"

"Super."

"How's Rau treating you?"

"Oh, fine, actually . . ."

"You don't sound too sure. Look, if he starts giving you a rough
time, let me know."

She managed a carefree laugh. "What *could* you do?"

"I don't know . . . but I'd make damned certain he'd know he had
me to deal with. God, I miss you . . . it's like the sun's been taken
away."

"Me, too, sugar . . ."

"Listen, my book's officially out in a couple of weeks. The
publisher's lining up a promotion tour and I swing through Salt Lake
City. I could take a little jaunt up your way for a couple days—"

"Sugar," she interrupted softly, "I'm just beginning to get the hang of things . . . this acting takes a whole lot of concentration. I'm afraid y'all distract me." She paused, then added, "When you're around, sugar, I'm always distracted."

"That so bad? I mean, hell, it won't be for a few weeks. Surely you'll be acclimated by then. I don't know if I can hang on even that long."

"Let's talk about it later, okay? I'd love to see y'all but, well, I just wouldn't want anything to spoil my chance of succeeding at this. It's all so . . . sort of new."

There was a long pause before he asked, "What're you wearing?"

"Right now? My nightie."

"Which one?"

"That sexy blue lace shorty," she fabricated. "Your birthday present, remember the one?"

He sighed sadly. "Man, would I love to have you here right now. I'd make you so hot and bothered, you'd never want to leave again."

She touched a breast under the silk of her full-length gold negligee. "That's unfair. You're making me bothered right now."

They spoke for a few minutes more before she yawned. "Sugar, I'm fading fast. I was up at five-thirty this morning and it'll be even earlier tomorrow. Just wanted to send my love . . ."

"Thanks, babe. Good night. I love you."

"Me too . . ." She hung up slowly, her hand still caressing her breast. Damn, damn, damn. It wasn't fair.

The next morning torrential rains cancelled the day's shooting schedule. Under the drumming eaves, she slept gratefully until noon, had breakfast sent up from the restaurant and tried to read James Dickey's *Deliverance,* one of several new novels that Erik had sent. The rain continued, lulling her in and out of sleep. From the bed, she could look out the window and over the dreary little town—old-fashioned false, second-story fronts lined the single main street. Everything was slate gray—clouds obscured the mountains which loomed over the valley. How could she possibly endure another three months in this godforsaken hole?

When she awoke, it was dark outside, still pouring down rain, and someone was tapping softly at her door. Hastily she pulled on a matching silk peignoir robe, fluffed her hair and opened the door. Instantly she tensed. David Rau nodded curtly, his hair wet and slicked back, making him look like an extra in a thirties movie. He attempted to smile but failed. "Have some dialogue changes for tomorrow's scene."

Wordlessly she let him in, shutting the door and turning on the desk lamp, speaking with what she felt was admirable control, "I didn't know y'all were back."

"Quick trip." His eyes darted around the room like dark moths seeking a secure place to land. "I found a solid young actor to play Billy. Very strong. He'll give the character a lot of zap."

She nodded disinterestedly. "Why do y'all keep changing my scenes?"

He opened his leather spiral notebook. "Get your script."

She sat next to him, tangibly feeling his unease. He bent over his script and began dictating in short clipped sentences the rewrites in Gretchen's dialogue. She hurriedly scribbled them in her script with a gold Mark Cross felt-tip. The changes were minor—a word deletion here, a new phrase there, nitpicking she thought, but they took close to a half-hour to complete.

The whole while Shelby was overly conscious of his presence—for the first time she noticed, as he printed a note neatly to himself, that he was left-handed. His hands were small, rather childlike, and he held his fountain pen in an odd manner, between his first and second fingers, the thumb overlapping. It looked awkward and added to the child image. There was a vague scent of musk lingering on him—she tried to place it. It didn't smell like aftershave or cologne, perhaps a shampoo.

David snapped closed the cover of his notebook and stood, as though itching to get away. "With our copier on the blink, these new changes won't be distributed until the first of the week," he said, looking through the rainstreaked window. "Can you believe this burg? Not a Xerox machine in the whole damned town. Fishtrap is right."

"I think it's rather quaint," she said. His tenseness made her extremely uncomfortable. Other than the one lunch back in New

York, and the screaming session in her trailer, she could not remember being completely alone with him before. "I do get terribly bored here, though," she offered quietly and crossed her legs.

"If I hadn't wanted absolute authenticity, I would have chosen another locale. Closer to civilization."

"Are you an only child, David?"

He seemed taken aback. "Why do you ask?"

"Curious, that's all. *I* am."

"I know." He looked down at his hands, flexing the fingers over the binder cover. "I have two half-sisters by my father's first wife. But I was raised pretty much by myself. Sometimes—holidays and the like—the others visited. Hated them. They were bigger, always hassling me."

She nodded thoughtfully. "Didn't I read somewhere that Cara Noor and your father got a divorce?"

He shot her a sour glance. "Yeah . . . look, do you have any questions on these changes?"

"No . . . but I'd like you to stay for a while."

"Why?"

She rose to pour a glass of Perrier water. "Would you like one?"

"No."

"You mean . . . no 'thank you,' " she teased and sipped. "Why don't y'all ever look at me directly?"

He hesitated. "Hadn't noticed."

"I do."

For several beats, the only sound was the rain beating on the shingled roof over their heads. But he was looking at her fully, locking onto her face with a strange determination. Slowly she moved across the room until she stood before him, his back against the window. Sweetly she peered over her glass of mineral water. "I don't like being called a cunt, David."

His eyes narrowed, catlike.

She leaned into him, placing the glass on the windowsill beside him. "I like to think of myself as a lady and to be treated as one. If we're going to be working together so closely, perhaps we should get

to know one another better. I, for one, would appreciate a cessation
to all this mutual hostility."

"I don't feel hostile toward you."

"Funny I should get those vibes."

"Perhaps you're just projecting your own." He made a move to
go around her, but she blocked his way.

"If that's true," she said, "I apologize profusely. Do you ever
apologize?"

"When I think it's necessary."

"Would you apologize to me? For calling me that terrible thing?"

"I apologize. It was a slip of anger."

"I accept. Thank you." She bent and kissed his lips. They were
much softer than they looked.

His head snapped away. "Why'd you do that?"

"I felt like it."

"Do you always do what you feel like?"

"As often as I can." She opened her robe. "Touch me . . . please."

He stalled, staring up into her eyes. She could see small beads of
perspiration forming on his upper lip. His touch on her breast was
cautious. She closed her eyes and arched her back, thrusting more
fully into his palm. His exploration was too brief.

She dropped her robe to the floor and in her pale gold satin
nightgown took his hand, leading him toward the bed. He opened his
mouth to speak and she touched his lips with a finger. "Shhhhh,
don't say anything."

She lay down, pulling him next to her. He leaned up, yanking off
his coat. She reached for the buttons of his shirt and he helped her
hands, a faint, quizzical smile on his lips. It made him look younger,
less severe, and she rose to kiss him again as he pulled off his shirt.
His chest was smooth under her fingertips, hairless, his nipples
small, brown buttons. She flicked them with her nails and his breath
deepened.

She waited for him to lift her nightgown, but he was too slow. She
pulled it over her head. For a long while, he stared at her body.
Anxiously she reached for him. She rolled over on her side, one
hand moving across his hip to the front of his slacks. She probed,
squeezed, discovering, much to her astonishment, he did not have an

erection. She undid his belt, unzipping him, opening his pants wide. She reached behind him, yanking at both his shorts and trousers. He struggled out of them, kicking to free his feet. His manhood was generous but totally unaroused. She fondled it expertly. The more she attended him, the more aroused she became.

Gradually, ever so slowly, her efforts were rewarded. His penis thickened, she could feel blood pumping into it. But David lay back against the pillow, his eyes tightly closed. He had barely touched her. She rose up to her knees and threw a leg over him. Slowly she sat on it, pushing down further and further until their pelvises touched. She began to rock up and down, watching his expression.

He reached up with both hands to catch her swinging breasts, hanging onto them like handles, increasing the pressure until it was just short of pain. Together they moved. The bed creaked beneath them, her gasps became louder, faster.

Later, on his ribcage, her head rocking up and down, she felt totally released and oddly triumphant. Quivering with delicious aftershocks, she rolled off him, curling up against his body, and after a long moment, asked, "What're y'all thinking?"

"Nothing much . . . except how surprised I am."

"Surprised—good or bad?"

"Definitely good."

She studied his profile. "What were you like as a kid?"

"Fat. Very fat."

"No . . . not you," she said, pinching his waist, barely able to find a roll. "I find that hard to believe."

"It's true. I was the shortest, fattest, ugliest little pig—all the way up into college. I had a mouthful of crooked teeth too. Until I wore braces in prep school. You should have seen me—a roly-poly turd with a mouthful of metal."

"Did you date much?"

He laughed softly, derisively. "Not for a long time. Always shorter than the girls. Still am to some, like you, right?"

"Y'all're not short. Werner's short. You're . . . well, you've just a slight frame." She lowered a hand to grab his slightly diminishing penis. "Except here, where it counts." He grinned at her, obviously pleased. It was such an engaging, boyish grin, she felt bolder. "David . . . are you gay?"

"No," he said emphatically.

She hesitated, running her fingers over the inside of his armpit—the hairs there were moist, long and silky. "I just thought . . . you weren't turned on by me."

When he finally spoke it was the softest, least forced she'd ever heard him sound. "You're so goddamned beautiful, Shelby . . . you scare me. I've never once—ever made it with someone as beautiful as you."

He looked at her oddly, then kissed her nose and her mouth. It was the first overt move on his part and it thrilled her, striking a responsive chord deep inside. He whispered, "What made you do it?"

"I like challenges."

"Thought you hated me."

"I did."

"Why'd you change your mind?"

She considered briefly, not really knowing. "I guess it was because you never looked at me. You'd be surprised at how boring it is to be ogled all your life."

"I was positive you were just leading me on to dump on me. Suppose that's why I was so tense . . ."

"You don't seem to have any problems now," she murmured and ran her hand over his hardness. It gave her a tremendous sense of victory, an exhilaration she had not experienced before in exactly that way.

He licked her nipples. "Me on top now?"

"Do I get extra sleep in the morning?"

"Only if it's raining . . ."

"Then let's pray for rain. 'Cause I may just want to keep y'all here for days and days."

Laughing sexily, he rolled on top of her.

REBECCA
August 1972
New York

"Then, when Miss Liberty melts to the pavement," Scooter was saying, "we all regroup and launch into a chorus of 'Nixon's the One.' "

"Damn, that's my song," she cried with more than mock anguish. In the rear alcove of Ada's lower East Village apartment, Rebecca hurriedly pulled on her new salmon-colored blouse and poked her head around the corner, moaning, "I want to be there." Scooter, Josh and Ada, each bent over a project, printing a placard, sewing a costume, pasting a prop, but all three grinned back at her. She tugged on her wraparound skirt and stepped fully into view. "After all, wasn't I the one who suggested all this?"

Josh lit his pipe, settled back. "Where you're going is important to your career as an actress. Our demonstration will be over and forgotten by the end of the week."

"Not if we're real lucky," Ada said with a nudge to his ribs.

Rebecca tied the skirt's belt. "What time is it?"

"Relax," Scooter said softly. "You've plenty of time."

She twirled, showing off her khaki skirt and blazer ensemble purchased especially for the interview and dipped into an exaggerated curtsy before Scooter. "So what do you think?"

He grinned. "Long ways from the Haight, huh?"

Their eyes connected and held, bonding together, once again reaffirming what she'd learned since his return—Scooter loved her, he truly did. She grinned back unashamedly. "Yes . . . a long ways."

"You want a cup of coffee?" he asked, refilling his own.

"No, thanks—I'm already so jangled I can't stand still."

"It's only an interview," he warned. "Don't put too many eggs in the basket."

"Listen to him," she threw at the couple on the couch. "Hired for one flick and he's talking like George C. Scott." She kissed him on the cheek. "But, I hear you, man—I hear you."

Ada asked the room, "You think we'll hit the national news before Tricky Dick's nomination?"

"If we're effective, yes," Josh said. "Carlos promises almost as much media exposure as the PLO massacre at the Munich Olympics."

Rebecca shuddered at the horrible memory and spoke softly but with conviction, "It seems so incongruous—here you people are bravely raising your voices for something you believe in and I'm flitting off to see an agent. Kind of frivolous, isn't it, for an adult of twenty-three years of age to be still seeking an agent?"

"You'll be there with us in spirit, I know," Ada furnished. "Besides, it was your idea to hit Nixon's largest contributor," Josh said. "Fresh ideas are the keystones for change."

"But still . . ." Rebecca protested.

Scooter stood. "May I walk Your Lateness to her golden coach?"

"The IND uptown? I'd be honored, sir. Good luck," she said to the couple on the couch and then added impassionedly, "Give 'em hell."

Scooter limped along beside, holding her hand, exploring ideas out loud on what the group could do to climax their guerrilla theater piece later that afternoon. He'd already come up with and rejected a dozen ideas Rebecca had thought sensational. "It's got to be something stark, theatrical—even explosive," he said energetically. "Maybe even shocking or gross. We have to show it hard or keep it in our pants."

She laughed, squeezing his fingers. "You'll come up with something terrific. Mark Spitz and all his medals has nothing on you."

He tilted his finely sculptured head. "*Muchas gracias, gordita.*"

She beamed. "*De nada.* Hey, what's this lady want? I don't have a clue what she's looking for in me."

"Just be yourself and she'll love it. Mo's one savvy lady."

"Are you sure you didn't ask her to interview me?"

He stopped walking. "Honest, I didn't. I told you—it's her idea. I didn't know a thing about it until you got that phone call. Don't look a gift horse in the mouth."

"My, aren't you full of wise old sayings today," she teased and slipped an arm around his waist, tucking her hand into his rear pocket. She loved the feeling of his tush as he moved—tight muscles, tight cheek.

They reached the underground entrance and he pulled her close. "Break a leg, kid."

They kissed until she pulled away reluctantly. "Can't wait to hear how your protest piece comes off. Surprise me."

He winked. "Surprise yourself, kid. See you at the theater."

As soon as she was ushered into Mo Engle's overflowing office, Rebecca lost a great deal of her nervousness. There was something so unassuming and genuine about the lady, Rebecca felt she was dealing with a high-school teacher—perhaps of earth sciences.

Settling into a chintz-covered easy chair, the roundish agent expelled air through her nose. It was a funny kind of sound and it amused Rebecca. They chatted in general about Rebecca's career. Then Mo observed her openly for a long moment. "What's more important to you, right now? Your career or Scooter?" Mo smiled, almost apologetically. "Hope you don't think that's too unfair to ask?"

Rebecca shook her head and tried to read the face before her. It wasn't a pretty face, or even attractive, but there was an intelligence that shone through and inquisitive, warm eyes. "No, it's a fair question—coming from an agent," she started gamely. "Acting is all I want to do. Scooter . . . ? Well, I guess you could say he's the fuel that keeps me going. It's difficult to separate them, they're both such an integral part of me. I can't think of my life without either one. And I . . . I . . . I guess I'm not making myself too clear, huh?"

"You're doing very well," Mo said, her sensible dress tight over her rounded stomach. "I'll level with you. I asked you in as a favor to a client."

"Scooter? He promised me . . ."

"Not Scooter," Mo said. "Robby. Robby Rhomann."

Rebecca felt a flurry of activity in her chest. "Robby?"

"Yes. You seemed surprised. I assumed you were old friends."

"We are . . . or *were*. I mean . . . well, I saw his picture hanging out there in the reception area so I assumed you represented him . . . but, wow, I haven't seen or talked with him in ages."

"He speaks very highly of you—thinks you're quite gifted."

"Really? Well, talk about gifted. He's the one."

"And the first to tell you, too." Mo laughed. "Have you seen the summer series he's in? On CBS?"

"Scooter and I don't have a TV. But I read about Robby's role."

"He plays this goofy kid Buster in a ghetto boys' club. Not a large part. But it's a beginning. So far CBS is pleased."

"Is he still living with his mother?"

"Yes, out in the Hollywood Hills. Strange little lady, isn't she?" Mo dumped the full ashtray into her wastebasket. "As I said, Robby asked a favor. I agreed. That night I saw Real Amerika's new show I was so dazzled by Scooter, I don't recall your performance very much. On the whole, I thought every one in the cast was quite good. But I was curious after Robby built you up so much. So here you are. And . . . to be frank, I don't think there is anything I can do for you."

Rebecca drooped with disappointment. "You don't?"

Mo shook her head. "If there were, I'd sign you. But I'm afraid it would only raise false hopes. I handle primarily TV and film actors. And in that end of the business, I just don't see a large demand for you."

"I think I'm really good."

"You could be one of the most talented actresses in the city and I'd still find you a tough sell."

"A tough sell?"

"To be frank, Rebecca—TV, film actresses your age have to have more than talent. They have to possess great looks and big boobs. Yes, I know, sexist as hell. But those are the facts. You're attractive, lord knows. But the competition's too keen with young women who fit the bill and the sweater more than you. Do you see what I'm saying?"

"I . . . I suppose so . . ." She reached for her shoulder bag.

Mo stood with an expression of maternal concern. "I don't believe in offering false hopes for something I know I won't be able to deliver. I'm sorry."

Rebecca rose. "Guess I'll have to work all the harder to prove myself."

"That's the attitude. All you need is one good theatrical showcase and your fortunes could change overnight," Mo said and dropped her voice to a confidential level. "Also, set realistic, step-by-step goals for yourself and work hard to achieve them. Like number one would be for you to get your Equity card, then a good part, then an agent. Understand? Those goals are important. If you're not absolutely sure of what you want, you'll never succeed. You have to know your goals."

Mo pushed herself up out of her chair, smiling warmly. "Is Scooter excited about his film?"

Rebecca nodded, edging toward the door. "He's so grateful you sent him up for the part."

"It could be his big break," Mo continued. "The part's meaty enough."

"Yes. I read it. He'll be sensational."

Mo snubbed out a cigarette and asked, "You sure you want to tag along for his shoot? It's only for four days, two for travel."

"Scooter says he wants me along," Rebecca replied simply. "And I sense he really does, so I'm going. Don't worry though. I won't get in his way."

Mo snorted again with amusement. "You're okay, Rebecca. I'm glad we had a chance to meet. He's going to be the next Paul Newman, I promise."

Rebecca grinned. "Only better. Well, thank you again for your time. And especially your honesty." She opened the hall door. "And thank Robby too, okay? Good-bye." She stepped out and closed the door. She walked deliberately to the sidewalk out front and then started to run. She didn't stop until she hit the subway turnstile. By then, her eyes were so flooded she could not find the slot for her token.

"I love your boobs," he whispered in the darkness and put his mouth over her right breast, sucking it in fully, letting it slip out.

She patted his head, trying to be funny. "Thank God for small favors, huh?"

Scooter rose on one elbow. "Don't ever put yourself down because you're not stacked," he said quietly. "You've more talent in your little fingers than all the thirty-eight-D cups in New York put together."

She smiled reflectively. "She said it wasn't just my boobs—it's my natural good looks too.

"Hey, you've got a great face." He kissed the tip of her nose. "And a schnozzle that drives me wild."

"A nose fetish, huh? Always knew there was something weird about you." She hugged his lean frame to her.

He laid his head on her breasts. "Don't listen to what Mo said, you need a male agent anyway. A woman couldn't possibly see your gifts."

He sounded as exhausted as she. His anti-Nixon demonstration performed by Real Amerika had been a rousing success in spite of a near violent encounter with some overeager policemen and some hard-hat construction workers.

When Rebecca had arrived back at the storefront theater after her depressing interview, she'd been relieved that the entire troop and dozens of other supporters had already regrouped and were so high on their own supercharged success no one had noticed how down she was. Not even Scooter. He had excitedly filled her in on the details, the huge crowd they'd attracted, the healthy turn out of news media and the explosive climax of the guerrilla theater piece— his throwing a bucket of pig's blood on the front doors of Allied Industries. That action had triggered the security guards from the giant corporation, who'd charged into the troop—which, in turn, sparked the police attack. Which legitimized the free-for-all thrown by the construction workers from a neighboring site. Though some of the acting troop had been struck, and some were bloodied or bruised, all had managed to slip away in the ensuing fracas.

There, at the theater, Rebecca had joined them before a portable TV set on the stage. All of the local news broadcasts had extensive footage of their protest, one station going so far as to label it a "riot in Wall Street." Much to their amazement and eventual ecstacy, even Cronkite, down in Miami for the Republican convention, had carried an excerpt of the highly visual theater piece. Scooter had been featured prominently, looking both possessed and extraordinarily handsome as he shouted before the microphones in front of the metal doors of Allied Industries, "Before we withdraw, a final quote from John F. Kennedy: 'Those who make peaceful revolution impossible will make violent revolution inevitable.'" With that Scooter had thrown the bucket of pig's blood.

When the TV coverage had finished airing, the members and friends of Real Amerika had cheered and screamed jubilantly. They had succeeded beyond their wildest dreams. Even Rebecca had been swept away by their contagious and overwhelming high.

Therefore, it wasn't until after she and Scooter had returned home, crawled into bed for a brief but tender bout of lovemaking, that she had worked up enough nerve to tell him about the interview.

Now, they were drifting closer to sleep and she curled tightly into him. "Scooter . . . do you really want me to tag along to Montana?"

"I've got two little scenes. And two whole days to hang around by myself. You just don't want to run into that Rau fellow."

"I'd like to run *over* him. With a Mack truck."

When she'd first learned that David Rau was producing Scooter's film debut, Rebecca had about fallen through the floor with shock— followed quickly by a deep dread. Scooter, to this day, insisted he didn't remember the screaming, shoving incident with Rau in Golden Gate Park. His days of drug haze, she chalked it up to. And he'd reported that upon meeting David personally at the audition Mo had set up, the producer, himself, gave no indication he'd remembered either. But somehow, Rebecca could not help but feel leery of seeing David again, or having Scooter working for him. Let alone meeting Erik's super *shiksah* wife. Rebecca eased into sleep's inky folds, wondering if Erik, himself, would be there in the mountains of Montana.

Rebecca fell in love with the mining village of Fishtrap the moment she laid eyes on it. From the rear seat of the production company's station wagon, which had picked them up and brought them from the airport in Butte, she gazed out in wonderment. She'd never seen any place so small, even the buildings seemed to be child-sized, none over two stories, snuggled in a steep green mountain valley. Their room on the second floor of the quaint old brick hotel offered stunning vistas of the surrounding majestic Rockies. While Scooter unpacked their jointly shared suitcase, she stood staring in awe at the craggy peaks. "Sure beats the concrete canyons." She turned to assess his mood. "You nervous?"

"Only to get started." He yawned. "Wanna take a nap?"

"Hmmmm . . . you say the sexiest things."

The van's headlights cut a wide swath through the darkness. An eerie blue-white glow materialized far in the distance, even further up the mountain. Gradually as they approached it, the glow brightened, revealing a good section of the production site set in a hollow of tall evergreens and craggy rocks, all lit by a stark white light. The van lurched to a stop, parking near dozens of other vehicles. The night smelled of pine and was crisply cold. But Rebecca was too keyed up to feel it. Her very first movie set did not disappoint her.

Huge floodlights illuminated the bustling activity: men were laying cables which twisted and snaked everywhere underfoot, another group was placing a large camera on a small, railroadlike track, technicians were mounting lights, huge generators hummed noisily, people shouted back and forth. Someone's portable tapedeck played nearby, Harry Chapin's new hit, "Taxi," which Rebecca was already tired of hearing.

The A.D., a friendly Southerner with too many suggestions in his eyes, plucked Scooter from her side and whisked him off to rehearsal with the director. Left on her own, Rebecca wandered about, noting the large tent which held the makeup and hairdressing facilities, and beyond, the two smaller tents used as dressing rooms for the handful of actors and actresses. Further away sat a snazzy-looking trailer. She figured it was for Shelby—La Star. Rebecca kept catching glimpses of David Rau, looking as young as ever and playing the same games, everywhere at once, barking orders. Purposefully, she steered clear of him.

Finally, after what seemed like ages, quiet was called for a runthrough rehearsal and miraculously all noise but the generators ceased. The director, a tiny, gray man bundled in several sweaters, led the actors through the action for the first shot. Scooter, in torn bib overalls and beat-up straw hat, looked like a hillbilly redneck but she was so proud of him she felt like busting.

At least an hour passed, before David indicated he wanted a take. Only then was Shelby Cale summoned out of the trailer. Dressed and looking like a 1950s high-school cheerleader, the famous model strolled leisurely into the midst of the actors, replacing her stand-in with a studied nonchalance. Rebecca had never seen anyone more beautiful—everything she'd always wanted to be—tall, blond, stacked and gorgeous. The additional fact that Shelby was married to Rebecca's favorite celebrity did not help either.

The director called, "Action" and Scooter limped into the foreground, waving a sawed-off shotgun, shouting his lines with a burning ferocity. The director called, "Cut," hurriedly conferred with David Rau and then spoke with Scooter, who nodded seriously. Again the sequence was begun. "Roll 'em," shouted the A.D. "Rolling," replied the soundmixer.

The night dragged on, becoming colder and more tedious for Rebecca. All sorts of technical adjustments seemed vital before each shot could be made and the repetition of the long waits exhausted her. When the activity moved inside the mouth of the mine-shaft, it was impossible to see much of anything. She waited in the large tent, sitting close to the row of portable electric heaters, nursing a cup of coffee, trying to look as if she belonged. Eventually the heat made her so drowsy she drifted off to sleep and dreamed of replacing Shelby due to a terrible mining accident. And Erik was behind the camera, directing the scene. Way after three in the morning, Scooter carried her to the van for the ride down the mountain.

The next morning, a ray of sunlight awoke her. Scooter wasn't in the hotel room but he'd left a note saying that he hadn't wanted to disturb her "beauty sleep" and for her to hitch a ride up that afternoon. Disappointed, she dressed and went downstairs to see about a ride. The desk clerk said a "go-fer" would be down at two for more sandwiches for the crew.

Disgruntled, Rebecca wandered into the hotel's cafe and stopped short. Shelby Cale was the only person in the knotty pine paneled room. Rebecca hesitated, then smiled and moved forward, speaking,

"Good morning. I'm so mad. I overslept. I wanted to see Scooter's scene being shot."

Shelby Cale merely tilted her perfect head, a light of recognition slowly dawning in the misty green eyes. "Oh, you're the girl with that New York actor."

"Yes, Scooter . . . Christopher Warren's his acting name."

"He's quite good . . . actually."

Rebecca grimaced inwardly—"actually" was one of her least favorite words. "Yes, he's terrific. I'm Rebecca Loren," she introduced herself, trying out a new stage name. "You're not shooting today?"

"No." Shelby raised her glass of iced tea. The gesture was as precise as a sales graph.

Tired of standing and waiting for an invitation to join her, Rebecca sat at an opposite table. "Don't you love this town?"

"Blistering each day," Shelby sighed. "Freezing each night. Actually, I detest this place."

"Well, I've never been in the mountains before. Or west of Pittsburgh for that matter. So I think it's the most beautiful scenery I've ever seen. And I can't believe there's no litter."

The blonde raised her shoulders wearily—they were bare under the halter of a simple but exquisite sundress. Rebecca rubbed her palms over the knees of her old jeans. "I met your husband once," she said. "Long, long ago."

"Really?" Shelby asked, obviously not giving a damn one way or the other.

"Yes," Rebecca continued, not knowing why. "I thought he was wonderful—warm and naturally bigger than life." That brought a small smile to Shelby's perfect lips but no comment.

"I read he has a new book out," Rebecca went on. "Can't wait to read it. I read his last one, *Rogues and Scoundrels,* three times. It was so complex and multilayered."

"Actually, I thought it was a big bore."

Rebecca was stunned into silence. Shelby eased her tall, perfect body out of the chair with a studied grace. "Very pleasant chatting with you," she said, without looking over, and walked out.

Rebecca grabbed the menu, muttering to herself, "Well, *actually*, I pity poor Erik . . . *reahlly*, I do, darhling."

Her eventual ride to the top of the mountain was breathtaking both in beauty and in terror—sheer vertical drops, so visible now in the light of day, fell away from the road with dizzying regularity. Rebecca clutched the arm of the van's door, ready to jump at the slightest provocation.

At the top, she searched the milling crowd of technicians and actors, finally locating Scooter under a tree with a borrowed copy of *Jonathan Livingston Seagull*, howling to himself. Once sprawled in the pine needles by his side, she mimicked Shelby's appraisal of his talent, "Actually, he's quite good."

Scooter laughed. "Hell, what does she know about acting? I can't for the life of me figure out why Rau cast her."

Rebecca thought for a moment, then said, "Probably because she looks like the girl he couldn't get in high school." They laughed together.

Later that afternoon, as Rebecca was watching from a distance, David interrupted the rehearsal, voicing sharply to Scooter, "The character would wave the dynamite there. He's threatening. Not prick teasing."

She knew at once that David's tone, let alone the artistic interference, would set Scooter's teeth on edge. For a few seconds, the two men stared at each other; the silence was charged with intensity.

David grabbed the bound sticks of dynamite and shouted Scooter's line of dialogue, "There's more than one way to skin a cat." And brandished the sticks over his head.

Scooter laughed. "That looks like the villain in a silent flick. Should I twirl a black cape too?"

The dynamite trembled noticeably in David's hand, but his expression remained unswerving. "Do it my way." He tossed forward the prop explosives. Scooter snatched them out of the air and bounced them in his hand a couple of times, as if weighing his options. "I believe I can imply it rather than underlining it in red."

Holding her breath, Rebecca eyed David for his reaction. His face clouded. "I don't want any Actors' Studio garbage. I want visible action." David turned to the director. "Again. *My way*." He moved to his position next to the camera.

Scooter shrugged. "You're the main man."

"Damned right I am," David said.

The sequence was shot according to his wishes.

After Scooter's last close-up had been completed and the still photographer had stepped in for a few shots of him in character, Rebecca looked around for David. She spotted him heading for the makeup tent. Quieting her nerves, she followed and entered the dim, sweltering, canvas-smelling interior.

He was alone, bent over blueprints on the makeup counter. Seeing her reflection in the mirrors, he frowned. "What do you want?"

"I just want to tell you something," she began, tentative. "I've seen Silver."

"Bully for you." He began rolling up the blueprints loudly.

"Yes, bully for me. And bully for Silver too. With a lot of luck, she's going to pull herself out of that hell."

"Never doubted it."

"Well, I sure did. You just about killed her, David."

He snapped a thick rubber band around the roll of papers. "I don't know what the hell you're talking about." He started to move toward the open tent flap. She held her ground, in front of his exit.

"I was there, David. Dallas? Doctor Feelgood? You had her shot up. She'd never touched any hard stuff before you—"

He slapped the cylinder of paper hard on the counter, cutting her off. "That's a pretty serious accusation, sister."

She held his gaze, too worked up to retreat. "She needs help. Badly. And she's not going to get the right kind in that cheap joint."

"So? She made her bucks."

"She's broke."

"That my fault? I warned her—quit blowing it away."

"She made millions for you. A measly few thousand for herself because of your contracts. Is that fair?"

He grabbed the roll of blueprints. "Let me tell you something, sister. Fair is what you make it. She made her bed, let her lie in it. And another thing—I don't like your kind. Sticking your nose in my business. You tried it before and you're doing it again. And I'm getting damned tired of it." He brushed past and stopped. "I want you and your boyfriend out of here by tonight. He's done his bit. You should be thanking me for giving the gimp a gig."

He was gone before she could find her voice.

Back at the hotel, when telling Scooter, she minimized the confrontation, but admitted the departure ultimatum. To her immense relief, he seemed pleased they would be leaving right away. "Let's blow this hicksville and catch the bus," Scooter urged. "Back to the real world, with neon and nightlife."

Quickly they finished packing, tore downstairs, checked out and just made the Greyhound bus bound for Butte. Scooter led her to the very rear seats. "See? This ain't so bad," he said, pulling her close. "We've a bigger chauffeured limousine than when we arrived."

They were settling into their seats as the engines started beneath them. Rebecca swiveled in her seat to peer out of the rear window, wanting to remember the town in spite of everything. A mud-splattered yellow cab was arriving in front of the quaint old hotel.

She craned her neck to see the disembarking passenger who had hired a cab in Butte to drive all the way here. A balloon of surprise expanded in her chest.

Scooter nudged her. "You know him?"

She nodded, unable to tear her eyes away as the bus pulled ahead. "That's Erik Lungren. You know, the writer."

"Shelby's husband?"

Erik's figure grew smaller and smaller. He was staring after the bus. She was positive—absolutely positive—that he had seen her. But even more joyously, she sensed that even after all these years, he had recognized her.

ERIK
August 1972
Montana

He stared after the departing bus's rear window, at the small face framed by the raven hair. With more than surprise, he was flooded with memories of their brief evening together. Keenly disappointed that their timing had been so off, he strode up the steps of the wide covered veranda and entered the small lobby of the solidly constructed 1890s hotel. In the rustic-furnished lobby, the only concession to modernity was a TV set in the corner.

The broad, jovial face behind the counter smiled. "Hope you don't want a room, sir. A big movie production's in town."

Erik shook his head. "I'm Shelby Cale's husband."

"Well, welcome," the desk clerk said. "Funny, she didn't mention your arrival or we'd've been expecting you."

"Thought I'd pop in and surprise her. Tell me . . . on that bus that just left here was a young lady. Her first name is Rebecca. Do you know her last?"

"Wonderful little lady. Wife of one of those film actors, Christopher Warren."

"Rebecca Warren," he echoed. "Thanks. One more question, do you know where Shelby is now?"

"The whole shebang of them's across the street. At the moving picture house. They're seeing what they call 'rushes.'"

Erik walked briskly across the empty street into the tiny movie theater. It looked like it hadn't been used since television hit the small town; the candy display case was empty, the glass dirty. The smell of stale popcorn hung in the air.

Film sounds drew him through the heavy velour curtains and into the auditorium. He paused, waiting for his eyes to adjust to the darkness, his anticipation rising.

On the screen an intense, strikingly good-looking young actor ranted at a group of startled teenagers. He waved a shotgun and spewed out his lines with realistic menace. Erik looked around—forty to fifty people were scattered about the small auditorium. The scene on the screen began to repeat, this time from another camera angle. He spotted her hair shimmering in the half light. She was seated two seats in from the aisle, next to a small guy.

Relishing the moment, Erik slipped into the vacant seat behind her and tapped her shoulder, whispering, "'Scuse me, miss. Mind removing your hat?"

Her head twisted around, her eyes popping open in shock.

"What're you doing here?" she whispered and cast a glance at her companion. It was then Erik recognized the producer, David Rau, who seemed to be pulling away, tilting toward the aisle. She hurriedly climbed over Rau and headed up the aisle. Erik followed eagerly and pushed through the dusty curtains. She was already outside, under the overhanging marquee, fumbling in her purse. He stepped out, grinning broadly. "Caught you, didn't I?"

"What?"

"Surprised the hell out of you. Come on, admit it." He pulled her close, kissing her fully on the mouth. "Oh god, Shelby," he breathed into her. "You can't imagine how I've missed you." Her body felt strangely unyielding against him. He relaxed his embrace. "You pissed?"

"No, no, not at all," she offered with a slightly strained smile and brought up a cigarette. "But y'all did give this girl one hell of a start." She leaned into his lighter, lit her cigarette, casting a worried glance toward the doors, then back at him. Her exquisite face softened. "You bastard, why didn't you tell me you were coming?"

"Didn't know until this morning," he said, studying her. "In Salt Lake City. My TV interview was finished. And the bookstore appearance. Decided what the hell? Look, if you have to be back in there, I understand."

"No, no, I don't. My scenes have already run." She filled her lungs and exhaled slowly, shaking her head. "Erik, what am I going to do with you?"

"I hope all sorts of devilishly erotic things."

She took his arm. "Well, sugar, we'll just have to iron out some of those nasty ol' kinks, won't we?" She started walking him across the street, leaning into him like old times, one arm draped around his.

He began to relax. "I caught some pretty strong stuff in there. That kid with the shotgun's really good."

"Christopher Warren." She noted his expression of surprise and added, "Know him?"

"No. But I met his wife, Rebecca, once a few years back."

"His wife?" She gave a short laugh. "Sugar, they're not married.

She's just his ol' girl friend. Odd little minx, isn't she? How did you meet her?''

"Can't really remember that," he said, not knowing why he didn't want to tell her about it. He squeezed her closer. "Do you realize, you've only four more days of this isolation?''

"Yes . . . I'm counting them off too . . ." She stopped, staring at the hotel doors. "Let's not go up right away. Do you mind?''

Hand in hand they wandered down the main street, looking into the lighted shop windows, talking quietly. She seemed to be over the initial shock but he sensed a reserve. She complained that she had been so cut off from what was happening. She told him she'd just learned of Bob Fosse's winning the last award in his triple crown of directing, an Emmy for *Liza* to add to his Tony for *Pippin* and Oscar for *Cabaret*.

In the grassy town square, complete with a covered octagonal bandstand, they sat on a bench watching fireflies dance through the rose bushes. Erik pulled out of his sports coat pocket a copy of his novel and laid it reverently in her hands "One of the primary reasons I am here." He watched her weigh the slim volume in her graceful hands.

"Oh, sugar, how sweet. I was wondering why you hadn't sent a copy. Sure's a lot smaller than the last one, isn't it?''

"Yeah . . . go on, open it.''

She turned to the title page, reading softly, "*Hidden Assets*—a memoir by Erik Lungren.''

"Lehmann-Haupt in the *New York Times* called it a 'masterful gem.' ''

"Oh, Erik . . . congratulations, darling . . .''

He flipped the page for her, pointing to the printed dedication which read, "For my sweet muse, Shelby.''

Her eyes misted. "How touching . . .''

Tenderly he pulled her close. "It's all yours . . . all the praise, all my gratitude. Without you, I would never have written it. It's the best I've ever done, thanks to you . . . my darling.''

She searched his face, shivering slightly under his arm. He wrapped both arms around her, asking, "You cold, babe?''

She shook her head and stood, looking back up the street.

For a moment he did not rise. He watched her staring at the hotel and wondered why her reaction to his offering had been so muted. Doubts began to plague him and he pushed himself to his feet feeling drained of the energy that had swept him to her side. He embraced her again, holding her crazily tight, crushing her breath, kissing her desperately, searchingly, regretfully until her body relaxed, blending into his.

In her small hotel room, he took her to bed, aching for release, reconnections. Slowly he explored her lovely body, her nearly flawless skin, kissing her tiny brown birthmark again and again. His fingers lightly traced the curves, the fullness of her breasts which swelled under his touch, the hard pliancy of her nipples, the tantalizing mystery of her vagina.

Only when he was certain that the heat of desire had flamed within her, did he enter her, watching her face contort with pleasure, becoming fuller, flatter, more flushed, her eyes glazing over with that unique combination of lust and distance, as though she were transported to some faraway place where he was unable to reach her. Again and again he teetered on the brink of climax, forcing himself to hold off until she was ready.

Her long legs locked behind his back and she held on until he was spent and drained. He stretched fully beside her, gasping for breath, smelling his own sweat and her sweetness. His heartbeat was just normalizing when she moved. "Don't go yet," he sighed, but it was too late. She threw herself over the edge of the bed and stood. "I'll be right back, sugar . . ."

He lay on his back. Listening to the tub fill, wanting her beside him, worried that somehow things had changed irrevocably. A heavy tiredness blanketed him. He strove to stay awake until she returned. Listening to the soft sounds of her bathing, he drifted reluctantly to sleep.

Even before sunrise, they were up and went down for breakfast in the hotel dining room. With a gaiety he sensed was forced, Shelby introduced him to various members of the cast and crew, chatting overanimatedly with them and in general working too hard to make him feel included. They rode up the side of the mountain with the elderly Austrian film director, whose films Erik had long admired. Shelby bantered non-stop. The more vivacious she became the more uneasy Erik felt. He concentrated on the rising sun. It bathed the valleys far below with a haze so lilac it looked scented.

At the mountain top location, she led him to her dressing-room trailer. He sat on the couch observing the exacting process of her being made up and coiffed by a busy team of three. Shelby kept up a stream of chatter.

The producer stopped by to explain the complicated special effects sequence which was to be shot that day. David Rau seemed surprised that she had company. While Erik made idle chatter, she fluttered around the cramped space, clearing off her makeup table for a roll of blueprints and site diagrams.

Erik lit a cigarette and smiled. "How do you feel the film's shaping up?"

"Very pleased," David said, casting a frown in his direction.

"And my sweetheart here is going to come out all right?"

"Definitely."

Erik caught hold of her wrist and tugged her close into a hug, voicing proudly, "I knew she would."

All efficiency, the producer unfurled the set of plans and in a dry, crisp voice began talking to Shelby, indicating the various factors she would have to be aware of in the complicated stunt. She kept nodding seriously, her brow creased. From the moment David had entered, Erik had sensed her unease and now easily could understand her feelings. Rau projected nothing but hard business and cold facts.

Erik stood. "I'll let you two shoptalk. I want to stretch my legs." He paused by the open door. "Hope this stunt of yours isn't dangerous."

Rau shook his head. "Not if it's timed down to the last degree."

"Good. Can't be too careful with dynamite." Erik ducked out into the hot sun and felt released from an inexplicable tension.

Within the hour, however, the more he watched the runthrough, the more concerned he became. Standing beside a camera which would be filming the stunt in slow motion, Erik observed again the split-second timing necessary to bring it off. He could not believe that Rau was not using a double for Shelby.

The sequence required her to dash from a hiding place high in the rocks, run down the steep, boulder-strewn slope, stop before the mouth of the mining tunnel, scoop up the lit sticks of dynamite and throw them deep into the shaft. She then had to dive for cover as the explosion would rip for real. She was practicing even how to shield and protect herself from the expected shower of rocks and debris.

While Shelby again practiced the run, the assistant director was shouting out each beat with the aid of a stopwatch and an amplified megaphone. Nearing the mine, she stumbled and fell. If it had been lit, she would not have reached the sputtering fuse in time.

Erik could not control his concern any longer. He sought out the producer and quietly explained his worry. "She's just too close at the end," he concluded. "Anything might happen. All it takes is one little thing to go wrong—just one. And you've got a goddamn disaster."

David glanced over at him and away. "I have the top explosives man in Hollywood handling it."

"Her life's in jeopardy. Why don't you use a double?"

"Because we can only shoot it once," David explained, tight-lipped. "It has to be Shelby or the verisimilitude is totally destroyed."

"To hell with verisimilitude. What about a little movie magic?"

"I *am* creating movie magic," David snapped. "Butt out." He whirled on his heel.

Erik caught his arm, spinning him around. "I don't want my wife going through this bullshit just so you can make an extra buck at the box office."

David wrenched his arm free, glaring. "For Shelby's sake, I'll forget you grabbed me."

"Okay, okay, I'm sorry. But I'm afraid I'll have to refuse to let Shelby do this. It's just too damned dangerous."

David replied grimly, "Shelby is under contract to me. What's more, she has agreed to do as I ask."

"We'll see about that," Erik said and turned to find her.

She stood at a distance watching them, one hand jutting flat from her brow to shield her eyes from the sun. She kept it there as he approached. He began gravely, "I don't want you to do this. It's too dangerous."

She tried to laugh, but it came out wrong, forced. "Aren't you being just a wee bit overprotective, sugar?"

"Maybe. Maybe not. All I know is that any time dynamite is used the unexpected can happen. Logging once, I saw a guy lose his arm—torn right off at the shoulder. And he'd been handling the stuff for twenty years and—"

"Don't," she interrupted. "Please . . . don't make a fuss. We've rehearsed this over and over and over."

"Look," he sighed. "I don't want to be demanding but I'm asking you—please, for my sake—don't go through with this."

"Sugar, I'm sure if there were any real danger of me getting even the slightest scratch on my person, David wouldn't allow it." She flashed a teasing sort of smile. "After all, I do have one more nude scene."

Erik hesitated, hating the feeling inside and yet powerless to stop it. "Shelby . . . do I have to put my foot down and forbid this?"

Her head rose stiffly on her long neck. "My, my what a loathsome word. Forbid. Y'all must have picked that up from Evangeline." She locked eyes with him.

Suddenly David was beside them. "We're ready, Shelby." He yelled over his shoulder, "Makeup!"

Erik tried another tack. "Couldn't it be shot in sections? Take it up to her throwing the dynamite and then setting up the explosion—"

"No," David cut it, cold and curt. "Can't you see what you're doing? You've upset her. If there is any danger it'll come from lack of concentration. Obviously with you around that's an impossibility. I want you to leave."

"Shelby, I—"

"Get off this mountain! *Now!*"

The outburst was so vitriolic Shelby grabbed Erik's hand, pulling him away, whispering, "Go . . . please, just go. I'll see you at the hotel later. Please, Erik . . ."

He hesitated, fighting the battle within, then kissed her cheek. "Good luck, champ."

"I'll have a car take you down," she called after him. He waved it off without turning and headed for the beginning of the dirt road. Each step he took he felt the distance growing between them.

He'd been walking barely twenty minutes when the explosion rocked the earth. It reverberated off the giant rocks around him, sending shock waves out over the valley below, frightening flocks of pheasant and other birds screeching skyward. He spun around to face the mountain. A large billowing cloud of smoke and dust rose to the heavens.

A muffled, distanced cheer filtered down to him. He halted, watching the dirty cloud smudging the clear sky. The shouting was obviously jubilant. Feeling like a damned fool, he turned and plunged into the tangled underbrush, heading straight down the mountain side. To hell with the road.

It took him over three sweat-filled hours to reach the hotel. In the cafe, Erik purchased a cold six-pack of beer and drinking one, headed upstairs, hoping she'd returned. She wasn't in her room, but she'd left a note: "Where are you, sugar? Waited forever. Am going to dinner in Anaconda about a half hour from here. Along with Lenore (the hair lady) and some others. I'll be back by eight. The stunt went gloriously."

He showered, grabbed a bite at the lunch counter and joined in a friendly poker game in the lobby with some of the crew. By eight that evening, she had still not returned. He eased out of the game, not caring too much that he lost over fifty bucks. But it didn't help that the kitchen radio was playing "Alone Again, Naturally."

Erik felt sufficiently lubricated to inquire at the desk if Rau were around. The young woman pointed to a bucket of ice and a tray of soft drinks that she hadn't found time to take up to the producer's room. Erik offered to make the delivery, sparing her a trip. He added a six-pack of beer, paid for it out of his own pocket and set off with the tray.

At the rear of the hotel's second floor, he knocked at Rau's door. There was no answer. A light shone through the glass transom above. He knocked again, calling out good-naturedly, "Room service." He heard muffled noises of someone moving inside and shortly the door opened an inch. Erik thrust the tray out. "Hi. Have come bearing a peace offering." Though he could only see part of Rau's face through the crack, it was enough to discern the sour surprise.

"What do you want?" Rau grumbled, making no move to take the tray.

"Thought we could share a few beers and—"

"I don't drink beer." The door started to close.

Erik put up a hand to stop it and pushed. "Hey, I just want to apologize." His pressure on the door was stronger than he thought, either that or Rau was fairly weak in the muscle department. Whatever, the door under Erik's hand gave way, opening partially, allowing him to see further into the room, beyond Rau's bathrobe-covered frame. It was only a glimpse, but it was more than enough.

Shelby sat in the bed, nude to the waist.

Rau threw his weight on the door, slamming it shut. Erik did not resist. He was too shocked to move. He stared at the wood panels as though his gaze alone would remove the barrier, allowing him access.

He turned, forgetting the tray balanced in one hand. It started to slip, startling him with its rattling of bottles. He spun around, hurling it at the door. The bottles smashed into the wood, shattering completely, spewing bits of glass and liquid all over him. The sound of the crash echoed down the hall. He stomped for the stairs.

Inside Shelby's room, Erik grabbed his suitcase. He finished tossing in his belongings, snapped it shut and reached for the phone. He offered the switchboard lady fifty bucks if she could round up a car for him to drive to the airport. She suggested hers. He told her he would be right down. He'd just hung up when Shelby entered.

He could not bring himself to look at her. He snatched up his bag and started out.

"Aren't you being a little bit melodramatic?" she asked.

He forced himself to glance in her direction. She had dressed completely—beige tailored slacks, a matching cashmere sweater, not a button undone, her hair brushed soft and flowing. She could have just returned from dinner in Anaconda.

She smiled tensely. "Aren't you going to say something?"

He shook his head and opened the hall door. Moving quickly, he reached the main stairs. Rounding the banister, he caught a glimpse of her silhouetted in the doorway. He almost turned back. Instead, he drove his boots downward.

The plump telephone operator with swept-wing eyeglasses was

waiting for him on the front porch. Eyes all fluttery, she handed him the keys and he gave her a hundred bucks. "I'll park it in the airport lot. Keys under the front mat," he said, already heading toward the small Falcon at the foot of the stairs.

"No problem," she answered shyly.

He opened the rear door, tossing in his suitcase and sports jacket. Shelby appeared on the porch. "I want to talk," she said, paying no attention to the young woman. The latter vanished inside as if sensing an impending accident.

He tore open the driver's door. "I can't. Not now," he managed to voice. "Later. Back home."

"No. *Now*. I'm not going to wait another minute longer."

The tone was so defiant it rekindled the deep anger. He shot around the front of the car and grabbed her arm. Without thinking, he yanked her down the stairs. "Erik," she warned, trying to twist away, but he did not heed. He ripped open the passenger door and shoved her roughly inside, slamming the door on her startled face. He was around the car and in behind the wheel before she could right herself from the unladylike sprawl. He reached across her and reslammed her partially opened door. "You wanted to talk, so talk," he said. Adjusting the bucket seat with one hand, he started the engine.

"Erik," she warned again, eyeing him warily. He jammed the car in gear and the compact shot ahead. "Let me out," she yelled.

"Talk."

"Not unless you stop and let me out."

He yanked the wheel, squealing the tires around the corner, heading out of town. "Where are you taking me?" she demanded. He did not respond but concentrated fully on the road ahead, not wanting to miss the turn-off. The headlights picked up the marker and he spun the wheel, sliding the car onto the gravel side road. He pressed the accelerator to the floor.

"Slow down for god's sake!"

Fiercely he hunched over the wheel, roaring the car forward until the road turned to dirt. Only then did he let up on the gas. The car bounced through the deep ruts, raising clouds of dust on both sides.

"You're behaving like an absolute idiot!" She clung to her door handle, fighting to remain upright. "Erik—please! For god's sake stop!" The road twisted and turned, climbing steeply up the dark mountain. "You want to kill us?" she shrieked above the motor's whine. "Is that it? Because that's what you're going to do if you—" She screamed as the car skidded around a hairpin bend, swerving dangerously close to the abrupt precipice dropping below now on her side. He ground the motor into a lower gear, not slowing, no thought in his mind except to reach the top of the mountain, the end of the road.

She began to cry. "Erik . . . please . . . for god's sake . . . please. I'm sorry. I didn't want you to find out that way . . . I was going to tell you. Really, truly I was. Please . . . you have to believe me." She let go of the door handle, covering her face with her hands. The car veered again, throwing her against him. He pushed her off and fought to keep the small car on the narrow logging road.

Higher and higher they climbed, the four-cylinders straining in the lowest gear to maintain the speed he dictated. Furious blows began raining on his arms and shoulders. "You crazy sonofabitch!" she screamed into his ear. She attempted to grab the keys from the ignition. His arm shot out, slamming her back against the seat.

The momentary break in his concentration came at the worng time. The front wheel missed the main ruts and hurtled toward the cliff. He slammed on the brakes, wrenching the wheel. The car shimmied, spinning sideways, and skidded to a grinding stop; the engine sputtered and conked out. The heavy thick dust swirled slowly in the headlights, enveloping the car, as though they had hurtled off the cliff and were sailing through roiling chalky clouds.

As the dust settled, he sat, his fingers still locked on the wheel. With difficulty he pried them loose. He became aware of her moans. She was curled into the far door, knees drawn up, her torso shaking. He opened his door and climbed out. In the night air, the headlights aimed out across the rocks and the valley below, cutting a wide swath of bright light into the darkness. He stumbled out of the light to the edge of the road, found a large rock and sank onto it, his back to the car.

The lights of Fishtrap twinkled below, a tiny cluster of bright glitter on black velvet. The night sky was overcast, no stars were out, no moon visible. Just outside of the car's high beams, he sat huddled into himself for warmth.

Her voice came softly from behind. "I didn't mean to hurt you."

She appeared beside him. She'd pulled on his sports coat—the sleeves hung below her hands, making her look like a small child. Her face was tearstained. "Really, truly, I didn't," she said. "It just happened—that's all. One minute I hated him—the next, I loved him."

He jerked his head toward her. "Loved?"

"Yes, loved," she murmured. "I love him, Erik. Really, I do."

"He can't love you any more than I do."

"It has nothing to do with that."

"Then *what* does it have to do with? Is he a better lay? Is it his money? His power? His promise to land you an Oscar? What is it? Tell me for chrissakes."

She shook her head stiffly. "I . . . I don't know . . . he . . . he just makes me feel different."

"That's *real* descriptive. Makes me feel a helluva lot better." He moved away, trying to get a grip on his scrambled emotions. When he turned, she'd sunk to the rock, her shoulders drooping forward under the oversized coat. She looked so forlorn his anguish began to take over. "Aw, Shelby . . . how could you do this to us?"

In her silence, he went to her and sat beside her on the rock. "Let's forget this. It didn't happen. From this moment on, it doesn't exist. I'll cut short my book tour. Meet you back in New York later this week. We'll fly somewhere. Anywhere you like. We just need time. We'll work together to make it all better. It's been so good for us, hasn't it?"

She stood. "You just don't understand." She faced him squarely. "I want a divorce."

He could only stare back at her, his tongue immobile.

"This isn't just some casual affair, Erik. I've never felt like this before. Never. Not with you. Not with anyone. I want to be with him. Always."

"That pompous little asshole," he growled. "How could you?"

Her cheeks flushed with anger. "Because he makes me feel like I'm the very core of his life."

"And I don't? Is that it?"

"Yes, yes, yes," she railed. "I was never more than a . . . a book in your library. Now and then you took me down from the shelf."

"That's bullshit."

"Is it? Is it really? We've been married fifty-four months and out of that, you've been writing on your ol' book for forty of them. Well, I'm sick and tired of playing second fiddle in your orchestra. Not when I can be the whole damned symphony for David."

"That little putz . . . he's his own symphony. You'll be lucky to carry his goddamned sheet music."

She rose on her toes, hissing, "I hate you for saying that!"

One side of her face was brightly lit by the beam of headlights, the other in total darkness. And her tone was just as harsh. "You're married to your writing, Erik. You don't need a wife. Just a mistress you can boff now and then."

"Don't tell me what I need."

"So don't *you* tell *me* what *I* need. I'm finishing this film and then filing for divorce. And there is nothing you can say that will change my mind." She turned to the car. "So you might as well take me back. Or do I have to walk?"

The drive down the mountain was in silence. Each of them sat tensely, staring ahead, making no effort to speak. The silence filled him with an emptiness he had never before experienced. He felt hollow—a pair of eyes watching the twisting road, a pair of hands turning the wheel mechanically and for the life of him, he couldn't think of words or arguments persuasive enough to assuage the terrible sense that he was guilty of all she had accused. And if he couldn't convince himself otherwise, he knew damned well he was in no shape to take her on at the height of her willfulness. Later, it would have to be later.

As he pulled the compact into the town's main street, Shelby leaned forward, spotting with him the small figure pacing in front of the illuminated hotel. "You better let me out here," she said thinly. "That's David."

Erik deliberately drove straight down the street, braking in front of the wide veranda. Immediately David leaped forward, a flurry of self-righteous anger, dashing to Shelby's door, flinging it open before the car had even stopped, hurling questions, "You all right? Did he hurt you?" He pulled her out of the car. "In five minutes I was calling the cops." He leaned inside the open doorway. "You cocksucking prick! I oughta have you arrested! You kidnapped her. I have witnesses!"

Shelby tried to restrain him with a hand to his arm but he shook her off, slamming the car door as hard as he could. David continued yelling through the closed windows, his face a mask of twisted rage. It triggered a burst of fury within Erik. He shot out of his door, looming up over the car. David rushed to him, screaming, "You shit! You want to make something out of it?"

Erik hauled back and smashed him with all his strength right in the jaw. Under his knuckles, he felt skin breaking, bone crunching. The blow sent David flying to the pavement several feet away. Shelby shrieked and darted to him, swooping down. "You didn't have to do that, Erik," she screamed. "We all know what a big, macho he-man you are!"

He rubbed his knuckles, feeling little satisfaction. He looked at her and felt suddenly helpless. "We'll talk more," he heard his voice say. "Back home." She wasn't listening.

He squeezed back behind the wheel and gunned the engine, heading out for the route to Butte. His last glimpse of her—in the rearview mirror—kneeling, cradling David's bloody head in her lap. Like a madonna, he thought—like a goddamned beautiful madonna.

DAVID
November 1972
Los Angeles

He nodded to the uniformed guard in the glass security booth and drove through the open main gates of Pacific Studios. Mentally ticking off a dozen matters to solve that day, David roared his new metallic silver Mercedes 450 SL convertible around the Mission-styled, stucco-and-tile administration buildings and slowed for the raised concrete bumps. In front of the producers' bungalows, he braked to a stop in his parking space and hopped out with a burst of satisfaction. Even though he had not left the lot until three that morning, he was the first of the studio producers to arrive for the day. He liked it that way.

The moment David strode into the outer office, his secretary reported, "Mister Shaw's New York office called twice already."

"Put a call in," he said and took the morning trade papers from her desk. "And get Sammy up here." He entered his office. "And set up a ten o'clock with Donaldson in Promotion and lunch with Wolf."

She followed, scribbling in her poised notepad. "You already have a luncheon scheduled. With Kenniston over at RPM."

"Change it. Later this week." He tossed her the cassette tape of notes he'd made while driving in on the Ventura Freeway from Malibu. "Transcribe these. A few on there for you." He glanced at the trade headlines, then looked up. "Well, get a move on it. The day's begun."

She hesitated. "Could I take off a half-hour early? To vote."

"The polls are open late."

"I have my yoga class."

He shrugged. "Make a choice. And take off that damn McGovern button. This is a film studio." He sat behind his desk, reaching for the full pot of hot coffee. Shortly she called into him that Shaw's office was on line one. He snatched up the receiver. "Rau, here. What's up?"

"Mister Shaw will be in L.A. for the weekend," the male secretary responded. "He'd like a screening of *Fool's Gold* on Saturday evening."

"It's not ready."

"Eight P.M. Saturday. His place."

"Let me speak to him."

"In conference. Do I have a confirmation?"

"No. Tell Dixon I'd like to explain personally."

"I'll relay your message." The receiver went dead in his hand.

David slammed it down and stood. Damned interfering sonofabitches. "Where's Sammy?" he shouted to his secretary.

"No answer."

David grabbed his notes and headed out. "If Shaw calls, I'll be with Sammy. And call Miss Cale. Time she woke up."

He took the shortcut through the alley between two sound stages and climbed the exterior stairs to the second-floor entrance of the editing facilities. Walking into the small room which had been his home for the last three months, he stopped short. "Where's Sammy?"

"Beats me," the stranger answered. "Who's Sammy?"

"Who the fuck are you? This room's off-limits." With a start, David noted that the metal wall-racks were only half full of canisters. "Where the hell's my film?"

"I don't know anything," the young man said. "I was told—"

David was already out in the hall, heading for the stairs. On the first floor, he barged into the Editing-Operations' office, startling the secretary. He brushed past her and threw open her boss's door. "Lyle, what the hell'd you do with my film?"

"Relax, David," the Operations' head man replied, offering a half conciliatory smile. "We've had to move you, that's—"

"Where?" David interrupted. "On whose orders?"

"You're in the second annex now. I told you we needed—"

"On whose orders, Lyle?"

Lyle smiled again, a shit-eating grin if David ever saw one. "David, *Fool's Gold* is six weeks overdue. We had to make room for . . ."

David walked out on him. There was no use wasting energy with a flunky. Irving was up to his old tricks—doing his damnedest to sabotage the film.

Fuming, David finally located the second annex—a corrugated-tin, World War Two Quonset hut next to the machine shop far off in a corner of the sixty-acre lot in old Hollywood. If he remembered correctly, the hut had been first erected to house the animal trainers for *Sins of Bathsheba*. Inside, he found Sammy and his assistant sweating in their efforts to sort through a floor-full of 35 mm. film canisters. The weary first-editor sighed, "It'll take us days to get reorganized. And look what we have to work on." Sammy indicated the dusty moviola in the corner.

"Jesus H. Christ," David said, "I haven't seen one of those since Cagney's last picture. You hold on."

It took him barely three minutes to race across the lot to Irving's suite of offices on the top floor of the administration building. He scorched past the receptionist and the outer secretaries, coming to a halt before the last barrier, a bleached blonde vaguely reminiscent of all of Irving's former secretaries. David leaned over her. "Buzz me in."

"I'm sorry, but he's—"

David's hand shot out, hitting the switch on the intercom box. "Irving! I want to talk to you."

"Get off this damn squawk box," came the raspy growl from the inner office. "Make an appointment like everyone else."

"*Now,*" David said.

Almost at once, the office door burst open, revealing a red-faced Irving. "Do I have to get Security up here?" he shouted. "I'm taking a meeting for chrissakes."

"I want my facilities back."

"Got a beef? Take it up with Operations." Irving started to shut the door.

David blocked it with his foot. "Shaw wants to see the film Saturday. He'll be pissed when he finds out why I can't deliver."

"Loraine, call Security. Get this schmuck outta here. As for you, Mister Big-Time Producer, you shoulda thought about Shaw a month ago."

"If I had a little cooperation around here, I'd be done."

"You couldn't finish that schmeer if God himself was editing."

"I'll move off the lot. Charge all my overhead to the studio."

"Go ahead. I'd love your ass off the lot," Irving said. "Now get your fuckin' foot outta my door before I squash it."

David barely had time to withdraw it before Irving slammed the door.

Back in his office, David made arrangements to have the latest in editing equipment delivered that same afternoon from an outside leasing firm. When he tried to lay off the additional expense onto the studio, he learned from Accounting that Irving had pulled the plug on the film's budget. The continual threats had been put into force. *Fool's Gold,* according to the studio, had been officially "wrapped." David was being boxed into a corner, but was determined that no one, not even Dixon Shaw, would view a single frame of the film until it was ready to be shown. He called his production accountant to juggle the figures, laying off all future post-production costs for the film onto RPM records, buried somewhere in the sound-track album costs.

The two calls David had been waiting for did not materialize. Shaw he could understand—a busy man playing the usual pressure politics. But Shelby was another matter. David personally put a call into her Reno hotel room, a private line he had had the hotel install for her. She answered on the fourth ring. "Where've you been?" he asked, his voice tinged with vexation.

"My hair, sugar."

"Shelby, how many times . . . I don't want to be called that."

A long silence followed on the other end. "I'm sorry, David. I'll try not to. I promise."

"Thought you had a meeting with your lawyer this morning?"

"I was just on my way."

"Call me as soon as you get out. And have him phone too."

"Sure enough. He promised this one should do it," she said brightly. "Y'all coming up this weekend?"

He ceased doodling on the notepad and explained rapidly about Shaw's intent to see the film. "You going to show it?" she asked.

"Not if I can help it."

"Then you'll be able to come up," she concluded cheerfully. "I'll just die if I have to spend another weekend alone in this dumpy ol' town. Nothing but frustrated gamblers, lonely ol' women and horny ol' cowboys. I detest it all."

"I'll try my damnedest." He switched topics, asking what she had had done to her hair. Shelby was rambling on when his secretary came in signaling. He stood in anticipation. "Shaw's on the other line. Phone me from the lawyer's. Bye-bye."

He disconnected her by punching up the second line. "Morning, Dixon."

"I'm making a special trip out to see your film, David. Right after the president's planned reelection celebration at the White House," the chairman said with hearty spirit. "McGovern thankfully will be sent to where he banished Thomas Eagleton. Political oblivion. The land of no clout."

"The film's not ready, Dixon. We're waiting for the remixed music—"

"I'll see it as it is," the chairman broke in bluntly. "I don't give a damn about the sound track."

"The fifties music sets the whole period, Dixon. You won't be able to judge it."

"I'm not going to judge it. I just want to see the damned thing."

Still standing, David rammed his thighs into the corner of the desk. "Has Irving been bad-mouthing it? If he has, he's blowing it out his ass. He hasn't seen jackshit of it."

"That's precisely why I'm asking to see it," Shaw said, coldly professional. "You have to let go of it sometime. You're booked for the Christmas season."

"It'll be ready on schedule. But it's *not* ready now."

"I'm coming out on Saturday. I intend to see it in whatever state it is." Shaw clicked off.

David hurled the receiver from him. It sailed the length of the cord, pulled up short and crashed to the floor.

For the rest of the week, David maneuvered desperately to get out of the screening, all the while editing furiously. He dictated an eight-page personal letter to Shaw which detailed precisely the reasons for the film's not being ready: studio interference, incompetent crews and studio lab delays. Although David did not come out and name Irving in the letter as the root of his problems, he made certain that the implication was clear. David sent the letter to be hand-delivered by special courier.

While waiting for Shaw's reply, David returned to the problems at hand—namely perfecting the sound-track to his film. For the background music, David had meticulously selected eleven top forty songs from the midfifties—from Fats Domino to the Everly Brothers. He had secured the rights, then had the standards rerecorded using

RPM artists to nearly duplicate the original sound. He planned a simultaneous release of the sound-track album with the film. He was carefully structuring *Fool's Gold* to be a smash hit on many fronts at once.

Several times a day and at night, whether in the editing room, in his Mercedes, or even in the bathroom, he kept in close touch with Shelby by phone. He wanted to know her every move, what she had to eat, what her weight was, what her mood was, even what she was thinking and dreaming. Enthusiastically she reported to him, obviously pleased at his continued interest. Every morning he had delivered to her suite in Reno a dozen long-stemmed roses. Every evening before her dinner, he had arranged to have Tiffany's, through a local Reno jeweler, deliver something glittering and expensive—a diamond pendant, a pearl drop on a platinum chain, an emerald dinner ring, a gold ankle bracelet with his initials engraved. For each of the presents, she thanked him, bubbling over the phone her delight and surprise.

"Oh, David," she exclaimed once, "you're spoiling me something terrible.

"Nothing I give you can match what you're worth. And don't you forget it."

"How sweet . . . I miss you desperately."

"Only a little while longer. Then you'll be free."

"If you had let me go to Mexico, it could've been done over a weekend and we wouldn't be apart."

"I want this permanent and legal. No quickies to be contested. Just hang on. You'll see it's for the best."

"Anything you say, darling . . . anything."

On Friday morning, David finally received a reply to his request for a postponement of the screening. It was a one-word telegram from Shaw. The word was "No." David sat, staring at it, knowing that he had been outgunned.

Precisely at seven-thirty that Saturday evening, David arrived by chauffeur-driven limousine at Shaw's discreetly guarded Bel Air estate. With him, he had brought an exhausted Sammy. David had insisted that his top editor be in the booth with Shaw's projectionist in case any of the splices on the workprint broke. Shaw did not greet them at the door, the English butler let them in. Hurriedly David, Sammy and the projectionist lugged the heavy cans into the luxuriously appointed screening room with a giant, gold-framed Thomas Hill oil of Yosemite Falls at one end.

On the stroke of eight, Shaw opened the hall door and strode in, wearing full boardroom gear of a three-piece suit. Politely but formally, Shaw greeted David, they shook hands, then sat. Immediately the lights dimmed out and the large framed nineteenth-century oil rose into the ceiling with the soft *whirr* of a concealed twentieth-century motor.

The projector's beam of white light cut over their heads filling the screen. The black-and-white leader numbers counted down to the top of the film—four, three, two, one. *Fool's Gold* began its first screening for an outsider.

As well as David knew every frame of the footage, he found himself becoming engrossed by the relatively large image projected on the screen. Yet out of the corner of his eye, he was conscious of the chairman. Shaw sat intently viewing, giving no outward indication of what he was thinking. The screen story unfolded quickly and when Shelby made her first appearance, he noted that Shaw settled back even further into his easy chair. Although the film was basically dramatic in intent, David had incorporated some comic relief. He was pleased when Shaw smiled at the first bit, chuckled softly at the second and laughed outright at the next.

The story had just begun the tension-filled incident introducing the story's heavy, the grandson of the original owner of the mine, when suddenly Shaw was sitting upright. David congratulated himself—the damned film was riveting Shaw's attention.

Ninety-six minutes after the lights had dimmed, the plot reached its explosive climax and the film was over. David could not wait until the lights had been brought back up. He swiveled in the darkness. "Well . . . ?"

Shaw buzzed the booth, "I'd like to see that last reel again." He turned to David. "Hope you don't mind."

"Of course not," David replied, mystified. "Would you tell me why though?"

"Afterward," the chairman said with the finality of a man who did not wish to talk any further. The lights went out and in silence, they waited for the reel to be reracked. The film began again, picking up the action at an awkward point, David thought. The last reel ran in its entirety without a comment from Shaw. Again the lights were brought up and David waited stonily, bitterly, for a clue.

"Care for a drink?" the chairman asked, polite, distant.

"No. But I'd like to know what you thought."

"The young actor with the limp. His name, please. You've no credits at this stage."

"Christopher Warren."

The chairman nodded. "Also goes by the name Scooter."

"He's extraordinarily powerful. Could be a new Brando."

"I'm afraid you've made a terrible blunder in casting him." Shaw read David's confusion and continued, "Remember that riot in Wall Street? Timed for the very night our president was being renominated in Miami this last July?"

"Can't say that I do."

The chairman sighed. "Don't you keep up on anything that's happening out there? Outside of the movie or record business?"

"Of course I do," David replied with barely controlled annoyance. "Nixon and Agnew were just reelected by a landslide. Kissinger is in Paris and says peace is at hand, so? So what?"

"Headlines. Nothing more."

"What the hell difference does it make?" David said heatedly. "Does it cut down on the profits I've brought in? And what the hell does it have to do with my film?"

"A very great deal."

"I don't read tea leaves, Dixon. What're you talking about? Do you like it or not? That's all I want to know." David was on his feet, pacing the carpet in front of the white screen.

The chairman remained seated, solid as a conference table. "I think you've made a nice little film, but unfortunately it can not be released in its present form."

David quivered, ready to erupt.

"Sit down," Shaw ordered. The tone was sharp, the expression filled with annoyance. David dropped back into his chair. Shaw appraised him coolly. "I repeat, this film cannot be released as is. I will not allow it. Either you cut that actor out entirely or I'll shelve it."

"Cut him out? His role is absolutely pivotal to the plot. We have no climax without him. I'd be a damned fool to cut him out."

"You'd be a damned fool to leave him in." Shaw stood, moving to the liquor cabinet. "Scooter Warren is a commie punk. He was the ring leader of a bunch of freaked-out radical actors that attacked our corporate world headquarters. Blood was thrown—pig's blood!—all over our doors, the windows. But what's worse, far worse, was the amount of press and airtime those punks were able to generate. And at a time when America's greatest president was sharing the very same public airwaves. A disgrace."

David stared in disbelief. "I had no idea . . ."

"Now you know the severity of your mistake," Shaw admonished. "I could not in all consciousness release a film that contained a performance by one of these commie bastards. Let them work elsewhere. Preferably Russia where they belong."

David stiffly bobbed his head. "But I'd have to recast, reshoot, reedit. It'll take more time, more money . . ."

"How much extra would it take?" Shaw asked.

"I've no idea," David said spiritlessly. "All of it was exteriors. And it's full-blast winter in Montana now. Let alone finding an actor as good as Warren."

"Actors are a dime a dozen," Shaw replied and stood. "I like your film, David. I'd hate to have to shelve it." Without any further comment, he started across the carpet. By the door, he paused. "Get me an estimate on what it would take. I'll see what I can do. Good night."

For a long while, David could only sit there in the large, empty screening room. For some strange reason, all he could think of was Shelby. He wondered what she was doing at the very moment.

REBECCA
December 1972
New York

Outside the small off-Broadway theater, into the dinner hour dusk, she emerged after a strenuous all-day rehearsal and paused only long enough to read the large poster announcing the play: *Mother Courage* by Bertolt Brecht. Her eyes danced over the cast list until she came to her own name—only four down from the lead actress. That fact never failed to bring on such a rush of satisfaction. Spinning on her toes, Rebecca skipped away, heading into the icy twilight.

Her landing the part of the mute daughter, Catherine, had been unexpected and thrilling. Now, only three weeks from opening, her excitement had not diminished. To make it all even sweeter, it was a full Equity production and at last, one of her primary goals had been reached. She was finally a full, card-carrying member of the actors' union.

She barreled up the stairs to their East Village apartment and burst through the door, calling out, "Did the tickets come? Oh my god . . . you look gorgeous!"

Scooter stood awkwardly in the center of the room dressed in a rented tuxedo, complete with bow tie, starched white shirt and shiny black shoes. She'd never seen him in a suit before, let alone so handsome and so classily attired. She wished for a camera.

He grumbled, "I feel like a queer monkey in a penguin suit."

"I'd be queer for you any day."

He cast another glum glance in the mirror. "Is this really necessary to get ahead?"

"Just another costume. For the hottest up-and-coming young actor in town?" She stood on tiptoes and pecked him on the cheek. "Hey, no shave?"

"Haven't even showered yet," he admitted, with a sly grin. "Seriously considering not to. Sort of a silent but smelly protest."

"Not on your life, mister. You take those duds off and march into that bathroom," she ordered with exaggerated threat. "Or I won't sit by you all night."

"We may have to stand."

"They didn't come?"

He shook his head, yanking loose the tie. "Another reason I may not shower. No tickee, no washee."

She groaned. "Bad joke, Scooter. Bad." She tore off her coat and began tugging at her clothes. She could tell that in spite of his attempt at humor, he was even more uptight than when she had left that morning. And he had been for weeks. So much was riding on tonight, she vowed silently to keep the mood light no matter what. "Did you get ahold of Mo?"

"Yeah. She doesn't know a damn thing either. Promised again she'd find out what's going on and call back." He threw off the dress shirt and stepped out of the shoes. He was barefoot.

"Where're your socks?"

"Forgot to buy 'em."

"You can't go to a world premiere like that, silly. I'll find you some. Who showers first? Me or the movie star?"

"Go ahead. Mo might call." He slumped into a chair.

Rebecca paused by the bathroom door. "Hey, Scooter, don't worry. The tickets'll show up. Just a stupid oversight, that's all."

He nodded as though he'd heard it all before—which he had. She ducked into the shower and turned on the faucet.

Who ever heard of an actor not being invited to his own film premiere? So his part was small, did that make any difference? Not according to Mo Engle.

Two months previously, while out in L.A., Mo had been able to talk herself into Rau's editing room when the producer wasn't there and had her own private sneak preview of Scooter's sequences. Her report back had been so full of praise, both Mo and Scooter had concluded that this film would launch his career like a skyrocket. So how could the studio overlook his invitation and tickets? It just didn't make sense.

Over the streaming water, Rebecca heard the phone ring. Keeping her fingers crossed, she rinsed her hair. The shower curtain parted and he stepped in, nude, lanky, feigning boredom. "That was Mo…"

"And…?"

"She harangued Rau's office out of a couple tickets."

"Whoopeee! *Now* tickee, *now* washee!" She handed him the bar of soap. Instead, he grabbed her, rubbing his lean frame over her slippery skin, holding her under the driving water, laughing with her.

A half hour later, after much scrambling, they were seated in the uptown subway, dressed to the hilt—Scooter in his rented tux under his baggy old overcoat, Rebecca bundled in her bulky winter coat over a new burgundy velvet cocktail dress which he'd bought her for Christmas. With tight long sleeves, a low-cut square neckline and flared skirt, it was the most beautiful dress she'd ever worn. Over her hair, which she had twisted into a sedate French roll, she'd thrown a white lace mantilla which Ada had given her just before leaving for Europe with Real Amerika. Rebecca felt like a princess stepping out to her first real ball accompanied by the most handsome prince in the world.

Climbing up from the subterranean Times Square stop, she jerked him to a halt. In wonderment she gazed upwards. Four giant arc lights in front of the theater swept the sides of the buildings and probed the night sky, crisscrossing overhead with fanciful patterns. "Oh, Lordee," she murmured, "a real, honest-to-god Hollywood premiere."

Scooter tugged her forward, his distaste a facade, she decided. He seemed as eager as she to get to the theater. The entire block in front of the giant movie house had been cordoned off, large black limousines inched forward in a long line, police were everywhere, some even on horseback, holding the crowds behind wooden barriers. Spectators, despite the frosty night, jammed the sidewalks, cheering the arriving stars. In large block metallic letters the marquee read *Fool's Gold—World Premiere*. She could not remember when she'd ever been so excited.

They darted across the street and entered the milling crowd at the end of the block. Their progress was so slow, Scooter pulled her into the street where they hustled along the gutter. The limousines passed by so closely she could peer into the rear windows. Finally she was lucky. "Scooter! Didja see who that was?"

"Where?"

"That car right up there," she exhaled. "Joey Heatherton. She even smiled at me. So close I could see lipstick on her teeth."

"Probably from kissing herself."

"Hold it right there." One of New York's finest was blocking them from slipping through the barriers.

"I'm in this film," Scooter said in his anti-uniform tone.

"Let's see your tickets."

"They're at the door."

She could tell the cop didn't believe him. "It's true, officer. This is Christopher Warren and he's really in the film. He's going to be a big star."

"Yeah and I'm Sportsman of the Year, Billie Jean King," the cop growled. "Now move back."

Rebecca smiled. "Officer, please. I'll wait right here. Couldn't he just go up and collect the tickets? You'll see. We're legit."

The policeman studied her for an agonizing moment. "Okay. Just him. Lady, you stay put."

"Gladly," she replied and pushed Scooter through the opening of the wooden barricades. "Go on. Just don't forget me?"

Scooter winked at her. "You look like a kid with a free pass to Coney Island."

"Better than that. I've got a free pass to you. So go, already."

He pushed through the mob of curious bystanders. She kept the top of his head in sight until it disappeared in the throng. Around her, over her, people were buzzing about the latest star to arrive— "Mia Farrow," "Elliot Gould," "Senator Javits," "George Segal," "Ingrid Bergman," "James Earl Jones"—the names were like peals of clarion bells to Rebecca, signaling the importance of the event and adding immeasurably to her excitement, her sense of unreality. A squeal of young voices broke out above the others, "Buster! Buster!"

It took her a moment to realize that they were yelling for Robby Rhomann. "Buster" was his TV character. Eagerly she made an extra effort to squeeze through the press of humanity and lunged for the red velvet covered rope.

On the far side of the red carpet, which stretched from the curb to the theater doors, Robby was surrounded by snapping photographers and a mob of awestruck, giggling, pre-teenagers who thrust out autograph books and slips of paper, some still chanting, "Buster, Buster!"

Jammed against the taut velvet rope, Rebecca gazed at him. Except for the sky blue tuxedo which made him appear more dapper, he looked the same, curly blond and devilishly cute. And he was obviously enjoying the adulation. It gave her an odd sensation. He was making it, she thought—just as she'd always known he would. It filled her with both pride and envy.

Rebecca spotted Mo, standing off to one side, grinning at her client's reception. "Mo, Mo!" she called above the noise, finally attracting her notice. Wrapped in a bulky mink coat, Mo ambled over like a friendly brown bear. "Hi, Rebecca . . . where's Scooter?"

"Trying to get our tickets."

Mo gave a stentorian honk through her nose. "I don't understand it. The bastard won't return my phone calls. In fact, the only communication I've had from Rau in the last two months was a terse note informing me that he was handling Shelby's career from now on. Her I can live without. Scooter—I'd sure as hell hate to lose him because of this foul-up."

"No way," Rebecca insisted. "Not after you got him this big break."

"Scooter could land a Best Supporting Actor nomination for this," Mo stated emphatically. "And look at Robby. Lapping this up like whipped cream. His mom refuses to come to his public appearances. I think she resents sharing him with strangers. Want me to call him over? Say hello?"

"No, I wouldn't want to butt into his glory."

Again Mo snorted, a cloud of vaporized air rushing from her nose. "Well, well, speak of the bastard himself."

Rebecca had already seen. David Rau had stepped out of the front limousine like a man who'd just conquered Mount Everest. He reached in and helped out a spectacular Shelby Cale. The crowd gasped, gaped and applauded. Her blond hair shimmered in the exploding light of dozens of flashbulbs. Wearing a low-cut, clinging jersey gown of soft green, a healthy expanse of pale bosom swelling out, a white ermine stole thrown carelessly over her bare shoulders,

Shelby turned this way and that for the press photographers, smiling, dazzling everyone into near silence.

So she's gorgeous, Rebecca thought, but she doesn't have Erik anymore. Imagine her dumping him for that runt David. Well, they deserve each other. Look at him—glowering at the press for getting too close—like he owned her or something.

Mo squared her shoulders. "I'm going to ask him about your tickets. And look, if there's further b.s., Scooter can have mine and sit with Robby. You and I can get a drink somewhere. I'd even prefer that. Lord, I hate these things. About as real as Shelby's smile."

Rebecca lost track of Mo in the ensuing crush. Doormen were hurrying people inside. Even Robby had vanished. Lights over the doors were flashing, the film was about to start. Halfway down the block, last-minute arrivals bustled out of their limousines and ran for the doors, not waiting for a more grand entrance on the red carpet.

Scooter appeared, surveying the crowd of spectators. Rebecca waved and hollered. He moved to her, shaking his head from side to side like a metronome beating out a funeral dirge. Reaching her, he muttered, "No soap."

"Oh, no! Did you see Mo? She said you could have her ticket."

"Not going in there without you."

"Go on, will you? She just left here. Catch her."

"No," he said dourly and grabbed her hand. "Let's split."

Rebecca ducked under the red rope. "Please, Scooter. For me. Go find her. Go see your film . . . please . . ."

"Dammit, no!" He yanked her off the curb, making a wide berth around the crowd, pulling her along behind him. In her high heels, she struggled to keep up. "What happened? Did you tell 'em you're in it?"

"No one seemed to give a shit."

They reached the end of the block where the mob had thinned out. He stepped back onto the sidewalk to wait for the "Walk" light to cross the street. His features were hard-set, his clenched jaw working furiously. She tugged at his sleeve. "Well, if they don't know you now, they sure will afterward. Why don't we hang around?"

"Too damned cold."

"Then let's go up to Howard Johnson's. Grab a bite. Wait until this crowd packs it in and heads home. The subways will be less jammed." She sensed his vacillation so took the lead, linking her arm through his, heading him up the street. "I'm freezing anyway," she said cheerfully. "Doesn't hot soup sound good?" He didn't respond, but he was beside her.

Inside the restaurant, they had to wait for a while but were eventually seated in a small booth way in the back. Scooter slouched over his food, his bow tie hanging loose, his shirt open at the collar. She could tell he barely listened to her stream of chatter. She reported in detail all the famous people she'd seen arrive, what the women were wearing, which male stars were shorter than their screen image, the crowd's reaction to each. She made a point of not mentioning Robby and the ruckus he'd raised.

"Did you see Shelby?" she asked casually. He shook his head, bending over his bowl of vegetable soup. "She looked sensational, Scooter. A real glamor queen. You think she's going to be a movie star?"

"If Rau has his way."

"Doesn't seem fair. Just because she's gorgeous . . ."

"Who said the world was fair?"

"I did," she joked, halfheartedly. "Don't you remember? The world is fair, I said back in sixty-six. It's not only fair, the good guys always win."

"Dreams, Rebecca. You live in dreams."

"Maybe so. But what else have I got?" She considered for a moment, chewing on her toasted cheese sandwich. It tasted like cardboard. "No, I take that back. I used to have only dreams. But now, I've got you. And I've got a juicy role to act. And I've got my Equity card. Really, what more could I ask for?"

"To be a star. To be beautiful like Shelby. To be rich like—"

"Okay, okay, I hear you," she interrupted with a wave of a hand. "But you can't tell me you don't want that too."

"To be beautiful?" A smile cracked his dour face.

"You're already that," she teased. "Now, come on, level with me. Don't you have an itch to be famous too? Like Dustin Hoffman?

He's a real New York actor, did a lot of stage, just like you and look at all the fun he's having.''

Scooter leaned back, stretching his arms behind him, locking them behind his head. "Yeah, I see certain advantages. Being able to pick and choose your roles. Not having to wait around for someone to ask you. Or have to audition for everything. To have a certain freedom to explore and to fail. What actor wouldn't mind that?''

She toyed with her spoon. "What are your dreams, Scooter? All the time we've been together...I don't remember you ever mentioning a single dream or fantasy. And here I am, blabbing them out all the time. Ol' motor-mouth with a head full of tinsel and stardust." She paused, smiling. "Give me just one little dream. Something you think'd be extra special to come true some day.''

He was silent for several beats, an odd, soft expression in his velvety eyes. "I'd like to have some kids.''

She nearly spilled her coffee. "I didn't even know you liked kids.''

"I do. At least, I think I do. Who knows until you have your own?" He leaned forward. "How 'bout you? Want kids?''

Confused, she stalled. "Sure . . . some day.''

"Want to have 'em by me?''

"I'd love to," she said, not having to think about it.

"Well, then, while we're on the subject, let me tell you another part of this little fantasy of mine, okay?''

"Sure. Shoot." Her breathing thinned.

"If this film tonight," he began seriously, "makes me as hot as Mo thinks it will, and I start getting work—regular like—what do you say we get married and start a family?''

He could have knocked her over with a dill pickle. The subject of marriage was one which she'd never dared broach before. He actually blushed, his chiseled cheekbones turning rosy. "Hell, I know I've treated you pretty rotten in the past . . . but . . . I hope I've made up a bit for that.''

Her head was bobbing, tears beginning to cloud her vision.

"I'm not asking you to give up your acting," he continued, boyishly earnest. "But maybe . . . just maybe, mind you, if everything clicks tonight—we could kind of take turns. You know, me watching the brood while you work and then you minding them when I've got a gig. I've seen other acting couples do that and they seem to manage pretty well . . . what do you say?''

Grinning like a fool, she wiped the tears from her chin. "When?"

He shrugged. "How 'bout after all the reviews are in and I've had my first offer? We could go down tomorrow, get our license and then see how the old cookie crumbles."

"Oh, Scooter . . ." She half rose and stretched across the table, throwing her arms around his neck, kissing him fully on the lips. "Yes!"

"Hey, com'on," he grumbled. "You're creating a scene."

"Isn't that what actresses are for?" She kissed him again and collapsed into her seat.

"Hell, if I'd known it's such a big deal, I'd've asked you before."

"So why didn't you, you big putz? You think I've been hanging around to do your laundry?"

He laughed, his mood definitely lighter. "Well, since we're sharing our little soap-opera dreams and all—I guess I was waiting for the future to look a bit brighter. A little more secure."

"It looks better than ever, doesn't it?" She blew her nose loudly into a paper napkin and stuffed a clean one into her pocket to keep as a memento.

How perfect, she thought as they left the restaurant—two New York actors getting engaged in Howard Johnson's on Times Square, right in the heart of the theater district. Hanging onto him, feeling happier than ever before, Rebecca floated beside him toward the subway.

On the corner, Scooter stopped, staring up at the news-reader lights which ran around one of the towers. "Look," he mumbled. "Peace at hand, huh?" She glanced up to read the words flashing by like a moving train: ". . . THE LARGEST AIRSTRIKE IN THE WAR'S HISTORY CONTINUES AGAINST NORTH VIETNAM . . ."

She looked away, not wanting to spoil the cloud she was walking on. "Hey, Scooter, check the time. Your flick's about ready to end. Let's just sort of stroll by."

"Naw, I'd feel like a dog waiting for a pat on the head."

"Com'on, it'll be a kick. Want to bet they recognize you now?"

He seemed to brighten at the thought and allowed himself to be tugged toward the theater on the next block. The cold air had driven most of the spectators away—only a few hearty souls remained behind the rope and wooden barricades. The line of waiting limousines parked along the curb stretched around the block and out of sight.

Before she and Scooter even reached halfway, the main entrance doors were thrown open, disgorging the first of the elegantly attired crowd. Rebecca hastened their pace. "Let's grab one of the programs. Start a scrapbook."

"Aren't you full of new traditions," he groused but ducked under the rope, beginning a search for an abandoned program. People streamed past him hurrying to reach their limos. With barely controlled anticipation, she watched them, waiting for someone to recognize him. More and more of the filmgoers walked by, and still no one did a doubletake. Rebecca could not believe it. What were they, blind? Scooter disappeared into the crowd.

Someone called her name and Rebecca turned, seeing Mo plowing toward her grimly. "Where's Scooter?" Her tone bordered on harshness.

"Just up there. He's getting a . . . what's wrong?"

"That bastard, that sonofabitch Rau."

"What?" Rebecca asked, apprehension mushrooming.

"He shafted Scooter. And royally. Cut him out. Totally."

Rebecca couldn't respond, her eyelids blinked rapid, frantic questions. Mo took her arm solicitously. "Oh, the character's still in. But some other actor's playing him."

"Oh, my god . . ."

"And what's even harder to take—he's carbon-copied Scooter's performance. Same inflections. Same quirky mannerisms. Right down to Scooter's limp. Lord, it's the most disgusting travesty ever witnessed."

"But . . . why? Why'd they do . . . ?"

"Damned if I know. Scooter was so much better—where're you going?"

"Have to find him and . . ." Rebecca's power of speech failed.

Scooter was heading slowly toward them, his eyes glazed, unfocused, in his hand dangled a printed program. The sight of his stricken face ripped her to shreds. A dozen paces away, he stopped, staring at them as if they were the last two people he wanted to see. The program dropped to the sidewalk. He jerked around and plunged into the crowd.

"Scooter!" Rebecca cried.

Mo caught her arm. "He may want to be alone."

Rebecca shook off the restraining grip and dashed forward, darting into the crowd where she'd last seen him. The theater patrons had moved down the block searching for their limousines. The jumble of humanity slowed her, but she kept moving, scrambling, pushing, shoving.

"Scooter!" she called and paused to jump up and down, hoping to see him. People stared at her, their eyes filled with amusement. She ran again, cursing the high heels. At the intersection, she slowed, looking in all directions, her heart sinking lower and lower. She did not see him anywhere. Choosing the most likely avenue of escape, she ran through the intersection and down the darkest sidewalk leading from Times Square.

Wearily using the banister, Rebecca pulled herself up the stairs to their apartment. Her search fruitless, she was hoping against hope that he had returned home, but she had an ominous feeling—an unnamed terror clutched at her throat. The apartment door was unlocked. She pushed through into the small living room. "Scooter? You here, man?"

There was no response.

Her eyes swept over the room. He'd been there. Under the glare of the overhead light, the rented tuxedo lay twisted on the area rug—the white dress shirt crumpled into a tight ball. She walked into the bathroom and switched on the light. Automatically she found herself checking for his shaving gear. All of it was there.

She returned to the main room and began picking up his things, putting them into the plastic bag from the rental shop. A stiff icy blast of air blew past her. She spun, trying to figure where it came from just as someone knocked on the hall door. Rebecca unlocked it, flinging it open.

Mo Engle, bundled in her fur coat, heaved a sigh of relief. "How's he doing?"

Again Rebecca felt the cold draft of air, stronger because of the open hall door. She whirled, zeroing in on the closed venetian blinds. They were steadily breathing in and out.

With a jolt, she knew. The window to the fire escape was open. She dashed for it. Pushing aside the dusty plastic blinds, she was halfway out the open window when Mo shouted, "Where're you going?"

The metal beneath her fingers was like ice, rusted and grimy with soot. In the near dark, Rebecca clambered one floor up the brownstone's steep ladder to the roof. She should've known. He often spent time up there when he wanted to be alone. She reached the top and pulled herself onto the bulging, warped tarpaper.

The floodlights from the apartment building next door partially lit the flat roof before her. She ran for the top of the stairwell which jutted up like a large, brick box—the opposite side was his favorite sanctuary. Vaguely conscious of a siren bleating in the distance, she rounded the corner of the brick rectangle and stopped to peer into the shadows. He was not there.

Disappointed, confused, she walked around the brick stairwell structure to the metal fire door. The siren was coming closer, its wail disturbing the relative quiet of the late night hour. She yanked on the cold handle of the roof's door. It was locked from the inside—as it always was. Scooter could not have gone down that way.

The mournful, shrill siren, now very close, cut into her consciousness. Flashing red reflected from windows across the street. She ran to the alley cornice. A police car—its top lights spinning, siren dying—was entering the darkened alley from the street. She leaned over the waist-high wall and looked straight down.

A bomb exploded in her heart. In the white spotlight from the police car, Scooter's pale naked form lay face down on the pavement—broken like a piece of discarded wood.

She began to scream—it welled from deep within her, rising up in anguish, higher and higher. She threw a leg over the wall, wanting to plunge down to join him.

Hands clutched at her, pulling her back, pushing her head into the soft fur. She fought to get loose from the tenacious grip but Mo held her tightly.

Rebecca's hysterical cries did not abate until a doctor injected her with a strong sedative. Even while she was blacking out, being held down by two paramedics on the black tarpaper, her last feeble cry was, "Scooter. . . ."

SHELBY
January 1973
Malibu

The phone rang continuously all morning at David's colony beach house. Last-minute acceptances were pouring in. Her private secretary, Judith, in the upstairs den, announced the latest by yelling down the hall. "That was Tatum. Both she and daddy, affirmative."

In her dressing room off the master suite, seated before her vanity-table mirrors, Shelby made a neat check beside the names on the master invitation list. So far, so good. With less than eight hours before the party, over ninety percent had responded—the majority positive. She carefully applied the last dusting of cheek blush and leaned back, narrowing her eyes slightly to view the overall effect. She was not totally satisfied but in too big a hurry to take more time.

"Charles and Jill Bronson," Judith shouted from the other room.

Another hasty checkmark and Shelby switched off the row of makeup lights and noticed the clock. Damn, she was running late—she rose to drop her dressing robe and caught a reflection of a youthful male in the doorway behind. She spun in surprise, holding her robe tightly closed. "What're you doing?"

Henry Mawson smiled lazily, his drooping, bedroom-lidded eyes rising from her covered breasts. "Need any help?"

For a second, she was affronted by his boldness, but something about his manner made her smile. Not to mention his tight designer jeans. "Yes, I desperately do need your help, *down*stairs. That's why I hired you, Henry Mawson. You're supposedly the best in Beverly Hills. But in mere hours, two hundred of Hollywood's finest will be arriving here and you still have painters in the sunroom, cooks behind schedule in the kitchen, gardeners still planting shrubs on the decks . . . get the picture?"

He winked lazily. "Pretty as . . ."

"Sam Ervin from D.C.," Judith screamed from down the hall. "Regretfully declines due to the senate hearings."

Henry raised his palms. "Another time? More personal help?"

"I'm strongly attached, remember?" Shelby voiced with promise.

"Lucky man—a hit movie and you too." He sighed ingenuously. "Some guys have it all." Henry slipped out as quietly as he'd entered.

After dressing in a lemon sorbet-colored afternoon dress by Ann Klein and giving voluminous last-minute instructions to Judith, Shelby descended the open staircase which swept down into the cathedral-ceilinged living room. The transformation was nearly complete—giant baskets of trailing fuchsia and varicolored orchids hung from the thick wood beams, the wood-paneled wall around the brick fireplace was strung with garlands of pink mimosa, small potted trees of camellias and gardenias clustered in the corners and along the French doors leading to the glass-screened beach deck were tubs full of blooming spring bulbs—daffodils, tulips, iris and hyacinths. The ocean air was heavy with sweet fragrances and delicious aromas drifted in from the kitchen. A dozen workers paused in setting up the round tables and matching white chairs to turn an admiring focus on her descent.

Aware of their attention, she smiled all the way to the bottom of the stairs. "Henry, it's looking superb."

On top of a ladder, fussing with a spray of forsythia, he grinned. "The only bash in town with jasmine and jonquils in January." She ignored his meaningful glance and started for the front door. Judith hollered from the top of the stairs. "Oh my god, Cary Grant! Just said yes! In person!"

The drive from Malibu Colony into downtown Hollywood usually took over an hour, depending on traffic. That afternoon, vehicles were minimal on the Pacific Coast Highway and she sped along, loving the sensation of driving David's holiday gift, a mint-colored Mercedes Benz 450 SL convertible. She felt in an exceptional mood and was positive David suspected nothing. On the radio, she tuned into Carly Simon singing "You're So Vain" and wondered if the gossip were true that it was about Warren Beatty and reminded herself to check first thing back to see if he'd accepted her invitation.

Deep in old Hollywood, below Sunset Boulevard, at Pacific Studios, Shelby presented herself to Irving R. Dyer's personal secretary. The dubious blonde rose grandly. "This way, please," she said in an affected manner and opened the double doors to the presidential office suite. "Miss Cale," she announced theatrically.

For the first time, Shelby swept into the spacious room which, with its green leather couches, framed English hunting scenes and brass lamps, looked more like a lodge room than a working office of a studio head. Irving stood at the far end, behind a mammoth slab of rosewood desk. His arms were crossed over his chest, like a buyer at a slave auction, his eye critically appraising her approach.

Shelby gave it her all, holding out a hand, greeting warmly, "Hello, Mister Dyer. I've been looking forward to meeting y'all for simply ages."

He took her hand formally and bent his nearly bald head, brushing his lips lightly over her knuckles. The contact made the back of her knees prickle with shivers.

"Miss Cale," he began with a strange, raspy voice. "What do I owe this unexpected and delightful visit? Please . . . sit." He waited until she'd sunk gracefully into the indicated chair, then lowered himself into the huge carved desk chair.

She presented her most dazzling smile. "I thought it high time we met, Irving. I may call you Irving, mightn't I?"

"Suits me fine, Shelby." His bushy gray brows drew together noticeably. "David send you?"

She laughed throatily and leaned back, crossing her long legs.

"He's in Chicago. Won't be back until seven tonight and hasn't an inkling that I'm here. Why'd you ask?"

He shrugged. The gesture was so reminiscent of David's she found herself trying to find other similarities. Unless she'd known for certain, she would never have guessed they were related. A shared crusty energy perhaps.

Irving lit a long thick cigar and blew a cloud of blue smoke out of the side of his mouth. "Curious, that's all."

"Or suspicious?" She had deliberately made it sound teasing and could tell he liked that approach. So far, he was not what she'd expected.

"Well, you gotta admit, Shelby, I've good cause to be a bit of both. David and I have not been exactly what you'd call close. No Andy Hardy and the Judge, right?"

She smiled in spite of not knowing to whom he was referring. "That's one of the reasons I'm here. I just can't understand why two such intelligent and obviously successful men should continue to remain at odds with each other." She paused to smooth the accordion pleats of her skirt, trying to recall the exact wording of her prepared spiel. "After all, here y'all are involved in the same profession—on the same lot—and working for the same team and y'all hardly speak to each other."

"But we yell a helluva lot." He smiled at his own humor.

Feeling more at ease, she asked suddenly, "What was David's mother like? He hardly mentions her at all and . . ." She swallowed the end of her sentence. Irving had flipped the cigar ash angrily into the ashtray. She rushed to make amends, turning on all her charm. "I surely don't mean to pry, Irving. I'm just curious."

"So we're both curious, huh?"

"Yes . . . I guess y'all could say that."

"Well, I'll make a deal with you," he said gruffly. "You tell me why you're here and I'll tell you about Nedra. Fair?"

"All right," she answered. "I'll go first. Fair?" His nod prodded her on. "I've been personally trying to reach you for days, Irving. But I didn't want to leave a message, so here I am. I would dearly love for y'all to come to my surprise party for David tonight."

He stared at her poker-faced. "That's it?"

"Cross my heart." Girlishly she wagged a forefinger over her left breast.

He chuckled. "I'm surprised."

"At what?"

"At David. Had no idea he had such good taste in girls."

"Why thank you," she murmured, looking up through her lashes.

"And not a bad little actress. On top of being such a looker."

"Y'all like my performance in *Fool's Gold*?"

"What's not to like? Who'd've thought a little story like that would make such box-office and get such notice?"

"David did," she said proudly.

Irving flipped the ash again and studied the end of the cigar. "So what's so important about me coming to your party?"

"It'd make the whole evening for me. And would mean a great deal to David."

"Ha!" he exploded with a burst of smoke. "That's a good one. You've got a sense of humor too. I like that in a girl."

"Why do you think he holds such a grudge against you?"

"Because he's an ungrateful schmuck."

She let her smile fade, wanting him to know she liked neither the language nor the thought behind it.

Irving shrugged a "what'd-I-say?" sort of gesture. "Okay, you tell me then. Why's he holding this grudge? For the life of me, I can't figure it. You know when he was a kid we had some good times together. He used to come sit on my desk—right here," he said, patting the polished wood beside him. "Course, I wasn't in this head office but it's the same damned desk. There he'd sit. Big as life. Watching me handle the boys and girls on the lot. Some free education he got. Never dawned on me he'd one day use it against me. Live and learn."

She tossed her hair back over her shoulders. "I always heard y'all were a man of your word."

"Who says otherwise?" he asked.

"Remember? About David's mother?"

"Oh, that. I don't like to speak disrespectful of the dead."

"I'm waiting . . ." She gave him a hint of future smiles.

Sighing, he shrugged broadly. "What can I say? Nedra was a

looker like you. Except dark. Foreign-looking. But from Walbash, Tennessee. She was under contract to the studio. Maybe a year before I saw her. I used her in a couple of films. Forgettable. She had a certain air of mystery about her. I liked that. Six years of marriage, she still was a mystery. I didn't like that. She drank too much, partied too much, ran with a wild crowd. Errol Flynn, those hopheads. Always partying. Lousy mother because of it. I wanted a homebody. With Nedra I had to call the clubs to find her. I divorced her. Won custody of David because she never contested. Mistake number two. Should have let her have him.'' He ground out his cigar. "She went off the deep end. Took her own life with drugs. No tragedy. Just a weak sister. Nobody missed her.''

"Except David,'' Shelby said quietly.

"Yeah, he would. They're two of a kind.''

"That's funny . . . I always thought he took after you.''

"I ain't flattered.''

"Not even a little?''

"Only 'cause it came out of such a pretty mouth.'' He smiled oddly. "Got anything else on your mind?''

"Not a thing,'' she replied. "Except to say, I'm grateful for your time and that I do wish you'd drop by tonight—even for a few minutes. You know, it seems you're the only one who hasn't congratulated David on his film.''

"That supposed to make me feel guilty or something?''

"Not at all. I'm so pleased we finally had a chance for a little private chat. I feel so much closer to you now.''

"Good. I like beautiful girls to feel close.''

Again she had the odd sensation he was hitting on her. As she stood, so did he. She offered a hand. "Good-bye, Irving. Hope to see you tonight.''

He held her hand longer than necessary. "Come in anytime you like. My door's always open to the likes of you.''

"I'll remember that. Bye now.'' She withdrew her hand, waved it gaily and made certain her exit was as provocative and full of promise as she could. In the elevator, she noticed her palms were perspiring.

Once back at the beach house, the afternoon fled. A million

details required her immediate attention. If it hadn't been for Henry, she was positive she'd have gone crazy. In the kitchen, looking over the buffet items—which included cracked crab, cold salmon, artichokes, caviar, baked potatoes—Shelby began to have serious doubts about her choices.

Dressed in a blue Adidas jogging suit, which she'd bought thinking she'd take up the new running fad on the beach, she moaned to Henry, "You just don't understand. David is the consummate producer. Every choice he makes is always right. I should never have dreamed I could do this. It's all wrong."

Henry threw an arm across the doorway, blocking her exit. "Now, you listen to me," he began sternly. "I am *the* professional party giver in L.A.—you can doubt yourself, but don't you dare doubt me. Every decision we've made is pluperfect. We're already the talk of the town."

She wilted. "I can't even decide what I should wear tonight. And the time! I have to leave in less than an hour to pick him up at the airport."

"Thought you'd bought a dress especially?"

"I did, but now it seems totally out of key."

"Let's see it and decide." All business, Henry turned to follow her upstairs to the master bedroom.

She brought the gown out of the walk-in closet. "I should never have chosen this—it'll clash with all the fuchsias." The dress was tangerine in color, a Halston original—soft chiffon layers cascaded down from thin, spaghetti straps.

Henry's sultry lids lowered even further. "You're absolutely right. It *is* all wrong. What else do you have?"

"Nothing that David hasn't seen," she snapped, wadding the dress and throwing it in the corner.

"Then pick one of his favorites. Better safe than sorry." He stuck something into his mouth, lit it, inhaled and held it out.

"Marijuana?" she asked, knowing full well what it was from just the smell—Erik often smoked the stuff. "No, thank you. It'll make me all the more crazed. I'll show you some more." She hurried back into the closet and surveyed the rows and rows of gowns, all organized by category and color. She began pawing through the short evening dress section, frantically slapping the hangers back, snatching a few possibilities and hurrying back into the bedroom.

Henry, looking more like a young parking valet than a successful businessman, was stretched out, propped up comfortably against the headboard pillows, finishing the joint. He smiled lazily at her armful. "Forget the black—they'll think you're in mourning for LBJ's death. And that shiny one—too Las Vegas."

Shelby threw the indicated outfits onto the floor, dumping the rest at his feet on the king-sized bed. One by one she held them up waiting for his reaction. Henry either nodded his approval or waved it away disdainfully. Soon she was down to only three. "Try that blue one first," he suggested, apparently getting a kick out of the proceedings.

Ducking back into her dressing room, she pulled off the jogging suit and was stepping into the blue crepe Mainbocher when a voice barked from the bedroom. "Who the hell're you?"

David! She snatched up the dressing robe and pulling it on, ran to the doorway. "David! What're you—"

"What the hell's going on?" he cut in sharply and dropped his suitcase onto the rug. "Who is this guy?"

Henry scrambled up. "Henry Mawson. The caterer."

David whipped around to her. "What the fuck?" Before she could reply, he swung back to Henry, sniffing the air. "Are you smoking shit? In *my* bedroom? Get out!"

Henry beat a hasty retreat, circling wide around David, who stood, glaring at her, his black eyes stark and accusing. She felt a souring in her stomach and wanted to move to him, throw her arms around him, welcome him home—however unexpected as it was. But he was so visibly angered, she longed for a sign of approbation.

David slammed the door, cutting off the rest of the house. "What the hell's going on? I come back and the house is crawling with strangers, the place decorated like a goddamned Busby Berkeley musical, a stoned asshole on my bed and you half-dressed in the closet."

She struggled to find her voice. "It . . . it was a surprise . . ."

"It sure as hell is."

". . . for you . . . a surprise party . . ." She couldn't help herself.

She began to weep—all her plans had been ruined and to top it off, he was raging mad at her. She collapsed on the bed, burying her face in a pillow.

"Why, Shelby?"

"To celebrate . . . your success," she sobbed. She rolled over to seek him out. "I wanted to give you something special . . ."

"What the hell for?"

"Because . . . you've given me so much . . . I just wanted to show you how much I loved you . . . now it's all spoiled . . . Why'd you come back so soon?"

He was stony silent for a couple of beats. "I didn't want you to drive to the airport by yourself."

"Oh, David," she cried and half sat up, holding out her arms to him. He did not make a move. It devastated her. She collapsed backward, her cries renewing. It seemed ages before she felt the bed side sag.

"I didn't want a party," he said earnestly. "Now or in the future. Understand?"

"But why?"

"I detest them. Everyone sucking up to anyone above them, the desperation, the scrambling, the lies. I want this canceled, Shelby."

"But . . . but how?" She sought out the clock on his dresser. "It's after six-thirty. Everyone's invited for eight."

"So un-invite them."

"We can't do that . . . absolutely everyone's coming . . . it'd . . ."

He took her hand, squeezing it just short of pain. "I don't want them in my house. Not one of them."

"We'll be the joke of Hollywood. It's—ouch! You're hurting!"

"Who gives a damn what others think?"

She yanked her wrist away and rubbing it, attempted to pull her swarming thoughts together. "We'll never reach them all in time."

"You have to. There's no choice. Move."

With an agonized effort, she heaved off the bed. Trancelike, she walked toward the hall door. His voice came to her from far away, "I'll get rid of the jokers downstairs."

She hesitated by the door. "What about the food? The flowers?"

"I'll send it to a hospital. You just do what you have to."

She moved into the hallway, holding onto the wall for support. This was crazy, totally crazy.

The next hour was frantic, desperate. Shelby, Judith and Henry, each with a third of the invitation list, each in a separate room, each on a separate outside line, dialed numbers hurriedly, trying to contact every last person, leaving messages with answering services when the individual or the household could not be reached directly. To the surprised few Shelby spoke with personally, she could only dully recite the same litany, "I deeply regret the inconvenience but something's come up and David and I are forced to cancel this evening's party." The painful process was the most excruciating, most embarrassing and most humiliating episode in her entire life. She did not know if she would ever recover.

Shut in David's downstairs' study, she postponed Irving's call to the last, eventually reaching him via his limo's phone. "What's up, doll?" he asked. Rapidly, she gave him the prepared excuse. Irving guffawed. "I was waiting for this. Figured it didn't sound like David. Live and learn, huh, Shelby? Listen, if he gives you any grief, you come straight to me, understand?" She mumbled her thanks and hung up.

Finally, blessedly, it was over. To double insure no one would show up at the front door, Henry notified the colony gatehouse and stationed one of the valet-parkers outside David's drive and another beachside to turn away any who appeared from within the colony itself.

Shelby sent Judith packing and scribbled the last check owed to Henry's company for his services. As she handed it to him, he smiled bravely. "You have my number in case you ever need my services again." Henry kissed her cheek and left.

She locked the front door behind him, turned off the outside lights and drifted back into the living room. Stripped of every last vestige of the festivities, it once more looked barren, cold, unlived in. The house was silent, only the sound of the waves lapping at the beach outside. In the damp night air, the scent of flowers had already faded.

Dreading any further emotional drains, she headed upstairs to the master bedroom. She opened the door quietly. The room was devoid of artificial light. In front of the windows, David stood in silhouette against the darkening sky, his back to her. He did not turn. She crossed quickly to him and put her arms around him, pressing her face against his shoulders.

"Did you fuck him?"

She pulled away. "What're you talking about?"

"Answer me, dammit." He faced her. "Did you fuck him?"

With difficulty she found her voice. "I don't know to whom you're referring, but the answer is a definite no."

"Your caterer," he spat out. "The stoned pretty boy on my bed."

"Henry? Don't be silly. He's just—"

"Don't lie to me, goddammit."

"I'm *not* lying."

"Then what *were* you doing? Half-dressed, hiding in the closet when I returned. Guilt plastered all over your face."

Reeling from his outburst, she rushed to reassure. "David, I swear to you nothing happened."

"You can't tell me you weren't screwing around. I've got eyes."

"They deceived you. Not me. You imagined it all. I was trying on dresses. He was helping me decide what to wear."

Abruptly he pushed past her and switched on the lamp by the bed. "Come here," he ordered curtly. "Look me in the eye and say that."

Leadenly she moved forward and met his accusatory glare. "I was trying on dresses, David. I swear. That's all. I respect his taste."

"You're lying."

"It's the truth, David. Look . . . here . . ." She darted to a crumpled gown on the floor. "See? This is the dress I bought to wear. But the color's all wrong. See . . . this orange. The flower scheme was—"

He snatched the dress out of her hands, flinging it away. "So you stripped down and changed in front of him."

"No, no," she cried. "I was changing in the closet! Out of sight! I never undressed in front of him. I wouldn't . . ."

"Except when you're stoned."

"I wasn't stoned," she screamed. "I didn't smoke any of that. I don't like it. You're jumping to conclusions. Why're you doing this?"

"Because I want the truth. So far you've done nothing but lie."

"David, David," she moaned, tears of anger and hurt flowing.

"Your acting needs work, Shelby."

"I'm *not* acting," she shouted. "I'm telling you the truth. You just refuse to believe it." She moved to turn away, but he grabbed her arms, shaking her roughly.

"You fucked him, didn't you? *Didn't you*?"

"No!"

"You were going to then, weren't you?"

"No! I wouldn't do that. I love you."

Painfully his fingers gouged into the flesh of her arms and he leaned into her. "You loved Erik once but were screwing me. How am I supposed to believe you now?"

She stared, stung. "Oh, god, is that it? Are you going to throw that in my face now?"

"Well, didn't you? You didn't love me when we first got it on. You did it for kicks. Because you were bored. And don't tell me differently." He pushed her away in disgust.

She crumpled on the rug, sobbing. Her cries grew and still he made no move to her. He stood rigidly, watching as though judging a performance. "David . . . please." She raised an abject face. "I love you. More than I loved anybody in my whole life. I need you, David. I would never, ever do anything to hurt you. Or to destroy our love. You've got to believe me. I'll just die if you don't." She was scooting on one haunch, pushing herself toward him by inches. "Please . . . believe me . . ."

He stared down and for a moment, she thought she had failed. Then, unexpectedly, abruptly, he sank to his knees in front of her, opening his arms. "See?" he asked, his voice suddenly soft. "See how much I love you? You'll just have to get used to it . . ." He pulled her into his arms, holding her tightly.

She wiped her eyes, amazed at his transformation. "As long as I know that you love me . . . I can . . . I swear I can get used to anything."

But she was not so certain she meant it.

ERIK
March 1973
New York

Straight from the airport, Erik checked into the Algonquin Hotel, not far from Times Square, dug out of his suitcase the fifth of tequila and began to drink from the bathroom's sanitized glass. He sat in the small affordable room, sipping slowly—in no hurry to reach inebriation. Ever since Shelby had left him, he had been drinking more, struggling through painfully lonely nights in endless motels, hoping her infatuation would burn itself out. Even after the final divorce papers had been served, he had fantasized that her film debut would turn out to be such a disaster, she would begin to see the truth behind the tinsel dreams.

But *Fool's Gold* was a gigantic, legitimate hit. In nearly every town in which Erik had stopped to promote his book, the movie was playing. To make matters even worse, every interview he had endured on the recent tour had included questions about the recent divorce and Shelby's subsequent and much publicized live-in relationship with Rau out in Malibu. Despite Erik's adamant refusals to discuss the matter, every article and TV host somehow had slipped in the topic, making him come across as a jilted cuckolded husband. One typical newspaper interview had headlined in Denver: SUNNY'S EX PUSHES BOOK.

But now that he was in New York, Erik regretted coming back. The city reminded him too much of Shelby—everywhere he could think of going only brought back memories of happier times. But he had returned for one vitally important reason—to convince his publisher to pump more money and energy into the promotion of

Hidden Assets, which was dying on the vine faster than strawberries in a snowstorm.

The phone rang across the room, startling him. Reluctantly he answered it. "You ol' reprobate," came the familiar, cheerful voice, "I've tracked you down. It's your buddy, Michael McKitrick."

Surprised, Erik sank to a chair. "Where the hell're you?"

"Montreal. We're partying up here over today's Watergate news. How about you?"

"I've been on a plane all day, what happened?"

"McCord charges Mr. Attorney General, John Mitchell himself, with the responsibility of the break-in." Michael laughed, a short, triumphant burst, on the other end of the line. "Looks like the shit's crept under the door of the Oval Office at last."

"As we long suspected it would," Erik replied, feeling his spirits struggling to revive. "What're you doing up there in Canada?"

"Trying to organize a U.S. amnesty for draft dodgers," Michael said and began waxing ardently about his plans. Erik listened with growing unease. It had been too long since he had shared with his longtime friend and now the telephone line only teased him with still more memories of happier, more fulfilling times.

"I was in New York last month," Michael said. "Hoped you'd be back by then but I couldn't wait around any longer. I took the boys up near Bearsville for a long weekend of camping. I think they dug it. They're good kids. And man, are they growing. Have you seen 'em lately?"

Erik muttered a weak apology about not keeping in touch with anyone.

Michael cut in with a slice of sarcasm, "Lord, Erik, you sound like an old man. I want you to ring Mo when we hang up and go over for dinner. They're moving to California soon."

"They are? Why?"

"I'll let her tell you," Michael said. "Now listen, buddy. Get off the pot and get to work on something new, okay? Your last book was your best by far. Just imagine what the next could be."

"Yeah, another no-seller," Erik groused.

"Man, you're too self-absorbed right now. Bust out, get some new energies coming in. Want to come up here and help me? No bread but some superfine folks committed to things we both believe in."

"Thanks for the thought, but I don't know what the hell I believe in anymore."

"Hell, that sounds like the bottle talking."

They talked for another few minutes, mainly political matters, the Vietnam ceasefire agreement worked out in Paris between Kissinger and Le Doc, the new battle of Wounded Knee being waged out in South Dakota between militant native Americans and overzealous Federal enforcers, Allende's problems in Chile, and whether Brando's *Last Tango in Paris* should be banned for boredom rather than obscenity. Michael did not ask about Shelby and Erik did not offer anything. But just before he signed off, Michael said, "I know it must be a rough time for you, Erik. But I want you to remember what Max kept telling you, 'It's not the destination that brings us joy, it's the journey.' So you've got to find it on the way, buddy. Because it ain't out there, it's right there with you. You'll see it soon. Now I'm going, you call Mo. God bless us all on this fiery planet. Bye."

Erik sat staring at the phone for a long while.

Riding up in the scarred, wood-paneled elevator of Michael's former apartment house on Washington Square, Erik sagged with more memories. Several cups of black coffee, a cold shower and fairly fresh clothes had done little to his state of mind. Nor was his mood enhanced at Mo's door. From inside, a hit song from *Fool's Gold* played loudly.

One of the twins answered his ring. Erik stared back at the maturing, but still freckled, twelve-year-old face. "Hi, Uncle Erik," the kid greeted shyly. "I'm Timmy. In case you're wondering."

"My god, you're taller by a half foot." Erik offered a hand, squelching the impulse to sweep the boy up in the air like old times.

"Mom's in the kitchen," Timmy said, ushering him politely into the cluttered living room. "It's the cook's night off so be prepared."

"Could you do something about that godawful record?"

"Tommy doesn't listen to anybody. Mom says he's entered a rebellious phase. But I'll try." Timmy fled down the hall.

Eyeing the full packing cartons stacked along one wall, Erik wandered into the kitchen. Mo perspired over a large pot on the stove, looking harried and plump in her apron-covered dark dress. She glanced up. "Well, the bushman cometh." She wiped her hands on Michael's old barbecue apron and hugged him briefly.

Then snorted her amusement at his appearance. "How am I going to keep the boys from turning hippie when you show up looking like Wolfman Jack? Added a few pounds too."

"I missed you too."

She chuckled appreciatively, returning to the pot. "I'm not guaranteeing this is spaghetti sauce. But the noodles, I can handle."

He removed a carton of dishes from a chair and sank gratefully beside the breakfast-nook table. "So you guys are moving?"

"Out to L.A.—California dreamin'."

"Thought you were a bonafide New Yorker?"

"Where've you been, Erik? Don't you watch TV?"

"First rule I learned as a writer. Turn off the damned tube."

"I've got the hottest TV star in America," she boasted. "Buster? Robby Rhomann? Those ring any bells in your pickled brain?"

"Yeah, sure," he muttered, wishing she'd offer a drink. The movie album continued from the back bedroom, a version of "Bye-Bye Love."

"My Robby is such a success with the kids, he's been handed his own spin-off series. Starts taping next month out there. So-o-o . . . I decided to make the move with him. Time I got into that Hollywood scene. That's where the real power is. I'm opening a branch of the agency out there. And guess what? I'm a full partner now. Officially it's The Hendricks-Engle Agency. How 'bout them apples?"

"Congratulations. You must be riding high. The twins too."

"Tommy, the noisy one in the backroom, he can't wait to try surfing; Timmy fears the change. But then he fears just about anything. TOMMY!" she shouted shrilly, splitting Erik's eardrums. "Lord, I'm sick of that music. Have you seen the film yet?"

"Tried to. In Boise. Couldn't take more than ten minutes." He avoided her gaze. "Should I've brownbagged this evening?"

"Sorry. A hostess, I'm not. There in the same old cupboard. You look two sheets to the wind already."

He ignored the observation and located the liquor. The stock was sorely depleted—a far cry from the days of Michael. He poured himself a double shot of Scotch.

"Hate to admit it," Mo was saying, "but *Fool's Gold* was really good. And Shelby's performance the biggest surprise of all. Course I realize it was made in the editing room, but even at that it was solid."

He nodded and sank into the chair. It had been such anguish seeing Shelby on the screen, he'd barely been able to judge her acting.

Mo started slapping down dinner plates around the table. "Hate to see that bastard Rau have a hit. After what he did to my client. Scooter Warren? You hear about that?"

"Yeah, I read about it," he said, suddenly remembering Rebecca. "I learned the facts but not the why. Was Scooter always that flaky?"

"Aren't all actors? Like little children. That's where their talent comes from. Along with mammoth insecurities. Scooter was banking on the film to launch his career." She paused, resting a thick hip against the counter. "I'm to blame for most of that. I built up his hopes. Added fuel to his fantasies. You know, all those dreams made in Hollywood." She lowered heavily into a chair.

"It's wanting too much from something, putting all that weight on the end of what we do," Erik said and lit one of Mo's cigarettes. "Like I did with *Rogues and Scoundrels*. I wanted that book to do so much, to win all the praise and glittering prizes, to sell the millions and catapult me back up there. Crashing reality set in. Hard lessons to be learned and relearned, I guess." He coughed a few times on the strength of her Gauloise.

Then asked, "How's Rebecca doing?"

Mo glanced away. "She was in a production here not long ago—some Brecht thing. Stayed in it in spite of Scooter's death. Best thing for her to keep working. She got some pretty good notices too. But it closed before I got my ass down to see her. And to tell the truth, I haven't seen her for a while. I feel so responsible myself about Scooter, and she's been consumed by guilt, feeling somehow she failed him." Mo stood, returning to the oven. "Together, we're not as gruesome as Alice Cooper, but close."

Erik sipped his Scotch thoughtfully. "Why did Rau cut Scooter out of the film?"

"There's the mystery. Plenty of rumors. The strongest being that Scooter was stealing the film away from Shelby." Mo slammed open the oven door. "Whatever the reason. It was Rau's not telling us before the premiere that I find unconscionable." She cursed under her breath and Erik could see why. The French bread was decidedly on the singed side. "Erik, you want to drain the noodles? I'll collar the boys."

Throughout the hastily prepared but substantial meal, Erik tried to maintain an agreeable front, listening to Mo's chatter about the move to L.A. and idly questioning the twins about their lives, hearing differing opinions on the success of the camping trip with their dad. Observing the boys, Erik grew even more depressed. Their gestures, mannerisms, vocal inflections reminded him too much of Michael and he began to respect Mo anew, wondering how she could face a daily double-image of her long-absent husband. Erik was relieved when the twins ran off to watch their new TV hero, the Fonz.

Erik poured another drink and began telling Mo about his conversation with Michael, eventually he asked if she thought there was a chance she and Michael would get back together.

"Who knows?" she said with a dismissing snort. "Michael's an eternal vagabond. Like you."

"I was settled down for a while, wasn't I?"

She tapped her cigarette thoughtfully. "Want to know what I think?"

"I've a feeling you're going to tell me regardless."

"Damn right. I think the only reason you're still hung up on Shelby is because she's the only lady who walked out on you. Not vice versa."

"Mo, you don't know a damn thing about it." He got up and

poured more Scotch into the glass. But he silently stored away that viewpoint, knowing he would now be compelled to bring it up for review and cross examination at a more sober and solitary occasion.

When Mo, with her usual bluntness, told him it was time to leave because she had too much to do in the morning, she handed him a slip of paper. "Our address out in L.A.," she explained. "I've leased a big house with a pool in Westwood. Near UCLA. Come out and visit. Hey, I meant to ask, has there been any movie interest in your new book?"

"Are you kidding? The best reviews of my career and the novel isn't selling worth piss. You know Hollywood only wants bestsellers."

"Your book's a terrific coming-of-age tale," she encouraged. "They always need good stories. Want me to shop it around out there?"

"I'd appreciate that. Could use the bucks."

Mo snorted again, good-naturedly. "When're you going to quit being such a snob and sell out? Write a movie or TV pilot. Have a chance at some real money."

"Hell, I'd love to have some big bucks," he admitted. "But it's those damned compromises to get it that throw me. You end up not writing for yourself, but to please others. I don't know how to do that."

"I'm not talking about art," she said dryly, "I'm talking about commerce, writing for money. Like you did for Cara Noor's beauty pageant introductions. Witty words for hire."

He tugged on his sports jacket. "Sell my novel to the movies and I'll be free to write for myself for a while longer." He started putting her address slip into his wallet.

"I jotted down something else on that," Mo said. "Rebecca's phone number and address here in the city."

He studied her for a moment before asking, "Why?"

Mo smiled toothily. "My dad used to say: When you're feeling down, help someone. You'd be surprised how it lifts your spirits."

At the nearest bar on MacDougal, while Peter, Paul and Mary sang from the jukebox, "Leaving on a Jet Plane," Erik thought about what Mo had said. She was a damned good woman, astute too, but he doubted she really understood his needs. Hell, he didn't even know. He felt spiritless, empty of all creativity. He longed for a sense of direction, a rededication to his writing. But his muse had flown. He honestly believed that.

By the time he staggered out of the bar, it was pouring down rain, making it impossible to find an available taxi. Determinedly he headed for the hotel on foot and soon was drenched to the skin. He stopped by a store window to count his money and caught his reflected image. He was a sorry sight if ever he had seen one: his long hair was as wet and bedraggled as a retriever dog's, dark circles under bloodshot eyes; his face puffy and red; his full beard wild and unkempt. Where the hell am I, he thought and turned away, slogging for the corner, looking for a street sign.

By the next evening, Erik was more sober than he'd been in a month. In the hall of the Upper West Side building, outside a fifth-floor walk-up apartment, he paused to catch his breath, then knocked on the door. It swung open, revealing an odd young woman, her head wrapped in a long colorful scarf and pale blue eyes peering over tinted eyeglasses.

She chuckled throatily. "Well, if you ain' the biggest hunk I seen in months."

"Is this Rebecca Parlato's apartment?"

"'Tis at that," she replied with zest. "Com'on in. Thought maybe that was her that buzzed. But it was you, right?"

"Right," he said and stepped into the room. Promptly the door was closed behind him and the lean-framed young woman stood openly appraising him. "I'm Sara Jane. An' you're Erik Lungren. You look jus' like that photo on the back of tha' last book o' yours." She smiled widely. "Com'on in an' sit a spell. She should be back 'fore you know it. Want some ginseng tea?"

He nodded and she bopped into the kitchen. He had the strange sensation he'd seen her somewhere before. He glanced around the living room—it was decorated in an eclectic style, part-hippie with a giant poster of the Maharishi, part-New York theater with a small stack of *Playbill*s on the apple-box coffee table. The room smelled like strawberry incense.

Sara Jane returned with a chipped Chinese teapot and three

mismatched ceramic cups. "Rebecca's at the laundromat doin' the weekly wash. Thank gawd. Nothin' more borin' than sittin' an' watchin' you rags tumblin' 'round an' 'round." She knelt and poured tea into two of the cups, grinning broadly. "Hot damn, I sure'm glad you came. She needs all the pick-me-ups she can get."

"How is she?"

The thin shoulders under the bright-beaded shawl rose and fell in resignation. "So-so. Some days better than others. I took it you done heard what happened to her ol' man."

He nodded, sipping the strong-tasting, steamy brew. Sara Jane jerked her head toward the bookshelf on the wall. "Recognize anythin'?"

He'd already seen them. Between Castaneda's *A Separate Reality* and *Be Here Now* by Baba Ram Dass, copies of his own three novels were set off by polished wood bookends.

Erik returned his gaze to the lively, unique being before him. "How long have you been living with her?"

"Couple months maybe. In fact, the same day ol' Timothy Leary got himself rearrested. When I heard about Scooter, I knew Rebecca'd need someone. Like when she was right there when I needed her. When no one else came to visit me in the funny farm, she made the trip a whole bunch. Showed me someone cared. That's wha' I love 'bout her. Her pure soul."

He nodded, enjoying Sara Jane's perceptions and energy.

"That's what I dig about life," she went on. "Circles. Some good—some not so good. But the magical, cyclical life force goes on. Took me a long spell to git my shit together, but I did. An' just in time to help Rebecca. I always figure life provides, dig? For the good folk anyway. You know, Rebecca always did think you two was somehow connected."

"She does?"

"You find that strange?"

"It was so long ago..."

"Don't make no difference, no how. Connections is connections. Bonds is bonds. Don't have to be conscious of 'em. They're still there. Now don' you go tellin' her I said any o' this. She'll get mighty flustered."

At that moment, the front door burst open and Rebecca struggled in under a heavy load of white laundry bags. Erik's rising to his feet drew her attention. She blanched under the black bangs, then instantly flushed. But her fragile smile was genuine.

"Hello, Rebecca," he said, realizing that his memory had not done her full justice. She was absolutely lovely—a dark-eyed kind of beauty that went beyond time, like a figure on a Greek vase.

"Surprise!" Sara Jane said, jumping up to retrieve the laundry bags. "Erik an' me is ol' friends now. Ain't that right, Erik?"

He nodded, still watching the shy young woman by the door. Not looking at him, Rebecca half-followed Sara Jane into the adjoining bedroom and backed out as her roommate hustled past. "Time for me to split," Sara Jane announced pointedly and yanked on a faded blue peacoat.

"You don't have to leave," Rebecca said, her voice barely a whisper. "Please . . ."

"Don't have to," Sara Jane replied at the hall door. "Want to. Goin' jammin' with some friends. Grand meetin' you, Erik. Have fun, hear? An' Erik, she's a helluva lot stronger than she looks." She picked up her guitar case, threw him a lewd wink over her glasses and bounced out.

"Bye, Sara Jane," he called as the door closed and then said to Rebecca, in the sudden quietness, "Very special, isn't she?"

"The best," Rebecca said, watching him through her long black bangs. "Did you recognize her? She used to be famous. A rock group called White Meat? Their lead singer, Silver?"

"I'll be damned. I did see them once. On TV . . . in a bar somewhere."

" 'The Smothers Brothers' Show,' " she said. "It was their only national TV appearance."

"Aren't you going to sit down?" he asked.

At once, she sank to her knees at the coffee table and busily poured herself a cup of tea and more for him. She was wearing a dark green turtleneck and tan corduroy jeans which emphasized her petite body. Her hair, clipped short, was as black as a raven's wing and set off her delicate profile.

He sank back onto the couch with growing concern. She had

barely spoken but he felt viscerally her great need. He did not know if he were capable of offering her anything but more pain. He considered whether he should cut short his visit.

"I'm sorry I'm so rude," she began breathlessly. "I have to admit I'm flabbergasted. You're the last person I figured on seeing again. So what've you been up to, Mister Lungren? Other than growing a beard. I think though, now seeing it in person, I liked your face better without all that hair. But it must be easier not having to shave, I bet."

She hesitated and slid down to sit on one hip, her feet tucked to one side. He couldn't think of anything to say and found himself longing for a drink.

"Congratulations for *Hidden Assets*," she began again spiritedly. "It still makes me cry when I read portions about that kid's sweet family, their close ties, their whole simple fisherman lifestyle. I think it's your best by far. I could almost smell the sea air and the fish being unloaded on the docks—that was your hometown? Sounds beautiful out there, Mister Lungren."

"Erik . . . please, call me Erik. After all, we did spend the night together once."

Her head rose. "You remember?"

"Yes. Always have. But I can't recall when it was."

"First week of July. Nineteen sixty-six. July fifth. That makes it —what? Going on seven years. Wow! Can you believe that?"

"My god, how old were you then?"

She blushed even more. "Seventeen. You're right, I lied. I told you I was nineteen. I didn't want to freak you out."

He shook his head. "I was pretty drunk, wasn't I?"

"No more so than I was terrified. Do you remember standing me up the next night?"

"Damn, did I really? Must've had a good reason."

Her face broke into an enchantingly innocent smile. "Hey! You owe me five bucks."

"I do? Here, let me pay you." He reached for his wallet.

"Oh no! I was just . . . I didn't mean to—No, really, I couldn't."

He pushed a ten at her. "I insist. With interest, okay? Please.

Seems only fair.'' She refused to even look at the bill so he put in next to the teapot.

She bit her lower lip. ''I . . . I don't know why I even mentioned that . . .''

''Please. Let me be the one to feel bummed out. I mean, hell, standing you up, forgetting I even borrowed bread. I was pretty full of hot air, wasn't I?''

She seemed to have sunk into herself, withdrawing, staring into her teacup as if all the answers of the world lay within. He felt disconcerted. He reached across and laid a hand on her arm. The contact caused her to jump slightly and her eyes flew to his. For a long moment, he gazed into them and felt a strange stirring in his chest, as though something were alive in there after all.

He asked quietly, ''How are you managing, Rebecca?''

''I'm in this therapy group. A lot of encounter work. It's been a big help . . . getting over . . . this pain. Scooter left me three times, the last was permanent. I'm learning to accept that.'' She reflected for a long moment, then raised her dark eyes. ''How about you? How're you holding up since . . . the divorce?''

''I don't know,'' he said. ''I haven't even tried to write anything.''

She nodded seriously. ''I understand . . . totally. After Scooter's death, I didn't think I could ever find strength again to act. When you lose someone as close as that, you feel incomplete. Like a big, major chunk of you is missing. There was no way I could go on living—let alone to get on a stage in front of strangers. It all seemed so frivolous . . .''

''But I understand you did. And very successfully too.''

''I was fortunate. Had the support of people that cared. You have to keep going. That's all. It's as simple as that. 'Life goes on, ob-lah-dee, ob-lah-dah.' ''

He sank back on the couch and stared at her.

''What're your plans now, Erik?'' she asked softly.

''Don't really know. Been thinking of home again. The Oregon coast. I haven't been back since my folks passed on. What about you?''

She shrugged. ''I'm just trying to get through each day. I did get an invitation to go out to Los Angeles . . . from Robby, you know,

Buster? He called last week. Blew my mind—hadn't talked to him in ages. He insisted I needed the change. Said I could live with him and his mom while I try to get some acting work.''

"Going to do it?''

"Maybe . . . I don't know. Don't think I'm ready yet.''

"The joy is in the doing, Rebecca . . . a very wise man told that to me once. I think it rings true.''

"Could be. But the idea of going out there . . . to lotus land. Starting in all over again, same old treadmill . . .''

He dug into his memory for something. "I remember reading once, somewhere . . . about a British explorer back in the mideighteen-hundreds. Went out to live with the Indians in the American Southwest. He was interested in their rituals, especially their raindance. After observing it for months, he wrote in his journal, 'The damn thing works, because the Indians keep dancing till it rains.' ''

He watched her face change ever so subtly. She was a marvelous listener—alive, responsive, expressive. A spirit that communicated warmth and understanding. He wanted to reach out and touch her but she spoke before he could.

"The raindance . . . I like that," she said, smiling. "A lot. I'll have to remember that.'' She brushed back her bangs. "Oh, damn, look at the time. I've my group at eight. I'd skip it, but . . .''

"Want some company on the way?''

She shook her head. "No thank you. I always need time by myself before I go. It can get pretty intense.''

"I understand,'' he said.

"Why are you smiling like that?''

"Because I think you're a rare treasure.''

The blush invaded her cheeks again, but this time she did not duck her head. "Well, I think you're kind of sharp yourself.'' She started to laugh. The outburst was so spontaneous, so unaffected, he began laughing with her.

Their laughter infused him with a sudden burst of energy, he stood and reached down, pulling her up—she seemed weightless in his arms. He held her close until their laughter faded. For a long moment, they clung to each other and when he leaned down to kiss her, he heard a sharp intake of breath. Her small, compact body melted into his. Before he wanted to end it, she rolled her head back, muttering, "Damn you . . ."

"Me? Why?"

"Because you kissed me once like that over six years ago and I never forgot it. Is it going to be another six before I can hope it'll happen again?"

He stared down at her surprisingly serious face and stammered, "I . . . I don't know."

She was all smiles again, her eyes flooding with amusement. She gave him a big squeeze around the middle before stepping back. "Hey, I was only kidding."

"I wasn't," he admitted. "In fact, I'd like to do it again." He pulled her back into his arms, kissing her again firmly. This time she let it ride the full course.

"That was nice," she murmured with another of those enchanting smiles. "And I promise . . . if that's all there is, I'm satisfied . . . sort of."

He couldn't help but laugh. It bubbled out of him with such an urgency, such a feeling of release, he felt light-headed. He gathered her to him and held her close. She fingered the buttons of his sports coat. "So this is it again? Another good-bye?"

"For now, yes." He hesitated, wanting to get the words right, "But I promise . . . after each of us gets rid of some of this excess baggage we're carrying around . . . our paths will cross again."

She took another quick, deep breath. "Look. Don't say that if you don't mean it. I'm tired of living in the past and waiting around for the future. Sara Jane keeps telling me—all we have is the now. Right now. This is it. So no false promises made with good intentions, okay? I'd just as soon leave it like this."

"But I do mean it," he said. "We'll see each other again. Maybe out in L.A. or wherever. But we will. Let Mo know if you move, okay?"

"Okay," she said and began walking him to the door. He had the odd feeling she didn't believe him. He kissed her again.

"I got the message," she said after they'd broken apart. "I'll remember it all . . . especially the raindance."

"Bye, Rebecca. Keep on dancing." With one last look, he

slipped out the open door and down the stairs, the vision of her shining gaze carried with him.

On the sidewalk, he put his hands in his coat pockets to find a cigarette. With surprise, he pulled out the loose ten-dollar bill he'd left for her by the teapot. He stared at it a long while.

Mystified, intrigued, exhilarated, he broke into a trot, heading for the lights of the intersection.

Book Four

1974-1976

DAVID
June 1974
Malibu

On toes and fingertips, he crabbed up the steep hill of mud, the rain slicing like sharp knives. He lost his balance and sprawled into the runny muck, sliding downward on the belly of his plastic rain poncho. Grunting with disgust, he hauled himself up and clambered back uphill with a gritty determination. Reaching the top, panting for breath, he bent into the rain, squinting to survey the chaos.

A mountain of wet earth had broken off the cliff, spilling onto the Pacific Coast Highway, blocking all four lanes. An angry river of muddy water disgorged from the collapsed face of the cliff, racing down the new mountain and raging out onto the beach. To the south of the slide, giant yellow earth-movers rumbled in the early morning light, scooping, scraping at the mud.

David headed down the hill for a car with an L.A. county engineer insignia on its door, the gooey mud burying his shoes to the ankles. He banged on the driver's window. The man rolled it down and David shouted, "How long is this goddamned mess going to take?"

"Can't say. Day or two."

David hollered, "I've got *People* Magazine coming out. How the hell're they going to get through?"

"Like everyone else. Park on the south side of this mess and walk around. Or drive out via Malibu Canyon."

"Damn shit," David hollered and attacked the mud again, crawling back up and sliding down the north side. At the bottom, on the windshield of his forest green Rolls Royce Corniche there was a parking ticket. He tore it from the wiper blade, throwing the pieces into the mud. Goddamned rain—fouling up his whole schedule.

He returned to his Malibu Colony home, parked in the drive behind the other cars and stalked into the house, tearing off his rain gear and shouting for his secretary, "Marge, Marge!"

On the living room tiles, he paused to step out of his muddy shoes. A phone was ringing somewhere. "Answer that, goddammit!"

In the dining room the stout Danish housekeeper was replenishing the coffee urn while Willie Radner—one of his screen writers who'd been forced to spend the night—looked up from the newspaper. "Morning. How's it look?"

"We're trapped. Like on a goddamned desert island." David poured coffee into his large china mug. "Harley up yet?"

"A late riser."

"Well, get him up," David urged. "As long as you're both stuck out here, you might as well be working. You're getting paid enough to." He started out.

"David," Willie said quickly, stopping him. "Got a great idea for a movie. Perfect for Shelby. Right out of the headlines. Heiress captured by radicals."

David stared at the pasty-faced, elderly writer. "Every schlock producer in town hustled that the day Patty Hearst was snatched. Stick with what I hired you for. You've got enough problems with that."

In his beachside den, David tugged off his soggy clothes, showered in the adjacent bath, and changing into a long brown robe, perused the morning trades which miraculously had been delivered. Almost at once, the three phones on his desk began ringing. "Marge," he screamed and punched the first button. "Rau, here."

"London calling," came the operator's reply. The day had begun and it was not yet seven A.M.

Around nine an already frazzled Marge slipped in from her apartment/office above the garage, handing him a stack of message slips announcing, "Can't get anyone at *People*." He covered one mouthpiece, burying the second receiver into his shoulder. "Keep on it. And put a call in to Misho in Tokyo. Also Angler in New York. I'm here, I'm here," he shouted into the third receiver. "Wilhelm, I don't know what the hell's the hold-up at Pacific. We had a firm go on Thursday. I'm just waiting for a confirmation." He paused, handing one receiver to Marge, whispering hoarsely, "Stall this one."

By ten, the *People* reporter had not called to confirm the interview and Shelby was still not up. During a lull, David bounded up the stairs and into the master bedroom, throwing open the drapes to the dripping eaves and the drizzling, gray beach. "Up, up," he said loudly. Curled on the king-sized bed, Shelby did not stir. He crawled onto the bed. "Up! You've only got an hour to get ready."

She groaned and flopped over on her back, one fleshy arm covering her eyes. He tore the covers from her and with one quick movement, hiked up her nightgown, spread her legs and burrowed his head into her crotch. She squealed with irritation and tried to roll away. Grabbing her arms, pinning her down, he continued mechanically tonguing. She began to moan, undulating her hips. Soon she was panting, squirming. He scooted up, unzipped his slacks and shoved into her, watching her face as he pumped.

A short time later, not bothering to come himself, he rolled off her and, in the bathroom, washed his cock. She was smiling cautiously when he walked back into the bedroom. He pulled on a fresh shirt and said, "I want you dressed and made up in exactly one hour. Wear what's on the hanger there. Helene is waiting to do your hair. And for godsakes do something about your chin line, shadow it or something, okay?"

Squealing in anger, she threw a pillow. He headed downstairs.

Around eleven, Marge poked her curly head in through his office doorway, interrupting his story meeting with Harley and Willie. "*People's* here," she said with a quiet urgency.

David bounded for her, throwing over his shoulder to his screenwriters, "That scene sucks. Think Hitchcock." In the hall, he pushed Marge toward the stairs. "I want Shelby down here in five flat."

Entering the living room, David pulled up short. "Where's Geduld?"

The damp stranger, with tie askew and wet, horned-rimmed glasses, smiled apologetically. "Last-minute assignment. Cover article on Nicholson and *Chinatown*. I'm Marty Lewskon—and this is our photographer, Jane Arpy." A rain disheveled young woman dripped by the window.

"I was promised Geduld," David said. "Not second-stringers."

The young reporter bristled. "Want to cancel?"

David considered his alternate game plans. For Shelby's first interview he had allowed in over a year, he wanted a *Time* cover but there were no guarantees, especially without a film to promote. His second choice, *Newsweek*, refused to deal with him after he had kicked their stringer off the set of *A Woman Alone*. That left *People* Magazine. Only a few months old, it was proving itself to be a popular choice. And that's what David needed, some mass publicity to launch his and Shelby's next film. But he needed it now, if it were to be effective in adding to the pressure on Pacific to schedule the production.

Displaying as much amiability as he could dredge up, David finally said, "Okay, it's a go. Did your editor give you the parameters?"

"Better run over them again," Marty replied, pulling out a small tape recorder.

David sank into an easy chair. "Miss Cale and I will only answer questions relating to our two films together and our impending project. Nothing about my relationship with Irving R. Dyer or hers to her former husband. Clear?"

"As mud," Marty replied with a side glance to his photographer. By the beach windows, the young woman smiled shyly and asked, "Do you mind if we open these drapes? It's sort of gloomy in here."

David nodded his approval and folded his arms across his chest. "Let's begin. Shelby'll be down soon."

Marty hit the record button and referred to a notepad. "Why do you feel *A Woman Alone* was such a flop?"

David masked his annoyance, having prepared himself for this kind of slant. "As far as the American audience—on a mass scale—they never got a chance to see it. Pacific yanked it out of distribution before it had a chance of finding its audience. Overseas, where they appreciate quality costume drama, it will do great."

"Will it make back its costs?"

"If they release it as I wanted."

"How much did it go overbudget?"

"Depends on who's doing the bookkeeping—me or Pacific," David replied with a boyish smile aimed at the snapping camera. "What counts for me is whether you see the money up on the screen—the size, the sweep, the grandeur . . ."

Marty was not listening—he was looking toward the stairs. David turned and swore silently. Shelby was descending, dressed as if for a funeral, all in black. Her cheekbones—no longer sharply defined—appeared artificially painted, her posture stiff, displaying none of her natural grace. He'd wanted her buoyant and bubbly, showing the world she was unaffected by the quick demise of their last film. And why the hell hadn't she worn the yellow dress he'd picked out?

The photographer moved forward to capture the entrance, but Shelby waved her away with a pained expression—promptly recorded on film. David stood and made a great show of embracing her. turning her toward the camera, whispering in one ear, "For chrissake, lighten up."

After the cursory introductions, David sat Shelby beside him on the beige couch, throwing a protective arm around her shoulders, crossing his legs and leaning into her. She clutched his hand.

The reporter began again. "Miss Cale, do you feel that the role of Hester Prynne was over your head?"

"No," she breathed and fell silent.

David rushed to expand her answer, explaining the difficulties of doing a historical drama for today's television-oriented movie goer. A *Woman Alone* had been a reworking of Hawthorne's *The Scarlet Letter* and as far as David was concerned, Shelby had pulled off the difficult role with flying colors. The critics, however, had focused on her lack of talent as being the major cause for the film's failure. Their criticism had ranged from condescending to vicious.

The bespectacled reporter asked her, "What was your reaction to the reviews?"

David leaped in. "Critics love your first time at bat, but as soon as you hit it big, they like to show they've got the power to unmake you. We hit a home run the first time at bat. They feel they've struck us out second time up. Well, here comes number three and we'll start even. I'm hoping some of their venom will have been spent and we can be judged fairly."

Shelby took a breath, beginning shakily, "I...I also feel there might be some sort of moral backlash from the silent majority. Because of our openly living together. Refusing to follow convention..."

David silently congratulated her on a point well-made. He was about to announce their new film project when Marty, the reporter, asked Shelby, "You and David have been together now for going on two years, any plans of marriage?"

Shelby turned to David and smiled, slyly. "He doesn't want kids so I don't know why we should. Times have changed since my grandmothers' day."

Marty glanced at his notes, then to Shelby. "How does it feel to be the heroine in your ex-husband's new novel?"

"What the——?" David was on his feet. "Where the hell did that come from? Turn off that damn recorder."

Marty complied with an apologetic shrug. "That's fair, isn't it?"

"This interview is over."

"David..." It was Shelby's voice, pleading. He ignored her and turned for the main entrance to show the amateurs out.

Shelby was on her feet. "I...I didn't know Erik had written a new one."

Marty was gathering his things. "Our book reviewer showed me a galley copy. Called *The Rainbow Shuttle* and it's a thinly disguised——"

"*Goddammit!*"

Shelby looked aghast at David for his explosion and fled for the stairs. David threw open the front door. "I'll be speaking to your editor. Consider yourselves off this assignment." He waited stonily for them to move past him and then slammed the door.

He found her in the master bedroom, facedown on the bed weeping. "How could you?" she sobbed into the pillow. "Throwing them out because of a stupid little question?"

"Just looking out for your interests."

"Ye gods, David, I'm twenty-six."

"Then for Chrissakes, act your age. I've got enough to worry about.'' She rolled over on her back, her jaw squared, her hands bunched into tight balls.

He sat on the edge of the bed, speaking quietly. ''Have you heard anything about this new book?''

''How could I?'' she muttered tearfully. ''You've canceled every subscription for fear I might read something bad about us. And you won't let me go out of the house alone. You follow me around like a goddamned prison warden.''

''Don't swear. It doesn't become you.''

''I'll swear if I goddamned please,'' she shouted. ''Fuck! Piss! Shit! Cock——''

''Stop it!'' he barked. ''You sound like a spoiled kid.''

''I'm not the child. *You* are.'' Her caterwauling resumed.

Impassively he watched her. He was certain that once into production and before the cameras again where she belonged, all this would change. It would have to. He didn't know if he could put up with much more. He left her hoping she would cry herself to sleep.

Minutes later, in his study, David was on the phone to Ian, his lawyer, trying to find out what the delay was at Pacific. ''They've been stalling since Thursday. My cofinancing in Germany is ready to yank. Italia is talking tough. I can't keep these balls up in the air much longer. We have to have an answer. Today. Understand?''

Unexpectedly Shelby appeared in the doorway, clutching her copy of their new script. David rang off from Ian and eyed her.

She had changed into a flowing caftan of deep violet that made her look even bigger—her hair was unbrushed, her face strangely tense, defiant. She tossed the script onto his desk. ''I loathe this script,'' she said sullenly. ''It's totally wrong for me.''

''I know better what you're capable of.''

''Like the last one? That was to be perfect for me too.''

Her tone was snide, cutting. He swallowed the urge to lash out and asked in his quietest manner, ''Why didn't you speak up earlier?''

''Because you never once solicited my opinion. Well, I'm giving it to you now. It's too heavy. I don't have the talent.''

He shook his head sadly. ''Shelby, it's tailor-made for you.'' He stood, going around the desk and knelt in front of her. ''I'm waiting to hear from Pacific any moment. Now is not the time for us to be divided. To win this one, we have to be united.''

"Why must everything always be a knockdown drag-out fight?"

"Because that's the only way I know to get what I want. You think it's easy getting Pacific to schedule this production? Face it. It's always been this way: You're only hot as your last film. Well, I groove on those odds, I dig that challenge. I know we can do it. Together, we can win.''

She sighed at length, closing her eyes. "I've the strongest feeling of *déjà vu* . . .''

"And you'll hear it until you get your head screwed on straight.''

"Why is it always my head—never yours?''

"Because your damned attitude stinks. You're letting them defeat you.''

"Them?" she asked caustically. "Who the hell's them?''

"Anyone outside of you and me.''

"I'm tired of fighting . . . I just want to go somewhere and lie in the sun and forget acting and interviews and . . . please, David. Can't we?" She read his expression and moaned, "Why not?''

"Because I don't quit until I win.''

She raised her head. "You'll never quit, David. There's always something more to win.''

"What else is there?''

"I wish I knew," she cried, her eyes tearing again. "I wish to God I did . . .'' She pushed herself upright and left the room.

He considered whether to follow. One of his lines rang. He reached for it. The call was from Ed Hume, Pacific's vice president of Production, second-in-command to Irving. David listened to the unexpected message, then rasped, "What do you mean?''

"It's off," came Hume's voice. "What more's there to say?''

"You could start telling me what the fuck?''

"Too iffy.''

David sank into his chair, pinching the bridge of his nose. "Hume, you sonofabitch, just last week you said—''

"The film's dead, David. Let it lie.''

"Goddamned Irving . . .''

"The entire board voted on this.''

"Then goddamn all of you," David railed and let the receiver fall back into place. For a long moment, all he could do was stare out the window at the falling rain. The ocean had turned a muddy gray brown, the sky a dirty gray. He hit Marge's button and lifted the receiver. "Track down Dixon Shaw."

On the Rolls's stereo, Elton John was singing "The Bitch is Back" and the irony did not escape David. He pulled the Rolls under the Grecian-styled portico of Shaw's Bel Air mansion. Night had fallen, the rain continued in sheets and his cluster migraine intensified. The aging butler, Holmes, answered his ring and ushered him, with dignified stoop, into a far backroom where David had never been.

The fumes of paint thinner hit him, increasing the pounding in his head. Off the unlit swimming pool, the large, nearly empty room was set up as a studio. Unfinished canvases, paintings in a very primitive style adorned the two walls that were not glass—a variety of Western scenes, landscapes, still lifes.

At a far casel, Dixon Shaw, wearing paint-smeared white coveralls and a Yankees' baseball cap, sat on a high stool before a large unfinished canvas. Concentrating on a single brushstroke, the chairman did not turn to greet him but said easily, "I was expecting to hear from you."

David hesitated, staring at Shaw's canvas—it looked like a kid's cowboy scene, a campfire, some misproportioned horses sketched in.

"Have you been following this Watergate affair?" Shaw asked.

"A bit."

"All politics, you know," Shaw continued, bending to his work. "Damned Democrats—trying to force out our great president. That goddamned weasel, Dean . . . treason, that's what it is. A mighty sad time for our country." He stabbed the brush at the canvas.

"Why, Dixon? That's all I want to know. Why was my new film dropped?"

Dixon swiveled to stare. "You're taking this much too personally. Care for a drink?"

"No."

The chairman gazed critically at him for a moment, then laid the color-dabbed palette on the pine table. "Pacific cannot afford another costly chancy production."

"Chancy?" David's voice rose with vexation. "Nothing chancy about it, compared to some of the drek Irving's produced."

"You're entitled to your opinion, of course; but hardly in the position to judge. *A Woman Alone* was seventeen million overbudget and four months late in delivery. Pacific and therefore AII had to eat close to thirty-five million because of your unbridled ego." Shaw waved his paintbrush, cutting off David's attempt to speak and continued with a clipped precision. "I do not want to go into your extensive defense again. I merely want to point out that there are several factors which make this last project of yours an extremely invalid proposition."

"If it's the budget, I can shave that."

"It's not just the proposed cost. There's something more." Shaw stuck his paintbrush carefully into the jar. "Your insistence on casting Miss Cale again."

Words fled and David felt only the throb in his temples.

The chairman's voice continued in a dry monotone. "I will be candid, David. You are making a complete ass of yourself over this girl. Your last homage to her cost us all far too much. I can no longer back you in board discussions. Now, in addition to being candid, I will be blunt and coarse. Take my advice. Fuck her but don't film her."

It took a while before David could find his voice but when he did it cracked with fire, "Irving put you up to this."

The chairman eased his girth off the stool and stood, his expression one of stern paternalism. "These are my decisions and mine alone. Hear them well before I lose patience with you completely. I *personally* will oversee your next film. You must receive my approval on any new script as well as budget and all of the above-the-line personnel. And if you insist on using Miss Cale, against my strong recommendation, then you better make damned certain it is a property she can handle. This is your last chance as far as AII is concerned."

"After . . . all the mega-millions . . . I brought into your coffers, I'm reduced to this? Kissing ass and waiting tables?"

Shaw carefully selected another brush from his jar. "Please send all proposed film properties to my assistant in New York," He concluded, again not looking at him, then glanced up with a smile. "My grandson had a terrific idea for a movie. Why don't you secure the rights to Evel Knievel's story? He's quite the rage with the young people now. Could be a giant hit with this Grand Canyon jump and all. Think about it. Let me know."

Quietly, with a minimum of movement, David disrobed in the darkness and slipped into bed. The Demerol had not kicked in yet. He laid his head on the pillow gingerly.

Shelby stirred and rolled into him. "Where'd you run off to?"

He could not respond.

She reached out and switched on her bed light. His eyes clamped shut. She turned the lamp off, murmuring, "Oh, poor baby." She brushed his forehead with a cool hand. "You take your pills?"

He managed a small nod. She snaked an arm under his neck and moved closer. "You've been pushing too hard. You must learn to ease up."

He sank into her arm and did not attempt to think or speak for a long, long while. Gradually he could feel the narcotic taking hold, layering the pain with a blessed thickness. "I've decided you're right," he whispered eventually. "The script. I'm junking it."

"You really mean that?"

"Tomorrow we'll start the search for something new—lighter."

"Oh, thank you, David, thank you, thank you." She smothered his face with kisses, her breasts pushing heavily into him.

"On one condition. I want you back in shape."

"It's a deal, darling." She slipped exploring fingers under the waistband of his jockey shorts.

"It's going to be a very tough climb," he said slowly. "But we're going to make it, Shelby . . . you and I . . . together."

He was conscious of the silence outside the deck windows.

The rain had stopped.

REBECCA
August 1974
Los Angeles

The audition had gone well. The casting director for "The ABC Movie-of-the-Week" said he had liked her reading. That raised her hopes until he added, "I'll keep you in mind for something else. You have a very special quality."

Covering her disappointment with a game smile, Rebecca stood. "Thanks but I'd rather have this role."

"Maybe next time," he said and bent over another girl's photo.

In the parking lot, Rebecca's bashed-in sixty-one VW bug would not start. Inside the broiling interior, she slapped the wheel, "Com'on, baby. If I can put up with this, you can." She tried the ignition again. Nothing. For a moment, she sat, staring at the tiny fur monkey taped to her dash. So far, after over a year on the Hollywood treadmill, Scooter's talisman had brought little success. Other than a small part Robby had gotten her on his hit TV-series, she had not been cast. But that one small break had provided two basic necessities in L.A.—a screen actors' union card plus enough bucks to buy a car. The union card hadn't gotten her a job yet and now the damned bug wouldn't start again. And yet another audition to add to her list of hits.

Rebecca clambered out and opened the rear-engine hood. Holding back her long hair, she stooped over the small motor, checking the parts which usually gave her trouble. The distributor cap was loose. She searched the pockets of her bushjacket and found one of the long bobby pins used to pile her hair up for dance-exercise class. Bending it, she slipped it over the cap, latching the free side tightly, then dropped the engine cover. Behind the wheel, she tried the motor. It choked to life. She kissed the end of a finger and planted it on the nose of the tiny monkey.

Sunset Boulevard was bumper-to-bumper, heavier than expected and she knew she'd be late. Robby had insisted she be back by three and she still had to drop by her agent's. The red light stopped her at the entrance to Laurel Canyon and she gazed down the strip at all the elaborate billboards for the summer's hit films, the biggest for *The Exorcist*. With a jolt of surprise, she discovered a brand-new huge billboard, for Erik's new novel, *The Rainbow Shuttle*. His name was prominent under the portrait of a blond that looked more than coincidentally like Shelby. Rebecca eased the car forward, wondering if Erik were even aware of such a rip-off advertising campaign.

Her stop at her agent's was just to drop off copies of her new photos and résumés. Rebecca couldn't get in to see Arnie Stuart, the man who handled her, but then she rarely could. She'd known when signing with Arnie that he was taking her only to get to Robby. But she knew the game well enough that, as little as Arnie did for her, he was better than no agent at all. At least, out there hustling auditions on her own, she could say she was represented by his agency. But someday, she kept telling herself, they're all going to see me as something other than Robby's little friend.

Ten minutes later, Rebecca turned her bug up Lexington, above the Beverly Hills Hotel, and once on the side street immediately caught sight of the fans cavorting and milling around outside Robby's main gate. "Busterites" the press called them—mainly preteen boys and young teen girls who were rabid and tenacious devotees to Robby's weekly character. Within days of his move to the huge mansion, word had leaked out and the vigil had begun. Day and night they were there, a constant source of irritation to Robby. And a continual obstacle course to get through.

Rebecca eased her car into the mob and pulled up to the massive iron gates equipped with the latest in electronic TV surveillance. One of the full-time guards unlocked the gate and opened it only wide enough for her car to squeeze through.

"Who's she?" a chubby girl screamed as if personally attacked.

"Ah, she's nobody," a young boy yelled back, dressed in Buster garb of yellow sweatshirt and red golf cap. "She's always going in and out. Just some maid or something."

Bitterly amused by the accuracy of the comment, Rebecca drove up the long drive and parked before the mammoth brick-and-wood Tudor-styled house, which once had been Charles Laughton's. Close to a dozen vehicles were in the visitors' lot. Inside chaos reigned: several phones were ringing at once; someone pounded the grand piano—a spirited version of "Angie Baby"; the carpenters hammering and sawing noisily. The interior decorator—a well-preserved, Beverly Hills matron with an air of bewildered detachment—wandered in from the dining room with several swatches of fabric. "I've been waiting since noon. Where is he?"

"No idea. Did you try the poolhouse?" Rebecca hurried into the office off the kitchen. Bulging mailbags full of fan letters were piled three-high along one wall, the four young women hired to sort and answer them were busy over their individual desks. Stacks of glossy photos of Robby as Buster covered one entire counter. She greeted the workers, dropped her things onto her desk and surveyed the disarray. Pink phone messages were scattered among the bills, personal mail and ritzy catalogs with items circled by Robby for purchase. Sorting with one hand, she answered a ringing phone.

For the next hour, Rebecca tried bringing some semblance of order to the confusion. Eventually she pulled over one of the fan-letter girls to answer the phone and hurried out to track down Robby. Rumors were that he was in the house. Everywhere she looked she found herself dealing with another urgent problem: in the kitchen, the cook and her helper huffily complained of being unprepared to cook dinner for twenty or more on such short notice—she told them to call Jurgenson's and have more food delivered; in the game room, several of Robby's hangers-on wanted the jukebox fixed—she told them to use the stereo instead; out by the pool, where several enviably attractive young ladies were sunning *sans* tops, the head groundskeeper harped to her about the side lawn which had been dug up by someone driving a car over it—Rebecca soothed, cajoled and promised to try to find the culprit, knowing full well it was Robby. In the TV room, the interior decorator cornered her again and Rebecca placated her again before slipping away upstairs, off-limits to everyone but the invited.

The exercise room, complete with Universal gym equipment, saunas and steam rooms, plus a large whirlpool tub, all were empty.

His door to the master bedroom suite was closed. She knocked loudly. "Robby? You in there?" She heard voices laughing. "Your highness," she called out in her loudest, toughest street-voice. "Get your ass out here."

"Go away," came his muffled reply.

"Now, Robby."

"Oh, for cripesakes!" Shortly the door flew open and he stuck out his tightly curled head. "Can't I get *any* privacy?"

"If you want privacy, how 'bout kicking out the freeloaders. *And* renting a separate office to handle your precious fan mail. *And* stopping all this damned remodeling and redecorating. *And*—"

He smiled his Buster-cute best and interrupted, "What's up?"

She was impervious, long aware that his charm was automatic, called up at will. She handed him the phone messages. "The decorator has been—"

Rifling through the stack of messages, he cut her off, "You make the decisions. I trust your taste."

"Until you see it—then you scream it's all in my mouth."

"Be a pal. It's my only day off in two weeks." His face folded into a perfect little pout. "Call Mo. I want her here by five."

"Give her a break, Robby. She's jammed, what with tonight's party and—"

"Call her," he insisted. "For what she makes off me, she can damn well come when I want. Five, got it?" He handed back the messages. "What happened to that White House confirmation? I thought they wanted Buster for next Sunday?"

"I tried again to reach that lady who wrote but she hasn't returned my call three times now."

"We'll keep trying. It may be my only chance to see the Oval Office. And here, you take care of these. And call the cops again. Get rid of those hordes at the gate. And everybody in the house. I can't even split for a Big Mac without being mobbed."

"Another reminder, Robby. As of Monday, my two weeks' notice is up and you're on your own." She turned away but his voice stopped her.

His tone was the old Robby. "Becks, you can't leave me. I'd never survive without you."

She felt a tug of sympathy for her friend, who was beleaguered and overworked. "Get your mom back here," she suggested. "Or let me help you find a replacement. But I have to leave. After six months with you, I'm verging on a Watts burnout."

"We'll talk," he said emotionlessly and stepped back into his room, guarding carefully how much she could see of his room.

She whispered playfully, "Who you hiding in there anyway?"

"None of your damned business," he snipped and started to close the door in her face.

Abruptly, she threw out a hand, blocking the door open. "Don't talk to me like that," she said in a sudden fury. "I'm not a servant and I sure as hell am not your mother."

She stopped in surprise, noting in the mirror behind Robby—a handsome young man, blushing nude, dashing into the bathroom. Robby sighed grandly, "So now you know."

"What? That you're gay? Or a swollen-headed, puny-hearted asshole? No surprise on either count." She flew away, fed up to her eyebrows again. The shit bag was more than full. And damned if she were going to get a bigger one.

Later, after kicking out everyone in the house, Rebecca wandered to the pool area. Relishing the sudden quiet and the rare privacy, she lay on a cushioned lounge chair and stared at the dazzling sunlight reflected off the blue water of the Olympic-sized pool. Her surroundings only underscored her feelings. Nothing seemed real in southern California, everything looked like a set for a movie. Too clean, too brightly colored, too perfectly beautiful—like the brilliant red poinsettia bushes hiding the tennis court's fence. The large-leafed, red-blossomed bushes stood motionless, unruffled by a breeze, like a painted backdrop. Or a Hockney painting, she thought. And again, her mind wandered to Scooter. And her heart ached anew.

Hearing the main doorbell, Rebecca pulled herself together and made her way to the front of the house. Mo Engle barged in wearing tight white slacks, platform cork heels and a plunging neckline that exposed a great deal of tanned bosom. "Where's the little putz?" Mo asked, good-humored in spite of her obvious haste.

"Upstairs. I'll get him."

"Hold on. You feeling okay?"

"Sure . . . sort of," Rebecca began, then let off a little steam. "No, I'm teed off. He's impossible. Expects everyone to say yes to his merest whim. He's surrounding himself with an entourage of sycophants who stroke and feed his ego until he thinks he's the second coming Himself."

Mo snorted sympathetically and plopped into a high-backed chair with ornately carved arms. "Sometimes I feel like Frankenstein. Such a monster I've created."

"Oh no, Robby's persona is all self-made," Rebecca commented and sat in a matching chair. "Even as a kid, he demanded and ordered his mother about, expecting her to wait on him like a servant. That's how he wants me to behave. Devoted and uncomplaining. Well, I love him but I mean it, Mo. Come Monday, I'm out the door and so long, Buster."

Rebecca began to feel uncomfortable with Mo's lack of response. Mo was rummaging through her large shoulder-strap handbag. And again Rebecca marveled at the astounding physical change. Deeply tanned, Mo had lost considerable weight and her short, swept-back auburn hair was highlighted with streaks of near blond. What was more noticeable, however, was Mo's entire manner of carrying herself. Here was a buxom, earthy, even flashy woman over forty with a distinct flair for the outlandish and hip. Her aura sparked with youth and vitality. Rebecca wondered if Robby's tidbit of gossip was the real reason behind the incredible metamorphosis, something about a twenty-five-year-old lover. Whatever the reason, Mo looked sensational.

Mo pulled out her tortoise-shell cigarette case and settled back. "I hate to think of you going. It'll sure mean more headaches for me. But that's what I'm paid for, right?" She lit a cigarette. "So, three guesses who might be there tonight."

"Erik?" Embarrassed, Rebecca fought to cover the sudden outburst of elation. "Out of hibernation? Why? He didn't come all the way down here for Robby's party?"

Mo grinned knowingly. "He asked after you."

"He did?"

"Wanted to know if I knew where you were. I told him you were living at Robby's. But note—I didn't say with Robby. Figured you'd want that clear. Right?"

"Maybe it'll be my only claim to fame," Rebecca said wryly. "Having lived with America's favorite teenager."

Mo reached for a large pewter ashtray. "Rebecca, I have a favor to ask. Erik won't let me sell the film rights to *The Rainbow Shuttle*. And out less than a month and climbing all the bestseller lists. He's being a damned fool. It's such a sexy, trashy little book, I could get him a cool million or more. He'd be set up for life. Would you put in a good word for me?"

Rebecca hesitated, torn between not wanting to alienate Mo but also wanting to respect Erik's choices. "I'd certainly like to find out his reasons for turning down all that money. Sure, I'll ask him."

Mo grinned her thanks. "How's your career going?"

"Don't ask," Rebecca quipped and headed for the doorway. " 'Ours is not to reason why, ours is just to do or die.' I'll summon his highness."

Suddenly a shriek, a strangled cry from a dying swan, broke from upstairs. Rebecca and Mo rushed for the hallway. Before they could reach the carpeted staircase, an angry Robby appeared, in a silk dressing gown, on the balcony. He shrilled down at them, "Goddammit, I can't go to the White House now. Nixon's just resigned! Who the hell do we know in Gerry Ford's circle?"

Rebecca turned for the kitchen. "How about Minnie Mouse?"

That night in the Crystal Room of the Beverly Hills Hotel, Mo went all out to honor Robby's recent Golden Globe Award as Most Popular Newcomer in Television. For four hundred of Hollywood's "almost-A list," there was a delicious buffet spread along one whole wall, three open bars and a top dance band playing all night. Nixon's resignation was definitely the topic of the night, the pros and cons were bandied about along with talk of percentage points and who's got what deal and who was screwing whom to get more.

Rebecca sought sanctuary in the shadows of a large potted fern and sipped from a glass of white wine. Watching the famous faces, listening to snatches of conversations, remembering too much from the days of Real Amerika's anti-Nixon demonstrations, she wondered where Ada and the others were right then, imagining how they would be taking the news. She caught sight of Jack Lord, barely four feet from her. And then, by the nearest bar, spotted Faye Dunaway. Rebecca faded further into the shadows. Even with her new dress of white moiré taffeta with a jagged, handkerchief skirt and her new hairstyle, piled high with loose tendrils of soft curls, she felt out of place. A nobody among somebodys. And Erik was nowhere to be seen.

Mo was bustling about the crowd, having a grand time. Dressed in sleek blue silk evening pajamas, which emphasized her newly found bustline, she sparkled bright as the diamonds glistening at her wrists and neck. She laughed now with a young trio of blond surfers. Rebecca recognized Mo's twin sons and wondered if the taller, more good-looking youth was the purported lover. Mo swooped to Gene Hackman, slapping him on the back like a drinking buddy.

Rebecca turned and slipped out the side doors into the balmy night air, inhaling the fragrant scent of gardenias blooming along the lanai. The band's music drifted out—a sedate version of Neil Sedaka's "Laughter in the Rain."

"Rebecca . . . is that you?"

The familiar, deep voice brought her around, sparks like fireflies dancing over her skin. He came to her out of the shadows, the light flickering across his rugged face, revealing not only an unexpected mustache but a welcoming expression. "My god, you look so different."

"Is that bad or good?" she asked.

He laughed and threw his arms around her, squeezing her tightly. "Sensational," he said and released her, keeping his hands on her bare shoulders. "I almost didn't recognize you."

"You look pretty spiffy yourself in that white suit." She wondered if it were the same one he'd gotten married in. For a brief moment, she ducked her head. Why had he not kissed her? She gazed up at him and tried to keep the tremble out of her voice, "Another bestseller, Mister Lungren. Congratulations. Dreams coming true for you? Why aren't you inside with all the other biggies?"

Wearily he dropped his hands. "If not for Mo I wouldn't've come."

"Me too . . . except with me it was for Robby."

"I understand you two are living together."

She threw an exploratory glance into his eyes. They were studying her seriously. "Basically as a nanny," she explained. "Room and board plus a hundred a week. But I retire Monday. Already found my own place down in Venice, near the beach."

"And more time for your own tap dance. Let's have a drink. To celebrate, paths crossing and Nixon resigning. Been in the Polo Lounge?"

"Once. The first day I arrived. Robby took me in there with his mother—I was still wearing my December woolies from New York. Sweated like a pig, if you'll pardon such a graphic description."

He laughed. "Then let's find someplace new."

"Be my guide . . ."

"With pleasure."

They ended up at Jack's on the Beach, a well-known seafood restaurant south of Santa Monica, perched over the ocean on pilings. The drive out in his rented Ford had held too many awkward silences for her to fully enjoy his sudden proximity. He'd probed her with questions about her career and she'd found herself spilling out the age-old frustrations of being an actress. She'd kept the tone light and he had been both amused by her delivery and understanding of her struggle. That pleased her greatly.

Now they were seated in a green leather circular booth by the expanse of window. Floodlights from under the restaurant cut out into the darkness, illuminating the frothy incoming waves. She stuck to white wine while he ordered tonic water. "Gave up booze," he explained. "Found it only augmented my neurosis."

"You, neurotic? Never."

Chuckling, he threw an arm over the back of her portion of the booth. "You just don't know me that well."

"Is that my fault? Hey, I've got a rude question. Mo wants me to find out why you won't let her sell your new book to the movies?"

"Have you read it?"

She nodded into her wineglass.

"What'd you think?"

With tact but with directness, Rebecca told him exactly what she felt about *The Rainbow Shuttle*, how she thought it was his weakest, not because of the subject matter, but because of the general, one-level tone. "I learned in acting," she concluded, "if a scene is supposed to be sad, it's better to play against the tears rather than giving into them. Go against the obvious grain. Somehow that makes it all the more sad. Am I making myself clear?"

"Yes—that I gave into the sentimentality rather than allowing the real sentiment to come out naturally."

"Gee," she teased broadly, "you sure have a way with words."

He laughed again, then toyed with his glass. "Your critique's about the most perceptive anyone's made. Don't you ever lie to make people feel good?"

"Sure. All the time."

"I doubt that. Seriously I do."

She glowed self-consciously. He wadded a cocktail napkin. "It's damned ironic, the success of this book. I wish to God I'd never written it. I tossed it off in less than a month. I was trying to work out some of that pain of the divorce . . . sent it off to my publisher thinking they'd reject it and I'd be free of my contractual obligations. Hell, they've spent a small fortune pushing it." He shook his head, not looking at her. "Who was it that said, 'beware of what you wish for because you just might get it'?"

She wanted to ask again why he wouldn't allow a film sale, but she felt she already knew. There was something in his eyes, a sort of lingering sadness. As if he were genuinely humiliated for so thinly disguising in his novel an obvious rehashing of his marriage to Shelby. It grieved Rebecca to think she would never have the opportunity of helping ease that pain, a subject she felt she knew a great deal about.

They left Jack's and he leisurely drove south to Marina del Rey. He parked near the boat-filled slips and led her out onto one of the docks, draping his coat over her shoulders. Dwarfed by the coat's size, she was talking a mile a minute, trying to fill completely the empty spaces. ". . . and I looked up and this guy was running toward me down the sidewalk totally nude. Like remember that streaker on the Oscars this year? What was it David Niven said right after? Some funny ad lib about displaying one's shortcomings. Remember?"

"Didn't see the show."

"You didn't? I thought everyone watched the Oscars. Don't think I've ever missed one in my whole life. Back in Buffalo, Robby and I used to play this game—our favorite. We'd take turns being the presenter for Best Actor or Actress. Make up lists of actors and their movies and add our own names—like Rebecca Parlato in *Donkeys Die at Dawn* . . . then 'the winner is . . .' Of course we'd win all the time. We alternated rushing up and giving an acceptance speech." She fell silent, feeling giddy and foolish and ten years younger than her age of twenty-five.

Erik was smiling down oddly at her. "Mo tells me you're going by the name Rebecca Warren. Why?"

"Oh, you know . . . Parlato sounds too ethnic."

"Wasn't Warren Scooter's last name?"

Flustered, Rebecca tugged his suit jacket closer. "Yes . . ." She wanted to tell him the reasons—that it was her small tribute to Scooter's memory, the least she could do for failing him that night—but she felt incapable at the moment of expressing it.

He pointed across the dark waters to the opposite boat dock. "See that one there? The two-masted job with the blue sail covers?"

"Oh yes . . . a beauty."

"A Sparkman-and-Stephens ketch, forty-five feet. Tomorrow, it's on auction . . . I'm going to make a bid for it."

"That's terrific. You must be an accomplished sailor then."

"As a kid, I dreamed of having a ketch, like Jack London. Always wanted to sail the Seven Seas."

"Would you believe, other than the Staten Island Ferry, I've never been on a boat? Let alone one with sails."

"Hell, when it's mine, I'll take you out. You'll love it."

Arm and arm, they walked back to the car and Erik deposited her inside. Once he'd started the engine, he asked simply, "Want to spend the night with me?"

Not far from the marina, he parked behind the guest house of a large walled mansion near the beach. The house was nothing more than a cottage. When they walked in, it was cold and dark, smelling of mildew and there was grit of tracked-in sand underfoot. Explaining that the estate belonged to a friend of Mo's, a producer who was off on location, Erik built a blazing fire in the fireplace. Rebecca began to feel a little more comfortable. The self-doubts, however, remained.

He sat beside her on the rug before the fire. In her stocking feet, she hugged her knees, watching the flames. A radio in a nearby house played soft music, James Taylor crooning from his new "Sweet Baby James" album.

Erik leaned into her, brushing his lips against hers. Disarmed, she melted, a swarm of feelings overwhelming her. His arms were around her and she sensed his urgency. She tried to relax. His caresses intensified. Soon he was disrobing her, pausing to plant kisses on strategic spots along the way, or whisper a phrase of poetry here, a snippet of a sonnet there. Her heart raced wildly. Dizzily, willingly, she gave herself to him there on the rug. But the sand ground into her backside, adding to her self-consciousness. Several times she felt she was going to reach some sort of climax, but it kept slipping away with a maddening elusiveness.

Afterward, he padded nude into the kitchen for a couple of cold beers and they sat wrapped in an old quilt before the dying embers, drinking the dark brew and talking quietly. Erik speaking at length of Mo's wandering husband and how much Michael McKitrick would be celebrating that evening over Nixon's political demise. She told him her similar thoughts about Ada and the others. The longer Rebecca stayed with him, the more at ease she felt. Soon, she suggested they move into his bedroom.

And that time was delicious, completely satisfying. She cried openly in his arms when it was over, unable to help it, feeling so released she did not care what he thought. It had been as if he had touched a long buried nerve deep within her most inner soul and had set free a well of feelings she thought had died long before. That both thrilled and mystified her.

She lay on his thick, strong arm, her chin resting on his chest, staring at his face, wondering if he felt something special too. He smiled contentedly and kneaded her back with his knuckles. "Hey, black eyes," he whispered. "You're thinking too much."

"How long're you going to be around?"

"Soon as I can work out the financing on that ketch. That's the main reason I came down. I've been looking for that ship for months.''

''Then what?''

''I'd like to test sail it to Hawaii,'' he said dreamily. ''Then if all checks out, down to the South Pacific and ports unknown.''

''You're so lucky being a writer, you can take your work with you, do it anywhere,'' she said, one cheek resting on his chest. ''I hope I see you again before you sail off into the sunset.''

''Count on it,'' he murmured and closed his eyes.

It seemed he fell asleep instantly, steadily. She did not move for a long time, her cheek pressed against his chestbone, listening to the dull, rhythmic beating of his heart. Hers had barely slowed and she did not feel sleepy at all. Her whole body tingled like millions of nerve endings reconnecting within. She felt very much alive. And very confused. Part of her heart had always been reserved for Erik and that part was now even more fully committed and in love. But the part of her being that was and always would be Scooter's cried out now, clawing at her insides for so quickly betraying his memory.

Torn by the conflict, exhilarated one moment, remorseful the next, Rebecca clung to Erik and waited for sleep to release her.

SHELBY
November 1974
Los Angeles

''Seven, Eight, Nine and Ten,'' Colleen shouted in cadence. ''Relax! Breathe. In-In. Fill the lungs. *Ex*-hale. Slowly. Again. Legs up!''

Shelby, in leotards, flat on her back and wringing wet, dropped her feet to the carpet with a loud, frustrated groan.

Colleen ceased her leg throws. ''No pain, no gain.''

"No guts, no glory," Shelby muttered and sat up, reaching for a towel. "What time is it?"

"We've been at it less than a half hour."

There in the fully equipped mini-gym, which David had built for her in the upstairs guest bedroom of his beach house, Shelby eyed the taut, lithe figure before her. Even in a sweatsuit and a good ten years older, Colleen looked like a walking advertisement for her exclusive, "in the privacy of your own home" exercise program. But Colleen had been David's choice and Shelby loathed the trainer's gung-ho enthusiasm and martinet manner.

"Colleen, darling," Shelby said petulantly, "it's now or never."

"I don't want any part of your little scheme."

Shelby stood with effort and turned on the portable radio to cover their voices; John Denver sang "Annie's Song." And Shelby walked to Colleen, pleading, "This is my only chance." She yanked the damp sweatshirt over her head, raising her bare breasts provocatively. "Y'all won't let me down, will you?"

Knowing full well what Colleen wanted, Shelby watched the stern face soften with desire and acquiescence. Slowly Colleen shrugged, giving in. Shelby leaned forward and kissed her cheek gratefully. "He's down in the screening room..."

Moments later, stepping from the shower, Shelby recoiled in shock. In the doorway, David frowned at her legs and asked, "What's wrong?"

She moaned and clutched a leg. "My thigh. Must have pulled something." Noting the suspicion in his eyes, she asked quickly, "My robe, please?"

He reached for it. "Colleen said it was your calf."

"She was mistaken." She hastily pulled on her robe.

He spun into the bedroom. "I'm phoning a specialist."

"Don't," she flared and added in a gentler tone, "Colleen's taking me to hers."

"You're not going to some stranger." He reached for the phone.

"David, please ... let Colleen handle this. Isn't that why you're paying these exorbitant rates? *She's* the expert." She limped effectively into the dressing room. Swiftly she began to pull on the tailored, peach-colored pants suit by Ralph Lauren. Holding her breath, she listened for the sound of his dialing. Not hearing anything, she ventured to the doorway. The bedroom was empty.

Momentarily relieved, she finished dressing, grabbed her purse, making certain it held keys, wallet and makeup. Spying his keys on top of his dresser, she made a quick decision and tossed them into her purse as well. With one last critical look in the full-length mirror, she hobbled into the hallway and headed for the stairs.

He appeared from the nearby den, holding his personal phone directory, scowling at her. She started down the stairs as fast as her "hurt" leg would permit, moaning, "I'm going with Colleen."

"Shelby," he warned, following her. "Why're you acting like this?"

She kept limping down the staircase. "I happen to be in great pain and don't want to argue all day."

"Who's arguing?"

"You are. Colleen? Where're you?"

"By the front door," came the reply.

"I'm on my way!" Shelby cried out.

At the bottom of the stairs, he caught her arm. "Wait. I'll get my keys and drive you." He dashed up the stairs.

As soon as he disappeared, she ran—as lightly and noiselessly as possible—to the main entrance. "Quick," she threw to a startled Colleen and yanked open the front door. "Follow me in your car. We'll rendezvous up the highway."

Disguised in oversized dark sunglasses and a short curly black wig, Shelby waited nervously in the parking lot of the Pacific Palisades Medical Clinic. In order to insure a believable cover story for David, she had undergone a quickly arranged examination by Colleen's doctor. Now, however, she searched anxiously each incoming car.

She saw him the moment he drove into the parking lot. Snatching off her sunglasses, she rapidly scanned her face in the rearview mirror, noting again the tiny lines at the corners of the eyes and mouth. Those minute cracks were growing reminders that time was running damned short.

Deliberately, she relaxed her face muscles, a trick learned modeling, then slipped on her glasses and eased out of the car. She struck a languid pose against the side of her Mercedes. Eyeing him as he emerged from his parked sedan, she was conscious of the low angle of the afternoon sun and what the light and shadows were doing to her face.

In his hurried survey of the lot, Erik glanced over at her. She deepened her smile, wistful, mysterious. His recognition came fast and hard and with a satisfying completeness. He flushed to a ruddy color and momentarily looked unsure of himself, uncertain. In that one instant, she knew she would get what she wanted.

He strode toward her, regaining his composure. She eased off the car. "Y'all've a new mustache, sugar," she commented, tossing him a welcoming smile. "Looks divine . . . very masculine."

"What the hell's going on?" he asked, not acknowledging the friendly little peck she planted on his cheek. "I've been babysitting the damned phone for nearly forty-eight hours." She kept smiling up at him waiting patiently for him to finish, smelling the alcohol on his breath.

"Y'all finished, sugar?" She asked sweetly. "If so, we'd better get out of here. I've a funny feeling David might show up any sec." She linked arms with him, steering him back to his rented Ford LTD.

"Dammit, Shelby, what's up? Where're we going?"

"Somewhere private. Where we can be alone for a while. Y'all drive. I'll navigate." Grumbling, he deposited her inside.

She waited until they were on the main street before beginning her carefully thought-out approach. "Sugar, I'm so grateful y'all're here. I can't tell you what it means—to have somebody you can trust no matter what—someone you can turn to for help. When you most need them. Make a left at the next light."

"I've come to the rather obvious conclusion—this is not a matter of life or death as you implied on the phone in that one, hasty, hysterical call over two days ago."

She laid a hand gently on his arm. "Sugar, I hope y'all know me well enough to realize, I wouldn't have called and asked you to fly down here from Oregon and wait at Mo's for my signal unless it was something terribly important. A girl has to have some pride."

"Well then, dammit, tell me."

"Isn't that just like you? Always anxious for the whole story. Look at this long line for gas, will you?" she said, indicating the cars waiting for the rationed gas at the corner station. "Honestly, those damn Arabs. I tell you OPEC is going to end up owning the world, just you watch."

Erik slapped the wheel vehemently. "Goddammit, if you knew the worry . . . the fears. What I've gone through since you called—you wouldn't be taking this all as a joy ride."

She caught his eye and began in her most womanly voice. "Erik, I am desperate. Really, truly, totally, unequivocally desperate. David has not left the house for almost six weeks. Think about that for a sec. I've not been able to leave without one of his flunkies tagging along. He screens all my phone calls, both incoming and outgoing. He listens in too. So y'all see . . . there was no way I could've gotten to you before now. I'm supposed to be taking a whirlpool bath back at the clinic right now—that's the only way we've got this little time."

He did not look at her. "How much *do* we have?"

"An hour. At the most. Pull into that alley there by the van."

"Dammit, why all the mystery? Where're you taking me?"

"The only place I could arrange on such short notice. Belongs to my exercise coach."

It was a plain, open room with a polished, hardwood floor, one mirrored wall and dance bar, the skylight filtered sunshine for the green, hanging plants. Near the desk fern, Shelby pulled off her wig, shaking loose her hair. "There now," she sighed. "I feel more like myself."

"The black hair really sets off your green eyes."

"Oh, hush," she teased. "Don't y'all know? Flattery won't get you anywhere."

"I don't want anything from you," he said quietly.

For a second, she considered whether he really believed that. Tossing the wig on the desk, she trailed a single finger over a frond of the fern and began to cry softly.

"Shelby? For god's sake, what is it?"

"This damn plant—it's so healthy," she wept. "Remember? All mine die. I'm a failure at everything."

"You're not a failure," he said softly, from too far away.

"Oh yes, I am. Washed up. Finished."

"How can you say that? You've your whole life ahead."

"Not in this town." Teary-eyed she turned, sagging onto the desk. "Oh, Erik, it's been horrible, absolutely horrible. Ever since the release of *A Woman Alone*. I'm the butt of every nasty, dirty vicious joke in this town. Heard the latest? The Shelby Cale doll? You wind her up and she lays the producer." She broke down completely, covering her face with her hands, sobbing into them.

"It's only a damned movie. Not your whole life."

"But what *is* my life?" she asked emotionally. "Who am I anyway? I don't even know anymore. Everything used to be so easy. All I had to do was smile. And now . . . wind-up doll jokes."

He was watching her, little crinkles of concern around his eyes, but still he made no overt action. "You're still truly beautiful . . ."

"Being beautiful means nothing in this town," she sobbed. "There's so much around, no one gives it a second glance. All it does is get you a seat at the table. From then on you have to have something more. Connections. Talent, luck . . . I haven't got any."

"A rough period, Shelby, but believe me, things'll look up."

"I've used up my luck—don't think I ever had any real talent for acting—just for being myself. As far as connections, the only one I've got is David and he . . . he's so loathed by everyone . . . I . . ." She noted his expression and decided not to mention David's name again.

"I know what failure is like, Shelby. I've had my share. You'll learn from this. Believe me. It hurts, but it forces you to grow."

"That's easy for you to say—you're a big success now. On your way to a giant bestseller. Congratulations."

He hesitated. "I'm not a success. Not by my standards."

"Why not?"

"You know why . . ."

The way he'd said it sent little flurries of gooseflesh along her arms. He grabbed one of the long, plastic exercise mats from the stack near the desk and sat down on it, cross-legged. He was wearing tan gabardine Western-styled slacks. They stretched tightly over his thighs, emphasizing his powerful legs. At that moment, she was aware of a strong sexual pull.

He held her eyes. "I . . . I feel I owe you an apology."

"What on earth for?"

"Among other things . . . for my novel."

"*The Rainbow Shuttle*? Sugar, I *love* your book. I think it's positively the best thing you've ever written . . . I cried and cried." She looked at him sincerely. "Sugar, if y'all think you owe me an apology for writing Savannah so much like me, why you're mistaken. I cherish Savannah. I think she's real and . . . and vivacious."

"You're not offended? Or feel I invaded your privacy? Embarrassed you at all for revealing intimacies that were real?"

"Why? Because everyone thinks Savannah's me?" She tossed her head. "Sugar, I'm flattered. Savannah's sort of a cross between Scarlet O'Hara and Eve Harrington . . . and I adore that mix. You know I've always admired girls who know what they want and go after it."

He stared with relief and curious appraisal. Girlishly she knelt on the other end of his mat and sank back onto her heels. "Y'all're just embarrassed for yourself. Your hero loves Savannah no matter what she does and people think the book's about me, so that has to make the hero you. And that's kind of awkward for you, isn't it, sugar? Telling the whole world you love me even though I left you." She batted her eyelashes, teasing with a broad parody of coyness. "Is my woman's intuition still functioning correctly?"

A smile flickered under his mustache—the first since their meeting. She sank to one hip and touched the back of his hand, tracking the thick blue veins. "I've missed you . . . honestly."

"If only I could believe that . . ."

She looked up through her lashes. "I never stopped loving you. I tried—honest to God, I tried. I thought I wanted to forget you. But I couldn't. Not a day goes by when I don't think of you—wishing you were close—that I could share something with you . . ." She let the tears begin again. He was holding her hand now.

"God, Shelby . . ." He raised her palm, kissing it tenderly. She caressed the back of his neck, wanting to speed things up.

Finally, he kissed her lips, gently at first, then with a growing passion. His arms slipped around her, pulling her close. Holding her tightly, he covered her face with kisses. She returned them, feeling the desire taking over.

Gradually he lowered her to the mat, his large hands, which seemed rougher than she remembered, tracing her neck, lightly touching her breasts. She pulled away slightly to allow more access. Slowly, almost maddeningly so, he began to unbutton her blouse. She waited until it was fully open before touching a button of his shirt.

She let him take his time disrobing her fully, then coveted the feel of his scarred, bulky body, now also nude against hers. The contrast with David's was so strong it intensified her heat all the more. She was ready for him to enter her long before he did and when he did, her back was to him and she was on her side, her top leg thrown back over his. He opened her wide, his hands roaming her front, squeezing her nipples, his strokes long, slow. She caught their reflection in the opposite mirrored-wall. His head rose above hers and he was watching her. She heightened her reactions, wanting him to realize how much pleasure he was bringing her.

He lay on top for a long while, kissing her until their breathing had quieted. When he stretched out beside her, it seemed a long while before he began talking quietly, about his own new life—the fishing town he lived in on the Oregon coast, his small house overlooking the harbor and the mountains, his new sailboat, the novel he'd begun.

"Sugar," she finally began, toying with his chest hair. "I've been thinking about *The Rainbow Shuttle* a lot since I read it . . . it would make a marvelous movie."

He looked at her sharply. "No way."

"Why not?"

"I just don't want it to have any more exposure."

"Why?"

"Let's not waste time talking of that, okay?"

She kissed him again, snuggling deep into the crook of his arm so she could observe his face. "Sugar . . . don't you think Savannah would be a perfect role for me?" His eyes narrowed drastically so she rushed on, "I mean—let's face it. I know it's a role I could handle really well. And damn, I need a part like that. Desperately." She could feel his body tense.

"What're you asking?"

"I'm asking . . . no, I'm pleading with you, Erik. Would you sell me the movie rights so I can—"

He sat up abruptly. "David put you up to this?"

"Oh, no," she cried. "How can you think of something like that? This is my own idea. And I think it's fabulous."

"So *this* is why you got me down here."

"I won't lie," she responded, rising up beside him. "Yes, that's what I had on my mind, but after seeing you . . . being with you again, it just sort of slipped away. Didn't seem important."

"But now it suddenly is?" He stood, reaching for his slacks.

"Oh, sugar, don't act like this. You make me feel terrible."

"How'd you think it makes me feel?" He jammed his legs into the trousers and yanked them on.

"I was hoping it would make you happy. That you'd want to help me."

"Just like that, huh? Lure me down here, keep me waiting on the hook for two days, then whisking me here to soften me up. Or should I say harden me up?" He yanked on his shirt.

"Y'all make it sound so calculated," she said, covering her breasts with her arms.

"Wasn't it?"

"No. Absolutely not. What happened here, happened because we both wanted it. Not just me. You can't deny that, Erik." Again the tears sprang forth. "I told you honestly, I need your help. Only you can help."

"You mean, only my book can help." He slammed into his boots. "I wish to God I'd never written it."

"Just because it didn't get the reviews you wanted? Sugar, it's selling because it touches people. They don't care about reviews, only what moves them, or titillates them."

"Shelby . . . I can't expect you to understand this . . . but it's something I feel strongly about. I don't want a movie—"

The phone on the desk rang, cutting him off. Both of them stared at it in surprise. Two rings, then silence. She darted to it, waiting for it to begin again. "That's Colleen's signal," she said tensely. On the next ring, she snatched up the receiver. "Yes?" The message was terse, expected. She replaced the phone and began pulling on her clothes in haste. "David called the clinic. He's on his way in by cab."

"Why the hell do you put up with him?"

She fumbled with the sleeves of her jacket, searching for an appropriate response. "I may not for long..." She noted Erik's guarded glance.

And he was glumly silent on the quick drive across town, staring stonily ahead at the traffic. A block from the clinic, she tugged on the black wig. "Better let me out on the corner."

He pulled in at the curb, stopped and swung to her. "You realize that if I do let you have the film rights, you're opening yourself up for even more unfavorable publicity. People wouldn't credit your acting—they'll say you're just playing yourself."

"It'll resurrect my career. Make a fortune for everybody. And free you, forever, from all sense of guilt that you have trashed the memory of our marriage." She reached over on the seat between them and squeezed his hand. "I know you'll do what's best. For both of us." She opened the door to slip out.

"Am I going to see you again?"

"I hope so... keep in touch with Mo. I'll see if I can arrange something. Real quick like. Bye, sugar. It's been divine." She popped out of the car and jauntily walked across the asphalt. At the side door of the clinic, she cast a glance over her shoulder. Through the windshield he stared at her, sadly, longingly. She entered the clinic, strangely unsettled.

Shelby was barely five minutes in the hot whirlpool, stainless steel tub when David barged into the muggy private room. She raised her head groggily. "Hello, darling. What'd you come in for?"

He was livid with anger. "I tried to reach you by phone."

"Really? I've been so out of it in here I wouldn't know." She stretched luxuriously in the steaming, vibrating waters. "Hmmmm, this feels so good. Makes a world of difference. Want to join me?"

He had grabbed her purse and was pawing through it. Triumphantly he pulled out his key ring. "I knew you had these."

"How'd they get in there?"

"You tell me. You left me stranded. With the house empty, no one at work. And that bitch, Colleen, taking off after you."

"Oh, darling, I am so sorry. I was in such pain, I guess I just grabbed them by mistake. Do forgive me, sugar . . . darling." She could not read his expression.

That evening, in the formal dining room looking out on the curved string of lights marking the coastline, they ate a nearly silent dinner of crab soufflé and endive salad served by the matronly housekeeper. Shelby ate ravenously but David picked at his food. She attempted conversation many times. However, he seemed to prefer remaining distant. After dinner he retired to the screening room, not even bothering to invite her in. She changed into a revealing, low-cut dressing gown of soft teal silk and slipped into the darkened room.

On the screen, a black-and-white film flickered away. She recognized it at a glance—one of Nedra Rau's films made for Pacific and produced by Irving. Shelby had seen it a half-dozen times with David and knew that he ran it often for himself. Quietly, she settled beside him on the huge pillowed couch and tried to enjoy the movie. It was a 1949 melodrama entitled *Wayward Girl*—the print was scratchy, the sound fuzzy, the plot creaked along like an old stagecoach, and she thought Nedra overacted like crazy, although she was rather pretty in a dark, vampy sort of way. And at times, the resemblance to David was astonishing.

When the film was over and the room's lights dimmed up, Shelby was disconcerted to note that David was misty-eyed. That oddity threw her so much she forgot the reason for her being there.

Collecting himself, he was silent for a long while, and when he began to speak, his tone bordered on reverential, "She was so talented and so damned beautiful." He paused, then added sullenly, "I'll never forgive Irving for what he did to her."

Shelby questioned with her eyes and David's voice hardened, becoming brittle, cold, "He destroyed her. After the divorce, he spread the rumor that she was a drug addict. Got her blacklisted, no studio would touch her. Without her career, she was lost. He might as well have taken a gun and shot her.''

"How did she die?''

"She fell in her apartment's bathroom, cut her head open on the tub,'' he said sullenly. "Bled to death. She'd been ostracized so no one missed her or even checked on her for six whole goddamned days. And when they found her, Irving told everyone she'd overdosed. The goddamned bastard . . .''

Strangely moved, she laid a hand across the back of his neck, massaging the tight muscles.

It wasn't until much later, after he had taken his nightly medication and they were in bed together, that she dared broach the subject. "Darling, as long as you're still undecided on our next project, I've been thinking. Since we need a guaranteed success—why don't we look for a property with a built-in box office? Like a hit play, a popular song, a bestseller book, like they just did with *All the President's Men?* Something that'll help insure your getting production approval.'' She rubbed his chest.

"Anything that's a hit will've been snapped up already.''

"Oh, I'm certain there must be something out there no producer or studio has an option on . . . if we just look.''

"Shelby, I wish you'd leave this end to me.''

She recognized the tone. "Of course, darling. It was just a suggestion…I leave it all in your capable hands…'' Seeds planted, she snuggled closer and with satisfaction thought back over her busy, busy, day.

DAVID
January 1975
Los Angeles

In his newly assigned office at Pacific Studios, his secretary rang again from the reception area, reporting *sotto voce*, "Maureen Engle is still waiting.''

"Where the hell's the maintenance crew?"

"I'll check again."

"Do that." David slammed the receiver down and stood to unstick his shirt. The damned air conditioner was on the fritz. The air was foul with rancid, stale cigar smoke from the previous occupant. David flopped into the desk chair, fuming at the tacky, small office and the studio pressure politics which had forced the move into it. He, however, had his own plans. And his every move inched him closer to ultimate victory.

Deliberately, he stalled several more minutes before buzzing to have the agent admitted. Mo Engle ambled in with a lot of clanking sounds from her bangling jewelry. Wearing a long colorful peasant skirt and a flower-embroidered white blouse, she looked tanner and fitter than David recalled. But the smirk on her face had not changed since his first dealings with her, nor her air of barely tolerant amusement.

Not rising, he offered his hand across the desk. Mo Engle shook it forcefully and lowered into the chair in front. "No air conditioning? Daddy not treating you well?"

Fighting the urge to lash out, David leaned back in his swivel chair, steepling his hands. "Why the hell has this taken so long? I wanted to be in production by May...June at the latest."

Mo dug into her leather attaché case and brought out several thick contracts, tossing them before him on the desk. "Signed, sealed and personally delivered."

He picked up the top copy, turned the pages, scanning the dated signatures. "You could've sent them by messenger."

The gypsy-attired agent snorted through her nose like a goose and settled back. "David, I wouldn't have missed this for anything." She held out a ring-covered hand. "Hand it over."

He did not like her present attitude and he certainly had not appreciated her bargaining skills. Mo Engle, in the previous two months' negotiations, had proved to be tougher than expected, a keenly focused and dogged game player. Locked in head-on, one-to-one negotiating, David had been surprised. What she had lacked in originality, Mo Engle more than made up with determination and toughness. He hated to admit it but she had forced him into a draw.

Now, she snapped her fingers across the desk, demanding satisfaction. David lifted the printed check from the leather folder and, with a show of nonchalance, handed it to her.

Snatching it, Mo stared at the check, a slow, self-satisfied grin forming. "This do make it all worthwhile." She folded it once and stuffed it into her attaché case with great care. "It's not every day I get a client a million-dollar downpayment."

"It's not every day I give in to outrageous demands."

Her jawline hardened. "And I feel just dandy about that, David. I can't tell you how much satisfaction this has given me. However, it does not vindicate Scooter's death."

He fixed his gaze on her and refused to show anything.

Leaning forward with a soft clink of displaced jewelry, Mo asked in a voice surprisingly devoid of bitterness, "David, please, tell me. Why did you do that? Why did you cut Scooter out? You know he was sensational."

David measured her stonily for several moments. "I've told you before, Mo, and I stick by it. His appearance in my film was detrimental to the project."

Unsatisfied with his response, she jerked back into her chair and reached for a cigarette. "Damn you, Rau."

"He got paid his full contract and you got your cut. So what're you bitchin' about?"

"I'll tell you what I'm bitching about," she challenged. "You didn't have the decency, the courage or the balls to inform me so I could warn him, let him down easy. I'll never forgive you for that, David. Never."

He was on his feet, pacing out from behind his desk and past her to the end of the room. "So it slipped my mind, I had a lot to do at the last minute. New location stuff to shoot in Mexico." He spun to face her. "Besides, I've more than made up for it on this one."

Again she snorted, this time with obvious derision. "*The Rainbow Shuttle* has been Number One for thirty weeks now. If my client would've allowed it to be put up for auction, like I wanted, even higher records would've been set. And this event would've been covered by hordes of press corps and news cameras. Which this circus so richly deserves."

He returned to his desk chair and said tightly, "But your client would sell only to Shelby. How fortunate for all of us." David tapped the toes of his shoes together, thinking.

That infuriating smirk again twisted her mouth as she began to talk, "Which brings us to page one, paragraph two of our contract. Erik is selling Shelby the film rights and she, in turn, is granting you fifty percent participation. And she is entitled to co-creative control. My client wants me to stress that again."

David rocked forward, implanting his elbows on the desk top. "Let's get one thing straight. I'm the producer. I'm writing the screenplay. It's my film. I'll make all the decisions. I'm giving her co-producer credit, but that's a mere formality. Shelby's contribution will be in the acting department only."

"Then you're sure to be up shit creek," Mo muttered and gathered her things. "But one way or the other, Erik washes his hands of this project."

"Smart of him to just take the money and run."

"David, he's not doing it for the money. The book sales alone have set him up for life."

He hesitated asking what he already knew. "Why then?"

"Thought that was apparent. Erik still loves Shelby."

"Listen, you tell Erik not to go seeking any favors in return. Shelby's off-limits. Absolutely no contact. Is that clear?"

Mo started for the door. "Well, that all depends now, doesn't it?"

"On what?"

"On Shelby. What *she* wants. These are liberated days."

"I know what she wants," David replied testily. "A hit movie. Nothing more."

"Well, you've just bought the hottest property in town. So go to it then. Make Erik and me some more money." Mo snorted and walked out, leaving the door open. He darted forward and slammed it behind her.

The days piled on top of one another, each filled with the myriad details of getting a major studio production off the ground. David spent long hours dictating his screenplay of the novel, concentrating on Shelby's character, making her less childish, more sympathetic and more mysterious. Concurrently, he scrambled to line up foreign money for co-production as Shaw had set Pacific's participation at only six million, a sum far below what David felt was needed—especially since purchase of Lungren's million-dollar novel had to be included in the production budget. Both in spite of the pressures and because of them, David felt energized again and relished each challenge, each battle, each decision.

He also continued to search the roster of available directors, wanting one talented enough to take advantage of Shelby's unique qualities. After much deliberation, he narrowed his list to three possibilities. Every night at home, he screened one of their films, weighing his options.

During a late-night screening of Cukor's *The Philadelphia Story*, long after David had assumed Shelby had retired for the evening, she appeared in her dressing gown, wanting to talk. Holding her hand, he waited until the film's conclusion before turning his attention fully to her.

"I've been thinking," she said, all coiled, soft and womanly, beside him on the couch. "Don't you think it'd be a good idea for me to take some acting lessons?"

"Absolutely not."

"I've got all this time on my hands. A few lessons a week wouldn't hurt, would it?"

"Shelby," he began patiently. "We've been through this before. You have a natural gift. I don't want it to become studied or mannered."

"But you're the one who keeps telling me artists must perfect their craft." Her lower lip protruded into a perfect little pout.

"Your naturalness *is* your art. It's a unique talent."

She clutched his hand. "David, I'm afraid. Really, truly I am. I don't want to fail again. I want to grow . . . as an actress."

"It's impossible for you to judge your own growth or merits." He eyed her petulant expression and continued, "Shelby, I don't want you turned into a carbon copy of every other actress in town. Believe me, with the right director you'll shine."

"David . . . please . . ."

"No," he said firmly. "Now you run along to bed and leave the worrying to me." He touched a finger to the space between her dusky brows. "If you don't stop frowning, these lines will become permanent." She pulled away from him. "I know what's best," he sighed. "Now give a kiss and off to bed."

She pecked his cheek. "Want me to wait up?"

"Not tonight. In the morning?"

"Not too early."

"Just before I leave for the studio."

She withdrew, leaving behind a scent of roses.

The following afternoon, at his studio office, David was in a meeting with his production supervisors when his secretary buzzed. "A Miss Colleen Stringfellow out here. Says it's urgent and *very* personal."

David recognized the name. "Tell her to wait."

"She insists it has to be now. Promises it'll take a minute."

"One minute, that's all she's got." He sent his production men into another office. Soon Shelby's former exercise instructor strode in like a WAC sergeant, her firm body tightly packed into electric blue hotpants and a skimpy tube-top. "Didn't you get the severance check?" he asked.

"That's not why I'm here. I've some information for sale."

Saying nothing, he surveyed her hard face.

Colleen went on flatly, "About Shelby and this other guy?"

A muscle began to twitch in the back of his neck.

She waved a slip of paper. "His address. She's there now."

"How much?"

"Ten grand."

He laughed.

She jammed the paper between her taut breasts. "*National Enquirer* will pay it. More if I get photos."

He considered for a moment, then brought out his checkbook. "If this turns out to be a con, I'll stop payment."

Smiling triumphantly, she traded his paper for hers.

David sat in the darkened living room, facing the front door. His mind too inflamed to think, his temples pounding like a drummer strung out on amphetamines. The Malibu house staff had been dismissed for the day, drapes closed, phones disconnected. He had been waiting, vibrating in pain for over two hours.

Finally, from the front of the house, the automatic garage-door opener whined into action. He could hear her car pulling in, the motor cutting off. One car door slammed. Then another. She'd brought her secretary back with her. High heels clicked on the outside brick entryway. A key in the lock. A shaft of light spilled into the entrance hall. Silhouettes of two women, carrying many packages, entering the house.

"Hello! We're back from shopping," came Shelby's cheerful lie. He did not answer.

"Why's it so dark?" That was Judith's voice.

"David? You here, darling?" Shelby switched on the overhead chandelier and caught sight of him. Her face flattened with shock.

"Get that bitch out of here," he rasped. "She's fired."

Shelby did not move. Judith blinked, not comprehending.

"You heard me. Get the fuck out and don't come back." His voice sounded strangulated and from far away. And every syllable hurt his head.

Judith moved for the staircase. "I . . . I'll just get my things."

"Now!"

She dumped the packages on the rug and fled, leaving Shelby by the wall switch. The front door slammed. Silence. Except for his own belabored breathing.

She took a hesitant step. "Darling . . . what is it? What's wrong?" He could barely bring himself to look at her.

She dropped her purse and packages onto the coffee table. "David? What is it? Why're you looking at me like that?"

"You cunt," he spewed out. "You two-timing, double-crossing cunt!"

"Wha' . . . what's . . . ?"

"How long've you been fucking him behind my back?"

Her head trembled from side to side, her eyes wide with fright. "No, no . . . it's not—"

He exploded to his feet, cutting her off. "Don't lie to me!"

She recoiled, shrinking from him. "I'm not—"

His hand shot out, slapping her across the cheek. "You can't lie your way out of this one. I saw with my own eyes."

"Where? What?" she moaned, rubbing her cheek.

"Hurricane Street. His garage. Your car!" He grabbed her wrist and yanked her close, twisting her arm behind her. "I could kill you!"

"David . . . you're hurting me . . ."

"How do you think I feel? You think I'm not hurting?" He twisted her arm harder, forcing her close.

Her eyes grew even larger. "David . . . please. That hurts!"

"Admit it."

"No—Owow!" she shrilled. "Yes . . . Yes . . . I—"

"How many times?"

"I don't know . . ."

"TELL ME!"

"Ouch, stop it!" she cried.

"How many? Six? A dozen? Hundred? How many times have you put out for that sonofabitch?"

"Let go, please . . . owow! Just a few times, I swear."

"You disgust me." With all his might, he threw her away from him. She fell on the rug by the fireplace.

Her hair tumbled over one blotched cheek and she sobbed, "I did it for us . . . you and me . . ."

"You fucked *him* for me?!"

She raised her eyes, they were swimming with tears. "Yes . . . to get what we needed. He wouldn't have sold the book . . . oh, David, don't do this."

"What do you want? Thanks? You think I give a rat's fuck for that piece of shit he's written? You fucked Erik because you wanted to."

"No," she moaned. "I had to . . ."

"Get up, you conniving bitch!" He kicked out at her.

She jerked away from his shoe. But she did not rise quickly enough for him. He reached down, grabbing the material of her silk blouse. With a wrench, he tore it from her. She yelped in fright, her heavy breasts falling free.

"I said *get up!*"

She lumbered to her feet, backing away. Black mascara made dirty tracks down her cheeks, her mouth hung open. "David . . . please . . . forgive me . . . you just don't understand . . ."

He took a step to her. "Get upstairs."

"What're you—"

"Now! *Move!*"

She backpedaled to the staircase, misjudged the distance and tripped on the bottom step with a helpless cry. He lunged for her. She clambered out of his path. "Move!" he barked, lashing out with his foot, catching her squarely on the rump. She screamed and scrambled up the stairs, bent low, her hands clawing at the carpet. He followed slowly, painfully pulling himself up by the banister, the roar in his temples near deafening.

At the top, she spun, hysterical. "David, for god's sake, listen!"

He shoved her down the hall and into the bedroom. Entering, he began removing his shirt. Cowering by the bed, she looked a mess and it disgusted him all the more. He yanked the belt from the loops of his pants. "Take off your slacks."

"No!"

He lashed out with the belt, it whipped across her thighs, a stinging blow. She screamed in pain and doubled over, clutching her legs. "Take 'em off. Everything," he said hoarsely and raised the belt.

She began unfastening her slacks. He watched through half-lidded eyes, his body coiled tight from the steel needles stabbing into temples. When she was nude, trembling, he dropped his pants, stepping out of them, shoving down his shorts. "On your knees."

"David, please . . . god, I said I was sorry," she wailed. "What do you want me to say?"

"On your knees!"

Slowly, with an agonized groan, she contorted, collapsing onto all fours, facing him, her breasts swaying between her arms.

"Turn around."

With a strangled cry, she swung around. Her soft, full ass pointed at him. He flicked out with the belt, catching her cheeks. She shrieked, crawling away. He pursued, cornering her, flailing away until her buttocks were crisscrossed with red welts. Her head dropped to the carpet, her screams became muffled, her fingers clutching at the deep pile.

He threw aside the belt. His cock was fully erect, straining. He sank to his knees behind her. Reaching over her back, he grabbed a fistful of hair and snapped her head up, bending it back on her long neck. He spat into his free hand and wiped spittle onto the head of his cock. He began pushing into her. Protesting violently, she struggled in his grasp.

He bent over her, croaking in her ear, "You think I'd shove it where *he's* been?" With a powerful thrust, he rammed into her. Her mouth flew open and she screamed. She tried flattening down on her stomach. He held her upright, yanking her head back, one arm tight around her middle.

It took him a long, long time to come.

Carefully he washed himself under the jets of water, toweled off, took two more Demerol and returned to the bedroom. She had crawled onto the bed. Curled on one side, she wept deep, hollow sobs into a pillow. He climbed beside her and lay down, his arms pulling her close. She resisted at first, but he held her so tightly she could not move. He whispered into her tangled, damp hair, "See how it feels to be violated?"

"I . . . I hurt all over," she cried. "Inside and out . . ."

"So do I . . ."

"I'm so sorry, David . . . you'll never forgive me, will you? Ever . . ."

"Have already," he said, kissing her wet cheek.

She turned into him, searching his face, her eyes red, tragic. "Swear . . . honest and truly . . . ?"

"I swear . . . honest and truly." He kissed her nose. "After all, we've got a lot of movies to make."

REBECCA
May 1975
Los Angeles

To shrieks of childish laughter, she pulled off the long braids made of thick yellow yarn and swept low from the waist in a grand bow. On the dusty, sunparched grass, the children—primarily minority kids—clapped and screamed for more. The few adults, lounging in the shade of the trees bordering the park, applauded with appreciation.

Rebecca grinned and bowed some more, hamming it up before signaling "enough" and began to speak in a firm, clear voice, "I want to thank each and every one of you for coming. And thanks to the Parks Department, I'll be back in two weeks. In the meantime, remember, each of you has special magic. So be magical! Bye!" With a wave, she gathered her sack of props and costumes and threw it over her shoulder. Before she'd walked two steps, she was surrounded by adoring kids.

One little black fellow of no more than seven grabbed her hand, walking her toward her nearby VW bug. "Say, you don' really believe in magic, do you?"

"Oh, absolutely," she said and tossed her prop sack into the rear seat. She climbed behind the wheel. "We all have magic, I believe that."

He leaned his head in through the window, pointing to her dash. "Say, wha's that?"

"That toy monkey is magical too. I can vouch for that."

"Aw, com'on, don' jive me."

Rebecca uprooted the talisman from its taped base, kissed the worn, shiny nose and handed the toy to the kid. "You find out. It sure worked for me." She started the engine. The boy was staring with wonderment at the unexpected gift. "Remember," she said. "The magic's inside you. The monkey just helps get it out. See you next time?" With a wave, she drove off, feeling good about letting go of that part of the past. Then she laughed, thinking she'd sounded just like Loretta Young on her old TV show.

Rebecca's one-woman story theater had been totally her idea. She'd worked up in mime and narration several well-known fairy tales, designed and made the colorful costumes and props. Auditioning for the board of L.A. parks, she'd met with instant approval and was hired on the spot. Each day of the week, she performed her sixty-minute show in a different park. The gig was a perfect part-time job, giving her a certain freedom, depending upon the distance to the park, to be available for auditions and interviews as well as providing a much needed outlet for her long-denied acting talents. Finances were always tight, but she was fairly resigned to that state, being broke came with the territory of being an actress.

On this day, however, Rebecca's high spirits emanated not just from her energizing performance. Today was an extra special day. After nearly a four-month absence, Erik was back for two weeks and today he was sailing her to Catalina Island for the first time. Two whole days by themselves—that alone made her joyous. Even the eye-burning smog and relentless dry heat of the Santa Ana winds did not abate her spirits on the congested drive to the marina. Singing "Mandy" at the top of her lungs, accompanying Barry Manilow on the radio, she parked hurriedly in the lot. She ran down the dock, out toward Erik's boat. Catching sight of him—coiling a rope on the aftdeck, wearing only ragged cutoffs, his skin burnished copper and his hair nearly blond—her heart skipped a beat or two. "Ahoy there, captain!"

He burst into a wide grin. "Get your landlubber legs aboard or we'll miss the tide."

She tossed him her bag and scrambled onto the highly polished teak deck. "Sorry I'm late. The kids were persistent little devils." He grabbed her playfully around the middle and planted a big kiss on her lips. "Welcome aboard."

Dazed by the sudden outburst of affection, she hugged him back, smelling the sea and sun on his chest. He released her, sending her below to stow her gear. She saluted with a comic, cockeyed expression. "Aye, aye, captain."

The first time Erik had taken her sailing on his new ketch, *The Dreamer,* she'd become deathly sick. She'd been so embarrassed by her lack of sea-worthiness regardless of how much she'd wanted to spend time with him, she had been secretly hoping he'd never ask her again. Though over the last months, he had been away most of the time, on each of his returns to L.A., he'd eased her into the joys of sailing. He had gotten a big kick out of teaching her the ropes and as she was always a fast study she soon had mastered the rudiments.

And now, halfway to Avalon, the coastline had receded until it was a mere sliver on the eastern horizon. Even the ugly, brownish yellow haze of the smogbank was slipping behind them, leaving the skies above clear and blue. Both of them had stripped down to their fair-weather sailing gear, the briefest of bikinis, and were sprawled in the cockpit, Erik at the helm.

As *The Dreamer* was on a long, southwesterly tack, there was nothing to do but lean back and unwind. Three of the sails—the jib, the main and the mizzen—were set and billowing full with the brisk wind. The sleek wood-hulled craft dipped and plunged into the swells. The hiss of the bow as it cut through the water and the gentle rolling motion lulled her into a blissful state. Lying on her back on the blue canvas cushions, she stretched lazily, her arms thrown over her head, arching her brown stomach up toward the hot sun.

"Lord," Erik murmured, "you've one helluva beautiful body."

She blushed in spite of herself. She never thought she possessed anything but a small, almost flat torso. Rolling over on her front, she grinned. "Thanks. You too."

"Me?" He chuckled heartily and slapped his belly.

"Beauty's in the eye of the beholder," she replied.

He gazed up at the top of the mainmast with a faraway expression. " 'Spanish sailors with bearded lips, and the beauty and mystery of the ships. And the magic of the sea.' "

"What's that from?"

"Poem by Longfellow—*My Lost Youth.*"

"Sometimes I feel so illiterate around you."

"Don't. Memorizing poems was just something I used to do. Guess it was because I never had any formal education beyond high school."

"And look where it's gotten you." She laughed. "On the *New York Times* bestseller list for ten months in a row." She surveyed his face, then joked quickly, "I won't hold it against you, I promise. Would you like a beer?"

"Hey, I was just going to ask for one."

"Intuition." She beamed and rose. "Just one of those basic tools of an actress. Like grace." With exaggerated nonchalance, she sashayed to the hatch door and purposely stumbled. His quick burst of laughter was the sweetest applause.

Avalon turned out to be straight from a fairy tale. The only inhabited portion of Catalina—a once private island, part of the vast Wrigley chewing-gum holdings—the small hilly village ringed a natural harbor filled with pleasure yachts and boats of all sizes and descriptions. A large, round art-deco building, from which the famed Big Bands were broadcast, capped a promontory like a giant, pink birthday cake, she thought.

After they had anchored in the harbor, showered and changed, Erik rowed them in the dinghy to the main dock. They ate fresh broiled abalone and drank dry white wine in a quaint second-story restaurant with a view of the twinkling lights of the harbor. Their talk, as usual, ranged wide, from Idi Amin's reported statue of Adolf Hitler, to Diana Ross's performance in *The Wiz,* from Gerry Ford's bungled handling of the *Mayagüez* incident to Baryshnikov's impact on the U.S. media. They also laughed a lot and held hands across the table.

Later that night, aboard *The Dreamer,* Erik made love to her with such tenderness and passion, she climaxed several times in a row. A first for her, an all-consuming pleasure ride of abandonment. She clung to him, kissing his neck and chest and eyes, repeating over and over, "Ohmygod, ohmygod, ohmygod . . ."

For a long while they were silent, except for their breathing, each winding down from different rhythms. She nuzzled her cheek against the damp, rough hairs of his chest. Then asked softly, "Do you believe in destiny?"

Tracing a delicious pattern on her back, he did not respond for a while but then said, "No, not in the 'fated' sense, or predetermined. But I do think character is destiny. What we choose to focus on, to believe in, our point of view—all that creates our future."

She nodded into him and began to laugh quietly with recognition.

"What's so funny?" he asked.

She said, "It's just like my mom used to chant at me: 'Sow a thought, you reap an act; sow an act, you reap a habit; sow a habit, you reap a character; sow a character, you reap a destiny.' "

He turned into her, wrapping a warm arm around her. "So dark eyes, what are you sowing for? Stardom?"

She chuckled huskily. "Survival."

"And so you reap. I'd say, you're more than surviving."

"But not winning yet," she added quickly.

"Winning, I've finally learned, is a state of mind." He blew a cool breeze over her brow and settled his head next to hers. "Like William Blake wrote, 'If a star should doubt, it would immediately go out.' "

She frowned in the dancing pattern of light bouncing around the teak walls, reflected off the water through the porthole. "But I've seen what happens when wanting it too much runs your whole life. Like to Sara Jane—remember Silver? And Scooter too. He always sought the limelight. And when it was snatched from him, he couldn't deal with it. And Robby? He wanted it more than any of us and got it. And now? He's miserable, bugging Mo all the time to get him out of the series, land him a movie."

"So they created their own destinies," he murmured sleepily into her hair. She could hear the sea lapping on the hull mere inches from her head. And in the distance, the faint sound of a dance band, as though from the past, beginning to play "Stardust" in swing-style.

Humming along to herself, she yawned, then said, "I'd certainly like to work more as an actress. To be paid for what you love doing, isn't that the ultimate success?"

"Amen," he voiced and held her tightly for a while.

"Or I guess even," she continued, "loving what you get paid to do, that's a kind of success too."

"What do you think drives people to seek to be famous, or special, is it insecurity, self-absorption?"

She considered for a few moments. "I think the drive to be the best you can be is one thing. The drive to be famous, another. For example, maybe my not getting enough love and attention at home when I was growing up—having to compete with my older brother, Tony, for everything—maybe that's what ran me for a long while. That need to be noticed and appreciated growing until it had to be the whole world that loved me. But now, I feel better about myself, more secure. I'm now more concerned with reaching my potential. Not needing now the whole world applauding." She paused, then added, half-joking, "But I wouldn't mind hearing that once in a while, if you could arrange it maybe?"

He laughed with her and she snuggled closer, saying, "You always make me feel so good."

"That's mutual, Rebecca . . . I mean that." He kissed her again and she returned it fully. They lay quietly, drifting closer to sleep. The gentle lap of the water on the hull near their heads was the last thing she was conscious of—other than the extraordinary glow enveloping her heart and the dance band still playing "Stardust" in the distance.

Sunday dawned with a blaze of golden light. She awone to the appetizing smells of fresh coffee brewing and bacon sizzling in the galley. Erik set up a table up in the cockpit, and they ate greedily, a radio on a nearby boat playing the Eagles' "One of These Nights." The morning L.A. Times, bought from a kid in a rowboat, front-paged the anti-busing riots by white neighborhoods in the Midwest. Over coffee, they talked leisurely and watched the surrounding boats come to life.

When the sun had climbed higher, Erik hauled up the anchor and under motor-power, they set off for the south end of the island. Once around the tip of the island, they cranked up the sails and caught a fresh breeze blowing north. Halfway up the island, he steered into a small, isolated cove where they dropped sails, anchored and went snorkeling in the crystal clear, blue-green waters. They raced and chased each other, ending up near the sandy beach, making love again in the shallow water.

Shortly they were under sail, paralleling the rugged shoreline. The wind picked up as they swung wide around the northern, most western portion of the island and soon they were making an estimated eight knots. The sense of speed was exhilarating. When the wind dropped, slowing them, he turned the wheel over to her and went forward to trim the mainsail. Returning, he kept her at the helm and stretched out with his head in her lap.

She leaned back against the cushion and concentrated on keeping the boat on its compass course. A sense of peace pervaded. Idly, with her free hand, she stroked his head, her fingers touseling his curly, thick hair. His eyes were closed, the long, nearly blond lashes a thick curtain over the top of his cheeks. She could not contain her feelings. She leaned down and kissed his lips. "I want you to know, I love you, Erik."

His eyes were upon her now and he smiled, raising the back of his hand to graze her cheek. "You are the dearest, sweetest . . . I don't think there is a mean, vindictive bone in you."

"You wanna see an X ray, maybe?"

He grinned. "You give without asking for anything in return."

His words warmed her more than the sun overhead. "But it's not true," she voiced softly. "I want you to love me. As much as I love you." His silence gave her doubts again. "I've always had a big mouth, right?"

"I love your big mouth."

"You do?" she asked, brightening. "What else?" She momentarily forgot the wheel. A sharp gust of wind wrenched it away from her and the boat veered suddenly. The sails began flapping, cracking loudly. He sat up, taking the helm. Soon the sails were as puffed as before.

He threw an arm around her, pulling her back against the cushion with him. For a long while, they just watched the sails and water, white and blue, each color intense, sparkling. And she waited for him. Finally he began to speak, quietly, thoughtfully, "Rebecca . . . I think I do love you. I really do. But . . . the love you were speaking of earlier, it requires a strong commitment. And that's something I can't give you at this time."

When she found her voice, it was small, unsure. "Why?"

"It's . . . I feel I'm in some sort of transitional period in my life. I'm going on thirty-nine and for the first time, I don't have to worry about the future financially."

"That must be freeing."

"It should be. But—I feel this . . . this guilt. Especially since it was made on the one book I'm ashamed of writing."

"You earned your rewards honestly. By the fruits of labor and talent. After all, you've had long periods of being broke."

"Still . . . it makes me uneasy. I'm free to do whatever I like— write whatever I wish without having to worry if it'll sell or be liked. And now I'm finding that freedom is only another curse."

"Well, take it from your Number One fan," she said unhesitatingly. "For *Hidden Assets* alone, you'd deserve all the awards."

He tugged her closer. "Thanks, number one fan."

She kneaded the strong bicep muscle of the arm that held her. "I cherish this right now, being here, with you."

"Then at this moment," he said quietly. "I love you and you love me. And that's enough." He reached up and pulled her head down to his, sealing her lips with a tender kiss.

As *The Dreamer* joined the steady stream of boats up the main channel of Marina del Rey, the sun began to sink, turning the sky a fiery orange—a condition, Erik had pointed out, brought on by the amount of smog in the air. Rebecca moved onto the bow to lower the jib on command. Legs braced apart, she watched the approaching slip. Beyond, on the dock, a blonde with large sunglasses, looking overdressed in a Pucci print dress and high heels, hurried along, waving frantically in their direction.

Rebecca recognized Shelby immediately and was so unsettled she almost missed Erik's shout to drop the jib. She snapped to attention, quickly untying and lowering the sail just as the bow pointed into the slip. Terribly aware of Shelby's gaze, she gathered in the folds of the stiff, white Dacron and dropped them onto the deck. The bow eased forward, bringing her closer and closer to Shelby near the piling.

Rebecca cast a glance back at Erik. He, too, had seen Shelby and was frowning. At the last instant, Rebecca hopped to the dock and leaned back over the water to catch the bow with her hands, preventing the dock from hitting the rubber-fenders too hard. She snatched up the bowline to tie it off. Straightening up, she saw him hurrying toward Shelby. Not wanting to be an unwelcome observer, Rebecca climbed on board and busied herself with freeing the jib sheets—all the while keenly aware.

Shelby was clinging to him, weeping openly. He took her into his arms, patting her back reassuringly, kissing the top of her head. The more Rebecca watched from under her bangs, the more the icy chill crept over her. It was his manner—at once solicitous and concerned, angry and disturbed. Unable to observe anymore, Rebecca slipped below.

As if by rote, she gathered her things and began stuffing them into her tote bag. Tears began blinding her, making it impossible to locate all her belongings. Hearing his footsteps above, she wiped her face and bent over her bag. He entered behind her, but she could not bring herself to turn around.

"I've got to go," he mumbled. "Won't be able to make it tonight."

She bent for her sandals, gritting out an unemotional, "Oh?"

"That bastard Rau slapped Shelby around because she criticized his damned screenplay of my book. He's delivered in person the final draft to Shaw in New York. She wants me to read it before he gets back tonight."

Rebecca forced herself to look at him. His face was clouded with dark emotions and he was changing into a clean pair of jeans.

"You still deeply love her, don't you?"

He stopped to stare. "Unfortunately for both of us . . . yes."

She nodded, a voice screaming inside, don't feel anything, don't feel it. "I guess that puts a lot of things into clearer perspective."

"Look, babe, I don't expect you to understand—"

"I don't," she broke in. "But enough. It was grand while it lasted. Thanks."

"Hey, wait!" He caught up to her in the stateroom. "Look, you're upset. I'm upset. Shelby's upset. It's not the time to make any rash moves."

"This isn't rash, Erik. It may be sudden, but it's not rash."

"Why, for god's sake? It doesn't change anything between us."

"It already has."

"I can't turn off my feelings for her, just because she divorced me. Just like I know you can't turn off your feelings for me now."

"Who said I was turning off my feelings? I love you, Erik. And I will probably for a long time. But I know one thing. I'm not getting the fair end of the stick. I'd rather say good-bye, right now. Right here, then go on fooling myself."

"Goddammit, she needs me right now. It's possible for me to love two people at once."

"I wouldn't know."

"Rebecca, dammit, please."

"I don't want to be in competition with Shelby. So please, let's just call it a day. Right here."

"No! Dammit!" He slammed a fist into a cupboard door. The wood cracked, splitting open. "I don't want that."

"But I do, Erik. I do. Thanks for the sail. Good-bye." Rebecca turned and fled up the steps. She tumbled out on deck and leaped onto the dock. Without looking at Shelby, she ran all the way to her VW bug in the parking lot. Proud that she had not cried in front of them, but too distraught now to contain the tears any longer, she bent over the steering wheel, the dam broke and the deep valley of her heart was flooded.

SHELBY
September 1975
Los Angeles

On hearing of the new pages, her portly director, Victor Craig, sighed, "Will David never stop rewriting?"

"Will Wilbur Mills stop drinking?" Shelby asked.

"When Fannie Fox stops stripping," Victor joshed then turned serious. "Mind if I check out these new pages?"

"Be my guest." She stood back, giving his wide frame space to enter her dressing room, a temporary wooden suite built at one end of Pacific Studios' cavernous sound stage nineteen. Inside was luxuriously opulent, decorated in delicate pastels, predominantly apricot. David had spent a small fortune for her comforts during the shooting of the interior scenes for *The Rainbow Shuttle*. Just a week into principal photography and she felt more at home there than out in Malibu.

She located the three new pink pages of her monologue and while Victor perused them, sat in her makeup chair, watching him. He was a genius—the daily rushes proved it. She had never been so good on film and attributed that totally to the talents of this gentle, soft-spoken Canadian. His thoughtful manner, backed by years of experience directing quality dramatic television, was providing her the freedom to explore her own talents. And he had found the key on the first day.

David's presence on the set had made her extremely uneasy. Victor had noticed it at once and privately had requested that David absent himself during her sequences. Much to her surprise, David had not put up much of a fuss and had stayed away from the set. But there was never any doubt whose picture it was. Though she was a co-partner in the production company, she had handed David total creative control many months before.

Victor lowered the pages, looking somewhat befuddled. "It is rather different than my version." He broke into a broad grin. "But not to worry."

"Do you think it's improved?"

"But of course," he replied jovially.

For the first time since working with him, Shelby did not trust what Victor Craig was saying.

During her lunch break, Shelby hurriedly slipped into her street clothes and, leaving her makeup intact, headed for the studio's cafeteria. She could have ordered lunch to be brought to her, but she enjoyed being seen on the lot—wanting everyone in the business to know that Shelby Cale was back at work and doing splendidly, thank you very much.

The commissary was disappointingly empty. She ate by herself, the pink pages beside her plate where she could test her memory on the troublesome, long monologue. She was just finishing when David appeared, slipping into the chair opposite, asking tensely, "How was it?"

"The salad tostada is lovely, but the iced tea's weak. I think they make it with that powdery imitation stuff."

"The *scene*, Shelby—how'd the goddamn scene go?"

"Fantastic."

"Did Craig do the bit I suggested?"

"Which was that?"

"The ninety-degree pan around to pick you up in the mirror?" She shook her head. He scowled. "Goddammit, I should've been there instead of writing."

"Oh no," she groaned. "Not more changes. Darling, you're polishing the script to death."

"Not polishing. Major rewriting."

"Why? The novel's story was good to begin with. Even Dixon—"

"I don't give a damn what Shaw thought. What the hell's he know about filmmaking? If I say the script's not good enough, it's not."

She managed a vague smile. "Whatever you say, darling."

He jerked his head around, surveying the empty tables. "Look at this place. Like a goddamned morgue. They used to have so many productions on the lot they had to have the lunch in shifts. Irving's running the studio all right—right into the ground."

It was such a tiresome old record, she tuned it out. Pushing back her chair, she stood. "I promised Victor some pie a la mode."

On the way back to the sound stage, David walked beside her with his hands crammed into his slacks pockets, staring at the asphalt. She chatted blithely about the crew's reaction to the SLA shootout and the recapture of Patty Hearst, hoping he would not follow her inside. She wanted time by herself to run over the monologue. Above the iron door to the stage, the red warning light flashed, indicating filming inside. She fell silent. They stood waiting, she with her back to the sun, holding the Styrofoam container away from her dress. The warning light blinked off. With relief, she reached for the door handle.

"Later," he said and turned away. She watched him move off—the forward thrust of his shoulders indicating he was still in a foul mood.

It was an extremely difficult sequence. Her character had several emotional transitions in a very short period of time. Savannah, a top-flight fashion model, returns to her home base—a stunning New York duplex—to tell her present lover she is leaving him for another man. In the novel, Erik had kept the dialogue to a minimum, concentrating on the tension and the subtext between the two principals. David had chosen—for some unfathomable reason—to have Savannah streak off on a talking jag. To top it off, he'd insisted that Victor film the monologue in one continuous take—nearly three minutes of screentime, an eternity. It also meant she had to be letter perfect with her lines.

The rehearsal had been proceeding fairly smoothly until she saw David standing on the fringes. Now her concentration fragmented and she began to blow lines and miss her marks. Again and again, Victor patiently asked her to start over—from her entrance into the apartment. Again and again, she breezed through the doorway. Her first emotional transition came when she discovered her live-in lover, played by newcomer Avery Daniels, waiting for her in the living room. From then on, it was nonstop movement and jumbled explanation on her part.

The camera followed her everywhere in the large ultramodern set, into the bedroom, the bath, to the kitchen where she poured herself a stiff drink, back into the living room, a return to the bedroom upstairs. There were takes where she would reach the final action, hitting her mark, but forgetting her lines, having to call for help from the script girl. Other times, she would remember her lines, but end up way off the spot where she should have landed in order to be properly lit and in focus. The more she rehearsed, the more scattered she became. Each time she muffed something she threw a little glance in David's direction.

Eventually, after nearly an hour of the torture, Victor called a break and she sank into her canvas-backed director's chair to pore over her lines, her face burning with embarrassment. Victor came to her and eased his hefty frame into a wide, specially constructed chair. "I've requested David to leave but he prefers staying," he began softly. "Would you object if I insisted he leave?"

"Oh, Victor, you're such a mind reader."

His round face smiled benignly. "And you, my dear, have enough to worry about." He paused a long beat. "I've been considering an alternative approach. What do you think of breaking up the scene? Doing it in several set-ups?"

"Victor, that would be heaven sent. Really."

"I'll see if I can convince our illustrious producer hyphen industrious writer." Victor struggled out of the chair and waddled his way to David, who paced on the far side of the sound stage.

Shelby returned to the script, not wanting to be witness to the sticky confrontation. Several moments passed, the subdued buzz and the general milling about of the crew covered any words being exchanged between Victor and David. She glanced up through her lashes. The two were off in a far corner of the sound stage. David's whole posture indicated resistance, he was stiff, woodenlike. Victor, however, was the picture of gentle persuasion—his face animated with good-natured charm, his bulky body surprisingly graceful as he moved about, his arms waving theatrically.

David's voice rose and she caught snatches of his argument, "integrity of the scene," "mandatory," something about "meeting the challenge." Victor persisted, David resisted. The exchange grew in intensity. The entire activity of the sound stage had come to a halt, the crew watching in fascination the unscripted scene playing before them. She found herself on her feet, moving rapidly toward them. David had whirled away, Victor laid a hand on his arm, David shook it off savagely. "We'll do it until she gets it right."

"But is it *so* important to the movement of the scene?" Victor responded. "I can visualize a definite rhythm being built up in a series of successively shorter cuts, underscoring Savannah's inner turmoil. Could be equally, if not *more* effective."

Flushed with concern, she reached them. "Please . . . you two—"

"Stay out of this," David shot at her.

"But is this necessary?" she asked with forced lightness. "Can't one express another opinion around here?"

"I told you to keep out of this."

"David, please, not so loud. Let's move this into my—"

"Goddammit, will you butt out? Go learn your lines for chrissakes. You're stumbling around up there like a ditzy dingbat."

His voice sliced through the sound stage with a caustic acidity. Mortified, she fled to her dressing room, slamming the door. She collapsed face down on the apricot velvet couch. How dare he treat her like that—in front of everyone—like she were a common, little two-bit walk on. She felt like strangling him.

An hour passed. Shelby grew weary of her anger. The tears had long dried up. She remained on the couch in hopes that when summoned she would be discovered prostrate with grief and humiliation. The problem was—no one came for her. The longer she lay there, the more curious she became. She rose, checked her reflection in the mirrors. Her eyes were appropriately red, the makeup smeared effectively, her hair in fetching disarray. She opened the door and stepped out slowly, making a grand show of her professionalism— her willingness to get on with the shoot in spite of what happened. She stopped short.

The large sound stage was empty of people. Only the string of worklights high in the rafters were on. They cast large, gloomy shadows everywhere. In the darkened, two-tier set, under a pool of light, David sat in a chair, his back to her. "David? Where is everybody?"

"I wrapped for the day."

She approached and stood in front of him. "Why?"

"Needed the time to bone up." He spoke without looking up from his script.

"I've been waiting to be called. Why didn't someone inform me?"

He shrugged. "Figured you'd come out when you got bored."

"Well, how thoughtful." She plopped onto the set's couch, crossing her arms and legs. "How'd you resolve your dispute with Victor?"

"Stupid question."

"Was he terribly upset?"

"No more than to be expected."

She eyed his bent head—the dark hair fell over his brow, concealing his features. "David, you're not telling me everything."

He looked up innocently. "I let him go."

"You what?!"

"Released him from his contract."

"Oh, no," she gasped. "How could you?"

"Easy. I told him to take a walk and not come back."

She clutched the cushions beneath her. "I can't . . . believe you'd do something . . . so foolish. So detrimental to both of us."

He slammed his script shut. "Listen, I gave him his chance. All the free rope he wanted. He just hanged himself, that's all."

"But he was doing a beautiful job," she cried.

"He was turning it into a goddamned soap opera."

She could only shake her head, feeling suddenly abandoned, alone, unprotected. "Wha' . . . what about me? We'll never find anyone as good as he was . . . for *me*, David. For *me*!"

"Already have."

She blinked back the salty tears. "Who?"

"Yours truly."

She could not find the strength to voice her shock and dismay.

"Don't look so blown," he said with a boyish grin. "Who knows this project better than me? Who knows your talents better than me? Your weaknesses? How to get the best out of you? I'm the perfect director for this. I should've hired myself from the very start."

"But . . . but you've never directed before . . ."

"Shelby, I've been directing all my life."

She could not look at him anymore and buried her face in her hands. A sob rent from her chest. Disaster hovered over her like a blade of guillotine.

"Hey, don't take this so hard," he said quietly. "Believe me . . . he was all wrong. Too dated. Old-fashioned."

"But I was good . . . dammit, I was really good."

"And you'll continue to be. I'm not going to change your performance that much. You're doing just fine. All I want to do is update the feel. Make it more contemporary. Compatible to the overall tone I've achieved in the script."

She stifled a sob. "It scares me, David. We're too close. I need a director who has some distance, some perspective . . . on who I am and who I'm not."

He frowned. "I know that better than anyone."

"Do you? Honestly?"

"Of course I do," he said and pulled away. "Don't be childish now. We're facing a huge challenge. And we're going to win. *And* have some fun. Aren't we?" His tone indicated he was through mollifying her. And in his expression, she read impatience, vexation. "Aren't we?" he repeated, his tone firming. She brushed the tears from her cheeks and managed a small nod. Piece by piece he was killing her, she knew for a fact.

He patted her shoulder. "The driver's waiting. Don't bother changing. We'll get a new costume tomorrow. Never liked it anyway. You run on home. We'll tackle this thing in the morning. Conquer it."

Like a sleepwalker, she moved outside and down the narrow, alleylike street between the towering, empty sound stages, unaware of the sun's glare on her face. Or the horn honking behind her. Not until the long black limousine pulled around her did she veer to one side.

"Shelby?" a gruff male voice called through an open rear window of the stopped limo. She pulled up and stared unseeingly at the face. It spoke again, "Wanna lift?"

She blinked in delayed recognition. "Oh, Mister Dyer . . . I'm just going to the parking lot."

He threw open his door. "Hop in. Save your pretty legs."

She bent and stepped in, sitting beside him. Irving reached across to slam the door, his arm brushing lightly across her breasts. "Hit it," he said to the chauffeur. The limo pulled slowly ahead, passed the false storefront facades of the Western street and into the European village square. Irving straightened his suit jacket, grinning. "You shouldn't have to walk anywhere, Shelby. If you was my girl, you'd be carried on a satin pillow. Everywhere you wanted to go."

"How sweet," she murmured. Unsuccessfully she tried to find

the button to turn on her charm. "Forgive me . . . I'm a little disoriented."

"Have every right to be. Considering."

"You heard?"

"There's nuthin' on this lot I don't know. Most of the time even before it happens."

"Is it legal? I mean . . . can he do it?"

Irving pulled a thick black cigar from the teak humidor built into the back of the driver's seat. "Any contract can be broken. You going out to the colony?" he asked, studying her through a sudden haze of smoke. She nodded and he tapped the cigar's ash onto the rug. "I'll take you out. We can have us a little chat."

Irving had his chauffeur pause by David's waiting Rolls and driver, long enough to announce the change of plans. She realized she was taking a great risk—David would be furious when he found out. But for some reason, she did not care. Not after what he had done.

"Irving," she began hesitantly, "can I trust you?"

He laughed, a harsh chest rattle that startled her. "Just because David thinks I'm a sonuvabitch doesn't make me one," he said. "In fact, I love the little putz."

"You do?"

He laughed again, this time bitter, sardonic. "I don't *like* him mind you. Never did. But he's still my son. My blood. Till I die. I can't change that."

"That's really . . . admirable."

"Admirable, schmadrable. It's life. So in answer to your previous question . . . yeah, you can trust me. We got that bond you and me. You *do* love my son, don't you?"

"Of course," she replied, somewhat defensive. "Would I put up with all . . . with everything if I didn't?"

He flicked the cigar again. "Now that's an interesting question. I've seen many a girl in this town, put up with a helluva lot—just because she wanted something."

She straightened her spine. "Well, you're partially right. I *do* want something from David. I want a successful picture."

"Don't we all. You, me, the board of Pacific, Shaw in New York. All of us want it, Shelby."

"Well then, are you going to allow him to direct?"

Irving ground his cigar into the ashtray near his elbow and broke the stub in half. "I don't have a damn thing to say on this film."

"What about Dixon Shaw? Will he allow this?"

"Funny you should ask." He reached into a coat pocket and unceremoniously handed over a white Telex copy. Quickly she read it. The message was just one sentence from Shaw: *"He sinks or swims on his own."* Disheartened, she handed it back.

"So you see, Shelby, we all know where we stand, right? On *very* shaky ground."

"I . . . I don't know if . . . if . . ." At once she was crying.

"There, there . . ." Irving's arm pulled her against him. "I know how you must feel. Terrified, right?"

Smelling his mixture of cologne and cigar smoke, she sobbed into his chest, "Isn't there something . . . *anything* you can do?"

"My hands are tied. We'll just have to make the best of this. We'll know soon enough if he's got what it takes."

Reluctantly she forced herself upright. "Do you think he has?"

"Who the hell knows? He's always been full of surprises."

When David returned home later that evening, Shelby was waiting for him in his study, a fire roaring in the fieldstone fireplace. She had bathed, changed into one of her most flattering dressing gowns—a sheer caftan of shimmering, iridescent blue. She was nude underneath. He glared suspiciously from the doorway. She glided to him. "Irving drove me home."

"So I heard."

"He told me Dixon's given you his blessing."

" 'Sink or swim' is a blessing?"

She put her arms around his neck. "How'd you know?"

"A guy in Telex slipped me a copy."

"Well, at least Dixon didn't prohibit you."

"He trusts me."

She kissed him fully on the lips, closing her eyes, rubbing her pelvis into him. When she'd finished the kiss, she clung to him, lying desperately, "So do I, darling . . . So do I . . ."

ERIK
November 1975
Los Angeles

The phone rang. He downed the shot of tequila, closed the new suitcase and answered on the third ring. "Greetings."

"Mo here. Got your message. What's up?"

"Splittin' tomorrow."

"You just sailed in."

"Only to install the new navigation system. The wiring's finished. A few tests tomorrow morning. That's it."

"Where to?"

"Maybe back to Oregon. Or Tahiti. Or Bali. Or Tangiers. Wherever *The Dreamer* takes me."

"Ah, to be rich and famous and footloose."

"Ah," he mimicked, "to be dedicated, disciplined and devoted."

"You drinking again? Listen, I'll buy you one. Pick you up in a half hour." Before he could respond, she'd hung up.

On the front porch of the small Marina guest house, which Erik used as a homebase for his rare visits back to Los Angeles, he sat in the hanging, oak-slat swing, smoking, staring up at the belt of Orion, thinking too much, feeling too much: how his life was drifting away, how he had no emotional anchors anymore, how he couldn't even count on his writing anymore to center him.

A fire-engine red Cadillac convertible, white top up, squealed to a stop at the sidewalk's curb. Erik recognized Mo's car, purchased the day G.M. announced discontinuation of all soft tops. The horn summoned him impatiently.

Tugging on his sports coat, he wavered to it. The passenger door opened and Mo slipped out. She was wearing tight designer jeans, platform wedgies and a bright green blouse tied under her ample bosom, displaying a swatch of tanned stomach. He whistled appreciatively. "Damn, Mo, what's your fountain of youth?"

She handed him an already lit jay. "Fast cars, hot sex and good dope. You ride shotgun." She crawled into the rear and Erik settled into the front, slamming the door and nodding to the youthful driver. From the rear seat, Mo leaned forward between them. "Erik, you remember Griff."

"Sure. How's it goin'?" Erik slapped the upturned palm of the handsome young man with a surfer's build, but an actor's haircut.

"Super. Try that shit, man," Griff said, gunning the car forward.

Erik took a toke, savoring the taste of resin. He shook his head. "I know Michael would dig your changes, Mo. Hey, I got a call from him yesterday. He's back in New York."

She snorted in bitter amusement. "How long have you known about his book?"

Shifting uneasily, he watched the skyline of Westwood approach. "Since he got the contract last August. It's coming out next spring."

She flopped back into the shadows. "I had to read about it in the trades. Did I tell you, Griff? My husband has edited and compiled a whole damned book of interviews with draft resisters and Viet vets."

"Who needs it?" Griff asked, passing the jay to his right.

Erik took a hit and said through held breath, "Michael did. And most likely all of us. One day that whole war will have to be put into some clearer perspective. I'm real proud of Michael."

Mo's voice came from the darkness behind him, sounding very tired, "Me too. God I hope it brings him some peace."

Erik swiveled to Griff. "She taking us any place special?"

"Don't tell him," Mo snapped from the rear seat, her energies revived. "Erik, did you hear what I'm making Pacific fork over for Robby's multi-picture deal?"

"Yes, Mo," he said wearily. "Have you seen Rebecca lately?"

"Last week up at Robby's. Not looking too chipper."

"Meaning?"

"Too thin, peaked. Seems to have lost lots of her old spark. Whatever happened to you two? Thought things were hot and heavy."

"That was finished months ago." He fished for a cigarette in his coat pocket. "You know me, once an ass, always an ass." He took his time lighting it. "She ask after me?"

"Sorry, sweets. Hey, what do you think of these Werner Erhardest Marathons? Griff's trying to talk me into going with him."

Erik made an innocuous comment, not caring if he sounded ill-informed, stoned or just plain dumb. Mo and her young beau began arguing about which of the new TV shows would hit hardest and last longest. Mo put a bet on "Mary Hartman, Mary Hartman," while Griff backed the late night entry, "Saturday Night Live." But Erik was still thinking about Rebecca. Wondering again what it was—or who—he was running away from. And he wondered if his running would ever stop.

Those thoughts were still brewing when he recognized their destination in Beverly Hills. Griff roared the Caddy past the famous iron lion gates. Erik groused, "Mo, what the hell're you up to now?"

"Lord, Erik. Get off the rag. Drop us over there, Griff." As the car headed for the front portico, she tapped Erik, passing over a gold compact mirror with six lines of cocaine already prepared. He took two toots and handed the compact to Griff. Soon Erik and she were out of the car. She leaned in through the open window to kiss Griff tenderly. "Have a blast, honey. My place, after midnight?"

"Ten-four, good buddy," Griff said and with a squeal of rubber, roared the convertible in a circle around the splashing fountain and back down the cobblestone driveway. Sourly, Erik watched the car disappear. "We walking back?"

"Irving's limo, dummy. Com'on." She linked arms and marched him toward the towering front doors. The night air smelled of jasmine and Erik inhaled deeply, steeling himself for whatever else was in the air.

A maid in starched black-and-white ushered them stiffly through the spacious entrance hall and into the mammoth, museumlike, overstuffed living room lit gloomily by a single brass floor torchier. "Mister Dyer will be down shortly," she said solemnly and withdrew.

Erik immediately sprawled onto a couch. "Remember, it's my last night in the fast lane, Mo. Don't bore me."

"Where's your sense of adventure?"

"In my other pair of boots."

"Check out the mantel," she said. Above the man-sized opening, a stone cornice held several gold Oscar statuettes, lined up like toy soldiers. Erik was impressed in spite of himself. "How long has he been divorced from Cara?"

Before she could reply, Irving burst into the room like a man with a mission. Short, much older than Erik's memory of him, yet possessing an internal electricity that instantly charged the room. "Mo," he greeted and turned with no sign of recognition. "Mister Lungren, thanks for coming."

Erik stood to shake hands. "Can't take any credit for that." He waited for any acknowledgment that the movie mogul might have recalled their brief, stormy encounter in Cara Noor's dressing room so many years before.

But Irving was busily pushing a button on an endtable. At the far end of the room, a large screen dropped from the ceiling, covering the French doors. At once, Erik felt he'd been suckered royally.

"What you're gonna see," Irving said dourly, "is my son's film of your book."

"Surprise," Erik mumbled and folded back into the couch.

Mo smiled toothily. "You've been bugging me to see it."

"Not for a long, long while."

"This is only a rough cut," Irving explained. "No opticals. Only a scratch sound track. But you'll get the general idea."

Erik sank lower into the cushions, preparing himself, feeling put upon. The white beam of light cut over their heads. The film began. A color closeup of someone's bare toes. He stared at them in shock. He would have known them anywhere. They were Shelby's—small, somewhat misshapen. He'd always teased her, calling them potato peelings, claiming they were her one imperfection.

What a way to start. A film supposedly about the world's most beautiful woman—beginning like this. Erik slouched further, his chin leaning into a palm, wishing he hadn't taken the hits of coke, for he was wide awake—there was no escaping.

The Rainbow Shuttle turned out to be over two hours of unmitigated boredom, silliness and self-indulgence. Scene after scene fell flat, the dialogue was unrecognizable to him, the plot of his novel had been gutted and reworked atrociously, making the simple love-triangle story almost incomprehensible. There was no drama, no tension, no conflict, no laughs, no style. Shot with artsy-fartsy camera angles and murky shadows, David had turned the light romance into a gothic horror show.

But Shelby was the worst. She moved through the film like a robot—dull, lifeless, awkward. In some sequences she looked so terrified and unsure, Erik could not watch. At other times, she was photographed as if David had purposely set out to deglamorize her. It might have worked if Shelby had the talent or the persona to carry it off. But she was lacking on all counts.

The film dragged tediously to a conclusion, ending with a sequence not from the novel—a scene which documented too graphically an attempted suicide by the supermodel. It was so absurd, Erik found himself laughing derisively as the brass torchier dimmed on again. But the laughter was short lived. It was immediately replaced with a sense of revulsion. And a sense of being violated.

"Unreleasable," Irving condemned and lit a fat cigar.

"Trash," Mo uttered. "Not even classy trash at that."

"Close to ten million down the toilet," Irving added and looked over. "Cat got your tongue?"

Erik straightened on the sofa. "No wonder you're shelving it."

"Big irony here," Irving said and blew a cloud of smoke.

"You're not going to release this abortion?"

Irving stood and began to pace in front of them. "What I'm about to tell you is strictly for us." He stopped in front of Erik, staring down solemnly. "You think New York City is down for the count, ready to default on loans? Well, believe me, Pacific is even more fucked. We need this product out. We've signed contracts with distributors. This film was to be our major Christmas release. I can get us out of that. Stall. Three, four months maybe. Beyond that?"

Again Irving paused, a small picture of dejection. "Not to mention our stockholders. We just wrapped our fall meeting. I was able to hold them off. Next spring, who knows? They could crucify me. What to do? The million-dollar question."

Mo leaned forward eagerly. "Obviously you have no choice—like you said—you *must* release this film to recoup some of your investment.''

"And be met by ridicule," Erik muttered. "And ignominious defeat.''

"Not if we can fix it," Irving said, with a strong burst of enthusiasm. "Any suggestions, Erik?''

"Shelve it or start over.''

"You could cut Shelby out completely," Mo cracked. "Release it as a short.''

Irving was not pleased. "Yeah, Shelby's scenes have to be whacked down. But then you'd have to replace them with new footage. That we could do. But what with?''

Mo slid to the edge of her seat. "How about devising a whole new story to be intercut with the old?'' Her voice was tinged with excitement, as if she were getting off on the challenge.

Irving stared at the lit end of his cigar. "But that wouldn't be kosher would it. The public—can't forget them. The novel's such a monster you'd be tampering with a modern classic. Could backfire.''

Mo stood, all energy. "So you keep enough of the old to satisfy those that read the book. But develop one of the subplots. From the novel. Like Savannah's sister? The ugly duckling story. That's always surefire. It's only a minor thread in the book, but it could add a whole new dimension to the plot. The trials and tribulations of Plain-Jane sister living in the shadow of the glamorous Savannah. I love it!''

"Me too," Irving said energetically. "What do you say, Erik?''

Erik downed his brandy. "I think I've been set up.'' They both looked shocked. Erik set the glass on the coffee table with deliberation. "You want me to dream up a new story to film. To bastardize my own novel.''

"Naturally I'd like your input," Irving answered evasively.

Mo shot a gleaming grin. "After all, sweets, it is *your* novel we're trying to save.''

"Well, don't," Erik growled. "For god's sake, let it die its own death.'' He lumbered to his feet. "I'd like to go home now.''

"Hold on, can'cha?" Irving asked. "I'm prepared to offer you anything—understand? If you help us out.''

"There's nothing I want from you. Or need, for that matter."

"How 'bout your reputation?" Mo asked. "Your name's on this piece of crap."

"First thing in the morning, I'll request my lawyer to begin proceedings to have it removed." He started for the door. "Where can I call a cab?"

"My car's available," Irving rushed to say. "But I sure as hell wish you'd let me finish."

"Sorry, Irving, but I've heard enough. Good luck and good night."

"Name your price."

Erik turned to him slowly. "Two years ago you could have had me for the price of a shoeshine. Now . . . I can easily say, fuck off."

"I'll double your points. Triple them. Make you executive producer. I'll even option your next three books sight unseen. Set you up in your own production company. No writer's ever had that."

Mo sidled forward, her round face flushed with the excitement of a sell. "Think of it, Erik. The once-in-a-lifetime chance to improve on your own novel. You could make something successful out of what you feel is a failure. It's a golden opportunity."

Erik smiled. "You two are quite a team. Should be in business together. Or are you already? You coming Mo?" He stepped into the hall, feeling like he'd flown over the cuckoo's nest.

In the rear seat of Irving's limousine, heading out to the marina, Mo electronically rolled up the window cutting off the chauffeur and continued her pitch. "Look, Erik, I'll level with you, okay?"

"A refreshing change."

"Be snide, be sarcastic, but Lord, don't be dumb. He's prepared to offer you the moon, sweets. You could write your own ticket."

"What's in this for you? Surely just not an agent's commission."

She tapped out a Gauloise and took her time lighting it. "Irving's offered me something I've wanted since hitting this town. A studio position: vice president of Creative Affairs."

"Sorry I can't be a steppingstone for your career."

"Okay," she sighed. "I deserved that. I'm not laying my goals off on you. What I'd like to lay on you is an opportunity for real power, Erik."

"Power?" The thought amused him.

"That's the name of the game, kiddo. Power. Who's got it. Who calls the shots. Who has final cut."

"What's this got to do with me?"

"Don't you see? Dyer is prepared to offer you a shot at it. If you play ball, you have it made. You could make a film of even *Hidden Assets*—your pet, right?"

He blew out a tired lungful of air. "I'll stick to writing. Hollywood doesn't turn me on. Power never has."

"Don't feed me that. Everyone gets off on power. You just haven't tasted enough of it. Once you nibble it, it's addictive."

"So I see."

"Sure, I get off on it. And dammit, Erik, this is my chance. Yours too. What would it take to come up with a new story for this film? Three weeks? A month?"

"It's not the time. It's the wasted energy. I don't want a damn thing to do with it." He stared out his window at the unseen horizon.

"Not even to save Shelby?"

The question caught him off-guard.

"Yes, Shelby," she said. "She's washed up if this film is released as is. If you thought she had it rough after *A Woman Alone*, you ain't seen nuthin' yet. She'll be lucky to get a pantyhose commercial."

He ground out his cigarette angrily. "That's her concern."

"You don't mean that, you know you don't."

"I don't? Hell, she's still with that asshole Rau." He was surprised at his vehemence. Its residue embarrassed him.

Mo studied him with a bemused expression. "Isn't it odd how we give ourselves away when we least want to?"

He cranked down his window, seeking some fresh air. He leaned into the stiff breeze, longing to be at sea again on *The Dreamer*. "I don't want anything to do with your scam," he said, exhausted. "Let it be, Mo."

He couldn't sleep. Couldn't turn off his mind. It raced in high gear, going around and around, over the same ground, until he knew the whole damned course by heart. But he couldn't get off the track.

Around three A.M., a knock on the backdoor brought him to a

sitting position. It came again, more insistent. He scrambled up and into a pair of jean cutoffs. Slapping barefoot through the kitchen, he unlocked the rear door of the beach house and opened it.

Shelby stumbled into his arms, reeking of booze. "Evenin', sugar," she slurred and kissed him wetly on the lips. She tasted of champagne, fruity and dry. She clung to him, pressing her breasts into his naked chest, then pulled away, waving a bottle he'd not noticed. "Grab a glass 'n join me."

"Looks like you've a head start." He tugged her inside and shut the door, switching on the overhead light.

She grimaced at the brightness, flopping a hand in the air for him to turn it off. "More fun in the dark."

"Is that the agenda? Fun and games?"

"Sure. Why the hell not? No one likes to have fun anymore." She wavered to the table, unaware of the dribbling champagne. It left a frothy trail behind her. Leaning on the table, she turned, pouting. "*S'il vous plaît, la lampe.*" He snapped it off. "*Merci,*" she murmured.

It was just as well he could not see her plainly. She did not look her best. Dressed in unpressed tailored slacks and a buttoned closed, red cardigan sweater, she looked like she'd been hitting the bottle all day. Puffy-eyed, her hair pulled back into a sloppy ponytail, she was giggling. "Bet you're surprised to see me, aren't you, sugar?"

"To put it mildly."

"Well, I kind of surprised myself, I did, I did." By the reflected light from the alley, he could see her. She was guzzling straight from the bottle. Lowering it, she hiccuped loudly. "Pardon my weak emotions, as Evangeline used to say." She giggled again before asking coyly, "What're y'all doing way over there? Can hardly make you out."

"I can't make you out either. Even in the light."

"Oh, oh, he's turning heavy on me. I better sit down. I don't think I'm ready for this." She plopped into a chair and banged the bottle on the table setting it down. "Don'cha wanta little bubbly?"

"Haven't you had enough for one night?"

"I'm not as drunk as I . . . as *you* think I am. *And* . . . I'm not as drunk as *you* used to get."

Suddenly she was sobbing, great gushes of sounds erupting from her. He pressed his back against the cool plaster wall. Her crying intensified. He took it as long as he could. Then, with two long strides, he was beside her, kneeling, his arms around her. She buried her face into his shoulder. "I'm ruined, ruined," she moaned, her tears wetting his skin. "I'll never work in this town . . . ever again."

"Of course you will."

"Don't!" She tried to push him away. "Don't! Don't baby me!" She managed to hold him at arm's length. "You think I'm just drunk. But I'm not too drunk to know. I tell you—I'm finished. It's the end of me."

"Shelby . . ."

"David's thrown me out."

His hand froze above her back.

Her head bobbed up. "It's true," she wailed. "He blames *me* for the film being yanked away by Shaw and Irving. Said it's all my fault that he can't finish it the way he wanted. That I wasn't even pretty anymore. Such awful . . . awful things. Just suddenly started attacking me. Calling me all sorts of despicable—" Her face contorted, twisted with pain. "He vowed . . . came right out and *vowed* that I'd never work in films again. That he'd tell everyone that I was unprofessional. Caused delays. Temperamental. Made extreme demands. He . . . he . . ." She collapsed over the back of the chair, sobbing, "Oh, Erik, what am I going to do?"

He watched her shoulders undulating under the thin wool of her sweater. He'd been set up once that evening. He didn't want to be a sucker twice. He took the bottle to the sink and poured out the remainder. When he turned, she was eyeing him over her shoulder. "I want you to make love to me," she whispered.

"Only make matters worse."

"Not for me."

"For me."

"I need you now."

"Only after David kicked you out?"

"Please, sugar . . ."

"So you come running to me. Good old Erik. Always there."

"Don't . . . don't say that . . . not that way . . ."

"I'll tell you what I'm feeling, Shelby. This has happened once too often. I'm damned tired of it."

"But . . . but don't you love me anymore?"

"Oh, god, Shelby . . . I wish it were that simple."

"Then you do . . . you still do."

He ran a hand through his hair, massaging the scalp roughly. "I don't know anymore . . . honest to god, I don't."

"Y'all don't want to help me?" she asked, her voice breathless. "How? Tell me how?"

She held his eyes. "Save the film for Irving."

The implication of her statement sank into his chest like a block of granite. "Did *he* send you here?"

"Of course not, don't be silly."

"Then it was Mo, wasn't it?"

"No."

"She's the only other person who knew. It had to be her."

"*All right*," she yelled. "What of it?" She softened, a pouty smile blurring her lips. "Y'all asked how you could help? I told you. Please . . . save that turkey from the trash heap. For all of us."

"Didn't Mo tell you? I don't give a damn what happens to it."

She glided to her feet, coming to him seductively. "Don't y'all care what happens to me?"

"Of course I do. That's why I sold you the film rights to begin with. But now it's just . . ."

"Just what?" She toyed with the top button of her sweater. "Shelby . . ."

She began unbuttoning the front, looking down at her hands. "Everytime I wear red now, I think of that Squeaky Fromme, you know, the lady in red who shot at Ford?" She opened her sweater, thrusting her bare breasts into the skin of his chest. "Am I your lady in red?"

Taking her shoulders, he held her off. "Don't do this, please."

She began toying with the top buttons of his cutoffs. "Won't y'all save the film for me? Please . . . pretty please." She ground her pelvis against him. "Y'all're my only hope."

"How 'bout Irving? He likes blondes."

Her head reared back, eyes narrowing. "That's disgusting."

"Sorry. It's been a long day."

"I don't understand you anymore, sugar," she said coldly. "Honest to god I don't." She whirled away, heading for the door, hastily buttoning up.

"Where're you going?"

"Someplace where I'm wanted." She tore open the door.

"Babe—"

"I hate that!" she screamed. "I'm *not* a babe—I can take care of myself." She lurched outside. "I don't need any of you."

He loped after her. "Shelby, wait!"

Not answering, she ran, disappearing behind the garage. The pavement was cold on his bare feet. "Shelby, please . . . don't leave like this." He rounded the garage corner. "Shelby!"

She roared the engine to life. It was a new Bentley. The white car shot forward up the alley, gravel spinning under its wheels. Helplessly, he watched it career away, striking a garbage can, overturning it with a horrendous clatter of metal. The large auto straightened in time to swing widely around the corner out of sight. He listened to the engine shift, whining into the night.

His shoulders and back were cold, exposed to the ocean's night air. He turned, started for his house. His steps were slow, measured, each hammering home his confusion. There did not seem to be a way out of it—no matter which way he chose. He was damned if he did, damned if he didn't—if he began, he would detest each moment; if he walked away, he would be opening himself up for more self-derision.

With a whole new set of concerns, he slouched into the house.

DAVID
December 1975
Los Angeles

"You wouldn't believe this guy at Stanford," Robert Loggins said to the assembled coterie around the dining-room table before the beach windows. He was speaking about David, who listened with a bemused, tolerant expression. "My freshman year," Loggins continued energetically, "we're in the same dorm, right? Most of us rinky-dinks couldn't afford a bicycle, right? And David here, shows up driving a brand new Stingray. He was always blowing our mind with some bitchin' rat fuck."

David's lawyer, Ian, spoke up, "Hasn't changed, has he? What's that new song called, 'Still Crazy After All These Years'?"

The tableful of men laughed. But not David. He had risen to retrieve the morning papers off the buffet. He figured he'd let them enjoy themselves, help solidify the recently formed corporation before getting down to business. He turned to the stock page, thinking that Loggins himself hadn't changed. A superficial jock then and still was—beefy, bovine and blustery. The only difference now was that Robert Loggins was worth hundreds of millions, head of a vast real-estate empire, responsible for over half the new shopping malls in southern California plus Nevada and New Mexico. However, if David hadn't needed Loggins's extra financial clout, he wouldn't have had a cup of coffee with the ex-frat jock, let alone invited Loggins into his Malibu home.

David glanced up from the paper to the half-dozen top flight lawyers and investment counselors. "Pacific lost another full point."

"What's it at now?" Loggins asked, instantly serious, as though teeing off for a championship golf match.

"Eleven-four," Loggins's lawyer furnished. "At this rate, we could wrap it all up by February."

"And I'll have me a movie studio," Loggins gloated.

"Correction," David said. "*We'll* have *us* a movie studio."

"Sure thing . . . partner." Loggins winked.

David managed a smile. Once Pacific was firmly in their hands, Loggins would find himself relegated to one step above a "yes" man. David turned to his main advisor. "Any further info on AII?"

"The street says," Ian began, "that Shaw plans on dumping their shares just prior to the July stockholders' meeting."

"And we'll grab enough to lock up controlling interest," Loggins said, then tossed around a triumphant glance. "Bitchin'."

Half-listening, David turned his attention to the morning trade papers. As the entire stock-buying take-over plan had been his conception, he knew precisely where every major chunk of Pacific stock lay. AII controlled the largest block with thirty-one percent. The rest was owned by private stockholders. David, himself, had inherited, through his mother's trust fund, three and a half percent. Already he personally had spent close to five million of his own resources to garner another five percent. Since the month-old partnership with Loggins, an additional eleven percent had been purchased in open-market S.E.C. approved purchases. His plan was to control thirty by the time AII dumped their shares, making it virtually impossible for anyone but himself to wrestle control away from Irving and the Pacific boys.

He turned the page of *Variety* and scanned the headlines. One caught his eye and he bolted into his study, closed the doors, dialed a number and stood, waiting, twisting the phone cord. "Good morning," answered the secretary. "Olson's Detective Agency."

"David Rau here. Put on Owen," he ordered and took a felt-tip pen, circling the article in bold red.

"Morning, David," came Olson's crisp voice.

"Where the hell is she?"

"I assume you're referring to Miss Cale?"

"You prick, she's in town."

There was a slight pause on the other end. "My sources clearly indicate that she left town in November for New—"

"Fuck your sources. Read today's goddamn *Variety*."

"I have it on my desk, but I haven't had—"

"Page two, third column," David snapped and began reading, " 'CALE INKS DYER'S REMAKE—The Engle Agency announced today that Shelby Cale has been signed by Irving R. Dyer, president of Pacific, to star in the studio's revamping of *The Rainbow Shuttle*. Miss Cale said over lunch at Scandia that she is looking forward to working with Dyer, who will be personally overseeing the new sequences.' " David slapped the paper onto his desk. "You hear that? Scandia. She's back in town."

"Not necessarily."

"You idiot, you think she would fly in for a two-sentence blurb?

For three fuckin' weeks all I've gotten are padded expense accounts and crybaby excuses.''

"Perhaps someone at the Engle Agency would know."

"If you don't deliver where Shelby is by five today, you're canned." David slammed down the receiver.

Near the top of Topanga Canyon, just before it intersected Mulholland Drive, a gravel road veered sharply to the right. David pulled his Rolls into it, doused the lights, drove slowly around the bend and parked where Olson had suggested—at the foot of the first driveway. He eased out of the car and stood staring up the hill toward the small, shake-shingled house nestled in the trees.

The night sky was dark, high clouds blotted out the stars. In the distance, a dog barked. He tensed. He'd forgotten to ask if Shelby had a guard dog. He moved forward, cautiously making his way up the drive. In front of the closed garage, a familiar-looking Porsche convertible was parked. He tried recalling where he'd seen it before. He knew it wasn't Lungren's. He wondered if Shelby had sold her Bentley.

No lights were on inside the house, but a bright flood illuminated the front walk. He skirted the light and darted toward the entrance around back. Olson had drawn a floor plan and provided him with a set of master keys, one of which was guaranteed to unlock the backdoor. The fifth one did the trick.

Silently he stepped inside, leaving the door ajar. He remained stationary until his eyes became accustomed to the darkness. Her bedroom lay just off the back hall, beyond the kitchen. Trailing a hand along the wall, he tiptoed forward, seeking the doorway. Once he found it, the going was easier—the hallway carpeted in thick shag. The first door would be the bath, the second hers. It was closed. He leaned into it, listening.

A soft murmur of voices, followed by the unmistakable trill of her laughter. She had someone in there. His jealousy rocketed. With a lunge, he burst open the door. She screamed in fright. His hand found the wall switch and he flicked on the overhead light.

Shelby squealed again, covering her nudity with a sheet. Sprawled naked next to her was that pretty-boy caterer, Henry Mawson, the one David had caught her messing around with the day of her aborted party. The color was draining fast from the guy's overly tanned face.

"David!" she gasped. "What the hell're—"

"Get the fuck out," he shouted at her bedmate.

"Now listen here," the jerk began, making an effort to control his astonishment. "This is—"

"Out you shithead," David growled and took a threatening step.

With a leap, Mawson was off the bed, groping on the floor for his clothes. She rolled toward him, pleading, "Don't go, Henry. He's only bluffing."

"Like hell I am," David snarled in his best Bogie voice. He stepped aside, freeing the doorway.

Mawson grabbed his shoes and holding the bunch of clothes close to his crotch, edged toward the door. "I'll call the cops, Shelby. From the station at—"

"Won't be necessary," she interrupted. "David's harmless as an ol' flea. And just about as irritating."

The caterer nodded in relief and darted out of the room. David could not help but smile as the guy's naked butt disappeared down the hall. But Shelby was glaring. She twitched at the sound of the front door banging shut and then reached, overly casual, for a cigarette. She steadied her hands to light it. Outside the Porsche roared to life and backed down the drive. Her icy facade did not crack.

David lowered himself into an armchair near the foot of the bed, trying to control his anger, the feeling of betrayal. She pushed up against the whitewood headboard and blew smoke in his direction. "What do you want now?" Her tone was weary but cautious.

"Why the fuck did you doublecross me?"

"Me? Doublecross you?" She attempted a burst of hard laughter. "*That's* the joke of the year."

"Signing on for this illegal version of *my* film."

"What's illegal about it? You don't deliver, they take it away. Happens all the time."

"I've slapped an injunction. Irving can't touch my film."

"*Half* of it's mine. Besides the courts haven't ruled yet. Irving told me there's no precedent in your favor. He has the right to—"

David broke in with a roar, "Irving doesn't know crap! Come July, he'll be damned lucky to hang onto his old-age pension."

She rearranged the covers over her, drawing up her knees as a barrier between them. "You're so full of bullshit, David. Bullshit, bile and hatred. Isn't there anything—one little thing you love that's living? Besides yourself?"

"I love you."

"Ha! You don't know the first thing about love." In spite of her vehement tone, he could tell she was pleased—a special glint highlighted her eyes.

He decided to pursue that same line for a while. "I may have a hard time showing them, but my feelings are there for you. Strong ones."

"Such as?"

"Wanting to protect you . . ."

"From what? The only protection I need is from being in one of your turkeys."

He bristled. "My *Rainbow Shuttle* would have established you as a major star—if Irving hadn't been so goddamned anxious to screw me."

"It's always someone else. The last time I saw you, you were screaming your head off that it was *my* fault."

He shrugged dejectedly. "I was upset. Thought Dixon would back me. I was pissed he didn't give me a chance to finish my cut of the film—to prove that my conception was valid."

"It's a turkey, David," she muttered and stubbed out her cigarette in the ashtray on the night table. "I was mortified by my performance." Her lower lip began to quiver. "I might have been really good if you'd kept on Victor Craig. You can't direct, David. Certainly not me."

"What the hell do you know about films? If it hadn't been for me, you'd be lucky now to be doing handshots for Villa Caesari."

"Meaning what?" she challenged. "That I've lost my looks, is that what you're saying? Because if it is, you're blind. I can get any man I put my mind to."

"Like the pansy food-pusher that just ran out on you? Some conquest. Every housewife in Beverly Hills has sampled *his* wares."

She snatched up the ashtray and hurled it at him. Cigarette butts and ash sprayed the bed, the heavy pottery missing him by a yard. It fell to the carpet harmlessly. He laughed—which made her turn pink with rage. "I'll tell you what still finds me beautiful," she sputtered. "*Erik*—that's who."

"Then why the hell isn't he in here?"

"He's not even in town. He's off writing somewhere. Trying the impossible. To save the pile of drek you call a film."

David blinked in surprise and his gaze hardened. "Lungren's rewriting *my* film?"

"Listen to yourself. You are sick, David, *sick!*"

"If we stuck together, against Irving, we'd win."

"Win what, for god's sakes?" Her voice cracked with emotion.

His voice grew even quieter. "I want you to come back, Shelby. Back home where you belong."

"Not after you said those hateful things. I could never forgive you. I'll never come back."

"Even if I told you how sorry I was?"

"You never said 'I'm sorry' once. Not since I've been with you."

"I'm telling you now. I've been looking for you ever since that night. To tell you. I'm sorry you believed those things. They were harsh, uncalled for . . . I . . . I guess I was crying out for some help." He lowered his eyes, as though he could hardly admit his failure. "I . . . I need you, Shelby. *You* need me . . ."

He heard the bed coverings rustle and when he looked up, her eyes were watering with tears, but in one hand, she held a snub-nosed revolver. It pointed directly at him. "I want you to leave," she said in a quaky voice.

"Shelby, where in the hell'd you get that?"

"I bought it. For protection. And I know how to use it too. I've taken lessons and everything."

"I don't believe this."

"I just want to be left alone." Tears moistened her sculptured cheekbones. Her lower lip trembled. "I'm so sick and tired of men trying to make me over . . . into something they wanted. First there was Caesari, then Erik—then you. Trying to mold me. Change me. I got so confused I didn't know who the hell I was. Well, I'm damned tired of being used. I want to be me. Just *me*!" Her voice broke and she sobbed, her gun hand sagging.

He jumped to his feet, lunging for the revolver. She snapped it up, inches from his chest, freezing him. He heard the *click* as she cocked it. There was a look of such grim determination, he backed away slowly. "Shelby . . . you'll never find anyone as good for you as I am."

"From now on, I'm doing what *I* want," she cried. "Now go on. Just leave me alone, will you? *Will you*?!"

He wavered indecisively, his fury mounting. "You and me . . . we're a good team."

"I'm my own team now!" She swung the gun toward the door, pointing. "Leave me alone, David . . . please . . ."

"After all I've done for you—"

"*I want you out of my life!* Do I have to kill you?"

"You'll be sorry, Shelby," he warned hoarsely and stepped into the hall. He stood in the darkness out of her line of vision. "When I win," he said, his voice choking with rage, "you'll come crawling back to me. See if you don't."

On his way out, he slammed the front door so hard it sounded like a gunshot.

REBECCA
January 1976
Los Angeles

She knelt before the shining, upturned faces. "Okay, gang, who wants to be the Beast?" Instantly several boys raised their hands, clamoring for her attention. "How about you, Mary?" Rebecca asked. The shy little girl smirked and said, "Beasts are for boys." Giggles erupted.

"Not always," Rebecca said and stood, moving to the covered windows. "Girls can be Beasts or anything they want to be. Especially when they grow up into women. It's their choice." She pulled open the sky blue, burlap drapes. The small storefront space flooded with buttery sunshine. "Let's try reversing the roles. Charlie, how about you being the Beauty?"

The boy shrank in embarrassment, crumbling further under the barrage of kidding and jeers from the other boys. Quieting them, Rebecca was just launching into a spirited definition of the word "stereotype" when Sara Jane, guitar in hand, stepped in from the music class room. "You gotta call, Becky."

"Can you take a message?"

"It's your agent," Sara Jane replied and jerked her curly head meaningfully, indicating "get your butt in there and answer it."

Rebecca turned to the semicircle of youngsters. "I'll be right back. Why don't you try the processional again?" She passed Sara Jane, who winked and whispered, "I'll keep an eye on the lil' mothers."

Rebecca dashed into the cramped rear office of the Raindance Academy of Drama and Music—a two-month-old school of the performing arts for children which Rebecca had established in partnership with Sara Jane. Their school was just two storefront rooms on a side street not far from the Venice beach and their combined student body numbered only twenty-two but for Rebecca the project had been a godsend, reinvolving her in life, giving her an outlet and a renewed sense of purpose after a particularly bleak period. But it had all started getting better the moment Sara Jane had waltzed back into her life. That had been the real beginning of the Raindance Academy, which Rebecca always joked should be subtitled, "For Survivors and Other Oddities."

Totaling a stack of utility bills, she waited for her agent to be put on. When he answered, she jumped right in, "Hi, Charlie, I got a class waiting. Is this about that commercial callback? I just don't think I'm a disco-dancer type, so—''

Her agent broke in, ''Do you know Irving R. Dyer?''

''Oh yeah, sure, we're real close. I call him Irv, he calls me Becks. But we've really never met, why'd you ask?''

''Well someone at Pacific knows you. Dyer's office called and wants you to audition tomorrow morning at ten.''

''For a movie?''

''The infamous remake of *The Rainbow Shuttle*.''

Rebecca sank to the chair, sitting on a pile of printed leaflets advertising the new school. Her agent's voice broke in, ''Rebecca? You there?''

''Yeah . . . sure . . .''

''They want to messenger a script right away. You want it delivered to the school?''

''Ahh . . . listen, Charlie, is David Rau still producing that film? Because if he's got *anything* to do with it, I pass.''

''From what I hear, he's out,'' Charlie said, then added sharply, ''But even if he's not, you're in no position to take that attitude.''

She hesitated a moment but when she spoke it was firm, committed. ''Charlie, I appreciate your opinion but I will never work for that man. So check it out thoroughly, okay? If he's out of the picture totally, tell them I'd be happy to read their script. And if the part's right for me, I'll audition.''

''Gee, that's mighty big of you.''

''I try to stand tall, Charlie.''

When the messenger arrived, Rebecca set the package aside, unopened. She finished her last mime class of the day and leaving Sara Jane to close up the studio, ran with the studio package to their nearby apartment. She had been sharing the space with her old friend ever since the previous Thanksgiving when Sara Jane had showed up on the doorstep with her guitar and healthy disposition. Curled on the couch, she finished Erik's new screen version of his novel. She had liked his first version but this script she dearly loved. It was even more satisfying than his book. And Erik had taken Savannah's non-glamorous sister, Summer, and had told the story from her point of view. Now the meteoric rise of the supermodel, her many love affairs, her dazzling but empty life was all the more moving because it was juxtaposed with the meaningful existence of the loving, younger sister, Summer. Erik had meshed the two stories seamlessly, integrating new, vivid scenes with already existing ones from Rau's movie version. What touched Rebecca most, however, was that by the end of the story, it was Summer who was the stronger, the more real, the more beautiful because of her inner strength. So moved by Summer's transformation, Rebecca was still worked up emotionally when Sara Jane strolled in, commenting at the sight of her, "The script that bad?"

"It's beautiful," Rebecca said, wiping her eyes. "And a part I can act the hell out of. Will you run lines with me later?"

"Happy to oblige. Can I help now?"

"No thanks. Have to learn these two scenes first." Rebecca retired to the bedroom, pored over the script—rereading it several times to get a surer feel for the character, noting some odd similarities about the shy, insecure Summer and herself. It was as though Erik had borrowed several of her own problems of identity. She wondered how intentional that had been and decided it was just an example of how a writer culled from his own range of experience. But still, she could not help thinking about him and that he had written the very words she was trying to memorize.

By eight that evening, Rebecca was running lines with Sara Jane. At one point, Sara Jane lowered the script and looked up over her glasses. "Gawd, if this here girl don' sound jus' like the ol' Rebecca."

Rebecca replied "in character" with a faint Southern accent, "Why, do y'all mean to compare me to that mealy-mouth, gutless wonder?"

Sara Jane laughed merrily. "Not anymore, chil', not anymore. An' thank the Lord for that."

"And his special emissaries," Rebecca said, squeezing Sara Jane's hand.

By eight-thirty the next morning, Rebecca had carefully dressed in character, an unflattering, brown shift under a baggy cardigan sweater, her hair pulled back into a tidy ponytail and her face free of makeup. She gulped a swallow of hot coffee, grabbed the script and blew Sara Jane a kiss. "Tell me to break a leg."

"What? Won't do no such thing."

"An old theatrical custom, darling. Means, good luck. But wishing good luck is bad luck so just wish me a broken leg."

"An' I thought rock 'n' rollers was crazy. So break a leg, will you? But how about just a simple fracture?"

Driving east on the Santa Monica freeway, Rebecca fell to thinking again of Erik. She wished he were still in town so she could drop him a note, telling him how much she loved his new script. But according to Mo, he'd left before Christmas, sailing *The Dreamer* through the Panama Canal toward the Caribbean, and points unknown.

She forced her mind into more placid waters and soon was trying to think up ways to increase the enrollment of the school. Twenty-two kids at five bucks a week was barely meeting expenses. By the time she approached the dusty pink stucco gates of Pacific Studios, she had thought of raffling off a free tuition scholarship at a buck a ticket.

Presenting herself on the executive floor to the receptionist behind a black marble desk, Rebecca was told to wait with the others. She took a seat on a maroon leather couch and eyed the half-dozen actresses nervously waiting their turn at bat. Several she recognized from previous auditions, but each was so wrapped up in her own anxiety, little was said between them.

Shortly after ten, her name was called and she was ushered into Irving R. Dyer's spacious office, the walls full of framed photos of some of her favorite stars. The mogul, himself, came forward—a short, bald, energetic-looking man with a magnetic smile. "Miss Rebecca Warren, a pleasure."

"Oh, excuse me, Mister Dyer, I know this is kind of silly at a time like this but I've . . . changed my name."

"Common enough," he said pleasantly. "What's the new handle?"

"My real one. Rebecca Parlato."

"Well, at least it ain't Carrie Snodgrass."

She laughed nervously with him, trying to find something that reminded her of David. There was nothing, except they were both short and possessed a similar high-strung energy. He waved a small hand to the corner where some video equipment was set up—a camera on a tripod, a recorder pack and a TV monitor. "We're auditioning on tape? Mind?"

"Never done it that way, but I'm game to grow."

He said he liked that attitude and introduced her to a buxom actress who was to read the other lines of dialogue. Rebecca was placed in a chair in front of the TV camera. He went behind his massive desk and sat, signaling the cameraman to hit the lights and roll. Irving began by asking a few personal questions, where she was from, how long she'd been acting, what some of her favorite roles were. She didn't have time to think so responded with straightforward answers, trying to muster as much animation as she could under the circumstances.

He asked if she were ready to begin. She closed her eyes briefly, concentrating on the internal core of the character, conjuring up the mental image of a lost puppy. Her body concaved, her head drooping lower, her shoulders rounding. She opened her eyes, nodding shyly that she was prepared. The first scene began.

Her audition took less than ten minutes. Before she knew it, she was being thanked by Dyer in a professionally polite manner and shown to the door. She walked through the maroon and gray waiting room, slightly stunned by the suddenness of it all. Barely conscious of the waiting actresses, she stepped out into the hallway and ducked into the nearest ladies' room.

Just opposite the door, by the sinks, a well-dressed young woman was hugging herself, sobbing uncontrollably. When Rebecca asked what was wrong, if there was something she could do to help, the young woman tearfully tried to pull herself together, crying, "I can't go in there. Audition for the head of a studio? I must be crazy."

Rebecca put her arm around the girl's shoulders, leading her to the sink. "I hear you, I hear you. Well, the first thing we have to do is wash that pretty face of yours. Too much makeup anyway. You're reading for Summer, right? I thought so. Well, listen, what's your name? Mine's Rebecca."

"Jill," the girl sniffled, looking even more confused.

Rebecca soaked a paper towel in cold water and began wiping Jill's running nose, talking all the while, "Well, listen, Jill, could I give you a little advice? Just from the point of view of one who has been doing this crazy old dance for over ten years."

"You mean auditioning?" Jill asked with a sniffle.

"This whole crazy dance we actresses have to go through. I used to fight it like crazy. Made myself miserable. Now I accept it for what it is. An opportunity to show my stuff. I do the best I can at the time. That's all. The rest is out of my hands. Like a dear friend told me, just before I left this morning, she said—worry is interest paid on the future before it's due. Isn't that terrific?"

Jill stopped scrubbing her face and tears clouded her eyes again. "But I want this part so bad. I'll die, honest to God I will, I'll just curl up and die if I don't get it."

"I used to think that too," Rebecca said. "But now, I try to keep it separate. How I'm doing in my career is not how I'm doing as a person."

Jill pulled away, her eyes narrowing suspiciously. "So you probably have a heavy romance to fall back on. Or piles of money."

Rebecca laughed softly. "Jill, it's just finding the balance between passion and persistence. And not be dazzled by the bright lights. You're going to do just fine."

The telephone call came to her apartment early the next morning. Her agent was beside himself, "It's yours, sweetheart. It's yours! They loved you. Dyer himself called. You start Monday. Congratulations!"

She began to scream.

Sara Jane had to wrestle the receiver away from her to hang up. Wild with uncontained joy, Rebecca grabbed her and danced her around and around the room. Both of them shrieking at the top of their lungs.

That very night, David Rau showed up at her door.

Sara Jane had left earlier to join a jam session of women musicians in a loft in Playa del Rey and Rebecca was alone diligently studying her lines. The radio was playing, Paul Simon singing softly "Fifty Ways to Leave Your Lover" when the door buzzer sounded. Thinking it might be Sara Jane who'd come back early without her key, Rebecca threw open the door. At the sight of him, her knees turned to liquid.

"May I come in?" David asked with a friendly smile.

"Why?"

"I'd like to talk with you."

"I haven't anything to say to you. Good-bye." She started to close the door.

He put out a hand, stopping it. "Please . . . ?"

"Look, David, I don't want anything to do with you. So get lost, okay? Before I get angry."

Casually he removed his hand from the door. "It'll be worth your while. I promise."

Warily she eyed him. There was something about his manner that gave her pause. It was boyish, ingratiating, low-keyed—none of the hypertension she so keenly remembered. Wearing a soft tan sports coat which looked like cashmere, over a hemp-colored silk shirt, he reeked of cologne and smiled as though they were old friends. She didn't trust him worth spit.

He must have read her leeriness for he stepped back. "May I buy you a drink somewhere?"

"No."

"A walk on the beach? A beautiful night out . . ."

"I'm working."

"On your new role?"

She hesitated, fighting to get a grip on her emotions. "So you heard?"

He shrugged easily. "Small town."

"Too small. Good night."

This time he caught the closing door with both hands and shoved it wider, slipping through into the living room. She whirled to him, venting some of her anger. "Get out, David. You're not welcome here."

"Hey, is that any way to—"

"I *mean* it," she blazed and threw wide the door, pointing to the outside hall. "I'm warning you, I'll call the cops."

He sauntered to the couch to sit. "Won't take five minutes."

"Damned right, it won't." She sped to the telephone.

"I wouldn't do that."

Facing him, she lifted the receiver and dialed the operator. It began to ring.

"I'll be gone before they get here."

"Terrific," she muttered, not taking her eyes off him. The line was still ringing.

"What've you got against me?"

"You've got to be kidding."

"So we've had a few run-ins. Nothing major."

"Maybe not for you . . ." Damn, where was the operator?

"Hang up and I'll tell you why I cut Scooter out of *Fool's Gold*." Her heart shifted into still higher gear. "Don't want to hear."

"Sure you do."

Someone answered on the other end of the line. Rebecca began breathlessly, "Operator? This is an emergency. Get me—"

Before she could finish, David shot across the room, snatching the receiver out of her hands. In fright, she fell back. He replaced it quietly and stood looking at her, his expression darkening. "You're a very dumb girl."

"I'm a *woman*, you peacock." She edged toward the open doorway.

"Don't run away," he said. "I'm not going to hurt you. Just give you a little friendly advice."

"You've brought nothing but pain and destruction to people I love."

"Which is what might happen if you don't follow my advice." His boyish charm had evaporated, his face became stone.

"I'm not afraid of you, David."

"You should be. I'm very powerful. I can ruin you."

"Oh yeah? How?"

"Be a shame if you met some sort of accident before Monday, wouldn't it? To your face maybe. You'd have to be replaced in the film."

"God," she groaned. "You cheap B-movie gangster."

"Don't do this film."

She drew herself up as tall as she could. "I'm going to do it, David. You can't stop me. Unless you carry out your threats. Which I think you're too chickenshit to do."

"Try me."

"No," she hurled. *"You* try me. Now beat it before I start screaming. They're two rugby players across the hall who'd just love to—"

"Is this the bastard's script?" He bent to pick it up.

Without blinking, she darted across the room, grabbed it out of his hands and dashed into the relative safety of the hall. *"Get out!"* she screamed at the top of her lungs. *"Now!"* One thing she knew she had in her favor—an extremely powerful voice. It echoed down the hall, but no doors opened on her floor.

Desperate, she pretended, half-turning to the far end of the hallway which was out of David's line of sight. "Hi, Pete," she greeted to an imaginary person. "Just throwing some dumb jerk out. I'll yell if I need help, okay? Thanks." She waved good-bye and turned to gaze sternly at David. "Now are you going to leave?"

He fumed for a moment, then started for her. She backed further into the hall out of his way. At the top of the stairs, he stopped, his mouth twitching with tightly controlled rage. "Drop out of this film and I'll pay you a hundred grand a year for five years. Cash."

"I'm not for sale."

"Then I'll see to it you'll never work in movies again."

She forced a laugh. "David, you're a cliché. Get lost, asshole."

Before he could retort, she stepped inside, slammed the door, locked it and immediately sank to the floor in shattered relief. Erik's script cradled to her like a baby.

SHELBY
March 1976
Los Angeles

With a grunt, Irving came.

In the reflected light from the bathroom, his fleshy face was splattered with color. His nearly bald head glistened with sweat, some dripped from his bushy eyebrows, falling on her breasts. His breath wheezed out in short gasps. She wondered seriously if he were having a heart attack on top of her.

Shelby unwrapped her long legs from around his paunchy middle, freeing him to roll off. But he remained inside, his whole weight upon her as he continued to struggle for breath. "Y'all okay?" she asked huskily.

His voice came out a rasping croak, "Sure."

She wanted him off. Since he hadn't bothered to bring her to climax, she was itching for relief. But not tonight, she sighed inwardly. Not with this old man. "Sugar," she murmured. "I can hardly breathe."

Without a word, Irving pulled out of her and eased off, rolling to his side, eyes shut, his thin chest heaving irregularly. Deciding to let him recover on his own, she stood and slipped into the bathroom, closing the door on him.

The large bath was all maroon tile with black trim. She spotted a matching porcelain bidet and quickly squatted on it, turning on a warm stream of water. A brass nautical clock on the towel shelf indicated it was barely past midnight.

And it had taken most of the evening to get him into bed. Irving had spent hours grumbling and bemoaning his run of bad luck at Pacific and cursing David's stock raid on the company. For the entire, brief, disgusting little affair, she had been the instigator—first proposing the intimate dinner at Ma Maison, later suggesting a nightcap back at his legendary home off Benedict Canyon, maneuvering him upstairs to this master bedroom suite on the pretext of wanting to see the rest of the house. He'd been reluctant to make a move even after she'd tugged him onto his Victorian four-poster bed. Why if she hadn't gone down on him, working like the dickens to arouse him, they'd most likely still be there, rolling around unproductively.

Recalling the first time she'd made it with David and noting the comparison of "like father, like son," Shelby used one of Irving's guest brushes to rearrange her hair and returned to the bedroom to conclude the business on her mind. He lay flat on his back, eyes closed—like a dead man, she thought.

Crawling in next to him, she cupped his genitals, giving them a little tug, hard enough to open his eyes. "That was wonderful, sugar," she purred. "I thoroughly enjoyed myself."

"You're a great lay," he mumbled, not looking at her. "I can see why David kept you around so long."

She frowned into the semidarkness. Obviously Irving could be as uncouth and thoughtless as his son. "Oh, he's not half as good."

"Oh, yeah?"

"You're much more virile, more masculine."

"You come?"

"Oh my yes, many times."

"You're quick too, huh?"

"Only with experienced men."

A smile tweaked the corners of his lips. She created a light laugh and ran her long nails up his pot-bellied trunk. "Irving, about that scene tomorrow . . ."

He flopped his head over, staring coldly at her.

"Do y'all really think it'll work?" she asked, as a doting daughter would ask her revered father. "I mean this other actress is fairly green and it's an extremely demanding scene."

"Rebecca's doing okay."

"So everyone keeps telling me. But actually, I'm more concerned about my part . . . it's so undeveloped. Y'll know what I mean?"

"I like it the way Lungren wrote it."

"But it's so similar to so many other scenes we shot last year. Savannah the self-centered bitch, Savannah the cold—"

"You want me to fatten up your part?"

His tone disturbed her—it was gruff, distant. She laid her head on his sunken chest. "I'm not after more lines, really, truly I'm not. Although Summer does seem to have a great deal more than Savannah now. Actually, what I'm looking for is a chance to demonstrate another quality. Another facet of my character's personality."

He shrugged. "Your ex-hubby ain't around to tinker with it."

"Isn't there some other writer?"

"I like it as it is," Irving said and yawned. "You got an early call. Gonna stay or want Wilson to drive you home?"

For a second she felt like telling him what a lousy fuck he was, but pulled away with a pout. "I'll go."

"Douse that light on the way."

In her tiny, stuffy, temporary dressing room behind Pacific's sound stage nineteen, Shelby shifted the phone receiver and batted away the makeup man's hand hovering over her face like an insistent fly. "Can't you see I'm on the phone," she hissed. "You've done enough damage for one morning. That goes for you too," she directed at the hairstylist. "Clear out—both of you." She waited, tapping her foot against the metal base of the makeup chair until they'd withdrawn. "Operator," she yelled into the receiver. "Have y'all forgotten me? My South American call?"

"I'm trying the connection again," the overseas operator replied.

"Well, I'm an extremely busy person," Shelby said and listened impatiently to the muffled ringing on the other end. She could also hear one of the crew in the alley loudly imitating Elton John's "Don't Go Breaking My Heart." Eventually on the other end of her line, a heavily accented male voice answered with the name of the hotel and the operator started to inquire. "Erik Lungren," Shelby shouted, interrupting the operator, and repeated, "Long distance calling for Erik Lungren."

"Mister Lungren, he checked out last night," came the reply.

The mirrors reflected her disappointment. "Did he leave a forwarding address? Where was he going?" The man knew nothing. She banged down the receiver and shot to her feet, throwing open the door.

"Lisa!" she screamed into the empty alleyway. Her temporary private secretary, wearing a "Welcome Back, Kotter" T-shirt, lumbered around the corner where she'd been banished for smoking a cigarette in the airless confines of the small dressing room.

"Get ahold of Mo Engle again," Shelby ordered. "Tell her Erik left Caracas for points unknown. If she hears from him, I want to know. Immediately. Got that?''

The overweight girl, in the extra-large T-shirt, nodded tightly and turned, bumping into the assistant director. He grimaced. "Ready for you, Miss Cale."

"Dandy. Just dandy."

Inside the cool interior of the sound stage, Shelby took up her indicated position in front of the camera. "Well, where is my co-star?" she asked, pointedly looking around. The crewman, who thought he could sing, was crooning in the rafters, his version of the Sondheim hit "Send in the Clowns." Shelby walked over to Victor Craig whom Irving had rehired to complete the film. The rotund director huddled with his cinematographer. "Victor," she said, sweetly, "are you *sure* you need me now?"

"But of course," he replied graciously.

She checked her irritation. She had nothing against Victor Craig— in fact, she knew all too well she was totally dependent upon his gifts to resurrect her career. "But where is Miss Parlato?" she asked.

"Here I am," came the actress's voice behind her. "Sorry. But Mister Dyer was explaining this scene's process shot."

"Mister Dyer?" Shelby echoed, her eyebrows arching skyward. She turned to behold the dark-eyed actress. Rebecca looked like she should have been selling matchsticks on a street corner. The frumpy costume, the hairstyle and makeup only emphasized her shortcomings. For the life of her, Shelby could not see what Erik had found so fascinating. Oh, the girl projected a certain air of innocence and vulnerability, but Shelby could read straight through that. Men might be fooled by it, but not another woman.

Rebecca came to her. "Want to run lines?"

"I know *mine* cold, thank you."

"I'd kind of like to, if you don't mind."

"I *do* mind. I find they get stale if I repeat them too much. Ask one of the script girls."

Rebecca stared back as though ready to fire off a retort, but then shrugged vaguely and left the area, walking to the leading man, Vince Brubrick, a curly-headed box-office draw whom David had cast in the first production. Shelby watched the two of them together—they were giggling over something like fast friends.

Someone touched her arm. "We should all offer her a little more support," the director said in his soft manner. "Rebecca's carrying an awfully heavy load for one so inexperienced."

Shelby huffed, "I didn't cast her. Irving should have thought of that before. There's no room in this business for incompetence."

"I didn't say she was incompetent," Victor replied smoothly. "Merely inexperienced. But quite a trooper."

Shelby sighed with a wistful smile. "Victor, she's been handed the meatiest role of the year on a silver platter. I would damned well expect her to be a pro."

After what seemed an interminable wait, the two principals were called onto the parklike setting. As Shelby and Rebecca stood before him, Victor explained quietly what he was after in the short scene and placed them on the park bench. Behind them was a large, blue cyclorama over which a shot of Central Park in the dead of winter would be superimposed in the lab processing.

The director rehearsed and coached the duo through a few runthroughs, then called for a take. Shelby blew her first line. "Keep rolling," Victor said. "Begin again, please."

Shelby pulled the black sable fur tighter around her throat. "Summer," she drawled, "y'all must not hang onto me so. Find your own life, for heavens' sake."

"But you are my life," Rebecca uttered. "My *whole* life. I don't have anyone or anything but you . . ."

"That's my very point. Summer, I'm getting married and . . . damn, what's that line?"

"Cut!"

It took eleven tries before Shelby managed to get through the short scene without stumbling over a line. Each time, Rebecca remained silent, indicating nothing, but Shelby felt judged nevertheless. Finally she managed to pull herself together and the brief sequence was "in the can." A break was called before the next setup. Rebecca hurried off to her dressing room. Momentarily Shelby shucked her fur and followed.

At the far end of the sound stage, she tapped on the door and entered. Curled up, barefoot on the apricot velvet pillow couch, Rebecca glanced up from her script. Shelby smiled. "Do you mind?"

"Not at all, please, come in."

Shelby closed the door softly behind her, glancing around. "David built this suite for me."

"Would you like to switch?"

"Darling, I've only a few more days. I can manage."

"I really wouldn't mind," Rebecca said. "I find it difficult to get into Summer's character in here. Too plush. Lovely but—"

"May I smoke?"

Rebecca stretched for an ashtray. "Here."

Shelby took her time lighting the cigarette, inhaling deeply then settling onto the arm of the makeup chair, all the while studying the dark eyes that held her gaze so steadily. She exhaled. "Mind if I ask you a personal question?"

The girl hesitated briefly before responding, "No."

"Have you heard from Erik lately?"

A bright red invaded the girl's cheeks but her voice was firmly in control, "No, I haven't."

Shelby pressed, "When was the last time?"

"Months ago."

"Mind telling me why y'all stopped seeing each other?"

The dark-haired actress shrugged. "I don't know if that's any of your business. But since you asked, I'll level with you. He was still hung up on you."

Shelby could not contain her pleasure. "Are y'all sure?"

"Look, Shelby, I've got no reason to play games with you. You asked, I told you. Anything else?"

"Maybe," Shelby said reflectively. "Perhaps I could tell you something. Something *you* don't know."

"I'm not sure if there's anything I need to know . . ."

"I'm sure you'll find this fascinating. Perhaps y'all already know? Erik wrote this part especially for you." Noting the alarm growing in the girl's eyes, Shelby pressed on with a casual, chatty manner. "Not only did he write it for you, he *insisted* Irving cast you. In fact, Erik made it the main stipulation of his second contract."

Rebecca began to move her head slowly from side to side, as if she were finding it impossible to believe.

"But it's true," Shelby continued. "Irving told me so himself. Last night. He said he had no choice if he wanted Erik to rework the film."

The girl's coloring had paled. "So why'd Irving go through all those auditions, if . . . if . . ." Her voice broke, giving away her uncertainty.

"To make the casting look legit, I suppose," Shelby responded and flicked the cigarette into the sink. "It's so like Erik to have insisted. Actually, you should feel flattered. It does mean he cared . . . in his own way. That scamp. He must have felt so guilty. Using you the way he did while we were still . . . how should I say it? Romantically involved? I suppose he felt it was one way of paying you off."

Observing that Rebecca was far less upset than she'd hoped, Shelby stood slowly, moving toward the door. "But darling, don't feel badly. Everyone knows we all have to get started somehow. If some can't get there on talent, it shouldn't be held against them. I keep telling Victor and the others—especially Vince—they shouldn't feel stuck with you. You're doing a lovely job for a beginner." She opened the door, smiling graciously. "Keep up the good work, darling." She started to step out.

"Shelby," came the sharp call, stopping her in the doorway. Rebecca rose from the couch, her small frame vibrant, her eyes shooting sparks of rebellion. "That crock sounds like something you'd dream up all right. Because that's the way you've gotten everything. Having men do it for you. Well, let me tell *you* something—I don't give a damn how I got this part. I auditioned and I was cast. What I care about is doing the job the best I can. You see, I came up the hard way. The regular way. By busting my ass—not selling it. Now I'm going to study my lines. I suggest you do the same."

Shelby was too stunned to think of a retort. She swept out, not bothering to close the door.

ERIK
June 1976
La Paz, Mexico

In the teak-lined galley of *The Dreamer*, Mo Engle downed the warm bottle of Mexican beer and sputtered wearily, "Lungren, I didn't fly for over seven hours on a pissing prop plane, not to mention an unscheduled two-hour layover in some godforsaken dirt mound called an airport, where the temperature in the tin shack they called a terminal, I swear, was over one hundred twenty degrees, and finally find your damned boat, the very last one on the longest dock in the harbor and then have you stand there, like an aging hippie and tell me you don't want to come to your own premiere. Listen asshole, it happens to be at this moment the hottest ticket in the world."

He chuckled dryly, shaking an unruly mane of beard and hair. "Mo, cool down, okay? You've barely arrived. Whole different rhythm of life down here."

With a huff, she exhaled in resignation and glanced out the open side windows of the raised, center cabin—the fading light of an early evening sky caught the mouth of the harbor and the sea beyond in degrees of blue and gray. "If you lived like a normal person for god's sake, with a phone," she began with renewed attack. "Or even an address. But oh no, the best-selling author of the decade is a goddamned romantic. Lives like a monk on a boat. This month, in some forgotten Mexican fishing village. Looking like a stranded beachcomber." She snorted ruefully. "And I always thought Baja California was just south of the L.A. airport."

"Sure you don't want anything to eat?"

"Take a look at me," Mo challenged. "Do I look like a person

517

who needs to eat? Not that I would eat anything down here. Unless it came out of a can. Got anything in a can?''

He shook his head, smiling at the pleasure of old friends. ''Some engine oil.''

''I'll pass.''

Lighting a small kerosene lantern, he said, ''Each morning of my daily ritual, very early, I go fishing for an hour or so. A time to think before I attack the writing. Today, I lucked out. Caught a pretty swordfish—gave most of it to the locals I went out with, but I've a couple of nice fillets for dinner.'' As soon as Mo had stepped out of the dusty cab at the end of his dock, along with his surprise at seeing her, he had been momentarily taken aback by the changes in her demeanor. Plump once more, dressed in a wrinkled, shapeless, ochre-colored pants-suit over a beige blouse, her short hair salted with gray, she had lost or had given up her former flash of tinsel town. She looked like she had been working too hard, or working too much. Maybe a lot of both.

He poured his one drink of the day and settled into his favorite blue canvas chair. Through the open aft-hatch, behind Mo, he could watch the waters of the Sea of Cortez through the masts of the fishing boats.

She nodded to his shot glass. ''Thought you'd given up both smoking and drinking.''

''Definite on the cigarettes, but . . .'' He sipped the straight tequila and winked at Mo. ''As old Ben Franklin said, everything in moderation, including moderation.''

She laughed and slipped off her sandals.

''How're the twins?''

''Tommy knocked up some beach bunny,'' she answered sourly. ''I paid for the abortion. And last month, Timmy got busted. Driving without a license, open bottle of Vodka, half-ounce of weed and some uppers. On probation now. Believe me, night court alone gives one a certain amount of humility. And a strong dose of reality. What a mess I've made of their lives.''

''The boys are almost seventeen, right? Old enough to begin assuming responsibility for their own lives.''

''I don't think they know how. No one ever taught them.''

"They'll learn. They'll have to. Hell, I hit the road at seventeen. You learn real fast when there's no one there to clean up after you. What about your young friend? What's his name?"

"Griff? I told him to *vamoose*," she reported matter-of-factly. "Like having another dependent. But it sure was sensational while it lasted."

In the gently rocking cabin, they listened for a while to the sounds of the crowded harbor and watched the boats being secured for the fast-approaching darkness. Crews shouted in Spanish across the waters and replies of laughter faded into the night. Mo lit another cigarette. "Know what I've decided? Whatever happens this Fourth of July on this vice president position Irving's offered—I'm going to track down that husband of mine and spell it out: Michael McKitrick either give me a divorce or preferably, get your Catholic ass back to me and the boys."

Erik rose to tug on a faded sweatshirt. "He wrote me he was going to cover both political conventions. For the *Village Voice*."

Mo nodded and exhaled. "Presently he's in Plains, Georgia, to interview the peanut farmer," she said with a smirk. "What a choice we'll have—the man who pardoned Nixon or the oldest son of Miss Lillian. Now *her* I'd vote for." She nodded to the corner counter, at his typewriter and a small, neat stack of manuscript pages. "Is there a movie in this one?"

"Never again."

"Had it with Hollywood?"

"Same old dancers in the same old shoes," he replied. "You still thriving on that game?"

"Ask me in three weeks," she said. "After *Rainbow*'s premiere and Pacific's stockholders' convention. Level with me. Aren't you even curious how your new version turned out?"

"A little, sure," he admitted. "But not enough to make a special trip up to see it. I'll catch it later. When I can observe without being observed."

Mo leaned forward over the gleaming teak tabletop. "Irving hasn't shown it to anyone. Not even me. That's just what David did. Playing his hand real tight to his chest." She studied his silence through her cigarette smoke. "But Irving said he'd screen it for you.

Get your opinion before he sends it to the lab.'' Again Erik did not respond, so she continued, ''He would also like to have you at the premiere, give it your blessings for the press, but more importantly for all the stockholders who'll be there.''

''That why you came all the way down here?''

''One of the reasons.''

''The other . . . ?''

Mo paused, then voiced, ''I've signed Shelby back on as a client. After *Rainbow*'s released, her career could have some real legs.''

He pushed to his feet, collected Mo's empty beer bottle and tossed it into the wastebasket. It sank into the crumpled papers of rejected pages. At the open hatch, he asked, ''What's she want?''

''For you to take her to the premiere.''

''Why the hell's Irving having the premiere on the Bicentennial? Who the hell's going to come?''

''Half of Hollywood, plus Pacific's stockholders. Their biannual meeting begins at the Beverly Wilshire the following day. Irving wants them to see the film before they vote.''

Erik avoided her direct stare, not knowing why he felt so angry. ''Isn't Rau within striking distance of acquiring Pacific?''

''David's closing in, to be sure. But Irving's counting on AII not dumping their shares on the market. That Dixon will support him.''

''Irving seems to be counting on a helluva lot falling his way in the final round. I hate to see you so closely allied with him,'' he said. ''Your career could go down the toilet with his.''

''Everything's a gamble, Erik. You win some, you lose some. But you gotta play your cards. That's the game, no?''

''Is it worth the bullshit?''

''To be a V.P. of a major studio? Damn tootin'.''

He smiled a slow grin. ''Know what I like best about you Mo?''

''My fab bod?'' she cracked.

''Your independence. If I could ever find a woman who had your strong sense of self—I'd settle down in a flash.''

''You're not looking hard enough.''

''I'm not looking.'' He listened to the internal echo of his voice and found the words strangely hollow, lacking in conviction.

She smiled knowingly. ''Erik, know what I like best about you?''

"My big head?"

"You are so damned easy to decipher." She snuffed her cigarette butt in the seashell ashtray. "Have you really given up on all of us?"

"I didn't say I'd given up on *all* of you. Just those so wrapped up in the fame game they don't know who the hell they are."

She smirked again. "So what'll I tell Irving?"

Erik scratched his beard. "Wish him luck for me. But I won't come see *The Rainbow Shuttle*. That's yesterday's newspaper blowing down Sunset."

"And Shelby?"

He stared out at the deepening gray of the water, not commenting for several beats. "Tell her I'll be holding my own Fourth celebration. Me, my typewriter and my muse."

"She'll be *desolé,* I'm sure."

He shrugged. "She'll get over it."

Later, after a hearty dinner of broiled swordfish and a fresh fruit salad loaded with mangoes, melons, tamarind, guava, coconut and pineapple, Erik and Mo moved up on the aftdeck. Sitting in the cockpit reveling in the cool night breeze off the water, they watched the lights of the harbor village and listened to the soft guitar music from a nearby boat. Mo spoke quietly, unwinding after the harried trip south. She told of Michael's invitation to the twins to join him at the upcoming Montreal Olympics and that the boys were jazzed up to go see this Nadia Comaneci whom they'd seen on television. Then Mo mentioned Rebecca, casually in connection with Robby Rhomann.

Erik concentrated on the rope splice in his hands and fought the desire to bum one of her cigarettes. "How'd she do in the film?"

"Hell, if you're curious, you'll just have to come up and judge for yourself. I've known her for so long, I can't wait to see her act myself. I told you her performing school folded, didn't I? Lord, if I'd known it was only a matter of money, I would've chipped in. She's trying to get Robby to become a highly visible backer so she and her partner can reopen. I've come to really admire that girl's spunk. After all that's happened to her, she's not a quitter."

Feet up on the railing, he nodded, conscious of the spontaneous grin that had crept upon his face. With a snort of recognition, she said, "I'm going to offer you a bit of unsolicited advice."

He groaned, but she proceeded anyway. "You're a fence sitter, Erik. Ever since I've known you, the only commitment you've ever followed through on is your writing. Oh, you may think you made a commitment to Shelby, but I think you were fooling yourself. Bamboozled by your overimaginative fantasy life. Well, I think it's time you made some choices in the real world and go after them."

"Mo . . ." he sighed, shaking his head.

"Hear me out, okay? I thought about this all the way down here and I won't be satisfied until I get it off my chest. You're a big success, Erik . . . all the money, all the glory, all the freedom in the world. But you're living on a goddamned boat in a foreign country and you're all by yourself."

He snapped taut the new splice. "By my choice."

"Sure it is," she said pointedly. "But coming from what? I say it's fear. You're a coward. Burned once, you're afraid to put yourself on the line again."

"Can't do anything until I finish the manuscript."

She snorted and stood. "There'll always be another book. You can keep postponing your personal life until you drop. You're just a chickenshit, Erik. Make up your mind about her and take some action. All she can do is turn you down."

He stared at her emptily. "Who the hell are you talking about now?"

"Well, if you don't know, how the hell am I supposed to?" She stood, stretching her arms out, looking back at the sleepy village. "Some weekend vacation hot spot, all right. I can hardly keep awake. If you'll show me where I bunk, I'll turn in. I've got a long return trip tomorrow."

After she'd retired in the fore cabin, Erik sat at his typewriter. Too many of her words ran like a tape-recording in his head, crowding out his own. He tried rereading the new pages, but his mind was roaming elsewhere. To one person in particular: Rebecca.

Grabbing the last beer, he stood up on deck in the darkness, sipping slowly, listening to the waves slap at the side of the boat, watching a pelican, like some prehistoric pterosaur in the midnight blue sky, swooping low to dive for dinner in the harbor. Erik swished the beer in his mouth and spat it over the railing. Lukewarm beer, lukewarm guts.

DAVID
July 1976
Los Angeles

Two days before the Bicentennial of the United States and the long-awaited, overhyped world premiere of Pacific Studios' *The Rainbow Shuttle*, David paid a polite but pointed call on Dixon Shaw.

"You're asking the impossible," the chairman said easily and slipped out of his white patent leather golf shoes. "I can't give you that information. Sure you don't want a drink?"

David declined with a curt nod of his head. They were standing in the sunlit library of Shaw's Bel Air mansion. At the built-in bar, Shaw, fresh from the estate's nine-hole golf course, tossed his cap into a chair and began pouring a straight whiskey, speaking easily as if there had been no professional strain between them for several months, ever since Dixon had yanked away David's version of *The Rainbow Shuttle*. David had never forgiven the chairman for being so gutless and giving into Irving's assessment of David's unfinished film. However, David had worked too hard, invested too much of his own personal resources, both financial and emotional, to allow personal feelings to get in the way of his goals. In fact, now more so than any period of his life, he was all consumed with winning.

Dixon capped the crystal decanter. "The whole nation seems to have closed up early for this weekend. So I have too." In a toast, he raised the glass. "Happy Bicentennial."

David barely acknowledged it. "Six months ago—yes. It would

have been ill-considered to ask you. But today, AII holds only four percent more of Pacific than I do.''

''I'm fully aware of that.''

There was a slight bite to Shaw's tone that cautioned David not to press too hard. ''Dixon, what's three days? As you said, everything is closing up early. There's nothing I could do with the information.''

Shaw stared back, poker-faced. David changed approaches. ''You and I—we go back a long way. I've always thought of you as my mentor. You gave me my first real break. When I was with your label, I think I amply demonstrated my gratitude.''

''You ran a tight ship for us. Generated a healthy profit,'' Shaw said, sinking his girth into a matching armchair. ''If you'd stayed on with RPM, we wouldn't have had to unload it. It would have continued to perform efficiently. As it was, we had no choice. We were losing millions.''

''Almost as much as you've lost on Pacific over the last three years.''

''Close, yes.'' Shaw ran a flat palm over his thinning red hair.

''One would assume then that AII would be more than happy to cut their losses on the market.''

The chairman, casual in golfing slacks and polyester knit shirt of pale blue, smiled cryptically. ''Surely you can wait until Tuesday when the rest of the stockholders find out.''

David shrugged boyishly. ''To be frank, my backers are getting antsy. I'd like to offer some reassurance over this three-day weekend. Something to ease their holiday anxieties.''

''How thoughtful.''

''Just keeping my eye on all the balls in the air.''

''You've always been a highly skilled juggler.''

''Thank you,'' David responded and freely looked around the book-lined room. The furniture and appointments were solid, masculine, expensive. A perfect setting for a corporate giant. But there was something that disturbed David about the room. His memory nagged him. Something was out of place or missing.

Shaw set his empty glass on the mahogany endtable, centering it on a cork coaster. ''I assume you're not going to the premiere.''

"Irving's office must have mislaid my invitation," David said with an engaging grin.

"He seems quite high on the film's prospects."

"Seeing how his whole future at Pacific is dependent upon it, Irving had damn well better have some professional enthusiasm."

Shaw's heavy jowls sank into sadness. "I'll never understand this bitterness between you two. Such a rivalry between father and son."

"I don't expect anyone to understand," David answered guardedly. "Except Irving and I."

"I'm certain you both must have legitimate reasons. Still . . . even Zanuck's made up with his son."

David stood. "I won't keep you any longer. I just wanted to wish you a happy Fourth."

"And do a little fishing, eh?" Shaw smiled pleasantly and shoved himself upright, adjusting the shirt over his bulk.

"Unsuccessfully, alas," David sighed and started out. He stopped by the curio cabinet, staring at the wall above it. "Wasn't there a small painting here? A Remington? An Indian spearing a buffalo?"

"Bravo. Excellent memory. It's been sent out to be cleaned."

David nodded and moved into the hallway. As Shaw relayed his own plans for celebrating the Bicentennial, they headed toward the main entrance. Passing the open double-doors of the living room, David glanced in. The walls, previously covered with large ornately framed oil paintings, were now totally bare, faded discolorations indicating where each had hung.

At the front door, David shook hands with the chairman and said, "I'll see you Tuesday at the convention. Ready for whatever surprises you have in store."

"Don't go expecting too much," Shaw cautioned.

David could not help his frown. He offered a cordial but reserved good-bye and quickly headed for his parked Rolls, just beyond the four-car garage. One of the garage doors was open. Something caught his eye and he strolled inside. Along one wall, large, flat, wooden packing crates of various sizes leaned against each other. They were obviously Shaw's extensive and priceless nineteenth-century American paintings crated for pick up.

What aroused his curiosity, however, were the labels. The crates were being shipped back to the AII headquarters in New York. David stared at the labels, feeling a distinct stirring in his chest. Surely there were reputable firms in Beverly Hills that could handle the cleaning job. Why would Shaw go to all the trouble of having his entire collection sent back East? Unless . . . A piece of the puzzle clicked into place.

Bursting with news, David pushed through the sauna-room door off his partner's master bedroom suite. "Loggins, good—" He pulled up short.

The head of Robert Loggins, ex-Stanford jock and present partner of the stock-purchasing plan, was buried between the open legs of a nearly ecstatic young woman. Naked, eyes now wide with astonishment rather than lust, the brunette lay on the wooden slats, her gourd-shaped breasts rising and falling rapidly, glistening with moisture. Loggins, also nude, on his knees before her, made greedy noises as he lapped. A piped-in stereo system played Dionne Warwick singing "Never Gonna Fall in Love Again."

The chick ceased writhing and Loggins's head rose questioningly. He caught sight of David. "Christ, Rau, how'd you get in here?"

"Lunch break's over. Have some news."

"Can't it wait?"

"It can. But I can't." Even from the open doorway, the dry heat of the all-wood sauna blazed into his skin, searing his nostrils. "I'll be out by the pool." With a wink at the girl, David turned on his heel and exited.

Shortly, the bovine Loggins appeared out of the side door of his sprawling, white stone, flat-roofed home situated high in the fashionable hills of Trousdale Estates. Pulling on a blue terry-cloth robe, he stomped toward the diving board on which David sat. "Can't a guy take a meeting with his secretary without being busted?"

"Your little girl told me where I could find you."

"Christ, she back?" Loggins grumbled and threw a guilty glance toward the house. "Thought the housekeeper took her to see *The Bad News Bears*." His head swiveled back. "So what's so goddamned important? It's a goddamned holiday, you know that?"

"Shaw's selling his house."

The broad, all-American face registered nothing. "So? Hell, David, I'm in real estate up to my ears. *Everyone's* selling. With these prices we're getting, I'm even thinking of selling this spread."

"He's not buying another out here."

Loggins screwed up his eyes, trying to fathom the relevance.

David sighed impatiently, explaining, "Listen, he's shipping all his paintings back to New York. So I called your Beverly Hills branch to see if someone there could find out if his house were up for sale. Fortunately one of your subordinates had the presence of mind to keep the office open during business hours. He had the information in a half hour. It's going on the market Wednesday morning. The day *after* Shaw's report to the stockholders."

"You think that means—"

"Damn right it does," David interrupted. "Why else would he leave L.A.? The corporation has no other business out here anymore. They dumped RPM last year. Pacific's next. He's pulling up stakes and packing out."

Loggins slapped his palms on the board. "Bitchin'! Wc'll make tham an offer they can't refuse."

David could not help but smile and turned for the gate to the drive. "You can go back to your snack now."

"Have a bitchin' Fourth, partner," Loggins called after him

David shouted over his shoulder, "It's going to be the very best . . . believe me."

Behind the wheel of his Rolls, driving to his lawyer's home in Palos Verdes, David tried reaching Shelby by the car phone. He would have preferred delivering his exultant message in person, but there were a thousand details to iron out before Tuesday. There was no answer at her Topanga Canyon house.

Again by car phone, he checked in with the detective agency. Owen Olson was not in the office and the man assigned to keep tabs on Shelby had not reported in. Pissed at not knowing exactly where she was, or with whom, David called Western Union and fired off a telegram to her. He left the same message on her service:

Our victory is in sight. Call me immediately. Love, David.

REBECCA
July 1976
Los Angeles

She woke up to a string of firecrackers going off beneath her Venice apartment window. In the bright patch of morning sunlight, she yawned, "Happy Birthday, America," and turned over for more sleep.

Suddenly she had to scramble out of bed, dashing into the bathroom to relieve herself. *The premiere!* Oh Lordee, how was she ever going to get through the day?

Sara Jane hollered raucously from her back bedroom. "She's up! She's up!" Soon, Rebecca heard her roomie knocking at the bathroom door, calling out, "But is she up for my ol' grandpop's special Arkansas breakfast?"

"And what, pray tell, would that be? Or dare I ask?"

On the other side of the door, Sara Jane laughed rawly. "Pickled possum on tater-bread toast, smothered with whole mess o' Chili-con-carni."

Tying her bathrobe belt, Rebecca fought the quease in her stomach and said primly to the door, "Thanks. You're such a help." By the time she joined Sara Jane in the kitchen, her stomach was calmer but not the nerves crackling under her skin. "Tea and toast will be about it for me today," she reported and mechanically set about filling the teakettle under the sink tap.

"Girl, open your eyes."

Blinking in discovery, Rebecca put down the teakettle and settled into a chair before the glazed pot of brewing tea and the plate o' buttered toast. But she sat staring at the two tickets to the premiere thumbtacked to the wall, alongside the printed invitation from Irving R. Dyer. "If only I could have seen the film all cut together," she began without energy, "I'd know better what to expect tonight."

"If only," Sara Jane mimicked broadly. "Those are just wishin' words. They haven't got nothin' to do with reality. You know that by now."

Rebecca poured a cup of tea and held it absently in both hands. "I've spent most my life dreaming things that began with 'if only.' If only I were prettier, or if only I were smarter, if only I were more talented, or more loved."

"An' what that get you?" Sara Jane asked, her pale eyes smiling over her cup. "All it got me was just a lot o' meaningless comparisons an' failed expectations."

"Like, if only Erik would show up tonight," Rebecca said and with her teacup, drifted into the living room to the bookshelf. She pulled out *Hidden Assets* and read again his hurried scrawl: "For Rebecca, whose tenacious and vivacious spirit has revived my own. May *your* assets soon no longer be hidden. Always, Erik."

For a long moment, she studied his photo on the back, remembering when he'd written that inscription, that same night in New York he had told her of the Raindance. And she thought back to the very beginning, when she had first seen him walking into Mac's Diner and had ended up taking him home. Almost ten years to the day, she reminded herself begrudgingly and replaced the book in its proper position. She returned to the kitchen and grabbed a piece of toast. "Okay, Miss Schermerhorn, what do you say to a little rollerskating before lunch?"

"Hot damn," Sara Jane said, jumping up with a wide grin. "Let's roller up to the pier an' buy some sparklers. I can dazzle an' delight my new drummer tonight."

Rebecca laughed, giving her friend a quick hug. "Sure wish you had wanted to go the premiere. I'll need moral support."

Sara Jane cackled throatily. "Tonight, this ol' gal is boogyin' to other beats, dig? Besides, ain't nothin' to worry about. The rainbow is more beautiful than any pot at the end of it."

*   *   *

Joining the celebrating throngs jamming the beachside serpentine and ocean front walks, they skated slowly up to Santa Monica, amused and exhilarated by the circuslike atmosphere. Later that morning, they returned to the apartment, exhausted by all the sunshine and unbounded energy of thousands of holiday revelers. Sara claimed the shower first. Rebecca sat at the kitchen table, poring over their new accountant's proposed budget for the reopening of the Raindance Academy when the phone rang. It was Robby.

"Are you all right?" he asked ominously.

"I can't believe it. It's not noon yet. And La Star is up? Robby, are *you* all right?"

"I couldn't sleep a wink. Such fears. Becks, I am so worried for you."

She couldn't help but laugh. "Robby, you're sounding more like your mother every day. I'm so glad you brought her back to give you such cheery thoughts. Did she wake you up?"

"No lie, Becks, all these rumors," he went on. "Did I tell you what I heard last night? A friend of mine has a cousin who works in the lab? Saw a color test of the whole film. Said it was worse than *Darling Lily*. Just told me that out of the blue. Without even knowing I—"

She broke in, "Why are you doing this? I had almost forgotten it all with my account books and here you are. Such a friend. Robby—"

"Rebecca," he interrupted testily, "how can you be so damned calm? This, in all probability, is the most important day of your life."

"Robin Rhomann," she said evenly, "if you don't lighten up, I'd rather go play on the freeway."

"You're not taking this all seriously enough."

She vented some of her exasperation. "Robby, if this film fails? So what? Is it going to stop me wanting to act? Or trying to find gigs? Not on your sweet booby. Just like your series being canceled, that's not going to stop you, right?"

He moaned, "I'm already the new Bob Denver. Next year they'll be asking, Robby who? Hey, I've been thinking. That dress we picked out. It's *all* wrong."

"Are you crazy? It took us a month to choose that dress."

"Too severe. Not appropriate. Should've picked that chiffon number."

Fighting a new bout of nerves, she responded with a tight control, "Why couldn't you've had these flashes last week? Or yesterday...?"

"Relax," he ordered. "We'll go pick out another this afternoon."

"Robby, it's the Bicentennial! What's going to be open?"

The pause was brief. "Oh damn..."

She replied with exaggerated concern, "Poor baby, you're not used to being up so early. You know what? You should go back to work instead of waiting around for Mo to close this movie deal. Why not go out on the road for some summer stock?"

"Shut up!" he snapped. "Let me think."

With firm resolve, she forced herself to sit in the straight-back chair next to the phone. Robby asked quickly, "What time is Freddie doing your hair and makeup?"

"He'll be here at three. Listen, if you want to get more press tonight, why don't you wear the dress?"

"Will you shut up? I'm trying to think."

"Well, think out loud for cripes'sake. I'm tired of listening to your defective conclusions. I could correct your reasoning as you go along."

"I'll call you right back," he said and hung up.

She glared at the dead receiver, then leaped to her feet. At the closet, she yanked out the hanger bag, opened it, brought out the dress and seriously considered it once more. Black taffeta, square neckline, little cap sleeves, trim skirt. No more than three yards of material in the entire thing and Robby had spent over six hundred for it. He'd insisted on buying it for her even though she had saved most of the money she had made on the film.

Now she held it up to her over the white robe and squinted at her reflection in the full-length mirror on the back of the bathroom door. Abruptly, the image swung away from her and Sara Jane stepped out of the bathroom, fully dressed in jeans and a Victorian, high-neck blouse.

"What do you think?" Rebecca asked, holding the dress up. "Too severe? Too mature? Like a kid playing dressup?"

Sara Jane nodded sagely. "It's real pretty. But if you're startin' that again, you're goin' to drive yourself crazy. Think I'll run over to

Keith's for a spell. See if we can nail down this Troubadour date. Take a long bath. That'll mellow you out.''

Long after Sara Jane had left and the soak in the tub had wrinkled her hands into pale prunes, there was a knock at the front door. "It's me, Robby. Hurry up for god's sake, I've got a load." Rebecca threw on a robe and opened the door. She was confronted by a mountain of colorful cloth, Robby struggling underneath. He squeezed past her, announcing, "There's more in the car."

"You rob a cleaners?"

He draped the pile over the arm of the couch and collapsed beside them. "Let's start with these."

She closed the door and stood gazing at her old friend, touched that he had driven out from Beverly Hills by himself. "You went to all this trouble, Robby. And here I've decided the dress will do. It's lovely, really. And thank you again for your generosity. Let's not make a big fuss over it, okay?"

He bolted upright, looking like she had just stuck him with a hatpin. "Ye gawds, Becks. I just went into hock getting my friend to open up his Rodeo Drive boutique. I optioned everything he had in your size." He stood excitedly and began to paw through the gowns. "He's got super taste."

"Oh, Robby," she murmured and went to him and put her arms around his slender torso. "Thank you, Robby, you're such a friend."

He squeezed her. "Tonight, Becks, let's make an entrance you'll never, ever forget. After all, it may be your one and only premiere."

Ignoring the overly sweet face he mugged, she turned to the dresses. "So, you bring anything in red, white and blue?"

SHELBY
July 1976
Los Angeles

Late that afternoon, in a nearly empty, downtown Beverly Hills, Shelby pulled her white Bentley into the underground garage and spotted Mo's red convertible with relief. Earlier, she had been surprised to learn that Mo was at her office, in spite of the holiday. Aware that both of them were working overtime, she swept out of her car and hurried toward the elevator, adjusting the skirt of her forest green, matte jersey, Halston street dress.

Rushing into the reception room, Shelby could hear loud voices coming from Mo's inner office. Perturbed that Mo was not alone to give her undivided attention, she hesitated outside Mo's closed door, listening to the angry exchange inside.

"Don't be such a tight old bitch," a young man's voice shouted. "Give it to me. Now!"

Shocked at the violent tone, Shelby strained to hear Mo's low-voiced reply, but could not make it out. Whatever it had been, it set off another string of abusive obscenities, ending with, "Fuck it. I'm warning you, Mom. I need the bread, you know? Like now."

Shelby tapped lightly at the door and pushed it open. "Y'all excuse me? I hate to interrupt but—"

"Goddammit," the teenager exploded, his sun-tanned face contorting with rage.

"Tommy, watch your mouth," Mo warned from behind her desk. Dressed in a baggy UCLA sweatshirt and jeans, she flushed. "Sorry, Shelby. A wee family argument."

Her son shouted, "Do I have to trash the place?"

Shelby was stunned. The blond youth, small but powerfully built in faded Hawaiian shirt and baggy surf-shorts, leaned over the desk as if he were about to strike his mother.

Mo begrudgingly opened her purse, extracting a wad of bills. "That's the *last* for this month. I promise," she uttered, not even convincing Shelby.

Tommy grabbed the money and flashed a vainglorious victory smile at Shelby. "Far out," he said and left the office, slamming both doors.

Mo shook her head, a collage of emotions filtering over her face, exhaustion, embarrassment, anger. Shelby had never seen Mo so perturbed, so totally without her usual "bulldog" control.

"What is it?" Mo asked irritably. One hand fumbled to light a cigarette. "I'm jammed right now. Irving's shindig. Overnight, I find myself completely in charge."

"Shindig?"

"A private reception at his Beverly Hills home after the screening. Just for the 'A' list. Don't worry, you're invited. The others'll have their own party in one of the sound stages."

"A victory celebration?" Shelby asked innocently.

"Maybe a wake. Who knows but Irving?"

Shelby settled into the chair next to the desk. "Have you heard anything from Erik? Is he coming?"

"Haven't heard a word since I left La Paz." Mo's head bent over a list of names as if she did not want to discuss the matter further.

Shelby took note of the dismissal and waved at Mo's list. "Well, why have a party if it's the bomb everybody claims it is?"

"Lord, Shelby, haven't you learned by now? Don't believe a damned thing you hear in this town. Or read for that matter. And don't count Irving out until the final bell."

"Y'all follow through on his offer to me?"

Mo's tone became blunt and accusatory, "*His* memory of the exchange is slightly different than yours."

"He *promised* me a film this fall."

"He told me he said he'd *think* about a film for you."

Shelby straightened her back, her tolerance fading. "I did not lie to you, Maureen. He promised emphatically a starring role. Nothing less."

With exasperation, Mo snorted through her nose and stubbed out the cigarette. "Look, can't this wait? I've a zillion—"

"No, it can't," Shelby interrupted. "My *whole* future is dependent upon this. I want you to nail down Irving. Tonight. If not sooner. If you won't, *I* will."

Mo leaned back in her swivel chair, her expression hardening. "Let me give you a little advice, Shelby. Lay off pressuring Irving today, tonight or tomorrow. In fact, lay off him totally until *I* make a move. And I'm not budging until after we know what the hell is happening to Pacific on Tuesday."

"*After* the stockholders' meeting? That's way too late," Shelby cried. "If Irving wins, I don't want to be lost in the shuffle. If he loses, I want my deal memorandum signed and in the files at Pacific."

"Covering all bases?"

"What do y'all mean by that?" She held Mo's direct gaze.

"If Irving loses, then David wins, correct? And aren't you assured of new films if David's in power? You told me yourself—"

"*Mo*," she exclaimed in vexation, "*whoever* is to head Pacific, I want a deal with. Now. Tonight. Before the screening. Is that clear?"

Mo rocked forward. "I don't need this. In fact, I don't need you. Since taking you back on as a client, you've been nothing but a royal pain in the ass. Get yourself a new screaming board. I'll send copies of your file material to your lawyer."

Shelby blinked rapidly in shock. This was not happening—not today of all days. Without Mo behind her, she was positive Irving's interest would wane. She retreated ino a placating smile. "Now, Mo, honestly . . . I'm sorry to have caught you at a bad time. Let's just forget I even stopped by." Gracefully, she rose to her feet. "I'll see y'all tonight. When some of this pressure is off both of us."

"I mean it," Mo said firmly. "Get yourself a new agent."

Her throat constricted. She wanted to scream back and cry at the same time. "Maureen . . ." she began, her voice quavering, "you've never cared for me, have you?"

"To be frank—no."

Shelby's lower lip quivered. "Why? I've never done anything to you, have I?"

"Not *to* me, no. But what have you done *for* me? Or for *anyone* for that matter. You're always so cocooned in your own self-importance."

"It's Erik, isn't it? You still blame me for *that*. You've always been on *his* side."

Mo wearily pushed herself to a standing position. "Shelby, this had nothing to do with Erik—you two were never right for each other anyway. What this *has* to do with is you and me. And I simply don't want to represent you anymore."

"If y'all think I'm washed up in this town, you've got another think coming."

"You could go on and win an Oscar for this film and I *still* wouldn't want to represent you. Life's too short. Like Ida Lupino once said, 'We all may be standing in the mud, but some of us are looking at the stars.' "

"And I'm *not* a star, is that it?"

Mo shook her head, snorting derisively. "You don't get it."

"I got one thing," Shelby burst out. "Your son *is* right. You *are* a tight old bitch! I wouldn't have you represent me if you were the last agent on earth." Head held high, she strode quickly from the room.

Still shaken by Mo's betrayal, Shelby kept her appointment at Jon Peters's salon and after five, returned to her temporary abode, the Beverly Hills Hotel, feeling abandoned and abused by everyone. Stopping by the front desk, she checked to see if she'd received any messages, particularly one from Erik. Devastated that there were none, that he had not bothered to send even a good-luck note or to phone to let her know where he was, Shelby strode petulantly through the lobby, past the Polo Lounge and outside again, following the meandering path through the blooming pink and white oleander bushes to bungalow twelve. Longing only for a hot bath, she unlocked the door to the pink stucco, self-contained unit and stepped inside the dim, cool interior.

David sat in a chair opposite the door. "I've been trying to reach you."

Quickly averting her face to find a light switch, she forced herself to recover from the initial shock. "How'd y'all know where I was?" She flicked on a table lamp and turned to assess his mood.

Hunched in the chair, he was strangely quiet. "Why'd you move in here?"

Still cautious, she tossed her purse on the green and white floral print couch. "Just for the weekend. I didn't want to get all dressed up and have that long ride into the screening." She stretched her arms over her head, arching her back. "My dress would've been positively ruined."

"Who's taking you tonight?"

Hands behind her head, she smiled coyly. But said nothing. If

Erik did not show up by showtime, she had Henry Mawson, the growing tiresome caterer, waiting on ice for her last-minute summons.

"You going alone?" David asked, very low-keyed.

"Maybe . . . maybe not." She glided into the bathroom and turned on the tub's faucets. He was up to something, she knew damn well. He was too quiet, too under control. It both unnerved and intrigued her. Sensing he was behind her in the doorway, she decided to play along for a while. "Y'all haven't said anything about my hair," she voiced. "You like?" She pirouetted gracefully under his scrutiny. The stylist had convinced her to cut it shorter and have it permed into a mass of tight curls, like Streisand in her new film, *A Star Is Born*. Shelby could tell by his eyes that the new hairstyle met his approval but he frowned anyway.

"You didn't answer me," he said. "Who's taking you to this fiasco?"

"What if I told you, I decided to go all by my lonesome?"

"I wouldn't believe you."

She stuck out her lower lip. "Well, it just might be true." She poured pink bath salts into the filling tub, pondering her next move. His intensity level seemed dangerously low. That always had preceded a vitriolic explosion. She did not want to take any chances of triggering anything. And yet she was all too aware that her options were damned few. "I just fired Mo," she announced, swishing a hand through the water to raise more bubbles.

"You never needed her."

"So you've always said . . ." She turned her back. "Unzip me, darling. I've a mad dash to get ready."

He obliged and she shrugged out of the jersey dress, dropping it to the floor. Languidly in her bra and panties, she bent over the tub to turn off the faucets, making certain he got a complete view of her new, trim figure. She'd been conscientiously following a rigorous diet-and-exercise program in order to look her very best for the premiere. So much was riding on this evening, she wanted to look every inch the reigning movie queen.

"Shaw's definitely dumping Pacific," he said.

She twirled. "How do you know? Did he tell you?"

"In his own way, yes."

"But, darling, that's wonderful. That means you've won, doesn't it? Pacific is yours?"

"A mere formality from here on out."

"Congratulations, darling!" She threw her arms around him, kissing him wetly on the lips, pressing her breasts into his silk shirt. "You've worked so hard for this."

She slipped off her bra and panties and stepped into the tub, sitting in the mounds of pink bubbles. The reassuring, sweet scent of rose petals filled her nostrils. She smiled up at him with lowered lids. "I've been on your side from the very beginning."

"Sure have a helluva funny way of showing it," he said. "Moving out on me. Acting in Irving's bastardization of *our* film. Taking up with every dick you could lay your hands on. Not to mention pulling that gun on me. That's being on my side?"

"Oh darling, y'all just don't understand women. Don't y'all realize I did all those things to regain your flagging interest? Y'all were so involved in besting Irving, you left me totally on the shelf. I was afraid of losing you . . . took desperate steps to win you back . . . that's all."

He shrugged, a half-smile forming. "You are the most beautiful liar I've ever met."

She blanched. "I'm not so certain that is a compliment . . ."

"If you're on my side, don't go tonight. Boycott it. I won't release this version anyhow."

"You'll need product to release just as much as Irving does," she said and casually raised a leg, running a hand over the calf, checking the smooth, taut skin.

He repeated dourly, "Don't go tonight."

"But I *have* to be there. It's the premiere. I'm the star . . ."

A corner of his mouth twitched. "Who *made* you a star, Shelby?"

"Why y'all did, darling . . . but I still have a responsibility to—"

He spun on his heel and disappeared.

"Darling?" she cried out. The front door of the bungalow banged shut with a terrifying finality. Damn, damn, damn, she moaned. Why was everyone walking out on her? Just when everything should be on the upswing. Tears welled and a sob rent from her throat.

What's going to happen to me, she cried inwardly . . . who's going to take care of me now?

Suddenly, the front door slammed again and she bolted up to a sitting position, grabbing a towel to wipe her face. "Who's there?" she cried out and then, through the open doorway, in walked the largest bouquet of yellow roses she'd ever seen. David grinned out from behind and with a flourish, dug out of the center of the bouquet, a flat black velvet box from Bulgari jewelers. He presented the slim case to her with a slight bow.

Stunned, expectant, she lifted the lid. And gasped with wonderment, "Oh, my . . . David, how exquisite." Spread out on black velvet, the diamond choker necklace winked brilliantly at her, at least a dozen rows of perfectly matched, one-carat, emerald-cut, rare yellow diamonds, all linked together on a wide gold mesh.

Tears reflooded her eyes and she looked up at him too overwhelmed by his ultraextravagant gesture to speak. With the golden roses on the vanity counter as background, David dropped to his knees on the bathmat, took the box from her hands and slipped the scintillating choker around her neck, fastening it, then settling back on his haunches to appraise her. There in the tub, with soap bubbles frothing her breasts, she delicately touched the wide band of diamonds snug around her throat. Under her fingertips, the gems' points were hard and jagged; on her neck, the mesh circle felt cold and stiff. But she knew positively, without a doubt, it was the most fabulous piece of jewelry she'd ever seen, let alone worn. She opened her mouth to thank him.

But he held out his hands flat, offering still another gift. It was a thick screenplay with a gold foil cover. "This will be my first production as head of Pacific," he said solemnly. "Mike Nichols is reading it now. The lead is yours. Director approval is yours. I will executive produce only. When you read it, you'll agree. The part is perfect for you. It's a snappy update of *Gentlemen Prefer Blondes*."

She sat up even further in the warm, soapy water. "I . . . I'm speechless," she breathed. "Y'all're just overwhelming me with all this—"

His lips cut off her words as he kissed her into silence. Their breaths intensified, mingling for several moments, then pulling back, he said softly, "Just one favor in return."

"Anything, darling," she whispered.

"I escort you tonight."

REBECCA
July 1976
Los Angeles

At seven-forty-five that night, exactly on schedule, Rebecca was whisked through the open gates of Pacific in a studio-provided, white stretch-limousine. Immediately bright lights engulfed the car as their chauffeur joined a line of limos inching forward. Beside her, Robby leaned forward in his powder blue tuxedo. "Look! Ol' man Dyer's gone all out."

She had already seen. Giant beams of brilliant white light swept the deepening night sky and flashed across the newly painted, sky blue facade of the lot's largest theater auditorium. Above the permanent bronze marquee, a huge, spangled, glittering, full-colored rainbow arched skyward. Inside its arc, neon lights colorfully announced, *The Rainbow Shuttle*.

"Lordee," Rebecca sighed and clutched Robby's hand. "Is this for real? Oh my god, look, there's Rosalind Russell. With David Niven!"

For several minutes, from the back seat of the slowly moving limousine, Rebecca and Robby ogled the famous faces alighting and gathering, chatting and mingling before the theater's entrances. John Huston was laughing with Paramount head, Barry Diller. And Sue Mengers, top agent, hustled Warren Beatty for a cigarette and Cybil Shepherd was straightening Peter Bogdanovich's collar. Rebecca felt so out of touch with reality, it was as if she were watching news footage of a Hollywood premiere.

Eventually, her limousine reached the front of the line and stopped beside the welcoming carpet, before crowds of gawking people. A livery-suited man opened her door. Robby winked at her. "Break a leg, Becks. And for heavens' sake smile. You look like a princess."

Tingling with anticipation, jittery with anxiety, Rebecca stepped out into the rainbow-colored carpet and into a barrage of exploding flashbulbs and bright television lights. Momentarily blinded, she turned to the blurry form next to her and smiled, pretending to recognize the large man—or woman. Only when the flashbulbs and TV lights left her and landed on Robby did Rebecca's vision return and she realized that she had been smiling foolishly at a potted Ficus. Embarrassed, she smoothed the soft yellow silk panels of her short, full-skirted evening gown and smiled at anything that moved, waiting nervously for Robby to reach her side, patting the back of her hairdo, making certain the modified Gibson-girl style was staying up. Loose curls hung down randomly. She could feel them bouncing off bare shoulders. And she remembered she'd left her matching stole in the limo.

She heard Irving's voice before seeing him, "Rebecca, you gorgeous girl, this way." In evening clothes, he materialized out of the glare and made a big show of kissing her for the cameras.

She thought he looked haggard and strained, dark circles underlined his eyes and his enthusiastic greetings seemed forced. Irving leaned his short frame into her, smelling of cigars and whiskey, telling her about a special gathering at his place afterward. She seized the moment. "Mister Dyer, I never got a chance to thank you for casting me in this. I just want you to know that I didn't know about Erik . . . Mister Lungren's ultimatum to you. I hope I delivered for you anyway."

Irving rubbed his chin, glowering. "Ultimatum? To me? No one gives me ultimatums. What the hell're you talking about?"

Her voice lost some of its strength. "Erik Lungren didn't insist I play this part? Made it a stipulation of his contract?"

A brittle laugh burst from his mouth. "Hell no. Who fed you that bullshit? Lungren just suggested I oughta try you out. But nothing..." Irving stopped talking. Coldly, he stared past her and muttered, "Well, I'll be a sonuvabitch."

She turned to see what held his stony gaze. Her jumpy stomach scrambled anew. At curbside, out of the back of a silver limousine climbed a cocky David Rau in black formal attire. Already before him, on the colorful carpet, stood a ravishing, newly coiffed Shelby Cale. Spectacular in a full-length, gold-threaded, skin-tight gown with one long sleeve, Shelby waved her bare arm at the phalanx of cameras. Their brilliant white flashes caught both the thick diamond choker at her neck and the metallic threads of her gown, her entire form radiated incandescence. In her element, she smiled and hugged the arm of David. What Rebecca thought was extraordinary, however, was the fact that David actually grinned. It was a sly, self-satisfied smirk, as if he knew something no one else did.

With an involuntary shudder, Rebecca looked away from him and took Robby's arm, saying to the studio head at her elbow, "We'll see you afterward, Mister Dyer. And thanks again for this break. Good show to us all, right?"

But Irving wasn't listening. He stared at his son with barely controlled contempt. Quickly Rebecca moved away through the throng, toward the entrance doors and Robby grumbled beside her, "What am I? Chopped liver? Irving didn't say two words to me. I don't even think he recognized me."

"Don't you find that strange?" she asked, glancing warily over her shoulder. "David being here?"

Robby beamed for an aiming camera, talking through his smile. "Maybe he's heard the film's a hit and wants the credit. There's Mo."

Sizing up the crowd, Mo stood by one of the doors, solid and flushed in an earth-toned, peasant-styled smock. Rebecca searched the people around the agent, hoping beyond hope to see the welcome face of Erik. But he wasn't there. And with the lights blinking, announcing the impending curtain, there was too much last-minute bustle for her to ask Mo about him. Within moments, Rebecca found herself hurrying down the aisle behind Robby, who in turn followed Mo to their row. Scooting sideways in front of a seated row of formally attired people, none of whom she could bring herself to look at, Rebecca offered soft apologies until reaching her assigned seat, smack in the middle of the house. At once she sank into it but

Robby stood, milking every moment of attention, waving to people he knew.

On the far side of him, Mo tugged at his coattail and muttered, "Sit down, squirt. This is not your night."

Robby plopped down and leaned to Rebecca, whispering, "Guess who's sitting right behind you? Don't look, you'll die. Henry Fonda!"

At the thought, Rebecca felt the skin on her neck crinkle up and she moaned softly, "Robby, be a friend and just shut up. I've got enough to worry about."

Within a little time, the lights were dimming and the grand drape over the movie screen began to rise silently. There was a last second excited buzz from the assembled crowd and Rebecca closed her eyes, saying a quick little prayer. When she opened her eyes again, the logo for Pacific Studios was filling the screen. A supportive burst of applause broke out from some of the gathered stockholders. The logo faded and the film began.

With mounting anxiety, Rebecca watched the opening few scenes leading up to her entrance. When she appeared on the screen, especially her first closeup, she felt numb, bewildered, the mere size of her features disturbing her. And then there was her acting, which, at the time of filming, had felt to be honest emotions. But up there on the screen, thirty feet high, it all rang false to her. Nothing seemed real. She was just an actress in costume and makeup, performing a role. And she had never known that her face, when she cried, twisted so absurdly. Almost comically. Agonizing, she scrunched down in her seat to wait out the ordeal.

Thankfully, the film moved quickly through its double-layered story and Rebecca became so caught up in its unraveling, she was surprised when the final sequence began and built to the climax of reunion between the two sisters. The camera, in a tight closeup, lingered on her tearful face and gradually pulled back into a long shot—she and Shelby huddled together on the expansive terrace, framed by the lights of the Manhattan skyline. The lush theme music came up, the screen faded to black, the final credits began to roll.

From the audience, a smattering of clapping. The grand drape started to close over the last of the credits, the house lights dimming up. Rebecca realized she had tears in her eyes and a soft glow of conviction dusting her heart. Robby turned, his bright blue eyes were overflowing. Then she knew—her judgment had been correct. The soft glow expanded, filling her with the sweet recognition of her own abilities.

Suddenly a thunderous ovation shook the floor. The explosion of clapping and cheers startled her. The house lights had reached their fullest intensity and wide-eyed, she looked around. People were beginning to stand, applauding, some even cheering.

Nonplused she turned to Robby. He beamed at her through his tears, joining in with enthusiastic clapping of his own. "*Brava!*" he shouted. Several turned to where she was seated, smiling their approval. Someone was shouting, "Bravo, Irving!" Others echoed the cry.

Mo, clapping energetically on the other side of Robby, winked at her and put two fingers to her mouth, letting loose with a loud whistle. Suddenly a pair of hands grabbed Rebecca from behind—it was Henry Fonda. He was leaning over the back of her seat. "God, kid, you're sensational!" He planted a friendly buss on her cheek.

Goose pimples flew over her skin. Robby was tugging on her arm, pulling her up. A new wave of acknowledgment poured loudly from the crowd. He turned her around. "Wave, dummy," he shouted in her ear. "Wave!" Her arm rose as if by its own accord.

Her head became so light she felt she were going to faint. She sank into her seat. Covering her face with her hands, she began to cry. Someone thrust a handkerchief into her hands. Mo sat next to her, ordering maternally, "Blow your nose, wipe your eyes."

Rebecca did so, her hands shaking. "Mo," she whispered, breathless with the revelation. "I'm good. I'm really good."

"Took the words right out of my mouth," Mo said with a wink. "I was a damned fool not to have signed you before. Listen, if I'm still an agent after all this studio politics, I'd love to represent you. But if Irving wins this stock fight and I'm Pacific's newest vice president, how about you and Robby in a picture together?"

"I'd be thrilled with either one."

"Scooter would've been so proud of you."

"Oh, Mo, that's the nicest thing you could've said. You know, I can't get over this . . . honest to God, it's a first . . . I knew before the applause, before anyone acknowledged it . . . I'm a *damned good actress.*''

Dazed, Rebecca peered around, trying to get a grip on her emotions. Some of the audience had begun moving out. A humming buzz of excited conversation hung in the air. She caught a glimpse of Shelby pushing up the aisle. When the blonde glanced over, Rebecca grinned openly, wanting to share their mutual triumph. Shelby's glare ricocheted away, her head rising on her long, diamond-studded neck. She tugged David up the crowded aisle. But he had locked eyes with Rebecca, who had the oddest, strangest feeling that he was really seeing her for the very first time. And she found she could not tear her eyes away from him. It was he who first broke their disturbing gaze. And again she felt a tremor pass through her body, a quaking of an unknown fear.

''Don't count on any acknowledgment from them,'' Mo said at her elbow. ''You stole Shelby's thunder.''

''But she did all right,'' Rebecca said. ''Didn't you think?''

''But it's no longer her film. *You* walked away with it.''

Robby rejoined them. ''Rebecca, you should be mingling.''

''I want to find Irving,'' Mo said, huffing to her feet. ''Congratulate the old man. This film's going to be a monster. Now you two should make an appearance at the party here on the lot. That's for the press and most of the guests and stockholders. Then in about an hour, find your limo and head for Irving's. That's where the real celebration'll be. Congratulations again, Rebecca. *Ciao.*''

Robby managed to get Rebecca out of her seat and up the jammed aisle. Every step she took, someone else approached, telling her how marvelous she'd been, how moved they were by her performance. Everything was a blur, as if in a dream.

He steered her proudly through the crowd, out into the lobby, across the street and toward the cavernous sound stage draped in Bicentennial bunting. Above her, fireworks began exploding, filling the night sky over the studio lot with brilliant bursts of color and pattern. The milling crowd *ooh*ed and *ahh*ed. To her eyes, the showering pyrotechnics were a natural extension of how she felt.

Every new explosion of sound and color shot her excitement higher and higher.

Inside the huge sound stage blazed more colored lights, sweeping spots and banners of red, white and blue. A dance band played loudly at one end, "I'm Easy" from the movie *Nashville,* around the walls several open bars were set up. The press swept down on her with such a crush she felt momentarily frightened, unable to breathe. Questions were hurled at her so fast she was confused which to answer first, flashbulbs went off in her face with such rapidity, she was again blinded, seeing dark spots everywhere. Robby handled the press with the aplomb of a seasoned veteran, making them stand back, insisting she was there to celebrate, not to answer questions. Promising them she would be available at an upcoming news conference after the holidays, Robby propelled her away.

By one of the bars, they stopped. "Thanks, Robby," she said. "I had no idea they attacked like that. Just when..." Her voice gave out, her eyes frozen on the back of a very familiar head across the way. *It was Erik.* There was no doubt in her mind. Her heart began to beat extraordinarily fast.

"Who'd you see?" Robby cracked. "Robert Redford?"

"Erik..." she whispered, standing on tiptoes to keep him in sight.

Robby took her hand. "Let's just amble by, okay?" Willingly, she allowed herself to be led away. By the time they reached the end of the bar where she'd spotted him, Erik was nowhere in sight. She searched the push of people. Robby led her on, making an ever widening circle around the immense sound stage. She was so intent upon seeing Erik again, the many people who stopped to congratulate her were barely noticed, although she murmured her thanks before pressing on with the search.

Eventually a weary Robby pulled her to one of the giant sliding doors which opened out onto the backlot. "This is a good vantage point," he insisted. "Let's just wait here. He's bound to walk by."

Reluctantly she agreed, wondering if her eyes hadn't deceived her, that she had made a mistake. Outside, a skyrocket flashed over the lot, bursting to life, illuminating the old exterior sets which stood in tired clusters. She watched the splotch of color fade and die away.

She felt stoned but hadn't had even a glass of champagne yet. She asked herself again if she had really seen Erik. Or had merely created what she had wanted to see. And again she wondered why she continued to feel so much apprehension about the evening, it was like a cold fog settling over her. And it gave her the willies.

DAVID
July 1976
Beverly Hills

He squinted in the bright floodlights and jerked down the leather sun visor, shielding his eyes from the painful glare. Behind the wheel of Shelby's Bentley, he waited impatiently for the uniformed security guard to cross her name off the exclusive invitation list. At the base of David's neck, a knot the size of a tight fist throbbed to life. Finally, the infuriatingly slow guard waved them through the open lion gates. David barreled her car up the cobblestones, anxious to get it over with, anticipating the reactions.

"Will y'all slow down?" Shelby voiced beside him.

Deliberately, he hit the brakes, halving their speed, throwing her forward enough for her to take note that he was listening. Through the floodlit trees, Irving's house appeared, every window brightly shining from within. David couldn't remember seeing so many lights on.

Shelby spoke again, "Why are we coming here, if you're in one of your moods?"

"I feel terrific."

She said, "I know y'all better than that. You've got something eating at you. You've barely said a word all night. And I'm dying to know what you thought of the film."

"Shelby, I'm cool. And as for that abortion we witnessed, Irving's swan song is a pathetic soap opera, a mindless comic book." He steered the car around the fountain and toward the front portico. Before the waiting valet parkers, he pulled up, braked to a stop and turned toward Shelby. She was surveying her face in a gold compact mirror and caught him looking at her. She smiled, clicked the compact shut. "Why're y'all acting so funny, David? Is there something I don't know?"

"No," he said. "In fact, you know more than anyone else." He eased out and waited for the valet to open her door. She stepped out, regally, he thought and watched her glide toward him. Again she smiled wistfully and took his arm. "Will y'all tell me? What's up your sleeve?"

Wordlessly, but with a winning smile, he put his arm around her and walked her up the front stairs to the open front doors. With each step, the throb in his temples increased. Uncle Sam, a costumed man on stilts, greeted them with a shower of patriotic-colored confetti. A typical Irving circus, David assessed and steered Shelby inside.

Surprisingly, the old mausoleumlike mansion was almost festive. From the center exterior courtyard, around which the house was built, came music of a small dance band playing "As Time Goes By." In the high-ceilinged living room and adjoining dining room, thick white candles flickered on ledges and cornices, sills and shelves that David had not known even existed. Pools of pale golden light warmed rooms long cold and dark. The massive antique beams and wood wainscoting, imported in the thirties from a seventeenth-century Belgium manor house, shone freshly oiled and polished. Bunches of white daisies tied with red, white and blue ribbons hung everywhere.

But David eyed only the party crowd, those he could see in his brief tour of the mammoth living room: no Irving, no Dixon Shaw, maybe forty people at the most, several studio execs and major stockholders on Irving's team, none of whom acknowledged David's presence, although many, especially the wives, were staring at Shelby.

She already had a glass of champagne and was edging him discreetly toward a dessert-laden table in the dining room. "Can y'all believe what he's done to this place? It looks just fabulous. Not the gloomy ol' . . ." She stopped because he had taken her elbow.

"When were you here?" David asked softly.

"Didn't y'all bring me here?"

"No. We've never been here together."

Lashes lowered, Shelby sipped from her glass and then looked up brightly. "I was here with Mo...one afternoon. About Irving's offer, I was telling y'all, remember?"

He studied her, the candlelight was very flattering to her face and, in the glistening diamond choker, she looked eighteen if a day. Very innocent. He tilted forward and kissed her lightly on the lips.

When he pulled back, Shelby was all aglow. "Why, what in the world's gotten into you?" she asked, casting delighted but embarrassed looks around the room. "Never have y'all kissed me in public, like that."

"Let's go find Irving," he said and started for the hallway.

At that moment, Dixon Shaw, in full evening attire but minus his cumberbund, stepped from the dining room, holding a plate of apple pie and ice cream. He seemed surprised to see David with Shelby and started toward them. They met halfway, by the Bechstein grand piano, draped with an antique-fringed shawl that David remembered had been there since his mother had lived in the house.

"Well, you are full of surprises," Shaw greeted and smiled paternally at Shelby. "Miss Cale, very fine performance."

"Why, thank y'all."

"David, as long as you're here, stick around," Shaw continued, his ice cream melting. "I have a little announcement later on. Should be of interest."

David shrugged, as if nothing really made any difference anymore and asked, "Have you seen Irving?"

"In the den with that Maureen Engle woman. Now, I have to eat this before my wife busts me. Isn't that what the kids say today?" Pleased with his hipness, Shaw nodded to them both and headed back to the kitchen.

Shelby made certain no one was in listening range and then bent toward David, whispering conspiratorially, "Do y'all think he'll announce he's dumping Pacific?"

"Why don't you go find out?"

Her eye lids narrowed. "Are y'all serious?"

"Yes. I want to speak to Irving alone."

She appraised him with caution. "David, are you all right?"

"Yes."

"Well, y'all have changed then, something major."

He held her gaze. "Who do you say that?"

Carefully, she set down her empty champagne glass on the piano's fringed shawl. Then said cautiously, "Because y'all have never let me out of your sight . . . except for the ladies' room."

He couldn't help but smile. "What I have to say to Irving won't take long. Meet you back here in five flat?"

Through a dubious, questioning expression, she nodded and blew him a kiss off her fingertips. He watched her move away, swaying her hips languidly toward the dining room. And the knot at the base of his neck constricted tighter, increasing the painful throb, the urgency to get the whole affair over with. Only when Shelby had turned the corner, out of sight toward the kitchen, did he head for the hallway.

In the center courtyard, a mini-Fourth of July picnic had been set up: bunting-draped picnic tables, a portable hardwood dancefloor on which a handful of brave souls boogied sedately to the band's version of "Afternoon Delight," beyond them a barbecue grilled hamburgers and hotdogs. At another large table groaning with imported delicacies, salads and fruits, David saw Rebecca. In a flattering, pale yellow dress, she was chatting animatedly with Ed Hume, one of Irving's flunkies. Beside her camped Robby Rhomann, an aging child actor whom David despised. For a moment, David watched Rebecca, not really knowing why or even aware that he was staring at her, but when Hume turned his way, he moved into the shadows again and hurried down the long corridor.

On the west terrace, outside the French doors leading to Irving's den, Hume caught up with him. "What the hell are you doing here?"

"That's none of your goddamned business."

"You're not only not invited, you're unwelcome. How'd you get through the gate?"

David managed a tight smile. "Better mind your manners, Hume. Never know what tomorrow may bring."

"Tomorrow brings tomorrow, Rau. Now take your butt on a long hike. Out of here. Or I'm calling Security."

David sighed, weary of minor irritants on the road to bigger ones. "Hume, don't be an ass. Just go in and tell him I want to talk to him. One on one. Two minutes. That's all."

Unloosening his bow tie, Hume considered for a few beats, his tennis-court tan veneering a weak, petty man. "I'll check it out first."

"Peachy keen, Hume," David said. Hume scurried to the den's door, knocked discreetly and slipped inside.

With his back to the house, David stood at the stone balustrade, trying to quiet the pounding in his head. He stared out over the gently rolling, lushly vegetated and manicured grounds, gazing down toward the lighted tennis courts and far beyond to the darkened, children's play area. He hadn't thought of it in years and wondered if it still existed. His mother had created it just for him. She'd brought in top studio designers and craftsmen to turn a secluded, forested area in the far corner of the estate into a whole little medieval village, on a child's scale, with moats and turret towers and slides and furnished, thatched-roof cottages with electricity and running water. He had spent some of the happiest hours of his life, alone there or playing royalty with his mother, there in his own private kingdom.

Suddenly he had the strangest desire, almost overwhelming in its intensity, to run down to the hollow and see for himself, right at that moment, if the little village still stood. But his head hurt too much to move. And he had more adult games to play. So, with rigid little motions, he tapped out three more pills into his palm and popped them deep into his throat. Head gently back, he swallowed them with difficulty.

Hume's voice brought him around. "You can go in now, Rau. Daddy's waiting for you."

Grimly, David nodded and waited until Hume had vanished on down the terrace. In spite of the steel vise clamping his head, he believed he was totally concentrated on the objective ahead. He turned the knob of the shuttered French door and walked in with assurance.

The repugnant sour smell of Irving's cigar wafted over him. David blinked in the smoky light and thick air. Mo Engle sat by the fireplace, her shoes off, her feet propped up on an ottoman. She raised a half-empty glass toward him in a silent but mocking gesture of welcome. Coatless, Irving stood by his desk, his dress shirt damp with sweat but a victorious, self-congratulating grin on his puss. "Com'on in, Davey. Mo mentioned she'd seen you arrive."

"This is between us, Irving," David said and stared at Mo pointedly.

Wheezing through her nostrils, she rolled forward, swinging her feet to the floor, searching for her shoes. "Well, David, I hope you congratulate Irving on his accomplishment. What a classic he's created."

David shrugged. "Won't be seen unless I drop my lawsuits."

Irving swung away with a derisive grunt. "He's blowin' it outta his ass, Mo. Don't listen to him."

Mo shot Irving a concerned glance. "I'll go round up the crowd for Dixon's little announcement." She hesitated by the doors to the interior hallway. "David, you should be falling all over yourself to get in on some of the box office this film will generate."

David said flatly, "Go get screwed, Mo. You need it bad."

"Shut your wiseass mouth," Irving growled and moved to close the door after Mo's sudden departure. He turned to David and took his time lighting another cigar, puffing a blue cloud between them. "So I saw you there tonight, Davey. Did you learn anything about making movies?"

"I got control of Pacific."

"Says you."

David nodded, half smiling. "And Shaw."

Irving stared in disbelief, wavered a moment, then moved to his desk. "He tell you something, he didn't tell me?"

David shrugged with a faint smile.

"So he didn't tell you," Irving erupted, his voice hoarse.

"Pacific's mine. It's only a matter of time now. I've won, Irving. I beat you at your own fucking game."

Irving puffed in silence, chewing the end of the cigar. Then said, gruffly, "What the hell do you know about running a studio? You couldn't even make a simple little love story. But then, hell, what's love to you? Crazed adoration from a dope-fiend mama. Hell, you couldn't even keep that *shiksa* of yours happy.''

"What the fuck's that mean?"

"Ask her. Ask that blond bimbo of yours."

"Ask her what?" David threatened.

"Ask her who *schtupped* her best—me or you."

The vise gripping David's head flashed white hot.

Irving was grinning lasciviously. "Sure did love that bitty brown birthmark on her tummy. Right down there by her—"

David slammed his forearm into Irving's chest, driving him back against the desk. Irving recoiled, arms flapping helplessly. David pushed away, the pressure in his head building. From the front of the house, far away, he could hear the band striking up a spirited march. Irving coughed on the other side of the desk, rasping, "You crazy sonuvabitch. Don't you ever touch me again or I'll throw the book at you."

Hovering near a wing chair, David fought to maintain his equilibrium. "You fucked Shelby?"

"Goddamned right I did. And she sure as hell was a better screw than Nedra."

David managed to straighten up and began steadily moving toward the terrace doors. The distant band music continued, the pounding of a bass drum, joining the mounting roar inside his skull. By keeping his head upright, he could maintain control. He tore open the French doors and plowed outside. Once in the night air, he moved unsteadily toward the lighted French windows of the living room at the far end. Band music still played, growing louder as he approached. Holding his head, he stumbled to the nearest open French door and sagged against the doorway. Near delirious with pain, he scanned the room, trying to locate Shelby in all the faces. He spotted Erik Lungren first, the only non-tuxedo male, in washpants and blue blazer just leaving the room. But then David noticed the chairman, Dixon Shaw, holding court in front of the band, ready to address the crowded room. When the band's march ended, David strained to focus, to hear Shaw's faint words above the roaring in his ears.

"My fellow stockholders and friends of Pacific Studio. It is no secret Allied Industries was considering getting out of the movie business," the chairman said glumly, then smiled. "But after seeing tonight's film, made under the genius of Irving R. Dyer, I am heartily recommending to the board that we hold onto Pacific's shares indefinitely. Now let's bring our host out here . . ." Shaw was drowned out by cheers and applause. The band struck up "For He's a Jolly Good Fellow."

The blaring brass section set off a shrill siren in David's head. He had lost. Everything. The siren exploded and the last vestige of reason was incinerated. Groaning, he reeled away down the terrace. Up ahead, even with blurring vision he could make out a young couple leaning on the stone railing, listening to the music inside. The dark-haired young woman, dressed all in glowing yellow, was staring open-mouthed at him. With a cry, he lunged for her. She screamed and tried to duck away. He clasped onto her wrist and with a powerful grip, yanked her down the stone stairs and onto the grass. She fought and nearly pulled him off balance but he fiercely held onto her and began running, dragging her across the lawn and into the night. She screamed his name, several times. But David could not distinguish her voice from all the other noises in his head. All he wanted was to get them both to safety before it was too late.

ERIK
July 1976
Los Angeles

Barely ten minutes before, Erik had been searching the living room for Rebecca. In fact, ever since the final scenes of the film back at the lot, he'd been looking for her. Foul weather off San Diego had delayed *The Dreamer* in reaching the marina in time for him to make the entire screening but Erik had not been too perturbed. He had preferred arriving late with no whoopla and had slipped into the back of the theater, catching the climax of the film and slipping out again before the final credits. Briefly he had seen her at the sound stage party but she had disappeared before he could reach her.

That was why he had come to Irving's in his tropical-weight blazer and unpressed Mexican wedding shirt. Seeing all the stuffed shirts in their high formal gear, he was glad that at least he'd found time to shave. Shortly after his arrival, Mo had swooped down on him, deriding his lack of evening attire but obviously pleased that he'd come. In exuberant spirits, Mo had told him Rebecca was somewhere in the house and Erik had set off to find her. But he had bumped into Shelby first.

He had stopped in the TV alcove, off the living room, where several men were watching a recap of the nationwide Bicentennial celebrations. For several moments, he lost himself in the spectacular sight of the tall ships entering New York Harbor and it stirred something deep and wondrous within him.

"Why, sugar," Shelby's voice breathed. He turned and there she was, moving to him, all tawny and gold, entwining one of his arms. "Y'all came after all." She offered a cheek for him to kiss and he found himself doing so. She still smelled of roses. She tugged him out of the alcove and to the nearby living-room piano.

In the warm glow of candlelight, she was dazzling, her golden gown clinging like a second skin and around her throat, a thick diamond band that looked like it could choke a horse. Hastily she surveyed the room, then returned her attention fully to him. "Were y'all there for the film?"

"Just the last two scenes," he said, not wanting to explain his lukewarm reactions to what little he had caught of her performance.

She drooped with sadness, leaning a bare elbow on the closed piano top. "I wish y'all had seen it. I just can't judge myself anymore. Y'all could get Irving to set up a screening, even tonight, if you'd like."

"There's no hurry, Shelby."

She looked at him strangely, then dropped her long lashes. "I wanted so much to go to the premiere tonight with you." She raised her eyes to his. "I tried and tried to find you. I finally had to fire Mo because she wouldn't relay my messages to you."

It surprised him that she was once again back in pursuit. And realized again that she never failed to amaze him. Her full, curly hair, backlit by glowing candles, created a golden halo. She was so damned beautiful. She moved a breath closer. "Who did y'all come with? Tonight, here?"

"Myself."

She raised her chin to him, whispering, "Let's you and me go, right now. Right this very minute, walk out that front door and never come back."

"Shelby," he began quietly, "I came to find someone else."

Her head reared back and she searched his face, seeking that which was not there. Her fingers sought her gold evening case. "Irving?" she asked hopefully and placed a cigarette between her lips.

He took her gold Dunhill lighter from her trembling hands. Raising it to the dangling cigarette, he lit the end and said, "No. Someone I want to reopen a dialogue with."

Mischievously, she blew smoke over his shoulder. "Write him a letter. It makes more of an impact."

"It's not a 'him.'" He held out her lighter.

She ignored his hand. Through the smoke, her eyes were squinting at him with stunned disbelief.

"It's over, Shelby. Has been for a long time. You just fail to recognize it. Hell, it's taken me a damned long . . ."

Abruptly, she pulled back from him as if he were carrying a dreaded disease. Like frantic searchlights, her eyes swept over his face. And this time, the meaning of his words finally registered. At once, she had tears in her eyes, a tremble to her lower lip.

Stuffing his hands into his pants pockets, he bent forward and chastely kissed her cheek. "Good-bye, Shelby. Don't worry. You'll get what you need. You always do."

He tore his gaze from her and stepped out into the crowded room, feeling surprisingly calm, readily accepting the end of that chapter of his life. But the open agony on her face had caused him more discomfort than he wanted to admit to himself.

From the hall, an explosion of music erupted—"Stars and Stripes Forever" with plenty of brass and snare drum—and soon the eight-man dance band marched into the living room led by the tall Uncle Sam, who had to bend to enter the room. Behind him, strutting like a matronly cheerleader, Mo was thoroughly enjoying herself, doffing to the clapping crowd her white straw boater with a red, white and blue ribbon. Erik forgot about Shelby. He'd never seen Mo to be such a ham before and it tickled him.

With Uncle Sam handing out small American flags to all the guests, Mo led the band once around the huge living room and then stopped, grouping them before the imposing stone fireplace at the far end. The infectious music, like a small town parade, had drawn everyone in to listen and participate. Clapping, waving flags in rhythm, their faces were bright, joyful, filled with unabashed patriotism. And that too made Erik feel good. But still he had not seen Rebecca among them.

He moved to the hall, excusing himself as he brushed through still clapping people. Just before leaving the living room, he cast a glance back over their heads toward Mo. She had handed Dixon Shaw her straw boater and was bringing him forward in front of the band. The march was reaching its rousing conclusion. And Shaw looked very serious, as if preparing himself to make a definitive statement.

The hallway was empty and Erik moved swiftly, checking through open doors the rooms off the central corridor, heading for Irving's den in the far wing. The further he walked, the more the band's music faded. When the Sousa march finally climaxed, he was too far away to hear if anyone were speaking. Just as Erik reached the den, Irving opened the door and, ashen faced, staggered into the hall.

Erik rushed to him. "What the . . . ?"

Frantically, Irving waved him away, rasping, "Outside. David . . . he's flipped out."

Hurriedly, Erik helped him to a straightback chair and took off running, through Irving's office and out the French doors onto the rear terrace that stretched the length of the mansion. Most of these rear windows were dark but at the far end, light spilled from the living room's French doors. A stone railing at the terrace edge cut off access to the yard, except in the middle of the house, where broad stairs swept down to the lawn. Running to that point, Erik almost collided with a figure hurtling out of the shadows with a terrified cry.

"Ohmygod, help!" It was Robby Rhomann and he was in a state of shock, clutching, babbling above the blaring band, pointing. "Rebecca! He's got her. Out there! He just grabbed her. Do something! David's got Rebecca!"

Erik bolted for the stairs to the grounds, yelling back over his shoulder, "Which way?!"

"Down there!" Robby shouted, pointing. "Past the tennis courts!"

The lawn banked sharply away from the terrace and Erik ran down it, toward the double tennis courts, which were brightly lit, empty and garishly surrealistic in the surrounding shades of darkness. He ran past the two-story tennis pavilion and around a neatly tended rose garden, heading to a clump of oaks, visible against the moonlit sky. Panting, he reached the top of a knoll and dropped to one knee next to a bushy camillia, blending into its shadowed silhouette while he caught his breath. And listened to the night.

From his viewpoint, he could not even see the house, and the lights of the tennis courts were only a glow in the sky behind him. But, looking around and remembering as best he could the rest of the grounds, Erik decided if they were out there at all, they had to be straight ahead. Everything else on this side of the house lay within open, partially lighted areas. But down there, in what looked like a wooden hollow at the far corner of the estate, anybody could be doing anything.

That thought chilled him and he called out, "Rebecca! You there?"

He listened to the slight echo in the night air and again the silence. Just as he was about to call again, brassy band music once more broke the stillness. A stately version of "America, the Beautiful." It sounded like the band had moved out on the terrace far up the hill. Suddenly, there was an explosion from over near the swimming pool, followed by several more loud pops and the whine of launched skyrockets. Momentarily they burst high over his head like warfare. The brilliantly colored flashes illuminated the terrain.

Without thinking, Erik ran down into the scrubby trees, using the rapidly fading light. He dodged a boulder, tripped on a root and sprawled face out into a shallow, smelly swamp; falling flat just as the last flare blinked out.

In the distance, the band played on. Erik raised his face out of the muck, sputtering and spewing slimy water from his mouth. Up at the house, he could hear voices joining in with the band for the finale—"And crown thy good with brotherhood, from sea to shining sea." As the impromptu chorus raggedly hit the final notes, a series of fireworks blasted into the air and began exploding. Low, on his knees, Erik looked up in amazement at what the colored flashes revealed: the stone walls of a Brueghelesque village, accurate down to a closed drawbridge and turreted watchtower.

For a moment, Erik thought he might be hallucinating. But when he scrambled to his feet in the ankle-deep muck and touched the stone, he realized that the wall was real. Not as large as it first had appeared, he could easily see over it and, in the final bursts of fireworks, he could discern a small village of several scale-model structures, some with their roofs caved in. The last note of music faded away and then the final chunks of falling light fizzled out. Erik quickly vaulted the wall, falling noiselessly into an interior courtyard. Again he caught his breath and listened.

It was distinct but very faint. He could hear whimpering. But in the darkness he couldn't tell from which direction. "Rebecca," he called out softly. "Where are you?"

He strained to hear. Not even whimpering. Tormented, Erik leaped to his feet, shouting in anger, "Rau, I know you're here." Again there was silence. Erik lunged forward in the darkness. "Goddammit, Rau, come out and fight like a man. What kind of balls do you have?"

Stumbling into a low wall, Erik crashed to his knees, groaning in pain. Leaning against the wall, he hugged his legs until he could think. Patting his muddy pants pockets, he came across Shelby's lighter. He had failed to give it back to her. Eagerly, he searched for a dry area of his clothing to wipe it on. A shirttail later, he tried the lighter, clicking it in the darkness. It burst into a small but welcoming flame. He held it up, lighting the area around him. He was on a cobblestone street lined with little shops. He stood up, feeling like Gulliver.

"Rebecca?"

Her voice answered, not too far away, but strangely emotionless. "Shhh, quiet."

He tempered his tone, asking softly, "Are you hurt?"

She did not answer. He crept forward, holding the lighter low, stepping carefully in the overgrown debris. Her voice whispered, very near, tense with urgency, "No closer."

Flicking the lighter closed, he crouched in the dark, urging quietly, "What is it? Is David there? Please, let me help."

He waited and soon could hear low moaning, a soft, helpless, repetitive sound. He couldn't take it any longer and bolted to his feet, holding the lighter's flame aloft. In front of him was a small, stone cottage, intact to a partially thatched roof. The front door was closed but as he stepped forward, he began to see inside through the holes in the rotting thatch. The whimpering came from within and increased the closer he got. He stood directly over a large gap in the roof and lowered his hand with the flickering lighter. The moans grew frantic.

Erik plunged the lighter down, ready to attack. Instead, he froze. In the corner, on the floor near a small fireplace, Rebecca sat, muddied, frightened, pinned against the walls and cradling in her lap a curled up David. Moaning, eyes tightly closed against the light, he held his head and rocked in her lap like a child. Beseechingly, Rebecca looked up at Erik, her eyes filled with barely controlled fear. Erik found his voice, a hoarse whisper, "How do you want to handle this?"

"Get help," she mouthed, barely audible.

Erik straightened, looking back in the direction of the house. It was a long way. He turned back to her, not wanting to leave her alone.

David had reacted to her voice and buried his head deeper into her lap, his tortured groans increasing in intensity. She stroked his head and jerked hers to Erik, indicating for him to split. Erik clicked the lighter off and in the darkness asked quietly, "Does he have any weapons on him?"

She pleaded softly, "No, just get me out of here."

Erik was off like a shot, running in the darkness from memory. He leaped over the village's outer wall and sloughed through the marshy moat, firming his stride on the far lawn. He ran full out, up toward the camillias, then stopped as he reached the bright lights of the tennis courts. Coming down the far hill, flashlights bobbing, dogs barking, was a veritable posse: several armed security guards, a brace of leashed weimaraners and four white-suited paramedics, two carrying a rolled-up, canvas stretcher. Urgently, Erik yelled, waving them on as he turned back, stopping only to gesture for them to move faster. At the edge of the moat he waited. As they reached him he quieted them, then speedily filled them in on the details.

As Erik whispered, he could hear Rebecca singing softly inside the walls. But it wasn't until he and two of the paramedics were within a few feet of the cottage that her words were clear. "Baby, I'm your mama/An' I'm your papa/an' I'm your sister too/So come an' get it/just grab hold of/your sweet . . ."

Erik interrupted softly, "I brought some help." He stood and shone a shielded flashlight, illuminating the interior dimly. Rebecca had not moved but David had his arms wrapped around her waist now. His eyes were still closed and his body was a tight coil. As the paramedic prepared the needle, Rebecca resumed singing, her voice quaking but resilient: "Baby/when you're feeling low/an' the floor's comin' up to greet you . . ."

At Erik's direction, the paramedic plunged the needle into David's arm, right through the jacket. David shrieked and jerked upright, slamming Rebecca against the wall in outrage. Reaching in through the roof, Erik grabbed him from behind and yanked him off her, tugging him out and over the roof with one angry pull. He threw David to the ground, fell on top of him, and held him like a squirming dog until the shot took hold. David's cries, like those of an enraged child, steadily faded and his writhing slowed enough for Erik to hand him over to the assembled ambulance team. He helped them strap David into a straitjacket. By the time David was trussed, sedated and on the stretcher, Rebecca had disappeared. Erik was told that the security guards had hustled her away. He ran back to the house to catch her.

The party was long over. A few servants cleaned up in the kitchen, and Irving, alone in the darkened living room, nursed a whiskey and explained hoarsely that he'd sent everybody home after the fireworks. When Erik asked after Rebecca, Irving said that Mo had driven off with her. Exhausted and drained, Erik looked at the mogul's haggard face and asked, "What the hell happened to David?"

Irving shrugged wearily and growled, "Life."

Erik spent the next several exasperating hours trying to track down Rebecca, or at least Mo. It wasn't until toward dawn that he learned from Timmy, one of her sons, that Mo had driven Rebecca to Palm Springs and had left no forwarding number. Feeling at loose ends and still a bit scrambled, Erik holed up on *The Dreamer*. He'd left messages all over town for Mo, asking her to call his temporary answering service the moment she got back to town. He debated with himself whether he should leave a similar message on Rebecca's line, but decided against it.

He slept late and when he awoke, he spent a lot of time thinking about why he'd come back to L.A. and what it was he thought he wanted in his life. He examined again the barriers he had constructed to keep people out. And what those choices had cost him. He looked at his loneliness again. And he knew that he wanted to change all that. But he wasn't sure of how. Again his thoughts drifted back to Rebecca.

That night he lay up on deck, reading Keats by lantern light. One stanza stuck with him: "When I have fears that I may cease to be/Before my pen has glean'd my teaming brain. . . . When I behold, upon the night's starr'd face,/Huge cloudy symbols of high romance, . . . /Then on the shore,/of the wide world I stand alone, and think/Till love and fame to nothingness do sink."

Late the following afternoon. he received a message at the marina's office. Slipping into a nearby phone booth, he quickly dialed Mo's home. She answered on the third ring.

His first words were, "How's Rebecca doing?"

Mo's voice sounded quiet but full of spirit. "She's really remarkable. Honestly, she spent more time shoring me up. I think she's the strongest of us all. Why the hell aren't you following through with her, anyway?''

"I'm trying my damnedest, Mo. But just where the hell is she?"

"I dropped her off at her Venice apartment not more than an hour ago. You heard what's happened to the film? Since David's incapacitated, his lawyer—"

Erik broke in, "What's that mean? Incapacitated?"

"He's in some form of catatonia, Erik. Won't respond to anything. The doctors think it's extremely serious. As long as he is out of it, the film could be held up from being released for months, maybe years. Shelby's so distraught she flew home to Virginia. That horse farm her grandmother owns.''

"One third is Shelby's," Erik recalled aloud. "But she swore she'd never return there.''

"We should all be so lucky. But not to worry about Rebecca. She's had two firm offers already for her talents. One major lead role from Zanuck and Brown. She may be the first star launched by a film that's never released.''

"She deserves it all," he said, anxiously rising to his feet. "Look, I can't talk all day. I've got something I've waited too long to do.''

"Well, hell, the least you could do is congratulate me, turkey. Didn't you read the trades today? Irving announced my vice presidency.''

"Mo, forgive me, I didn't know. Yes, by all means, congratulations. When do you start?''

Much later than he wanted, he finally was able to extricate himself and he raced by car the few blocks to Venice, parking near Rebecca's apartment building. The orange-red sun sank toward the water, casting a fiery glow on the stucco facade. Upstairs, on her apartment door, was a tacked-up note in Rebecca's handwriting. Erik read the message to Sara Jane, telling her that the paint had been delivered and to meet at the school. It was signed with an enthusiastic flourish, *Rebecca*.

He jogged down the sidewalk, catching glimpses between the buildings of the red sun fattening out like a flat tire on the waterline.

Reaching the block of the Raindance Academy, he slowed to a walk, feeling eager, hopeful. The front windows were papered with newsprint but the lights were on and the front door ajar. Inside, a radio played. Paul and Linda McCartney were singing "Silly Love Songs." It felt right to him. He walked in.

REBECCA AND ERIK
July 1976
Los Angeles

Under the glare of a bare lightbulb, high on a ladder, her hair up under a Rams' cap, Rebecca stretched out, rolling glossy white paint on a corner of the tin, patterned ceiling. She attacked the job with vigor and determination, singing along under her breath with Paul and Linda, concentrating on the lyrics. She was trying desperately to burn off some of the confusion of energies coursing through her system ever since the premiere. And work—hard, tiring, monotonous, brain-draining manual labor had been her only release. It kept her mind relatively free from the unanswered questions still haunting her.

Her back was to him, and for several moments he watched her, admiring the almost choreographed physicality of her energetic painting. In a baggy man's workshirt, a pair of paint-smeared jeans and that cap, she looked like a little street kid. Suddenly, quite vividly, he had a flash image of her that first morning he had awakened in her one-room New York apartment. And with the sweet glow of recognition, he realized something he had instinctively known for over ten years. He did love her, deeply and truly, and he had loved her from that very first moment. A love buried within him. But she had been there all along, deep within his heart, only a dream away. He bent to the radio.

In the middle of a paint stroke, in the middle of her song, the radio cut out on her. In annoyance, she swung around and caught sight of him. Her heart bloomed with love and in that instant, that eternity, when her eyes met his, she knew that something major had changed. She dared not guess what it was. But she was full of hope.

"Congratulations," he began, somewhat shyly. "Mo tells me you're an overnight star in this town."

Pleased, she shrugged. "Yes, it looks like I've finally graduated from my apprenticeship." Her eyes twinkling with humor, she wiped her nose on the sleeve of her workshirt. "Another ten years at my craft, I might even be ready to graduate out of the journeyman stage."

He discovered that he was smiling at her. She had a smudge of white on her nose. "I only saw two scenes of the film, but from what I did catch, Rebecca, you brought it alive—more than I ever dreamed possible. Thank you."

"Shouldn't I be thanking you?" she asked, wondering why he was still standing so far across the room. Heart pounding, she came down the ladder a step.

He was smiling again at her. "You want to go for a sail?"

"For how long?"

"However long you want."

Holding his eyes, reading them, liking what she saw, she took a long moment before she replied, "How about a short trip to start with?"

He frowned, not breaking her gaze. "How short?"

"Well," she started thoughtfully, feeling a tickle of laughter in her throat, "I've an audition on Friday morning . . . so how about just an overnighter? If that's not too bold of a request?"

His face brightened and with two strides, he was across the strewn newspapers and stopped before the ladder, staring deeply into her eyes. With her on the first rung, their eyes were level and he slowly slipped his arms about her waist. They each felt the electricity of a completed, satisfying connection. He reached up and took off her cap. Her raven hair tumbled to her shoulders. He leaned his nose into hers, touching the smudge of white paint. "I love you, Rebecca. With all my heart."

She no longer felt the paint roller in her hand. It slipped to the floor unnoticed. He pulled her into him. Their breaths mingled. And just before he kissed her, he remembered the first words she'd uttered to him that morning so long ago. Their noses still touching, he laughed softly. "Hey, it's my turn to ask you. Could I have your autograph?"